A HAROLD BELL WRIGHT TRILOGY

The Shepherd of the Hills

The Calling of Dan Matthews

God and the Groceryman

A HAROLD BELL WRIGHT TRILOGY

The Shepherd of the Hills

The Calling of Dan Matthews

God and the Groceryman

PELICAN PUBLISHING COMPANY
GRETNA 2007

The Shepherd of the Hills was first published in 1907.
The Calling of Dan Matthews was first published in 1909.
God and the Groceryman was first published in 1927.

First printing, August 2007
Second printing, April 2014

ISBN-13: 978-1-58980-512-5
E-book ISBN: 978-1-45560-556-9

Printed in the United States of America

Published by Pelican Publishing Company, Inc.
1000 Burmaster Street, Gretna, Louisiana 70053

CONTENTS

A HAROLD BELL WRIGHT TRILOGY

The Shepherd of the Hills

The Calling of Dan Matthews

God and the Groceryman

THE SHEPHERD OF THE HILLS

To Frances, my wife
In memory of that beautiful summer in the Ozark Hills, when, so often, we followed the old trails around the rim of Mutton Hollow—
the trail that is nobody knows how old—
and from Sammy's Lookout watched the day go over the western ridges

"That all with one consent praise new-born gawds,
Tho they are made and moulded of things past,
And give to dust that is a little gilt
More laud than gilt o'er-dusted."

TROILUS AND CRESSIDA. ACT 3: SC. 8.

CONTENTS

THE SHEPHERD OF THE HILLS

INTRODUCTORY.

THE TWO TRAILS.

This, my story, is a very old story. In the hills of life there are two trails. One lies along the higher sunlit fields where those who journey see afar, and the light lingers even when the sun is down; and one leads to the lower ground, where those who travel, as they go, look always over their shoulders with eyes of dread, and gloomy shadows gather long before the day is done.

This, my story, is the story of a man who took the trail that leads to the lower ground, and of a woman, and how she found her way to the higher sunlit fields.

In the story, it all happened in the Ozark Mountains, many miles from what we of the city call civilization. In life, it has all happened many, many times before, in many, many places. The two trails lead afar. The story, so very old, is still in the telling.

"Preachin' Bill" who runs the ferry says, "When God looked upon th' work of his hands an' called hit good, he war sure a lookin' at this here Ozark country. Rough? Law yes! Hit war made that a way on purpose. Ain't nothin' to a flat country nohow. A man jest naturally wear hisself plumb out a walkin' on a level 'thout ary down hill t' spell him. An' then look how much more there is of hit! Take forty acres o' *flat* now an' hit's jest a forty, but you take forty acres o' this here Ozark country an' God 'lmighty only knows how much 'twould be if hit war rolled out flat. 'Taint no wonder 't all, God rested when he made these here hills; he jest naturally *had* t' quit, fer he done his beatenest an' war plumb gin out."

Of all the country Bill had seen, "from Ant Creek Head t' the mouth of James an' plumb to Pilot Knob," he "lowed the Mutton Hollow neighborhood was the prettiest."

From the Matthews place on the ridge that shuts in the valley on the north and east, there is an Old Trail leading down the mountain. Two hundred yards below the log barn, the narrow path finds a bench on the steep slope of the hillside, and, at that level, follows around the rim of the Hollow. Dipping a little at the head of the ravine east of the spring, then lifting itself over a low, heavily timbered spur of one of the higher hills, it comes out again into the open. Following a rocky ledge, the way, further on, leads through a clump of sumac bushes, and past the deer lick in the big low gaps, then around the base of Boulder Bald, along another ledge, and out on the bare shoulder of Dewey Bald, which partly shuts in the little valley on the south.

From the big rock that Sammy Lane calls her Lookout, the Old Trail leaves the rim of Mutton Hollow and slips easily down into the lower valleys; down past the little cabin on the southern slope of the mountain where Sammy lived with her father; down to the banks of Fall Creek and to the distant river bottom. Here the thread-like path finds a wider way, leading, somehow, out of the wilderness to the great world that lies miles, and miles, beyond the farthest blue line of hills; the world that Sammy said "seemed mighty fine to them that knowed nothin' about it."

No one seems to know how long that narrow path has lain along the mountain; but it must be very long for it is deeply worn at places.

Often, in the years of our story, swift leaping deer would cross the ridge at the low gap and follow along the benches to the spring. And sometimes a lithe bodied panther, in the belt of timber, watched hungrily for their coming, or a huge-pawed catamount on some over-hanging rock would lie in wait for fawn or doe. Or perhaps a gaunt timber wolf would sniff the trail, and with wild echoing howls call his comrades to the chase.

Jim Lane, young then, followed that winding way from the distant river, and from nobody knows where beyond, when he came to build his lonely hunter's shack by the spring on the southern slope of Dewey. And later, when the shack in the timber was replaced by a more substantial settler's cabin, Jim led Sammy's mother along the same old way. Then came the giant Grant Matthews with Aunt Mollie and their little family. They followed the path three miles farther and built their home where the trail climbs over the ridge.

When Grant Matthews, Jr., was eighteen, his father mortgaged the hard-won homestead to purchase the sheep ranch in Mutton Hollow. Then it was that another path was made, branching off in the belt of timber from the Old Trail and following the spur down into the little valley where the corral was snuggly sheltered from the winter winds.

So the Lane cabin, the Matthew's homestead, and the sheep ranch in Mutton Hollow were all connected by well-marked paths; but it is the trail that leads from Sammy Lane's home to the big log house where young Matthews lives, that is, nobody knows, how old.

CHAPTER I.

THE STRANGER.

It was corn-planting time, when the stranger followed the Old Trail into the Mutton Hollow neighborhood.

All day a fine rain had fallen steadily, and the mists hung heavy over the valley. The lower hills were wrapped as in a winding sheet; dank and cold. The trees were dripping with moisture. The stranger looked tired and wet.

By his dress, the man was from the world beyond the ridges, and his carefully tailored clothing looked strangely out of place in the mountain wilderness. His form stooped a little in the shoulders, perhaps with weariness, but he carried himself with the unconscious air of one long used to a position of conspicuous power and influence; and, while his well-kept hair and beard were strongly touched with white, the brown, clear lighted eyes, that looked from under their shaggy brows, told of an intellect unclouded by the shadows of many years. It was a face marked deeply by pride; pride of birth, of intellect, of culture; the face of a scholar and poet; but it was more—it was the countenance of one fairly staggering under a burden of disappointment and grief.

As the stranger walked, he looked searchingly into the mists on every hand, and paused frequently as if questioning the proper course. Suddenly he stepped quickly forward. His ear had caught the sharp ring of a horse's shoe on a flint rock somewhere in the mists on the mountain side above. It was Jed Holland coming down the trail with a week's supply of corn meal in a sack across his horse's back.

As the figure of the traveler emerged from the mists, the native checked his horse to greet the newcomer with the customary salutation of the backwoods, "Howdy."

The man returned Jed's greeting cordially, and, resting his satchel on a rock beside the narrow path, added, "I am very glad to meet you. I fear that I am lost."

The voice was marvelously pure, deep, and musical, and, like the brown eyes, betrayed the real strength of the man, denied by his gray hair and bent form. The tones were as different from the high keyed, slurring speech of the backwoods, as the gentleman himself was unlike any man Jed had ever met. The boy looked at the speaker in wide-eyed wonder; he had a queer feeling that he was in the presence of a superior being.

Throwing one thin leg over the old mare's neck, and waving a long arm up the hill and to the left, Jed drawled, "That thar's Dewey Bal'; down yonder's Mutton Holler." Then turning a little to the right and pointing into the mist with the other hand, he continued, "Compton Ridge is over thar. Whar was you tryin' to git to, Mister?"

"Where am I trying to get to?" As the man repeated Jed's question, he drew his hand wearily across his brow; "I—I—it doesn't much matter, boy. I suppose I must find some place where I can stay to- night. Do you live near here?"

"Nope," Jed answered, "Hit's a right smart piece to whar I live. This here's grindin' day, an' I've been t' mill over on Fall Creek; the Matthews mill hit is. Hit'll be plumb dark 'gin I git home. I 'lowed you was a stranger in these parts soon 's I ketched sight of you. What might YER name be, Mister?"

The other, looking back over the way he had come, seemed not to hear Jed's question, and the native continued, "Mine's Holland. Pap an' Mam they come from Tennessee. Pap he's down in th' back now, an' ain't right peart, but he'll be 'round in a little, I reckon. Preachin' Bill he 'lows hit's good fer a feller t' be down in th' back onct in a while; says if hit warn't fer that we'd git to standin' so durned proud an' straight we'd go plumb over backwards."

A bitter smile crossed the face of the older man. He evidently applied the native's philosophy in a way unguessed by Jed. "Very true, very true, indeed," he mused. Then he turned to Jed, and asked, "Is there a house near here?"

"Jim Lane lives up the trail 'bout half a quarter. Ever hear tell o' Jim?"

"No, I have never been in these mountains before." "I 'lowed maybe you'd heard tell o' Jim or Sammy. There's them that 'lows Jim knows a heap more 'bout old man Dewey's cave than he lets on; his place bein' so nigh. Reckon you know 'bout Colonel Dewey, him th' Bal' up thar's named fer? Maybe you come t' look fer the big mine they say's in th' cave? I'll hep you hunt hit, if you want me to, Mister."

"No," said the other, "I am not looking for mines of lead or zinc; there is greater wealth in these hills and forests, young man."

"Law, you don't say! Jim Wilson allus 'lowed thar must be gold in these here mountains, 'cause they're so dad burned rough. Lemme hep you, Mister. I'd like mighty well t' git some clothes like them."

"I do not speak of gold, my boy," the stranger answered kindly. "But I must not keep you longer, or darkness will overtake us. Do you think this Mr. Lane would entertain me?"

Jed pushed a hand up under his tattered old hat, and scratched awhile before he answered, "Don't know 'bout th' entertainin', Mister, but 'most anybody would take you in." He turned and looked thoughtfully up the trail. "I don't guess Jim's to home though; 'cause I see'd Sammy a fixin' t' go over t' th' Matthews's when I come past. You know the Matthews's, I reckon?"

There was a hint of impatience now in the deep voice. "No, I told you that I had never been in these mountains before. Will Mr. Matthews keep me, do you think?"

Jed, who was still looking up the trail, suddenly leaned forward, and, pointing into the timber to the left of the path, said in an exciting whisper, "Look at that, Mister; yonder thar by that big rock."

The stranger, looking, thought he saw a form, weird and ghost-like in the mist, flitting from tree to tree, but, even as he looked, it vanished among the hundreds of fantastic shapes in the gray forest. "What is it?" he asked.

The native shook his head. "Durned if I know, Mister. You can't tell. There's mighty strange things stirrin' on this here mountain, an' in the Holler down yonder. Say, Mister, did you ever see a hant?"

The gentleman did not understand.

"A hant, a ghost, some calls 'em," explained Jed. "Bud Wilson he sure seed old Matt's—"

The other interrupted. "Really, young man, I must go. It is already late, and you know I have yet to find a place to stay for the night."

"Law, that's alright, Mister!" replied Jed. "Ain't no call t' worry. Stay anywhere. Whar do you live when you're to home?"

Again Jed's question was ignored. "You think then that Mr. Matthews will keep me?"

"Law, yes! They'll take anybody in. I know they're to home 'cause they was a fixin' t' leave the mill when I left 'bout an hour ago. Was the river up much when you come acrost?" As the native spoke he was still peering uneasily into the woods.

"I did not cross the river. How far is it to this Matthews place, and how do I go?"

"Jest foller this Old Trail. Hit'll take you right thar. Good road all th' way. 'Bout three mile, I'd say. Did you come from Springfield or St. Louis, maybe?"

The man lifted his satchel from the rock as he answered: "No, I do not live in either Springfield or St. Louis. Thank you, very much, for your assistance. I will go on, now, for I must hurry, or night will overtake me, and I shall not be able to find the path."

"Oh, hit's a heap lighter when you git up on th' hill 'bove th' fog," said Jed, lowering his leg from the horse's neck, and settling the meal sack, preparatory to moving. "But I'd a heap rather hit was you than me a goin' up on Dewey t'night." He was still looking up the trail. "Reckon you must be from Kansas City or Chicago? I heard tell they're mighty big towns."

The stranger's only answer was a curt "Good-by," as his form vanished in the mist.

Jed turned and dug his heels vigorously in the old mare's flanks, as he ejaculated softly, "Well, I'll be dod durned! Must be from New York, sure!"

Slowly the old man toiled up the mountain; up from the mists of the lower ground to the ridge above; and, as he climbed, unseen by him, a shadowy form flitted from tree to tree in the dim, dripping forest.

As the stranger came in sight of the Lane cabin, a young woman on a brown pony rode out of the gate and up the trail before him; and when the man reached the open ground on the mountain above, and rounded the shoulder of the hill, he saw the pony, far ahead, loping easily along the little path. A moment he watched, and horse and rider passed from sight.

The clouds were drifting far away. The western sky was clear with the sun still above the hills. In an old tree that leaned far out over the valley, a crow shook the wet from his plumage and dried himself in the warm light; while far below the mists rolled, and on the surface of that gray sea, the traveler saw a company of buzzards, wheeling and circling above some dead thing hidden in its depth.

Wearily the man followed the Old Trail toward the Matthews place, and always, as he went, in the edge of the gloomy forest, flitted that shadowy form.

CHAPTER II.

SAMMY LANE.

Preachin' Bill, says, "Hit's a plumb shame there ain't more men in th' world built like old man Matthews and that thar boy o' his'n. Men like them ought t' be as common as th' other kind, an' would be too if folks cared half as much 'bout breeding folks as they do 'bout raising hogs an' horses."

Mr. Matthews was a giant. Fully six feet four inches in height, with big bones, broad shoulders, and mighty muscles. At log rollings and chopping bees, in the field or at the mill, or in any of the games in which the backwoodsman tries his strength, no one had ever successfully contested his place as the strongest man in the hills. And still, throughout the country side, the old folks tell with pride tales of the marvelous feats of strength performed in the days when "Old Matt" was young.

Of the son, "Young Matt," the people called him, it is enough to say that he seemed made of the same metal and cast in the same mold as the father; a mighty frame, softened yet by young manhood's grace; a powerful neck and well poised head with wavy red-brown hair; and blue eyes that had in them the calm of summer skies or the glint of battle steel. It was a countenance fearless and frank, but gentle and kind, and the eyes were honest eyes.

Anyone meeting the pair, as they walked with the long swinging stride of the mountaineer up the steep mill road that gray afternoon, would have turned for a second look; such men are seldom seen.

When they reached the big log house that looks down upon the Hollow, the boy went at once with his axe to the woodpile, while the older man busied himself with the milking and other chores about the barn.

Young Matt had not been chopping long when he heard, coming up the hill, the sound of a horse's feet on the Old Trail. The horse stopped at the house and a voice, that stirred the blood in the young man's veins, called, "Howdy, Aunt Mollie."

Mrs. Matthews appeared in the doorway; by her frank countenance and kindly look anyone would have known her at a glance as the boy's mother. "Land sakes, if it ain't Sammy Lane! How are you, honey?"

"I am alright," answered the voice; "I've come over t' stop with you tonight; Dad's away again; Mandy Ford staid with me last night, but she had to go home this evenin'." The big fellow at the woodpile drove his axe deeper into the log.

"It's about time you was a comin' over," replied the woman in the doorway; "I was a tellin' the menfolks this mornin' that you hadn't been nigh the whole blessed week. Mr. Matthews 'lowed maybe you was sick."

The other returned with a gay laugh, "I was never sick a minute in my life that anybody ever heard tell. I'm powerful hungry, though. You'd better put in another pan of corn bread." She turned her pony's head toward the barn.

"Seems like you are always hungry," laughed the older woman, in return. "Well just go on out to the barn, and the men will take your horse; then come right in and I'll mighty soon have something to fill you up."

Operations at the woodpile suddenly ceased and Young Matt was first at the barn-yard gate.

Miss Sammy Lane was one of those rare young women whose appearance is not to be described. One can, of course, put it down that she was tall; beautifully tall, with the trimness of a young pine, deep bosomed, with limbs full-rounded, fairly tingling with the life and strength of perfect womanhood; and it may be said that her face was a face to go with one through the years, and to live still in one's dreams when the sap of life is gone, and, withered and old, one sits shaking before the fire; a generous, loving mouth, red lipped, full arched, with the corners tucked in and perfect teeth between; a womanly chin and nose, with character enough to save them from being pretty; hair dark, showing a touch of gold with umber in the shadows; a brow, full broad, set over brown eyes that had never been taught to hide behind their fringed veils, but looked always square out at you with a healthy look of good comradeship, a gleam of mirth, or a sudden, wide, questioning gaze that revealed depth of soul within.

But what is the use? When all this is written, those who knew Sammy will say, "'Tis but a poor picture, for she is something more than all this." Uncle Ike, the postmaster at the Forks, did it much better when he said to "Preachin' Bill," the night of the "Doin's" at the Cove School, "Ba thundas! That gal o' Jim Lane's jest plumb fills th' whole house. *What!* An' when she comes a ridin' up t' th' office on that brown pony o' hern, I'll be dad burned if she don't pretty nigh fill th' whole out doors, ba thundas! What!" And the little shrivelled up old hillsman, who keeps the ferry, removed his cob pipe long enough to reply, with all the emphasis possible to his squeaky voice, "She sure do, Ike. She sure do. I've often thought hit didn't look jest fair fer God 'lmighty t' make sech a woman 'thout ary man t' match her. Makes me feel plumb 'shamed o' myself t' stand 'round in th' same county with her. Hit sure do, Ike."

Greeting the girl the young man opened the gate for her to pass.

"I've been a lookin' for you over," said Sammy, a teasing light in her eyes. "Didn't you know that Mandy was stoppin' with me? She's been a dyin' to see you."

"I'm mighty sorry," he replied, fastening the gate and coming to the pony's side. "Why didn't you tell me before? I reckon she'll get over it alright, though," he added with a smile, as he raised his arms to assist the girl to dismount.

The teasing light vanished as the young woman placed her hands on the powerful shoulders of the giant, and as she felt the play of the swelling muscles that swung her to the ground so easily, her face flushed with admiration. For the fraction of a minute she stood facing him, her hands still on his arms, her lips parted as if to speak; then she turned quickly away, and without a word walked toward the house, while the boy, pretending to busy himself with the pony's bridle, watched her as she went.

When the girl was gone, the big fellow led the horse away to the stable, where he crossed his arms upon the saddle and hid his face from the light. Mr. Matthews coming quietly to the door a few minutes later saw the boy standing there, and the rugged face of the big mountaineer softened at the sight. Quietly he withdrew to the other side of the barn, to return later when the saddle and bridle had been removed, and the young man stood stroking the pony, as the little horse munched his generous feed of corn.

The elder man laid his hand on the broad shoulder of the lad so like him, and looked full into the clear eyes. "Is it alright, son?" he asked gruffly; and the boy answered, as he returned his father's look, "It's alright, Dad."

Then let's go to the house; Mother called supper some time ago."

Just as the little company were seating themselves at the table, the dog in the yard barked loudly. Young Matt went to the door. The stranger, whom Jed had met on the Old Trail, stood at the gate.

CHAPTER III.

THE VOICE FROM OUT THE MISTS.

While Young Matt was gone to the corral in the valley to see that the sheep were safely folded for the night, and the two women were busy in the house with their after-supper work, Mr. Matthews and his guest sat on the front porch.

"My name is Howitt, Daniel Howitt," the man said in answer to the host's question. But, as he spoke, there was in his manner a touch of embarrassment, and he continued quickly as if to prevent further question, "You have two remarkable children, sir; that boy is the finest specimen of manhood I have ever seen, and the girl is remarkable—remarkable, sir. You will pardon me, I am sure, but I am an enthusiastic lover of my kind, and I certainly have never seen such a pair."

The grim face of the elder Matthews showed both pleasure and amusement. "You're mistaken, Mister; the boy's mine alright, an' he's all that you say, an' more, I reckon. I doubt if there's a man in the hills can match him to-day; not excepting Wash Gibbs; an' he's a mighty good boy, too. But the girl is a daughter of a neighbor, and no kin at all."

"Indeed!" exclaimed the other, "you have only one child then?"

The amused smile left the face of the old mountaineer, as he answered slowly, "There was six boys, sir; this one, Grant, is the youngest. The others lie over there." He pointed with his pipe to where a clump of pines, not far from the house, showed dark and tall, against the last red glow in the sky.

The stranger glanced at the big man's face in quick sympathy. "I had only two; a boy and a girl," he said softly. "The girl and her mother have been gone these twenty years. The boy grew to be a man, and now he has left me." The deep voice faltered. "Pardon me, sir, for speaking of this, but my lad was so like your boy there. He was all I had, and now—now—I am very lonely, sir."

There is a bond of fellowship in sorrow that knows no conventionalities. As the two men sat in the hush of the coming night, their faces turned toward the somber group of trees, they felt strongly drawn to one another.

The mountaineer's companion spoke again half to himself; "I wish that my dear ones had a resting place like that. In the crowded city cemetery the ground is always shaken by the tramping of funeral professions." He buried his face in his hands.

For some time the stranger sat thus, while his host spoke no word. Then lifting his head, the man looked away over the ridges just touched with the lingering light, and the valley below wrapped in the shadowy mists. "I came away from it all because they said I must, and because I was hungry for this." He waved his hand toward the glowing sky and the forest clad hills. "This is good for me; it somehow seems to help me know how big God is. One could find peace here—surely, sir, one could find it here—peace and strength."

The mountaineer puffed hard at his pipe for a while, then said gruffly, "Seems that way, Mister, to them that don't know. But many's the time I've wished to God I'd never seen these here Ozarks. I used to feel like you do, but I can't no more. They 'mind me now of him that blackened my life; he used to take on powerful about the beauty of the country and all the time he was a turnin' it into a hell for them that had to stay here after he was gone."

As he spoke, anger and hatred grew dark in the giant's face, and the stranger saw the big hands clench and the huge frame grow tense with passion. Then, as if striving to be not ungracious, the woodsman said in a somewhat softer tone, "You can't see much of it, this evening, though, 'count of the mists. It'll fair up by morning, I reckon. You can see a long way from here, of a clear day, Mister."

"Yes, indeed," replied Mr. Howitt, in an odd tone. "One could see far from here, I am sure. We, who live in the cities, see but a little farther than across the street. We spend our days looking at the work of our own and our neighbors' hands. Small wonder our lives have so little of God in them, when we come in touch with so little that God has made."

"You live in the city, then, when you are at home?" asked Mr. Matthews, looking curiously at his guest.

"I did, when I had a home; I cannot say that I live anywhere now."

Old Matt leaned forward in his chair as if to speak again; then paused; someone was coming up the hill; and soon they distinguished the stalwart form of the son. Sammy coming from the house with an empty bucket met the young man at the gate, and the two went toward the spring together.

In silence the men on the porch watched the moon as she slowly pushed her way up through the leafy screen on the mountain wall. Higher and higher she climbed until her rays fell into the valley below, and the drifting mists from ridge to ridge became a sea of ghostly light. It was a weird scene, almost supernatural in its beauty.

Then from down at the spring a young girl's laugh rose clearly, and the big mountaineer said in a low tone, "Mr. Howitt, you've got education; it's easy to see that; I've always wanted to ask somebody like you, do you believe in hants? Do you reckon folks ever come back once they're dead and gone?"

The man from the city saw that his big host was terribly in earnest, and answered quietly, "No, I do not believe in such things, Mr. Matthews; but if it should be true, I do not see why we should fear the dead."

The other shook his head; "I don't know—I don't know, sir; I always said I didn't believe, but some things is mighty queer." He seemed to be shaping his thought for further speech, when again the girl's laugh rang clear along the mountain side. The young people were returning from the spring.

The mountaineer relighted his pipe, while Young Matt and Sammy seated themselves on the step, and Mrs. Matthews coming from the house joined the group.

"We've just naturally got to find somebody to stay with them sheep, Dad," said the son; "there ain't nobody there to-night, and as near as I can make out there's three ewes and their lambs missing. There ain't a bit of use in us trying to depend on Pete."

"I'll ride over on Bear Creek to-morrow, and see if I can get that fellow Buck told us about," returned the father.

"You find it hard to get help on the ranch?" inquired the stranger.

"Yes, sir, we do," answered Old Matt. "We had a good 'nough man 'till about a month ago; since then we've been gettin' along the best we could. But with some a stayin' out on the range, an' not comin' in, an' the wolves a gettin' into the corral at night, we'll lose mighty nigh all the profits this year. The worst of it is, there ain't much show to get a man; unless that one over on Bear Creek will come. I reckon, though, he'll be like the rest." He sat staring gloomily into the night.

"Is the work so difficult?" Mr. Howitt asked.

"Difficult, no; there ain't nothing to do but tendin' to the sheep. The man has to stay at the ranch of nights, though."

Mr. Howitt was wondering what staying at the ranch nights could have to do with the difficulty, when, up from the valley below, from out the darkness and the mists, came a strange sound; a sound as if someone were singing a song without words. So wild and weird was the melody; so passionately sweet the voice, it seemed impossible that the music should come from human lips. It was more as though some genie of the forest-clad hills wandered through the mists, singing as he went with the joy of his possessions.

Mrs. Matthews came close to her husband's side, and placed her hand upon his shoulder as he half rose from his chair, his pipe fallen to the floor. Young Matt rose to his feet and moved closer to the girl, who was also standing. The stranger alone kept his seat and he noted the agitation of the others in wonder.

For some moments the sound continued, now soft and low, with the sweet sadness of the wind in the pines; then clear and ringing, it echoed and reechoed along the mountain; now pleadings, as though a soul in darkness prayed a gleam of light; again rising, swelling exultingly, as in glad triumph, only to die away once more to that moaning wail, seeming at last to lose itself in the mists.

Slowly Old Matt sank back into his seat and the stranger heard him mutter, "Poor boy, poor boy." Aunt Mollie was weeping. Suddenly Sammy sprang from the steps and running down the walk to the gate sent a clear, piercing call over the valley: "O—h—h, Pete." The group on the porch listened intently. Again the girl called, and yet again: "O—h—h, Pete." But there was no answer.

"It's no use, honey," said Mrs. Matthews, breaking the silence; "it just ain't no use;" and the young girl came slowly back to the porch.

CHAPTER IV.

A CHAT WITH AUNT MOLLIE.

When the stranger looked from his window the next morning, the valley was still wrapped in its gray blanket. But when he and his host came from the house after breakfast, the sun had climbed well above the ridge, and, save a long, loosely twisted rope of fog that hung above the distant river, the mists were gone. The city man exclaimed with delight at the beauty of the scene.

As they stood watching the sheep—white specks in the distance— climbing out of the valley where the long shadows still lay, to the higher, sunlit pastures, Mr. Matthews said, "We've all been a talkin' about you this mornin', Mr. Howitt, and we'd like mighty well to have you stop with us for a spell. If I understood right, you're just out for your health anyway, and you'll go a long ways, sir, before you find a healthier place than this right here. We ain't got much such as you're used to, I know, but what we have is yourn, and we'd be proud to have you make yourself to home for as long as you'd like to stay. You see it's been a good while since we met up with anybody like you, and we count it a real favor to have you."

Mr. Howitt accepted the invitation with evident pleasure, and, soon after, the mountaineer rode away to Bear Creek, on his quest for a man to herd sheep. Young Matt had already gone with his team to the field on the hillside west of the house, and the brown pony stood at the gate ready for Sammy Lane to return to her home on Dewey Bald.

"I'd like the best in the world to stay, Aunt Mollie," she said, in answer to Mrs. Matthews' protest; "but you know there is no one to feed the stock, and besides Mandy Ford will be back sometime to-day."

The older woman's arm was around the girl as they went down the walk. "You must come over real often, now, honey; you know it won't he long 'til you'll be a leavin' us for good. How do you reckon you'll like bein' a fine lady, and livin' in the city with them big folks?"

The girl's face flushed, and her eyes had that wide questioning look, as she answered slowly, "I don't know, Aunt Mollie; I ain't never seen a sure 'nough fine lady; I reckon them city folks are a heap different from us, but I reckon they're just as human. It would be nice to have lots of money and pretties, but somehow I feel like there's a heap more than that to think about. Any how," she added brightly, "I ain't goin' for quite a spell yet, and you know 'Preachin' Bill' says, 'There ain't no use to worry 'bout the choppin' 'til the dogs has treed the coon.' I'll sure come over every day."

Mrs. Matthews kissed the girl, and then, standing at the gate, watched until pony and rider had disappeared in the forest.

Later Aunt Mollie, with a woman's fondness for a quiet chat, brought the potatoes she was preparing for dinner, to sit with Mr. Howitt on the porch. "I declare I don't know what we'll do without Sammy," she said; "I just can't bear to think of her goin' away."

The guest, feeling that some sort of a reply was expected, asked, "Is the family moving from the neighborhood?"

"No, sir, there ain't no family to move. Just Sammy and her Pa, and Jim Lane won't never leave this country again. You see Ollie Stewart's uncle, his father's brother it is, ain't got no children of his own, and he wrote for Ollie to come and live with him in the city. He's to go to school and learn the business, foundry and machine shops, or something like that it is; and if the boy does what's right, he's to get it all some day; Ollie and Sammy has been promised ever since the talk first began about his goin'; but they'll wait now until he gets through his schoolin'. It'll be mighty nice for Sammy, marryin' Ollie, but we'll miss her awful; the whole country will miss her, too. She's just the life of the neighborhood, and everybody 'lows there never was another girl like her. Poor child, she ain't had no mother since she was a little trick, and she has always come to me for everything like, us bein' such close neighbors, and all. But law! sir, I ain't a blamin' her a mite for goin', with her Daddy a runnin' with that ornery Wash Gibbs the way he does."

Again the man felt called upon to express his interest; "Is Mr. Lane in business with this man Gibbs?"

"Law, no! that is, don't nobody know about any business; I reckon it's all on account of those old Bald Knobbers; they used to hold their meetin's on top of Dewey yonder, and folks do say a man was burned there once, because he told some of their secrets. Well, Jim and Wash's daddy, and Wash, all belonged, 'though Wash himself wasn't much more than a boy then; and when the government broke up the gang, old man Gibbs was killed, and Jim went to Texas. It was there that Sammy's Ma died. When Jim come back it wasn't long before he was mighty thick again with Wash and his crowd down on the river, and he's been that way ever since. There's them that says it's the same old gang, what's left of them, and some thinks too that Jim and Wash knows about the old Dewey mine."

Mr. Howitt, remembering his conversation with Jed Holland, asked encouragingly, "Is this mine a very rich one?"

"Don't nobody rightly know about that, sir," answered Aunt Mollie. "This is how it was: away back when the Injuns was makin' trouble 'cause the government was movin' them west to the territory, this old man Dewey lived up there somewhere on that mountain. He was a mighty queer old fellow; didn't mix up with the settlers at all, except Uncle Josh Hensley's boy who wasn't right smart, and didn't nobody know where he come from nor nothing; but all the same, 'twas him that warned the settlers of the trouble, and helped them all through it, scoutin' and such. And one time when they was about out of bullets and didn't have nothin' to make more out of, Colonel Dewey took a couple of men and some mules up on that mountain yonder in the night, and when they got back they was just loaded down with lead, but he wouldn't tell nobody where he got it, and as long as he was with them, the men didn't dare tell. Well, sir, them two men was killed soon after by the Injuns, and when the trouble was finally over, old Dewey disappeared, and ain't never been heard tell of since. They say the mine is somewhere's in a big cave, but nobody ain't never found it, 'though there's them that says the Bald Knobbers used the cave to hide their stuff in, and that's how Jim Lane and Wash Gibbs knows where it is; it's all mighty queer. You can see for yourself that Lost Creek down yonder just sinks clean out of sight all at once; there must be a big hole in there somewhere."

Aunt Mollie pointed with her knife to the little stream that winds like a thread of light down into the Hollow. "I tell you, sir, these hills is pretty to look at, but there ain't much here for a girl like Sammy, and I don't blame her a mite for wantin' to leave. It's a mighty hard place to live, Mr. Howitt, and dangerous, too, sometimes."

"The city has its hardships and its dangers too, Mrs. Matthews; life there demands almost too much at times; I often wonder if it is worth the straggle."

"I guess that's so," replied Aunt Mollie, "but it don't seem like it could be so hard as it is here. I tell Mr. Matthews we've clean forgot the ways of civilized folks; altogether, though, I suppose we've done as well as most, and we hadn't ought to complain."

The old scholar looked at the sturdy figure in its plain calico dress; at the worn hands, busy with their homely task; and the patient, kindly face, across which time had ploughed many a furrow, in which to plant the seeds of character and worth. He thought of other women who had sat with him on hotel verandas, at fashionable watering places; women gowned in silks and laces; women whose soft hands knew no heavier task than the filmy fancy work they toyed with, and whose greatest care, seemingly, was that time should leave upon their faces no record of the passing years. "And this is the stuff," said he to himself, "that makes possible the civilization that produces them." Aloud, he said, "Do you ever talk of going back to your old home?"

"No, sir, not now;" she rested her wet hands idly on the edge of the pan of potatoes, and turned her face toward the clump of pines. "We used to think we'd go back sometime; seemed like at first I couldn't stand it; then the children come, and every time we laid one of them over there I thought less about leavin', until now we never talk about it no more. Then there was our girl, too, Mr. Howitt. No, sir, we won't never leave these hills now."

"Oh, you had a daughter, too? I understood from Mr. Matthews that your children were all boys."

Aunt Mollie worked a few moments longer in silence, then arose and turned toward the house. "Yes, sir, there was a girl; she's buried under that biggest pine you see off there a little to one side. We—we—don't never talk about her. Mr. Matthews can't stand it. Seems like he ain't never been the same since—since—it happened. 'Tain't natural for him to be so rough and short; he's just as good and kind inside as any man ever was or could be. He's real taken with you, Mr. Howitt, and I'm mighty glad you're goin' to stop a spell, for it will do him good. If it hadn't been for Sammy Lane runnin' in every day or two, I don't guess he could have stood it at all. I sure don't know what we'll do now that she's goin' away. Then there's—there's—that at the ranch in Mutton Hollow; but I guess I'd better not try to tell you about that. I wish Mr. Matthews would, though; maybe he will. You know so much more than us; I know most you could help us or tell us about things.

CHAPTER V.

"JEST NOBODY."

After the midday meal, while walking about the place, Mr. Howitt found a well worn path; it led him to the group of pines not far from the house, where five rough head stones marked the five mounds placed side by side. A little apart from these was another mound, alone.

Beneath the pines the needles made a carpet, firm and smooth, figured by the wild woodbine that clambered over the graves; moss had gathered on the head stones, and the wind, in the dark branches above, moaned ceaselessly. About the little plot of ground a rustic fence of poles was built, and the path led to a stile by which one might enter the enclosure.

The stranger seated himself upon the rude steps. Below and far away he saw the low hills, rolling ridge on ridge like the waves of a great sea, until in the blue distance they were so lost in the sky that he could not say which was mountain and which was cloud. His poet heart was stirred at sight of the vast reaches of the forest all shifting light and shadows; the cool depths of the near-by woods with the sunlight filtering through the leafy arches in streaks and patches of gold on green; and the wide, wide sky with fleets of cloud ships sailing to unseen ports below the hills.

The man sat very still, and as he looked the worn face changed; once, as if at some pleasing memory, he smiled. A gray squirrel with bright eyes full of curious regard peeped over the limb of an oak; a red bird hopping from bush to bush whistled to his mate; and a bob-white's quick call came from a nearby thicket.

The dreamer was aroused at last by the musical tinkle of a bell. He turned his face toward the sound, but could see nothing. The bell was coming nearer; it came nearer still. Then he saw here and there through the trees small, moving patches of white; an old ewe followed by two lambs came from behind a clump of bushes, and the moving patches of white shaped themselves into other sheep feeding in the timber.

Mr. Howitt sat quite still, and, while the old ewe paused to look at him, the lambs took advantage of the opportunity, until their mother was satisfied with her inspection, and by moving on, upset them. Soon the whole flock surrounded him, and, after the first lingering look of inquiry, paid no heed to his presence.

Then from somewhere among the trees came the quick, low bark of a dog. The man looked carefully in every direction; be could see nothing but the sheep, yet he felt himself observed. Again came the short bark; and this time a voice—a girl's voice, Mr. Howitt thought—said, "It's alright, Brave; go on, brother." And from behind a big rock not far away a shepherd dog appeared, followed by a youth of some fifteen years.

He was a lightly built boy; a bit tall for his age, perhaps, but perfectly erect; and his every movement was one of indescribable grace, while he managed, somehow, to wear his rough backwoods garments with an air of distinction as remarkable as it was charming. The face was finely molded, almost girlish, with the large gray eyes, and its frame of yellow, golden hair. It was a sad face when in repose, yet wonderfully responsive to every passing thought and mood. But the eyes, with their strange expression, and shifting light, proclaimed the lad's mental condition.

As the boy came forward in a shy, hesitating way, an expression of amazement and wonder crept into the stranger's face; he left his seat and started forward. "Howard," he said; "Howard."

"That ain't his name, Mister; his name's Pete," returned the youth, in low, soft tones.

In the voice and manner of the lad, no less than in his face and eyes, Mr. Howitt read his story. Unconsciously he echoed the words of Mr. Matthews, "Poor Pete."

The dog lifted his head and looked into the man's face, while his tail wagged a joyful greeting, and, as the man stooped to pat the animal and speak a few kind words, a beautiful smile broke over the delicate features of the youth. Throwing himself upon the ground, he cried, "Come here, Brave"; and taking the dog's face between his hands, said in confidential tones, ignoring Mr. Howitt's presence, "He's a good man, ain't he, brother?" The dog answered with wagging tail. "We sure like him, don't we?" The dog gave a low bark. "Listen, Brave, listen." He lifted his face to the tree tops, then turned his ear to the ground, while the dog, too, seemed to hearken. Again that strange smile illuminated his face; "Yes, yes, Brave, we sure like him. And the tree things like him, too, brother; and the flowers, the little flower things that know everything; they're all a singin' to Pete 'cause he's come. Did you see the flower things in his eyes, and hear the tree things a talkin' in his voice, Brave? And see, brother, the sheep like him too!" Pointing toward the stranger, he laughed aloud. The old ewe had come quite close to the man, and one of the lambs was nibbling at his trousers' leg.

Mr. Howitt seated himself on the stile again, and the dog, released by the youth, came to lie down at his feet; while the boy seemed to forget his companions, and appeared to be listening to voices unheard by them, now and then nodding his head and moving his lips in answer.

The old man looked long and thoughtfully at the youth, his own face revealing a troubled mind. This then was Pete, Poor Pete. "Howard," whispered the man; "the perfect image;" then again he said, half aloud, "Howard."

The boy turned his face and smiled; "That ain't his name, Mister; his name's Pete. Pete seen you yesterday over on Dewey, and Pete he heard the big hills and the woods a singin' when you talked. But Jed he didn't hear. Jed he don't hear nothin' but himself; he can't. But Pete he heard and all Pete's people, too. And the gray mist things come out and danced along the mountain, 'cause they was so glad you come. And Pete went with you along the Old Trail. Course, though, you didn't know. Do you like Pete's people, Mister?" He waved his hands to include the forest, the mountains and the sky; and there was a note of anxiety in the sweet voice as he asked again: "Do you like Pete's friends?"

"Yes, indeed, I like your friends," replied Mr. Howitt, heartily; "and I would like to be your friend too, if you will let me. What is your other name?"

The boy shook his head; "Not me; not me;" he said; "do you like Pete?"

The man was puzzled. "Are you not Pete?" he asked. The delicate face grew sad: "No, no, no," he said in a low moaning tone; "I'm not Pete; Pete, he lives in here;" he touched himself on the breast. "I am—I am—" A look of hopeless bewilderment crept into his eyes; "I don't know who I am; I'm jest nobody. Nobody can't have no name, can he?" He stood with downcast head; then suddenly he raised his face and the shadows lifted, as he said, "But Pete he knows, Mister, ask Pete."

A sudden thought came to Mr. Howitt. "Who is your father, my boy?"

Instantly the brightness vanished; again the words were a puzzled moan; "I ain't got no father, Mister; I ain't me; nobody can't have no father, can he?"

The other spoke quickly; "But Pete had a father; who was Pete's father?" Instantly the gloom was gone and the face was bright again. "Sure, Mister, Pete's got a father; don't you know? Everybody knows that. Look!" He pointed upward to a break in the trees, to a large cumulus cloud that had assumed a fantastic shape. "He lives in them white hills, up there. See him, Mister? Sometimes he takes Pete with him up through the sky, and course I go along. We sail, and sail, and sail, with the big bird things up there, while the sky things sing; and sometimes we play with the cloud things, all day in them white hills. Pete says he'll take me away up there where the star things live, some day, and we won't never come back again; and I won't be nobody no more; and Aunt Mollie says she reckons Pete knows. 'Course, I'd hate mighty much to go away from Uncle Matt and Aunt Mollie and Matt and Sammy, 'cause they're mighty good to me; but I jest got to go where Pete goes, you see, 'cause I ain't nobody, and nobody can't be nothin', can he?"

The stranger was fascinated by the wonderful charm of the boy's manner and words. As the lad's sensitive face glowed or was clouded by each wayward thought, and the music of his sweet voice rose and fell, Mr. Howitt told himself that one might easily fancy the child some wandering spirit of the woods and hills. Aloud, he asked, "Has Pete a mother, too?"

The youth nodded toward the big pine that grew to one side of the group, and, lowering his voice, replied, "That's Pete's mother."

Mr. Howitt pointed to the grave; "You mean she sleeps there?"

"No, no, not there; there!" He pointed up to the big tree, itself. "She never sleeps; don't you hear her?" He paused. The wind moaned through the branches of the pine. Drawing closer to the stranger's side, the boy whispered, "She always talks that a way; always, and it makes Pete feel bad. She wants somebody. Hear her callin', callin', callin'? He'll sure come some day, Mister; he sure will. Say, do you know where he is?"

The stranger, startled, drew back; "No, no, my boy, certainly not; what do you mean; who are you?"

Like the moaning of the pines came the reply, "Nothin', Mister, nobody can't mean nothin', can they? I'm jest nobody. But Pete lives in here; ask Pete."

"Is Pete watching the sheep?" asked Mr. Howitt, anxious to divert the boy's mind to other channels.

"Yes, we're a tendin' 'em now; but they can't trust us, you know; when they call Pete, he just goes, and course I've got to go 'long."

"Who is it calls Pete?" "Why, they, don't you know? I 'lowed you knowed about things. They called Pete last night. The moonlight things was out, and all the shadow things; didn't you see them, Mister? The moonlight things, the wind, the stars, the shadow things, and all the rest played with Pete in the shiny mists, and, course, I was along. Didn't you hear singin'? Pete he always sings that a way, when the moonlight things is out. Seems like he just can't help it."

"But what becomes of the sheep when Pete goes away?"

The boy shook his head sadly; "Sometimes they get so lost that Young Matt can't never find 'em; sometimes wolves get 'em; it's too bad, Mister, it sure is." Then laughing aloud, he clapped his hands; "There was a feller at the ranch to keep 'em, but he didn't stay; Ho! Ho! he didn't stay, you bet he didn't. Pete didn't like him, Brave didn't like him, nothing didn't like him, the trees wouldn't talk when he was around, the flowers died when he looked at 'em, and the birds all stopped singin' and went away over the mountains. He didn't stay, though." Again he laughed. "You bet he didn't stay! Pete knows."

"Why did the man go?" asked Mr. Howitt, thinking to solve a part of the mystery, at least. But the only answer he could draw from the boy was, "Pete knows; Pete knows."

Later when the stranger returned to the house, Pete went with him; at the big gate they met Mr. Matthews, returning unsuccessful from his trip.

"Hello, boy!" said the big man; "How's Pete to-day?"

The lad went with glad face to the giant mountaineer. It was clear that the two were the warmest friends. "Pete's mighty glad to-day, 'cause he's come." He pointed to Mr. Howitt. "Does Pete like him?"

The boy nodded. "All Pete's people like him. Ask him to keep the sheep, Uncle Matt. He won't be scared at the shadow things in the night."

Mr. Matthews smiled, as he turned to his guest. "Pete never makes a mistake in his judgment of men, Mr. Howitt. He's different from us ordinary folks, as you can see; but in some things he knows a heap more. I'm mighty glad he's took up with you, sir. All day I've been thinking I'd tell you about some things I don't like to talk about; I feel after last night like you'd understand, maybe, and might help me, you having education. But still I've been a little afraid, us being such strangers. I know I'm right now, 'cause Pete says so. If you weren't the kind of a man I think you are, he'd never took to you like he has."

That night the mountaineer told the stranger from the city the story that I have put down in the next chapter.

CHAPTER VI.

THE STORY.

Slowly the big mountaineer filled his cob pipe with strong, home grown tobacco, watching his guest keenly the while, from under heavy brows. Behind the dark pines the sky was blood red, and below, Mutton Hollow was fast being lost in the gathering gloom.

When his pipe was lighted, Old Matt said, "Well, sir, I reckon you think some things you seen and heard since you come last night are mighty queer. I ain't sayin', neither, but what you got reasons for thinkin' so."

Mr. Howitt made no reply. And, after puffing a few moments in silence, the other continued, "If it weren't for what you said last night makin' me feel like I wanted to talk to you, and Pete a takin' up with you the way he has, I wouldn't be a tellin' you what I am goin' to now. There's some trails, Mr. Howitt, that ain't pleasant to go back over. I didn't 'low to ever go over this one again. Did you and Pete talk much this afternoon?"

In a few words Mr. Howitt told of his meeting with the strange boy, and their conversation. When he had finished, the big man smoked in silence. It was as if he found it hard to begin. From a tree on the mountain side below, a screech owl sent up his long, quavering call; a bat darted past in the dusk; and away over on Compton Ridge a hound bayed. The mountaineer spoke; "That's Sam Wilson's dog, Ranger; must a' started a fox." The sound died away in the distance. Old Matt began his story.

"Our folks all live back in Illinois. And if I do say so, they are as good stock as you'll find anywhere. But there was a lot of us, and I always had a notion to settle in a new country where there was more room like and land wasn't so dear; so when wife and I was married we come out here. I recollect we camped at the spring below Jim Lane's cabin on yon side of Old Dewey, there. That was before Jim was married, and a wild young buck he was too, as ever you see. The next day wife and I rode along the Old Trail 'til we struck this gap, and here we've been ever since.

"We've had our ups and downs like most folks, sir, and sometimes it looked like they was mostly downs; but we got along, and last fall I bought in the ranch down there in the Hollow. The boy was just eighteen and we thought then that he'd be makin' his home there some day. I don't know how that'll be now, but there was another reason too why we wanted the place, as you'll see when I get to it.

"There was five other boys, as I told you last night. The oldest two would have been men now. The girl"—his voice broke—"the girl she come third; she was twenty when we buried her over there. That was fifteen year ago come the middle of next month.

"Everybody 'lowed she was a mighty pretty baby, and, bein' the only girl, I reckon we made more of her than we did of the boys. She growed up into a mighty fine young woman too; strong, and full of fire and go, like Sammy Lane. Seems to wife and me when Sammy's 'round that it's our own girl come back and we've always hoped that she and Grant would take the ranch down yonder; but I reckon that's all over, now that Ollie Stewart has come into such a fine thing in the city. Anyway, it ain't got nothing to do with this that I'm a tellin' you.

"She didn't seem to care nothin' at all for none of the neighbor boys like most girls do; she'd go with them and have a good time alright, but that was all. 'Peared like she'd rather be with her brothers or her mother or me.

"Well, one day, when we was out on the range a ridin' for stock— she'd often go with me that way—we met a stranger over there at the deer lick in the big low gap, coming along the Old Trail. He was as fine a lookin' man as you ever see, sir; big and grand like, with lightish hair, kind, of wavy, and a big mustache like his hair, and fine white teeth showing when he smiled. He was sure good lookin', damn him! and with his fine store clothes and a smooth easy way of talkin' and actin' he had, 'tain't no wonder she took up with him. We all did. I used to think God never made a finer body for a man. I know now that Hell don't hold a meaner heart than the one in that same fine body. And that's somethin' that bothers me a heap, Mr. Howitt.

"As I say, our girl was built like Sammy Lane, and so far as looks go she was his dead match. I used to wonder when I'd look at them together if there ever was such another fine lookin' pair. I ain't a goin' to tell you his name; there ain't no call to, as I can see. There might be some decent man named the same. But he was one of these here artist fellows and had come into the hills to paint, he said."

A smothered exclamation burst from the listener.

Mr. Matthews, not noticing, continued: "He sure did make a lot of pictures and they seemed mighty nice to us, 'though of course we didn't know nothin' about such things. There was one big one he made of Maggie that was as natural as life. He was always drawin' of her in one way or another, and had a lot of little pictures that didn't amount to much, and that he didn't never finish. But this big one he worked at off and on all summer. It was sure fine, with her a standin' by the ranch spring, holdin' out a cup of water, and smilin' like she was offerin' you a drink."

It was well that the night had fallen. At Old Matt's words the stranger shrank back in his chair, his hand raised as if to ward off a deadly blow. He made a sound in his throat as if he would cry out, but could not from horror or fear. But the darkness hid his face, and the mountaineer, with mind intent upon his story, did not heed.

"He took an old cabin at the foot of the hill near where the sheep corral is now, and fixed it up to work in. The shack had been built first by old man Dewey, him that the mountain's named after. It was down there he painted the big picture of her a standin' by the big spring. We never thought nothin' about her bein' with him so much. Country folks is that way, Mr. Howitt, 'though we ought to knowed better; we sure ought to knowed better." The old giant paused and for some time sat with his head bowed, his forgotten pipe on the floor.

"Well," he began again; "he stopped with us all that summer, and then one day he went out as usual and didn't come back. We hunted the hills out for signs, thinkin' maybe he met up with some trouble. He'd sent all his pictures away the week before, Jim Lane haulin' them to the settlement for him.

"The girl was nigh about wild and rode with me all durin' the hunt, and once when we saw some buzzards circlin', she gave a little cry and turned so white that I suspicioned maybe she got to thinkin' more of him than we knew. Then one afternoon when we were down yonder in the Hollow, she says, all of a sudden like, 'Daddy, it ain't no use a ridin' no more. He ain't met up with no trouble. He's left all the trouble with us.' She looked so piqued and her eyes were so big and starin' that it come over me in a flash what she meant. She saw in a minute that I sensed it, and just hung her head, and we come home.

"She just kept a gettin' worse and worse, Mr. Howitt; 'peared to fade away like, like I watched them big glade lilies do when the hot weather comes. About the only time she would show any life at all was when someone would go for the mail, when she'd always be at the gate a waitin' for us.

"Then one day, a letter come. I brung it myself. She give a little cry when I handed it to her, and run into the house, most like her old self. I went on out to the barn to put up my horse, thinkin' maybe it was goin' to be alright after all; but pretty soon, I heard a scream and then a laugh. 'Fore God, sir, that laugh's a ringin' in my ears yet. She was ravin' mad when I got to her, a laughin', and a screechin', and tryin' to hurt herself, all the while callin' for him to come.

"I read the letter afterwards. It told over and over how he loved her and how no woman could ever be to him what she was; said they was made for each other, and all that; and then it went on to say how he couldn't never see her again; and told about what a grand old family his was, and how his father was so proud and expected such great things from him, that he didn't dare tell, them bein' the last of this here old family, and her bein' a backwoods girl, without any schoolin' or nothin'."

"My God! O, my God!" faltered the stranger's voice in the darkness.

Old Matt talked on in a hard easy tone. "Course it was all wrote out nice and smooth like he talked, but that's the sense of it. He finished it by sayin' that he would be on his way to the old country when the letter reached her, and that it wouldn't be no use to try to find him.

"The girl quieted down after a spell, but her mind never come back. She wasn't just to say plumb crazy, but she seemed kind o' dazed and lost like, and wouldn't take no notice of nobody. Acted all the time like she was expectin' him to come. And she'd stand out there by the gate for hours at a time, watchin' the Old Trail and talkin' low to herself.

"Pete is her boy, Mr. Howitt, and as you've seen he ain't just right. Seems like he was marked some way in his mind like you've seen other folks marked in their bodies. We've done our best by the boy, sir, but I don't guess he'll ever be any better. Once for a spell we tried keepin' him to home, but he got right sick and would o' died sure, if we hadn't let him go; it was pitiful to see him. Everybody 'lows there won't nothin' in the woods hurt him nohow; so we let him come and go, as he likes; and he just stops with the neighbors wherever he happens in. Folks are all as good to him as they can be, 'cause everybody knows how it is. You see, sir, people here don't think nothin' of a wood's colt, nohow, but we was raised different. As wife says, we've most forgot civilized ways, but I guess there's some things a man that's been raised right can't never forget.

"She died when Pete was born, and the last thing she said was, 'He'll come, Daddy, he'll sure come.' Pete says the wind singin' in that big pine over her grave is her a callin' for him yet. It's mighty queer how the boy got that notion, but you see that's the way it is with him.

"And that ain't all, sir." The big man moved his chair nearer the other, and lowered his voice to a hoarse whisper; "Folks say she's come back. There's them that swears they've seen her 'round the old cabin where they used to meet when he painted her picture, the big one, you know. Just before I bought the ranch, it was first; and that's why we can't get no one to stay with the sheep.

"I don't know, Mr. Howitt; I don't know. I've thought a heap about it, I ain't never seen it myself, and it 'pears to me that if she *could* come back at all, she'd sure come to her old Daddy. Then again I figure it that bein' took the way she was, part of her dead, so to speak, from the time she got that letter, and her mind so set on his comin' back, that maybe somehow—you see—that maybe she is sort a waitin' for him there. Many's the time I have prayed all night that God would let me meet him again just once, or that proud father of his'n, just once, sir; I'd glad go to Hell if I could only meet them first. If she is waitin' for him down there, he'll come; *he'll sure come. Hell couldn't hold him against such as that, and when he comes—"*

Unconsciously, as he spoke the last sentences, the giant's voice took a tone of terrible meaning, and he slowly rose from his seat. When he uttered the last word he was standing erect, his muscles tense, his powerful frame shaken with passion.

There was an inarticulate cry of horror, as the mountaineer's guest started to his feet. A moment he stood, then sank back into his chair, a cowering, shivering heap.

Long into the night, the stranger walked the floor of his little room under the roof, his face drawn and white, whispering half aloud things that would have startled his unsuspecting host. *"My* boy—*my* boy—*mine!* To do such a thing as that! Howard—Howard. O Christ! that I should live to be glad that you are dead! And that picture! His masterpiece, the picture that made his fame, the picture he would never part with, and that we could never find! I see it all now! Just God, what a thing to carry on one's soul!"

Once he paused to stand at the window, looking down upon the valley. The moon had climbed high above the mountain, but beneath the flood of silver light the shadows lay dark and deep in Mutton Hollow. Then as he stood there, from out the shadowy gloom, came the wild, weird song they had heard the evening before. The man the window groaned. The song sank to a low, moaning wail, and he seemed to hear again the wind in the pine above the grave of the murdered girl. She was calling, calling—would he come back? Back from the grave, could he come? The words of the giant mountaineer seemed burned into the father's brain; *Hell couldn't hold him against such as that."*

Then the man with the proud face, the face of a scholar and poet, drew back from the window, shaking with a fear he could not control. He crept into a corner and crouched upon the floor. With wide eyes, he stared into the dark. He prayed.

And this is how it came about that the stranger, who followed the Old Trail along the higher sunlit ground, followed, also, the other trail down into the valley where the gloomy shadows are; there to live at the ranch near the haunted cabin—the shepherd of Mutton Hollow.

CHAPTER VII.

WHAT IS LOVE?

Sammy Lane rode very slowly on her way home from the Matthews place that morning after the stranger had arrived. She started out at her usual reckless gait, but that was because she knew that Young Matt was watching her.

Once in the timber, the brown pony was pulled to a walk, and by the time they came out into the open again, the little horse, unrebuked by his mistress, was snatching mouthfuls of grass as he strolled along the trail. Sammy was thinking; thinking very seriously. Aunt Mollie's parting question had stirred the girl deeply.

Sammy had seen few people who did not belong to the backwoods. The strangers she had met were hunters or cattlemen, and these had all been, in dress and manner, not unlike the natives themselves. This man, who had come so unexpectedly out of the mists the night before, was unlike anyone the young woman had ever known. Like Jed Holland, she felt somehow as if he were a superior being. The Matthews family were different in many ways from those born and raised in the hills. And Sammy's father, too, was different. But this stranger—it was quite as though he belonged to another world.

Coming to the big, low gap, the girl looked far away to the blue line of hills, miles, and miles away. The stranger had come from over these, she thought; and then she fell to wondering what that world beyond the farthest cloud-like ridge was like.

Of all the people Sammy had ever known, young Stewart was the only one who had seen even the edge of that world to tell her about it. Her father and her friends, the Matthews's, never talked of the old days. She had known Ollie from a child. With Young Matt they had gone to and from the log school house along the same road. Once, before Mr. Stewart's death, the boy had gone with his father for a day's visit to the city, and ever after had been a hero to his backwoods schoolmates. It was this distinction, really, that first won Sammy's admiration, and made them sweethearts before the girl's skirts had touched the tops of her shoes. Before the woman in her was fairly awake she had promised to be his wife; and they were going away now to live in that enchanted land.

Spying an extra choice bunch of grass a few steps to one side of the path, Brownie turned suddenly toward the valley; and the girl's eyes left the distant ridge for the little cabin and the sheep corral in Mutton Hollow. Sammy always spoke of that cabin as "Young Matt's house." And, all unbidden now, the thought came, who would live with the big fellow down there in the valley when she had gone far away to make her home with Ollie and his people in the city?

An impatient tug at the reins informed Brownie that his mistress was aware of his existence, and, for a time, the pony was obliged to pass many a luscious bunch of grass. But soon the reins fell slack again. The little horse moved slowly, and still more slowly, until, by the relaxed figure of his rider, he knew it was safe to again browse on the grass along the path.

So, wondering, dreaming, Sammy Lane rode down the trail that morning—the trail that is nobody knows how old. And on the hill back of the Matthews house a team was standing idle in the middle of the field.

At the big rock on the mountain side, where the trail seems to pause a moment before starting down to the valley, the girl slipped from her saddle, and, leaving Brownie to wander at will, climbed to her favorite seat. Half reclining in the warm sunshine, she watched the sheep feeding near, and laughed aloud as she saw the lambs with wagging tails, greedily suckling at their mother's sides; near by in a black-haw bush a mother bird sat on her nest; a gray mare, with a week old colt following on unsteady legs, came over the ridge; and not far away; a mother sow with ten squealing pigs came out of the timber. Keeping very still the young woman watched until they disappeared around the mountain. Then, lifting her arms above her head, she stretched her lithe form out upon the warm rocky couch with the freedom and grace of a wild thing of the woods.

Sammy Lane knew nothing of the laws and customs of the, so-called, best society. Her splendid young womanhood was not the product of those social traditions and rules that kill the instinct of her kind before it is fairly born. She was as free and as physically perfect as any of the free creatures that lived in the hills. And, keenly alive to the life that throbbed and surged about her, her woman's heart and soul responded to the spirit of the season. The droning of the bees in the blossoms that grew in a cranny of the rock; the tinkle, tinkle of the sheep bells, as the flock moved slowly in their feeding; and the soft breathing of Mother Earth was in her ears; while the gentle breeze that stirred her hair came heavy with the smell of growing things. Lying so, she looked far up into the blue sky where a buzzard floated on lazy wings. If she were up there she perhaps could see that world beyond the hills. Then suddenly a voice came to her, Aunt Mollie's voice, "How do you reckon you'll like bein' a fine lady, Sammy, and a livin' in the city with the big folks?"

The girl turned on her side and rising on one elbow looked again at

Mutton Hollow with its little cabin half hidden in the timber. And, as she looked, slowly her rich red life colored cheek, and neck, and brow. With a gesture of impatience, Sammy turned away to her own home on the southern slope of the mountain, just in time to see a young woman ride into the clearing and dismount before the cabin door. It was her friend, Mandy Ford. The girl on the rock whistled to her pony, and, mounting, made her way down the hill.

All that day the strange guest at the Matthews place was the one topic of conversation between the two girls.

"Shucks," said Mandy, when Sammy had finished a very minute description of Mr. Howitt; "he's jest some revenue, like's not."

Sammy tossed her head; "Revenue! you ought to see him! Revenues don't come in no such clothes as them, and they don't talk like him, neither."

"Can't tell 'bout revenues," retorted the other. "Don't you mind how that'n fooled everybody over on th' bend last year? He was jest as common as common, and folks all 'lowed he was just one of 'em."

"But this one ain't like anybody that we ever met up with, and that's jest it," returned Sammy.

Mandy shook her head; "You say he ain't huntin'; he sure ain't buyin' cattle this time o' year; and he ain't a wantin' t' locate a comin' in on foot; what else can he be but a revenue?"

To which Sammy replied with an unanswerable argument; "Look a here, Mandy Ford; you jest tell me, would a low down revenue ask a blessin' like Parson Bigelow does?"

At this Mandy gave up the case, saying in despair, "Well, what is he a doin' here then? 'Tain't likely he's done come into th' woods fer nothin'."

"He told Old Matt that he was sick and tired of it all," answered the other.

"Did he look like he was ailin'?"

Sammy replied slowly, "I don't reckon it's that kind of sickness he meant; and when you look right close into his eyes, he does 'pear kind o' used up like."

In connection with this discussion, it was easy to speak of Miss Lane's fairy prospects, for, was not the stranger from the city? and was not Sammy going to live in that land of wonders? The two girls were preparing for the night, when Sammy, who was seated on the edge of the bed, paused, with one shoe off, to ask thoughtfully, "Mandy, what is love, anyhow?"

Mandy looked surprised. "I reckon you ought to know," she said with a laugh; "Ollie's been a hangin' 'round you ever since I can remember."

Sammy was struggling with a knot in the other shoe lace; "Yes," she admitted slowly; "I reckon I had ought to know; but what do you say it is, Mandy?"

"Why, hit's—hit's—jest a caring fer somebody more'n fer ary one else in th' whole world."

"Is that all?" The knot was still stubborn.

"No, hit ain't all. Hit's a goin' t' live with somebody an' a lettin' him take care o' you, 'stead o' your folks." Sammy was still struggling with the knot. "An' hit's a cookin' an' a scrubbin' an' a mendin' fer him, an'—an'—sometimes hit's a splittin' wood, an' a doin' chores, too; an' I reckon that's all."

Just here the knot came undone, and the shoe dropped to the floor with a thud. Sammy sat upright. "No, it ain't, Mandy; it's a heap more'n that; it's a nursin' babies, and a takin' care of 'em 'till they're growed up, and then when they're big enough to take care o' themselves, and you're old and in the way, like Grandma Bowles, it's a lookin' back over it all, and bein' glad you done married the man you did. It's a heap more'n livin' with a man, Mandy; it's a doin' all that, without ever once wishin' he was somebody else."

This was too much for Mandy; she blushed and giggled, then remarked, as she gazed admiringly at her friend, "You'll look mighty fine, Sammy, when you get fixed up with all them pretties you'll have when you an' Ollie git married. I wish my hair was bright an' shiny like yourn. How do you reckon you'll like bein' a fine lady anyhow?"

Here it was again. Sammy turned upon her helpless friend, with, "How do I know if I would like it or not? What is bein' a fine lady, anyhow?"

"Why, bein' a fine lady is—is livin' in a big house with carpets on th' floor, an' lookin' glasses, an' not havin' no work t' do, an' wearin' pretty clothes, with lots of rings an' things, an'— an'," she paused; then finished in triumph, "an' a ridin' in a carriage."

That wide questioning look was in Sammy's eyes as she returned, "It's a heap more'n that, Mandy. I don't jest sense what it is, but I know 'tain't all them things that makes a sure 'nough lady. 'Tain't the clothes he wears that makes Mr. Howitt different from the folks we know. He don't wear no rings, and he walks. He's jest different 'cause he's different; and would be, no matter what he had on or where he was."

This, too, was beyond Mandy. Sammy continued, as she finished her preparations for retiring; "This here house is plenty big enough for me, least wise it would be if it had one more room like the cabin in Mutton Hollow; carpets would be mighty dirty and unhandy to clean when the men folks come trampin' in with their muddy boots; I wouldn't want to wear no dresses so fine I couldn't knock 'round in the brush with them; and it would be awful to have nothin' to do; as for a carriage, I wouldn't swap Brownie for a whole city full of carriages." She slipped into bed and stretched out luxuriously. "Do you reckon I could be a fine lady, and be as I am now, a livin' here in the hills?"

The next day Mandy went back to her home on Jake Creek. And in the evening Sammy's father, with Wash Gibbs, returned, both men and horses showing the effects of a long, hard ride.

CHAPTER VIII.

"WHY AIN'T WE GOT NO FOLKS."

Preachin' Bill says "There's a heap o' difference in most men, but Jim Lane now he's more different than ary man you ever seed. Ain't no better neighbor'n Jim anywhere. Ride out o' his way any time t' do you a favor. But you bet there ain't ary man lives can ask Jim any fool questions while Jim's a lookin' at him. Tried it onct myself. Jim was a waitin' at th' ferry fer Wash Gibbs, an' we was a talkin' 'long right peart 'bout crops an' th' weather an' such, when I says, says I, like a dumb ol' fool, 'How'd you like it down in Texas, Jim, when you was there that time?' I gonies! His jaw shet with a click like he'd cocked a pistol, an' that look o' hisn, like he was a seein' plumb through you, come int' his eyes, an' he says, says he, quiet like, 'D' you reckon that rain over on James yesterday raised th' river much?' An' 'fore I knowed it, I was a tellin' him how that ol' red bull o' mine treed th' Perkins' boys when they was a possum huntin'."

Many stories of the Bald Knobber days, when the law of the land was the law of rifle and rope, were drifting about the country side, and always, when these tales were recited, the name of Jim Lane was whispered; while the bolder ones wondered beneath their breath where Jim went so much with that Wash Gibbs, whose daddy was killed by the Government.

Mr. Lane was a tall man, well set up, with something in his face and bearing that told of good breeding; southern blood, one would say, by the dark skin, and the eyes, hair, and drooping mustache of black.

His companion, Wash Gibbs, was a gigantic man; taller and heavier, even, than the elder Matthews, but more loosely put together than Old Matt; with coarse, heavy features, and, as Grandma Bowles said, "the look of a sheep killin' dog." Grandma, being very near her journey's end, could tell the truth even about Wash Gibbs, but others spoke of the giant only in whispers, save when they spoke in admiration of his physical powers.

As the two men swung stiffly from their saddles, Sammy came running to greet her father with a kiss of welcome; this little exhibition of affection between parent and child was one of the many things that marked the Lanes as different from the natives of that region. Your true backwoodsman carefully hides every sign of his love for either family or friends. Wash Gibbs stood looking on with an expression upon his brutal face that had very little of the human in it.

Releasing his daughter, Mr. Lane said, "Got anything to eat, honey? We're powerful hungry. Wash 'lowed we'd better tie up at the river, but I knew you'd be watching for me. The horses are plumb beat." And Gibbs broke in with a coarse laugh, "I wouldn't mind killin' a hoss neither, if I was t' git what you do at th' end o' th' ride."

To this, Jim made no reply; but began loosening the saddle girths, while Sammy only said, as she turned toward the house, "I'll have supper ready for you directly, Daddy."

While the host was busy caring for his tired horse, the big man, who did not remove the saddle from his mount, followed the girl into the cabin. "Can't you even tell a feller, Howdy?" he exclaimed, as he entered the kitchen.

"I did tell you, Howdy," replied the girl sharply, stirring up the fire.

" 'Pears like you might o' been a grain warmer about hit," growled the other, seating himself where he could watch her. "If I'd been Young Matt er that skinny Ollie Stewart, you'd a' been keen enough."

Sammy turned and faced him with angry eyes; "Look a here, Wash Gibbs, I done tol' you last Thursday when you come for Daddy that you'd better let me alone. I don't like you, and I don't aim to ever have anything to do with you. You done fixed yourself with me that time at the Cove picnic. I'll tell Daddy about that if you don't mind. I don't want to make no trouble, but you just got to quit pestering me."

The big fellow sneered. "I 'lowed you might change your mind 'bout that some day. Jim ain't goin' t' say nothin' t' me, an' if he did, words don't break no bones. I'm a heap th' best man in this neck o' th' woods, an' your Paw knows hit. You know it, too."

Under his look, the blood rushed to the girl's face in a burning blush. In spite of her anger she dropped her eyes, and, without attempting a reply, turned to her work.

A moment later, Mr. Lane entered the room; a single glance at his daughter's face, a quick look at Wash Gibbs, as the bully sat following with wolfish eyes every movement of the girl, and Jim stepped quietly in front of his guest. At the same moment, Sammy left the house for a bucket of water, and Wash turned toward his host with a start to find the dark faced man gazing at him with a look that few men could face with composure. Without a word, Jim's right hand crept stealthily inside his hickory shirt, where a button was missing.

For a moment Gibbs tried to return the look. He failed. Something he read in the dark face before him—some meaning light in those black eyes—made him tremble and he felt, rather than saw, Jim's hand resting quietly now inside the hickory shirt near his left arm pit. The big man's face went white beneath the tan, his eyes wavered and shifted, he hung his head and shuffled his feet uneasily, like an overgrown school-boy brought sharply to task by the master.

Then Jim, his hand still inside his shirt, drawled, softly, but with a queer metallic ring in his voice, "Do you reckon it's a goin' t' storm again?"

At the commonplace question, the bully drew a long breath and looked around. "We might have a spell o' weather," he muttered; "but I don't guess it'll be t'night."

Then Sammy returned and they had supper.

Next to his daughter, Jim Lane loved his violin, and with good reason, for the instrument had once belonged to his great- grandfather, who, tradition says, was a musician of no mean ability.

Preachin' Bill "'lowed there was a heap o' difference between a playin' a violin an' jest fiddlin'. You wouldn't know some fellers was a makin' music, if you didn't see 'em a pattin' their foot; but hit ain't that a way with Jim Lane. He sure do make music, real music." As no one ever questioned Bill's judgment, it is safe to conclude that Mr. Lane inherited something of his great- grandfather's ability; along with his treasured instrument.

When supper was over, and Wash Gibbs had gone on his way; Jim took the violin from its peg above the fireplace, and, tucking it lovingly under his chin, gave himself up to his favorite pastime, while Sammy moved busily about the cabin, putting things right for the night.

When her evening tasks were finished, the girl came and stood before her father. At once the music ceased and the violin was laid carefully aside. Sammy seated herself on her father's knee.

"Law', child, but you're sure growin' up," said Jim, with a mock groan at her weight.

"Yes, Daddy, I reckon I'm about growed; I'll be nineteen come Christmas."

"O shucks!" ejaculated the man. "It wasn't more'n last week that you was washin' doll clothes, down by the spring."

The young woman laughed. "I didn't wash no doll clothes last week," she said. Then her voice changed, and that wide, questioning look, the look that made one think so of her father, came into her eyes. "There's something I want to ask you, Daddy Jim. You—you know—Ollie's goin' away, an'—an'—an' I was thinkin' about it all day yesterday, an', Daddy, why ain't we got no folks?"

Mr. Lane stirred uneasily. Sammy continued, "There's the Matthews's, they've got kin back in Illinois; Mandy Ford's got uncles and aunts over on

Lang Creek; Jed Holland's got a grandad and mam, and even Preachin' Bill talks about a pack o' kin folks over in Arkansaw. Why ain't we got no folks, Daddy?"

The man gazed long and thoughtfully at the fresh young face of his child; and the black eyes looked into the brown eyes keenly, as he answered her question with another question, "Do you reckon you love him right smart, honey? Are you sure, dead sure you ain't thinkin' of what he's got 'stead of what he is? I know it'll be mighty nice for you to be one of the fine folks and they're big reasons why you ought, but it's goin' to take a mighty good man to match you—a mighty good man. And it's the man you've got to live with, not his money."

"Ollie's good, Daddy," she returned in a low voice, her eyes fixed upon the floor.

"I know, I know," replied Jim. "He wouldn't do nobody no harm; he's good enough that way, and I ain't a faultin' him. But you ought to have a *man,* a sure enough good man."

"But tell me, Daddy, why ain't we got no folks?"

The faintest glimmer of a smile came into the dark face; "You're sure growed up, girl; you're sure growed up, girl; you sure are. An' I reckon you might as well know." Then he told her.

CHAPTER IX.

SAMMY LANE'S FOLKS.

It began on a big southern plantation, where there were several brothers and sisters, with a gentleman father of no little pride, and a lady mother of equal pride and great beauty.

With much care for detail, Jim drew a picture of the big mansion with its wide lawns, flower gardens and tree bordered walks; with its wealth of culture, its servants, and distinguished guests; for, said he, "When you get to be a fine lady, you ought to know that you got as good blood as the best of the thorough-breds." And Sammy, interrupting his speech with a kiss, bade him go on with his story.

Then he told how the one black sheep of that proud southern flock had been cast forth from the beautiful home while still hardly grown; and how, with his horse, gun and violin, the wanderer had come into the heart of the Ozark wilderness, when the print of moccasin feet was still warm on the Old Trail. Jim sketched broadly here, and for some reason did not fully explain the cause of his banishment; neither did he comment in any way upon its justice or injustice.

Time passed, and a strong, clear-eyed, clean-limbed, deep-bosomed mountain lass, with all the mastering passion of her kind, mated the free, half wild, young hunter; and they settled in the cabin by the spring on the southern slope of Dewey. Then the little one came, and in her veins there was mingled the blue blood of the proud southerners and the warm red life of her wilderness mother.

Again Jim's story grew rich in detail. Holding his daughter at arm's length, and looking at her through half-closed eyes, he said, "You're like her, honey; you're mighty like her; same eyes, same hair, same mouth, same build, same way of movin', strong, but smooth and free like. She could run clean to the top of Dewey, or sit a horse all day. Do you ever get tired, girl?"

Sammy laughed, and shook her head; "I've run from here to the signal tree, lots of times, Daddy."

"You're like the old folks, too," mused Jim; "like them in what you think and say."

"Tell me more," said the girl. "Seems like I remember bein' in a big wagon, and there was a woman there too; was she my mother?"

Jim nodded, and unconsciously lowered his voice, as he said, "It was in the old Bald Knobber time. Things happened in them days, honey. Many's the night I've seen the top of old Dewey yonder black with men. It was when things was broke up, that—that your mother and me thought we could do better in Texas; so we went," Jim was again sketching broadly.

"Your mother left us there, girl. Seemed like she couldn't stand it, bein' away from the hills or somethin', and she just give up. I never did rightly know how it was. We buried her out there, way out on the big plains."

"I remember her a little," whispered Sammy. Jim continued; "Then after a time you and me come back to the old place. Your mother named you Samantha, girl, but bein' as there wasn't no boy, I always called you Sammy. It seems right enough that way now, for you've sure been more'n a son to me since we've been alone; and that's one reason why I learned you to ride and shoot with the best of them.

"There's them that says I ain't done right by you, bringing you up without ary woman about the place; and I don't know as I have, but somehow I couldn't never think of no woman as I ought, after living with your mother. And then there was Aunt Mollie to learn you how to cook and do things about the house. I counted a good bit, too, on the old stock, and it sure showed up right. You're like the old folks, girl, in the way you think, but you're like your mother in the way you look."

Sammy's arms went around her father's neck, "You're a good man, Daddy Jim; the best Daddy a girl ever had; and if I ain't all bad, it's on account of you." There was a queer look on the man's dark face. He had sketched some parts of his tale with a broad hand, indeed.

The girl raised her head again; "But, Daddy, I wish you'd do something for me. I—I don't like Wash Gibbs to be a comin' here. I wish you'd quit ridin' with him, Daddy. I'm—I'm afeared of him; he looks at me so. He's a sure bad one—I know he is, Daddy."

Jim laughed and again there was that odd metallic note in his voice; "I've knowed him a long time, honey. Me and his daddy was— was together when he died; and you used to sit on Wash's knee when you was a little tad. Not that he's so mighty much older than you, but he was a man's size at fifteen. You don't understand, girl, but I've got to go with him sometimes. But don't you fret; Wash Gibbs ain't goin' to hurt me, and he won't come here more'n I can help, either." Then he changed the subject abruptly. "Tell me what you've been doin' while I was away."

Sammy told of' her visit to their friends at the Matthews place, and of the stranger who had come into the neighborhood. As the girl talked, her father questioned her carefully, and several times the metallic note crept into his soft, drawling speech, while into his eyes came that peculiar, searching look, as if he would draw from his daughter even more than she knew of the incident. Once he rose, and, going to the door, stood looking out into the night.

Sammy finished with her answer to Mandy Ford's opinion of the stranger; "You don't reckon a revenue would ask a blessin', do you, Daddy? Seems like he just naturally wouldn't dast; God would make the victuals stick in his throat and choke him sure."

Jim laughed, as he replied, "I don't know, girl; I never heard of a revenue's doin' such. But a feller can't tell."

When Sammy left him to retire for the night, her father picked up the violin again, and placed it beneath his chin as if to play; but he did not touch the strings, and soon hung the instrument in its place above the mantel. Then, going to the doorway, he lighted his pipe, and, for a full hour, sat, looking up the Old Trail toward the Matthews place, his right hand thrust into the bosom of his hickory shirt, where the button was missing.

CHAPTER X.

A FEAT OF STRENGTH AND A CHALLENGE.

What the club is to the city man, and the general store or postoffice to the citizens of the country village, the mill is to the native of the backwoods.

Made to saw the little rough lumber he needs in his primitive building, or to grind his corn into the rough meal, that is his staff of life, the mill does more for the settler than this; it brings together the scattered population, it is the news center, the heart of the social life, and the hub of the industrial wheel.

On grinding day, the Ozark mountaineer goes to mill on horse-back, his grist in a sack behind the saddle, or, indeed, taking place of the saddle itself. The rule is, first come, first served. So, while waiting his turn, or waiting for a neighbor who will ride in the same direction, the woodsman has time to contribute his share to the gossip of the country side, or to take part in the discussions that are of more or less vital interest. When the talk runs slow, there are games; pitching horse shoes, borrowed from the blacksmith shop—there is always a blacksmith shop near by; running or jumping contests, or wrestling or shooting matches.

Fall Creek Mill, owned and operated by Mr. Matthews and his son, was located on Fall Creek in a deep, narrow valley, about a mile from their home.

A little old threshing engine, one of the very first to take the place of the horse power, and itself in turn already pushed to the wall by improved competitors, rolled the saw or the burr. This engine, which had been rescued by Mr. Matthews from the scrap-pile of a Springfield machine shop, was accepted as evidence beyond question of the superior intelligence and genius of the Matthews family. In fact, Fall Creek Mill gave the whole Mutton Hollow neighborhood such a tone of up-to-date enterprise, that folks from the Bend, or the mouth of the James, looked upon the Mutton Hollow people with no little envy and awe, not to say even jealousy.

The settlers came to the Matthews mill from far up the creek, crossing and recrossing the little stream; from Iron Spring and from Gardner, beyond Sand Ridge, following faint, twisting bridle paths through the forest; from the other side of Dewey Bald, along the Old Trail; from the Cove and from the Postoffice at the Forks, down the wagon road, through the pinery; and from Wolf Ridge and the head of Indian Creek beyond, climbing the rough mountains. Even from the river bottoms they came, yellow and shaking with ague, to swap tobacco and yarns, and to watch with never failing interest the crazy old engine, as Young Matt patted, and coaxed, and flattered her into doing his will.

They began coming early that grinding day, two weeks after Mr. Howitt had been installed at the ranch. But the young engineer was ready, with a good head of steam in the old patched boiler, and the smoke was rising from the rusty stack, in a long, twisting line, above the motionless tree tops.

It was a great day for Young Matt; great because he knew that Sammy Lane would be coming to mill; he would see her and talk with her; perhaps if he were quick enough, he might even lift her from the brown pony.

It was a great day, too, because Ollie Stewart would be saying good-by, and before to-morrow would be on his way out of the hills. Not that it mattered whether Ollie went or not. It was settled that Sammy was going to marry young Stewart; that was what mattered. And Young Matt had given her up. And, as he had told his father in the barn that day, it was alright. But still—still it was a great day, because Ollie would be saying good-by.

It was a great day in Young Matt's life, too, because on that day he would issue his challenge to the acknowledged champion of the country-side, Wash Gibbs. But Young Matt did not know this until afterwards, for it all came about in a very unexpected way.

The company had been discussing the new arrival in the neighborhood, and speculating as to the probable length of Mr. Howitt's stay at the ranch, and while Young Matt was in the burr- house with his father, they had gone over yet again the familiar incidents of the ghost story; how "Budd Wilson seen her as close as from here t' th' shop yonder." How "Joe Gardner's mule had gone plumb hog-wild when he tried to ride past the ol' ruins near th' ranch." And "how Lem Wheeler, while out hunting that roan steer o' hisn, had heard a moanin' an' a wailin' under the bluff."

Upon Young Matthews returning to his engine, the conversation had been skilfully changed, to Ollie Stewart and his remarkable good fortune. From Ollie and his golden prospects, it was an easy way to Sammy Lane and her coming marriage.

Buck Thompson was just concluding a glowing tribute to the girl's beauty of face and form when Young Matt reached for an axe lying near the speaker. Said Buck, "Preachin' Bill 'lowed t'other day hit didn't make no difference how much money th' ol' man left Ollie he'd be a poor sort of a man anyhow; an' that there's a heap better men than him right here in th' hills that Sammy could a' had fer th' askin'."

"How 'bout that, Matt?" called a young fellow from the river.

The big man's face flushed at the general laugh which followed, and he answered hotly, as he swung his axe, "You'd better ask Wash Gibbs; I hear he says he's the best man in these woods."

"I reckin as how Wash can back his jedgment there," said Joe.

"Wash is a sure good man," remarked Buck, "but there's another not so mighty far away that'll pretty nigh hold, him level." He looked significantly to where Young Matt was making the big chips fly.

"Huh," grunted Joe. "I tell you, gentlemen, that there man, Gibbs, is powerful; yes, sir, he sure is. Tell you what I seed him do." Joe pulled a twist of tobacco from his hip pocket, and settled down upon his heels, his back against a post. "Wash an' me was a goin' to th' settlement last fall, an' jest this side th' camp house, on Wilderness Road, we struck a threshin' crew stuck in th' mud with their engine. Had a break down o' some kind. Somethin' th' matter with th' hind wheel. And jest as Wash an' me drove up, th' boss of th' outfit was a tellin' 'em t' cut a big pole for a pry t' lift th' hind ex, so's they could block it up, an' fix th' wheel.

"Wash he looked at 'em a minute an' then says, says he, 'Hold on, boys; you don't need ary pole.'

" 'What do you know 'bout an engine, you darned hill billy,' says th' old man, kind o' short.

" 'Don't know nothin' 'bout an engine, you prairie hopper,' says Wash, 'but I know you don't need no pole t' lift that thing.'

" 'How'd you lift it then?' says t'other.

" 'Why I'd jest catch holt an' lift,' says Wash.

"The gang like t' bust themselves laughin'. 'Why you blame fool,' says the boas; 'do you know what that engine'll weigh?"

" 'Don't care a cuss *what* she'll weigh,' says Wash. 'She ain't *planted* there, is she?' An' with that he climbs down from th' wagon, an' dad burn me if he didn't take holt o' that hind ex an' lift one whole side o' that there engine clean off th' ground. Them fellers jest stood 'round an' looked at him t' beat th' stir. 'Well,' says Wash, still a keepin' his holt; slide a block under her an' I'll mosey along!

"That boss didn't say a word 'till he'd got a bottle from a box on th' wagon an' handed, hit t' Wash; then he says kind o' scared like, 'Where in hell are you from, Mister?'

" 'Oh, I'm jest a kid from over on Roark,' says Wash, handin' th' bottle t' me. 'You ought t' see some o' th' *men* in my neighborhood!' Then we went on."

When the speaker had finished, there was quiet for a little; then the young man from the river drawled, "How much did you say that there engine 'd weigh, Joe?"

There was a general laugh at this, which the admirer of Gibbs took good naturedly; "Don't know what she'd weigh but she was 'bout the size o' that one there," he answered.

With one accord everyone turned to inspect the mill engine. "Pretty good lift, Joe. Let's you an' me take a pull at her, Budd," remarked Lem Wheeler.

The two men lifted and strained at the wheel. Then another joined them, and, amid the laughter and good natured raillery of the crowd, the three tried in vain to lift one of the wheels; while Mr. Matthews, seeing some unusual movement, came into the shed and stood with his son, an amused witness of their efforts.

"Sure this engine ain't bigger'n t'other, Joe?" asked one of the group.

"Don't believe she weighs a pound more," replied the mountaineer with conviction. "I tell you, gentlemen, that man Gibbs is a wonder, he sure is."

Old Matt and his son glanced quickly at each other, and the boy shook his head with a smile. This little by-play was lost on the men who were interested in the efforts of different ones, in groups of three, to move the wheel. When they had at last given it up, the young man from the river drawled, "You're right sure hit weren't after th' boas give you that bottle that Wash lifted her, are you Joe? Or wasn't hit on th' way home from th' settlement?"

When the laugh at this insinuation had died out, Buck said thoughtfully, "Tell you what, boys; I'd like t' see Young Matt try that lift."

Mr. Matthews, who was just starting back to the burr-house, paused in the doorway. All eyes were fixed upon his son. "Try her, Matt. Show us what you can do," called the men in chorus. But the young man shook his head, and found something that needed his immediate attention.

All that morning at intervals the mountaineers urged the big fellow to attempt the feat, but he always put them off with some evasive reply, or was too busy to gratify them.

But after dinner, while the men were pitching horse shoes in front of the blacksmith shop, Buck Thompson approached the young engineer alone. "Look a here, Matt," he said, "why don't you try that lift? Durned me if I don't believe you'd fetch her."

The young giant looked around; "I know I can, Buck; I lifted her yesterday while Dad fixed the blockin'; I always do it that way."

Buck looked at him in amazement. "Well, why in thunder don't you show th' boys, then?" he burst forth at last.

" 'Cause if I do Wash Gibbs'll hear of it sure, and I'll have to fight him to settle which is th' best man."

"Good Lord!" ejaculated Buck, with a groan. "If you're afraid o' Wash Gibbs, it's th' first thing I ever knowed you t' be scared o'."

Young Matt looked his friend steadily in the eyes, as he replied; "I ain't afraid of Wash Gibbs; I'm afraid of myself. Mr. Howitt says, 'No man needn't be afraid of nobody but himself.' I've been a thinkin' lately, Buck, an' I see some things that I never see before. I figure it that if I fight Wash Gibbs or anybody else just to see which is th' best man, I ain't no better'n he is. I reckon I'll have to whip him some day, alright, an' I ain't a carin' much how soon it comes; but I ain't a goin' to hurt nobody for nothin' just because I can."

Buck made no reply to this. Such sentiment was a little too much for his primitive notions. He went back to the men by the blacksmith shop.

It was not long, however, until the players left their game, to gather once more about the engine. Lem Wheeler approached Young Matt with a serious air; "Look a here," he said; "we all want t' see you try that lift."

"I ain't got no time for foolin'," replied the young man; "Dad's just pushin' to get done before dark."

"Shucks!" retorted the other; "Hit won't take a minute t' try. Jest catch hold an' show us what you can do."

"What are you all so keen about my liftin' for, anyhow?" demanded the big fellow, suspiciously. "I ain't never set up as the strong man of this country."

"Well, you see it's this way; Buck done bet me his mule colt agin mine that you could lift her; an' we want you to settle th' bet!" exclaimed Lem.

Young Matthews shot a glance at the mountaineer, who grinned joyously. "Yep," said Buck, "that's how it is; I'm a backin' you. Don't want you t' hurt yourself for me, but I sure do need that colt o' Lem's; hit's a dead match for mine."

The giant looked at his friend a moment in silence, then burst into a laugh of appreciation at Buck's hint. "Seein' as how you're backin' me, Buck, I'll have t' get you that mule if I can."

He shut off steam, and, as the engine came to a stop, stooped, and, with apparent ease, lifted the rear wheel a full four inches from the ground.

Loud exclamations of admiration came from the little group of men in the shed. Lem turned with a long face, "Them colts 'll make a fine team, Buck;" he said.

"You bet; come over an' hep me break 'em," replied Buck, with another grin of delight.

"Wait 'till Wash Gibbs hears 'bout this, an' he'll sure be for breakin' Young Matt," put in another.

"Better get your fightin' clothes on, Matt; Wash'll never rest easy until you've done showed him." These and similar remarks revealed the general view of the situation.

While the men were discussing the matter, a thin, high-pitched voice from the edge of the crowd, broke in, "That there's a good lift alright, but hit ain't nothin' t' what I seed when I was t' th' circus in th' city."

Young Matt, who had started the engine again, turned quickly. Ollie Stewart was sitting on a horse near by, and at his side, on the brown pony, was Miss Sammy Lane. They had evidently ridden up just in time to witness the exhibition of the giant's strength.

CHAPTER XI.

OLLIE STEWART'S GOOD-BY.

Beside the splendidly developed young woman, Ollie Stewart appeared but a weakling. His shoulders were too narrow and he stooped; his limbs were thin; his hair black and straight; and his eyes dull.

As Young Matt stepped forward, Ollie dismounted quickly, but the big fellow was first at the brown pony's side. Sammy's eyes shone with admiration, and, as the strong man felt their light, he was not at all sorry that he had won the mule colt for Buck.

"No," she said, declining his offered assistance; she did not wish to get down; they were going to the postoffice and would call for the meal on their way home.

Young Matt lifted the sack of corn from Brownie's back and carried it into the shed. When he returned to the group, Ollie was saying in his thin voice, "In th' circus I seen in the city there was a feller that lifted a man, big as Jed here, clean above his head with one hand."

Buck turned to his big friend. His look was met by a grim smile that just touched the corners of the lad's mouth, and there was a gleam in the blue eyes that betrayed the spirit within. The lean mountaineer again turned to the company, while the boy glanced at Sammy. The girl was watching him and had caught the silent exchange between the two friends.

"Shucks!" said Buck; "Matt could do that easy." "Try it, Matt." "Try Jed here." "Try hit once," called the chorus.

This time the big fellow needed no urging. With Sammy looking on, he could not resist the opportunity which Ollie himself had presented. Without a word, but with a quick tightening of the lips, he stepped forward and caught Jed by the belt with his right hand; and then, before anyone could guess his purpose, he reached out with his other hand, and grasped Ollie himself in the same manner. There was a short step forward, a quick upward swing, and the giant held a man in each hand at full arm's length above his head. Amid the shouts of the crowd, still holding the men, he walked deliberately to the blacksmith shop and back; then lowering them easily to their feet, turned to his engine.

Ollie and Sammy rode away together, up the green arched road, and the little company in the mill shed stood watching them. As the finely formed young woman and her inferior escort passed from sight, a tall mountaineer, from the other side of Compton Ridge, remarked, "I done heard Preachin' Rill say t'other day, that 'mighty nigh all this here gee-hawin', balkin', and kickin' 'mongst th' married folks comes 'cause th' teams ain't matched up right.' Bill he 'lowed God 'lmighty 'd fixed hit somehow so th' birds an' varmints don't make no mistake, but left hit plumb easy for men an' women t' make durned fools o' theirselves."

Everybody grinned in appreciation, and another spoke up; "According t' that, I'll bet four bits if them two yonder ever do get into double harness, there'll be pieces o' th' outfit strung from th' parson's clean t' th' buryin' ground."

When the laughter had subsided, Buck turned to see Young Matt standing just outside the shed, ostensibly doing something with the belt that led to the burr, but in reality looking up the creek.

"Law!" ejaculated Buck, under his breath; "what a team *they'd* make!"

"Who?" said Lem, who was standing near by.

"Them mule colts," returned Buck with a grin.

"They sure will, Buck. There ain't two better in the country; they're a dead match. I'll come over an' hep you break 'em when they're big 'nough." And then he wondered why Buck swore with such evident delight.

One by one the natives received their meal, and, singly, or in groups of two or three, were swallowed up by the great forest. Already the little valley was in the shadow of the mountain, though the sun still shone brightly on the tree tops higher up, when Ollie and Sammy returned from the Forks. Mr. Matthews had climbed the hill when the last grist was ground, leaving his son to cool down the engine and put things right about the mill.

"Come on, Matt," said Ollie, as the big fellow brought out the meal; "It's time you was a goin' home."

The young giant hung back, saying, "You folks better go on ahead. I'll get home alright."

"Didn't think nothin' would get you," laughed Ollie. "Come on, you might as well go 'long with us."

The other muttered something about being in the way, and started back into the shed.

"Hurry up," called Sammy, "we're waitin'."

After this there was nothing else for the young man to do but join them. And the three were soon making their way up the steep mountain road together.

For a time they talked of commonplace things, then Young Matt opened the subject that was on all their hearts. "I reckon, Ollie, this is the last time that you'll ever be a climbin' this old road." As he spoke he was really thinking of the time to come when Sammy would climb the road for the last time.

"Yes," returned Stewart; "I go to-morrow 'fore sun up."

The other continued; "It'll sure be fine for you to live in the city and get your schoolin' and all that. Us folks here in the woods don't know nothin'. We ain't got no chance to learn. You'll be forgettin' us all mighty quick, I reckon, once you get to livin' with your rich kin."

" 'Deed, I won't!" returned Ollie warmly. "Sammy an' me was a talkin' 'bout that this evenin'. We aim t' always come back t' Mutton Holler onct a year, an' be just like other folks; don't we, Sammy?"

The brown pony, stepping on a loose stone, stumbled toward the man walking by his side. And the big fellow put out his hand quickly to the little horse's neck. For an instant, the girl's hand rested on the giant's shoulder, and her face was close to his. Then Brownie recovered his footing, and Young Matt drew farther away.

Ollie continued; "We aim t' have you come t' th' city after a while. I'm goin' t' get Uncle Dan t' give you a job in th' shops, an' you can get out o' these hills an' be somebody like we'uns."

The tone was unmistakably patronizing. The big mountaineer lifted his head proudly, and turned toward the speaker; but before he could reply, Sammy broke in eagerly, "Law! but that would sure be fine, wouldn't it, Matt? I'd know you'd do somethin' big if you only had the chance. I just know you would. You're so—so kind o' big every way," she laughed. "It's a plumb shame for you to be buried alive in these hills."

There was nothing said after this, until, coming to the top of the ridge, they stopped. From here Ollie and Sammy would take the Old Trail to the girl's home. Then, with his eyes on the vast sweep of forest-clad hills and valleys, over which the blue haze was fast changing to purple in the level rays of the sun, Young Matt spoke.

"I don't guess you'd better figure on that. Some folks are made to live in the city, and some ain't. I reckon I was built to live in these hills. I don't somehow feel like I could get along without them; and besides, I'd always be knockin' against somethin' there." He laughed grimly, and stretched out his huge arms. "I've got to have room. Then there's the folks yonder." He turned his face toward the log house, just showing through the trees. "You know how it is, me bein' the only one left, and Dad gettin' old. No, I don't guess you need to count on me bein' more than I am."

Then suddenly he wheeled about and looked from one face to the other; and there was a faint hint of defiance in his voice, as he finished; "I got an idea, too, that the backwoods needs men same as the cities. I don't see how there ever could *be* a city even, if it wasn't for the men what cleared the brush. Somebody's got to lick Wash Gibbs some day, or there just naturally won't be no decent livin' in the neighborhood ever."

He held up his big hand to the man on the horse; "Good-by, and good luck to you, Ollie." The horses turned down the Old Trail and with their riders, passed from sight.

That night Sammy Lane said farewell to her lover, and, with many promises for the future, Ollie rode away to his cabin home, to leave the next morning for that world that lies so far—so far away from the world of Young Matt and his friends, the world that is so easy to get into after all, and so impossible to get out of ever.

CHAPTER XII.

THE SHEPHERD AND HIS FLOCK.

All that spring and summer things went smoothly in the Mutton Hollow neighborhood. The corn was ready to gather, and nothing had happened at the ranch since Mr. Howitt took charge, while the man, who had appeared so strangely in their midst, had made a large place for himself in the hearts of the simple mountaineers.

At first they were disposed to regard him with some distrust, as one apart; he was so unlike themselves. But when he had changed his dress for the rough garb of the hillsman, and, meeting them kindly upon their own ground, had entered so readily into their life, the people by common consent dropped the distinguishing title "Mister" for the more familiar one of the backwoods, "Dad." Not that they lacked in respect or courtesy; it was only their way. And the quiet shepherd accepted the title with a pleased smile, seeming to find in the change an honor to be received not lightly. But while showing such interest in all that made up their world, the man never opened the door for anyone to enter his past. They knew no more of his history than the hints he had given Mr. Matthews the night he came out of the mists.

At the occasional religious meetings in the school house at the Forks, Mr. Howitt was always present, an attentive listener to the sermons of the backwoods preacher. And then, seeing his interest, they asked him to talk to them one day when Parson Bigelow failed to make his appointment. "He don't holler so much as a regular parson," said Uncle Josh Hensley, "but he sure talks so we'uns can understand." From that time they always called upon him at their public gatherings.

So the scholar from the world beyond the ridges slipped quietly into the life of the mountain folk, and took firm root in their affections. And in his face, so "Preachin' Bill" said, was the look of one who had "done fought his fight to a finish, an' war too dead beat t' even be glad it war all over."

Between the giant Mr. Matthews and his shepherd, the friendship, begun that night, grew always stronger. In spite of the difference in education and training, they found much in common. Some bond of fellowship, unknown to the mountaineer, at least, drew them close, and the two men spent many evenings upon the front porch of the log house in quiet talk, while the shadows crept over the valley below; and the light went from the sky back of the clump of pines.

From the first Young Matt was strongly drawn to the stranger, who was to have such influence over his life, and Pete—Pete said that "God lived with Dad Howitt in Mutton Hollow."

Pete somehow knew a great deal about God these days. A strange comradeship had come to be between the thoughtful gentleman, who cared for the sheep, and the ignorant, sorely afflicted, and nameless backwoods boy. The two were always together, out on the hillside and in the little glens and valleys, during the day with the sheep, or at the ranch in the Hollow, when the flock was safely folded and the night slipped quietly over the timbered ridges. Mr. Howitt had fixed a bunk in his cabin for the boy, so that he could come and go at will. Often the shepherd awoke in the morning to find that some time during the night his strange friend had come in from his roving. Again, after seeing the boy soundly sleeping, the shepherd would arise in the morning to find the bunk empty.

Sammy Lane, too, had fallen under the charm of the man with the white hair and poet's face.

Sammy was not so often at the Matthews place after Ollie had gone to the city. The girl could not have told why. She had a vague feeling that it was better to stay away. But this feeling did not prevent her climbing the Old Trail to the Lookout on the shoulder of Dewey, and she spent hours at the big rock, looking over the valley to where the smoke from Aunt Mollie's kitchen curled above the trees. And sometimes, against the sky, she could see a man and a team moving slowly to and fro in the field back of the house. When this happened, Sammy always turned quickly away to where the far off line of hills lay like a long, low cloud against the sky.

Every week the girl rode her brown pony to the Postoffice at the Forks; and when she had a letter, things were different. She always stopped then at the Matthews home.

One day when this happened, Dad and Pete were on the ridge above the Old Trail, just where the north slope of Dewey shades into the rim of the Hollow. The elder man was seated on the ground in the shade of an oak, with his back against the trunk of the tree, while the boy lay full length on the soft grass, looking up into the green depths of foliage where a tiny brown bird flitted from bough to bough. In his quaint way, Pete was carrying on a conversation with his little friend in the tree top, translating freely the while for his less gifted, but deeply interested, companion on the ground below, when Brave, the shepherd dog, lying near, interrupted the talk by a short bark. Looking up, they saw Young Matt riding along the summit of the ridge.

The young man paused when he heard the dog, and caught sight of the two under the tree; then he came to them, and seated himself on the grass at Pete's side. He spoke no word of greeting, and the look on his face was not good to see.

Pete's eyes went wide with fear at the manner of his big friend, and he drew back as if to run, but when Young Matt, throwing himself over on the grass, had hidden his face, a half sad, half knowing look came into the lad's delicate features; reaching forth a hand, as slim as a girl's, he stroked the shaggy, red brown head, as he murmured softly, "Poor Matt. Poor Matt. Does it hurt? Is Matt hurt? It'll be better by-and-by."

The great form on the grass stirred impatiently. The shepherd spoke no word. Pete continued, stroking the big head, and talking in low, soothing tones, as one would hush a child, "Pete don't know what's a hurtin' Young Matt, but it'll be alright, some day. It'll sure grow over after awhile. Ain't nothing won't grow over after awhile; 'cause God he says so."

Still the older man was silent. Then the giant burst forth in curses, and the shepherd spoke, "Don't do that, Grant. It's not like you, lad. You cannot help your trouble that way."

Young Matt turned over to face his friend; "I know it, Dad;" he growled defiantly; "but I just got to say somethin'; I ain't meanin' no disrespect to God 'lmighty, and I reckon He ought to know it; but—" he broke forth again.

Pete drew back in alarm. "Look your trouble in the face, lad," said the shepherd; "don't let it get you down like this."

"Look it in the face!" roared the other. "Good God! that's just it! ain't I a lookin' it in the face every day? You don't know about it, Dad. If you did, you—you'd cuss too." He started in again.

"I know more than you think, Grant," said the other, when the big fellow had stopped swearing to get his breath. While he spoke, the shepherd was looking away along the Old Trail. "There comes your trouble now," he added, pointing to a girl on a brown pony, coming slowly out of the timber near the deer lick. The young man made no reply. Pete, at sight of the girl, started to his feet, but the big fellow pulled him down again, and made the boy understand that he must not betray their position.

When Sammy reached the sheep, she checked her pony, and searched the hillside with her eyes, while her clear call went over the mountain, "Oh—h—h—Dad!"

Young Matt shook his head savagely at his companion, and even Brave was held silent by a low "Be still" from his master.

Again Sammy looked carefully on every side, but lying on the higher ground, and partly hidden by the trees, the little group could not be seen. When there was no answer to her second call, the girl drew a letter from her pocket, and, permitting the pony to roam at will, proceeded to read.

The big man, looking on, cursed again beneath his breath. "It's from Ollie," he whispered to his companions. "She stopped at the house. He says his uncle will give me a job in the shops, and that it'll be fine for me, 'cause Ollie will be my boss himself. He my boss! Why, dad burn his sneakin' little soul, I could crunch him with one hand. I'd see him in hell before I'd take orders from him. I told her so, too," he finished savagely.

"And what did she say?" asked the shepherd quietly, his eyes on the girl below.

"Just said, kind o' short like, that she reckoned I could. Then I come away."

The girl finished her letter, and, after another long call for Dad, moved on over the shoulder of the mountain. Pete, who had withdrawn a little way from his companions, was busily talking in his strange manner to his unseen friends.

Then Young Matt opened his heart to the shepherd and told him all. It was the old, old story; and, as Mr. Howitt listened, dreams that he had thought dead with the death of his only son, stirred again in his heart, and his deep voice was vibrant with emotion as he sought to comfort the lad who had come to him.

While they talked, the sun dropped until its lower edge touched the top of the tallest pine on Wolf Ridge, and the long shadows lay over the valley below. "I'm mighty sorry I let go and cuss, Dad," finished, the boy. "But I keep a holdin' in, and a holdin' in, 'til I'm plumb wild; then something happens like that letter, and I go out on the range and bust. I've often wished you knowed. Seems like your just knowin' about it will help me to hold on. I get scared at myself sometimes, Dad, I do, honest."

"I'm glad, too, that you have told me, Grant. It means more to me than you can guess. I—I had a boy once, you know. He was like you. He would have come to me this way, if he had lived."

The sheep had begun working toward the lower ground. The shepherd rose to his feet. "Take them home, Brave. Come on, boys, you must eat with me at the ranch, to-night." Then the three friends, the giant mountaineer, the strangely afflicted youth, and the old scholar went down the mountain side together.

As they disappeared in the timber on the lower level, the bushes, near which they had been sitting, parted silently, and a man's head and shoulders appeared from behind a big rook. The man watched the strange companions out of sight. Then the bushes swayed together, and the mountain seemed to have swallowed him up.

The three friends had just finished their supper when Pete saw Sammy entering the ranch clearing. Young Matt caught up his hat. At the rear door he paused. "I've got to go now, Dad," he said awkwardly. "I can't see her any more to-day. But if you'll let me, I'll come again when things get too hot."

The shepherd held out his hand, "I understand. Come always, my boy."

The big fellow, with Pete, skipped away into the timber at the rear of the cabin, a moment before Sammy appeared at the open door in front.

CHAPTER XIII.

SAMMY LANE'S AMBITION.

"Law sakes!" cried Sammy, looking at the table. "You don't use all them dishes, do you, Dad? You sure must eat a lot."

"Oh, I eat enough," laughed Mr. Howitt; "but it happens that I had company this evening. Young Matt and Pete were here for supper." He brought two chairs outside the cabin.

"Shucks!" exclaimed Sammy, as she seated herself, and removed her sunbonnet; "they must've eat and run. Wish'd I'd got here sooner. Young Matt run away from me this afternoon. And I wanted to see him 'bout Mandy Ford's party next week. I done promised Mandy that I'd bring him. I reckon he'd go with me if I asked him."

"There is not the least doubt about that," observed the man; "I'm sure anyone would be glad for such charming company."

The girl looked up suspiciously; "Are you a jokin'?" she said.

"Indeed, I am not; I am very much in earnest. Then, taking a cob pipe from his pocket, he added, politely, "May I smoke?"

"Heh? O law! yes. What you ask me for?" She watched him curiously, as he filled and lighted the pipe. "I reckon that's because you was raised in the city," he added slowly; "is that the way folks do there?"

"Folks smoke here, sometimes, do they not?" he returned between puffs.

"I don't mean that. Course they smoke and chew, too. And the women dip snuff, some of 'em. Aunt Mollie Matthews don't, though, and I ain't never goin' to, 'cause she don't. But nobody don't ask nobody else if they can. They just go ahead. That ain't the only way you're different from us, though," she continued, looking at Mr. Howitt, with that wide questioning gaze. "You're different in a heap o' ways. 'Tain't that you wear different clothes, for you don't, no more. Nor, 'taint that you act like you were any better'n us. I don't know what it is, but it's somethin'. Take your stayin' here in Mutton Hollow, now; honest, Dad, ain't you afear'd to stay here all alone at nights?"

"Afraid? afraid of what?" he looked at her curiously.

"Hants," said the girl, lowering her voice; "down there." She pointed toward the old ruined cabin under the bluff. "*She's* sure been seen there. What if *he* was to come, too? Don't you believe in hants?"

The shepherd's face was troubled, as he answered, "I don't know, Sammy. I scarcely know what I believe. Some marvelous experiences are related by apparently reliable authorities; but I have always said that I could not accept the belief. I—I am not so sure now. After all, the unseen world is not so very far away. Strange forces, of which we know nothing, are about us everywhere. I dare not say that I do not believe."

"But you ain't scared?"

"Why should I fear?"

Sammy shook her head. "Ain't 'nother man or woman in the whole country would dast spend the night here, Dad; except Pete, of course. Not even Young Matt, nor my Daddy would do it; and I don't guess they're afraid of anything—anything that's alive, I mean. You're sure different, Dad; plumb different. I reckon it must be the city that does it. And that's what I've come to see you about this evenin'. You see Ollie's been a tellin' me a lot about folks and things way over there." She waived her hand toward the ridges that shut in the Hollow. "And Ollie he's changed a heap himself since he went there to live. I got a letter to-day, and, when I went home, I hunted up the first one he wrote, and I can tell there's a right smart difference already. You know all about Ollie and me goin' to get married, I reckon?"

Mr. Howitt admitted that he had heard something of that nature; and Sammy nodded, "I 'lowed you'd know. But you don't know how mighty proud and particular Ollie always is. I figure that bein' in the city with all them one folks ain't goin' to make him any less that way than he was. And if he stays there and keeps on a changin', and I stay here, and don't change none, why it might be that I—I—" She faltered and came to a dead stop, twisting her bonnet strings nervously in her confusion. "Ollie he ain't like Young Matt, nohow," she said again. "Such as that wouldn't make no difference with him. But Ollie—well you see—"

There was a twinkle, now, in the shepherd's eye, as he answered; "Yes, I see; I am quite sure that I see."

The girl continued; "You know all about these things, Dad. And there ain't nobody else here that does. Will you learn me to be a sure 'nough lady, so as Ollie won't—so he won't—" Again she paused in confusion. It was evident, from the look on Mr. Howitt's face, that, whatever he saw, it was not this.

"I feel somehow like I could do it, if I had a chance," she murmured.

There was no answer. After a time, Sammy stole a look at her quiet companion. What could the man in the chair be thinking about? His pipe was neglected; his gray head bowed.

"Course," said the young woman, with just a little lifting of her chin; "Course, if I couldn't never learn, there ain't no use to try."

The old scholar raised his head and looked long at the girl. Her splendid form, glowing with the rich life and strength of the wilderness, showed in every line the proud old southern blood. Could she learn to be a fine lady? Mr. Howitt thought of the women of the cities, pale, sickly, colorless, hot-house posies, beside this mountain flower. What would this beautiful creature be, had she their training? What would she gain? What might she not lose? Aloud he said, "My dear child, do you know what it is that you ask?'

Sammy hung her head, abashed at his serious tone. "I 'lowed it would be right smart trouble for you," she said. "But I could let you have Brownie in pay; he ain't only five year old, and is as sound as a button. He's all I've got, Mr. Howitt. But I'd be mighty proud to swap him to you."

"My girl, my girl," said the shepherd, "you misunderstand me. I did not mean that. It would be a pleasure to teach you. I was thinking how little you realized what the real life of the city is like, and how much you have that the 'fine ladies,' as you call them, would give fortunes for, and how little they have after all that could add one ray of brightness to your life."

Sammy laughed aloud, as she cried, "Me got anything that anybody would want? Why, Dad, I ain't got nothin' but Brownie, and my saddle, and—and that's all. I sure ain't got nothing to lose."

The man smiled in sympathy. Then slowly a purpose formed in his mind. "And if you should lose, you will never blame me?" he said at last.

"Never, never," she promised eagerly.

"Alright, it is a bargain. I will help you."

The girl sprang to her feet. "I knew you would. I knew you would. I was plumb sure you would," she cried, fairly quivering with life and excitement. "It's got to be a sure 'nough lady, Dad. I want to be a really truly fine lady, like them Ollie tells about in his letters, you know."

"Yes, Sammy. I understand, a 'sure enough' lady, and we will do it, I am sure. But it will take a great deal of hard work on your part, though."

"I reckon it will," she returned soberly, coming back to her seat. Then drawing her chair a little closer, she leaned toward her teacher, "Begin now," she commanded. "Tell me what I must do first."

Mr. Howitt carefully searched his pockets for a match, and lighted his pipe again, before he said, "First you must know what a 'sure enough' lady is. You see, Sammy, there are several kinds of women who call themselves ladies, but are not real ladies after all; and they all look very much like the 'sure enough' kind; that is, they look like them to most people."

Sammy nodded, "Just like them Thompsons down by Flat Rock. They're all mighty proud, 'cause they come from Illinois the same as the Matthews's. You'd think to hear 'em that Old Matt couldn't near run the ranch without 'em, and some folks, strangers like, might believe it. But we all know they ain't nothing but just low down trash, all the time, and no better than some of them folks over on the Bend."

The shepherd smiled, "Something like that. I see you understand. Now a real lady, Sammy, is a lady in three ways: First, in her heart; I mean just to herself, in the things that no one but she could ever know. A 'sure enough' lady does not *pretend* to be; she *is*."

Again the girl broke in eagerly, "That's just like Aunt Mollie, ain't it? Couldn't no one ever have a finer lady heart than her."

"Indeed, you are right," agreed the teacher heartily. "And that is the thing that lies at the bottom of it all, Sammy. The lady heart comes first."

"I won't never forget that," she returned. "I couldn't forget Aunt Mollie, nohow. Tell me more, Dad."

"Next, the 'sure enough' lady must have a lady mind. She must know how to think and talk about the things that really matter. All the fine dresses and jewels in the world can't make a real lady, if she does not think, or if she thinks only of things that are of no value. Do you see?"

Again the girl nodded, and, with a knowing smile, answered quickly, "I know a man like that. And I see now that that is what makes him so different from other folks. It's the things he thinks about all to himself that does it. But I've got a heap to learn, I sure have. I could read alright, if I had something to read, and I reckon I could learn to talk like you if I tried hard enough. What else is there?"

Then, continued the shepherd, "A lady will keep her body as strong and as beautiful as she can, for this is one way that she expresses her heart and mind. Do you see what I mean?"

Sammy answered slowly, "I reckon I do. You mean I mustn't get stooped over and thin chested, and go slouching around, like so many of the girls and women around here do, and I mustn't let my clothes go without buttons, 'cause I am in a hurry, and I must always comb my hair, and keep my hands as white as I can. Is that it?"

"That's the idea," said the shepherd.

Sammy gazed ruefully at a large rent in her skirt, and at a shoe half laced. Then she put up a hand to her tumbled hair. "I—I didn't think it made any difference, when only home folks was around," she said.

"That's just it, my child," said the old man gently. "I think a 'sure enough' lady would look after these things whether there was anyone to see her or not; just for herself, you know. And this is where you can begin. I will send for some books right away, and when they come we will begin to train your mind."

"But the heart, how'll I get a lady heart, Dad?"

"How does the violet get its perfume, Sammy?" Where does the rose get its color? How does the bird learn to sing its song?"

For a moment she was puzzled. Then her face lighted; "I see!" she exclaimed. "I'm just to catch it from folks like Aunt Mollie, and— and someone else I know. I'm just to *be,* not to make believe or let on like I was, but to *be* a real lady inside. And then I'm to learn how to talk and look, like I know myself to be." She drew a long breath as she rose to go. "It'll be mighty hard, Dad, in some ways; but it'll sure be worth it all when I get out 'mong the folks. I'm mighty thankful to you, I sure am. And I hope you won't never be sorry you promised to help me."

As the girl walked swiftly away through the thickening dusk of the evening, the shepherd watched her out of sight; then turned toward the corral for a last look at the sheep, to see that all was right for the night. "Brave, old fellow," he said to the dog who trotted by his side; "are we going to make another mistake, do you think? We have made so many, so many, you know." Brave looked up into the master's face, and answered with his low bark, as though to declare his confidence. "Well, well, old dog, I hope you are right. The child has a quick mind, and a good heart; and, if I am not mistaken, good blood. We shall see. We shall see."

Suddenly the dog whirled about, the hair on his back bristling as he gave a threatening growl. A man on a dun colored mule was coming up the road.

CHAPTER XIV.

THE COMMON YELLER KIND.

Mr. Howitt stood quietly by the corral gate when the horseman rode up. It was Wash Gibbs, on his way home from an all day visit with friends on the river.

When the big mountaineer took the short cut through Mutton Hollow, he thought to get well past the ranch before the light failed. No matter how well fortified with the courage distilled by his friend, Jennings, the big man would never have taken the trail by the old ruined cabin alone after dark. He had evidently been riding at a good pace, for his mule's neck and flanks were wet with sweat. Gibbs, himself, seemed greatly excited, and one hand rested on the pistol at his hip, as be pulled up in front of the shepherd.

Without returning Mr. Howitt's greeting, he pointed toward the two empty chairs in front of the house, demanding roughly, "Who was that with you before you heard me comin'?"

"Sammy Lane was here a few minutes ago," replied the shepherd.

Gibbs uttered an oath, "She was, was she? Well, who was th' man?"

"There was no man," returned the other. "Young Matt and Pete were here for supper, but they went as soon as the meal was finished, before Sammy came."

"Don't you try to lie to me!" exclaimed the big man, with another burst of language, and a threatening movement with the hand that rested on the pistol.

Mr. Howitt was startled. Never in his life before had such words been addressed to him. He managed to reply with quiet dignity, "I have no reason for deceiving you, or anyone else, Mr. Gibbs. There has been no man here but myself, since Matt and Pete left after supper." The shepherd's manner carried conviction, and Gibbs hesitated, evidently greatly perplexed. During the pause, Brave growled again, and faced toward the cliff below the corral, his hair bristling.

"What's th' matter with that dog?" said Gibbs, turning uneasily in his saddle, to face in the direction the animal was looking.

"What is it, Brave?" said Mr. Howitt. The only answer was an uneasy whine, followed by another growl, all of which said plainly, in dog talk, "I don't know what it is, but there is something over there on that cliff that I don't like."

"It must be some animal," said the shepherd.

"Ain't no animal that makes a dog act like that. Did any body pass while you was a sittin' there, jest before I come in sight?"

"Not a soul," answered the other. "Did you meet someone down the road?"

The big man looked at the shepherd hard before he answered, in a half-frightened, half-bullying tone, "I seed something in th' road yonder, an' hit disappeared right by th' old shack under th' bluffs." He twisted around in his saddle again, facing the cliff with its dense shadows and dim twilight forms, as he muttered, "If I was only right sure, I—" Then swinging back he leaned toward the man on the ground; "Look a here, Mister. There's them that 'lows there's things in this here Holler t' be afeared of, an' I reckon hit's so. There's sure been hell t' pay at that there cabin down yonder. I ain't a sayin' what hit was I seed, but if hit war anywhere else, I'd a said hit was a man; but if hit was a man, I don't know why you didn't see him when he come past; er else you're a lyin'. I jest want t' tell you, you're right smart of a stranger in these here parts, even if you have bean a workin' for Ol' Matt all summer. You're too blame careful 'bout talkin' 'bout yourself, or tellin' whar you come from, t' suit some folks. Some strangers are alright, an' again some ain't. But we don't aim t' have nobody in this here neighborhood what jumps into th' brush when they see an honest man a comin'."

As he finished speaking, Gibbs straightened himself in the saddle, and before Mr. Howitt could reply, the dun mule, at a touch of the spur, had dashed away up the road in the direction taken by Sammy Lane.

It was quite dark in the heavy timber of the Hollow by the time Sammy had reached the edge of the open ground on the hill side, but once on the higher level, clear of the trees, the strong glow of the western sky still lighted the way. From here it was not far to the girl's home, and, as she climbed a spur of Dewey, Sammy saw the cabin, and heard distinctly the sweet strain's of her father's violin. On top of the rise, the young woman paused a moment to enjoy the beauties of the evening, which seemed to come to her with a new meaning that night. As she stood there, her strong young figure was clearly outlined against the sky to the man who was riding swiftly along the road over which she had just passed.

Sammy turned when she heard the quick beating of the mule's feet; then, recognizing the huge form of the horseman, as he came out of the woods into the light, she started quickly away towards her home; but the mule and its rider were soon beside her.

"Howdy, Sammy." Gibbs leaped from the saddle, and, with the bridle rein over his arm, came close to the girl. "Fine evening for a walk."

"Howdy," returned the young woman, coolly, quickening her pace.

"You needn't t' be in such a powerful hurry," growled Wash. "If you've got time t' talk t' that old cuss at th' ranch, you sure got time t' talk t' me."

Sammy turned angrily. "You'd better get back on your mule, and go about your business, Wash Gibbs. When I want you to walk with me, I'll let you know."

"That's alright, honey," exclaimed the other insolently. "I'm a goin' your way just th' same; an' we'll mosey 'long t'gether. I was a goin' home, but I've got business with your paw now."

"Worse thing for Daddy, too," flashed the girl. "I wish you'd stay away from him."

Wash laughed; "Your daddy couldn't keep house 'thout me, nohow. Who was that feller talkin' with you an' th' old man down yonder?"

"There wasn't nobody talkin' to us," replied Sammy shortly.

"That's what he said, too," growled Gibbs; "but I sure seed somebody a sneakin' into th' brush when I rode up. I thought when I was down there hit might o' been a hant; but I know hit was a man, now. There's somethin' mighty funny a goin' on around here, since that feller come int' th' neighborhood; an' he'll sure find somethin' in Mutton Holler more alive than Ol' Matt's gal if he ain't careful."

The girl caught her breath quickly. She knew the big ruffian's methods, and with good reason feared for her old friend, should he even unconsciously incur the giant's displeasure.

As they drew near the house, Wash continued, "Young Matt he was there too. Let me tell you I ain't forgot 'bout his big show at th' mill last spring; he'll have t' do a heap better'n he done then, when I get 'round t' him."

Sammy laughed scornfully, "'Pears like you ain't been in no hurry t' try it on. I ain't heard tell of Young Matt's leaving th' country yet. You'd better stay away from Jennings' still though, when you do try it." Then, while the man was tying his mule to the fence, she ran into the cabin to greet her father with a hysterical sob that greatly astonished Jim. Before explanations could be made, a step was heard approaching the door, and Sammy had just time to say, "Wash Gibbs," in answer to her father's inquiring look, when the big man entered. Mr. Lane arose to hang his violin on its peg.

"Don't stop fer me, Jim," said the newcomer. "Jest let her go. Me an' Sammy's been havin' a nice little walk, an' some right peart music would sound mighty fine." Gibbs was angered beyond reason at Sammy's last words, or he would have exercised greater care.

Sammy's father made no reply until the girl had left the room, but whatever it was that his keen eye read in his daughter's face, it made him turn to his guest with anything but a cordial manner, and there was that in his voice that should have warned the other.

"So you and Sammy went for a walk, did you?"

"She was comin' home from th' sheep ranch, an' I caught up with her," explained Gibbs. "I 'lowed as how she needed company, so I come 'long. I seemed t' be 'bout as welcome as usual," he added with an ugly grin.

"Meanin' that my girl don't want your company, and told you so?" asked the other softly.

Wash answered with a scowl; "Sammy's gettin' too dad burned good fer me since Ollie's uncle took him in. An' now, this here old man from nowhere has come, it's worse than ever. She'll put a rope 'round our necks th' first thing you know."

Jim's right hand slipped quietly inside his hickory shirt, where the button was missing, as he drawled, "My girl always was too good for some folks. And it's about time you was a findin' it out. She can't help it. She was born that way. She's got mighty good blood in her veins, that girl has; and I don't aim to ever let it be mixed up with none of the low down common yeller kind."

The deliberate purpose of the speaker was too evident to be mistaken. The other man's hand flew to his hip almost before Mr. Lane had finished his sentence. But Wash was not quick enough. Like a flash Jim's hand was withdrawn from inside the hickory shirt, and the giant looked squarely into the muzzle of Jim Lane's ever ready, murderous weapon.

In the same even voice, without the slightest allusion to the unfinished movement of the other, Mr. Lane continued, "I done told you before that my girl would pick her own company, and I ain't never feared for a minute that she'd take up with such as you. Ollie Stewart ain't so mighty much of a man, maybe, but he's clean, he is, and the stock's pretty good. Now you can just listen to me, or you can mosey out of that door, and the next time we meet, we will settle it for good, without any further arrangement."

As Sammy's father talked, the big figure of his visitor relaxed, and when Jim had finished his slow speech, Wash was leaning forward with his elbows on his knees, his hands clasped in front. "We ain't got no call t' fight, now, Jim," he said in a tone of respect. "We got something else t' think about; an' that's what I come here fer t'night. I didn't aim t', 'til I seed what I did at th' ranch down yonder. I tell you hit's time we was a doin' somethin'."

At this, Mr. Lane's face and manner changed quickly. He put up his weapon, and the two men drew their chairs close together, as though Death had not a moment before stretched forth his hand to them.

For an hour they sat talking in low tones. Sammy in the next room had heard the conversation up to this point, but now only an occasional word reached her ears. Gibbs seemed to be urging some action, and her father was as vigorously protesting. "I tell you, Jim, hit's th' only safe way. You didn't use t' be so squeamish. Several times the old shepherd was mentioned, and also the stranger whom Wash had seen that evening. And once, the trembling girl heard Young Matt's name. At length the guest rose to go, and Mr.

Lane walked with him to the gate. Even after the big man was mounted, the conversation still continued; Wash still urging and Jim still protesting.

When his visitor was gone, Mr. Lane came slowly back to the house. Extinguishing the light, he seated himself in the open doorway, and filled his pipe. Sammy caught the odor of tobacco, and a moment later Jim heard a light, quick step on the floor behind him. Then two arms went around his neck; "What is it, Daddy? What is it? Why don't you drive that man away?"

"Did you hear us talkin'?" asked the man, an anxious note in his voice.

"I heard you talkin' to him about pesterin' me, but after that, you didn't talk so loud. What is the matter, Daddy, that he could stay and be so thick with you after the things you said? I was sure he'd make you kill him."

Jim laughed softly; "You're just like your mother, girl. Just like her, with the old blood a backin' you up." Then he asked a number of questions about Mr. Howitt, and her visit to the ranch that evening.

As Sammy told him of her ambition to fit herself for the place that would be hers, when she married, and repeating the things that Mr. Howitt had told her, explained how the shepherd had promised to help, Jim expressed his satisfaction and delight. "I knowed you was a studyin' about something, girl," he said, "but I didn't say nothin', 'cause I 'lowed you'd tell me when you got ready."

"I didn't want to say nothing 'til I was sure, you see," replied the daughter. "I aimed to tell you as soon as I got home to-night, but Wash Gibbs didn't give me no chance."

The man held her close "Dad Howitt sure puts the thing just right, Sammy. It'll be old times come back, when you're a lady in your own house with all your fine friends around; and you'll do it, girl; you sure will. Don't never be afraid to bank on the old blood. It'll see you through." Then his voice broke; "You won't never be learned away from your old Daddy, will you, honey? Will you always stand by Daddy, like you do now? Will you let me and Young Matt slip 'round once in a while, just to look at, you, all so fine?"

"Daddy Jim, if you don't—hush—I'll—I'll—" she hid her face on his shoulder.

"There, there, honey; I was only funnin'. You'll always be my Sammy; the only boy I ever had. You just naturally couldn't be nothin' else."

Long after his daughter had gone to her room and to her bed, the mountaineer sat in the doorway, looking into the dark. He heard the short bark of a fox in the brush back of the stable; and the wild cry of a catamount from a cliff farther down the mountain was answered by another from the timber below the spring. He saw the great hills heaving their dark forms into the sky, and in his soul he felt the spirit of the wilderness and the mystery of the hour. At last he went into the house to close and bar the door.

Away down in Mutton Hollow a dog barked, and high up on Old Dewey near Sammy's Lookout, a spot of light showed for a moment, then vanished.

CHAPTER XV.

THE PARTY AT FORD'S.

Young Matt would have found some excuse for staying at home the night of the party at Ford's, but the shepherd said he must go.

The boy felt that the long evening with Sammy would only hurt. He reasoned with himself that it would be better for him to see as little as possible of the girl who was to marry Ollie Stewart. Nevertheless, he was singing as he saddled the big white faced sorrel to ride once more over the trail that is nobody knows how old.

Mr. Lane was leading the brown pony from the stable as Young Matt rode up to the gate; and from the doorway of the cabin Sammy called to say that she would be ready in a minute.

"Ain't seen you for a coon's age, boy," said Jim, while they were waiting for the girl. "Why don't you never come down the Old Trail no more?"

The big fellow's face reddened, as he answered, "I ain't been nowhere, Jim. 'Pears like I just can't get away from the place no more; we're that busy."

Sammy's father looked his young neighbor squarely in the eye with that peculiar searching gaze; "Look a here, Grant. I've knowed you ever since you was born, and you ought to know me a little. 'Tain't your way to dodge, and 'tain't mine. I reckon you know you're welcome, same as always, don't you?"

Young Matt returned the other's look fairly; "I ain't never doubted it, Jim. But things is a heap different now, since it's all done and settled, with Ollie gone."

The two understood each other perfectly. Said Jim, drawing a long breath, "Well I wish you'd come over just the same, anyway. It can't do nobody no harm as I can see."

"It wouldn't do me no good," replied the young man.

"Maybe not," assented Jim. "But I'd like mighty well to have you come just the same." Then he drew closer to his young friend; "I've been aimin' to ride over and see you, Matt; but Sammy said you was a comin' this evenin', and I 'lowed this would be soon enough. I reckon you know what Wash Gibbs is tellin' he aims to do first chance he gets."

The giant drew himself up with a grim smile, "I've heard a good bit, Jim.

But you don't need to mind about me; I know I ain't quite growed, but I am a growin'."

The older man surveyed the great form of the other with a critical eye, as he returned, "Durned if I don't believe you'd push him mighty close, if he'd only play fair. But—but I 'lowed you ought to know it was a comin'."

"I have knowed it for a long time," said the other cheerfully; "but I heard 'Preachin' Bill' say once, that if a feller don't fuss about what he knows for sure, the things he don't know ain't apt to bother him none. It's this here guessin' that sure gets a man down."

" 'Preachin' Bill' hits it every pop, don't he?" exclaimed Jim, admiringly. "But there's somethin' else you ought to know, too, Matt. Wash has done made his threats agin the old man down there."

"You mean Dad Howitt?" said Young Matt, sharply. "What's Wash got agin Dad, Jim?"

Mr. Lane shifted uneasily, "Some fool notion of hisn. You mind old man Lewis, I reckon?"

The big man's muscles tightened. "Dad told us about his stoppin' at the ranch the other night. Wash Gibbs better keep his hands off Mr. Howitt."

"I ain't told nobody about this, Grant, and you can do as you like about tellin' your father, and the old man. But if anything happens, get word to me, quick."

Before more could be said, Sammy appeared in the doorway, and soon the two young people were riding on their way. Long after they had passed from sight in the depth of the forest, the dark mountaineer stood at the big gate, looking in the direction they had gone.

Young Matt was like a captive, tugging at his bonds. Mr. Lane's words had stirred the fire, and the girl's presence by his side added fuel to the flame. He could not speak. He dared not even look at her, but rode with his eyes fixed upon the ground, where the sunlight fell in long bars of gold. Sammy, too, was silent. She felt something that was strangely like fear, when she found herself alone with her big neighbor. Now and then she glanced timidly up at him and tried to find some word with which to break the silence. She half wished that she had not come. So they rode together through the lights and shadows down into the valley, the only creatures in all the free life of the forest who were not free.

At last the girl spoke, "It's mighty good of you to take me over to Mandy's to-night. There ain't no one else I could o' gone with." There was no reply, and Sammy, seeming not to notice, continued talking in a matter-of-fact tone that soon—for such is the way of a woman—won him from his mood, and the two chatted away like the good comrades they had always been.

Just after they had crossed Fall Creek at Slick Rock Ford, some two miles below the mill, Young Matt leaned from his saddle, and for a little way studied the ground carefully. When he sat erect again, he remarked, with the air of one who had reached a conclusion, "Wouldn't wonder but there'll be doin's at Ford's to- night, sure enough."

"There's sure to be," returned the girl; "everybody'll be there. Mandy's folks from over on Long Creek are comin', and some from the mouth of the James. Mandy wanted Daddy to play for 'em, but he says he can't play for parties no more, and they got that old fiddlin' Jake from the Flag neighborhood, I guess."

"There'll be somethin' a heap more excitin' than fiddlin' and dancin', accordin' to my guess," returned Young Matt.

"What do you mean?" asked Sammy.

Her escort pointed to the print of a mule's shoe in the soft soil of the low bottom land. "That there's Wash Gibbs's dun mule, and he's headed down the creek for Jennings's still. Wash'll meet a lot of his gang from over on the river, and like's not they'll go from there to the party. I wish your dad was goin' to do the playin' to-night."

It was full dark before they reached the Ford clearing. The faint, far away sound of a violin, seeming strange and out of place in the gloomy solitude of the great woods, first told them that other guests had already arrived. Then as they drew nearer and the tones of the instrument grew louder, they could hear the rhythmic swing and beat of heavily shod feet upon the rough board floors, with the shrill cries of the caller, and the half savage, half pathetic sing-song of the backwoods dancers, singing, "Missouri Gal."

Reaching the edge of the clearing, they involuntarily checked their horses, stopping just within the shadow of the timber. Here the sound of the squeaking fiddle, the shouting caller, the stamping feet, and the swinging dancers came with full force; and, through the open door and windows of the log house, they could see the wheeling, swaying figures of coatless men and calico gowned women, while the light, streaming out, opened long lanes in the dusk. About them in the forest's edge, standing in groups under the trees, were the shadowy forms of saddle horses and mules, tied by their bridle reins to the lower branches; and nearer to the cabin, two or three teams, tied to the rail-fence, stood hitched to big wagons in which were splint-bottom chairs for extra seats.

During the evening, the men tried in their rough, good natured way, to joke Young Matt about taking advantage of Ollie Stewart's absence, but they very soon learned that, while the big fellow was ready to enter heartily into all the fun of the occasion, he would not receive as a jest any allusion to his relation to the girl, whom he had escorted to the party. Sammy, too, when her big companion was not near, suffered from the crude wit of her friends.

"Ollie Stewart don't own me yet," she declared with a toss of the head, when someone threatened to write her absent lover.

"No," replied one of her tormentors, "but you ain't aimin' to miss your chance o' goin' t' th' city t' live with them big-bugs."

In the laugh that followed, Sammy was claimed by a tall woodsman for the next dance, and escaped to take her place on the floor.

"Well, Ollie'll sure make a good man for her," remarked another joker; "if he don't walk th' chalk, she can take him 'cross her knee an' wallop him."

"She'll surely marry him, alright," said the first, "'cause he's got th' money, but she's goin' t' have a heap o' fun makin' Young Matt play th' fool before she leaves th' woods. He ain't took his eyes off her t'night. Everybody's laughin' at him."

"I notice they take mighty good care t' laugh behind his back," flashed little black-eyed Annie Brooke from the Cove neighborhood.

Young Matt, who had been dancing with Mandy Ford, came up behind the group just in time to hear their remarks. Two or three who saw him within hearing tried to warn the speakers, but while everybody around them saw the situation, the two men caught the frantic signals of their friends too late. The music suddenly stopped. The dancers were still. By instinct every eye in the room was fixed upon the little group, as the jokers turned to face the object of their jests.

The big mountaineer took one long step toward the two who had spoken, his brow dark with rage, his huge fists clenched. But, even as his powerful muscles contracted for the expected blow, the giant came to a dead stop. Slowly his arm relaxed. His hand dropped to his side. Then, turning deliberately, he walked to the door, the silent crowd parting to give him way.

As the big man stepped from the room, a gasp of astonishment escaped from the company, and the two jokers, with frightened faces, broke into a shrill, nervous laughter. Then a buzz of talk went round; the fiddlers struck up again; the callers shouted; the dancers stamped, and bowed, and swung their partners as they sang.

And out in the night under the trees, at the edge of the gloomy forest, the strongest man in the hills was saying over and over to the big, white faced sorrel, "I don't dare do it. I don't dare. Dad Howitt wouldn't. He sure wouldn't."

Very soon two figures left the house, and hurried toward a bunch of saddle horses near by. They had untied their animals, and were about to mount, when suddenly a huge form stepped from the shadows to their horses' heads. "Put up your guns, boys," said Young Matt calmly. "I reckon you know that if I'd wanted trouble, it would o' been all over before this."

The weapons were not drawn, and the big man continued, "Dad Howitt says a feller always whips himself every time he fights when there ain't no—no principle evolved. I don't guess Dad would see ary principle in this, 'cause there might be some truth in what you boys said. I reckon I am somethin' at playin' a fool, but it would o' been a heap safer for you to let folks find it out for themselves."

"We all were jest a foolin', Matt," muttered one.

"That's alright," returned the big fellow; "But you'd better tie up again and go back into the house and dance a while longer. Folks might think you was scared if you was to leave so soon."

CHAPTER XVI.

ON THE WAY HOME.

Not until the party was breaking up, and he saw Sammy in the doorway, did Young Matt go back to the house.

When they had ridden again out of the circle of light, and the laughter and shouting of the guests was no longer heard, Sammy tried in vain to arouse her silent escort, chatting gaily about the pleasures of the evening. But all the young man's reserve had returned. When she did force him to speak, his responses were so short and cold that at last the girl, too, was silent. Then, man- like, he wished she would continue talking.

By the time they reached Compton Ridge the moon was well up. For the last two miles Sammy had been watching the wavering shafts of light that slipped through tremulous leaves and swaying branches. As they rode, a thousand fantastic shapes appeared and vanished along the way, and now and then as the sound of their horses' feet echoed through the silent forest, some wild thing in the underbrush leaped away into the gloomy depth.

Coming out on top of the narrow ridge, the brown pony crowded closer to the big, white faced sorrel, and the girl, stirred by the weird loveliness of the scene, broke the silence with an exclamation, "O Matt! Ain't it fine? Look there!" She pointed to the view ahead. "Makes me feel like I could keep on a goin', and goin', and never stop."

The man, too, felt the witchery of the night. The horses were crowding more closely together now, and, leaning forward, the girl looked up into his face; "What's the matter, Matt? Why don't you talk to me? You know it ain't true what them folks said back there."

The sorrel was jerked farther away. "It's true enough, so far as it touches me," returned the man shortly. "When are you goin' to the city?"

"I don't know," she replied. "Let's don't talk about that to- night. I don't want even to think about it, not to-night. You—you don't believe what they was a sayin', Matt; you know you don't. You mustn't ever believe such as that. I—I never could get along without you and Aunt Mollie and Uncle Matt, nohow." The brown pony was again crowding closer to his mate. The girl laid a hand on her companion's arm. "Say you don't blame me for what they said, Matt. You know I wouldn't do no such a thing even if I could. There mustn't anything ever come between you and me; never—never. I—I want us always to be like we are now. You've been so good to me ever since I was a little trick, and you whipped big Lem Wheeler for teasin' me. I—I don't guess I could get along without knowin' you was around somewhere." She finished with a half sob.

It was almost too much. The man swung around in his saddle, and the horses, apparently of their own accord, stopped. Without a word, the big fellow stretched forth his arms, and the girl, as if swept by a force beyond her control, felt herself swaying toward him.

The spell was broken by the trampling of horses and the sound of loud voices. For a moment they held their places, motionless, as if rudely awakened from a dream. The sound was coming nearer. Then Young Matt spoke, "It's Wash Gibbs and his crowd from the still. Ride into the brush quick."

There was no time for flight. In the bright moonlight, they would have been easily recognized, and a wild chase would have followed. Leaving the road, they forced their horses into a thick clump of bushes, where they dismounted, to hold the animals by their heads. Scarcely had they gained this position when the first of the crowd reached the spot where they had been a moment before. Wash Gibbs was easily distinguished by his gigantic form, and with him were ten others, riding two and two, several of whom were known to Young Matt as the most lawless characters in the country. All were fired by drink and were laughing and talking, with now and then a burst of song, or a vulgar jest.

"I say, Wash," called one, "What'll you do if Young Matt's there?" The unseen listeners could not hear the leader's reply; but those about the speaker laughed and shouted with great glee. Then the two in the bushes distinctly heard the last man in the line ask his companion, "Do you reckon he'll put up a fight?" and as they passed from sight, the other answered, "Wash don't aim t' give him no show."

When the sounds had died away; Young Matt turned to the girl; "Come on; we've got to keep 'em in sight."

But Sammy held back. "Oh, Matt, don't go yet. We must not. Didn't you hear what that man said? It's you they're after. Let's wait here until they're clean gone."

"No, 'tain't; they ain't a wantin' me," the big fellow replied. And before the young woman could protest further, he lifted her to the saddle as easily as if she were a child. Then, springing to the back of his own horse, he led the way at a pace that would keep them within hearing of the company of men.

"Who is it, Matt? Who is it, if it ain't you?" asked the girl.

"Don't know for sure yet, but I'll tell you pretty soon."

They had not gone far when Young Matt stopped the horse to listen intently; and soon by the sound he could tell that the party ahead had turned off the ridge road and were following the trail that leads down the eastern side of the mountain. A moment longer the mountaineer listened, as if to make sure; then he spoke; "Them devils are goin' to the ranch after Dad Howitt. Sammy, you've got to ride hard to-night. They won't hear you now, and they're getting farther off every minute. There ain't no other way, and, I know you'll do it for the old man. Get home as quick as you can and tell Jim what's up. Tell him I'll hold 'em until he gets there." Even as he spoke, he sprang from his horse and began loosening the saddle girths.

"But, Matt," protested the girl; "how can you? You can't get by them. How're you goin' to get there in time?"

"Down the mountain; short cut;" he answered as he jerked the heavy saddle from his horse and threw it under some nearby bushes.

"But they'll kill you. You can't never face that whole crowd alone."

"I can do it better'n Dad, and him not a lookin' for them."

Slipping the bridle from the sorrel, he turned the animal loose, and, removing his coat and hat, laid them with the saddle. Then to the girl on the pony he said sharply o on, Sammy. Why don't you go on? Don't you see how you're losin' time? Them devils will do for Dad Howitt like they done for old man Lewis. Your father's the only man can stop 'em now. Ride hard, girl, and tell Jim to hurry. And—and, good-by, Sammy." As he finished, he spoke to her horse and struck him such a blow that the animal sprang away.

For a moment Sammy attempted to pull up her startled pony. Then Young Matt saw her lean forward in the saddle, and urge the little horse to even greater speed. As they disappeared down the road, the giant turned and ran crashing through the brush down the steep side of the mountain. There was no path to follow. And with deep ravines to cross, rocky bluffs to descend or scale, and, in places, wild tangles of vines and brush and fallen trees, the trip before him would have been a hard one even in the full light of day. At night, it was almost impossible, and he must go like a buck with the dogs in full cry.

When Sammy came in sight of her home, she began calling to her father, and, as the almost exhausted horse dashed up to the big gate, the door of the cabin opened, and Jim came running out. Lifting his daughter from the trembling pony, he helped her into the house, where she sobbed out her message.

At the first word, "Wash Gibbs," Jim reached for a cartridge belt, and, by the time Sammy had finished, he had taken his Winchester from its brackets over the fireplace. Slipping a bridle on his horse that was feeding in the yard, he sprang upon the animal's back without waiting for a saddle. "Stay in the cabin, girl, put out the light, and don't open the door until I come," he said and he was gone.

As Sammy turned back into the house, from away down in Mutton Hollow, on the night wind, came the sound of guns.

CHAPTER XVII.

WHAT HAPPENED AT THE RANCH.

It was after midnight when Mr. Howitt was rudely awakened. The bright moon shining through the windows lit up the interior of the cabin and he easily recognized Young Matt standing by the bed, with Pete, who was sleeping at the ranch that night, near by.

"Why, Matt, what is the matter?" exclaimed the shepherd, sitting up. He could not see that the big fellow's clothing was torn, that his hat was gone, and that he was dripping with perspiration; but he could hear his labored breathing. Strong as he was, the young giant was nearly exhausted by the strain of his race over the mountains.

"Get up quick, Dad; I'll tell you while you're puttin' on your clothes," the woodsman answered; and while the shepherd dressed, he told him in a few words, finishing with, "Call Brave inside, and get your gun, with all the shells you can find. Don't show a light for a minute. They'll be here any time now, and it'll be a good bit yet before Sammy can get home." He began fastening the front door.

The peaceful minded scholar could not grasp the meaning of the message; it was to him an impossible thought; "You must be mistaken, Grant," he said. "Surely you are excited and unduly alarmed. Wash Gibbs has no reason to attack me."

Young Matt replied gruffly, "I ain't makin' no mistake in the woods, Dad. You ain't in the city now, and there ain't no one can hear you holler. Don't think I am scared neither, if that's what you mean. But there's ten of them in that bunch, and they're bad ones. You'd better call Brave, sir. He'll be some help when it comes to the rush."

But the other persisted, "You must be mistaken, lad. Why should any one wish to harm me? Those men are only out fox hunting, or something like that. If they should be coming here, it is all a mistake; I can easily explain."

"Explain, hell!" ejaculated the mountaineer. "I ask your pardon, Dad; but you don't know, not being raised in these woods like me. Old man Lewis hadn't done nothing neither, and he explained, too; only he never got through explainin'. They ain't got no reason. They're drunk. You've never seen Wash Gibbs drunk, and to-night he's got his whole gang with him. I don't know why he's comin' after you, but, from what you told me 'bout his stoppin' here that evenin', and what I've heard lately, I can guess. I know what he'll do when he gets here, if we don't stop him. It'll be all the same to you whether he's right or wrong."

Brave came trotting into the cabin through the rear door, and lay down in his corner by the fireplace. "That's mighty funny," said Young Matt. Then, as he glanced quickly around, "Where's Pete?"

The boy had slipped away while the two men were talking. Stepping outside they called several times; but, save the "Wh-w-h-o—w-h-o- o-o" of an owl in a big tree near the corral, there was no answer.

"The boy's alright, anyway," said the young man; "nothin' in the woods ever hurts Pete. He's safer there than he would be here, and I'm glad he's gone."

The shepherd did not reply. He seemed not to hear, but stood as though fascinated by the scene. He still could not grasp the truth of the situation, but the beauty of the hour moved him deeply. "What a marvelous, what a wonderful sight!" he said at last in a low tone. "I do not wonder the boy loves to roam the hills a night like this. Look, Grant! See how soft the moonlight falls on that patch of grass this side of the old tree yonder, and how black the shadow is under that bush, like the mouth of a cave, a witch's cave. I am sure there are ghosts and goblins in there, with fairies and gnomes, and perhaps a dragon or two. And see, lad, how the great hills rise into the sky. How grand, how beautiful the world is! It is good to live, Matt, though life be sometimes hard, still—still it is good to live."

At the old scholar's words and manner, the mountaineer, too, forgot for a moment the thing that had brought him there, and a look of awe and wonder came over his rugged features, as the shepherd, with his face turned upward and his deep voice full of emotion, repeated, "The heavens declare the glory of God; and the firmament showeth his handiwork. Day unto day uttereth speech, and night unto night showeth knowledge."

The owl left his place in the old tree and flew across the moonlit clearing into the deeper gloom of the woods. Inside the cabin the dog barked, and through the still night, from down the valley, where the ranch trail crosses the creek, came the rattle of horses' feet on the rocky floor of the little stream, and the faint sound of voices. Young Matt started, and again the man of the wilderness was master of the situation. "They're comin', Dad. We ain't got no time to lose."

Re-entering the cabin, Mr. Howitt quieted the dog, while his companion fastened the rear door, and, in the silence, while they waited, a cricket under the corner of the house sang his plaintive song. The sound of voices grew louder as the horses drew nearer. Brave growled and would have barked again, but was quieted by the shepherd, who crouched at his side, with one hand on the dog's neck.

The older man smiled to himself. It all seemed to him so like a child's game. He had watched the mountaineer's preparation with amused interest, and had followed the young woodsman's directions, even to the loaded shotgun in his hand, as one would humor a boy in his play. The scholar's mind, trained to consider the problems of civilization, and to recognize the dangers of the city, refused to entertain seriously the thought that there, in the peaceful woods, in the dead of night, a company of ruffians was seeking to do him harm.

The voices had ceased, and the listeners heard only the sound of the horses' feet, as the party passed the ruined cabin under the bluff. A moment or two later the riders stopped in front of the ranch house. Brave growled again, but was silenced by the hand on his neck.

Young Matt was at the window. "I see them," he whispered. "They're gettin' off their horses, and tyin' them to the corral fence." The smile on the shepherd's face vanished, and he experienced a queer sensation; it was as though something gripped his heart.

The other continued his whispered report; "They're bunchin' up now under the old tree, talkin' things over. Don't know what to make of the dog not bein' around, I reckon. Now they're takin' a drink. It takes a lot of whiskey to help ten men jump onto one old man, and him a stranger in the Woods. Now Wash is sendin' two of them around to the back, so you can't slip out into the brush. Sh—h— h, here comes a couple more to try the front door." He slipped quietly across the room to the shepherd's side. The visitors came softly up to the front door, and tried it gently. A moment later the rear door was tried in the same way.

"Let Brave speak to them," whispered Young Matt; and the dog, feeling the restraining hand removed, barked fiercely.

Mr. Howitt, following his companion's whispered instructions, spoke aloud, "What's the matter, Brave?"

A bold knock at the front door caused the dog to redouble his efforts, until his master commanded him to be still. "Who is there?" called the shepherd.

"Young Matt's took powerful bad," answered a voice; "an' they want you t' come up t' th' house, an' doctor him." A drunken laugh came from the old tree, followed by a smothered oath.

The giant at Mr. Howitt's side growled under his breath, "Oh, I'm sick, am I? There's them that'll be a heap sicker before mornin'. Keep on a talkin', Dad. We've got to make all the time we can, so's Jim can get here."

The shepherd called again, "I do not recognize your voice. You must tell me who you are."

Outside there was a short consultation, followed by a still louder knock; "Open up. Why don't you open up an' see who we are?" while from under the tree came a call, "Quit your foolin' an' bring him out o' there, you fellers." This command was followed by a still more vigorous hammering at the door, and the threats, "Open up ol' man. Open up, or we'll sure bust her in." Mr. Howitt whispered to his companion, "Let me open the door and talk to them, Grant. Surely they will listen to reason."

But the woodsman returned, "Talk to a nest of rattlers! Jim Lane's the only man that can talk to them now. We've got to stand them off as long as we can." As he spoke he raised his revolver, and was about to fire a shot through the door, when a slight noise at one side of the room attracted his attention. He turned just in time to catch a glimpse of a face as it was withdrawn from one of the little windows. The noise at the door ceased suddenly, and they heard the two men running to join the group under the tree.

"They've found you ain't alone," whispered the big fellow, springing to the window again. And, as a wild drunken yell came from the visitors, he added, "Seems like they're some excited about it, too. They're holdin' a regular pow-wow. What do you reckon they're thinkin'? Hope they'll keep it up 'till Jim—Sh—h- -h Here comes another. It's that ornery Jim Bowles from the mouth of Indian Creek."

The man approached the cabin, but stopped some distance away and called, "Hello, ol' man!"

"Well, what do you want?" answered Mr. Howitt.

"Who's that there feller you got with you?"

"A friend."

"Yes! We all 'lowed hit war a friend, an' we all want t' see him powerful bad. Can't he come out an' play with us, Mister?" Another laugh came from the group under the tree.

Young Matt whispered, "Keep him a talkin', Dad;" and Mr. Howitt called, "He doesn't feel like playing to-night. Come back to- morrow."

At this the spokesman dropped his bantering tone, "Look a here, ol' man. We'uns ain't got no time t' be a foolin' here. We know who that feller is, an' we're a goin' t' have him. He's been a sneakin' 'round this here neighborhood long enough. As fer you, Mister, we 'low your health'll be some better back where you come from; an' we aim t' hep you leave this neck o' th' woods right sudden. Open up, now, an' turn that there feller over t' us; an' we'll let you off easy like. If you don't, we'll bust in th' door, an' make you both dance t' th' same tune. There won't be ary thing under you t' dance on, nuther."

The old shepherd was replying kindly, when his speech was interrupted by a pistol shot, and a command from the leader, at which the entire gang charged toward the cabin, firing as they came, and making the little valley hideous with their drunken oaths and yells.

From his window, Young Matt coolly emptied his revolver, but even as the crowd faltered, there came from their leader another volley of oaths. "Go on, go on," yelled Wash. "Their guns are empty, now. Fetch 'em out 'fore they can load again." With an answering yell, the others responded. Carrying a small log they made for the cabin at full speed. One crashing blow—the door flew from its hinges, and the opening was filled with the drunken, sweating, swearing crew. The same instant, Young Matt dropped his useless revolver, and, springing forward, met them on the threshold. The old shepherd—who had not fired a shot—could scarcely believe his eyes, as he saw the giant catch the nearest man by the shoulder and waist, and, lifting him high above his head, fling him with terrific force full into the faces of his bewildered companions.

Those who were not knocked down by the strange weapon scattered in every direction, crouching low. For a moment the big fellow was master of the situation, and, standing alone in the doorway, in the full light of the moon, was easily recognized.

"Hell, boys! Hit's Young Matt hisself!" yelled the one who had raised a laugh, by saying that Young Matt was sick and the shepherd was wanted to doctor.

"Yes! It's me, Bill Simpson. I'm sure ailin' to-night. I need somebody to go for a doctor powerful bad," returned the young giant.

"We never knowed it war you," whined the other carefully lengthening the distance between the big man on the doorstep and himself.

No, I reckon not. You all played to find an old man alone, and do for him like you've done for others. A fine lot you are, ten to one, and him not knowin' the woods."

While he was speaking, the men slowly retreated, to gather about their big leader under the tree, two of them being assisted by their companions, and one other limping painfully. Young Matt raised his voice, "I know you, Wash Gibbs, and I know this here is your dirty work. You've been a braggin' what you'd do when you met up with me. I'm here now. Why don't you come up like a man? Come out here into the light and let's you and me settle this thing right now. You all—" *Crack!* A jet of flame leaped out of the shadow, and the speaker dropped like a log.

With a cry the shepherd ran to the side of his friend; but in a moment the crowd had again reached the cabin, and the old man was dragged from his fallen companion. With all his strength, Mr. Howitt struggled with his captors, begging them to let him go to the boy. But his hands were bound tightly behind his back, and when he still plead with those who held him, Wash Gibbs struck him full in the mouth, a blow that brought the blood.

They were leading the stunned and helpless old man away, when someone, who was bending over Young Matt, exclaimed, "You missed him, Wash!

Jest raked him. He'll be up in a minute. An' hell 'll be to pay in th' wilderness if he ain't tied. Better fix him quick."

The big fellow already showed signs of returning consciousness, and, by the time they had tied his arms, he was able to struggle to his feet. For a moment he looked dizzily around, his eyes turning from one evil, triumphant face to another, until they rested upon the bleeding countenance of his old friend. The shepherd's eyes smiled back a message of cheer, and the kind old man tried to speak, when Wash Gibbs made another threatening motion, with his clenched fist.

At this, a cry like the roar of a mad bull came from the young giant. In his rage, he seemed suddenly endowed with almost superhuman strength. Before a man of the startled company could do more than gasp with astonishment, he had shaken himself free from those who held him, and, breaking the rope with which he was bound, as though it were twine, had leaped to the shepherd's side.

But it was useless. For a moment, no one moved. Then a crashing blow, from the butt of a rifle in the hands of a man in the rear of the two prisoners, sent Young Matt once more to the ground. When he again regained consciousness, he was so securely bound, that, even with his great strength, he was helpless.

Leading their captives to the old tree, the men withdrew for a short consultation, and to refresh themselves with another drink. When they had finished, Gibbs addressed the two friends; "We'uns didn't aim to hurt you, Young Matt, but seein' how you're so thick with this here feller, an' 'pear to know so much 'bout him, I reckon we can't hep ourselves nohow." He turned to the shepherd; "There's been too dad burned much funny work, at this ranch, since you come, Mister, an' we'uns 'low we'll just give warnin' that we don't want no more strangers snoopin' 'round this neighborhood, an' we don't aim t' have 'em neither. We'uns 'low we can take care o' ourselves, without ary hep from th' dad burned government."

The shepherd tried to speak, but Gibbs, with an oath, roared, "Shut up, I tell you. Shut up. I've been a watchin', an' I know what I know. Fix that there rope, boys, an we'll get through, an' mosey 'long out o' here. Ain't no use to palaver, nohow."

A rope was thrown over a limb above their heads, and a man approached the shepherd with the noose. Young Matt struggled desperately. With an evil grin, Gibbs said, "Don't you worry, sonny; you're a goin', too." And at his signal another rope was fixed, and the noose placed over the young man's head. The men took their places, awaiting the word from their leader.

The shepherd spoke softly to his companion, "Thank you, my boy." The giant began another desperate struggle.

Wash Gibbs, raising his hand, opened his lips to give the signal. But no word came. The brutal jaw dropped. The ruffian's eyes fairly started from his head, while the men who held the ropes, stood as if turned to stone, as a long wailing cry came from the dark shadows under the bluff. There was a moment of death-like silence. Then another awful, sobbing groan, rising into a blood curdling scream, came from down the road, and, from the direction of the ruined cabin, advanced a ghostly figure. Through the deep shadows and the misty light, it seemed to float toward them, moaning and sobbing as it came.

A shuddering gasp of horror burst from the frightened crew under the tree. Then, at a louder wail from the approaching apparition, they broke and ran. Like wild men they leaped for their horses, and, flinging themselves into their saddles, fled in every direction.

Young Matt and the shepherd sank upon the ground in helpless amazement.

As the outlaws fled, the spectre paused. Then it started onward toward the two men. Again it hesitated. For a moment it remained motionless, then turned and vanished, just as Jim Lane came flying out of the timber, into the bright light of the little clearing.

CHAPTER XVIII.

LEARNING TO BE A LADY.

The books sent for by Mr. Howitt came a few days after the adventure at the ranch, and Sammy, with all the intensity of her nature, plunged at once into the work mapped out for her by the shepherd.

All through the long summer and autumn, the girl spent hours with her teacher out on the hillside. Seated on some rocky bench, or reclining on the grassy slope, she would recite the lessons he gave her, or listen to him, as he read aloud from character forming books, pausing now and then to slip in some comment to make the teaching clear, or to answer her eager questions.

At other times, while they followed the sheep, leisurely, from one feeding ground to another, he provoked her to talk of the things they were reading, and, while he thus led her to think, he as carefully guarded her speech and language.

At first they took the old familiar path of early intellectual training, but, little by little, he taught her to find the way for herself. Always as she advanced, he encouraged her to look for the life that is more than meat, and always, while they read and talked together, there was opened before them the great book wherein God has written, in the language of mountain, and tree, and sky, and flower, and brook, the things that make truly wise those who pause to read.

From her mother, and from her own free life in the hills, Sammy had a body beautiful with the grace and strength of perfect physical womanhood. With this, she had inherited from many generations of gentle-folk a mind and spirit susceptible of the highest culture. Unspoiled by the hot-house, forcing process, that so often leaves the intellectual powers jaded and weak, before they have fully developed, and free from the atmosphere of falsehood and surface culture, in which so many souls struggle for their very existence, the girl took what her teacher had to offer and made it her own. With a mental appetite uninjured by tit-bits and dainties, she digested the strong food, and asked eagerly for more.

Her progress was marvelous, and the old scholar often had cause to wonder at the quickness with which his pupil's clear mind grasped the truths he showed her. Often before he could finish speaking, a bright nod, or word, showed that she had caught the purpose of his speech, while that wide eager look, and the question that followed, revealed her readiness to go on. It was as though many of the things he sought to teach her slept already in her brain, and needed only a touch to arouse them to vigorous life.

In time, the girl's very clothing, and even her manner of dressing her hair, came to reveal the development and transformation of her inner self; not that she dressed more expensively; she could not do that; but in the selection of materials, and in the many subtle touches that give distinction even to the plainest apparel, she showed her awakening. To help her in this, there was Aunt Mollie and a good ladies' magazine, which came to her regularly, through the kindness of her teacher.

Sammy's father, too, came unconsciously under the shepherd's influence. As his daughter grew, the man responded to the change in her, as he always responded to her every thought and mood. He talked often now of the old home in the south land, and sometimes fell into the speech of other days, dropping, for a moment, the rougher expressions of his associates. But all this was to Sammy alone. To the world, there was no change in Jim, and he still went on his long rides with Wash Gibbs. By fall, the place was fixed up a bit; the fence was rebuilt, the yard trimmed, and another room added to the cabin.

So the days slipped away over the wood fringed ridges. The soft green of tree, and of bush, and grassy slope changed to brilliant gold, and crimson, and russet brown, while the gray blue haze that hangs always over the hollows took on a purple tone. Then in turn this purple changed to a deeper, colder blue, when the leaves had fallen, and the trees showed naked against the winter sky.

With the cold weather, the lessons were continued in the Lane cabin on the southern slope of Dewey. All day, while the shepherd was busy at the ranch, Sammy pored over her books; and every evening the old scholar climbed the hill to direct the work of his pupil, with long Jim sitting, silent and grim, by the fireside, listening to the talk, and seeing who knows what visions of the long ago in the dancing flame.

And so the winter passed, and the spring came again; came, with its soft beauty of tender green; its wealth of blossoms, and sweet fragrance of growing things. Then came the summer; that terrible summer, when all the promises of spring were broken; when no rain fell for weary months, and the settlers, in the total failure of their crops, faced certain ruin.

CHAPTER XIX.

THE DROUGHT.

It began to be serious by the time corn was waist high. When the growing grain lost its rich color and the long blades rustled dryly in the hot air, the settlers looked anxiously for signs of coming rain. The one topic of conversation at the mill was the condition of the crops. The stories were all of past drought or tales of hardship and want.

The moon changed and still the same hot dry sky, with only now and then a shred of cloud floating lazily across the blue. The grass in the glades grew parched and harsh; the trees rattled their shriveled leaves; creek beds lay glaring white and dusty in the sun; and all the wild things in the woods sought the distant river bottom. In the Mutton Hollow neighborhood, only the spring below the Matthews place held water; and all day the stock on the range, crowding around the little pool, tramped out the narrow fringe of green grass about its edge, and churned its bright life into mud in their struggle.

Fall came and there was no relief. Crops were a total failure. Many people were without means to buy fed for themselves and their stock for the coming winter and the months until another crop could be grown and harvested. Family after family loaded their few household goods into the big covered wagons, and, deserting their homes, set out to seek relief in more fortunate or more wealthy portions of the country.

The day came at last when Sammy found the shepherd in the little grove, near the deer lick, and told him that she and her father were going to move.

"Father says there is nothing else to do. Even if we could squeeze through the winter, we couldn't hold out until he could make another crop."

Throwing herself on the ground, she picked a big yellow daisy from a cluster, that, finding a little moisture oozing from a dirt- filled crevice of the rock, had managed to live, and began pulling it to pieces.

In silence the old man watched her. He had not before realized how much the companionship of this girl was to him. To the refined and cultivated scholar, whose lot had been cast so strangely with the rude people of the mountain wilderness, the companionship of such a spirit and mind was a necessity. Unconsciously Sammy had supplied the one thing lacking, and by her demands upon his thought had kept the shepherd from mental stagnation and morbid brooding. Day after day she had grown into his life—his intellectual and spiritual child, and though she had dropped the rude speech of the native, she persisted still in calling him by his backwoods title, "Dad." But the little word had come to hold a new meaning for them both. He saw now, all at once, what he would lose when she went away.

One by one, the petals from the big daisy fell from the girl's hand, dull splashes of gold against her dress and on the grass.

"Where will you go?" he asked at last.

Sammy shook her head without looking up; "Don't know; anywhere that Daddy can earn a livin'—I mean living—for us."

"And when do you start?"

"Pretty soon now; there ain't nothin'—there is nothing to stay for now. Father told me when he went away day before yesterday that we would go as soon as he returned. He promised to be home sometime this evening. I—I couldn't tell you before, Dad, but I guess you knew."

The shepherd did know. For weeks they had both avoided the subject.

Sammy continued; "I—I've just been over to the Matthews place. Uncle Matt has been gone three days now. I guess you know about that, too. Aunt Mollie told me all about it. Oh, I wish, I wish I could help them." She reached for another daisy and two big tears rolled from under the long lashes to fall with the golden petals. "We'll come back in the spring when it's time to plant again, but what if you're not here?"

Her teacher could not answer for a time; then he said, in an odd, hesitating way, "Have you heard from Ollie lately?"

The girl raised her head, her quick, rare instinct divining his unspoken thought, and something she saw in her old friend's face brought just a hint of a smile to her own tearful eyes. She knew him so well. "You don't mean that, Dad," she said. "We just couldn't do that. I had a letter from him yesterday offering us money, but you know we could not accept it from him." And there the subject was dropped.

They spent the afternoon together, and in the evening, at Sammy's Lookout on the shoulder of Dewey, she bade him good-night, and left him alone with his flocks in the soft twilight.

That same evening Mr. Matthews returned from his trip to the settlement.

CHAPTER XX.

THE SHEPHERD WRITES A LETTER.

To purchase the sheep and the ranch in the Hollow, Mr. Matthews placed a heavy mortgage not only upon the ranch land but upon the homestead as well. In the loss of his stock the woodsman would lose all he had won in years of toil from the mountain wilderness.

When the total failure of the crops became a certainty, and it was clear that the country could not produce enough feed to carry his flock through the winter until the spring grass, Mr. Matthews went to the settlement hoping to get help from the bank there, where he was known.

He found the little town in confusion and the doors of the bank closed. The night before a band of men had entered the building, and, forcing the safe, had escaped to the mountains with their booty.

Old Matt's interview with the bank official was brief. "It is simply impossible, Mr. Matthews," said the man; "as it is, we shall do well to keep our own heads above water."

Then the mountaineer had come the long way home. As he rode slowly up the last hill, the giant form stooped with a weariness unusual, and the rugged face looked so worn and hopelessly sad, that Aunt Mollie, who was waiting at the gate, did not need words to tell her of his failure. The old man got stiffly down from his horse, and when he had removed saddle and bridle, and had turned the animal into the lot, the two walked toward the house. But they did not enter the building. Without a word they turned aside from the steps and followed the little path to the graves in the rude enclosure beneath the pines, where the sunshine fell only in patches here and there.

That night after supper Mr. Matthews went down into the Hollow to see the shepherd. "It's goin' to be mighty hard on Mollie and me a leavin' the old place up yonder," said the big man, when he had told of his unsuccessful trip. "It won't matter so much to the boy, 'cause he's young yet, but we've worked hard, Mr. Howitt, for that home—Mollie and me has. She's up there now a sittin' on the porch and a livin' it all over again, like she does when there ain't no one around, with her face turned toward them pines west of the house. It's mighty nigh a breakin' her heart just to think of leavin', but she'll hide it all from me when I go up there, thinkin' not to worry me—as if I didn't know. An' it's goin to be mighty hard to part with you, too, Mr. Howitt. I don't reckon you'll ever know, sir, how much you done for us; for me most of all."

The shepherd made as if to interrupt, but the big man continued; "Don't you suppose we can see, sir, how you've made over the whole neighborhood. There ain't a family for ten miles that don't come to you when they're in trouble. An' there's Sammy Lane a readin', an' talkin' just about the same as you do yourself, fit to hold up her end with anybody what's got education, and Jim himself's changed something wonderful. Same old Jim in lots of ways, but something more, somehow, though I can't tell it. Then there's my boy, Grant. I know right well what he'd been if it wasn't for you to show him what the best kind of a man's like. He'd a sure never knowed it from me. I don't mean as he'd a ever been a bad man like Wash Gibbs, or a no account triflin' one, like them Thompsons, but he couldn't never a been what he is now, through and through, if he hadn't a known you. There's a heap more, too, all over the country that you've talked to a Sunday, when the parson wasn't here. As for me, you—you sure been a God's blessin' to me and Mollie, Mr. Howitt."

Again the shepherd moved uneasily, as if to protest, but his big friend made a gesture of silence; "Let me say it while I got a chance, Dad." And the other bowed his head while Old Matt continued; "I can't tell how it is, an' I don't reckon you'd understand any way, but stayin' as you have after our talk that first night you come, an' livin' down here on this spot alone, after what you know, it's—it's just like I was a little kid, an' you was a standin' big and strong like between me an' a great blackness that was somethin' awful. I reckon it looks foolish, me a talkin' this way. Maybe it's because I'm gettin' old, but anyhow I wanted you to know."

The shepherd raised his head and his face was aglow with a glad triumphant light, while his deep voice was full of meaning as he said gently, "It has been more to me, too, than you think, Mr. Matthews. I ought to tell you—I—I will tell you—" he checked himself and added, "some day." Then he changed the topic quickly.

"Are you sure there is no one who can help you over this hard time? Is there *no* way?"

The mountaineer shook his head. "I've gone over it all again an' again. Williams at the bank is the only man I know who had the money, an' he's done for now by this robbery. You see I can't go to strangers, Dad; I ain't got nothin' left for security."

"But, could you not sell the sheep for enough to save the homestead?"

"Who could buy? or who would buy, if they could, in this country, without a bit of feed? And then look at 'em, they're so poor an' weak, now, they couldn't stand the drivin' to the shippin' place. They'd die all along the road. They're just skin an' bones, Dad; ain't no butcher would pay freight on 'em, even."

Mr. Howitt sat with knitted brow, staring into the shadows. Then he said slowly, "There is that old mine. If this man Dewey were only here, do you suppose—?"

Again the mountaineer shook his head. "Colonel Dewey would be a mighty old man now, Dad, even if he were livin.' 'Tain't likely he'll ever come back, nor tain't likely the mine will ever be found without him. I studied all that out on the way home."

As he finished speaking, he rose to go, and the dog, springing up, dashed out of the cabin and across the clearing toward the bluff by the corral, barking furiously.

The two men looked at each other. "A rabbit," said Mr. Howitt. But they both knew that the well trained shepherd dog never tracked a rabbit, and Old Matt's face was white when he mounted to ride away up the trail.

Long the shepherd stood in the doorway looking out into the night, listening to the voices of the wilderness. In his life in the hills he had found a little brightness, while in the old mountaineer's words that evening, he had glimpsed a future happiness, of which he had scarcely dared to dream. With the single exception of that one wild night, his life had been an unbroken calm. Now he was to leave it all. And for what?

He seemed to hear the rush and roar of the world beyond the ridges, as one in a quiet harbor hears outside the thunder of the stormy sea. He shuddered. The gloom and mystery of it all crept into his heart. He was so alone. But it was not the wilderness that made him shudder. It was the thought of the great, mad, cruel world that raged beyond the hills; that, and something else.

The dog growled again and faced threateningly toward the cliff. "What is it, Brave?" The only answer was an uneasy whine as the animal crouched close to the man's feet. The shepherd peered into the darkness in the direction of the ruined cabin. "God," he whispered, "how can I leave this place?"

He turned back into the house, closed and barred the door. With the manner of one making a resolution after a hard struggle, he took writing material from the top shelf of the cupboard, and, seating himself at the table, began to write. The hours slipped by, and page after page, closely written, came from the shepherd's pen, while, as he wrote, the man's face grew worn and haggard. It was as though he lifted again the burden he had learned to lay aside. At last it was finished. Placing the sheets in an envelope, he wrote the address with trembling hand.

While Mr. Howitt was writing his letter at the ranch, and Old Matt was tossing sleeplessly on his bed in the big log house, a horseman rode slowly down from the Compton Ridge road. Stopping at the creek to water, he pushed on up the mountain toward the Lane cabin. The horse walked with low hung head and lagging feet; the man slouched half asleep in the saddle. It was Jim Lane.

CHAPTER XXI.

GOD'S GOLD.

The troubled night passed. The shepherd arose to see the sky above the eastern rim of the Hollow glowing with the first soft light of a new day. Away over Compton Ridge one last, pale star hung, caught in the upper branches of a dead pine. Not a leaf of the forest stirred. In awe the man watched the miracle of the morning, as the glowing colors touched cloud after cloud, until the whole sky was aflame, and the star was gone.

Again he seemed to hear, faint and far away, the roar and surge of the troubled sea. With face uplifted, he cried aloud, "O God, my Father, I ask thee not for the things that men deem great. I covet not wealth, nor honor, nor ease; only peace; only that I may live free from those who do not understand; only that I may in some measure make atonement; that I may win pardon. Oh, drive me not from this haven into the world again!"

"Again, again," came back from the cliff on the other side of the clearing, and, as the echo died away in the silent woods, a bush on top of the bluff stirred in the breathless air; stirred, and was still again. Somewhere up on Dewey a crow croaked hoarsely to his mate; a cow on the range bawled loudly and the sheep in the corral chorused in answer.

Re-entering the cabin, the old man quickly built a fire, then, taking the bucket, went to the spring for water. He must prepare his breakfast. Coming back with the brimming pail, he placed it on the bench and was turning to the cupboard, when he noticed on the table a small oblong package. "Mr. Matthews must have left it last night," he thought. "Strange that I did not see it before."

Picking up the package he found that it was quite heavy, and, to his amazement, saw that it was addressed to himself, in a strange, cramped printing, such letters as a child would make. He ripped open the covering and read in the same crude writing: "This stuff is for you to give to the Matthews's and Jim Lane, but don't tell anyone where you got it. And don't try to find out where it come from either, or you'll wish you hadn't. You needn't be afraid. It's good money alright." The package contained gold pieces of various denominations.

With a low exclamation, the shepherd let the parcel slip, and the money fell in a shining heap on the floor. He stood as in a dream, looking from the gold to the letter in his hand. Then, going to the door, he gazed long and searchingly in every direction. Nothing unusual met his eye. Turning back into the cabin again, he caught up the letter he had written, and stepped to the fireplace, an expression of relief upon his face. But with his hand outstretched toward the flames, he paused, the letter still in his grasp, while the expression of relief gave way to a look of fear.

"The bank," he muttered; "the robbery." The shining pieces on the floor seemed to glisten mockingly; "No, no, no," said the man. "Better the other way, and yet—" He read the letter again. "It's good money, alright; you needn't be afraid."

In his quandary, he heard a step without and looking up saw Pete in the open door.

The boy's sensitive face was aglow, as he said; "Pete's glad this morning; Pete saw the sky. Did Dad see the sky?"

Mr. Howitt nodded; then, moved by a sudden impulse, pointed to the money, and said, "Does Pete see this? It's gold, all gold."

The boy drew near with curious eyes. "Dad doesn't know where it came from," continued the shepherd. "Does Pete know?"

The youth gave a low laugh of delight; "Course Pete knows. Pete went up on Dewey this morning; 'way up to the old signal tree, and course he took me with him. The sky was all soft and silvery, an' the clouds was full, plumb full of gold, like that there." He pointed to the yellow coins on the floor. "Didn't Dad see? Some of it must o' spilled out."

"Ah, yes, that was God's gold," said the older man softly.

The lad touched his friend on the arm, and with the other hand again pointed to the glittering heap on the floor. "Pete says that there's God's gold too, and Pete he knows."

The man started and looked at the boy in wonder; "But why, why should it come to me at such a time as this?" he muttered.

" 'Cause you're the Shepherd of Mutton Hollow, Pete says. Don't be scared, Dad. Pete knows. It's sure God's gold."

The shepherd turned to the fireplace and dropped the letter he had written upon the leaping flames.

CHAPTER XXII.

A LETTER FROM OLLIE STEWART.

The Postoffice at the Forks occupied a commanding position in the northeast corner of Uncle Ike's cabin, covering an area not less than four feet square.

The fittings were in excellent taste, and the equipment fully adequate to the needs of the service: an old table, on legs somewhat rickety; upon the table, a rude box, set on end and divided roughly into eight pigeon holes, duly numbered; in the table, a drawer, filled a little with stamps and stationery, filled mostly with scraps of leaf tobacco, and an odd company of veteran cob pipes, now on the retired list, or home on furlough; before the table, a little old chair, wrought in some fearful and wonderful fashion from hickory sticks from which the bark had not been removed.

With every change of the weather, this chair, through some unknown but powerful influence, changed its shape, thus becoming in its own way a sort of government weather bureau. And if in all this "land of the free and home of the brave" there be a single throne, it must be this same curiously changeable chair. In spite of, or perhaps because of, its strange powers, that weird piece of furniture managed to make itself so felt that it was religiously avoided by every native who called at the Forks. Not the wildest "Hill-Billy" of them all dared to occupy for a moment this seat of Uncle Sam's representative. Here Uncle Ike reigned supreme over his four feet square of government property. And you may be very sure that the mighty mysterious thing known as the "gov'ment" lost none of its might, and nothing of its mystery, at the hands of its worthy official.

Uncle Ike left the group in front of the cabin, and, hurriedly entering the office, seated himself upon his throne. A tall, thin, slow moving mule, brought to before a certain tree with the grace and dignity of an ocean liner coming into her slip. Zeke Wheeler dismounted, and, with the saddle mail pouch over his arm, stalked solemnly across the yard and into the house, his spurs clinking on the gravel and rattling over the floor. Following the mail carrier, the group of mountaineers entered, and, with Uncle Ike's entire family, took their places at a respectful distance from the holy place of mystery and might, in the north east corner of the room.

The postmaster, with a key attached by a small chain to one corner of the table, unlocked the flat pouch and drew forth the contents- -five papers, three letters and one postal card.

The empty pouch was kicked contemptuously beneath the table. The papers were tossed to one side. All eyes were fixed on the little bundle of first class matter. In a breathless silence the official cut the string. The silence was broken. "Ba thundas! Mary Liz Jolly'll sure be glad t' git that there letter. Her man's been gone nigh onto three months now, an' ain't wrote but once. That was when he was in Mayville. I see he's down in th' nation now at Auburn, sendin' Mary Liz some money, I reckon. Ba thundas, it's 'bout time! What!"

"James Creelman, E-S-Q., Wal, dad burn *me* Jim done wrote t' that there house in Chicago more'n three weeks ago, 'bout a watch they're a sellin' fer fo' dollars. Ba thundas! They'd sure answer *me* quicker'n that, er they'd hear turkey. What! I done tole Jim it was only a blamed ol' fo' dollar house anyhow."

At this many nods and glances were exchanged by the group in silent admiration of the "gov'ment," and one mountaineer, bold even to recklessness, remarked, "Jim must have a heap o' money t' be a buyin' four dollar watches. Must er sold that gray mule o' hisn; hit'd fetch 'bout that much, I reckon."

"Much you know 'bout it, Buck Boswell. Let me tell you, Jim he works, he does. He's the workingest man in this here county, ba thundas! What! Jim he don't sit 'round like you fellers down on th' creek an' wait fer pawpaws to git ripe, so he can git a square meal, ba thundas!" The bold mountaineer wilted.

Uncle Ike proceeded with the business of his office. "Here's Sallie Rhodes done writ her maw a card from th' Corners. Sallie's been a visitin' her paw's folks. Says she'll be home on th' hack next mail, an' wants her maw t' meet her here. You can take th' hack next time, Zeke. An' ba thundas! Here's 'nother letter from that dummed Ollie Stewart. Sammy ain't been over yet after th' last one he wrote. Ba thundas! If it weren't for them blamed gov'-ment inspectors, I'd sure put a spoke in his wheel. What! I'd everlastin'ly seva' th' connections between that gentleman an' these here Ozarks. Dad burn me, if I wouldn't. He'd better take one o' them new fangled women in th' city, where he's gone to, an' not come back here for one o' our girls. I don't believe Sammy'd care much, nohow, ba thundas! What!" The official tossed the letter into a pigeon hole beside its neglected mate, with a gesture that fully expressed the opinion of the entire community, regarding Mr. Stewart and his intentions toward Miss Lane.

Sammy got the letters the next day, and read them over and over, as she rode slowly through the sweet smelling woods. The last one told her that Ollie was coming home on a visit. "Thursday, that's the day after to-morrow," she said aloud. Then she read the letter again.

It was a very different letter from those Ollie had written when first he left the woods. Most of all it was different in that indefinable something by which a man reveals his place in life in the letters he writes, no less than in the words he speaks, or the clothing he wears. As Sammy rode slowly through the pinery and down the narrow Fall Creek valley, she was thinking of these things, thinking of these things seriously.

The girl had been in a way conscious of the gradual change in Ollie's life, as it had been revealed in his letters, but she had failed to connect the change with her lover. The world into which young Stewart had gone, and by which he was being formed, was so foreign to the only world known to Sammy, that, while she realized in a dim way that he was undergoing a transformation, she still saw him in her mind as the backwoods boy. With the announcement of his return, and the thought that she would soon meet him face to face, it burst upon her suddenly that her lover was a stranger. The man who wrote this letter was not the man whom she had promised to marry. Who was he?

Passing the mill and the blacksmith shop, the brown pony with his absorbed rider began to climb the steep road to the Matthews place. Half way up the hill, the little horse, stepping on a loose stone, stumbled, catching himself quickly.

As a flash of lightning on a black night reveals well known landmarks and familiar objects, this incident brought back to Sammy the evening when, with Ollie and Young Matt, she had climbed the same way; when her horse had stumbled and her face had come close to the face of the big fellow whose hand was on the pony's neck. The whole scene came before her with a vividness that was startling; every word, every look, every gesture of the two young men, her own thoughts and words, the objects along the road, the very motion of her horse; she seemed to be actually living again those moments of the past. But more than this, she seemed not only to live again the incidents of that evening, but in some strange way to possess the faculty of analyzing and passing judgment upon her own thoughts and words.

Great changes had come to Sammy, too, since that night when her lover had said good-by. And now, in her deeper life, the young woman felt a curious sense of shame, as she saw how trivial were the things that had influenced her to become Ollie's promised wife. She blushed, as she recalled the motives that had sent her to the shepherd with the request that he teach her to be a fine lady.

Coming out on top of the ridge, Brownie stopped of his own accord, and the girl saw again the figure of a young giant, standing in the level rays of the setting sun, with his great arms outstretched, saying, "I reckon I was built to live in these hills. I don't guess you'd better count on me ever bein' more'n I am." Sammy realized suddenly that the question was no longer whether Ollie would be ashamed of her. It was quite a different question, indeed.

CHAPTER XXIII.

OLLIE COMES HOME.

The day that Ollie was expected at the cabin on Dewey Bald, Mr. Lane was busy in the field.

"I don't reckon you'll need me at th' house nohow," he said with a queer laugh, as he rose from the dinner table; and Sammy, blushing, told him to go on to his work, or Young Matt would get his planting done first.

Jim went out to get his horse from the stable, but before he left, he returned once more to the house.

"What is it, Daddy? Forget something?" asked Sammy, as her father stood in the doorway.

"Not exactly," drawled Jim. "I ain't got a very good forgetter.

Wish I had. It's somethin' I can't forget. Wish I could."

In a moment the girl's arms were about his neck, "You dear foolish old Daddy Jim. I have a bad forgetter, too. You thought when I began studying with Dad Howitt that my books would make me forget you. Well, have they?" A tightening of the long arm about her waist was the only answer. "And now you are making yourself miserable trying to think that Ollie Stewart and his friends will make me forget you; just as if all the folks in the world could ever be to me what you are; you, and Dad, and Uncle Matt, and Aunt Mollie, and Young Matt. Daddy, I am ashamed of you. Honest, I am. Do you think a real genuine lady could ever forget the father who had been so good to her? Daddy, I am insulted. You must apologize immediately."

She pretended to draw away, but the long arm held her fast, while the mountaineer said in a voice that had in it pride and pain, with a world of love, "I know, I know, girl. But you'll be a livin' in the city, when you and Ollie are married, and these old hills will be mighty lonesome with you gone. You see I couldn't never leave the old place. 'Tain't much, I know, so far as money value goes. But there's some things worth a heap more than their money value, I reckon. If you was only goin' t' live where I could ride over once or twice a week to see you, it would be different."

"Yes, Daddy; but maybe I won't go after all. I'm not married, yet, you know."

Something in her voice or manner caused Jim to hold his daughter at arm's length, and look full into the brown eyes; "What do you mean, girl?"

Sammy laughed in an uneasy and embarrassed way. She was not sure that she knew herself all that lay beneath the simple words. She tried to explain. "Why, I mean that—that Ollie and I have both grown up since we promised, and he has been living away out in the big world and going to school besides. He must have seen many girls since he left me. He is sure to be changed greatly, and— and, maybe he won't want a backwoods wife."

The man growled something beneath his breath, and the girl placed a hand over his lips; "You mustn't say swear words, Daddy Jim. Indeed, you must not. Not in the presence of ladies, anyway."

"You're changed a heap in some ways, too," said Jim.

"Yes, I suppose I am; but my changes are mostly on the inside like; and perhaps he won't see them."

"Would you care so mighty much, Sammy?" whispered the father.

"That's just it, Daddy. How can I tell? We must both begin all over again, don't you see?" Then she sent him away to his work.

Sammy had finished washing the dinner dishes, and was putting things in order about the house, when she stopped suddenly before the little shelf that held her books. Then, with a smile, she carried them every one into her own room, placing them carefully where they could not be seen from the open door. Going next to the mirror, she deliberately took down her hair, and arranged it in the old careless way that Ollie had always known. "You're just the same backwoods girl, Sammy Lane, so far as outside things go," she said to the face in the glass; "but you are not quite the same all the way through. We'll see if he—" She was interrupted by the loud barking of the dog outside, and her heart beat more quickly as a voice cried, "Hello, hello, I say; call off your dog!"

Sammy hurried to the door. A strange gentleman stood at the gate. The strangest gentleman that Sammy had ever seen. Surely this could not be Ollie Stewart; this slender, pale-faced man, with faultless linen, well gloved hands and shining patent leathers. The girl drew back in embarrassment.

But there was no hesitation on the part of the young man. Before she could recover from her astonishment, he caught her in his arms and kissed her again and again, until she struggled from his embrace. "You—you must not," she gasped.

"Why not?" he demanded laughingly. "Has anyone a better right? I have waited a long while for this, and I mean to make up now for lost time."

He took a step toward her again, but Sammy held him off at arm's length, as she repeated, "No—no—you must not; not now." Young Stewart was helpless. And the discovery that she was stronger than this man brought to the girl a strange feeling, as of shame.

"How strong you are," he said petulantly; ceasing his efforts. Then carefully surveying the splendidly proportioned and developed young woman, he added, "And how beautiful!"

Under his look, Sammy's face flushed painfully, even to her neck and brow; and the man, seeing her confusion, laughed again. Then, seating himself in the only rocking-chair in the room, the young gentleman leisurely removed his gloves, looking around the while with an amused expression on his face, while the girl stood watching him. At last, he said impatiently, "Sit down, sit down, Sammy. You look at me as if I were a ghost."

Unconsciously, she slipped into the speech of the old days, "You sure don't look much like you used to. I never see nobody wear such clothes as them. Not even Dad Howitt, when he first come. Do you wear 'em every day?"

Ollie frowned; "You're just like all the rest, Sammy. Why don't you talk as you write? You've improved a lot in your letters. If you talk like that in the city; people will know in a minute that you are from the country."

At this, Sammy rallied her scattered wits, and the wide, questioning look was in her eyes, as she replied quietly, "Thank you. I'll try to remember. But tell me, please, what harm could it do, if people did know I came from the country?"

It was Ollie's turn to be amazed. "Why you can talk!" he said. "Where did you learn?" And the girl answered simply that she had picked it up from the old shepherd.

This little incident put Sammy more at ease, and she skilfully led her companion to speak of the city and his life there. Of his studies the young fellow had little to say, and, to her secret delight, the girl found that she had actually made greater progress with her books than had her lover with all his supposed advantages.

But of other things, of the gaiety and excitement of the great city, of his new home, the wealth of his uncle, and his own bright prospects, Ollie spoke freely, never dreaming the girl had already seen the life he painted in such glowing colors through the eyes of one who had been careful to point out the froth and foam of it all. Neither did the young man discover in the quiet questions she asked that Sammy was seeking to know what in all this new world he had found that he could make his own as the thing most worth while.

The backwoods girl had never seen that type of man to whom the life of the city, only, is life. Ollie was peculiarly fitted by nature to absorb quickly those things of the world, into which he had gone, that were most different from the world he had left; and there remained scarcely a trace of his earlier wilderness training.

But there is that in life that lies too deep for any mere change of environment to touch. Sammy remembered a lesson the shepherd had given her:

gentle spirit may express itself in the rude words of illiteracy; it is not therefore rude. Ruffianism may speak the language of learning or religion; it is ruffianism still. Strength may wear the garb of weakness, and still be strong; and a weakling may carry the weapons of strength, but fight with a faint heart." So, beneath all the changes that had come to her backwoods lover, Sammy felt that Ollie himself was unchanged. It was as though he had learned a new language, but still said the same things.

Sammy, too, had entered a new world. Step by step, as the young man had advanced in his schooling, and, dropping the habits and customs of the backwoods, had conformed in his outward life to his new environment, the girl had advanced in her education under the careful hand of the old shepherd. Ignorant still of the false standards and the petty ambitions that are so large a part of the complex world, into which he had gone, she had been introduced to a world where the life itself is the only thing worth while. She had seen nothing of the glittering tinsel of that cheap culture that is death to all true refinement, But in the daily companionship of her gentle teacher, she had lived in touch with true aristocracy, the aristocracy of heart and spirit.

Young Matt and Jim had thought that, in Sammy's education, the bond between the girl and her lover would be strengthened. They had thought to see her growing farther and farther from the life of the hills; the life to which they felt that they must always belong. But that was because Young Matt and Jim did not know the kind of education the girl was getting.

So Ollie had come back to his old home to measure things by his new standard; and he had come back, too, to be measured according to the old, old standard. If the man's eyes were dimmed by the flash and sparkle that play upon the surface of life, the woman's vision was strong and clear to look into the still depths.

Later in the day, as they walked together up the Old Trail to Sammy's Lookout, the girl tried to show him some of the things that had been revealed to her in the past months. But the young fellow could not follow where she led, and answered her always with some flippant remark, or with the superficial philosophy of his kind.

When he tried to turn the talk to their future, she skillfully defeated his purpose, or was silent; and when he would claim a lover's privileges, she held him off. Upon his demanding a reason for her coldness, she answered, "Don't you see that everything is different now? We must learn to know each other over again."

"But you are my promised wife."

"I promised to be the wife of a backwoodsman," she answered. "I cannot keep that promise, for that man is dead. You are a man of the city, and I am scarcely acquainted with you."

Young Stewart found himself not a little puzzled by the situation. He had come home expecting to meet a girl beautiful in face and form, but with the mind of a child to wonder at the things he would tell her. He had found, instead, a thoughtful young woman trained to look for and recognize truth and beauty. Sammy was always his physical superior. She was now his intellectual superior as well. The change that had come to her was not a change by environment of the things that lay upon the surface, but it was a change in the deeper things of life—in the purpose and understanding of life itself. Like many of his kind, Ollie could not distinguish between these things.

CHAPTER XXIV.

WHAT MAKES A MAN.

Mr. Matthews and his son finished their planting early in the afternoon and the boy set out to find old Kate and the mule colt. Those rovers had not appeared at the home place for nearly two weeks, and some one must bring them in before they forgot their home completely.

"Don't mind if I ain't back for supper, Mother," said Young Matt. "I may eat at the ranch with Dad. I ain't been down there for quite a spell now, an' I'd kind o' like to know if that panther we've been a hearin' is givin' Dad any trouble."

"Dad told me yesterday that he thought he heard old Kate's bell over on yon side of Cox's Bald," said Mr. Matthews; "I believe if I was you I'd take across Cox's, along the far side of th' ridge, around Dewey an' down into the Hollow that way. Joe Gardner was over north yesterday, an' he said he didn't see no signs on that range. I reckon you'll find 'em on Dewey somewheres about Jim Lane's, maybe. You'd better saddle a horse."

"No, I'll take it a foot. I can ride old Kate in, if I find them," replied the big fellow; and, with his rifle in the hollow of his arm, he struck out over the hills. All along the eastern slope of the ridge, that forms one side of Mutton Hollow, he searched for the missing stock, but not a sound of the bell could he hear; not a trace of the vagabonds could he find. And that was because old Kate and the little colt were standing quietly in the shade in a little glen below Sand Ridge not a quarter of a mile from the barn.

The afternoon was well on when Young Matt gave up the search, and shaped his course for the sheep ranch. He was on the farther side of Dewey, and the sun told him that there was just time enough to reach the cabin before supper.

Pushing straight up the side of the mountain, he found the narrow bench, that runs like a great cornice two-thirds of the way around the Bald Knob. The mountaineer knew that at that level, on the side opposite from where he stood, was Sammy's Lookout, and from there it was an easy road down to the sheep ranch in the valley. Also, he knew that from that rocky shelf, all along the southern side of the mountain, he would look down upon Sammy's home; and, who could tell, he might even catch a glimpse of Sammy herself. Very soon he rounded the turn of the hill, and saw far below the Lane homestead; the cabin and the barn in the little clearing looking like tiny doll houses.

Young Matt walked slowly now. The supper was forgotten. Coming to the clump of cedars just above the Old Trail where it turns the shoulder of the hill from the west, he stopped for a last look. Beyond this point, he would turn his back upon the scene that interested him so deeply.

The young man could not remember when he had not loved Sammy Lane. She seemed to have been always a part of his life. It was the season of the year when all the wild things of the forest choose their mates, and as the big fellow stood there looking down upon the home of the girl he loved, all the splendid passion of his manhood called for her. It seemed to him that the whole world was slipping away to leave him alone in a measureless universe. He almost cried aloud. It is the same instinct that prompts the panther to send his mating call ringing over the hills and through the forest, and leads the moose to issue his loud challenge.

At last Young Matt turned to go, when he heard the sound of voices. Someone was coming along the Old Trail that lay in full view on the mountain side not two hundred yards away. Instinctively the woodsman drew back into the thick foliage of the cedars.

The voices grew louder. A moment more and Sammy with Ollie Stewart appeared from around the turn of the hill. They were walking side by side and talking earnestly. The young woman had just denied the claims of her former lover, and was explaining the change in her attitude toward him; but the big fellow on the ledge above could not know that. He could not hear what they were saying. He only saw his mate, and the man who had come to take her from him.

Half crouching on the rocky shelf in the dark shadow of the cedar, the giant seemed a wild thing ready for his spring; ready and eager, yet held in check by something more powerful still than his passion. Slowly the two, following the Old Trail, passed from sight, and Young Matt stood erect. He was trembling like a frightened child. A moment longer he waited, then turned and fairly ran from the place. Leaving the ledge at the Lookout, he rushed down the mountain and through the woods as if mad, to burst in upon the shepherd, with words that were half a cry, half a groan. "He's come, Dad; he's come. I've just seen him with her."

Mr. Howitt sprang up with a startled exclamation. His face went white. He grasped the table for support. He tried to speak, but words would not come. He could only stare with frightened eyes, as though Young Matt himself were some fearful apparition.

The big fellow threw himself into a chair, and presently the shepherd managed to say in a hoarse whisper, "Tell me about it, Grant, if you can."

"I seen them up on Dewey just now, goin' down the Old Trail from Sammy's Lookout to her home. I was huntin' stock."

The old scholar leaned toward his friend, as he almost shouted, "Saw them going to Sammy's home! Saw whom, lad? Whom did you see?"

"Why—why—Sammy Lane and that—that Ollie Stewart, of course. I tell you he's come back. Come to take her away."

The reaction was almost as bad as the shock. Mr. Howitt gasped as he dropped back into his seat. He felt a hysterical impulse to laugh, to cry out. Young Matt continued; "He's come home, Dad, with all his fine clothes and city airs, and now she'll go away with him, and we won't never see her again."

As he began to put his thoughts into words, the giant got upon his feet, and walked the floor like one insane. "He shan't have her," he cried, clenching his great fists; "he shan't have her. If he was a man I could stand it, Dad. But look at him! Look at him, will you? The little white-faced, washed out runt, what is he? He ain't no man, Dad. He ain't even as much of a man as he was. And Sammy is—God! What a woman she is! You've been a tellin' me that I could be a gentleman, even if I always lived in the backwoods. But you're wrong, Dad, plumb wrong. I ain't no gentleman. I can't never be one. I'm just a man. I'm a—a savage, a damned beast, and I'm glad of it." He threw back his shaggy head, and his white teeth gleamed through his parted lips, as he spoke in tones of mad defiance.

"Dad, you say there's some things bigger'n learnin', and such, and I reckon this here's one of them. I don't care if that little whelp goes to all the schools there is, and gets to be a president or a king; I don't care if he's got all the money there is between here and hell; put him out here in the woods, face to face with life where them things don't count, and what is he? What is he, Dad? He's nothin'! plumb nothin'!"

The old shepherd waited quietly for the storm to pass. The big fellow would come to himself after a time; until then, words were useless. At last Young Matt spoke in calmer tones; "I run away, Dad. I had to. I was afraid I'd hurt him. Something inside o' me just fought to get at him, and I couldn't a held out much longer. I don't want to hurt nobody, Dad. I reckon it was a seein' 'em together that did it. It's a God's blessin' I come away when I did; it sure is." He dropped wearily into his chair again.

Then the teacher spoke, "It is always a God's blessing, lad, when a man masters the worst of himself. You are a strong man, my boy. You hardly know your strength. But you need always to remember that the stronger the man, the easier it is for him to become a beast. Your manhood depends upon this, and upon nothing else, that you conquer and control the animal side of yourself. It will be a sad moment for you, and for all of us who love you, if you ever forget. Don't you see, lad, it is this victory only that gives you the right to think of yourself as a man. Mind, I say to think of yourself, as a man. It doesn't much matter what others think of you. It is what one can honestly think of one's self that matters."

So they spent the evening together, and the big mountaineer learned to see still more deeply into the things that had come to the older man in his years of study and painful experience.

When at last Young Matt arose to say good-night, the shepherd tried to persuade him to sleep at the ranch. But he said, no, the folks at home would be looking for him, and he must go. "I'm mighty glad I come, Dad," he added; "I don't know what I'd do if it wasn't for you; go plumb hog wild, and make a fool of myself, I reckon. I don't know what a lot of us would do, either. Seems like you're a sort of shepherd to the whole neighborhood. I reckon, though, I'm 'bout the worst in the flock," he finished with a grim smile.

Mr. Howitt took his hat from the nail. "If you must go, I will walk a little way with you. I love to be out such nights as this. I often wish Pete would take me with him."

"He's out somewhere to-night, sure," replied the other, as they started. "We heard him a singin' last night." Then he stopped and asked, "Where's your gun, Dad? There's a panther somewhere on this range."

"I know," returned the shepherd; "I heard it scream last night; and I meant to go up to the house to-day for a gun. I broke the hammer of mine yesterday."

"That's bad," said Young Matt. "But come on, I'll leave mine with you until to-morrow. That fellow would sure make things lively, if he should come to see you, and catch you without a shootin' iron."

Together the two walked through the timber, until they came to where the trail that leads to the Matthews place begins to climb the low spur of the hill back of the house. Here Mr. Howitt stopped to say good-night, adding, as the young man gave him the rifle, "I don't like to take this, Grant. What if you should meet that panther between here and home?"

"Shucks!" returned the other; "you're the one that'll need it. You've got to take care of them sheep. I'll get home alright."

"Don't forget the other beast, lad. Remember what it is that makes the man."

CHAPTER XXV.

YOUNG MATT REMEMBERS.

After parting with his friend, Young Matt continued on his way until he reached the open ground below the point where the path from the ranch joins the Old Trail. Then he stopped and looked around.

Before him was the belt of timber, and beyond, the dark mass of the mountain ridge with the low gap where his home nestled among the trees. He could see the light from the cabin window shining like a star. Behind him lay the darker forest of the Hollow, and beyond, like a great sentinel, was the round, treeless form of Dewey Bald. From where he stood, he could even see clearly against the sky the profile of the mountain's shoulder, and the ledge at Sammy's Lookout. Another moment, and the young man had left the path that led to his home, and was making straight for the distant hill. He would climb to that spot where he had stood in the afternoon, and would look down once more upon the little cabin on the mountain side. Then he would go home along the ridge.

Three quarters of an hour later, he pushed up out of a ravine that he followed to its head below the Old Trail, near the place where, with Pete and the shepherd, he had watched Sammy reading her letter. He was climbing to the Lookout, for it was the easiest way to the ledge, and, as his eye came on a level with the bench along which the path runs, he saw clearly on the big rock above the figure of a man. Instantly Young Matt stopped. The moon shone full upon the spot, and he easily recognized the figure. It was Ollie Stewart.

Young Stewart had been greatly puzzled by Sammy's attitude. It was so unexpected, and, to his mind, so unreasonable. He loved the girl as much as it was possible for one of his weak nature to love; and he had felt sure of his place in her affections. But the door that had once yielded so readily to his touch he had found fast shut. He was on the outside, and he seemed somehow to have lost the key. In this mood on his way home, he had reached the spot that was so closely associated with the girl, and, pausing to rest after the sharp climb, had fallen to brooding over his disappointment. So intent was he upon his gloomy thoughts that he had not heard Young Matt approaching, and was wholly unconscious of that big fellow's presence in the vicinity.

For a time the face at the edge of the path regarded the figure on the rock intently; then it dropped from sight. Young Matt slipped quietly down into the ravine, and a few moments later climbed again to the Old Trail at a point hidden from the Lookout. Here he stepped quickly across the narrow open space and into the bushes on the slope of the mountain above. Then with the skill of one born and reared in the woods, the mountaineer made his way toward the man on the shoulder of the hill.

What purpose lay under his strange movement Young Matt did not know. But certainly it was not in his mind to harm Ollie. He was acting upon the impulse of the moment; an impulse to get nearer and to study unobserved the person of his rival. So he stalked him with all the instinct of a creature of the woods. Not a twig snapped, not a leaf rustled, as from bush to fallen log, from tree trunk to rock, he crept, always in the black shadows, or behind some object.

But there were still other eyes on Old Dewey that night, and sharp ears heard the big woodsman climbing out of the ravine, if Ollie did not. When the young man in the clear light of the moon crossed the Old Trail, a figure near the clump of trees, where he had sat with his two friends that day, dropped quietly behind a big rock, half hidden in the bushes. As the giant crept toward the Lookout, this figure followed, showing but little less skill than the mountaineer himself. Once a loose stone rattled slightly, and the big fellow turned his head; but the figure was lying behind a log that the other had just left. When Young Matt finally reached the position as close to Ollie as he could go without certain discovery, the figure also came to a rest, not far away.

The moments passed very slowly now to the man crouching in the shadows. Ollie looked at his watch. It was early yet to one accustomed to late hours in the city. Young Matt heard distinctly the snap of the case as the watch was closed and returned to its owner's pocket. Then Stewart lighted a cigar, and flipped the burned out match almost into his unseen companion's face.

It seemed to Young Matt that he had been there for hours. Years ago he left his home yonder on the ridge, to look for stray stock. They must have forgotten him long before this. The quiet cabin in the Hollow, and his friend, the shepherd, too, were far away. In all that lonely mountain there was no one—no one but that man on the rock there; that man, and himself. How bright the moon was!

Suddenly another form appeared upon the scene. It came creeping around the hill from beyond the Lookout. It was a long, low, lithe-bodied, form that moved with the easy, gliding movements of a big cat. Noiselessly the soft padded feet fell upon the hard rock and loose gravel of the old pathway; the pathway along which so many things had gone for their kill, or had gone to be killed.

Young Matt saw it the moment it appeared. He started in his place. He recognized it instantly as the most feared of all the wild things in the mountain wilderness—a panther. He saw it sniff the footprints on the trail—Ollie's footprints. He saw it pause and crouch as it caught sight of the man on the rock.

Instantly wild and unwelcome thoughts burned within the strong man's brain. The woodsman knew why that thing had come. Against such a foe the unconscious weakling on the rock there, calmly puffing his cigar, would have no chance whatever. He would not even know of its presence, until it had made its spring, and its fangs were in his neck. The man of the wilderness knew just how it would be done. It would be over in a minute.

The giant clenched his teeth. Why had he not gone on to his home after leaving the shepherd? Why had he followed that impulse to stand again where he had stood that afternoon? Above all, what had possessed him—what had led him to creep to his present position? He shot a quick glance around. How bright—how bright the moon was!

The panther turned aside from the trail and with silent grace leaped to the ledge, gaining a position on a level with Ollie— still unconscious of its presence. A cold sweat broke out on the big man's forehead. The great hands worked. His breath came in quick gasps. It could not be laid to his door. He had only to withdraw, to stop his ears and run, as he had fled that afternoon. God! How slowly that thing crept forward, crouching low upon its belly, its tail twitching from side to side, nearer, nearer. Young Matt felt smothered. He loosened the collar of his shirt. The moon—the moon was so bright! He could even see the muscles in the beast's heavy neck and shoulders working under the sleek skin.

Suddenly the words of the shepherd came to him, as though shouted in his ears, *"Remember the other beast, lad. Don't you see it is this victory only that gives you the right to think of yourself as a man?"*

Ollie was almost brushed from his place as the big mountaineer sprang from the shadow, while the panther, startled by the appearance of another man upon the rock, paused. An exclamation of fright burst from young Stewart, as he took in the situation. And the giant by his side reached forth a hand to push him back, as he growled, "Shut up and get out of the way! This here's my fight!"

At the movement the wild beast seemed to understand that the newcomer was there to rob him of his prey. With a snarl, it crouched low again, gathering its muscles for the spring. The giant waited. Suddenly the sharp crack of a rifle rang out on the still night, echoing and echoing along the mountain.

The panther leaped, but fell short. The startled men on the rock saw it threshing the ground in its death struggle.

"That was a lucky shot for you," said Ollie.

"Lucky for me," repeated Young Matt slowly, eyeing his well dressed companion; "Well, yes, I reckon it was."

"Who fired it?"

The big fellow shook his head in a puzzled way.

Stewart looked surprised. "Wasn't it someone hunting with you?"

"With me? Huntin'? Not to-night;" muttered the other still searching the hill side.

"Well, I'd like to know what you were doing here alone, then;" said Ollie suspiciously.

At his tone, Young Matt turned upon him savagely, "'Tain't none of your business, what I was a doin' here, that I can see. I reckon these hills are free yet. But it's mighty lucky for us both that someone was 'round, whoever he is. Maybe you ain't thankful that that critter ain't fastened on your neck. But I am. An' I'm goin' to find out who fired that shot if I can."

He started forward, but Ollie called imperiously, "Hold on there a minute, I want to say something to you first." The other paused, and young Stewart continued; "I don't know what you mean by prowling around this time of night. But it looks as though you were watching me. I warn you fairly, don't try it again. I know how you feel toward Miss Lane, and I know how you have been with her while I was away. I tell you it's got to stop. She is to be my wife, and I shall protect her. You may just as well—"

He got no further. The big man sprang forward to face him with a look that made the dandy shrink with fear. "Protect Sammy Lane from me! Protect her, you! You know what I feel toward her? You!" He fairly choked with his wild rage.

The frightened Ollie drew a weapon from his pocket, but, with a snarling laugh, the big fellow reached out his great hand and the shining toy went whirling through the air. "Go home," said the giant. "Damn you, go home! Don't you hear? For God's sake get out o' my sight 'fore I forget again!"

Ollie went.

CHAPTER XXVI.

OLLIE'S DILEMMA.

As "Preachin' Bill" used to say, "Every hound has hits strong pints, but some has more of 'em."

Young Stewart was not without graces pleasing to the girl whom he hoped to make his wife. He seemed to know instinctively all those little attentions in which women so delight, and he could talk, too, very entertainingly of the things he had seen. To the simple girl of the backwoods, he succeeded in making the life in the city appear very wonderful, indeed. Neither was Sammy insensible to the influence of his position, and his prospective wealth, with the advantages that these things offered. Then, with all this, he loved her dearly; and when, if you please, was ever a woman wholly unmoved by the knowledge that she held first place in a man's heart?

For two weeks they were together nearly every day, sometimes spending the afternoon at the girl's home on the side of Dewey, or roving over the nearby hills; sometimes going for long rides through the great woods to pass the day with friends, returning in the evening to find Jim smoking in the doorway of the darkened cabin.

When Mr. Lane, at the end of the first week, asked his daughter, in his point blank fashion, what she was going to do with young Stewart, the girl answered, "He must have his chance, Daddy. He mast have a good fair chance. I—I don't know what it is, but there is—I—I don't know, Daddy. I am sure I loved him when he want away, that is, I think I am sure." And Jim, looking into her eyes, agreed heartily; then he took down his violin to make joyful music far into the night.

Ollie did not see Young Matt after their meeting on the Lookout. The big fellow, too, avoided the couple, and Sammy, for some reason, carefully planned their rides so that they would not be likely to meet their neighbor an the ridge. Once, indeed, they called at the Matthews place, walking over in the evening, but that was when Sammy knew that Young Matt was not at home.

Day after day as they talked together, the girl tried honestly to enter into the life of the man she had promised to marry. But always there was that feeling of something lacking. Just what that something was, or why she could not feel completely satisfied, Sammy did not understand. But the day was soon to come when she would know the real impulses of her heart.

Since that first afternoon, Ollie had not tried to force his suit. While, in a hundred little ways, he had not failed to make her feel his love, he had never openly attempted the role of lover. He was conscious that to put the girl constantly upon the defensive would be disastrous to his hopes; and in this, he was wise. But the time had come when he must speak, for it was the last day of his visit. He felt that he could not go back to the city without a definite understanding.

Sammy, too, realized this, but still she was not ready to give an answer to the question he would ask. They had been to the Forks, and were on their way home. As they rode slowly under the trees, the man pleaded his cause, but the woman could only shake her head and answer quite truthfully, "Ollie, I don't know."

"But tell me, Sammy, is there any one in the way?"

Again she shook her head, "I—I think not."

"You think not! Don't you know?" The young man reined his horse closer to the brown pony. "Let me help you decide, dear. You are troubled because of the change you see in me, and because the life that I have tried to tell you about is so strange, so different from this. You need not fear. With me, you will very soon be at home there; as much at home as you are here. Come, dear, let me answer for you."

The girl lifted her face to his; "Oh, if you only could!" But, even as she spoke, there came to her the memory of that ride home from the party at Ford's, when her pony had crowded close to the big white faced sorrel. It was Brownie this time who was pulled sharply aside. The almost involuntary act brought a quick flush to the young man's cheek, and he promptly reined his own horse to the right, thus placing the full width of the road between them. So they went down the hill into the valley, where Fall Creek tumbled and laughed on its rocky way.

A thread of blue smoke, curling lazily up from the old stack, and the sound of a hammer, told them that some one was at the mill. Sammy was caught by a sudden impulse. "Why, that must be Young Matt!" she exclaimed. "Let us stop. I do believe you haven't seen him since you came home."

"I don't want to see him, nor any one else, now," returned Ollie. "This is our last evening together, Sammy, and I want you all to myself. Let us go up the old Roark trail, around Cox's Bald, and home through the big, low gap." He checked his horse as he spoke, for they had already passed the point where the Roark trail leaves Fall Creek.

But the girl was determined to follow her impulse. "You can stop just a minute," she urged. "You really ought to see Matt, you know. We can ride back this way if you like. It's early yet."

But the man held his place, and replied shortly, "I tell you I don't want to see anybody, and I am very sure that Young Matt doesn't want to see me, not with you, anyway."

Sammy flushed at this, and answered with some warmth, "There is no reason in the world why you should refuse to meet an old friend; but you may do as you please, of course. Only I am going to the mill." So saying, she started down the valley, and as there was really nothing else for him to do, the man followed.

As they approached the mill, Sammy called for Young Matt, who immediately left his work, and came to them. The big fellow wore no coat, and his great arms were bare, while his old shirt, patched and faded and patched again, was soiled by engine grease and perspiration. His trousers, too, held in place by suspenders repaired with belt lacing and fastened with a nail, were covered with sawdust and dirt. His hands and arms and even his face were treated liberally with the same mixture that stained his clothing; and the shaggy red brown hair, uncovered, was sadly tumbled. In his hand he held a wrench. The morrow was grinding day, and he had been making some repairs about the engine.

Altogether, as the backwoodsman came forward, he presented a marked contrast to the freshly clad, well groomed gentleman from the city. And to the woman, the contrast was not without advantages to the man in the good clothes. The thought flashed through her mind that the men who would work for Ollie in the shops would look like this. It was the same old advantage; the advantage that the captain has over the private; the advantage of rank, regardless of worth.

Sammy greeted Young Matt warmly. "I just told Ollie that it was too bad he had not seen you. You were away the night we called at your house, you know; and he is going home to-morrow."

The giant looked from one to the other. Evidently Sammy had not heard of that meeting at the Lookout, and Stewart's face grew red as he saw what was in the big fellow's mind. "I'm mighty glad to see you again," he said lamely. "I told Sammy that I had seen you, but she has forgotten."

"Oh, no, I haven't," replied the girl. "You said that you saw him in the field as you passed the first day you came, but that you were in such a hurry you didn't stop."

At this Ollie forced a loud laugh, and remarked that he was in something of a hurry that day. He hoped that in the girl's confusion the point might be overlooked.

But the mountaineer was not to be sidetracked so easily. Ollie's poor attempt only showed more clearly that he had purposely refrained from telling Sammy of the might when Young Matt had interfered to save his life. To the simple straight-forward lad of the woods, such a course revealed a spirit most contemptible. Raising his soiled hands and looking straight at Ollie, he said, deliberately, "I'm sorry, seein' as this is the first time we've met, that I can't shake hands with you. This here's *clean* dirt, though."

Sammy was puzzled. Ollie's objection to their calling at the mill, his evident embarrassment at the meeting, and something in Young Matt's voice that hinted at a double meaning in his simple words, all told her that there was something beneath the surface which she did not understand.

After his one remark to her escort, the woodsman turned to the girl, and, in spite of Sammy's persistent attempts to bring the now sullen Ollie into the conversation, ignored the man completely. When they had talked for a few moments, Young Matt said, "I reckon you'll have to excuse me a minute, Sammy; I left the engine in such a hurry when you called that I'll have to look at it again. It won't take more'n a minute."

As he disappeared in the mill shed, the young lady turned to her companion, "What's the matter with you two? Have you met and quarreled since you came home?"

Fate was being very unkind to Ollie. He replied gruffly, "You'll have to ask your friend. I told you how it would be. The greasy hobo doesn't like to see me with you, and hasn't manners enough even to hide his feelings. Come, let us go on."

A look that was really worth seeing came into the girl's fine eyes, but she only said calmly; "Matt will be back in a minute."

"All the more reason why we should go. I should think you have had enough. I am sure I have."

The young woman was determined now to know what lay at the bottom of all this. She said quietly, but with a great deal of decision, "You may go on home if you wish; I am going to wait here until Young Matt comes back."

Ollie was angry now in good earnest. He had not told Sammy of the incident at the Lookout because he felt that the story would bring the backwoodsman into a light altogether too favorable. He thought to have the girl safely won before he left the hills; then it would not matter. That Young Matt would have really saved Ollie's life at the risk of his own there was no doubt. And Stewart realized that his silence under such circumstances would look decidedly small and ungrateful to the girl. To have the story told at this critical moment was altogether worse than if he had generously told of the incident at once. He saw, too, that Sammy guessed at some thing beneath the surface, and he felt uneasy in remaining until Young Matt came back to renew the conversation. And yet he feared to leave. At this stage of his dilemma, he was relieved from his plight in a very unexpected manner.

CHAPTER XXVII.

THE CHAMPION.

A big wagon, with two men on the seat, appeared coming up the valley road. It was Wash Gibbs and a crony from the river. They had stopped at the distillery on their way, and were just enough under the influence of drink to be funny and reckless.

When they caught sight of Ollie Stewart and Miss Lane, Wash said something to his companion, at which both laughed uproariously. Upon reaching the couple, the wagon came to a stop, and after looking at Ollie for some moments, with the silent gravity of an owl, Gibbs turned to the young lady, "Howdy, honey. Where did you git that there? Did your paw give hit to you fer a doll baby?"

Young Stewart's face grew scarlet, but he said nothing.

"Can't hit talk?" continued Gibbs with mock interest.

Glancing at her frightened escort, the girl replied, "You drive on, Wash Gibbs. You're in no condition to talk to anyone."

An ugly leer came over the brutal face of the giant; "Oh, I ain't, ain't I? You think I'm drunk. But I ain't, not so mighty much. Jest enough t' perten me up a pepper grain." Then, turning to his companion, who was grinning in appreciation of the scene, he continued, "Here, Bill; you hold th' ribbens, an' watch me tend t' that little job I told you I laid out t' do first chance I got." At this, Ollie grew as pale as death. Once he started as if to escape, but he could not under Sammy's eyes.

As Wash was climbing down from the wagon, he caught sight of Young Matt standing in the door of the mill shed. "Hello, Matt," he called cheerfully; "I ain't a lookin' fer you t' day; 'tend t' you some other time. Got more important business jest now."

Young Matt made no reply, nor did he move to interfere. In the backwoods every man must fight his own battles, so long as he fights with men. When Stewart was in danger from the panther, it was different. This was man to man. Sammy, too, reared in the mountains, and knowing the code, waited quietly to see what her lover would do.

Coming to Ollie's side, Gibbs said, "Git down, young feller, an' look at yer saddle."

"You go on, and let me alone, Wash Gibbs. I've never hurt you." Ollie's naturally high pitched voice was shrill with fear.

Wash paused, looked back at his companion in the wagon; then to Young Matt, and then to the girl on the horse. "That's right," he said, shaking his head with ponderous gravity. "You all hear him. He ain't never hurted me, nary a bit. Nary a bit, ladies an' gentlemen. But, good Lord! look at him! Hain't hit awful!" Suddenly he reached out one great arm, and jerked the young man from his horse, catching him with the other hand as he fell, and setting him on his feet in the middle of the road.

Ollie was like a child in the grasp of his huge tormentor, and, in spite of her indignation, a look of admiration flashed over Sammy's face at the exhibition of the bully's wonderful physical strength; an admiration, that only heightened the feeling of shame for her lover's weakness.

Gibbs addressed his victim, "Now, dolly, you an' me's goin' t' play a little. Come on, let's see you dance." The other struggled feebly a moment and attempted to draw a pistol, whereupon Wash promptly captured the weapon, remarking in a sad tone as he did so, "You hadn't ought t' tote such a gun as that, sonny; hit might go off. Hit's a right pretty little thing, ain't hit?" he continued, holding his victim with one hand, and examining the pearl handled, nickel plated weapon with great interest. "Hit sure is. But say, dolly, if you was ever t' shoot me with that there, an' I found hit out, I'd sure be powerful mad. You hear me, now, an' don't you pack that gun no more; not in these mountains. Hit ain't safe."

The fellow in the wagon roared with delight at these witticisms, and looked from Young Matt to Sammy to see if they also appreciated the joke.

"Got any more pretties?" asked Gibbs of his victim. "No? Let's see." Catching the young man by the waist, he lifted him bodily, and, holding him head downward, shook him roughly. Again Sammy felt her blood tingle at the feat of strength.

Next holding Ollie with one huge hand at the back of his neck, Wash said, "See that feller in th' wagon there? He's a mighty fine gentleman; friend o' mine. Make a bow t' him." As he finished, with his free hand he struck the young man a sharp blow in the stomach, with the result that Stewart did make a bow, very low, but rather too suddenly to be graceful.

The fellow in the wagon jumped up and bowed again and again; "Howdy, Mr. City Man; howdy. Mighty proud t' meet up with you; mighty proud, you bet!"

The giant whirled his captive toward the mill. "See that feller yonder? I'm goin' t' lick him some day. Make a face at him." Catching Ollie by the nose and chin, he tried to force his bidding, while the man in the wagon made the valley ring with his laughter. Then Wash suddenly faced the helpless young man toward Sammy. "Now ladies and gentlemen," he said in the tones of a showman addressing an audience, "this here pretty little feller from th' city's goin' t' show us Hill-Billies how t' spark a gal."

The bully's friend applauded loudly, roaring at the top of his voice, "Marry 'em, Wash. Marry 'em. You can do hit as good as a parson! You'd make a good parson. Let's see how'd you go at hit."

The notion tickled the fancy of the giant, for it offered a way to make Sammy share the humiliation more fully. "Git down an' come here t' yer honey," he said to the girl. "Git down, I say," he repeated, when the young woman made no motion to obey.

"Indeed, I will not," replied Sammy shortly.

Her tone and manner angered Gibbs, and dropping Ollie he started toward the girl to take her from the horse by force. As he reached the pony's side, Sammy raised her whip and with all her strength struck him full across the face. The big ruffian drew back with a bellow of pain and anger. Then he started toward her again. "I'll tame you, you wild cat," he yelled. And Sammy raised her whip again.

But before Gibbs could touch the girl, a powerful hand caught him by the shoulder. "I reckon you've had fun enough, Wash Gibbs," remarked Young Matt in his slow way. "I ain't interfering between man and man, but you'd best keep your dirty hands off that lady."

The young woman's heart leaped at the sound of that deep calm voice that carried such a suggestion of power. And she saw that the blue eyes under the tumbled red brown locks were shining now like points of polished steel. The strong man's soul was rejoicing with the fierce joy of battle.

The big bully drew back a step, and glared at the man who had come between him and his victim; the man whom, for every reason, he hated. Lifting his huge paws, he said in a voice hoarse with deadly menace, "Dirty, be they? By hell, I'll wash 'em. An' hit won't be water that'll clean 'em, neither. Don't you know that no man ever crosses my trail an' lives?"

The other returned easily, "Oh, shucks! Get into your wagon and drive on. You ain't on Roark now. You're on Fall Creek, and over here you ain't no bigger'n anybody else."

While Young Matt was speaking, Gibbs backed slowly away, and, as the young man finished, suddenly drew the pistol he had taken from Ollie. With a quickness and lightness astonishing in one of his bulk and usually slow movements, the mountaineer leaped upon his big enemy. There was a short, sharp struggle, and Wash staggered backward, leaving the shining weapon in Young Matt's hand. "It might go off, you know," said the young fellow quietly, as he tossed the gun on the ground at Ollie's feet.

With a mad roar, Gibbs recovered himself and rushed at his antagonist. It was a terrific struggle; not the skillful sparring of trained fighters, but the rough and tumble battling of primitive giants. It was the climax of long months of hatred; the meeting of two who were by every instinct mortal enemies. Ollie shrank back in terror, but Sammy leaned forward in the saddle, her beautiful figure tense, her lips parted, and her face flushed with excitement.

It was soon evident that the big champion of the hills had at last met his match. As he realized this, a look of devilish cunning crept into the animal face of Gibbs, and he maneuvered carefully to bring his enemy's back toward the wagon.

Catching a look from his friend, over Young Matt's shoulder, the man in the wagon slipped quickly to the ground, and Sammy saw with horror a naked knife in his hand. She glanced toward Ollie appealingly, but that gentleman was helpless. The man with the knife began creeping cautiously toward the fighting men, keeping always behind Young Matt. The young woman felt as though an iron band held her fast. She could not move. She could not speak. Then Gibbs went down, and the girl's scream rang out, *"Behind you, Matt! Look quick!"*

As he recovered his balance from the effort that had thrown Wash, Young Matt heard her cry, saw the girl's look of horror, and her outstretched hand pointing. Like a flash he whirled just as the knife was lifted high for the murderous blow. It was over in an instant. Sammy saw him catch the wrist of the uplifted arm, heard a dull snap and a groan, saw the knife fall from the helpless hand, and then saw the man lifted bodily and thrown clear over the wagon, to fall helpless on the rocky ground. The woman gave a low cry, "Oh, *what a man!*"

Wash Gibbs, too, opened his eyes, just in time to witness the unheard-of feat, and to see the bare-armed young giant who performed it turn again, breathing heavily with his great exertion, but still ready to meet his big antagonist.

The defeated bully rose from the ground. The other stepped forward to meet him. But without a word, Gibbs climbed into the wagon and took up the reins. Before they could move, Young Matt had the mules by their heads. "You have forgotten something," he said quietly, pointing to the man on the ground, who was still unconscious from his terrible fall. "That there's your property. Take it along. We ain't got no use for such as that on Fall Creek."

Sullenly Wash climbed down and lifted his companion into the wagon. As Young Matt stood aside to let him go, the bully said, "I'll see you agin fer this."

The strong man only answered, "I reckon you'd better stay on Roark, Wash Gibbs. You got more room there."

CHAPTER XXVIII.

WHAT PETE TOLD SAMMY.

No word was spoken by either Sammy or her lover, while their horses were climbing the mill road, and both were glad when they reached the top of the ridge, and turned into the narrow path where they would need to ride one before the other. It was not easy to ride side by side, when each was busy with thoughts not to be spoken.

At the gate, Ollie dismounted to help the girl from her horse. But before he could reach the pony's side, Sammy sprang lightly to the ground, unassisted. Opening the big gate, she turned Brownie loose in the yard, while the man stood watching her, a baffled look upon his face. He had always done these little things for her. To be refused at this time was not pleasant. The feeling that he was on the outside grew stronger.

Turning to his own horse, Ollie placed his foot in the stirrup to mount, when Sammy spoke,—perhaps she felt that she had been a little unkind—"You were going to stay to supper," she said.

"Not to-night," he answered, gaining his seat in the saddle, and picking up the reins.

"But you are going to leave in the morning, are you not? You—you must not go like this."

He dropped the reins to the horse's neck again, "Look here, Sammy, do you blame me because I did not fight that big bully?"

Sammy did not reply.

"What could I do? You know there is not another man in the mountains beside Young Matt who could have done it. Surely you cannot blame me."

The young woman moved uneasily, "No, certainly not. I do not blame you in the least. I—but it was very fortunate that Young Matt was there, wasn't it?" The last sentence slipped out before she knew.

Ollie retorted angrily, "It seems to be very fortunate for him. He will be a greater hero than ever, now, I suppose. If he is wise, he will stay in the backwoods to be worshipped for he'll find that his size won't count for much in the world. He's a great man here, where he can fight like a beast, but his style wouldn't go far where brains are of value. It would be interesting to see him in town; a man who never saw a railroad."

Sammy lifted her head quickly at this, and fixed her eyes on the man's face with that wide, questioning gaze that reminded one so of her father, "I never saw a railroad, either; not that I can remember; though, I suppose we must have crossed one or two on our way to Texas when I was a baby. Is it the railroads then that makes one so—so superior?"

The man turned impatiently in the saddle, "You know what I mean."

"Yes," she answered slowly. "I think I do know what you mean."

Ollie lifted the reins again from his horse's neck, and angered them nervously. "I'd better go now; there's no use talking about this to-night. I won't leave in the morning, as I had planned. I— I can't go like this." There was a little catch in his voice. "May I come again to-morrow afternoon, Sammy?"

"Yes, you had better go now, and come back to-morrow."

"And Sammy, won't you try to think that I am not altogether worthless, even if I am not big enough to fight Wash Gibbs? You are sure that you do not blame me for what happened at the mill?"

"No," she said; "of course not. You could not help it. Why should I blame anyone for that which he cannot help?"

Then Ollie rode away, and Sammy, going to her pony, stood petting the little horse, while she watched her lover up the Old Trail, and still there was that wide, questioning look in her eyes. As Ollie passed from sight around the hill above, the girl slipped out of the gate, and a few minutes later stood at the Lookout, where she could watch her lover riding along the ridge. She saw him pass from the open into the fringe of timber near the big gap; and, a few minutes later, saw him reappear beyond the deer lick. Still she watched as he moved along the rim of the Hollow, looking in the distance like a toy man on a toy horse; watched until he passed from sight into the timber again, and was gone. And all the time that questioning look was in her eyes.

Did she blame Ollie that he had played so poorly his part in the scene at the mill. No, she told herself over and over again, as though repeating a lesson; no, Ollie was not to blame, and yet—

She knew that he had spoken truly when he said that there were things that counted for more than brute strength. But was there not something more than brute strength in the incident? Was there not that which lay deeper? something of which the brute strength, after all, was only an expression? The girl stamped her foot impatiently, as she exclaimed aloud, "Oh, why did he not *try* to do something? He should have forced Wash Gibbs to beat him into insensibility rather than to have submitted so tamely to being played with."

In the distance she saw the shepherd following his flock down the mountain, and the old scholar, who always watched the Lookout, when in the vicinity, for a glimpse of his pupil, waved his hand in greeting as he moved slowly on after his charges. It was growing late. Her father, too, would be coming home for his supper. But as she rose to go, a step on the mountain side above caught her attention, and, looking up, she saw Pete coming toward the big rock. Sammy greeted the youth kindly, "I haven't seen Pete for days and days; where has he been?"

"Pete's been everywhere; an' course I've been with him," replied the lad with his wide, sweeping gesture. Then throwing himself at full length at the girl's feet, he said, abruptly, "Pete was here that night, and God, he was here, too. Couldn't nobody else but God o' done it. The gun went bang, and a lot more guns went bang, bang, all along the mountains. And the moonlight things that was a dancin' quit 'cause they was scared; and that panther it just doubled up and died. Matt and Ollie wasn't hurted nary a bit. Pete says it was God done that; He was sure in the hills that night."

Sammy was startled. "Matt and Ollie, a panther? What do you mean, boy?"

The troubled look shadowed the delicate face, as the lad shook his head; "Don't mean nothin', Sammy, not me. Nobody can't mean nothin', can they?"

"But what does Pete mean? Does Pete know about it?"

"Oh, yes, course Pete knows everything. Don't Sammy know 'bout that night when God was in the hills?" He was eager now, with eyes wide and face aglow.

"No," said Sammy, "I do not know. Will Pete tell me all about it?"

The strange youth seated himself on the rock, facing the valley below, saying in a low tone, "Ollie was a settin' like this, all still; just a smokin' and a watchin' the moonlight things that was dancin' over the tops of the trees down there." Then leaping to his feet the boy ran a short way along the ledge, to come stealing back, crouching low, as he whispered, "It come a creepin' and a creepin' towards Ollie, and he never knowed nothin' about it. But Matt he knowed, and God he knowed too." Wonderingly, the girl watched his movement. Suddenly he sprang to the rock again, and facing the imaginary beast, cried in childish imitation of a man's deep voice, "Get out of the way. This here's my fight." Then in his own tones, "It was sure scared when Young Matt jumped on the rock. Everything's scared of Matt when he talks like that. It was mad, too, 'cause Matt he wouldn't let it get Ollie. And it got ready to jump at Matt, and Matt he got ready for a tussle, and Ollie he got out of the way. And all the moonlight things stopped dancin', and the shadow things come out to see the fight." He had lowered his voice again almost to a whisper. Sammy was breathless. "Bang!" cried the lad, clapping his hands and shouting the words; "Bang! Bang! God, he fired and all the guns in the hills went off, and that panther it just doubled up and died. It would sure got Ollie, though, if Matt hadn't a jumped on the rock when he did. But do you reckon it could o' got Matt, if God hadn't been here that night?"

It was all too clearly portrayed to be mistaken. "Sammy needn't be afeared," continued Pete, seeing the look on the girl's face. "It can't come back no more. It just naturally can't, you know, Sammy; 'cause God he killed it plumb dead. And Pete dragged it way over on yon side of the ridge and the buzzards got it."

CHAPTER XXIX.

JIM LANE MAKES A PROMISE.

Sammy went home to find her father getting supper. Rushing into the cabin, the girl gave him a hug that caused Jim to nearly drop the coffee pot. "You poor abused Daddy, to come home from work, all tired and find no supper, no girl, no nothing. Sit right down there, now, and rest, while I finish things."

Jim obeyed with a grin of appreciation. "I didn't fix no taters; thought you wasn't comin'."

"Going to starve yourself, were you? just because I was gone," replied the girl with a pan of potatoes in her hand. "I see right now that I will have to take care of you always—always, Daddy Jim."

The smile suddenly left the man's face. "Where's Ollie Stewart? Didn't he come home with you?"

"Ollie's at home, I suppose. I have been up to the Lookout talking to Pete."

"Ain't Ollie goin' back to the city to-morrow?"

"No, not to-morrow; the next day. He's coming over here to-morrow afternoon. Then he's going away." Then, before Jim could ask another question, she held up the half of a ham; "Daddy, Daddy! How many times have I told you that you must not—you must not slice the ham with your pocket knife? Just look there! What would Aunt Mollie say if she saw that, so haggled and one sided?"

All during the evening meal, the girl kept up a ceaseless merry chatter, changing the subject abruptly every time it approached the question that her father was most anxious to ask. And the man delighted with her gay mood responded to it, as he answered to all her moods, until they were like two school children in their fun. But, when supper was over and the work done, and Jim, taking down his violin, would have made music, Sammy promptly relieved him of his instrument, and seated herself on his knee. "Not to-night, Daddy. I want to talk to-night, real serious."

She told him then of the encounter with Wash Gibbs and his friend at the mill, together with the story that Pete had illustrated so vividly at the Lookout. "And so, Daddy," she finished; "I know now what I shall do. He will come to-morrow afternoon to say good-by, and then he will go away again back to the city and his fine friends for good. And I'll stay and take care of my Daddy Jim. It isn't that he is a bad man like Wash Gibbs. He couldn't be a bad man like that; he isn't big enough. And that's just it. He is too little—body, soul and spirit—he is too little. He will do well in the world; perhaps he will even do big things. But I heard dear old Preachin' Bill say once, that 'some fellers can do mighty big things in a durned little way.' So he is going back to the city, and I am going to stay in the hills."

Jim took no pains to hide his delight. "I knowed it, girl. I knowed it. Bank on the old blood every time. There ain't a drop of yeller in it; not a drop, Sammy. Ollie ain't to say bad, but he ain't just our kind. Lord! But I'd like to o' seen Young Matt a givin' it to Wash Gibbs!" He threw back his head and roared with delight. "Just wait 'till I see Wash. I'll ask him if he thinks Young Matt would need a pry for to lift that mill engine with, now." Then all of a sudden the laugh died out, and the man's dark face was serious, as he said, slowly, "The boy'll have to watch him, though. It'll sure be war from this on; the worst kind of war."

"Daddy, what do you think Wash would have done to me, if Young Matt had not been there?"

That metallic ring was in Jim's voice, now, as he replied, "Wash Gibbs ought to knowed better than to done that. But it was a blessin' Young Matt was there, wasn't it? He'd take care of you anywhere. I wouldn't never be afraid for you with him."

The girl hid her face on her father's shoulder, as she said, "Daddy, will Wash Gibbs come here any more now? It seems to me he wouldn't dare meet you after this."

Jim answered uneasily, "I don't know, girl. I reckon he'll be around again after a time."

There was a pause for a little while; then Sammy, with her arms still about his neck, said, "Daddy, I'm going to stay in the hills with you now. I am going to send Ollie away to-morrow, because as you say, he isn't our kind. Daddy, Wash Gibbs is not our kind either, is he?"

"You don't understand, girl, and I can't tell you now. It all started way back when you was a little trick."

The young woman answered very gently, "Yes, I know. You have told me that often. But, Daddy, what will—what will our friends think, if you keep on with Wash Gibbs now, after what happened at the mill to-day? Young Matt fought Gibbs because he insulted me and was going to hurt me. You say yourself that it will be war between them now? Will you side with Wash? And if you do, won't it look like there was just a little, tiny streak of yellow in us?"

This side of the situation had not struck Jim at first. He got up and walked the floor, while the girl, standing quietly by the fireplace, watched him, a proud, fond light in her eyes. Sammy did not know what the bond between her father and the big ruffian was, but she knew that it was not a light one. Now that the issue was fairly defined, she felt confident that, whatever the cost, the break would be made. But at this time it was well that she did not know how great the cost of breaking the bond between the two men would be.

Jim stopped before his daughter, and, placing a hand upon each shoulder, said, "Tell me, girl; are you so powerful anxious to have me and Young Matt stay good friends like we've always been?"

"I—I am afraid I am, Daddy."

And then, a rare smile came into the dark face of Jim Lane. He kissed the girl and said, "I'll do it, honey. I ain't afraid to, now."

CHAPTER XXX.

SAMMY GRADUATES

The next day when young Stewart came, the books were all back on the shelf in the main room of the cabin, and Sammy, dressed in a fresh gown of simple goods and fashion, with her hair arranged carefully, as she had worn it the last two months before Ollie's coming, sat at the window reading.

The man was surprised and a little embarrassed. "Why, what have you been doing to yourself?" he exclaimed.

"I have not been doing anything to myself. I have only done some things to my clothes and hair," returned the girl.

Then he saw the books. "Why, where did these come from? He crossed the room to examine the volumes. "Do you—do you read all these?"

"The shepherd has been helping me," she explained.

"Oh, yes. I understood that you were studying with him." He looked at her curiously, as though they were meeting for the first time. Then, as she talked of her studies, his embarrassment deepened, for he found himself foundering hopelessly before this clear-eyed, clear-brained backwoods girl.

"Come," said Sammy at last. "Let us go for a walk." She led the way to her favorite spot, high up on the shoulder of Dewey, and there, with Mutton Hollow at their feet and the big hills about them, with the long blue ridges in the distance beyond which lay Ollie's world, she told him what he feared to learn. The man refused to believe that he heard aright. "You do not understand," he protested, and he tried to tell her of the place in life that would be hers as his wife. In his shallowness, he talked even of jewels, and dresses, and such things.

"But can all this add one thing to life itself?" she asked. "Is not life really independent of all these things? Do they not indeed cover up the real life, and rob one of freedom? It seems to me that it must be so."

He could only answer, "But you know nothing about it. How can you? You have never been out of these woods."

"No," she returned, "that is true; I have never been out of these woods, and you can never, now, get away from the world into which you have gone."

She pointed to the distant hills. "It is very, very far over there to where you live. I might, indeed, find many things in your world that would be delightful; but I fear that I should lose the things that after all are, to me, the really big things. I do not feel that the things that are greatest in your life could bring happiness without that which I find here. And there is something here that can bring happiness without what you call the advantages of the world to which you belong."

"What do you know of the world?" he said roughly.

"Nothing," she said. "But I know a little of life. And I have learned some things that I fear you have not. Beside, I know now that I do not love you. I have been slow to find the truth, but I have found it. And this is the one thing that matters, that I found it in time."

"Did you reach this conclusion at the mill yesterday?" he asked with a sneer.

"No. It came to me here on the rock last evening after you were gone. I heard a strange story; the story of a weak man, a strong man, and a God who was very kind."

Ollie saw that further persuasion was of no avail, and as he left her, she watched him out of sight for the last time—along the trail that is nobody knows how old. When he was gone, in obedience to an impulse she did not try to understand, she ran down the mountain to the cabin in the Hollow—Young Matt's cabin. And when the shepherd came in from the hills with his flock he found the house in such order as only a woman's hand can bring. The table was set, and his supper cooking on the stove.

"Dad," she asked, "Do you think I know enough now to live in the city?"

The old man's heart sank. It had come then. Bravely he concealed his feelings, as he assured her in the strongest terms, that she knew enough, and was good enough to live anywhere.

"Then," said Sammy; "I know enough, even if I am not good enough, to live in the hills."

The brown eyes, deep under their shaggy brows, were aglow with gladness, and there was a note of triumph in the scholar's voice as he said, "Then you do not regret learning the things I have tried to teach you? You are sure you have no sorrow for the things you are losing."

"Regret? Dad. Regret?" The young woman drew herself up and lifted her arms. "Oh, Dad, I see it all, now; all that you have been trying in a thousand ways to teach me. You have led me into a new world, the real world, the world that has always been and must always be, and in that world man is king; king because he is a man. And the treasure of his kingdom is the wealth of his manhood."

"And the woman, Sammy, the woman?"

" 'And they twain shall be one flesh.'"

Then the master knew that his teaching had not been in vain. "I can lead you no farther, my child," he said with a smile. "You have passed the final test."

She came close to him, "Then I want my diploma," she said, for he had told her about the schools.

Reverently the old scholar kissed her brow. "This is the only diploma I am authorized to give—the love and homage of your teacher."

"And my degree?" She waited with that wide, questioning look in her eyes.

"The most honorable in all the world—a sure enough lady."

CHAPTER XXXI.

CASTLE BUILDING.

The corn was big enough to cultivate the first time, and Young Matt with Old Kate was hard at work in the field west of the house.

It was nearly three weeks since the incident at the mill, since which time the young fellow had not met Sammy Lane to talk with her. He had seen her, though, at a distance nearly every day, for the girl had taken up her studies again, and spent most of her time out on the hills with the shepherd. That day he saw her as she turned into the mill road at the lower corner of the field, on her way to the Forks. And he was still thinking of her three hours later, as he sat on a stump in the shade of the forest's edge, while his horse was resting.

Young Matt recalled the fight at the mill with a wild joy in his heart. Under any circumstances it was no small thing to have defeated the champion strong man and terror of the hills. It was a glorious thing to have done the deed for the girl he loved, and under her eyes. Sammy might give herself to Ollie, now, and go far away to the great world, but she could never forget the man who had saved her from insult, when her lover was far too weak to save even himself. And Young Matt would stay in the hills alone, but always he would have the knowledge and the triumph of this thing that he had done. Yes, it would be easier now, but still—still the days would be years when there was no longer each morning the hope that somewhere before the day was gone he would see her.

The sun fell hot and glaring on the hillside field, and in the air was the smell of the freshly turned earth. High up in the blue a hawk circled and circled again. A puff of air came sighing through the forest, touched lightly the green blades in the open, slipped over the ridge, and was lost in the sky beyond. Old Kate, with head down, was dreaming of cool springs in shady dells, and a little shiny brown lizard with a bright blue tail crept from under the bottom rail of the fence to see why the man was so still.

The man turned his head quickly; the lizard dodged under the rail; and old Kate awoke with a start. Someone was coming along the road below.

Young Matt knew the step of that horse, as well as he knew the sound of old Kate's bell, or the neigh of his own sorrel.

The brown pony stopped at the lower corner of the field, and a voice called, "You'd better be at work. I don't believe you have ploughed three rows since I passed."

The big fellow went eagerly down the hill to the fence. "I sure ought to o' done better'n that, for it's been long enough since you went by. I always notice, though, that it gets a heap farther to the other side of the field and back about this time o' day. What's new over to the Forks?"

Sammy laughed, "Couldn't hear a thing but how the champion strong man was beaten at his own game. Uncle Ike says, 'Ba thundas! You tell Young Matt that he'd better come over. A man what can ride Wash Gibbs a bug huntin' is too blamed good a man t' stay at home all th' time. We want him t' tell us how he done it. Ba thundas! He'll be gittin' a job with th' gov'ment next. What!'"

The man crossed his arms on the top rail of the worm fence, and laughed. It was good to have Sammy deliver her message in just that way. "I reckon Uncle Ike thinks I ought to go dancin' all over the hills now, with a chip on my shoulder," he said.

"I don't think you'll do that," she returned. "Dad Howitt wouldn't, would he? But I must hurry on now, or Daddy's supper won't be ready when he comes in. I stopped to give you these papers for your father." She handed him the package. "And—and I want to thank you, Matt, for what you did at the mill. All my life you have been fighting for me, and—and I have never done anything for you. I wish I could do something—something that would show you how—how I care."

Her voice faltered. He was so big and strong, and there was such a look of hopeless love and pain on his rugged face—a face that was as frank and open as a child's. Here was a man who had no need for the shallow cunning of little fox-like men. This one would go open and bold on his way, and that which he could not take by his strength he would not have. Had she not seen him in battle? Had she not seen his eyes like polished steel points? Deep down in her heart, the woman felt a thrill of triumph that such a man should stand so before her. She must go quickly.

Young Matt climbed slowly up the hill again to his seat on the stump. Here he watched until across the Hollow he saw the pony and his rider come out of the timber and move swiftly along the ridge; watched until they faded into a tiny spot, rounded the mountain and disappeared from sight. Then, lifting his eyes, he looked away beyond the long blue line that marked the distant horizon. Some day he would watch Sammy ride away and she would go on, and on, and on, beyond that blue line, put of his life forever.

Ollie had gone over there to live, and the shepherd had come from there.

What was that world like, he wondered. Between the young man of the mountains and that big world yonder there had always been a closely shut door. He had seen the door open to Ollie, and now Sammy stood on the threshold. Would it ever open for him? And, if it did, what? Then came a thought that made his blood leap. Might he not force it open? The shepherd had told him of others who had done so.

Young Matt felt a strong man's contempt for the things Ollie had gotten out of the world, but he stood in awe before Mr. Howitt. He told himself, now, that he would look for and find the things yonder that made Dad the man he was. He would carry to the task his splendid strength. Nothing should stop him. And Sammy, when she understood that he was going away to be like the shepherd, would wait awhile to give him his chance. Surely, she would wait when he told her that. But how should he begin?

Looking up again, his eye caught a slow, shifting patch of white on the bench above Lost Creek, where the little stream begins its underground course. The faint bark of a dog came to him through the thin still air, and the patch of white turned off into the trail that leads to the ranch. "Dad!" exclaimed the young man in triumph. Dad should tell him how. He had taught Sammy.

And so while the sunlight danced on the green field, and old Kate slept in the lengthening shadows of the timber, the lad gave himself to his dreams and built his castles—as we all have builded.

His dreaming was interrupted as the supper bell rang, and, with the familiar sound, a multitude of other thoughts came crowding in; the father and mother—they were growing old. Would it do to leave them alone with the graves on the hill yonder, and the mystery of the Hollow? And there was the place to care for, and the mill. Who but Young Matt could get work from the old engine?

It was like the strong man that the fight did not last long. Young Matt's fights never lasted very long. By the time he had unhitched old Kate from the cultivator, it was finished. The lad went down the hill, his bright castles in ruin—even as we all have gone, or must sometime go down the hill with our brightest castles in ruin.

CHAPTER XXXII.

PREPARATION.

That same night, Mr. Lane told his daughter that he would leave home early the next morning to be gone two days. Jim was cleaning his big forty-five when he made the announcement.

Sammy paused with one hand on the cupboard door to ask, "With Wash Gibbs, Daddy?"

"No, I ain't goin' with Wash; but I'll likely meet up with him before I get back." There was a hint of that metallic ring in the man's voice.

The girl placed her armful of dishes carefully on the cupboard shelf; "You're—you're not going to forget your promise, are you, Daddy Jim?"

The mountaineer was carefully dropping a bit of oil into the lock of his big revolver. "No, girl, I ain't forgettin' nothin'. This here's the last ride I aim to take with Wash. I'm goin' to see him to,"—he paused and listened carefully to the click, click, click, as he tested the action of his weapon—"to keep my promise."

"Oh, Daddy, Daddy, I'm so glad! I wanted this more than I ever wanted anything in all my life before. You're such a good Daddy to me, I never could bear to see you with that bad, bad man." She was behind his chair now, and, stooping, laid her fresh young cheek against the swarthy, furrowed face.

The man sat like a grim, stone image, his eyes fixed on the gun resting on his knees. Not until she lifted her head to stand erect behind his chair, with a hand on each shoulder, did he find words. "Girl, there's just one thing I've got to know for sure before I go to-morrow. I reckon I'm right, but somehow a man can't never tell about a woman in such things. Will you tell your Daddy, Sammy?"

"Tell what, Daddy Jim?" the girl asked, her hands stealing up to caress her father's face.

"What answer will you give to Young Matt when he asks you what Ollie did?"

"But why must you know that before you go to-morrow?"

" 'Cause I want to be plumb sure I ain't makin' no mistake in sidin' with the boy in this here trouble."

"You couldn't make a mistake in doing that, Daddy, no matter whether I—no matter what—but perhaps Matt will not ask me what Ollie did."

Just a ray of humor touched the dark face. "I ain't makin' no mistake there. I know what the man will do." He laid the gun upon the table, and reaching up caught the girl's hand. "But I want to know what you'll say when he asks you. Tell me, honey, so I'll be plumb certain I'm doin' right."

Sammy lowered her head and whispered in his ear.

"Are you sure this time, girl, dead sure?"

"Oh, I'm so sure that it seems as if I—I couldn't wait for him to come to me. I never felt this way before, never."

The mountaineer drew his daughter into his arms, and held her close, as he said, "I ain't afraid to do it, now, girl."

The young woman was so occupied with her own thoughts and the emotions aroused by her father's question, that she failed to note the ominous suggestion that lay under his words. So she entered gaily into his plans for her during his two days' absence.

Jim would leave early in the morning, and Sammy was to stay with her friend, Mandy Ford, over on Jake Creek. Mr. Lane had arranged with Jed Holland to do the milking, so there would be no reason for the girl's return until the following evening, and she must promise that she would not come home before that time. Sammy promised laughingly. He need not worry; she and Mandy had not had a good visit alone for weeks.

When his daughter had said good-night, Jim extinguished the light, and slipping the big gun inside his shirt went to sit outside the cabin door with his pipe. An hour passed. Sammy was fast asleep. And still the man sat smoking. A half hour more went by. Suddenly the pipe was laid aside, and Jim's hand crept inside his shirt to find the butt of the revolver. His quick ear had caught the sound of a swiftly moving horse coming down the mountain.

The horse stopped at the gate and a low whistle came out of the darkness. Leaving his seat, Sammy's father crossed the yard, and, a moment later, the horse with its rider was going on again down the trail toward the valley below and the distant river.

Jim waited at the gate until the sound of the horse's feet had died away in the night. Then he returned to the cabin. But even as he walked toward the house, a dark figure arose from a clump of bushes within a few feet of the spot where Jim and the horseman had met. The figure slipped noiselessly away into the forest.

The next morning Jim carefully groomed and saddled the brown pony for Sammy, then, leading his own horse ready for the road, he came to the cabin door. "Going now, Daddy?" said the girl, coming for the good-by kiss.

"My girl, my girl," whispered the man, as he took her in his arms. Sammy was frightened at the sight of his face, so strange and white. "Why Daddy, Daddy Jim, what is the matter?"

"Nothin', girl, nothin'. Only—only you're so like your mother, girl. She—she used to come just this way when I'd be leavin'. You're sure like her, and—and I'm glad. I'm glad you're like the old folks, too. Remember now, stay at Mandy's until to-morrow evenin'. Kiss me again, honey. Good-by."

He mounted hurriedly and rode away at a brisk gallop. Pulling up a moment at the edge of the timber, he turned in the saddle to wave his hand to the girl in the cabin door.

CHAPTER XXXIII.

A RIDE IN THE NIGHT.

Sammy arrived at the Ford homestead in time for dinner, and was joyfully received by her friend, Mandy. But early in the afternoon, their pleasure was marred by a messenger from Long Creek on the other side of the river. Mrs. Ford's sister was very ill, and Mrs. Ford and Mandy must go at once.

"But Sammy can't stay here alone," protested the good woman. "Mandy, you'll just have to stay."

"Indeed, she shall not," declared their guest. "I can ride up Jake Creek to the Forks and stay all night at Uncle Ike's. Brownie will make it easily in time for supper. You just get your things on and start right away."

"You'd better hurry; too," put in Mr. Ford. "There's a storm comin' 'fore long, an' we got t' git across th' river 'fore hit strikes. I'll be here with th' horses by the time you get your bonnets on." He hurried away to the barn for his team, while the women with Sammy's assistance made their simple preparation.

As mother Ford climbed into the big wagon, she said to Sammy, "Hit's an awful lonely ol' trip fer you, child; an' you must start right away, so's t' be sure t' get there 'fore hit gets plumb dark," while Mr. Ford added, as he started the team, "Your pony's ready saddled, an' if you'll hurry along, you can jest 'bout make hit. Don't get catched on Jakey in a big rain whatever you do."

"Don't you worry about me," returned the girl, "Brownie and I could find the way in the dark."

But when her friends were gone, Sammy, womanlike, busied herself with setting the disordered house aright before she started on her journey. Watching the clouds, she told herself that there was plenty of time for her to reach the Postoffice before the storm. It might not come that way at all, in fact.

But the way up Jake Creek was wild and rough, and along the faint trail, that twisted and wound like a slim serpent through the lonely wilderness, Brownie could make but slow time. As they followed the little path, the walls of the narrow valley grew steeper, more rocky, and barren; and the road became more and more rough and difficult, until at last the valley narrowed to a mere rocky gorge, through which the creek ran, tumbling and foaming on its way.

It was quite late when Sammy reached the point near the head of the stream where the trail leads out of the canon to the road on the ridge above. It was still a good two miles to the Forks. As she passed the spring, a few big drops of rain came pattering down, and, looking up, she saw, swaying and tossing in the wind, the trees that fringed the ledges above, and she heard the roar of the oncoming storm.

A short way up the side of the mountain at the foot of a great overhanging cliff, there is a narrow bench, and less than a hundred feet from where the trail finds its way through a break in the rocky wall, there is a deep cave like hollow. Sammy knew the spot well. It would afford excellent shelter.

Pushing Brownie up the steep path, she had reached this bench, when the rushing storm cloud shut out the last of the light, and the hills shook with a deafening crash of thunder. Instinctively the girl turned her pony's head from the trail, and, following the cliff, reached the sheltered nook, just as the storm burst in all its wild fury.

The rain came down in torrents; the forest roared; and against the black sky, in an almost continuous glare of lightning, the big trees tugged and strained in their wild wrestle with the wind; while peal after peal of thunder, rolling, crashing, reverberating through the hills, added to the uproar.

It was over in a little while. The wind passed; the thunder rumbled and growled in the distance; and the rain fell gently; but the sky was still lighted by the red glare. Though it was so dark that Sammy could see the trees and rocks only by the lightning's flash, she was not frightened. She knew that Brownie would find the way easily, and, as for the wetting, she would soon be laughing at that with her friends at the Postoffice.

But, as the girl was on the point of moving, a voice said, "It's a mighty good thing for us this old ledge happened to be here, ain't it?" It was a man's voice, and another replied, "Right you are. And it's a good thing, too, that this blow came early in the evening."

The speakers were between Sammy and the trail. They had evidently sought shelter from the storm a few seconds after the girl had gained her position. In the wild uproar she had not heard them, and, as they crouched under the cliff, they were hidden by a projection of the rock, though now and then, when the lightning flashed, she could see a part of one of the horses. They might be neighbors and friends. They might be strangers, outlaws even. The young woman was too wise to move until she was sure.

The first voice spoke again. "Jack got off in good time, did he?"

"Got a good start," replied the other. "He ought to be back with the posse by ten at the latest. I told him we would meet them at nine where this trail comes into the big road."

"And how far do you say it is to Jim Lane's place, by the road and the Old Trail?" asked the first voice.

At the man's words a terrible fear gripped Sammy's heart. *"Posse,"* that could mean only one thing,—officers of the law. But her father's name and her home—in an instant Jim's strange companionship with Wash Gibbs, their long mysterious rides together, her father's agitation that morning, when he said good- by, with a thousand other things rushed through her mind. What terrible thing was this that she had happened upon in the night? What horrible trap had they set for her Daddy, her Daddy Jim? For trap it was. It could be nothing else. At any risk she must hear more. She had already lost the other man's reply. Calming herself, the girl listened eagerly for the next word.

A match cracked. The light flared out, and a whiff of tobacco smoke came curling around the rock, as one of the men said: "Are you sure there is no mistake about their meeting at Lane's to- night?"

"Can't possibly be," came the answer. "I was lying in the brush, right by the gate when the messenger got there, and I heard Jim give the order myself. Take it all the way through, unless we make a slip to-night, it will be one of the prettiest cases I ever saw."

"Yes," said the other; "but you mustn't forget that it all hinges on whether or not that bank watchman was right in thinking he recognized Wash Gibbs."

"The man couldn't be mistaken there," returned the other. "There is not another man in the country the size of Gibbs, except the two Matthews's, and of course they're out of the question. Then, look! Jim Lane was ready to move out because of the drought, when all at once, after being away several days the very time of the robbery, he changes his mind, and stays with plenty of money to carry him through. And now, here we are to-night, with that same old Bald Knobber gang, what's left of them, called together in the same old way by Jim himself, to meet in his cabin. Take my word for it, we'll bag the whole outfit, with the rest of the swag before morning. It's as sure as fate. I'm glad that girl is away from home, though."

Sammy had heard enough. As the full meaning of the officers' words came to her, she felt herself swaying dizzily in the saddle and clung blindly to the pony's mane for support. Then something in her brain kept beating out the words, "Ride, Ride, Ride."

Never for an instant did Sammy doubt her father. It was all some horrible mistake. Her Daddy Jim would explain it all. Of course he would, if—if she could only get home first. But the men were between her and the path that led to the road.

Then all at once she remembered that Young Matt had told her how Sake Creek hollow headed in the pinery below the ridge along which they went from Fall Creek to the Forks. It might be that this bench at the foot of the ledge would lead to a way out.

As quick as thought the girl slipped to the ground, and taking Brownie by the head began feeling her way along the narrow shelf. Dead leaves, tangled grass and ferns, all wet and sodden, made a soft carpet, so that the men behind the rock heard no sound. Now and then the lightning revealed a glimpse of the way for a short distance, but mostly she trusted blindly to her pony's instinct. Several times she stumbled over jagged fragments of rock that had fallen from above, cutting her hand and bruising her limbs cruelly. Once, she was saved from falling over the cliff by the little horse's refusal to move. A moment she stood still in the darkness; then the lightning showed a way past the dangerous point.

After a time that seemed hours, she noticed that the ledge had become no higher than her head, and that a little farther on the bench was lost in the general slope of the hill. She had reached the head of the hollow. A short climb up the side of the mountain, and, pushing through the wet bushes, she found herself in the road. She had saved about three miles. It was still nearly five to her home. An instant later the girl was in her saddle, and the brown pony was running his best.

Sammy always looked back upon that ride in the darkness, and, indeed, upon all that happened that night, as to a dream of horror. As she rode, that other night came back to her, the night she had ridden to save the shepherd, and she lived over again that evening in the beautiful woods with Young Matt. Oh, if he were only with her now! Unconsciously, at times, she called his name aloud again and again, keeping time to the beat of her pony's feet. At other times she urged Brownie on, and the little horse, feeling the spirit of his mistress, answered with the best he had to give. With eager, outstretched head, and wide nostrils, he ran as though he understood the need.

How dark it was! At every bound they seemed plunging into a black wall. What if there should be a tree blown across the road? At the thought she grew faint. She saw herself lying senseless, and her father carried away to prison. Then rallying, she held her seat carefully. She must make it as easy as possible for Brownie, dear little Brownie. How she strained her eyes to see into the black night! How she prayed God to keep the little horse!

Only once in a lifetime, it seemed to her, did the pony's iron shoe strike sparks of fire from the rocks, or the lightning give her a quick glimpse of the road ahead. They must go faster, faster, faster. Those men should not—they should not have her Daddy Jim; not unless Brownie stumbled.

Where the road leaves the ridge for Fall Creek Valley, Sammy never tightened the slack rein, and the pony never shortened his stride by so much as an inch. It was well that he was hill bred, for none but a mountain horse could have kept his feet at such a terrific pace down the rocky slope. Down the valley road, past the mill, and over the creek they flew; then up the first rise of the ridge beyond. The pony was breathing hard now, and the girl encouraged him with loving words and endearing terms; pleading with him to go on, go on, go on.

At last they reached the top of the ridge. The way was easier now. Here and there, where the clouds were breaking, the stars looked through; but over the distant hills, the lightning still played, showing which way the storm had gone; and against the sky, now showing but dimly under ragged clouds and peeping stars, now outlined clearly against the flashing light, she saw the round treeless form of Old Dewey above her home.

CHAPTER XXXIV.

JIM LANE KEEPS HIS PROMISE.

Sammy, on her tired pony, approached the Lookout on the shoulder of Dewey. As they drew near a figure rose quickly from its place on the rock, and, running swiftly along the ledge, concealed itself in the clump of cedars above the trail on the southern side of the mountain. A moment later the almost exhausted horse and his rider passed, and the figure, slipping from the ledge, followed them unobserved down the mountain.

Nearing the house Sammy began to wonder what she should do next. With all her heart the girl believed in her father's innocence. She did not know why those men were at her home. But she did know that the money that helped her father over the drought had come through the shepherd; the Matthews family, too, had been helped the same way. Surely Dad Howitt was incapable of any crime. It was all some terrible mistake; some trap from which her father must be saved. But Sammy knew, too, that Wash Gibbs and his companions were bad men, who might easily be guilty of the robbery. To help them escape the officers was quite a different matter.

Leaving the trembling Brownie in a clump of bushes a little way from the clearing, the girl went forward on foot, and behind her still crept the figure that had followed from the Lookout. Once the figure paused as if undecided which course to pursue. Close by, two saddle horses that had carried their riders on many a long ride were tied to a tree a few feet from the corner of the barn. Sammy would have recognized these, but in her excitement she had failed to notice them.

At first the girl saw no light. Could it be that the officers were wrong? that there was no one at the cabin after all? Then a little penciled gleam set her heart throbbing wildly. Blankets were fastened over the windows.

Sammy remembered that a few days before a bit of chinking had fallen from between the logs in the rear of the cabin. She had spoken to her father about it, but it was not likely that he had remembered to fix it. Cautiously she passed around the house, and, creeping up to the building, through the crevice between the logs, gained a clear view of the interior.

Seated or lounging on chairs and on the floor about the room were eleven men; one, the man who had been with Wash Gibbs at the mill, carried his arm in a sling. The girl outside could hear distinctly every word that was spoken. Wash, himself, was speaking. "Well, boys, we're all here. Let's get through and get away. Bring out the stuff, Jim."

Mr. Lane went to one corner of the cabin, and, pulling up a loose board of the flooring, drew out two heavy sacks. As he placed the bags on the table, the men all rose to their feet. "There it is just as you give it to me," said Jim. "But before you go any farther, men, I've got something to say."

The company stirred uneasily, and all eyes turned from Jim to their big leader, while Sammy noticed for the first time that the table had been moved from its usual place, and that her father had taken such a position that the corner of the cabin was directly behind him, with the table in front. For her life the girl could not have moved.

Slowly Jim swept the group of scowling, wondering faces on the other side of the table. Then, in his slow drawling speech, he said, "Most of you here was in the old organization. Tom and Ed and me knows how it started away back, for we was in it at the beginnin'. Wash, here, was the last man to join, 'fore we was busted, and he was the youngest member, too; bein' only a boy, but big for his age. You remember how he was taken in on account of his daddy's bein' killed by the gov'ment.

"Didn't ary one of us fellers that started it ever think the Bald Knobber's would get to be what they did. We began it as a kind of protection, times bein' wild then. But first we knowed some was a usin' the order to protect themselves in all kinds of devilment, and things went on that way, 'cause nobody didn't dare say anything; for if they did they was tried as traitors, and sentenced to the death.

"I ain't a sayin', boys, that I was any better than lots of others, for I reckon I done my share. But when my girl's mother died, away down there in Texas, I promised her that I'd be a good daddy to my little one, and since then I done the best I know.

"After things quieted down, and I come back with my girl, Wash here got the old crowd, what was left of us, together, and wanted to reorganize again. I told you then that I'd go in with you and stand by the old oath, so long as it was necessary to protect ourselves from them that might be tryin' to get even for what had been done, but that I wouldn't go no farther. I don't mind tellin' you now, boys—though I reckon you know it—that I went in because I knowed what you'd do for me if I didn't. And I didn't dare risk leaving my girl all alone then. I've 'tended every meetin', and done everything I agreed, and there ain't a man here can say I ain't."

Some of the men nodded, and "That's so," and "You're right, Jim" came from two or three.

Jim went on, "You know that I voted against it, and tried to stop you when you hung old man Lewis. I thought then, and I think yet, that it was spite work and not protection; and you know how I was against goin' for the shepherd, and you went when I didn't know it. As for this here bank business, I didn't even know of it, 'till you give me this stuff here for me to keep for you. I had to take it 'count of the oath.

"It's got to be just like it was before. We come together first to keep each other posted, and save ourselves if there was any call to, and little by little you've been led into first one thing and then another, 'till you're every bit and grain as bad as the old crowd was, only there ain't so many of you, and you've kept me in it 'cause I didn't dare leave my girl." Jim paused. There was an ominous silence in the room.

With his eyes covering every scowling face in the company, Jim spoke again, "But things has changed for me right smart, since our last meetin', when you give me this stuff to hold. You boys all know how I've kept Wash Gibbs away from my girl, and there ain't one of you that don't know I'm right, knowin' him as we do. More'n two weeks ago, when I wasn't around, he insulted her, and would have done worse, if Young Matt hadn't been there to take care of her. I called you here to-night, because I knowed that after what happened at the mill, Wash and Bill would be havin' a meetin' as soon as they could get around, and votin' you all to go against Young Matt and his people. But I'm goin' to have my say first."

Wash Gibbs reached stealthily for his weapon, but hesitated when he saw that the dark faced man noted his movement.

Jim continued, in his drawling tones, but his voice rang cold and clear, "I ain't never been mealy mouthed with no man, and I'm too old to begin now. I know the law of the order, and I reckon Gibbs there will try to have you keep it. You boys have got to say whether you'll stand by him or me. It looks like you was goin' to go with him alright. But whether you do or don't, I don't aim to stay with nobody that stands by such as Wash Gibbs. I'm goin' to side with decent folks, who have stood by my girl, and you can do your damnedest. You take this stuff away from here. And as for you, Wash Gibbs, if you ever set foot on my place again, if you ever cross my path after to-night I'll kill you like the measly yeller hound you are." As he finished, Jim stood with his back to the corner of the room, his hand inside of the hickory shirt where the button was missing.

While her father was speaking, Sammy forgot everything, in the wild joy and pride of her heart. He was her Daddy, her Daddy Jim; that man standing so calmly there before the wild company of men. Whatever the past had been, he had wiped it clean to-night. He belonged to her now, all to her. She looked toward Wash Gibbs. Then she remembered the posse, the officers of the law. They could not know what she knew. If her father was taken with the others and with the stolen gold, he would be compelled to suffer with the rest. Yet if she called out to save him, she would save Wash Gibbs and his companions also, and they would menace her father's life day and night.

The girl drew back from the window. She must think. What should she do? Even as she hesitated, a score of dark forms crept swiftly, silently toward the cabin. At the same moment a figure left the side of the house near the girl, and, crouching low, ran to the two horses that were tied near the barn.

Sammy was so dazed that for a moment she did not grasp the meaning of those swiftly moving forms. Then a figure riding one horse and leading another dashed away from the barn and across a corner of the clearing. The silence was broken by a pistol shot in the cabin. Like an echo came a shot from the yard, and a voice rang out sharply, *"Halt!"* The figure reeled in the saddle, as if to fall, but recovered, and disappeared in the timber. The same instant there was a rush toward the house—a loud call to surrender—a woman's scream—and then, came to Sammy, blessed, kindly darkness.

CHAPTER XXXV.

"I WILL LIFT UP MINE EYES UNTO THE HILLS."

When Sammy opened her eyes, she was on the bed in her own room. In the other room someone was moving about, and the light from a lamp shone through the door.

At first the girl thought that she had awakened from a night's sleep, and that it was her father whom she heard, building the fire before calling her, as his custom was. But no, he was not building the fire, he was scrubbing the floor. How strange. She would call presently and ask what he meant by getting up before daylight, and whether he thought to keep her from scolding him by trying to clean up what he had spilled before she should see it.

She had had a bad dream of some kind, but she could not remember just what it was. It was very strange that something seemed to keep her from calling to her father just then. She would call presently. She must remember first what that dream was. She felt that she ought to get up and dress, but she did not somehow wish to move. She was strangely tired. It was her dream, she supposed. Then she discovered that she was already fully dressed, and that her clothing was wet, muddy and torn. And with this discovery every incident of the night came vividly before her. She hid her face.

After awhile, she tried to rise to her feet, but fell back weak and dizzy, Who was that in the other room? Could it be her father? Would he never finish scrubbing the floor in that corner? When she could bear the suspense no longer, she called in a voice that sounded weak and far away; "Daddy, Oh, Daddy."

Instantly the noise ceased; a step crossed the room; and the shepherd appeared in the doorway. Placing the lamp on a little stand, the old man drew a chair to the side of the bed, and laid his hand upon her forehead, smoothing back the tangled hair. He spoke no word, but in his touch there was a world of tenderness.

Sammy looked at him in wonder. Where had he come from? Why was he there at all? And in her room? She glanced uneasily about the apartment, and then back to the kind face of her old teacher. "I— don't think I understand."

"Never mind, now, dear. Don't try to understand just yet. Aunt Mollie will be here in a few minutes. Matt has gone for her. When she comes and you are a little stronger, we shall talk."

The girl caught his hand; "You—you won't leave me, Dad? You won't leave me alone? I'm afraid, Dad. I never was before."

"No, no, my child; I shall not leave you. But you must have something warm to drink. I have been preparing it." He stepped into the other room, soon returning with a steaming cup. When she had finished the strengthening draught, Young Matt, with his mother and father, arrived.

While helping the girl into clean, dry clothing, Aunt Mollie spoke soothingly to her, as one would reassure a frightened child. But Sammy could hear only the three men, moving about in the other room, doing something and talking always in low tones. She did not speak, but in her brown eyes, that never left the older woman's face, was that wide, questioning look.

When Mrs. Matthews had done what she could for the comfort of the girl, and the men had finished whatever they were doing in the other room, Sammy said, "Aunt Mollie, I want to know. I must know. Won't you tell Dad to come, please?" Instinctively she had turned to her teacher.

When the shepherd came, she met him with the old familiar demand, "Tell me everything, Dad; everything. I want to be told all about it."

"You will be brave and strong, Sammy?"

Instantly, as ever, her quick mind grasped the meaning that lay back of the words and her face grew deathly white. Then she answered, "I will be brave and strong. But first, please open the window, Dad." He threw up the sash. It was morning, and the mists were over the valley, but the mountain tops were bathed in light.

Sammy arose, and walked steadily to a chair by the open window. Looking out upon the beautiful scene, her face caught the light that was on the higher ground, and she said softly, "'I will lift up mine eyes unto the hills.' That's our word, now, isn't it, Dad? I can share it with you, now." Then the shepherd told her. Young Matt had been at the ranch with Mr. Howitt since early in the evening, and was taking his leave for the night when they heard horses stopping at the corral, and a voice calling. Upon their answering, the voice said, "There is trouble at Jim Lane's. Take these horses and go quick." And then as they had run from the house, the messenger had retreated into the shadow of the bluff, saying, "Never mind me. If you love Sammy, hurry." At this they mounted and had ridden as fast as possible.

The old man did not tell the girl that he had found his saddle wet and slippery, and that when he reached the light his hands were red.

They had found the officers ready to leave with their prisoners. All but two of the men were captured with their booty—Wash Gibbs alone escaping badly hurt, they thought, after killing one of the posse.

When they had asked for Sammy, one of the officers told them that she was at Ford's over on Jake Creek, but another declared that he had heard a woman scream as they were making the attack. Young Matt had found her unconscious on the ground behind the cabin.

When the shepherd finished his brief account, the girl said, "Tell me all, Dad. I want to know all. Did—did they take Daddy away?"

The old man's eyes were dim as he answered gently, "No, dear girl; *they* did not take him away." Then Sammy knew why Dad had scrubbed the cabin floor, and what the three men who talked so low had been doing in the other room.

She made no outcry, only a moan, as she looked away across the silent hills and the valley, where the mists were slowly lifting; lifting slowly like the pale ghost of the starlight that was. "Oh, Daddy, Daddy Jim. You *sure* kept your promise. You sure did. I'm glad—glad they didn't get you, Daddy. They never *would* have believed what I know; never—never."

But there were no tears, and the shepherd, seeing after a little touched her hand. "Everything is ready, dear; would you like to go now?"

"Not just yet, Dad. I must tell you first how I came to be at home, and why I am glad—oh, so glad, that I was here. But call the others, please; I want them all to know."

When the three, who with her teacher loved her best, had come, Sammy told her story; repeating almost word for word what she had heard her father say to the men. When she had finished, she turned her face again to the open window. The mists were gone. The landscape lay bright in the sun. But Sammy could not see.

"It is much better, so much better, as it is, my child," said the old scholar. "You see, dear, they would have taken him away. Nothing could have saved him. It would have been a living death behind prison walls away from you."

"Yes, I know, Dad. I understand. It is better as it is. Now, we will go to him, please." They led her into the other room. The floor in the corner of the cabin where the shepherd had washed it was still damp.

Through it all, Sammy kept her old friend constantly by her side. "It is easier, Dad, when you are near." Nor would she leave the house until it was all over, save to walk a little way with her teacher.

Young Matt and his father made the coffin of rough boards, sawed at the mill; and from the country round about, the woods-people came to the funeral, or, as they called it in their simple way, the "burying." The grave was made in a little glen not far from the house. When some of the neighbors would have brought a minister from the settlement, Sammy said, "No." Dad would say all that was necessary. So the shepherd, standing under the big trees, talked a little in his simple kindly way, and spoke the words, "Earth to earth, dust to dust, ashes to ashes." "As good," declared some, "as any preacher on earth could o' done hit;" though one or two held "it warn't jest right to put a body in th' ground 'thout a regular parson t' preach th' sermon."

When the last word was spoken, and the neighbors had gone away over the mountains and through the woods to their homes, Aunt Mollie with her motherly arm about the girl, said, "Come, honey; you're our girl now. As long as you stay in the hills, you shall stay with us." And Old Matt added, "You're the only daughter we've got, Sammy; and we want you a heap worse than you know."

When Sammy told them that she was not going to the city to live, they cried in answer, "Then you shall be our girl always," and they took her home with them to the big log house on the ridge.

For a week after that night at the Lane cabin, Pete was not seen. When at last, he did appear, it was to the shepherd on the hill, and his voice and manner alarmed Dad. But the boy's only reply to Mr. Howitt's question was, "Pete knows; Pete knows." Then in his own way he told something that sent the shepherd to Young Matt, and the two followed the lad to a spot where the buzzards were flying low through the trees.

By the shreds of clothing and the weapons lying near, they knew that the horrid thing, from which as they approached, carrion birds flapped their wings in heavy flight, was all that remained of the giant, Wash Gibbs.

Many facts were brought out at the trial of the outlaws and it was made clear that Jim Lane had met his death at the hands of Wash Gibbs, just at the beginning of the attack, and that Gibbs himself had been wounded a moment later by one of the attacking posse.

Thus does justice live even in the hills.

CHAPTER XXXVI.

ANOTHER STRANGER.

Mr. Matthews and his son first heard of the stranger through Lou Gordon, the mail carrier, who stopped at the mill on his way to Flag with the week's mail.

The native rode close to the shed, and waited until the saw had shrieked its way through the log of oak, and the carriage had rattled back to first position. Then with the dignity belonging to one of his station, as a government officer, he relieved his overcharged mouth of an astonishing quantity of tobacco, and drawled, "Howdy, men."

"Howdy, Lou," returned Young Matt from the engine, and Old Matt from the saw.

"Reckon them boards is fer a floor in Joe Gardner's new cabin?"

"Yes," returned Old Matt; "we ought to got 'em out last week, but seems like we couldn't get at it with the buryin' an' all."

" 'Pears like you all 'r gettin' mighty proud in this neighborhood. *Puncheon* floors *used* t' be good enough fer anybody t' dance on. Be a buildin' board houses next, I reckon."

Mr. Matthews laughed, "Bring your logs over to Fall Creek when you get ready to build, Lou; we'll sure do you right."

The representative of the government recharged his mouth. "'Lowed as how I would," he returned. "I ain't one o' this here kind that don't want t' see no changes. Gov'ment's all th' time makin' 'provements. Inspector 'lowed last trip we'd sure be a gettin' mail twice a week at Flag next summer. This here's sure bound t' be a big country some day.

"Talkin' 'bout new fangled things, though, men! I seed the blamdest sight las' night that ever was in these woods, I reckon. I gonies! Hit was a plumb wonder!" Kicking one foot from the wooden stirrup and hitching sideways in the saddle, he prepared for an effort.

"Little feller, he is. Ain't as tall as Preachin' Bill even, an' fat! I gonies! he's fat as a possum 'n 'simmon time. *He* don't walk, can't; just naturally waddles on them little duck legs o' hisn. An' he's got th' prettiest little ol' face; all red an' white, an' as round's a walnut; an' a fringe of th' whitest hair you ever seed. An' clothes! Say, men." In the pause the speaker deliberately relieved his overcharged mouth. The two in the mill waited breathlessly. "Long tailed coat, stove pipe hat, an' cane with a gold head as big as a 'tater. 'Fo' God, men, there ain't been ary such a sight within a thousand miles of these here hills ever. An' doin's! My Lord, a'mighty!"

The thin form of the native doubled up as he broke into a laugh that echoed and re-echoed through the little valley, ending in a wild, "Whoop-e-e-e. Say! When he got out of th' hack last night at th' Forks, Uncle Ike he catched sight o' him an' says, says he t' me, 'Ba thundas! Lou, looky there! Talk 'bout prosperity. I'm dummed if there ain't ol' Santa Claus a comin' t' th' Forks in th' summa time. 'Ba thundas! What!'

"An' when Santa come in, he—he wanted—Now what d' you reckon he wanted? A *bath!* Yes, sir-e-e. Dad burn me, 'f he didn't. A bath! Whoop-e-e, you ought t' seen Uncle Ike! He told him, 'Ba thundas!' he could give him a bite to eat an' a place to sleep, but he'd be pisined bit by rattlers, clawed by wild cats, chawed by the hogs, et by buzzards, an' everlastin'ly damned 'fore he'd tote water 'nough fer anybody t' swim in. 'Ba thundas! What!'

"What's he doin' here?" asked Mr. Matthews, when the mountaineer had recovered from another explosion.

Lou shook his head, as he straightened himself in the saddle. "Blame me 'f I kin tell. Jest wouldn't tell 't all last night. Wanted a *bath.* Called Uncle Ike some new fangled kind of a savage, an' th' old man 'lowed he'd show him. He'd sure have him persecuted fer 'sultin' a gov'ment servant when th' inspector come around. Yes he did. Oh, thar was doin's at the Forks last night!"

Again the mail carrier's laugh echoed through the woods. "Well, I must mosey along. He warn't up this mornin' when I left. Reckon he'll show up 'round here sometime 'fore sun down. Him an' Uncle Ike won't hitch worth a cent an' he'll be huntin' prouder folks. I done told th' old man he'd better herd him fer a spell, fer if he was t' get loose in these woods, there wouldn't be nary deer er bear left come Thanksgivin' time. Uncle Ike said 'Ba thundas!' he'd let me know that he warn't runnin' no dummed asylum. He 'lowed he was postmaster, 'Ba thundas!' an' had all he could do t' keep th' dad burned gov'ment straight."

Late that afternoon Lou's prophecy was fulfilled. A wagon going down the Creek with a load of supplies for the distillery stopped at the mill shed and the stranger began climbing carefully down over the wheels. Budd Wilson on his high seat winked and nodded at Mr. Matthews and his son, as though it was the greatest joke of the season.

"Hold those horses, driver. Hold them tight; tight, sir."

"Got 'em, Mister," responded Budd promptly. The mules stood with drooping heads and sleepy eyes, the lines under their feet.

The gentleman was feeling carefully about the hub of the wheel with a foot that, stretch as he might, could not touch it by a good six inches.

"That's right, man, right," he puffed. "Hold them tight; tight. Start now, break a leg sure, sure. Then what would Sarah and the girls do? Oh, blast it all, where is that step? Can't stay here all day. Bring a ladder. Bring a high chair, a table, a box, a big box, a—heh—heh—Look out, I say, look out! Blast it all, what do you mean?" This last was called forth by Young Matt lifting the little man bodily to the ground, as an ordinary man would lift a child.

To look up at the young giant, the stranger tipped back his head, until his shining silk hat was in danger of falling in the dirt. "Bless my soul, what a specimen! What a specimen!" Then with a twinkle in his eye, "Which one of the boys are you, anyway?"

At this the three mountaineers roared with laughter. With his dumpy figure in the long coat, and his round face under the tall hat, the little man was irresistible. He fairly shone with good humor; his cheeks were polished like big red apples; his white hair had the luster of silver; his blue eyes twinkled; his silk hat glistened; his gold watch guard sparkled; his patent leathers glistened; and the cane with the big gold head gleamed in the sunlight.

"That's him, Doc," called the driver. "That's the feller what wallered Wash Gibbs like I was a tellin' ye. Strongest man in the hills he is. Dad burn me if I believe he knows how strong he is."

"Doc—Doc—Dad burned—Doc," muttered the stranger. "What would Sarah and the girls say!" He waddled to the wagon, and reached up one fat hand with a half dollar to Budd, "Here, driver, here. Get cigars with that; cigars, mind you, or candy. I stay here. Mind you don't get anything to drink; nothing to drink, I say."

Budd gathered up the reins and woke the sleepy mules with a vigorous jerk. "Nary a drink, Doc; nary a drink. Thank you kindly all the same. Got t' mosey 'long t' th' still now; ought t' o' been there hour ago. 'f I can do anything fer you, jest le' me know. I live over on Sow Coon Gap, when I'm 't home. Come over an' visit with me. Young Matt there'll guide you."

As he watched the wagon down the valley, the stranger mused. "Doc—Doc—huh. Quite sure that fellow will buy a drink; quite sure."

When the wagon had disappeared, he turned to Mr. Matthews and his son; "According to that fellow, I am not far from a sheep ranch kept by a Mr. Howitt. That's it, Mr. Daniel Howitt; fine looking man, fine; brown eyes; great voice; gentleman, sir, gentleman, if he is keeping sheep in this wilderness. Blast it all, just like him, just like him; always keeping somebody's sheep; born to be a shepherd; born to be. Know him?"

At mention of Mr. Howitt's name, Young Matt had looked at his father quickly. When the stranger paused, he answered, "Yes, sir. We know Dad Howitt. Is he a friend of yourn?"

"Dad—Dad Howitt. Doc and Dad. Well, what would Sarah and the girls say? Friend of mine? Young man Daniel and David, I am David; Daniel and David lay on the same blanket when they were babies; played in the same alley; school together same classes; colleged together; next door neighbors. Know him! Blast it all, where *is* this sheep place?"

Again the two woodsmen exchanged glances. The elder Matthews spoke, "It ain't so far from here, sir. The ranch belongs to me and my son. But Mr. Howitt will be out on the hills somewhere with the sheep now. You'd better go home with us and have supper, and the boy will take you down this evenin'."

"Well, now, that's kind, sir; very kind, indeed. Man at the Postoffice is a savage, sir; blasted, old incorrigible savage. My name is Coughlan; Dr. David Coughlan, of Chicago; practicing physician for forty years; don't do anything now; not much, that is. Sarah and the girls won't let me. Your name, sir?"

"Grant Matthews. My boy there has the same. We're mighty glad to meet any friend of Dad's, I can tell you. He's sure been a God's blessin' to this neighborhood."

Soon they started homeward, Young Matt going ahead to do the chores, and to tell his mother of their coming guest, while Mr. Matthews followed more slowly with the doctor. Shortening his stride to conform to the slow pace of the smaller man, the mountaineer told his guest about the shepherd; how he had come to them; of his life; and how he had won the hearts of the people. When he told how Mr. Howitt had educated Sammy, buying her books himself from his meager wages, the doctor interrupted in his quick way, "Just like him! just like him. Always giving away everything he earned. Made others give, too. Blast it all, he's cost me thousands of dollars, thousands of dollars, treating patients of his that never paid a cent; not a cent, sir. Proud, though; proud as Lucifer. Fine old, family; finest in the country, sir. Right to be proud, right to be."

Old Matt scowled as he returned coldly, "He sure don't seem that way to us, Mister. He's as common as an old shoe." And then the mountaineer told how his son loved the shepherd, and tried to explain what the old scholar's friendship had meant to them.

The stranger ejaculated, "Same old thing; same old trick. Did me that way; does everybody that way. Same old Daniel. Proud, though; can't help it; can't help it."

The big man answered with still more warmth, "You ought to hear how he talks to us folks when we have meetin's at the Cove school house. He's as good as any preacher you ever heard; except that he don't put on as much, maybe. Why, sir, when we buried Jim Lane week before last, everybody 'lowed he done as well as a regular parson."

At this Dr. Coughlan stopped short and leaned against a convenient tree for support, looking up at his big host, with merriment he could not hide; "Parson, parson! Daniel Howitt talk as good as a parson! Blast it all! Dan is one of the biggest D. D.'s in the United States; as good as a parson, I should think so! Why, man, he's my pastor; my pastor. Biggest church, greatest crowds in the city. Well what would Sarah and the girls say!" He stood there gasping and shaking with laughter, until Old Matt, finding the ridiculous side of the situation, joined in with a guffaw that fairly drowned the sound of the little man's merriment.

When they finally moved on again, the Doctor said, "And you never knew? The papers were always full, always. His real name is—"

"Stop!" Old Matt spoke so suddenly and in such a tone that the other jumped in alarm. "I ain't a meanin' no harm, Doc; but you oughtn't to tell his name, and—anyway I don't want to know. Preacher or no preacher, he's a man, he is, and that's what counts in this here country. If Dad had wanted us to know about himself, I reckon he'd a told us, and I don't want to hear it until he's ready."

The Doctor stopped short again, "Right, sir; right. Daniel has his reasons, of course. I forgot. That savage at the Postoffice tried to interrogate me; tried to draw me. I was close; on guard you see. Fellow in the wagon tried; still on guard. You caught me. Blast it all, I like you! Fine specimen that boy of yours; fine!"

When they reached the top of the ridge the stranger looked over the hills with exclamations of delight, "Grand, sir; grand! Wish Sarah and the girls could see. Don't wonder Daniel staid. That Hollow down there you say; way down there? Mutton—Mutton Hollow? Daniel lives there? Blast it all; come on, man; come on."

As they drew near the house, Pete came slowly up the Old Trail and met them at the gate.

CHAPTER XXXVII.

OLD FRIENDS.

After supper Young Matt guided the stranger down the trail to the sheep ranch in Mutton Hollow.

When they reached the edge of the clearing, the mountaineer stopped. "Yonder's the cabin, sir, an' Dad is there, as you can see by the smoke. I don't reckon you'll need me any more now, an' I'll go back. We'll be mighty glad to see you on the ridge any time, sir. Any friend of Dad's is mighty welcome in this neighborhood."

"Thank you; thank you; very thoughtful; very thoughtful, indeed; fine spirit, fine. I shall see you again when Daniel and I have had it out. Blast it all; what is he doing here? Good night, young man; good-night." He started forward impetuously. Matt turned back toward home.

The dog barked as Dr. Coughlan approached the cabin, and the shepherd came to the open door. He had been washing the supper dishes. His coat was off, his shirt open at the throat, and his sleeves rolled above his elbows. "Here, Brave." The deep voice rolled across the little clearing, and the dog ran to stand by his master's side. Then, as Mr. Howitt took in the unmistakable figure of the little physician, he put out a hand to steady himself.

"Oh, it's me, Daniel; it's me. Caught you didn't I? Blast it all; might have known I would. Bound to; bound to, Daniel; been at it ever since I lost you. Visiting in Kansas City last week with my old friends, the Stewarts; young fellow there, Ollie, put me right. First part of your name, description, voice and all that; knew it was you; knew it. Didn't tell them, though; blasted reporters go wild. Didn't tell a soul, not a soul. Sarah and the girls think I am in Kansas City or Denver. Didn't tell old man Matthews, either; came near, though, very near. Blast it all; what does it mean? what does it all mean?"

In his excitement the little man spoke rapidly as he hurried toward the shepherd. When he reached the cabin, the two friends, so different, yet so alike, clasped hands.

As soon as the old scholar could speak, he said, "David, David! To think that this is really you. You of all men; you, whom I most needed."

"Huh!" grunted the other. "Look like you never needed me less. Look fit for anything, anything; ten years younger; every bit of ten years. Blast it all; what have you done to yourself? What have you done?" He looked curiously at the tanned face and rude dress of his friend. "Bless my soul, what a change! What a change! Told Matthews you were an aristocrat. He wouldn't believe it. Don't wonder. Doubt it myself, now."

The other smiled at the Doctor's amazement. "I suppose I have changed some, David. The hills have done it. Look at them!" He pointed to the encircling mountains. "See how calm and strong they are; how they lift their heads above the gloom. They are my friends and companions, David. And they have given me of their calmness and strength a little. But come in, come in; you must be very tired. How did you come?"

The doctor followed him into the cabin. "Railroad, hack, wagon, walked. Postoffice last night. Man there is a savage, blasted incorrigible savage. Mill this afternoon. Home with your friends on the ridge. Old man is a gentleman, a gentleman, sir, if God ever made one. His boy's like him. The mother, she's a real mother; made to be a mother; couldn't help it. And that young woman, with the boy's name, bless my soul, I never saw such a creature before, Daniel, never! If I had I—I—Blast it all; I wouldn't be bossed by Sarah and the girls, I wouldn't. See in that young man and woman what God meant men and women to be. Told them they ought to marry; that they owed it to the race. You know my ideas, Daniel. Think they will?"

The shepherd laughed, a laugh that was good to hear.

"What's the matter now, Daniel? What is the matter? Have I said anything wrong again? Blast it all; you know how I always do the wrong thing. Have I?"

"No, indeed, David; you are exactly right," returned Mr. Howitt. "But tell me, did you see no one else at the house? There is another member of the family."

The doctor nodded. "I saw him; Pete, you mean. Looked him over. Mr. Matthews asked me to. Sad case, very sad. Hopeless, absolutely hopeless, Daniel."

"Pete has not seemed as well as usual lately. I fear so much night roaming is not good for the boy," returned the other slowly. "But tell me, how are Sarah and the girls? Still looking after Dr. Davie, I suppose."

"Just the same; haven't changed a bit; not a bit. Jennie looks after my socks and handkerchiefs; Mary looks after my shirts and linen; Anna looks after my ties and shoes; Sue looks after my hats and coats; and Kate looks after the things I eat; and Sarah, Sarah looks after everything and everybody, same as always. Blast it all! If they'd give me a show, I'd be as good as ever; good as ever, Daniel. What can a man do; what can a man do, with an only sister and her five old maid daughters looking after him from morning until night, from morning until night, Daniel? Tell them I am a full grown man; don't do no good; no good at all. Blast it all; poor old things, just got to mother something; got to, Daniel."

While he was speaking, his eyes were dancing from one object to another in the shepherd's rude dwelling, turning for frequent quick glances to Dad himself. "You live here, you? You ought not, Daniel, you ought not. What would Sarah and the girls say? Blast it all; what do you mean by it? I ordered you away on a vacation. You disappear. Think you dead; row in the papers, mystery; I hate mystery. Blast it all; what does it mean, what does it all mean? Not fair to me, Daniel; not fair."

By this time the little man had worked himself up to an astonishing pitch of excitement; his eyes snapped; his words came like pistol shots; his ejaculations were genuine explosions. He tapped with his feet; rapped with his cane; shook his finger; and fidgeted in his chair. "We want you back, Daniel. I want you. Church will want you when they know; looking for a preacher right now. I come after you, Daniel. Blast it all, I'll tell Sarah and the girls, and they'll come after you, too. Chicago will go wild when they know that Daniel Howitt Cha—"

"Stop!" The doctor bounced out of his chair. The shepherd was trembling, and his voice shook with emotion. "Forgive me, David. But that name must never be spoken again, never. My son is dead, and that name died with him. It must be forgotten."

The physician noted his friend's agitation in amazement. "There, there, Daniel. I didn't mean to. Thought it didn't matter when we were alone. I—I—Blast it all! Tell me Daniel, what do you mean by this strange business, this very strange business?"

A look of mingled affection, regret and pain, came into the shepherd's face, as he replied, "Let me tell you the story, David, and you will understand."

When he had finished, Mr. Howitt asked gently, "Have I not done right, David? The boy is gone. It was hard, going as he did. But I am glad, now, for Old Matt would have killed him, as he would kill me yet, if he knew. Thank God, we have not also made the father a murderer. Did I not say rightly, that the old name died with Howard? Have I not done well to stay on this spot and to give my life to this people?"

"Quite right, Daniel; quite right. You always are. It's me that goes wrong; blundering, bumping, smashing into things. Blast it all! I—I don't know what to say. B—B—Blast it all!"

The hour was late when the two men finally retired for the night. Long after his heavy, regular breathing announced that the doctor was sleeping soundly, the shepherd lay wide awake, keenly sensitive to every sound that stirred in the forest. Once he arose from his bed, and stepping softly left the cabin, to stand under the stars, his face lifted to the dark summit of Old Dewey and the hills that rimmed the Hollow. And once, when the first light of day came over the ridges, he went to the bunk where his friend lay, to look thoughtfully down upon the sleeping man.

Breakfast was nearly ready when Dr. Coughlan awoke. The physician saw at once by the worn and haggard look on his friend's face that his had been a sleepless night. It was as though all the pain and trouble of the old days had returned. The little doctor muttered angrily to himself while the shepherd was gone to the spring for water. "Blast it all, I'm a fool, a meddlesome, old fool. Ought to have let well enough alone. No need to drag him back into it all again; no need. Do no good; no good at all."

When the morning meal was finished, Mr. Howitt said, "David, will you think me rude, if I leave you alone to-day? The city pavement fits one but poorly to walk these hills of mine, and you are too tired after your trip and the loss of your regular sleep to go with me this morning. Stay at the ranch and rest. If you care to read, here are a few of your favorites. Will you mind very much? I should like to be alone to-day, David."

"Right, Daniel, right. I understand. Don't say another word; not a word. Go ahead. I'm stiff and sore anyway; just suit me."

The shepherd arranged everything for his friend's comfort, putting things in readiness for his noonday meal, and showing him the spring. Then, taking his own lunch, as his custom was, he went to the corral and released the sheep. The doctor watched until the last of the flock was gone, and he could no longer hear the tinkle of the bells and the bark of the dog.

CHAPTER XXXVIII.

I AIN'T NOBODY NO MORE.

With the coming of the evening, the shepherd returned to his guest. Dr. Coughlan heard first the bells on the leaders of the flock, and the barking of the dog coming nearer and nearer through the woods. Soon the sheep appeared trooping out of the twilight shadows into the clearing; then came Brave followed by his master.

The countenance of the old scholar wore again that look of calm strength and peace that had marked it before the coming of his friend. "Have you had a good rest, David? Or has your day been long and tiresome? I fear it was not kind of me to leave you alone in this wilderness."

The doctor told how he had passed the time, reading, sleeping and roaming about the clearing and the nearby woods. "And you," he said, looking the other over with a professional eye, "you look like a new man; a new man, Daniel. How do you do it? Some secret spring of youth in the wilderness? Blast it all, wish you would show me. Fool Sarah and the girls, fool them, sure."

"David, have you forgotten the prescription you gave me when you ordered me from the city? You took it you remember from one of our favorite volumes." The shepherd bared his head and repeated,

"If thou art worn and hard beset,
With sorrows, that thou wouldst forget;
If thou wouldst read a lesson, that will keep
Thy heart from fainting and thy soul from sleep,
Go to the woods and hills! No tears
Dim the sweet look that Nature wears."

"David, I never understood until the past months why the Master so often withdrew alone into the wilderness. There is not only food and medicine for one's body; there is also healing for the heart and strength for the soul in nature. One gets very close to God, David, in these temples of God's own building."

Dr. Coughlan studied his old friend curiously; "Change; remarkable change in you! Remarkable! Never said a thing like that in all your life before, never."

The shepherd smiled, "It's your prescription, Doctor," he said.

They retired early that evening, for the physician declared that his friend must need the rest. "Talk to-morrow," he said; "all day; nothing else to do." He promptly enforced his decision by retiring to his own bunk, leaving the shepherd to follow his example. But not until the doctor was sure that his friend was sleeping soundly did he permit himself to sink into unconsciousness.

It was just past midnight, when the shepherd was aroused by the doctor striking a match to light the lamp. As he awoke, he heard Pete's voice, "Where is Dad? Pete wants Dad."

Dr. Coughlan, thinking it some strange freak of the boy's disordered brain, and not wishing to break his friend's much needed rest, was trying in low tones to persuade the boy to wait until morning.

"What does Pete want?" asked the shepherd entering the room.

"Pete wants Dad; Dad and the other man. They must sure go with Pete right quick."

"Go where with Pete? Who told Pete to come for Dad?" asked Mr. Howitt.

"He told Pete. Right now, he said. And Pete he come. 'Course I come with him. Dad must go, an' the other man too, 'cause he said so."

In sickness or in trouble of any kind the people for miles around had long since come to depend upon the shepherd of Mutton Hollow. The old man turned now to the doctor. "Someone needs me, David. We must go with the boy."

"But, Daniel, Daniel! Blast it all! The boy's not responsible. Where will he take us? Where do you want us to go, boy?"

"Not me; not me; nobody can't go nowhere, can they? You go with Pete, Mister."

"Yes, yes; go with Pete; but where will Pete take us?" persisted the Doctor.

"Pete knows."

"Now, look at that, Daniel! Look at that. Blast it all; we ought not go; not in the night this way. What would Sarah and the girls say?" Notwithstanding his protests, the doctor was ready even before the shepherd. "Take a gun, Daniel; take a gun, at least," he said.

The other hesitated, then asked, "Does Pete want Dad to take a gun?"

The youth, who stood in the doorway waiting impatiently, shook his head and laughed, "No, no; nothing can't get Dad where Pete goes. God he's there just like Dad says."

"It's all right, David," said the shepherd with conviction. "Pete knows. It is safe to trust him to-night."

And the boy echoed, as he started forward, "It's alright, Mister; Pete knows."

"I wish you had your medicine case, though, David," added Mr. Howitt, as they followed the boy out into the night.

"Got one, Daniel; got one. Always have a pocket case; habit."

Pete led the way down the road, and straight to the old cabin ruin below the corral. Though the stars were hidden behind clouds, it was a little light in the clearing; but, in the timber under the shadow of the bluff, it was very dark. The two men were soon bewildered and stood still. "Which way, Pete?" said the shepherd. There was no answer. "Where's Pete? Tell Pete to come here," said Mr. Howitt again. Still there was on reply. Their guide seemed to have been swallowed up in the blackness. They listened for a sound. "This is strange," mused the shepherd.

A grunt of disgust came from the doctor, "Crazy, man, crazy. There's three of us. Which way is the house? Blast it all, what would—" A spot of light gleamed under the bushes not fifty feet away.

"Come, Dad. Come on, Pete's ready."

They were standing close to the old cabin under the bluff. In a narrow space between the log wall of the house and the cliff, Pete stood with a lighted lantern. The farther end of the passage was completely hidden by a projection of the rock; the overhanging roof touched the ledge above; while the opening near the men was concealed by the heavy growth of ferns and vines and the thick branches of a low cedar. Even in daylight the place would have escaped anything but a most careful search.

Dropping to his knees and to one hand the shepherd pushed aside the screen of vines and branches with the other, and then on all fours crawled into the narrow passage. The Doctor followed. They found their guide crouching in a small opening in the wall of rock. Mr. Howitt uttered an exclamation, "The lost cave! Old man Dewey!"

The boy laughed, "Pete knows. Come, Dad. Come, other man. Ain't nothin' can get you here." He scrambled ahead of them into the low tunnel. Some twenty feet from the entrance, the passage turned sharply to the left and opened suddenly into a hallway along which the shepherd could easily walk erect. Pete went briskly forward as one on very familiar ground, his lantern lighting up the way clearly for his two companions.

For some distance their course dipped downward at a gentle angle, while the ceilings and sides dripped with moisture. Soon they heard the sound of running water, and entering a wider room saw sparkling in the lantern's light a stream that came from under the rocky wall, crossed their path, and disappeared under the other wall of the chamber. "Lost Creek!" ejaculated the shepherd, as he picked his way over the stream on the big stones. And the boy answered, "Pete knows. Pete knows."

From the bank of the creek the path climbed strongly upward, the footing grew firmer, and the walls and ceiling drier; as they went on, the passage, too, grew wider and higher, until they found themselves in a large underground hallway that echoed loudly as they walked. Overhead, pure white stalactites and frost-like formations glittered in the light, and the walls were broken by dark nooks and shelf-like ledges with here and there openings leading who could tell where?

At the farther end of this hallway where the ceiling was highest, the guide paused at the foot of a ledge against which rested a rude ladder. The shepherd spoke again, "Dewey Bald?" he asked. Pete nodded, and began to climb the ladder.

Another room, and another ledge; then a long narrow passage, the ceiling of which was so high that it was beyond the lantern light; then a series of ledges, and they saw that they were climbing from shelf to shelf on one side of an underground canon. Following along the edge of the chasm, the doctor pushed a stone over the brink, and they heard it go bounding from ledge to ledge into the dark heart of the mountain. "No bottom, Daniel. Blast it all, no bottom to it! What would Sarah and the girls say?"

They climbed one more ladder and then turned from the canon into another great chamber, the largest they had entered. The floor was perfectly dry; the air, too, was dry and pure; and, from what seemed to be the opposite side of the huge cavern, a light gleamed like a red eye in the darkness. They were evidently nearing the end of their journey. Drawing closer they found that the light came from the window of a small cabin built partly of rock and partly of logs.

Instinctively the two men stopped. Pete said in a low tone, as one would speak in a sacred presence, *"He* is there. Come on, Dad. Come, other man. Don't be scared."

Still the boy's companions hesitated. Mr. Howitt asked, "Who, boy? who is there? Do you know who it is?"

"No, no, not me. Nobody can't know nothin', can they?"

"Hopeless case, Daniel; hopeless. Too bad, too bad," muttered the physician, laying his hand upon his friend's shoulder.

The shepherd tried again, "Who does Pete say it is?"

"Oh, Pete says it's him, just him."

"But who does Pete say he is?" suggested Dr. Coughlan.

Again the boy's voice lowered to a whisper, "Sometimes Pete says it must be God, 'cause he's so good. Dad says God is good an' that he takes care of folks, an' *he* sure does that. 'Twas him that scared Wash Gibbs an' his crowd that night. An' he sent the gold to you, Dad; God's gold it was; he's got heaps of it. He killed that panther, too, when it was a goin' to fight Young Matt. Pete knows. You see, Dad, when Pete is with him, I ain't nobody no more.

I'm just Pete then, an' Pete is me. Funny, ain't it? But he says that's the way it is, an' he sure knows."

The two friends listened with breathless interest. "And what does Pete call him?" asked the doctor.

"Pete calls him father, like Dad calls God. He talks to God, too, like Dad does. Do you reckon God would talk to God, mister?"

With a cry the shepherd reeled. The doctor caught him. "Strong, Daniel, strong." Pete drew away from the two men in alarm.

The old scholar's agitation was pitiful. "David, David; tell me, what is this thing? Can it be—my boy—Howard, my son—can it be? My God, David, what am I saying? He is dead. Dead, I tell you. Can the dead come back from the grave, David?" He broke from his friend and ran staggering toward the cabin; but at the door he stopped again. It was as if he longed yet feared to enter, and the doctor and the boy came to his side. Without ceremony Pete pushed open the door.

The room was furnished with a cupboard, table and small cook stove. It was evidently a living room. Through a curtained opening at the right, a light showed from another apartment, and a voice called, "Is that you, Pete?"

A look of pride came into the face of the lad, "That's me," he whispered. "I'm Pete here, an' Pete is me. It's always that way with him." Aloud, he said, "Yes, Father, it's Pete. Pete, an' Dad, an' the other man." As he spoke he drew aside the curtain.

For an instant the two men paused on the threshold. The room was small, and nearly bare of furniture. In the full glare of the lamp, so shaded as to throw the rest of the room in deep shadow, hung a painting that seemed to fill the rude chamber with its beauty. It was the picture of a young woman, standing by a spring of water, a cup brimming full in her outstretched hand.

On a bed in the shadow, facing the picture, lay a man. A voice faltered, "Father. Dr. Coughlan."

CHAPTER XXXIX.

A MATTER OF HOURS.

Father—Father; can—you—can—you—forgive me?"

The man on his knees raised his head.

"Forgive you, my son? Forgive you? My dear boy, there has never been in my heart a thought but of love and sympathy. Pain there has been, I can't deny, but it has helped me to know what you have suffered. I understand it now, my boy. I understand it all, for I, too, have felt it. But when I first knew, even beneath all the hurt, I was glad—glad to know, I mean. It is a father's right to suffer with his child, my son. It hurt most, when the secret stood between us, and I could not enter into your life, but I understand that, too. I understand why you could not tell me. I, too, came away because I was not strong enough."

"I—I thought it would be easier for you never to know," said the son as he lay on the bed. "I am—sorry, now. And I am glad that you know. But I must tell you all about it just the same. I must tell you myself, you see, so that it will be all clear and straight when I—when I go." He turned his eyes to the picture on the wall.

"When you go?"

Howard laid a hand upon the gray head. "Poor father; yes, I am going. It was an accident, but it was a kindness. It will be much better that way—only—only I am sorry for you, father. I thought I could save you all this. I intended to slip quietly away without your ever knowing, but when Pete said that Dr. Coughlan was here, I could not go without—without—"

The little doctor came forward. "I am a fool, Howard, an old fool. Blast it all; no business to go poking into this; no business at all! Daniel would have sent if he had wanted me. Ought to have known. Old native can give me lessons on being a gentleman every time. Blast it all! What's wrong, Howard? Get hurt? Now I am here, might as well be useful."

"Indeed, Doctor, you did right to come. You will be such a help to father. You will help us both, just as you have always done. Will you excuse us, father, while Dr. Coughlan looks at this thing here in my side?"

The physician arranged the light so that it shone full upon the man on the bed, then carefully removed the bandages from an ugly wound in the artist's side. Dr. Coughlan looked very grave. "When did this happen, Howard?"

"I—I can't tell exactly. You see I thought at first I could get along with Pete to help, and I did, for a week, I guess. Then things—didn't go so well. Some fever, I think, for she—she came." He turned his eyes toward the picture again. "And I—I lost all track of time. It was the night of the eighteenth. Father will know."

"Two weeks," muttered the physician.

A low exclamation came from the shepherd. "It was you—you who brought the horses to the ranch that night?"

The artist smiled grimly. "The officers saw me, and thought that I was one of the men they wanted. It's alright, though." The old scholar instinctively lifted his hands and looked at them. He remembered the saddle, wet with blood.

Making a careful examination, the doctor asked more questions. When he had finished and had skilfully replaced the bandages, the wounded man asked, "What about it, Dr. Coughlan?" The kind hearted physician jerked out a volley of scientific words and phrases that meant nothing, and busied himself with his medicine case.

When his patient had taken the medicine, the doctor watched him for a few minutes, and then asked, "Feel stronger, Howard?"

The artist nodded. "Tell me the truth, now, Doctor. I know that I am going. But how long have I? Wait a minute first. Where's Pete? Come here, my boy." The lad drew near. "Father." Mr. Howitt seated himself on the bedside. "You'll be strong, father? We are ready now, Dr. Coughlan."

"Yes, tell us, David," said the shepherd, and his voice was steady.

The physician spoke, "Matter of hours, I would say. Twenty-four, perhaps; not more; not more."

"There is no possible chance, David?" asked the shepherd.

Again the little doctor took refuge behind a broadside of scientific terms before replying, "No; no possible chance."

A groan slipped from the gray bearded lips of the father. The artist turned to the picture and smiled. Pete looked wonderingly from face to face.

"Poor father," said the artist. "One thing more, Doctor; can you keep up my strength for awhile?"

"Reasonably well, reasonably well, Howard."

"I am so glad of that because there is much to do before I go. There is so much that must be done first, and I want you both to help me."

CHAPTER XL.

THE SHEPHERD'S MISSION.

During the latter part of that night and most of the day, it rained; a fine, slow, quiet rain, with no wind to shake the wet from burdened leaf or blade. But when the old shepherd left the cave by a narrow opening on the side of the mountain, near Sammy's Lookout, the sky was clear. The mists rolled heavily over the valley, but the last of the sunlight was warm on the knobs and ridges.

The old man paused behind the rock and bushes that concealed the mouth of the underground passage. Not a hundred feet below was the Old Trail; he followed the little path with his eye until it vanished around the shoulder of Dewey. Along that way he had come into the hills. Then lifting his eyes to the far away lines of darker blue, his mind looked over the ridge to the world that is on the other side, the world from which he had fled. It all seemed very small and mean, now; it was so far—so far away.

He started as the sharp ring of a horse's iron shoe on the flint rocks came from beyond the Lookout, and, safely hidden, be saw a neighbor round the hill and pass on his way to the store on Roark. He watched, as horse and rider followed the Old Trail around the rim of the Hollow; watched, until they passed from sight in the belt of timber. Then his eyes were fixed on a fine thread of smoke that curled above the trees on the Matthews place; and, leaving the shelter of rock and bush, he walked along the Old Trail toward the big log house on the distant ridge.

Below him, on his left, Mutton Hollow lay submerged in the drifting mists, with only a faint line of light breaking now and then where Lost Creek made its way; and on the other side Compton Ridge lifted like a wooded shore from the sea. A black spot in the red west shaped itself into a crow, making his way on easy wing toward a dead tree on the top of Boulder Bald. The old shepherd walked wearily; the now familiar objects wore a strange look. It was as though he saw them for the first time, yet had seen them somewhere before, perhaps in another world. As he went his face was the face of one crushed by shame and grief, made desperate by his suffering.

Supper was just over and Young Matt was on the porch when Mr. Howitt entered the gate. The young fellow greeted his old friend, and called back into the house, "Here's Dad, Father." As Mr. Matthews came out, Aunt Mollie and Sammy appeared in the doorway. How like it all was to that other evening.

The mountaineer and the shepherd sat on the front porch, while Young Matt brought the big sorrel and the brown pony to the gate, and with Sammy rode away. They were going to the Postoffice at the Forks. "Ain't had no news for a week," said Aunt Mollie, as she brought her chair to join the two men. "And besides, Sammy needs the ride. There's goin' to be a moon, so it'll be light by the time they start home."

The sound of the horses' feet and the voices of the young people died away in the gray woods. The dusk thickened in the valley below, and, as the light in the west went out, the three friends saw the clump of pines etched black and sharp against the blood red background of the sky.

Old Matt spoke, "Reckon everything's alright at the ranch, Dad. How's the little doctor? You ought to brung him up with you." He watched the shepherd's face curiously from under his heavy brows, as he pulled at his cob pipe.

"Tired out trampin' over these hills, I reckon," ventured Aunt Mollie. Mr. Howitt tried to answer with some commonplace, but his friends could not but note his confusion. Mrs. Matthews continued, "I guess you'll be a leavin' us pretty soon, now. Well, I ain't a blamin' you; and you've sure been a God's blessin' to us here in the woods. I don't reckon we're much 'long 'side the fine friends you've got back where you come from in the city; and we—we can't do nothin' for you, but—but—" The good soul could say no more.

"We've often wondered, sir," added Old Matt, "how you've stood it here, an educated man like you. I reckon, though, there's somethin' deep under it all, keepin' you up; somethin' that ignorant folks, without no education, like us, can't understand."

The old scholar could have cried aloud, but he was forced to sit dumb while the other continued, "You're goin' won't make no difference, though, with what you've done. This neighborhood won't never go back to what it was before you come. It can't with all you've taught us, and with Sammy stayin' here to keep it up. It'll be mighty hard, though, to have you go; it sure will, Mr. Howitt."

Looking up, the shepherd said quietly, "I expect to live here until the end if you will let me. But I fear you will not want me to stay when you know what I've come to tell you this evening."

The mountaineer straightened his huge form as he returned, "Dad, there ain't nothin' on earth or in hell could change what we think of you, and we don't want to hear nothin' about you that you don't like to tell us. We ain't a carin' what sent you to the hills. We're takin' you for what you are. And there ain't nothin' can change that."

"Not even if it should be the grave under the pine yonder?" asked the other in a low voice.

Old Matt looked at him in a half frightened way, as though, without knowing why, he feared what the shepherd would say next. Mr. Howitt felt the look and hesitated. He was like one on a desperate mission in the heart of an enemy's country, feeling his way. Was the strong man's passion really tame? Or was his fury only sleeping, waiting to destroy the one who should wake it? Who could tell?

The old scholar looked away to Dewey Bald for strength. "Mr. Matthews," he said, "you once told me a story. It was here on this porch when I first came to you. It was a sad tale of a great crime. To-night I know the other aide of that story. I've come to tell you."

At the strange words, Aunt Mollie's face turned as white as her apron. Old Matt grasped the arms of his chair, as though he would crush the wood, as he said shortly, "Go on."

At the tone of his voice, the old shepherd's heart sank.

CHAPTER XLI.

THE OTHER SIDE OF THE STORY.

With a prayer in his heart for the boy who lay dying in that strange underground chamber, the artist's father began.

"It is the story, Mr. Matthews, of a man and his only son, the last of their family. With them will perish—has perished one of the oldest and proudest names in our country.

"From his childhood this man was taught the honored traditions of his people, and, thus trained in pride of ancestry, grew up to believe that the supreme things of life are what his kind call education, refinement, and culture. In his shallow egotism, he came to measure all life by the standards of his people.

"It was in keeping with this that the man should enter the pulpit of the church of his ancestors, and it was due very largely, no doubt, to the same ancestral influence that he became what the world calls a successful minister of the gospel. But Christianity to him was but little more than culture, and his place in the church merely an opportunity to add to the honor of his name. Soon after leaving the seminary, he married. The crowning moment of his life was when his first born—a boy—was laid in his arms. The second child was a girl; there were no more.

"For ten years before her death the wife was an invalid. The little girl, too, was never strong, and six months after they buried the mother the daughter was laid beside her.

"You, sir, can understand how the father lavished every care upon his son. The first offspring of the parents' love, the sole survivor of his home, and the last to bear the name of a family centuries old, he was the only hope of the proud man's ambition.

"The boy was a beautiful child, a delicate, sensitive soul in a body of uncommon physical grace and strength, and the proud father loved to think of him as the flower of long ages of culture and refinement. The minister, himself, jealously educated his son, and the two grew to be friends, sir, constant companions. This, also, *you* will understand—you and your boy. But with all this the young man did not follow his father in choosing his profession. He—he became an artist."

Old Matt started from his seat. Aunt Mollie uttered an exclamation. But the shepherd, without pausing, continued: "When his schooling was completed the boy came into the Ozarks one summer to spend the season painting. The man had expected to go with his son. For months they had planned the trip together, but at last something prevented, and the father could not go—no, he could not go—" The speaker's voice broke; the big mountaineer was breathing hard; Aunt Mollie was crying.

Presently Mr. Howitt went on. "When the young artist returned to his father, among many sketches of the mountains, he brought one painting that received instant recognition. The people stood before it in crowds when it was exhibited in the art gallery; the papers were extravagant in their praise; the artist became famous; and wealthy patrons came to his studio to sit for their portraits. The picture was of a beautiful girl, standing by a spring, holding out a dripping cup of water."

At this a wild oath burst from the giant. Springing to his feet, he started toward the speaker. Aunt Mollie screamed, "Grant, oh Grant! Think what Dad has done for us." The mountaineer paused.

"Mr. Matthews," said the shepherd, in trembling tones, "for my sake, will you not hear me to the end? for my sake?"

The big man dropped back heavily into his chair. "Go on," he said. But his voice was as the growl of a beast.

"The boy loved your girl, Mr. Matthews. It was as though he had left his soul in the hills. Night and day he heard her calling. The more his work was praised, the more his friends talked of honors and planned his future, the keener was his suffering, and most of all there was the shadow that had come between him and his father, breaking the old comradeship, and causing them to shun each other; though the father never knew why. The poor boy grew morose and despondent, giving way at times to spells of the deepest depression. He tried to lose himself in his work. He fled abroad and lived alone. It seemed a blight had fallen on his soul. The world called him mad. Many times he planned to take his life, but always the hope of meeting her again stopped him.

"At last he returned to this country determined to see her at any cost, and, if possible, gain her forgiveness and his father's consent to their marriage. He came into the hills only to find that the mother of his child had died of a broken heart.

"Then came the end. The artist disappeared, leaving a long, pitiful letter, saying that before the word reached his father, he would be dead. The most careful investigation brought nothing but convincing evidence that the unhappy boy had taken his own life. The artist knew that it would be a thousand times easier for the proud man to think his son dead than for him to know the truth, and he was right. Mr. Matthews, he was right. I cannot tell you of the man's suffering, but he found a little comfort in the reflection that such extravagant praise of his son's work had added to the honor of the family, for the lad's death was held by all to be the result of a disordered mind. There was not a whisper of wrong doing. His life, they said, was without reproach, and even his sad mental condition was held to be evidence of his great genius.

"The minister was weak, sir. He knew something of the intellectual side of his religion and the history of his church, but he knew little, very little, of the God that could sustain him in such a trial. He was shamefully weak. He tried to run away from his trouble, and, because the papers had made so much of his work as a preacher, and because of his son's fame, he gave only the first part of his name, thinking thus to get away from it all for a season.

"But God was to teach the proud man of culture and religious forms a great lesson, and to that end directed his steps. He was led here, here, sir, to your home, and you—you told him the story of his son's crime."

The shepherd paused. A hoarse whisper came from the giant in the chair, "You—you, Dad, your—name is—"

The other threw out his hand, as if to guard himself, and shrank back; "Hush, oh hush! I have no name but the name by which you know me. The man who bore that name is dead. In all his pride of intellect and position he died. Your prayers for vengeance were answered, sir. You—you killed him; killed him as truly as if you had plunged a knife into his heart; and—you—did—well."

Aunt Mollie moaned.

"Is that all?" growled the mountaineer.

"All! God, no! I—I must go on. I must tell you how the man you killed staid in the hills and was born again. There was nothing else for him to do but stay in the hills. With the shame and horror of his boy's disgrace on his heart, he could not go back— back to the city, his friends and his church—to the old life. He knew that he could not hope to deceive them. He was not skilled in hiding things. Every kind word in praise of himself, or in praise of his son, would have been keenest torture. He was a coward; he dared not go back. His secret would have driven him mad, and he would have ended it all as his son had done. His only hope for peace was to stay here; here on the very spot where the wrong was done, and to do what little he could to atone for the crime.

"At first it was terrible; the long, lonely nights with no human friend near; the weight of shame; the memories; and the lonely wind—always the wind—in the trees—her voice, Pete said, calling for him to come. God, sir, I wonder the man did not die under his punishment!

"But God is good, Mr. Matthews. God is good and merciful. Every day out on the range with the sheep, the man felt the spirit of the hills, and little by little their strength and their peace entered into his life. The minister learned here, sir, what he had not learned in all his theological studies. He learned to know God, the God of these mountains. The hills taught him, and they came at last to stand between him and the trouble from which he had fled. The nights were no longer weary and long. He was never alone. The voices in the wilderness became friendly voices, for he learned their speech, and the poor girl ceased to call in the wailing wind. Then Dr. Coughlan came, and—"

Again the shepherd stopped. He could not go on. The light was gone from the sky and he felt the blackness of the night. But against the stars he could still see the crown of the mountain where his son lay. When he had gathered strength, he continued, saying simply, "Dr. Coughlan came, and—last night we learned that my son was not dead but living."

Again that growl like the growl of a wild beast came from the mountaineer. Silently Mr. Howitt prayed. "Go on," came the command in hoarse tones.

In halting, broken words, the shepherd faltered through the rest of his story as he told how, while using the cabin under the cliff as a studio, the artist had discovered the passage to the old Dewey cave; how, since his supposed death, he had spent the summers at the scene of his former happiness; how he had met his son roaming the hills at night, and had been able to have the boy with him much of the time; how he had been wounded the night Jim Lane was killed; and finally how Pete had led them to his bedside.

"He is dying yonder. Dr. Coughlan is with him—and Pete—Pete is there, too. I—I came for you. He is calling for you. I came to tell you. All that a man may suffer here, he has suffered, sir. Your prayer has been doubly answered, Mr. Matthews. Both father and son are dead. The name—the old name is perished from the face of the earth. For Christ's dear sake, forgive my boy, and let him go. For my sake, sir, I—I can bear no more."

Who but He that looketh upon the heart of man could know the battle that was fought in the soul of that giant of the hills? He uttered no sound. He sat in his seat as if made of stone; save once, when he walked to the end of the porch to stand with clenched hands and passion shaken frame, facing the dark clump of pines on the hill.

Slowly the moon climbed over the ridge and lighted the scene. The mountaineer returned to his chair. All at once he raised his head, and, leaning forward, looked long and earnestly at the old shepherd, where he sat crouching like a convict awaiting sentence.

From down the mill road came voices and the sound of horses' feet. Old Matt started, turning his head a moment to listen. The horses stopped at the lower gate.

"The children," said Aunt Mollie softly. "The children. Grant, Oh, Grant! Sammy and our boy."

Then the shepherd felt a heavy hand on his shoulder, and a voice, that had in it something new and strange, said, "Dad,—my brother,—Daniel, I—I ain't got no education, an' I—don't know rightly how to say it—but, Daniel, what these hills have been to you, you—you have been to me. It's sure God's way, Daniel. Let's- -let's go to the boy."

CHAPTER XLII.

THE WAY OF THE LOWER TRAIL.

Fix—the—light, as it was—please? That's—it. Thank you, Doctor. How beautiful she is—how beautiful!" He seemed to gather strength, and looked carefully into the face of each member of the little group about the bed; the shepherd, Old Matt, Aunt Mollie, Pete, and the physician. Then he turned his eyes back to the painting. To the watchers, the girl in the picture, holding her brimming cup, seemed to smile back again.

"I loved her—I loved—her. She was my natural mate—my other self. I belonged to her—she to me. I—I can't tell you of that summer—when we were together—alone in the hills—the beautiful hills—away from the sham and the ugliness of the world that men have made. The beauty and inspiration of it all I put into my pictures, and I knew because of that they were good—I knew they would win a place for me—and—they did. Most of all—I put it there," (He pointed to the painting on the wall) "and the crowd saw it and felt it, and did not know what it was. But I knew—I knew—all the time, I knew. Oh!—if that short summer could have been lengthened—into years, what might I not have done? Oh, God! That men—can be—so blind—so blind!"

For a time he lay exhausted, his face still turned toward the picture, but with eyes closed as though he dreamed. Then suddenly, he started up again, raising himself on his elbows, his eyes opened wide, and on his face a look of wondering gladness. They drew near.

"Do—do—you—hear? She is calling—she is calling again. Yes— sweetheart—yes, dear. I—I am—com—"

Then, Old Matt and Aunt Mollie led the shepherd from the room.

And this way runs the trail that follows the lower level, where those who travel, as they go, look always over their shoulders with eyes of dread, and the gloomy shadows gather long before the day is done.

CHAPTER XLIII.

POOR PETE.

They buried the artist in the cave as he had directed, close under the wall on the ledge above the canon, with no stone or mark of any sort to fix the place. The old mine which he had discovered was reached by one of the side passages far below in the depth of the mountain. The grave would never be disturbed.

For two weeks longer, Dr. Coughlan staid with his friend; out on the hills with him all day, helping to cook their meals at the ranch, or sitting on the porch at the Matthews place when the day was gone. When the time finally came that he must go, the little physician said, as he grasped the shepherd's hand, "You're doing just right, Daniel; just right. Always did; always did. Blast it all! I would stay, too, but what would Sarah and the girls do? I'll come again next spring, Daniel, sure, sure, if I'm alive. Don't worry, no one will ever know. Blast it all! I don't like to leave you, Daniel. Don't like it at all. But you are right, right, Daniel."

The old scholar stood in the doorway of his cabin to watch the wagon as it disappeared in the forest. He heard it rattle across the creek bottom below the ruined cabin under the bluff. He waited until from away up on Compton Ridge the sound of wheels came to him on the breeze that slipped down the mountain side. Still he waited, listening, listening, until there were only the voices of the forest and the bleating of the sheep in the corral. Slipping a book in his pocket, and taking a luncheon for himself and Pete he opened the corral gate and followed his flock to the hills.

All that summer Pete was the shepherd's constant companion. At first he seemed not to understand. Frequently he would start off suddenly for the cave, only to return after a time, with that look of trouble upon his delicate face. Mr. Howitt tried to help the boy, and he appeared gradually to realize in part. Once he startled his old friend by saying quietly, "When are you goin', Dad?"

"Going where? Where does Pete think Dad is going?"

The boy was lying on his back on the grassy hillside watching the clouds.

He pointed upward, "There, where *he* went; up there in the white hills. Pete knows."

The other looked long at the lad before answering quietly, "Dad does not know when he will go. But he is ready any time, now."

"Pete says better not wait long, Dad; 'cause Pete he's a goin' an' course when he goes I've got to go 'long. Do you reckon Dad can see Pete when he is up there in them white hills? Some folks used to laugh at Pete when he told about the white hills, the flower things, the sky things, an' the moonlight things that play in the mists. An' once a fellow called Pete a fool, an' Young Matt he whipped him awful. But folks wasn't really to blame, 'cause they couldn't see 'em. That's what *he* said. An' *he* knew, 'cause he could see 'em too. But Aunt Mollie, an' Uncle Matt, an' you all, they don't never laugh. They just say, 'Pete knows.' But they couldn't see the flower things, or the tree things neither. Only *he* could see."

The summer passed, and, when the blue gray haze took on the purple touch and all the woods and hills were dressed with cloth of gold, Pete went from the world in which he had never really belonged, nor had been at home. Mr. Howitt, writing to Dr. Coughlan of the boy's death, said:

"Here and there among men, there are those who pause in the hurried rush to listen to the call of a life that is more real. How often have we seen them, David, jostled and ridiculed by their fellows, pushed aside and forgotten, as incompetent or unworthy. He who sees and hears too much is cursed for a dreamer, a fanatic, or a fool, by the mad mob, who, having eyes, see not, ears and hear not, and refuse to understand.

"We build temples and churches, but will not worship in them; we hire spiritual advisers, but refuse to heed them; we buy bibles, but will not read them; believing in God, we do not fear Him; acknowledging Christ, we neither follow nor obey Him. Only when we can no longer strive in the battle for earthly honors or material wealth, do we turn to the unseen but more enduring things of life; and, with ears deafened by the din of selfish war and cruel violence, and eyes blinded by the glare of passing pomp and folly, we strive to hear and see the things we have so long refused to consider.

"Pete knew a world unseen by us, and we, therefore, fancied ourselves wiser than he. The wind in the pines, the rustle of the leaves, the murmur of the brook, the growl of the thunder, and the voices of the night were all understood and answered by him. The flowers, the trees, the rocks, the hills, the clouds were to him, not lifeless things, but living friends, who laughed and wept with him as he was gay or sorrowful.

" 'Poor Pete,' we said. Was he in truth, David, poorer or richer than we?"

They laid the boy beside his mother under the pines on the hills; the pines that showed so dark against the sky when the sun was down behind the ridge. And over his bed the wild vines lovingly wove a coverlid of softest green, while all his woodland friends gathered about his couch. Forest and hill and flower and cloud sang the songs he loved. All day the sunlight laid its wealth in bars of gold at his feet, and at night the moonlight things and the shadow things came out to play.

Summer and autumn slipped away; the winter passed; spring came, with all the wonder of the resurrection of flower and leaf and blade. So peace and quiet came again into the shepherd's life. When no answer to his letter was received, and the doctor did not return as he had promised, the old man knew that the last link connecting him with the world was broken.

CHAPTER XLIV.

THE TRAIL ON THE SUNLIT HILLS.

When Young Matt first knew that Sammy had sent Ollie back to the city with no promise to follow, he took to the woods, and returned only after miles of tramping over the wildest, roughest part of the country. The big fellow said no word, but on his face was a look that his father understood, and the old mountaineer felt his own blood move more quickly at the sight.

But when Sammy with her books was fully established in the Matthews home, and Young Matt seemed always, as the weeks went by, to find her reading things that he could not understand, he was made to realize more fully what her studies with the shepherd meant. He came to feel that she had already crossed the threshold into that world where Mr. Howitt lived. And, thinking that he himself could never enter, he grew lonely and afraid.

With the quickness that was so marked in her character, Sammy grasped the meaning of his trouble almost before Young Matt himself knew fully what it was. Then the girl, with much care and tact, set about helping him to see the truths which the shepherd had revealed to her.

All through the summer and fall, when the day's work was done, or on a Sunday afternoon, they were together, and gradually the woods and the hills, with all the wild life that is in them, began to have for the young man a new meaning; or, rather, he learned little by little to read the message that lay on the open pages; first a word here and there, then sentences, then paragraphs, and soon he was reading alone, as he tramped the hills for stray stock, or worked in the mountain field. The idle days of winter and the long evenings were spent in reading aloud from the books that had come to mean most to her.

So she led him on slowly, along the way that her teacher had pointed out to her, but always as they went, he saw her going before, far ahead, and he knew that in the things that men call education, he could never hope to stand by her side. But he was beginning to ask, are there not after all things that lie still deeper in life than even these?

Often he would go to his old friend in the Hollow with some thought, and the shepherd, seeing how it was, would smile as he helped the lad on his way. The scholar looked forward with confidence to the time when young Matt would discover for himself, as Sammy had found for herself, that the only common ground whereon men and women may meet in safety is the ground of their manhood and womanhood.

And so it was, on that spring morning when the young giant felt the red life throbbing strongly in his great limbs, as he followed his team to and fro across the field. And in his voice, as he shouted to his horses at the end of the furrow, there was something under the words, something of a longing, something also of a challenge.

Sammy was going to spend the day with her friends on Jake Creek. She had not been to see Mandy since the night of her father's death. As she went, she stopped at the lower end of the field to shout a merry word to the man with the plow, and it was sometime later when the big fellow again started his team. The challenge in his tone had grown bolder.

Sammy returned that afternoon in time for the evening meal, and Aunt Mollie thought, as the girl came up the walk, that the young woman had never looked so beautiful. "Why, honey," she said, "you're just a bubblin' over with life. Your cheeks are as rosy; your eyes are as sparklin', you're fairly shinin' all over. Your ride sure done you good."

The young woman replied with a hug that made her admirer gasp. "Law, child; you're strong as a young panther. You walk like one too; so kind of strong, easy like."

The girl laughed. "I hope I don't impress everybody that way, Aunt Mollie. I don't believe I want to be like a panther. I'd rather be like—like—"

"Like what, child?"

"Like you, just like you; the best, the very best woman in the whole world, because you've got the best and biggest heart." She looked back over her shoulder laughing, as she ran into the house.

When Young Matt came in from the field, Sammy went out to the barn, while he unharnessed his team. "Are you very tired to- night?" she asked.

The big fellow smiled, "Tired? Me tired? Where do you want to go? Haven't you ridden enough to-day? I should think you'd be tired yourself."

"Tired? Me tired?" said the girl. "I don't want to ride. I want to walk. It's such a lovely evening, and there's going to be a moon. I have been thinking all day that I would like to walk over home after supper, if you cared to go."

That night the work within the house and the chores about the barn were finished in a remarkably short time. The young man and woman started down the Old Trail like two school children, while the father and mother sat on the porch and heard their voices die away on the mountain side below.

The girl went first along the little path, moving with that light, sure step that belongs only to perfect health, the health of the woods and hills. The man followed, walking with the same sure, easy step; strength and power revealed in every movement of his body. Two splendid creatures they were—masterpieces of the Creator's handiwork; made by Him who created man, male and female, and bade them have dominion "over every living thing that moveth upon the earth;" kings by divine right.

In the belt of timber, where the trail to the ranch branches off, they met the shepherd on his way to the house for an evening visit. The old man paused only long enough to greet them, and pushed on up the hill, for he saw by their faces that the time was come.

Sammy had grown very quiet when they rounded the shoulder of Dewey, and they went in silence down to the cabin on the southern slope of the mountain. The girl asked Young Matt to wait for her at the gate, and, going to the house, she entered alone.

A short time she remained in the familiar rooms, then, slipping out through the rear door, ran through the woods to the little glen back of the house. Dropping beside the mound she buried her face in the cool grass, as she whispered, "Oh, Daddy, Daddy Jim! I wish you were here to-night; this night that means so much to me. Do you know how happy I am, Daddy? Do you know, I wonder?" The twilight deepened, "I must go now, Daddy; I must go to him. You told me you would trust me anywhere with him. He is waiting for me, now; but I wish—oh, I wish that you were here to-night, Daddy Jim!"

Quickly she made her way back to the cabin, passed through the house, and rejoined Young Matt. The two returned silently up the mountain side, to the higher levels, where the light still lingered, though the sun was down. At the Lookout they stopped.

"We'll wait for the moon, here," she said; and so seated on a big rock, they watched the last of the evening go out from the west. From forest depth and mountain side came the myriad voices of Nature's chorus, blending softly in the evening hymn; and, rising clear above the low breathed tones, yet in perfect harmony, came a whip-poor-will's plaintive call floating up from the darkness below; the sweet cooing of a wood-dove in a tree on the ridge, and the chirping of a cricket in a nearby crevice of the ledge. Like shadowy spirits, the bats flitted here and there in the gathering gloom. The two on the mountain's shoulder felt themselves alone above it all; above it all, yet still a part of all.

Then the moon looked over the mountain behind them turning Mutton Hollow into a wondrous sea of misty light out of which the higher hills lifted their heads like fairy islands. The girl spoke, "Come, Matt; we must go now. Help me down."

He slipped from his seat and stood beside the rock with uplifted arms.

Sammy leaned forward and placed her hands upon his shoulders. He felt her breath upon his forehead. The next instant he held her close.

So they went home along the trail that is nobody knows how old, and the narrow path that was made by those who walked one before the other, they found wide enough for two.

Dad Howitt, returning to the ranch, saw them coming so in the moonlight, and slipped aside from the path into the deeper shadows. As they passed, the old shepherd, scholar and poet stood with bowed, uncovered head. When they were gone and their low voices were no longer heard, he said aloud, "What God hath joined; what God hath joined."

And this way runs the trail that lies along the higher, sunlit hills where those who journey see afar and the light lingers even when the day is done.

CHAPTER XLV.

SOME YEARS LATER.

A wandering artist, searching for new fields, found his way into the Ozark country. One day, as he painted in the hills, a flock of sheep came over the ridge through a low gap, and worked slowly along the mountain side. A few moments later, the worker at the easel lifted his eyes from the canvas to find himself regarded by an old man in the dress of a native.

"Hello, uncle. Fine day," said the artist shortly, his eyes again upon his picture.

"The God of these hills gives us many such, young sir, and all His days are good."

The painter's hand paused between palette and canvas, and his face was turned toward the speaker in wonder. Every word was perfect in accent of the highest culture, and the deep musical tone of the voice was remarkable in one with the speaker's snowy hair and beard. The young man arose to his feet. "I beg your pardon, sir. I thought—" He hesitated, as he again took in the rude dress of the other. The brown eyes, under their white shaggy brows, lighted with good nature. "You mean, young sir, that you did not think. 'Tis the privilege of youth; make the most of it. Very soon old age will rob you of your freedom, and force you to think, whether you will or no. Your greeting under the circumstance is surely excusable. It is I who should beg pardon, for I have interrupted your study, and I have no excuse; neither my youth nor my occupation will plead for me."

The charm of his voice and manner were irresistible. The painter stepped forward with outstretched hand, "Indeed, sir; I am delighted to meet you. I am here for the summer from Chicago. My camp is over there."

The other grasped the offered hand cordially, "I am Daniel Howitt, young sir; from the sheep ranch in Mutton Hollow. Dad Howitt, the people call me. So you see you were not far wrong when you hailed me 'Uncle.' Uncle and Dad are 'sure close kin,' as Preachin' Bill would say."

Both men laughed, and the painter offered his folding easel chair. "Thank you, no. Here is a couch to which I am more accustomed. I will rest here, if you please." The old man stretched himself upon the grassy slope. "Do you like my hills?" he asked. "But I am sure you do," he added, as his eye dwelt fondly upon the landscape.

"Ah, you are the owner of this land, then? I was wondering who—"

"No, no, young sir," the old man interrupted, laughing again. "Others pay the taxes; these hills belong to me only as they belong to all who have the grace to love them. They will give you great treasure, that you may give again to others, who have not your good strength to escape from the things that men make and do in the restless world over there. One of your noble craft could scarcely fail to find the good things God has written on this page of His great book. Your brothers need the truths that you will read here; unless the world has greatly changed."

"You are not then a native of this country?"

"I was a native of that world yonder, young sir. Before your day, they knew me; but long since, they have forgotten. When I died there, I was born again in these mountains. And so," he finished with a smile, "I am, as you see, a native. It is long now since I met one from beyond the ridges. I will not likely meet another."

"I wonder that others have not discovered the real beauty of the Ozarks," remarked the painter.

The old shepherd answered softly, "One did." Then rising to his feet and pointing to Roark valley, he said, "Before many years a railroad will find its way yonder. Then many will come, and the beautiful hills that have been my strength and peace will become the haunt of careless idlers and a place of revelry. I am glad that I shall not be here. But I must not keep you longer from your duties."

"I shall see you again, shall I not?" The painter was loath to let him go.

"More often than will be good for your picture, I fear. You must work hard, young sir, while the book of God is still open, and God's message is easily read. When the outside world comes, men will turn the page, and you may lose the place."

After that they met often, and one day the old man led the artist to where a big house looked down upon a ridge encircled valley. Though built of logs without, the house within was finished and furnished in excellent taste. To his surprise, the painter found one room lined with shelves, and upon the shelves the best things that men have written for their fellows. In another room was a piano. The floors were covered with rugs. Draperies and hangings softened the atmosphere; and the walls were hung with pictures; not many, but good and true; pictures that had power over those who looked upon them. The largest painting hung in the library and was veiled.

"My daughter, Mrs. Matthews," said the old shepherd, as he presented the stranger to the mistress of the house. In all his search for beauty, never had the artist looked upon such a form and such a face. It was a marvelous blending of the physical with the intellectual and spiritual. A firm step was heard on the porch. "My husband," said the lady. And the stranger rose to greet—the woman's MATE. The children of this father and mother were like them; or, as the visitor afterwards said in his extravagant way, "like young gods for beauty and strength."

The next summer the painter went again to the Ozarks. Even as he was greeted by the strong master of the hills and his charming wife, there fell upon his ears a dull report as of distant cannon; then another, and another. They led him across the yard, and there to the north on the other side of Roark, men were tearing up the mountain to make way for the railroad. As they looked, another blast sent the rocks flying, while the sound rolled and echoed through the peaceful hills.

The artist turned to his friends with questioning eyes; "Mr. Howitt said it would come. Is he—is he well?"

Mrs. Matthews answered softly, "Dad left us while the surveyors were at work. He sleeps yonder." She pointed to Dewey Bald.

Then they went into the library, where the large picture was unveiled. When the artist saw it, he exclaimed, "Mad Howard's lost masterpiece! How—where did you find it?"

"It was Father Howitt's request that I tell you the story," Sammy replied.

And then she told the artist a part of that which I have set down here.

THE END.

THE CALLING OF DAN MATTHEWS

TO
WILLIAM WILLIAMS, M.D.

"Tecolote," February Fifteenth, 1909.

CONTENTS

THE CALLING OF DAN MATTHEWS

CHAPTER I.

THE HOME OF THE ALLY.

> "And because the town of this story is what it is, there came to dwell in it a Spirit—a strange, mysterious power—playful, vicious, deadly; a Something to be at once feared and courted; to be denied—yet confessed in the denial; a deadly enemy, a welcome friend, an all-powerful Ally."

This story began in the Ozark Mountains. It follows the trail that is nobody knows how old. But mostly this story happened in Corinth, a town of the middle class in a Middle Western state.

There is nothing peculiar about Corinth. The story might have happened just as well in any other place, for the only distinguishing feature about this town is its utter lack of any distinguishing feature whatever. In all the essential elements of its life, so far as this story goes, Corinth is exactly like every other village, town or city in the land. This, indeed, is why the story happened in this particular place.

Years ago, when the railroad first climbed the backbone of the Ozarks, it found Corinth already located on the summit. Even before the war, this county-seat town was a place of no little importance, and many a good tale might be told of those exciting days when the woods were full of guerrillas and bushwhackers, and the village was raided first by one side, then by the other. Many a good tale is told, indeed; for the fathers and mothers of Corinth love to talk of the war times, and to point out in Old Town the bullet-marked buildings and the scenes of many thrilling events.

But the sons and daughters of the passing generation, with their sons and daughters, like better to talk of the great things that are going to be—when the proposed shoe-factory comes, the talked-of mills are established, the dreamed-of electric line is built out from the city, or the Capitalist from Somewhere-else arrives to invest in vacant lots, thereon to build new hotels and business blocks.

The Doctor says that in the whole history of Corinth there are only two events. The first was the coming of the railroad; the second was the death of the Doctor's good friend, the Statesman.

The railroad did not actually enter Corinth. It stopped at the front gate.

But with Judge Strong's assistance the fathers and mothers recognized their "golden opportunity" and took the step which the eloquent Judge assured them would result in a "glorious future." They left the beautiful, well-drained site chosen by those who cleared the wilderness, and stretched themselves out along the mud-flat on either side of the sacred right-of-way—that same mud-flat being, incidentally, the property of the patriotic Judge.

Thus Corinth took the railroad to her heart, literally. The depot, the yards, the red section-house and the water-tank are all in the very center of the town. Every train while stopping for water (and they all stop) blocks two of the three principal streets. And when, after waiting in the rain or snow until his patience is nearly exhausted, the humble Corinthian goes to the only remaining crossing, he always gets there just in time to meet a long freight backing onto the siding. Nowhere in the whole place can one escape the screaming whistle, clanging bell, and crashing drawbar. Day and night the rumble of the heavy trains jars and disturbs the peacefulness of the little village.

But the railroad did something for Corinth; not too much, but something. It did more for Judge Strong. For a time the town grew rapidly. Fulfillment of the Judge's prophecies seemed immediate and certain. Then, as mysteriously as they had come, the boom days departed. The mills, factories and shops that were going to be, established themselves elsewhere. The sound of the builder's hammer was no longer heard. The Doctor says that Judge Strong had come to believe in his own prediction, or at least, fearing that his prophecy might prove true, refused to part with more land except at prices that would be justified only in a great metropolis.

Neighboring towns that were born when Corinth was middle-aged, flourished and have become cities of importance. The country round about has grown rich and prosperous. Each year more and heavier trains thunder past on their way to and from the great city by the distant river, stopping only to take water. But in this swiftly moving stream of life Corinth is caught in an eddy. Her small world has come to swing in a very small circle—it can scarcely be said to swing at all. The very children stop growing when they become men and women, and are content to dream the dreams their fathers' fathers dreamed, even as they live in the houses the fathers of their fathers built. Only the trees that line the unpaved streets have grown—grown and grown until overhead their great tops touch to shut out the sky with an arch of green, and their mighty trunks crowd contemptuously aside the old sidewalks, with their decayed and broken boards.

Old Town, a mile away, is given over to the negroes. The few buildings that remain are fallen into ruin, save as they are patched up by their dusky tenants. And on the hill, the old Academy with its broken windows, crumbling walls, and fallen chimneys, stands a pitiful witness of an honor and dignity that is gone.

Poor Corinth! So are gone the days of her true glory—the glory of her usefulness, while the days of her promised honor and power are not yet fulfilled.

And because the town of this story is what it is, there came to dwell in it a Spirit—a strange, mysterious power—playful, vicious, deadly; a Something to be at once feared and courted; to be denied—yet confessed in the denial; a dreaded enemy, a welcome friend, an all-powerful Ally.

But, for Corinth, the humiliation of her material failure is forgotten in her pride of a finer success. The shame of commercial and civic obscurity is lost in the light of national recognition. And that self-respect and pride of place, without which neither man nor town can look the world in the face, is saved to her by the Statesman.

Born in Corinth, a graduate of the old Academy, town clerk, mayor, county clerk, state senator, congressman, his zeal in advocating a much discussed issue of his day, won for him national notice, and for his town everlasting fame.

In this man unusual talents were combined with rare integrity of purpose and purity of life. Politics to him meant a way whereby he might serve his fellows. However much men differed as to the value of the measures for which he fought, no one ever doubted his belief in them or questioned his reasons for fighting. It was not at all strange that such a man should have won the respect and friendship of the truly great. But with all the honors that came to him, the Statesman's heart never turned from the little Ozark town, and it was here among those who knew him best that his influence for good was greatest and that he was most loved and honored. Thus all that the railroad failed to do for Corinth the Statesman did in a larger, finer way.

Then the Statesman died.

It was the Old Town Corinth of the brick Academy days that inspired the erection of a monument to his memory. But it was the Corinth of the newer railroad days that made this monument of cast-iron; and under the cast-iron, life-sized, portrait figure of the dead statesman, this newer Corinth placed in cast-iron letters a quotation from one of his famous speeches upon an issue of his day.

The Doctor argues in language most vigorous that the broken sidewalks, the permitted insolence of the railroad, the presence and power of that Spirit, the Ally, and many other things and conditions in Corinth, with the lack of as many other things and conditions, are all due to the influence of what he calls "that hideous, cast-iron monstrosity." By this it will be seen that the Doctor is something of a philosopher.

The monument stands on the corner where Holmes Street ends in Strong Avenue. On the opposite corner the Doctor lives with Martha, his wife. It is a modest home for there are no children and the Doctor is not rich. The house is white with old-fashioned green shutters, and over the porch climbs a mass of vines. The steps are worn very thin and the ends of the floor-boards are rotted badly by the moisture of the growing vines. But the Doctor says he'll "be damned" if he'll pull down such a fine old vine to put in new boards, and that those will last anyway longer than either he or Martha. By this it will be seen that the Doctor is something of a poet.

On the rear of the lot is the wood-shed and stable; and on the east, along the fence in front, and down the Holmes Street side, are the Doctor's roses—the admiration and despair of every flower-growing housewife in town.

Full fifty years of the Doctor's professional life have been spent in active practice in Corinth and in the country round about. He declares himself worn out now and good for nothing, save to meddle in the affairs of his neighbors, to cultivate his roses, and—when the days are bright—to go fishing. For the rest, he sits in his chair on the porch and watches the world go by.

"Old Doctors and old dogs," he growls, "how equally useless we are, and yet how much—how much we could tell if only we dared speak!"

He is big, is the Doctor—big and fat and old. He knows every soul in Corinth, particularly the children; indeed he helped most of them to come to Corinth. He is acquainted as well with every dog and cat, and horse and cow, knowing their every trick and habit, from the old brindle milker that unlatches his front gate to feed on the lawn, to the bull pup that pinches his legs when he calls on old Granny Brown. For miles around, every road, lane, by-path, shortcut and trail, is a familiar way to him. His practice, he declares, has well-nigh ruined him financially, and totally wrecked his temper. He can curse a man and cry over a baby; and he would go as far and work as hard for the illiterate and penniless backwoodsman in his cabin home as for the president of the Bank of Corinth or even Judge Strong himself.

No one ever thinks of the Doctor as loving anyone or anything, and that is because he is so big and rough on the outside: but every one in trouble goes to him, and that is because he is so big and kind on the inside. It is a common saying that in cases of trying illness or serious accident a patient would rather "hear the Doctor cuss, than listen to the parson pray." Other physicians there are in Corinth, but every one understands when his neighbor says: "The Doctor." Nor does anyone ever, ever call him "Doc"!

After all, who knows the people of a community so well as the physician who lives among them? To the world the Doctor's patients were laborers, bankers, dressmakers, scrub-women, farmers, servants, teachers, preachers; to the Doctor they were men and women. Others knew their occupations—he knew their lives. The preachers knew what they professed—he knew what they practiced. Society saw them dressed up—he saw them—in bed. Why, the Doctor has spent more hours in the homes of his neighbors than ever he passed under his own roof, and there is not a skeleton closet in the whole town to which he has not the key.

On Strong Avenue, across from the monument, is a tiny four-roomed cottage. In the time of this story it wanted paint badly, and was not in the best of repair. But the place was neat and clean, with a big lilac bush just inside the gate, giving it an air of home-like privacy; and on the side directly opposite the Doctor's a fair-sized, well-kept garden, giving it an air of honest thrift. Here the widow Mulhall lived with her crippled son, Denny. Denny was to have been educated for the priesthood, but the accident that left him such a hopeless cripple shattered that dream; and after the death of his father, who was killed while discharging his duties as the town marshal, there was no money to buy even a book.

When there was anything for her to do, Deborah worked out by the day. Denny, in spite of his poor, misshapen body, tended the garden, raising such vegetables as no one else in all Corinth could—or would, raise. From early morning until late evening the lad dragged himself about among the growing things, and the only objects to mar the beauty of his garden, were Denny himself, and the great rock that crops out in the very center of the little field.

"It is altogether too bad that the rock should be there," the neighbors would say as they occasionally stopped to look over the fence or to order their vegetables for dinner. And Denny would answer with his knowing smile, "Oh, I don't know! It would be bad, I'll own, if it should ever take to rollin' 'round like. But it lays quiet enough. And do you see, I've planted them vines around it to make it a bit soft lookin'. And there's a nice little niche on yon side, that does very well for a seat now and then, when I have to rest."

Sometimes, when the Doctor looks at the monument—the cast-iron image of his old friend, in its cast-iron attitude, forever delivering that speech on an issue as dead today as an edict of one of the Pharaohs—he laughs, and sometimes, even as he laughs, he curses.

But when, in the days of the story, the Doctor would look across the street to where Denny, with his poor, twisted body, useless, swinging arm, and dragging leg, worked away so cheerily in his garden, the old physician, philosopher, and poet, declared that he felt like singing hymns of praise.

And it all began with a fishing trip.

CHAPTER II.

A REVELATION.

"And because of these things, to the keen old physician and student of life, the boy was a revelation of that best part of himself—that best part of the race."

It happened on the Doctor's first trip to the Ozarks.

Martha says that everything with the Doctor begins and ends with fishing. Martha has a way of saying such things as that. In this case she is more than half right for the Doctor does so begin and end most things.

Whenever there were grave cases to think out, knotty problems to solve, or important decisions to make, it was his habit to steal away to a shady nook by the side of some quiet, familiar stream. And he confidently asserts that to this practice more than to anything else he owes his professional success, and his reputation for sound, thoughtful judgment on all matters of moment.

"And why not?" he will argue when in the mood. "It is your impulsive, erratic, thoughtless fellow who goes smashing, trashing and banging about the field and woods with dogs and gun. Your true thinker slips quietly away with rod and line, and while his hook is down in the deep, still waters, or his fly is dancing over the foaming rapids and swiftly swirling eddies, his mind searches the true depths of the matter and every possible phase of the question passes before him."

For years the Doctor had heard much of the fishing to be had in the more unsettled parts of the Ozarks, but with his growing practice he could find leisure for no more than an occasional visit to nearby streams. But about the time that Martha began telling him that he was too old to stay out all day on the wet bank of a river, and Dr. Harry had come to relieve him of the heavier and more burdensome part of his practice, a railroad pushed its way across the mountain wilderness. The first season after the road was finished the Doctor went to cast his hook in new waters.

In all these after years those days so full of mystic beauty have lived in the old man's memory, the brightest days of all his life. For it was there he met the Boy—there in the Ozark hills, with their great ridges clothed from base to crest with trees all quivering and nodding in the summer breeze, with their quiet valleys, their cool hollows and lovely glades, and their deep and solemn woods. And the streams! Those Ozark streams! The Doctor wonders often if there can flow anywhere else such waters as run through that land of dreams.

The Doctor left the train at a little station where the railroad crosses White River, and two days later he was fishing near the mouth of Fall Creek. It was late in the afternoon. The Boy was passing on his way home from a point farther up the stream. Not more than twelve, but tall and strong for his age, he came along the rough path at the foot of the bluff with the easy movement and grace of a young deer. He checked a moment when he saw the Doctor, as a creature of the forest would pause at first sight of a human being. Then he came on again, his manner and bearing showing frank interest, and the clear, sunny face of him flushing a bit at the presence of a stranger.

"Hello," said the Doctor, with gruff kindness, "any luck?"

The boy's quick smile showed a set of teeth—the most perfect the physician had ever seen, and his young voice was tuned to the music of the woods, as he answered, "I have caught no fish, sir."

By these words and the light in his brown eyes the philosopher knew him instantly for a true fisherman. He noted wonderingly that the lad's speech was not the rude dialect of the backwoods, while he marveled at the depth of wisdom in one so young. How incidental after all is the catching of fish, to the one who fishes with true understanding. The boy's answer was both an explanation and a question. It explained that he did not go fishing for fish alone; and it asked of the stranger a declaration of his standing—why did he go fishing? What did he mean by fisherman's luck?

The Doctor deliberated over his reply, while slowly drawing in his line to examine the bait. Meanwhile the boy stood quietly by regarding him with a wide, questioning look. The man realized that much depended upon his next word.

Then the lad's youth betrayed him into eagerness. "Have you been farther up the river just around the bend, where the giant cottonwoods are, and the bluffs with the pines above, and the willows along the shore? Oh, but it's fine there! Much better than this."

He had given the stranger his chance. If the Doctor was to be admitted into this boy's world he must now prove his right to citizenship. Looking straight into the boy's brown eyes, the older fisherman asked, "A better place to catch fish?"

He laughed aloud—a clear, clean, boyish laugh of understanding, and throwing himself to the ground with the easy air of one entirely at home, returned, "No, sir, a better place to fish." So it was settled, each understanding the other.

An hour later when the shadow of the mountain came over the water, the boy sprang to his feet with an exclamation, "It's time that I was going, mother likes for me to be home for supper. I can just make it."

But the Doctor was loath to let him go. "Where do you live?" he asked. "Is it far?"

"Oh, no, only about six miles, but the trail is rough until you strike the top of Wolf Ridge."

"Humph! You can't walk six miles before dark."

"My horse is only a little way up the creek," he answered, "or at least he should be." Putting his fingers to his lips he blew a shrill whistle, which echoed and re-echoed from shore to shore along the river, and was answered by a loud neigh from somewhere in the ravine through which Fall Creek reaches the larger stream. Again the boy whistled, and a black pony came trotting out of the brush, the bridle hanging from the saddle horn. "Tramp and I can make it all right, can't we old fellow?" said the boy, patting the glossy neck, as the little horse rubbed a soft muzzle against his young master's shoulder.

While his companion was making ready for his ride the Doctor selected four of the largest of his catch—black bass they were—beauties. "Here," he said, when the lad was mounted, "take these along."

He accepted graciously without hesitation, and by this the Doctor knew that their fellowship was firmly established. "Oh, thank you! Mother is so fond of bass, and so are father and all of us. This is plenty for a good meal." Then, with another smile, "Mother likes to fish, too; she taught me."

The Doctor looked at him wistfully as he gathered up the reins, then burst forth eagerly with, "Look here, why can't you come back tomorrow? We'll have a bully time. What do you say?"

He lowered his hand. "Oh, I would like to." Then for a moment he considered, gravely, saying at last, "I think I can meet you here day after tomorrow. I am quite sure father and mother will be glad for me to come when I tell them about you."

Was ever a fat old Doctor so flattered? It was not so much the boy's words as his gracious manner and the meaning he unconsciously put into his exquisitely toned voice.

He had turned his pony's head when the old man shouted after him once more. "Hold on, wait a moment, you have not told me your name. I am Dr. Oldham from Corinth. I am staying at the Thompson's down the river."

"My name is Daniel Howitt Matthews," he answered. "My home is the old Matthews place on the ridge above Mutton Hollow."

Then he rode away up the winding Fall Creek trail.

The Doctor spent the whole of the next day near the spot where he had met the boy, fearing lest the lad might come again and not find him. He even went a mile or so up the little creek half expecting to meet his young friend, wondering at himself the while, that he could not break the spell the lad had cast over him. Who was he? He had told the Doctor his name, but that did not satisfy. Nor, indeed, did the question itself ask what the old man really wished to know. The words persistently shaped themselves—*What* is he? To this the physician's brain made answer clearly enough—a boy, a backwoods boy, with unusual beauty and strength of body, and uncommon fineness of mind; yet with all this, a boy.

But that something that sits in judgment upon the findings of our brain, and, in lofty disregard of us, accepts or rejects our most profound conclusions, refused this answer. It was too superficial. It was not, in short, an answer. It did not in any way explain the strange power that this lad had exerted over the Doctor.

"Me," he said to himself, "a hard old man calloused by years of professional contact with mankind and consequent knowledge of their general cussedness! Huh! I have helped too many hundreds of children into this world, and have carried too many of them through the measles, whooping-cough, chicken-pox and the like to be so moved by a mere boy."

The Thompsons could have told him about the lad and his people, but the Doctor instinctively shrank from asking them. He felt that he did not care to be told about the boy—that in truth no one could tell him about the boy, because he already knew the lad as well as he knew himself. Indeed the feeling that he already knew the boy was what troubled the Doctor; more, that he had always lived with him; but that he had never before met him face to face. He felt as a blind man might feel if, after living all his life in closest intimacy with someone, he were suddenly to receive his sight and, for the first time, actually look upon his companion's face.

In the years that have passed since that day the Doctor has learned that the lad was to him, not so much a mystery as a revelation—the revelation of an unspoken ideal, of a truth that he had always known but never fully confessed even to himself, and that lies at last too deeply buried beneath the accumulated rubbish of his life to be of any use to him or to others. In the boy he met this hidden, secret, unacknowledged part of himself, that he knows to be the truest, most precious and most sacred part, and that he has always persistently ignored even while always conscious that he can no more escape it than he can escape his own life. In short, Dan Matthews is to the Doctor that which the old man feels he ought to have been; that which he might have been, but never now can be.

It was still early in the forenoon of the following day when the Doctor heard a cheery hail, and the boy came riding out of the brush of the little ravine to meet his friend who was waiting on the river bank. As the lad sprang lightly to the ground, and, with quick fingers, took some things from the saddle, loosed the girths and removed the pony's bridle, the physician watched him with a slight feeling of—was it envy or regret? "You are early," he said.

The boy laughed. "I would have come earlier if I could," Then, dismissing the little horse, he turned eagerly, "Have you been there yet—to that place up the river?" "

Indeed I have not," said the Doctor, "I have been waiting for you to show me."

He was delighted at this, and very soon was leading the way along the foot of the bluff to his favorite fishing ground.

It is too much to attempt the telling of that day: how they lay on the ground beneath the giant-limbed cottonwoods, and listened to the waters going past; how they talked of the wild woodland life about them, of flower and tree, and moss and vine, and the creatures that nested and denned and lived therein; how they caught a goodly catch of bass and perch, and the Doctor, pulling off his boots, waded in the water like another boy, while the hills echoed with their laughter; and how, when they had their lunch on a great rock, an eagle watched hungrily from his perch on a dead pine, high up on the top of the bluff.

When the shadow of the mountain was come once more and in answer to the boy's whistle the black pony had trotted from the brush to be made ready for the evening ride, the Doctor again watched his young companion wistfully.

When he was ready, the boy said, "Father and mother asked me to tell you, sir, that they—that we would be glad to have you come to see us before you leave the hills." Seeing the surprise and hesitation of the Doctor, he continued with fine tact, "You see I told them all about you, and they would like to know you too. Won't you come? I'm sure you would like my father and mother, and we would be so glad to have you. I'll drive over after you tomorrow if you'll come."

Would he *go!* Why the Doctor would have gone to China, or Africa, or where would he not have gone, if the boy had asked him.

That visit to the Matthews' place was the beginning of a friendship that has never been broken. Every year since, the Doctor has gone to them for several weeks and always with increasing delight. Among the many households that, in his professional career, he has been privileged to know intimately, this home stands like a beautiful temple in a world of shacks and hovels. But it was not until the philosopher had heard from Mrs. Matthews the story of Dad Howitt that he understood the reason. In the characters of Young Matt and Sammy, in their home life and in their children, the physician found the teaching of the old Shepherd of the Hills bearing its legitimate fruit. Most clearly did he find it in Dan—the first born of this true mating of a man and woman who had never been touched by those forces in our civilization which so dwarf and cripple the race, but who had been taught to find in their natural environment those things that alone have the power to truly refine and glorify life.

Understanding this, the Doctor understood Dan. The boy was well born; he was natural. He was what a man-child ought to be. He did not carry the handicap that most of us stagger under so early in the race. And because of these things, to the keen old physician and student of life, the boy was a revelation of that best part of himself—that best part of the race. With the years this feeling of the Doctor's toward the boy has grown even as their fellowship. But Dan has never understood; how indeed could he?

It was always Dan who met the Doctor at the little wilderness station, and who said the last good-bye when the visit was over. Always they were together, roaming about the hills, on fishing trips to the river, exploring the country for new delights, or revisiting their familiar haunts. Dan seemed, in his quiet way, to claim his old friend by right of discovery and the others laughingly yielded, giving the Doctor—as Young Matt, the father, put it—"a third interest in the boy."

And so, with the companionship of the yearly visits, and frequent letters in the intervening months, the Doctor watched the development of his young friend, and dreamed of the part that Dan would play in life when he became a man. And often as he watched the boy there was, on the face of the old physician, that look of half envy, half regret.

In addition to his training at the little country school, Dan's mother was his constant teacher, passing on to her son as only a mother could, the truths she had received from her old master, the Shepherd. But when the time came for more advanced intellectual training the choice of a college was left to their friend. The Doctor hesitated. He shrank from sending the lad out into the world. He foolishly could not bear the thought of that splendid nature coming in touch with the filth of life as he knew it. "You can see," he argued gruffly, "what it has done for me."

But Sammy answered, "Why, Doctor, what is the boy for?" And Young Matt, looking away over Garber where an express train thundered over the trestles and around the curves, said in his slow way, "The brush is about all cleared, Doctor. The wilderness is going fast. The boy must live in his own age and do his own work." When their friend urged that they develop or sell the mine in the cave on Dewey Bald, and go with the boy, they both shook their heads emphatically, saying, "No, Doctor, we belong to the hills."

When the boy finally left his mountain home for a school in the distant city, he had grown to be a man to fill the heart of every lover of his race with pride. With his father's powerful frame and close-knit muscles, and the healthy life of the woods and hills leaping in his veins, his splendid body and physical strength were refined and dominated by the mind and spirit of his mother. His shaggy, red-brown hair was like his father's but his eyes were his mother's eyes, with that same trick of expression, that wide questioning gaze, that seemed to demand every vital truth in whatever came under his consideration. He had, too, his mother's quick way of grasping your thoughts almost before you yourself were fully conscious of them, with that same saving sense of humor that made Sammy Lane the life and sunshine of the countryside.

"Big Dan," the people of the hills had come to call him and "Big Dan" they called him in the school. For, in the young life of the schools, as in the country, there is a spirit that names men with names that fit.

Secretly the Doctor had hoped that Dan would choose the profession so dear to him. What an ideal physician he would make, with that clean, powerful, well balanced nature; and above all with that love for his race, and his passion to serve mankind that was the dominant note in his character. The boy would be the kind of a physician that the old Doctor had hoped to be. So he planned and dreamed for Dan as he had planned and dreamed for himself, thinking to see the dreams that he had failed to live, realized in the boy.

It was a severe shock to the Doctor when that letter came telling him of Dan's choice of a profession. For the first time the boy had disappointed him, disappointed him bitterly.

Seizing his fishing tackle the old man fled to the nearest stream. And there gazing into the deep, still waters, where he had cast his hook, he came to understand. It was that same dominant note in the boy's life, that inborn passion to serve, that fixed principle in his character that his life must be of the greatest possible worth to the world, that had led him to make his choice. With that instinct born in him, coming from the influence of the old Shepherd upon his father and mother, the boy could no more escape it than he could change the color of his brown eyes.

"But," said the Doctor to his cork, that floated on the surface in a patch of shadow, "what does he know about it, what does he really know? He's been reading history—that's what's the matter with him. He sees things as they were, not as they are. He should have come to me, I could have—" Just then the cork went under. The Doctor had a bite. "I could have told him," repeated the fisherman softly, "I—" The cork bobbed up again—it was only a nibble. "He'll find out the truth of course. He's that kind. But when he finds it!" The cork bobbed again—"He'll need me, he'll need me bad!" The cork went under for good this time. Zip—and the Doctor had a big one!

With fresh bait and his hook once more well down toward the bottom the Doctor saw the whole thing clearly, and so planned a way by which, as he put it, he might, when Dan needed him, "*stand by.*"

CHAPTER III.

A GREAT DAY IN CORINTH.

"'Talk of the responsibilities of age; humph! They are nothing compared to the responsibilities of youth. There's Dan, now—'"

Corinth was in the midst of a street fair. The neighboring city held a street fair that year, therefore Corinth. All that the city does Corinth imitates, thereby with a beautiful rural simplicity thinking herself metropolitan, just as those who take their styles from the metropolis feel themselves well dressed. The very Corinthian clerks and grocery boys, lounging behind their counters and in the doorways, the lawyer's understudy with his feet on the window sill, the mechanic's apprentice, the high school youths and the local sporting fraternity—all imitated their city kind and talked smartly about the country "rubes" who came to town; never once dreaming that they themselves, when they "go to town," are as much a mark for the like wit of their city brothers. So Corinth was in the midst of a street fair.

On every vacant lot in the down town section were pens, and stalls, and cages, wherein grunted, squealed, neighed, bellowed, bleated, cackled and crowed, exhibits from the neighboring farms. In the town hall or opera house (it was both) there were long tables covered with almost everything that grows on a farm, or is canned, baked, preserved, pickled or stitched by farmers' wives. The "Art Exhibit," product mainly of Corinth, had its place on the stage. Upon either side of the main street were booths containing the exhibits of the local merchants; farm machinery, buggies, wagons, harness and the like being most conspicuous. The chief distinction between the town and country exhibits were that the farmer displayed his goods to be looked at, the merchant his to be sold. It was the merchants who promoted the fair.

In a vacant store room the Memorial Church was holding its annual bazaar. On different corners other churches were serving chicken dinners, or ice cream, or in sundry ways were actively engaged for the conversion of the erring farmer's cash to the coffers of the village sanctuaries. In this way the promoters of the fair were encouraged by the churches. From every window, door, arch, pole, post, corner, gable, peak, cupola—fluttered, streamed and waved, decorations—banners mostly, bearing advertisements of the enterprising merchants and of the equally enterprising churches.

Afternoons there would be a baseball game between town and country teams, foot races, horseback riding, a greased pig to catch, a greased pole to climb and other entertainments too exciting to think about, too attractive to be resisted.

From the far backwoods districts, from the hills, from the creek bottoms and the river, the people came to crowd about the pens, and stalls and tables; to admire their own and their neighbors' products and possessions, that they had seen many times before in their neighbors' homes and fields. They visited on the street corners. They tramped up and down past the booths. They yelled themselves hoarse at the games and entertainments, and in the intoxication of their pleasures bought ice cream, chicken dinners and various other things of the churches, and much goods of the merchants who promoted the fair.

The Doctor was up that day at least a full hour before his regular time. At breakfast Martha looked him over suspiciously, and when he folded his napkin after eating only half his customary meal she remarked dryly, "It's three hours yet till train time, Doctor."

Without answer the Doctor went out on the porch.

Already the country people, dressed in their holiday garb, bright-faced, eager for the long looked for pleasures, were coming in for the fair. Many of them catching sight of the physician hailed him gaily, shouting good natured remarks in addition to their salutations, and laughing loudly at whatever he replied.

It may be that the good Lord had made days as fine as that day, but the Doctor could not remember them. His roses so filled the air with fragrance, the grass in the front yard was so fresh and clean, the flowers along the walk so bright and dainty, and the great maples, that make a green arch of the street, so cool and mysterious in their leafy depths, that his old heart fairly ached with the beauty of it. The Doctor was all poet that day. Dan was coming!

It had worked out just as the Doctor had planned it on that fishing trip some three months before. At first Martha was suspicious when he broached the subject. Mostly Martha is suspicious when her husband offers suggestions touching certain matters, but the wise old philosopher knew what strings to pull, and so it all came out as he had planned. Sammy had written him expressing her gladness, that her boy in the beginning of his work was to be with the friend whose counsel and advice they valued so highly. The Doctor had growled over the letter, promising himself that he would "stand by" when the boy needed him, but that was all he or an angel from heaven could do now. And the Doctor had written Dan at length about Corinth, but never a word about his thoughts regarding the boy's choice, or his fears for the outcome.

"There are some things," he reflected, "that every man must find out for himself. To some kinds of people the finding out doesn't matter much. To other kinds, it is well for them if there are those who love them to stand by." Dan was the kind to whom the finding out would mean a great deal, so the Doctor would "stand by."

There on his vine covered porch that morning, the old man's thoughts went back to that day when the boy first came to him on the river bank, and to all the bright days of Dan's boyhood and youth that he had passed with the lad in the hills. "His life—" said he, talking to himself, as he has a way of doing—"His life is like this day, fresh and clean and—". He looked across the street to the monument that stood a cold, lifeless mask in a world of living joy and beauty; from the monument he turned to Denny's garden. "And," he finished, "full of possibilities."

"Whatever are you muttering about now?" said Martha, who had followed him out after finishing her breakfast.

"I was wishing," said the Doctor, "that I—that it would be always morning, that there was no such thing as afternoon, and evening and night."

His wife replied sweetly, "For a man of your age, you do say the most idiotic things! Won't you ever get old enough to think seriously?"

"But what could be more serious, my dear? If it were morning I would always be beginning my life work, and never giving it up. I would be always looking forward to the success of my dreams, and never back to the failures of my poor attempts."

"You haven't failed in everything, John," protested Martha in softer tones.

"If it were morning," the philosopher continued, with a smile, "I would be always making love to the best and prettiest girl in the state."

Martha tossed her head and the ghost of an old blush crept into her wrinkled cheeks. "There's no fool like an old fool," she quoted with a spark of her girlhood fire.

"But a young fool gets so much more out of his foolishness," the man retorted. "Talk of the responsibilities of age; humph! They are nothing compared to the responsibilities of youth. There's Dan now—" He looked again toward the monument. "My goodness me, yes!" ejaculated Martha. "And I've got a week's work to do before I even begin to get dinner. You go right off this minute and kill three of those young roosters—three, mind you."

"But, my dear, he will only be here for dinner."

"Never you mind, the dinner's my business. Kill three, I tell you. I've cooked for preachers before. I hope to the Lord he'll start you to thinking of your eternal future, 'stead of mooning about the past." She bustled away to turn the little home upside down and to prepare dinner sufficient for six.

When the Doctor had killed the three roosters, and had fussed about until his wife ordered him out of the kitchen, he took his hat and stick and started down town, though it was still a good hour until train time. As he opened the front gate Denny called a cheery greeting from his garden across the street, and the old man went over for a word with the crippled boy.

"It's mighty fine you're lookin' this mornin', Doctor," said Denny pausing in his work, and seating himself on the big rock. "Is it the ten-forty he's comin' on?"

The Doctor tried to appear unconcerned. He looked at his watch with elaborately assumed carelessness as he answered: "I believe it's ten-forty; and how are you feeling this morning, Denny?"

The lad lifted his helpless left arm across his lap. "Oh I'm fine, thank you kindly, Doctor. Mother's fine too, and my garden's doing pretty good for me." He glanced about. "The early things are all gone, of course, but the others are doing well. Oh, we'll get along; I told mother this morning the Blessed Virgin hadn't forgotten us yet. I'll bet them potatoes grew an inch some nights this summer. And look what a day it is for the fair, and the preacher a comin' too."

The Doctor looked at his watch again, and Denny continued: "We're all so pleased at his comin'. People haven't talked of anything else for a month now, that and the fair of course. Things in this town will liven up now, sure. Seems to me I can feel it—yes sir, I can. Something's goin' to happen, sure."

"Humph," grunted the Doctor, "I rather feel that way myself." Then, "I expect you two will be great friends, Denny."

The poor little fellow nearly twisted himself off the rock. "Oh Doctor, really why I—the minister'll have no time for the likes of me. And is he really goin' to live at Mrs. Morgan's there?" He nodded his head toward the house next to his garden.

"That's his room," the other answered, pointing to the corner window. "He'll be right handy to us both."

Denny gazed at the window with the look of a worshiper. "Oh now, isn't that fine, isn't it grand! That's such a nice room, Doctor, it has such a fine view of the monument."

"Yes," the Doctor interrupted, "the monument and your garden." And then he left abruptly lest he should foolishly try to explain to the bewildered and embarrassed Denny what he meant.

It seemed to the Doctor that nearly every one he met on the well-filled street that morning, had a smile for him, while many stopped to pass a word about the coming of Dan. When he reached the depot the agent hailed him with, "Good morning, Doctor; looking for your preacher?"

"*My* preacher!" The old physician glared at the man in the cap, and turned his back with a few energetic remarks, while two or three loafers joined in the laugh, and a couple of traveling men who were pacing the platform with bored expressions on their faces, turned to stare at him curiously.

At the other end of the platform was a group of women, active members of the Memorial Ladies' Aid who had left their posts of duty at the bazaar, to have a first look at the new pastor. The old Elder, Nathan Jordan, with Charity, his daughter, was just coming up.

"Good morning, good morning, Doctor," said Nathan grasping his friend's hand as if he had not seen him for years. "Well I see we're all here." He turned proudly about as the group of women came forward, with an air of importance, the Doctor thought, as though the occasion required their presence. "Reckon our boy'll be here all right," Nathan continued.

"*Our* boy!" The Doctor caught a naughty word between his teeth—a feat he rarely accomplished.

The ladies all looked sweetly interested. One of them putting her arm lovingly about Charity cooed: "So nice of you to come, dear." She had remarked to another a moment before, "that a fire wouldn't keep the girl away from the depot that morning."

The Doctor felt distinctly the subtle, invisible presence of the Ally, and it was well that someone just then saw the smoke from the coming train two or three miles away, around the curve beyond the pumping station.

The negro porter from the hotel opposite the depot, came bumping across the rails, with the grips belonging to the two traveling men, in his little cart; the local expressman rattled up with a trunk in his shaky old wagon; and the sweet-faced daughter of the division track superintendent hurried out of the red section-house with a bundle of big envelopes in her hand. The platform was crowded with all kinds of people, carrying a great variety of bundles, baskets and handbags, asking all manner of questions, going to and from all sorts of places. The train drew rapidly nearer.

The Doctor's old heart was thumping painfully. He forgot the people, he forgot Corinth, he forgot everything but the boy who had come to him that day on the river bank.

Swiftly the long train with clanging bell and snorting engine came up to the depot. The conductor swung easily to the platform, and, watch in hand, walked quickly to the office. Porters and trainmen tumbled off, and with a long hiss of escaping air and a steady puff-puff, the train stopped.

In the bustle and confusion of crowding passengers getting on and off, tearful good-byes and joyful greetings, banging trunks, rattling trucks, hissing steam, the doctor watched. Then he saw him, his handsome head towering above the pushing, jostling crowd. The Doctor could not get to him, and with difficulty restrained a shout. But Dan with his back to them all pushed his way to an open window of the car he had just left, where a woman's face turned to him in earnest conversation.

"There he is," said the Doctor, "that tall fellow by the window there."

At his words the physician heard an exclamation, and, glancing back, saw the women staring eagerly, while Charity's face wore a look of painful doubt and disappointment. The Elder's countenance was stern and frowning.

"Seems mightily interested," said one, suggestively.

"What a pretty face," added another, also suggestively.

The Doctor spoke quickly, "Why that's—" Then he stopped with an expression on his face that came very near being a malicious grin.

The conductor, watch again in hand, shouted, the porters stepped aboard, the bell rang, the engineer, with his long oil-can, swung to his cab, slowly the heavy train began to gather headway. As it went Dan walked along the platform beside that open window, until he could no longer keep pace with the moving car. Then with a final wave of his hand he stood looking after the train, seemingly unconscious of everything but that one who was being carried so quickly beyond his sight.

He was standing so when his old friend grasped his arm. He turned with a start. "Doctor!"

What a handsome fellow he was, with his father's great body, powerful limbs and shaggy red-brown hair; and his mother's eyes and mouth, and her spirit ruling within him, making you feel that he was clean through and through. It was no wonder people stood around looking at him. The Doctor felt again that old, mysterious spell, that feeling that the boy was a revelation to him of something he had always known, the living embodiment of a truth never acknowledged. And his heart swelled with pride as he turned to lead Dan up to Elder Jordan and his company.

The church ladies, old in experience with preachers, seemed strangely embarrassed. This one was somehow so different from those they had known before, but their eyes were full of admiration. Charity's voice trembled as she bade him welcome. Nathaniel's manner was that of a judge. Dan himself, was as calm and self possessed as if he and the Doctor were alone on the bank of some river, far from church and church people. But the Doctor thought that the boy flinched a bit when he introduced him as Reverend Matthews. Perhaps, though, it was merely the Doctor's fancy. The old man felt too, even as he presented Dan to his people, that there had come between himself and the boy a something that was never there before, and it troubled him not a little. But perhaps this, too, was but a fancy.

At any rate the old man must have been somewhat excited for when the introductions were over, and the company was leaving the depot, he managed to steer Dan into collision with a young woman who was standing nearby. She was carrying a small grip, having evidently arrived on the same train that brought the minister. It was no joke for anyone into whom Big Dan bumped, and a look of indignation flashed on the girl's face. But the indignant look vanished quickly in a smile as the big fellow stood, hat in hand, offering the most abject apology for what he called *his* rudeness.

The Doctor noted a fine face, a strong graceful figure, and an air of wholesomeness and health that was most refreshing. But he thought that Dan took more time than was necessary for his apology.

When she had assured the young fellow several times that it was nothing, she asked: "Can you tell me, please, the way to Dr. Abbott's office?"

Dr. Abbott! The Doctor's own office—Dr. Harry's and his now. He looked the young woman over curiously, while Dan was saying: "I'm sorry, but I cannot. I am a stranger here, but my friend—"

The older man interrupted gruffly with the necessary directions and the information that Dr. Abbott was out of town, and would not be back until four o'clock. "Will you then direct me to a hotel?" she asked. The Doctor pointed across the track. Then he got Dan away.

The church ladies, with Charity and her father, were already on their way back to the place where the bazaar was doing business. Half way down the block the Doctor and Dan were checked by a crowd. There seemed to be some excitement ahead. But in the pause, Dan turned to look back toward the young woman who had arrived in Corinth on the same train that had brought him. She was coming slowly down the street toward them.

Again the thought flashed through the Doctor's mind that the boy had taken more time than was necessary for his apology.

CHAPTER IV.

WHO ARE THEY?

"And the old man pointed out to Dan his room across the way—the room that looked out upon the garden and the monument."

Jud Hardy, who lives at Windy Cove on the river some eighteen miles "back" from Corinth, had been looking forward to Fair time for months. Not that Jud had either things to exhibit or money to buy things exhibited. For while Jud professed to own, and ostensibly to cultivate a forty, he gained his living mostly by occasional "spells of work" on the farms of his neighbors. In lieu of products of his hand or fields for exhibition at the annual fair, Jud invariably makes an exhibition of himself, never failing thus to contribute his full share to the "other amusements," announced on the circulars and in the Daily Corinthian, as "too numerous to mention."

The citizens of the Windy Cove country have a saying that when Jud is sober and in a good humor and has money, he is a fairly good fellow, if he is not crossed in any way. The meat of which saying is in the well known fact, that Jud is never in a good humor when he is not sober, that he is never sober when he has money; and that with the exception of three or four kindred spirits, whose admiration for the bad man is equaled only by their fear of him, no one has ever been able to devise a way to avoid crossing him when he is in his normal condition.

With three of the kindred spirits, Jud arrived in Corinth that day, with the earliest of the visitors, and the quartette proceeded, at once, to warm up after their long ride. By ten o'clock they were well warmed. Just as the ten-forty train was slowing up at the depot, Jud began his exhibition. It took place at the post office where the crowd was greatest, because of the incoming mail. Stationing himself near the door, the man from Windy Cove blocked the way for everyone who wanted to pass either in or out of the building. For the women and young girls he stepped aside with elaborate, drunken politeness and maudlin, complimentary remarks. For the men who brushed him he had a scowling curse and a muttered threat. Meanwhile, his followers nearby looked on in tipsy admiration and "'lowed that there was bound to be somethin' doin', for Jud was sure a-huntin' trouble."

Then came one who politely asked Jud to move. He was an inoffensive little man, with a big star on his breast, and a big walking stick in his hand—the town marshal. Jud saw an opportunity to give an exhibition worth while. There were a few opening remarks—mostly profane—and then the representative of the law lay in a huddled heap on the floor, while the man from the river rushed from the building into the street.

The passing crowd stopped instantly. Scattered individuals from every side came running to push their way into the mass of men and women, until for a block on either side of the thoroughfare there was a solid wall of breathless humanity. Between these walls strolled Jud, roaring his opinion and defiance of every one in general, and the citizens of Corinth in particular.

It could not last long, of course. There were many men in the crowd who did not fear to challenge Jud, but there was that inevitable hesitation, while each man was muttering to his neighbor that this thing ought to be stopped, and they were waiting to see if someone else would not start first to stop it.

Nearly the length of the block, Jud made his triumphant way; then, at the corner where the crowd was not so dense, he saw a figure starting across the street.

"Hey there," he roared, "get back there where you belong! What th' hell do you mean? Don't you see the procession's a comin'?"

It was Denny. He had left his garden to go to the butcher's for a bit of meat for dinner. The crippled lad had just rounded the corner, and, forced to give all his attention to his own halting steps, did not grasp the situation but continued his dragging way across the path of the drunken and enraged bully. The ruffian, seeing the lad ignore his loud commands, strode heavily forward with menacing fists, heaping foul epithets upon the head of the helpless Irish boy.

The crowd gasped.

"Oh, why does someone not do something!" moaned a woman. A girl screamed.

Several men started, but before they could force their way through the press, the people saw a stranger, a well-dressed young giant, spring from the sidewalk, and run toward the two figures in the middle of the street. But Dan had not arrived upon the scene soon enough. Almost as he left the pavement the blow fell, and Denny lay still—a crumpled, pitiful heap in the dirt.

Jud, flushed with this second triumph, turned to face the approaching stranger.

"Come on, you pink-eyed dude! I've got some fer you too. Come git your medicine, you—"

Dan was coming—coming so quickly that Jud's curses had not left his lips when the big fellow reached him. With one clean, swinging blow the man from Windy Cove was lifted fairly off the ground to fall several feet away from his senseless victim.

There was an excited yell from the crowd. But Jud, lean, loose-jointed and hard of sinew, had the physical toughness of his kind. Almost instantly he was on his feet again, reaching for his hip pocket with a familiar movement. And there was a wild scramble as those in front sought cover in the rear.

"Look out! Look out!"—came from the crowd.

But the mountain bred Dan needed no warning. With a leap, cat-like in its quickness, he was again upon the other. There was a short struggle, a sharp report, a wrenching twist, a smashing blow, and Jud was down once more, this time senseless. The weapon lay in the dust. The bullet had gone wide.

The crowd yelled their approval, and, even while they applauded, the people were asking each of his neighbor: "Who is he? Who is he?"

Several men rushed in, and Dan, seeing the bully safe in as many hands as could lay hold of him, turned to discover the young woman whom he had met at the depot kneeling in the street over the still unconscious Denny. With her handkerchief she was wiping the blood and dirt from the boy's forehead. Dan had only time to wonder at the calmness of her face and manner when the crowd closed in about them.

Then the Doctor pushed his way through the throng, and the people, at sight of the familiar figure, obeyed his energetic orders and drew aside. A carriage was brought and Dan lifted the unconscious lad in his arms. The Doctor spoke shortly to the young woman, "You come too." And with the Doctor the two strangers in Corinth took Denny to his home.

In the excitement no one thought of introductions, while the people seeing their hero driving in the carriage with a young woman, also a stranger, changed their question from, "Who is he?" to "Who are they?"

When Denny had regained consciousness, and everything possible for his comfort and for the assistance of his distracted mother, had been done; and the physician had assured them that the lad would be as good as ever in a day or two, the men crossed the street to the little white house.

"Well," ejaculated Martha when Dan had been presented, and the incident on the street briefly related, "I'm mighty glad I cooked them three roosters."

Dan laughed his big, hearty laugh, "I'm glad, too," he said. "Doctor used to drive me wild out in the woods with tales of your cooking."

The Doctor could see that Martha was pleased at this by the way she fussed with her apron.

"We always hoped that he would bring you with him on some of his trips," continued Dan, "we all wanted so much to meet you."

To the Doctor's astonishment, Martha stammered, "I—maybe I will go some day." Then her manner underwent a change as if she had suddenly remembered something. "You'll excuse me now while I put the dinner on," she said stiffly. "Just make yourself to home; preachers always do in this house, even if Doctor don't belong." She hurried away, and Dan looked at his host with his mother's questioning eyes. The Doctor knew what it was. Dan had felt it even in the house of his dearest friend. It was the preacher Martha had welcomed, welcomed him professionally because he was a preacher. And the Doctor felt again *that* something that had come between him and the lad.

"Martha doesn't care for fishing," he said gently.

Then they went out on the porch, and the old man pointed out to Dan his room across the way—the room that looked out upon the garden and the monument.

"Several of your congregation wanted to have you in their homes," he explained. "But I felt—I thought you might like to be—it was near me you see—and handy to the church." He pointed to the building up the street.

"Yes," Dan answered, looking at his old friend curiously—such broken speech was not natural to the Doctor—"You are quite right. It was very kind of you; you know how I will like it to be near you." Then looking at the monument he asked whose it was.

The Doctor hesitated again. Dan faced him waiting for an answer.

"That—oh, that's our statesman. You will need time to fully appreciate that work of art, and what it means to Corinth. It will grow on you. It's been growing on me for several years."

The young man was about to ask another question regarding the monument, when he paused. The girl who had gone to Denny in the street was coming from the little cottage. As she walked away under the great trees that lined the sidewalk, the two men stood watching her. Dan's question about the monument was forgotten.

"I wonder who she is," he said in a low voice.

The Doctor recalled the meeting at the depot and chuckled, and just then Martha called to dinner.

And the people on the street corners, at the ladies' bazaar, in the stores, the church booths and in the homes, were talking; talking of the exhibition of the man from Windy Cove, and asking each of his neighbor: "Who are they?"

CHAPTER V.

HOPE FARWELL'S MINISTRY.

"Useful hands they were, made for real service."

After dinner was over and they had visited awhile, the Doctor introduced Dan to his landlady across the way and, making some trivial excuse about business, left the boy in his room. The fact is that the Doctor wished to be alone. If he could have done it decently, he would have gone off somewhere with his fishing tackle. As he could not go fishing, he did the next best thing. He went to his office.

The streets were not so crowded now, for the people were at the ball game, and the Doctor made his way down town without interruption. As he went he tried to think out what it was that had come between him and the boy whom he had known so intimately for so many years. Stopping at the post office, he found a letter in his care addressed to "Rev. Daniel H. Matthews." In his abstraction he was about to hand the letter in at the window with the explanation that he knew no such person, when a voice at his elbow said: "Is Brother Matthews fully rested from his tiresome journey, Doctor?"

The Doctor's abstraction vanished instantly, he jammed that letter into his pocket and faced the speaker.

"Yes," he growled, "I think Brother Matthews is fully rested. As he is a grown man of unusual strength, and in perfect health of body at least, and the tiresome journey was a trip of only four hours, in a comfortable railway coach, I think I may say that he is fully recovered."

Then the Doctor slipped away. But he had discovered what it was that had come between the boy and himself. The *man*, Dan Matthews, was no longer the Doctor's boy. He was "Reverend," "Brother," the *preacher*. All the morning it had been making itself felt, that something that sets preachers apart. The Doctor wondered how his young hill-bred giant would stand being coddled and petted and loved by the wives and mothers of men who, for their daily bread, met the world bare-handed, and whose hardships were accepted by them and by these same mothers and wives as a matter of course.

By this time the Doctor had reached his office, and the sight of the familiar old rooms that had been the scene of so many revelations of real tragedies and genuine hardships, known only to the sufferer and to him professionally, forced him to continue his thought.

"There was Dr. Harry, for instance. Who, beside his old negro housekeeper, ever petted and coddled *him?* Who ever thought of setting him apart? Whoever asked if he were rested from his tiresome journey—journeys made not in comfortable coaches on the railroad, but in his buggy over all kinds of roads, at all times of day or night, in all sorts of weather winter and summer, rain and sleet and snow? Whoever 'Reverended' or 'Brothered' him? Oh no, he was only a man, a physician. It was his business to kill himself trying to keep other people alive."

Dr. Harry Abbott had been first, the Doctor's assistant, then his partner, and now at last his successor. Of a fine old Southern family, his people had lost everything in the war when Harry was only a lad. The father was killed in battle and the mother died a year later, leaving the boy alone in the world. Thrown upon his own resources for the necessities of life, he had managed somehow to live and to educate himself, besides working his way through both preparatory and medical schools, choosing his profession for love of it. He came to Dr. Oldham from school, when the Doctor was beginning to feel the burden of his large practice too heavily, and it was while he was the old physician's assistant that the people learned to call him Dr. Harry. And Dr. Harry he is to this day. How that boy has worked! His profession and his church (for he is a member, a deacon now, in the Memorial Church) have occupied every working minute of his life, and many hours beside that he should have given to sleep.

As the months passed Dr. Oldham placed more and more responsibilities upon him, and at the end of the second year took him into full partnership. It was about this time that Dr. Harry bought the old Wilson Carter place, and brought from his boyhood home two former slaves of his father to keep house for him, Old Uncle George and his wife Mam Liz.

Every year the younger man took more and more of the load from his partner's shoulders, until the older physician retired from active practice; and never has there been a word but of confidence and friendship between them. Their only difference is, that Harry will go to prayer meeting, when the Doctor declares he should go to bed; and that he will not go fishing. Always he has been the same courteous, kindly gentleman, intent only upon his profession, keeping abreast of the new things pertaining to his work, but ever considerate of the old Doctor's whims and fancies. Even now that Dr. Oldham has stepped down and out Harry insists that he leave his old desk in its place, and still talks over his cases with him.

The Doctor was sitting in his dilapidated office chair thinking over all this, when he heard his brother physician's step on the stairs. Harry came in, dusty and worn, from a long ride in the country on an all-night case. His tired face lit up when he saw his friend.

"Hello, Doctor! Glad to see you. Has he come? How is he?" While he was speaking the physician dropped his case, slipped out of his coat, and was in the lavatory burying his face in cold water by the time the other was ready to answer. That was Harry, he was never in a hurry, never seemed to move fast, but people never ceased to wonder at his quickness.

"He's all right," the Doctor muttered, his mind slipping back into the channel that had started him off to thinking of his fellow physician. "Got in on the ten-forty. But you look fagged enough. Why the devil don't you rest, Harry?"

Standing in the doorway rubbing his face, neck, and chest, with a coarse towel the young man laughed, "Rest, what would I do with a vacation? I'll be all right, when I get outside of one of Mam Liz's dinners. It was that baby of Jensen's that kept me. Poor little chap. I thought, two or three times he was going to make a die of it sure, but I guess he'll pull through now."

Dr. Oldham knew the Jensens well, eighteen miles over the worst roads in the country. He growled hoarsely: "It'll be more years than there are miles between here and Jensen's before you get a cent out of that case. You're a fool for making the trip; why don't you let 'em get that old bushwhacker at Salem, he's only three miles away?"

Harry pulled on his coat and dropped into his chair with a grin. "What'll you give me to collect some of your old accounts, Doctor? The Jensens say that the reason they have me is because you have always been their physician."

Then the Doctor in characteristic language expressed his opinion of the whole Jensen tribe, while Harry calmly glanced through some letters on his desk.

"See here, Doctor," he exclaimed, wheeling around in his chair and interrupting the old man's eloquent discourse. "Here is a letter from Dr. Miles—says he is sending a nurse; just what we want." He tossed the letter to the other. "There'll be the deuce to pay at Judge Strong's when she arrives. Whew! I guess I better trot over home and get a bite and forty winks. A Jensen breakfast, as you may remember, isn't just the most staying thing for a civilized stomach, and I need to be fit when I call at the Strong mansion. Wonder when the nurse will get here."

"She's here now," said the old Doctor, and he then told him about the meeting at the depot and the fight on the street. "But go on and get your nap," he finished. "I'll look after her."

Harry had just taken his hat when there came a knock on the door leading into the little waiting room. He hung his hat back in the closet, and dropped into his chair again with a comical expression of resignation on his face. But his voice was cheerful, when he said: "Come in."

The door opened. The young lady of the depot entered. The old physician took a good look at her this time. He saw a girl of fine, strong form and good height, with clear skin, showing perfect health, large, gray eyes—serious enough, but with a laugh back of all their seriousness, brown hair, firm, rounded chin and a generous sensitive mouth. Particularly he noticed her hands—beautifully modeled, useful hands they were, made for real service. Altogether she gave him the impression of being very much alive, and very much a woman.

"Is this Dr. Abbott?" she asked, looking at Harry, who had risen from his chair. When she spoke the old man again noted her voice, it was low and clear.

"I am Dr. Abbott," replied Harry.

"I am Hope Farwell," she answered. "Dr. Miles, you know, asked me to come. You wanted a nurse for a special case, I believe."

"Oh, yes," exclaimed Harry, "we have the letter here. We were just speaking of you, Miss Farwell. This is Dr. Oldham; perhaps Dr. Miles told you of him."

She turned with a smile, "Yes indeed, Dr. Miles told me. I believe we have met before, Doctor."

The girl broke into a merry laugh, when the old man answered, gruffly: "I should think we had. I was just telling Harry there when you came in."

Then the younger physician asked, "How soon can you be ready to go on this case, Nurse?" She looked at him with a faint expression of surprise. "Why I'm ready now, Doctor."

And the old Doctor broke in so savagely that they both looked at him in astonishment as he said: "But this is a hard case. You'll be up most of the night. You're tired out from your trip."

"Why, Doctor," said the young woman, "it is my business to be ready at any time. Being up nights is part of my profession. Surely you know that. Besides, that trip was really a good rest, the first good rest I've had for a long time."

"I know, of course," he answered. "I was thinking of something else. You must pardon me, Miss. Harry there will explain that I am subject to these little attacks."

"Oh, I know already," she returned smiling. "Dr. Miles told me all about you." And there was something in her laughing gray eyes that made the rough old man wonder just what it was that his friend Miles had told her.

"All right, get back to business you two," he growled. "I'll not interrupt again. Tell her about the case, Harry."

The young woman's face was serious in a moment, and she gave the physician the most careful attention as he explained the case for which he had written Dr. Miles to send a trained nurse of certain qualifications.

The Judge Strong of this story is an only son of the old Judge who moved Corinth. He is a large man—physically, as large as the Doctor, but where the Doctor is fat the Judge is lean. He inherited, not only his father's title (a purely honorary one) but his father's property, his position as an Elder in the church, and his general disposition; together with his taste and skill in collecting mortgages and acquiring real estate. The old Judge had but the one child. The Judge of this story, though just passing middle age, has no children at all. Seemingly there is no room in his heart for more than his church and his properties—his mind being thus wholly occupied with titles to heaven and to earth. With Sapphira, his wife, he lives in a big house on Strong Avenue, beyond the Strong Memorial Church, with never so much as a pet dog or cat to roughen the well-kept lawn or romp, perchance, in the garden. The patient whom Miss Farwell had come to nurse, was Sapphira's sister, a widow with neither child nor home. The Judge had been forced by his fear of public sentiment to give her shelter, and he had been compelled by Dr. Oldham and Dr. Harry to employ a nurse. The case would not be a pleasant one; Miss Farwell would need all that abundant stock of tact and patience which Dr. Miles had declared she possessed.

All this Dr. Harry explained to her, and when he had finished she asked in the most matter-of-fact tone: "And what are your instructions, Doctor?"

That caught Harry. It caught the old Doctor, too. Not even a comment on the disagreeable position she knew she would have in the Strong household, for Harry had not slighted the hard facts! She understood clearly what she was going into.

A light came into the young physician's eyes that his old friend liked to see. "I guess Miles knew what he was talking about in his letter," said the old Doctor. And the young woman's face flushed warmly at his words and look.

Then in his professional tones Dr. Harry instructed her more fully as to the patient's condition—a nervous trouble greatly aggravated by the Judge's disposition.

"Nice job, isn't it, Miss Farwell?" Harry finished.

She smiled. "When do I go on, Doctor?"

Harry stepped to the telephone and called up the Strong mansion. "This you, Judge?" he said into the instrument. "The nurse from Chicago is here; came today. We want her to go on the case at once. Can you send your man to the depot for her trunk?"

By the look on his face the old Doctor knew what Harry was getting. The younger physician's jaw was set and his eyes were blazing, but his voice was calm and easy. "But Judge, you remember the agreement. Dr. Oldham is here now if you wish to speak to him. We shall hold you to the exact letter of your bargain, Judge. I am very sorry but—. Very well sir. I will be at your home with the nurse in a few moments. Please have a room ready. And by the way, Judge, I must tell you again that my patient is in a serious condition. I warn you that we will hold you responsible if anything happens to interfere with our arrangements for her treatment. Good-bye."

He turned to the nurse with a wry face. "It's pretty bad, Miss Farwell."

Then, ringing up the village drayman, he arranged to have the young woman's trunk taken to the house. When the man had called for the checks Harry said: "Now, Nurse, my buggy is here, and if you are ready I guess we had better follow your trunk pretty closely."

From the window the old Doctor watched them get into the buggy, and drive off down the street. Mechanically he opened the letter from Dr. Miles, which he still held in his hand. "An ideal nurse, who has taken up the work for love of it,—have known the family for years—thoroughbreds—just the kind to send a Kentuckian like you—I warn you look out,—I want her back again."

The Doctor chuckled when he remembered Harry's look as he talked to the young woman. "If ever a man needed a wife Harry does," he thought. "Who knows what might happen?"

Who knows, indeed?

Then the Doctor went home to Dan. He found him in Denny's garden, with Denny enthroned on the big rock—listening to his fun, while Deborah, from the house, looked on, unable to believe that it was "the parson sure enough out there wid Denny,"—Denny who was to have been a priest himself one day, but who would never now be good for much of anything.

CHAPTER VI.

THE CALLING OF DAN MATTHEWS.

"'In the battle of life we cannot hire a substitute; whatever work one volunteers to make his own he must look upon as his ministry to the race.'"

Dan, with the Doctor and Mrs. Oldham were to take supper and spend the evening at Elder Jordan's. Martha went over early in the afternoon, leaving the two men to follow.

As they were passing the monument, Dan stopped. "Did you know him?" he asked curiously, when he had read the inscription. It was not like Dan to be curious.

The Doctor answered briefly: "I was there when he was born and was his family physician all his life, and I was with him when he died."

Something in the doctor's voice made Dan look at him intently for a moment, then in a low tone: "He was a good man?"

"One of the best I ever knew, too good for this town. Look at that thing. They say that expressed their appreciation of him—and it does," he finished grimly.

"But," said Dan, in a puzzled way, turning once more to the monument, "this inscription—" he read again the sentence from the statesman's speech on the forgotten issue of his passing day.

The Doctor said nothing.

Then gazing up at the cast-iron figure posed stiffly with outstretched arm in the attitude of a public speaker, Dan asked: "Is that like him?"

"Like him! It's like nothing but the people who conceived it," growled the Doctor indignantly. "If that man were living he would not be always talking about issues that have no meaning at this day. He would be giving himself to the problems that trouble us now. This thing," he rapped the monument with his stick until it gave forth a dull, hollow sound, "this thing is not a memorial to the life and character of my friend. It memorializes the dead issue to which he gave himself at one passing moment of his life, and which, had he lived, he would have forgotten, as the changing times brought new issues to be met as he met this old one. He was too great, too brave, to ever stand still and let the world go by. He was always on the firing line. This thing—" he rapped the hollow iron shaft again contemptuously, and the hollow sound seemed to add emphasis to his words—"this is a dead monument to a dead issue. Instead of speaking of his life, it cries aloud in hideous emphasis that he is dead."

They stood silently for a moment then Dan said, quietly: "After all, Doctor, they meant well."

"And that," retorted the old man grimly, "is what we doctors say when we see our mistakes go by in the hearse."

They went on up the street until they reached the church. Here Dan stopped again. He read the inscription cut large in the stone over the door, "The Strong Memorial Church." Again Dan turned to his friend inquiringly.

"Judge Strong, the old Judge," explained the Doctor. "That's his picture in the big stained-glass window there."

In all his intentions Nathaniel Jordan was one of the best of men. Surely, if in the hereafter, any man receives credit for always doing what his conscience dictates, Nathan will. He was one of those characters who give up living ten years before they die. Nathan stayed on for the church's good.

Miss Charity, the Elder's only child is—well, she was born, raised and educated for a parson's wife. The Doctor says that she didn't even cry like other babies. At three she had taken a prize in Sunday school for committing Golden texts, at seven she was baptized, and knew the reason why, at twelve she played the organ in Christian Endeavor. At fourteen she was teaching a class, leading prayer meeting, attending conventions, was president of the Local Union, and pointed with pride to the fact that she was on more committees than any other single individual in the Memorial Church. The walls of her room were literally covered with badges, medals, tokens, prizes and emblems, with the picture of every conspicuous church worker and leader of her denomination. Between times the girl studied the early history of her church, read the religious papers and in other ways fitted herself for her life work. Poor Charity! She was so cursed with a holy ambition, that to her men were not men, they simply *were* or were *not* preachers.

When Dan and the Doctor reached the Jordan home they found this daughter of the church at the front gate watching for them, a look of eager hope and expectancy on her face. The Elder himself with his wife and Mrs. Oldham were on the front porch. Martha could scarcely wait for the usual greeting and the introduction of Dan to Mrs. Jordan, before she opened on the Doctor with, "It's a great pity Doctor, that you couldn't bring Brother Matthews here before the last possible minute; supper is ready right now. A body would think you had an important case, if they didn't know that you were too old to do anything any more."

"We did have an important case, my dear," the Doctor replied, "and it was Dan who caused our delay."

"That's it; lay it on to somebody else like you always do. What in the world could poor Brother Matthews be doing to keep him from a good meal?"

"He was studying—let me see, what was it, Dan? Art, Political Economy—or Theology?"

Dan smiled. "I think it might have been the theory and practice of medicine," he returned. At which they both laughed and the others joined in, though for his life the Doctor couldn't see why.

"Well," said the Elder, when he had finished his shrill cackle, "we better go in and discuss supper awhile; that's always a satisfactory subject at least." Which was a pretty good one for Nathaniel.

When the meal was finished, they all went out on the front porch again, where it soon became evident that Nathaniel did not propose to waste more time in light and frivolous conversation. By his familiar and ponderous "Ahem—ahem!" even Dan understood that he was anxious to get down to the real business of the evening, and that he was determined to do his full duty, or—as he would have said—"to keep that which was committed unto him."

"Ahem—ahem!" A hush fell upon the little company, the women turned their chairs expectantly, and the Doctor slipped over to the end of the porch to enjoy his evening cigar. The Elder had the field.

With another and still louder "Ahem!" he began. "I am sorry that Brother Strong is not here this evening. Judge Strong that is, Brother Matthews; he is our other Elder, you understand. I expected him but he has evidently been detained."

The Doctor, thinking of Dr. Harry and the nurse, chuckled, and Nathan turned a look of solemn inquiry in his direction.

"Ahem—ahem,—you did not come to Corinth directly from your home, I understand, Brother Matthews?"

The Doctor could see Dan's face by the light from the open window. He fancied it wore a look of amused understanding.

"No," answered the minister, "I spent yesterday in the city."

"Ahem—ahem," coughed the Elder. "Found an acquaintance on the train coming up, didn't you? We noticed you talking to a young woman at the car window."

Dan paused a moment before answering, and the Doctor could feel the interest of the company. Then the boy said, dryly, "Yes, I may say though, that she is something more than an acquaintance."

Smothered exclamations from the women. "Ah hah," from the Elder. The Doctor grinned to himself in the dark. "The young scamp!"

"Ahem! She had a pretty face, we noticed; are you—that is, have you known her long?"

"Several years, sir; the lady you saw is my mother. I went with her to the city day before yesterday, where she wished to do some shopping, and accompanied her on her way home as far as Corinth."

More exclamations from the women.

"Why, Doctor, you never told us it was his mother," cried Martha, and Nathaniel turned toward the end of the porch with a look of righteous indignation.

"You never asked me," chuckled the Doctor.

After this the two older women drifted into the house. Charity settled herself in an attitude of rapt attention, and the program was continued.

"Ahem. You may not be aware of it Brother Matthews, but I know a great deal about your family, sir."

"Indeed," exclaimed Dan.

"Yes sir. You see I have some mining interests in that district, quite profitable interests I may say. Judge Strong and I together have quite extensive interests. Two or three years ago we made a good many trips into your part of the country, where we heard a great deal of your people. Your mother seems to be a remarkable woman of considerable influence. Too bad she is not a regular member of the church. Our preachers often tell us, and I believe it is true, that people who do so much good out of the church really injure the cause more than anything else."

Dan made no answer to this, but as the Doctor saw his face in the light it wore a mingled expression of astonishment and doubt.

The Elder proceeded, "They used to tell us some great stories about your father, too. Big man, isn't he?"

"Yes sir, fairly good size."

"Yes, I remember some of his fights we used to hear about; and there was another member of the family, they mentioned a good deal. Dad—Dad—"

"Howitt," said Dan softly.

"That's it, Howitt. A kind of a shepherd, wasn't he? Discovered the big mine on your father's place. One of your father's fights was about the old man. Ahem—ahem—I judge you take after your father. I don't know just what to think about your whipping that fellow this morning. Someone had to do something of course, but—ahem, for a minister it was rather unusual. I don't know how the people will take it."

"I'm afraid that I forgot that I was a minister," said Dan uneasily. "I hope, sir, you do not think that I did wrong."

"Ahem—ahem, I can't say that it was wrong exactly, but as I said, we don't know how the people will take it. But there's one thing sure," and the Elder's shrill cackle rang out, "it will bring a big crowd to hear you preach. Well, well, that's off the subject. Ahem—Brother Matthews, why haven't your people opened that big mine in Dewey Bald?"

"I expect it would be better for me to let father or mother explain that to you, sir," answered Dan, as cool and calm as the evening.

"Yes, yes of course, but it's rather strange, rather unusual you know, to find a young man of your make-up and opportunities for wealth, entering the ministry. You could educate a great many preachers, sir, if you would develop that mine."

"Father and mother have always taught us children that in the battle of life one cannot hire a substitute; that whatever work one volunteers to make his own he must look upon as his ministry to the race. I believe that the church is an institution divinely given to serve the world, and that, more than any other, it helps men to the highest possible life. I volunteered for the work I have undertaken, because naturally I wish my life to count for the greatest possible good; and because I feel that I can serve men better in the church than in any other way."

"Whew!" thought the Doctor, "that was something for Nathan to chew on." The lad's face when he spoke made his old friend's nerves tingle. His was a new conception of the ministry, new to the Doctor at least. Forgetting his cigar he awaited the Elder's reply with breathless interest.

"Ahem—ahem, you feel then that you have no special Divine call to the work?"

"I have always been taught at home, sir, that every man is divinely called to his work, if that work is for the good of all men. His faithfulness or unfaithfulness to the call is revealed in the *motives* that prompt him to choose his field." The boy paused a moment and then added slowly—and no one who heard him could doubt his deep conviction—"Yes sir, I feel that I am divinely called to preach the gospel."

"Ahem—ahem, I trust, Brother Matthews, that you are not taken up with these new fads and fancies that are turning the minds of the people from the true worship of God."

"It is my desire, sir, to lead people to the true worship of God. I believe that nothing will accomplish that end but the simple old Jerusalem gospel."

The Doctor lit his cigar again. They seemed to be getting upon safer ground.

"I am glad to hear that—" said the Elder heartily—"very glad. I feared from the way you spoke, you might be going astray. There is a great work for you here in Corinth—a great work. Our old brother who preceded you was a good man, sound in the faith in every way, but he didn't seem to take somehow. The fact is the other churches—ahem—are getting about all our congregation."

Then for an hour or more, Elder Jordan, for the new minister's benefit, discussed in detail the religious history of Corinth, with the past, present and future of Memorial Church; while Charity, drinking in every word of the oft-heard discussion, grew ever more entranced with the possibilities of the new pastor's ministry, and the Doctor sat alone at the farther end of the porch. The Elder finished with: "Well, well, Brother Matthews, you are young, strong, unmarried, and with your reputation as a college man and an athlete you ought to do great things for Memorial Church. We are counting on you to build us up wonderfully. And let me say too, that we are one of the oldest and best known congregations in our brotherhood here in the state. We have had some great preachers here. You can make a reputation that will put you to the top of your—ah, calling."

Dan was just saying, "I hope I will please you, sir," when the women appeared in the doorway. Martha had her bonnet on.

"Come, come Nathan," said Mrs. Jordan, "you mustn't keep poor Brother Matthews up another minute. He must be nearly worn out with his long journey and all the excitement."

The Doctor thought again of the girl who had made the same journey in the car behind Dan, and who had also shared the excitement. He wondered how the nurse was enjoying her evening and when she would get to bed. "That's so," exclaimed the Doctor, rising to his feet. "We're all a lot of brutes to treat the poor boy so."

Dan whirled on him with a look that set the old man to laughing, "That's all right, sonny," he chuckled. "Come on, I've been asleep for an hour."

CHAPTER VII.

FROM DEBORAH'S PORCH.

"'With nothin' to think of all the time but the Blessed Jesus an' the Holy Mother; an' all the people so respectful, an' lookin' up to you. Sure 'tis a grand thing, Doctor, to be a priest.'"

Nathaniel Jordan's prediction proved true.

In the two days between Dan's arrival and his first Sunday in Corinth, the Ally was actively engaged in making known the identity of the big stranger, who had so skillfully punished the man from Windy Cove. Also the name and profession of the young woman who had gone to Denny's assistance were fully revealed.

The new minister of the Memorial Church was the sensation of the hour. The building could scarcely hold the crowd, while the rival churches were deserted, save only by the few faithful "pillars" who were held in their places by the deep conviction that heaven itself would fall should they fail to support their own particular faith. With the people who had attended the fair, the Ally journeyed far into the country, and the roads being good with promise of a moon to drive home by, the country folk for miles around came to worship God, and, incidentally, to see the preacher who had fought and vanquished the celebrated Jud. Many were there that day who had not been inside a church before for years. The Ally went also, but then the Ally, they say, is a regular attendant at all the services of every church.

Judge Strong, with an expression of pious satisfaction on his hard face, occupied his own particular corner. From another corner Elder Jordan watched for signs of false doctrine. Charity, except when busy at the organ, never took her adoring eyes from the preacher's face. At the last moment before the sermon, Dr. Harry slipped into the seat beside the Doctor. And many other earnest souls there were who depended upon the church as the only source of their life's inspiration and strength.

Facing this crowd that even in the small town of Corinth represented every class and kind, Dan felt it all; the vulgar curiosity, the craving for sensation, the admiration, the suspicion, the true welcome, the antagonism, the spiritual dependence. And the young man from the mountains and the schools, who had entered the ministry from the truest motives, with the highest ideals, shrank back and was afraid.

Dan was, literally, to this church and people a messenger from another world. It was not strange that many of the people thought, "How out of place this big fellow looks in the pulpit." Many of them felt dimly, too, that which the Doctor had always felt, that this man was somehow a revelation of something that might have been, that ought to be. But no one tried to search out the reason why.

The theme of the new minister's sermon was, "The Faith of the Fathers," and it must have been a good one, because Martha said the next day, that it was the finest thing she had ever heard; and she had it figured out somehow that the members of neighboring churches, who were there, got some straight gospel for once in their lives. Elder Jordan assured the Doctor in a confidential whisper, that it was a splendid effort. The Doctor knew that Dan was splendid, and he could see that the boy had fairly hypnotized the crowd, but he could not understand why it should have been much of an effort. He confided to Martha that "so far as he could see, the sermon might have been taken from the barrel of any one of the preachers that had served the Memorial Church since its establishment." But the sermon was new and fresh to Dan, and so gained something of interest and strength from the earnestness and personality of the speaker. "The boy had only to hold that gait," reflected the Doctor, "and he would, as Nathan had said, land at the very top of his profession."

In the evening, the Doctor slipped away from church as soon as the services were over, leaving Dan with those who always stay until the janitor begins turning out the lights. Martha would walk home with fellow workers in the Ladies' Aid, who lived a few doors beyond, and the Doctor wished to be alone.

Crossing the street to avoid the crowd, he walked slowly along under The big trees, trying to accustom himself to the thought of his boy dressed in the conventional minister's garb, delivering time worn conventionalities in a manner as conventional. It was to this strange thinking old man, almost as if he had seen Dan behind the grated doors of a prison cell.

Very slowly he went along, unmindful of aught but the thoughts that troubled him, until, coming to the Widow Mulhall's little cottage, where Deborah and Denny were sitting on the porch, he paused. Across the street in front of his own home, Martha and her friends were holding an animated conversation.

"Come in, come in, Doctor," called Deborah's cheery voice, "it's a fine evenin' it is and only beginnin'. I was just tellin' Denny that 'tis a shame folks have to waste such nights in sleep. Come right in, I'll fetch another chair—take the big rocker there, Doctor, that's right. And how are you? Denny? Oh the bye is all right again just as you said; sure the minister had him out in the garden that same afternoon. 'Twas the blessin' of God, though, that his Reverence was there to keep that devil from batin' the poor lad to death. I hope you'll not be forgettin' the way to our gate entirely now, Doctor, that you'll be crossin' the street so often to the house beyond the garden there."

In the Widow's voice there was a hint of her Irish ancestry, as, in her kind blue eyes, buxom figure and cordial manner, there was more than a hint of her warm-hearted, whole-souled nature.

"How do you like your new neighbor, Deborah?" asked the Doctor.

"Ah, Doctor, it's a fine big man he is, a danged fine man inside an' out. Denny and me are almighty proud, havin' him so close. He's that sociable, too, not at all like a priest. It's every blessed day since he's been here he's comin' over to Denny in the garden, and helpin' him with the things, a-talkin' away all the time. ''Tis the very exercise I need,' says he. 'And it's a real kindness for ye to let me work a bit now and then,' says he. But sure we kin see, 'tis the big heart of him, wishful to help the bye. But it's queer notioned he is fer a preacher."

"Didn't I see you and Denny at church this evening?" asked the Doctor.

"You did that, sir. You see not havin' no church of our own within reach of our legs, an' bein' real wishful to hear a bit of a prayer and a sermon like, Denny an' me slips into the protestant meetings now and then. After all there's no real harm in it now, do you think, Doctor?"

"Harm to you and Denny, or the church?" the Doctor asked.

"Aw, go on now, Doctor you do be always havin' your joke," she laughed. "Harm to neither or both or all, I mane, for, of course—well, let it go. I guess that while Denny and me do be sayin' our prayers in our little cabin on this side of the street, and you are a-sayin' yours in your fine house across the way, 'tis the same blessed Father of us all gets them both. I misdoubt if God had much to do wid layin' out the streets of Corinth anyhow. I've heard how 'twas the old Judge Strong did that."

"And what do you think of Mr. Matthews' sermon?"

"It's ashamed I am to say it, Doctor, but I niver heard him."

"Never heard him? But I thought you were there."

"And we was, sir, so we was. And Denny here can tell you the whole thing, but for myself I niver heard a blessed word, after the singin' and the preacher stood up."

"Why, what was the matter?"

"The preacher himself."

"The preacher?"

"Yes sir. 'Twas this way, Doctor, upon my soul I couldn't hear what he was a-sayin' for lookin' at the man himself. With him a-standin' up there so big an' strong an'—an' clean like through an' through an' the look on his face! It set me to thinkin' of all that I used to dream fer—fer my Denny here. Ye mind what a fine lookin' man poor Jack was, sir, tho' I do say it, and how Denny here, from a baby, was the very image of him. I always knowed he was a-goin' to grow up another Jack for strength an' looks. And you know yourself how our hearts was set on havin' him a priest, him havin' such a turn that way, bein' crazy on books and studyin' an' the likes—an' now—now here we are, sir. My man gone, an' my boy just able to drag his poor broken body around, an' good fer nothin' but to dig in the dirt. No sir, I couldn't hear the sermon fer lookin' at the preacher an' thinkin'."

Denny moved his twisted, misshapen body uneasily, "Oh, come now, mother," he said, "let's don't be spoilin' the fine night fer the Doctor with our troubles."

"Indade, that we will not," said Deborah cheerfully. "Don't you think Denny's garden's been doin' fine this summer, Doctor?"

"Fine," said the Doctor heartily. "But then it's always fine. There's lots of us would like to know how he makes it do so well."

Denny gave a pleased laugh.

"Aw now Doctor you're flatterin' me. They have been doin' pretty well though—pretty well fer me."

"I tell you what it is, Doctor," said Deborah, "the bye naturally loves them things into growin'. If people would be takin' as good care of their children as Denny does for his cabbage and truck it would be a blessin' to the world."

"It is funny, Doctor," put in Denny, "but do you know those things out there seem just like people to me. I tell mother it ain't so bad after all, not bein' a priest. The minister was a-sayin' yesterday, that the people needed more than their souls looked after. If I can't be tellin' people how to live, I can be growin' good things to keep them alive, and maybe that's not so bad as it might be."

"I don't know what we'd be doin' at all, if it wasn't fer that same garden," added Deborah, "with clothes, and wood and groceries to buy, to say nothin' of the interest that's always comin' due. We—"

"Whist," said Denny in a low tone as a light flashed up in the corner window of the house on the other side of the garden. "There's the minister come home."

Reverently they watched the light and the moving shadow in the room. The moon, through the branches of the trees along the street, threw waving patches of soft light over the dark green of the little lawn. Martha's friends had moved on. Martha herself had retired. The street was seemingly deserted and very still.

Leaning forward in her chair Deborah spoke in a whisper. "We can always tell when he's in of nights, and when he goes to bed. Ye see it's almost like we was livin' in the same house with him. An' a great comfort it is to us too, wid him such a good man, our havin' him so near. Poor bye I'll warrant he's tired tonight. But oh, it must be a grand thing, Doctor, to be doin' such holy work, an' a livin' with God Almighty like, with nothin' to think of all the time but the Blessed Jesus and the Holy Mother; an' all the people so respectful, an' lookin' up to you. Sure 'tis a grand thing, Doctor, to be a priest, savin' your presence sir, for I know how you've little truck wid churches, tho' the lady your wife does enough fer two."

The Doctor rose to go for he saw that the hour was late. As he stood on the steps ready to depart the steady flow of Deborah's talk continued, when Denny interrupted again, pointing toward a woman who was crossing to the other side of the street. She walked slowly, and, reaching the sidewalk in front of the Doctor's house, hesitated, in a troubled, undecided way. Approaching the gate, she paused, then drew back and moved on slowly up the street. Her movements and manner gave the impression that she was in trouble, perhaps in pain.

"There's something wrong there," said the Doctor. "Who is it? Can you see who it is, Denny?"

"Yes, sir," he answered, and Deborah broke in, "it's that poor girl of—of Jim Conner's, sir."

The Doctor, at once nervous and agitated, was not a little worried and could make no reply, knowing that it was Jim Conner who had killed Deborah's husband.

"Poor thing," murmured Deborah. "For the love of God, look at that now, Doctor!"

The girl had reached the corner, and had fallen or thrown herself in a crouching heap against the monument.

The widow was starting for the street, but Denny caught her arm: "No—no mother, you mustn't do that, you know how she's scared to death of you; let the Doctor go."

The physician was already on his way as fast as his old legs would take him.

CHAPTER VIII.

THE WORK OF THE ALLY.

"In the little room that looked out upon the Monument and the garden, Dan—all unknowing—slept. And over all brooded the spirit that lives in Corinth—the Ally—that dread, mysterious thing that never sleeps."

Grace Conner is a type common to every village, town and city in the land, the saddest of all sad creatures—a good girl with a bad reputation.

Her reputation Grace owed first to her father's misdeeds, for which the girl could in no way be to blame, and second, to the all-powerful Ally, without whom the making of any reputation, good or bad, is impossible.

The Doctor knew the girl well. When she was a little tot and a member of Martha's Sunday school class, she was at the house frequently. Later as a member of the church she herself was a teacher and an active worker. Then came the father's crime and conviction, followed soon by the mother's death, and the girl was left to shift for herself. She had kept herself alive by working here and there, in the canning factory and restaurants, and wherever she could. No one would give her a place in a home.

The young people in the church, imitating their elders, shunned her, and it was not considered good policy to permit her to continue teaching in the Sunday school. No mother wanted her child to associate with a criminal's daughter; naturally she drifted away from the regular services, and soon it was publicly announced that her name had been dropped from the roll of membership. After that she never came.

It was not long until the girl had such a name that no self respecting man or woman dared be caught recognizing her on the street.

The people always spoke of her as "that Grace Conner."

The girl, hurt so often, grew to fear everyone. She strove to avoid meeting people on the street, or meeting them, passed with downcast eyes, not daring to greet them. Barely able to earn bread to keep life within her poor body, her clothing grew shabby, her form thin and worn; and these very evidences of her goodness of character worked to accomplish her ruin. But she was a good girl through it all, a good girl with a bad reputation.

She was cowering at the foot of the monument, her face buried in her hands, when the Doctor touched her on the shoulder. She started and turned up to him the saddest face the old physician had ever seen.

"What's the matter, my girl?" he said as kindly as he could.

She shook her head and buried her face in her hands again.

"Please go away and let me alone."

"Come, come," said the Doctor laying his hand on her shoulder again. "This won't do; you must tell me what's wrong. You can't stay out here on the street at this time of the night."

At his tone she raised her head again. "This time of the night! What difference does it make to anyone whether I am on the street or not?"

"It makes a big difference to you, my girl," the Doctor answered. "You should be home and in bed."

God! What a laugh she gave!

"Home! In bed!" She laughed again.

"Stop that!" said the physician sharply, for he saw that just a touch more, and she would be over the line. "Stand up here and tell me what's the matter; are you sick?"

She rose to her feet with his help.

"No sir."

"Well, what have you been doing?"

"Nothing, Doctor. I—I was just walking around."

"Why don't you go back to the Hotel? You are working there, are you not?"

At this she wrung her hands and looked about in a dazed way, but answered nothing.

"See here, Grace," said the physician, "you know me, surely—old Doctor Oldham, can't you tell me what it is that's wrong?"

She made no answer.

"Come, let me take you to the Hotel," he urged; "it's only a step."

"No—no," she moaned, "I can't go there. I don't live there any more."

"Well where do you live now?" he asked.

"Over in Old Town."

"But why did you leave your place at the Hotel?"

"A—a man there said something that I didn't like, and then the proprietor told me that I must go, because some of the people were talking about me, and I was giving the Hotel a bad name. Oh, Doctor, I ain't a bad girl, I ain't never been, but folks are driving me to it. That or—or—" she hesitated.

What could he say?

"It's the same everywhere I try to work," she continued in a hopeless tone. "At the canning factory the other girls said their folks wouldn't let them work there if I didn't go. I haven't been able to earn a cent since I left the Hotel. I don't know what to do,—oh, I don't know what to do!" She broke down crying.

"Look here, why didn't you come to me?" the Doctor asked roughly. "You knew you could come to me. Didn't I tell you to?"

"I—I was afraid. I'm afraid of everybody." She shivered and looked over her shoulder.

The Doctor saw that this thing had gone far enough. "Come with me," he said. "You must have something to eat."

He started to lead her across the street toward Mrs. Mulhall whom he could see at the gate watching them. But the girl hung back.

"No, no," she panted in her excitement. "Not there, I dare not go there." The Doctor hesitated.

"Well, come to my house then," he said. She went as far as the gate then she stopped again.

"I can't, Doctor. Mrs. Oldham, I can't—" The girl was right. The Doctor was never so ashamed in all his life. After a little, he said with decision, "Look here, Grace, you sit down on the porch for a few minutes. Martha is in bed and fast asleep long ago." He stole away as quietly as possible, and in a little while returned with a basket full of such provisions as he could find in the pantry. He was chuckling to himself as he thought of Martha when she discovered the theft in the morning, and cursing half aloud the thing that made it necessary for him to steal from his own pantry for the girl whom he would have taken into his home so gladly, if—

He made her eat some of the cold chicken and bread and drink a glass of milk. And when she was feeling better, walked with her down the street a little way, to be sure that she was all right.

"I can't thank you enough, Doctor," she said, "you have saved me from—"

"Don't try," he broke in. He did not want her to get on that line again. "Go on home like a good girl now, and mind you look carefully in the bottom of that basket." He had put a little bill there, the only money he had in the house. "This will help until times are better for you, and mind now, if you run against it again, come to me or go to Dr. Harry at the office, and tell him that you want me."

He watched her down the street and then went home, stopping for a word of explanation to Deborah and Denny, who were waiting at the gate.

The light was still burning in Dan's window when the Doctor again entered his own yard. He thought once that he would run in on the minister for a minute, and then remembered that "the boy would be tired after his great effort defending the faith of Memorial Church." It was long past the old man's bed time. He told himself that he was an old fool to be prowling about so late at night, and that he would hear from Martha all right tomorrow. Then, as he climbed into bed, he chuckled again, thinking of the empty kitchen pantry and that missing basket.

The light in Dan's room went out. Some belated person passed, going home for the night; a little later, another. Then a man and woman, walking closely, talking in low tones, strolled slowly by in the shadow of the big trees. The quick step of a horse and the sound of buggy-wheels came swiftly nearer and nearer, passed and died away in the stillness. It was Dr. Harry answering a call. In Judge Strong's big, brown house, a nurse in her uniform of blue and white, by the dim light of a night-lamp, leaned over her patient with a glass of water. In Old Town a young woman in shabby dress, with a basket on her arm, hurried—trembling and frightened—across the lonely, grass-grown square. Under the quiet stars in the soft moonlight, the cast-iron monument stood—grim and cold and sinister. In the peace and quiet of the night, Denny's garden wrought its mystery. In the little room that looked out upon the monument and the garden, Dan—all unknowing—slept.

And over all brooded the spirit that lives in Corinth—the Ally—that dread, mysterious thing that never sleeps.

CHAPTER IX.

THE EDGE OF THE BATTLEFIELD.

"But it was as if his superior officers had ordered him to mark time, while his whole soul was eager for the command to charge."

Dan was trying to prepare his evening sermon for the third Sunday of what the old Doctor called his Corinthian ministry. The afternoon was half gone, when he arose from his study table. All day he had been at it, and all day the devils of dissatisfaction had rioted in his soul—or wherever it is that such devils are supposed to riot.

The three weeks had not been idle weeks for Dan. He had made many pastoral calls at the homes of his congregation; he had attended numberless committee meetings. Already he was beginning to feel the tug of his people's need—the world old need of sympathy and inspiration, of courage and cheer; the need of the soldier for the battle-cry of his comrades, the need of the striving runner for the lusty shout of his friends, the need of the toiling servant for the "well-done" of his master.

Keenly sensitive to this great unvoiced cry of life, the young man answered in his heart, "Here am I, use me." Standing before his people he felt as one who, on the edge of a battlefield longs, with all his heart, to throw himself into the fight. But it was as if his superior officers had ordered him to mark time, while his whole soul was eager for the command to charge.

Why do people go to church? What do men ask of their religion? What have they the right to expect from those who assume to lead them in their worship? Already these questions were being shouted at him from the innermost depths of his consciousness. He felt the answer that his Master would give. But always between him and those to whom he would speak there came the thought of his employers. And he found himself, while speaking to the people, nervously watching the faces of the men by whose permission he spoke. So it came that he was not satisfied with his work that afternoon, and he tossed aside his sermon to leave his study for the fresh air and sunshine of the open fields. From his roses the Doctor hailed him as he went down the street, but the boy only answered with a greeting and a wave of his hand.

Dan did not need the Doctor that day. Straight out into the country he went walking fast, down one hill—up another, across a creek, over fences, through a pasture into the woods. An hour of this at a good hard pace, and he felt better. The old familiar voices of hill and field and forest and stream soothed and calmed him. The physical exercise satisfied to some extent his instinct and passion for action.

Coming back through Old Town, and leisurely climbing the hill on the road that leads past the old Academy, he paused frequently to look back over the ever widening view, and to drink deep of the pure, sun-filled air. At the top of the hill, reluctant to go back to the town that lay beyond, he stood contemplating the ancient school building that held so bravely its commanding position, and looked so pitiful in its shabby old age. Then passing through a gap in the tumble-down fence, and crossing the weed-filled yard, he entered the building.

For a while he wandered curiously about the time-worn rooms, reading the names scratched on the plaster walls, cut in the desks and seats, on the window casing, and on the big square posts that, in the lower rooms, supported the ceiling. He laughed to himself, as he noticed how the sides of these posts facing away from the raised platform at the end of the room were most elaborately carved. It suggested so vividly the life that had once stirred within the old walls.

Several of the names were already familiar to him. He tried to imagine the venerable heads of families he knew, as they were in the days when they sat upon these worn benches. Did Judge Strong or Elder Jordan, perhaps, throw one of those spit-balls that stuck so hard and fast to the ceiling? And did some of the grandmothers he had met giggle and hide their faces at Nathaniel's cunning evasion of the teacher's quick effort to locate the successful marksman? Had those staid pillars of the church ever been swayed and bent by passions of young manhood and womanhood? Had their minds ever been stirred by the questions and doubts of youth? Had their hearts ever throbbed with eager longing to know—to feel life in its fullness?

Seating himself at one of the battered desks he tried to bring back the days that were gone, and to see about him the faces of those who once had filled the room with the strength and gladness of their youth. He felt strangely old in thus trying to feel a boy among those boys and girls of the days long gone.

Who among the boys would be his own particular chum? Elder Jordan? He smiled. And who, (the blood mounted to his cheek at the thought) who among the girls would be— Out of the mists of his revery came a face—a face that was strangely often in his mind since that day when he arrived in Corinth. Several times he had caught passing glimpses of her; once he had met her on the street and ventured to bow. And Dr. Harry, with whom he had already begun an enduring friendship, had told him much to add to his interest in her. But to dream about the stranger in this way—

"What nonsense!" he exclaimed aloud, and rising, strode to the window to clear his mind of those too strong fancies by a sight of the world in which he lived and to which he belonged.

The next moment he drew back with a start—a young woman in the uniform of a trained nurse was entering the yard.

CHAPTER X.

A MATTER OF OPINION.

"'Who spoke of condemnation? Is that just the question? Are you not unfair?'"

Miss Farwell had heard much of the new pastor of the Memorial Church. Dr. Harry frequently urged her to attend services; Deborah, when Hope had seen her was eloquent in his praise. Mrs. Strong and the ladies who called at the house spoke of him often. But for the first two weeks of her stay at Judge Strong's the nurse had been confined so closely to the care of her patient that she had heard nothing to identify the preacher with the big stranger whom she had met at the depot the day of her arrival.

By the time Miss Farwell began hearing of the new preacher the interest occasioned by his defense of Denny had already died down, and it chanced that no one mentioned it in her presence when speaking of him, while each time he had called at the Strong home the nurse had been absent or busy. Thus it happened that so far as she knew, Miss Farwell had never met the minister about whom she had heard so much. But she had several times seen the big fellow, who had apologized at such length for running into her at the depot, and who had gone so quickly to the assistance of Denny. It was natural, under such conditions, that she should remember him. It was natural, too, that she never dreamed of connecting the young hero of the street fight with the Reverend Matthews of the Memorial Church.

Her patient had so far improved that the nurse was now able to leave her for an hour or two in the afternoon, and the young woman had gone for a walk just beyond the outskirts of the village. Coming to the top of the hill she had turned aside from the dusty highway, thinking to enjoy the view from the shade of a great oak that grew on a grassy knoll in the center of the school grounds.

Dan watched her as she made her way slowly across the yard, his eyes bright with admiration for her womanly grace as she stopped, here and there, to pick a wild flower from the tangle of grass and weeds. Reaching the tree she seated herself and, laying her parasol on the grass by her side, began arranging the blossoms she had gathered—pausing, now and then, to look over the rolling country of field and woods that, dotted by farm houses with their buildings and stacks, stretched away into the blue distance.

The young fellow at the window gazed at her with almost superstitious awe. That her face had come before him so vividly, as he sat dreaming in the old school-room, at the very moment when she was turning into the yard, moved him greatly. His blood tingled at the odd premonition that this woman was somehow to play a great part in his life. Nothing seemed more natural than that he should have come to this spot this afternoon. Neither was it at all strange that, in her walk, she too, should be attracted by the beauty of the place. But the feeling forced itself upon him nevertheless that this perfectly natural incident was a great event in his life. He knew that he would go to her presently. He was painfully aware that he ought not to be thus secretly watching her, but he hesitated as one about to take a step that could never be retraced.

She started when he appeared in the doorway of the building and half-arose from her place. Then recognizing him she dropped back on the grass; and there was a half-amused frown on her face, though her cheeks were red. She was indignant with herself that she should be blushing like a schoolgirl at the presence of this stranger whose name even she did not know.

"I beg your pardon, Miss Farwell, I fear that I startled you," he said, hat in hand. Already Dan had grown so accustomed to being greeted by strangers, that it never occurred to him that this lady did not know who he was.

She saw the sunlight on his shaggy red-brown hair, and the fine poise of the well-shaped head, as she answered shortly, "You did."

Woman-like she was making him feel her anger at herself; and also woman-like, when she saw his embarrassment at her blunt words and manner, she smiled.

"I am sorry," he said, but he did not offer to go on his way.

When she made no reply but began rearranging her handful of blossoms, he spoke again, remarking on the beauty of the view before them; and ventured to ask if the knoll was to her a favorite spot, adding that it was his first visit to the place.

"I have never been here before either," she answered. The brief silence that followed was broken by Dan.

"We seem to have made a discovery," he said, wondering why she should seem confused at his simple remark. "I know I ought to go," he continued. "I will if you say the word, but—" he paused.

"You were here first," she returned with a smile. Really, she thought, there was no reason why she should drive him away. He was so evidently a gentleman, and the place was on the public thoroughfare.

"Then I may stay?" He dropped on the grass at her feet with an exclamation of satisfaction and pleasure.

Looking away over the landscape where the clouds and shadows were racing, and the warm autumn light lay on the varying shades of green and brown, he remarked: "Do you know when I see a bit of out-doors like that, on such a day as this, or when I am out in the woods or up in the hills, I wonder what men build churches for, anyway. I fear I must be something of a pagan, for I often feel that I can worship God best in his own temple. Quite heathenish isn't it?" He laughed, but under the laugh there was a note of troubled seriousness.

She looked at him curiously. "And is it heathenish to worship God outside of a church? If it is I fear that I, too, am a heathen."

He noted the words "I, too," and saw instantly that she did not know him but had understood from his words that he was not a church man. He felt that he ought to correct her false impression, that he ought to tell her who and what he was, but he was possessed of a curious feeling of reluctance to declare his calling.

The truth is, Dan Matthews did not want to meet this woman as a priest, but as a man. He had already learned how the moment the preacher was announced the man was pushed into the background.

While he hesitated she watched him with increasing interest. His words had pleased her; she waited for him to speak again.

"I suppose your profession does keep you from anything like regular church attendance," he said.

"Yes," she answered, "I have found that sick people do not as a rule observe a one-day-in-seven religion. But it is not my professional duties that keep me from church."

"You are not then—"

"Decidedly I am not," she answered.

"Really, you surprise me. I thought of course you were a member of some church."

There was a touch of impatience in her quick reply. "You thought 'of course'? And why of course, please?"

He started to answer, but she went on quickly, "I know why; because I am a woman, *the weaker sex!*"

It is not possible to describe the fine touch in her voice when she said "the weaker sex." It was so delicately done, that it had none of the coarseness that commonly marks like expressions, when used by some women. Dan was surprised to feel that it emphasized the fineness of her character, as well as its strength.

"Because I am not a man must I be *useless?"* she continued. "Is a woman's life of so little influence in the world that she can spend it in *make-believe living* as little girls play at being grown up? Have I not as great a right to my paganism as you call it, as you have to yours?"

Again he saw his opportunity and realized that he ought to correct her mistake in assuming from his words that he was not a man of church affiliation, but again he passed it by saying slowly, instead: "I think your kind of paganism must be a very splendid thing; no one could think of one in that dress as useless."

"I did not mean—"

"I understand I think," he said earnestly, "but won't you tell me why you feel so about the church?"

She laughed as she returned, "One might think from your awful seriousness that you were a preacher. Father Confessor, if you please—" she began mockingly, then stopped—arrested by the expression of his face. "Oh I beg your pardon, have I been rude?"

With a forced laugh he answered, "Oh no, indeed, not at all. It is only that your views of the Christian religion surprise me."

"My views of the Christian religion," she repeated, very serious now. "I did not know that my views of Christianity were mentioned."

He was bewildered. "But the church! You were speaking of the church."

"And the church and Christianity are one and the same of course." Again with a touch of sarcasm, more pronounced, "You will tell me next, I suppose, that a minister really ministers."

Dan was astonished and hurt. He had learned much of the spirit of Christianity in his backwoods home, but he knew nothing of churches except that which the school had taught him. He had accepted the church to which he belonged at its own valuation, highly colored by biased historians. Such words as these were to his ears little less than sacrilege. He was shocked that they should come from one whose personality and evident character had impressed him so strongly. His voice was doubtful and perplexed as be said: "But is not that true church of Christ, which is composed of his true disciples, Christian? Surely, they can no more be separated than the sun can be separated from the sunshine; and is not the ministry a vital part of that church?"

Miss Farwell, seeing him so troubled, wondered whether she understood him. She felt that she was talking too freely to this stranger, but his questions drew her on, and she was curiously anxious that he should understand her.

"I was not thinking of that true church composed of the true disciples of Christ," she returned. "And that is just it, don't you see? *This true church that is so inseparable from the religion of Christ is so far forgotten that it never enters into any thought of the church at all.* The sun always shines, it is true, but we do not always have the sunshine. There are the dark and stormy days, you know, and sometimes there is an eclipse. To me these are the dark days, so dark that I wonder sometimes if it is not an eclipse." She paused then added deliberately, "This selfish, wasteful, cruel, heartless thing that men have built up around their opinions, and whims, and ambitions, has so come between the people and the Christianity of the Christ, that they are beginning to question if, indeed, there is anywhere such a thing as the true church."

Again Dan was startled at her words and by her passionate earnestness; the more so that, in the manner of her speaking as in her words, there was an impersonal touch very unusual to those who speak on religious topics. And there was a note of sadness in her voice as well. It was as if she spoke to him professionally of the sickness of some one dear to her and sought to keep her love for her patient from influencing her calm consideration of the case.

His next words were forced from him almost against his will. And his eyes had that wide questioning look so like that of his mother. "And the ministry," he said.

She answered, "You ask if the ministry is not a vital part of the church, and your very question expresses conditions clearly. What conception of Christianity is it that makes it possible for us to even think of the ministry as a part of the church? Why, the true church is a ministry! There can be no other reason for its existence. But don't you see how we have come to think of the ministry as we have come to think of the church? It is to us, as you say, a part of this great organization that men have created and control, and in this we are right, for this church has made the minister, and this minister has in turn made the church. They are indeed inseparable."

Dan caught up a flower that she had dropped and began picking it to pieces with trembling fingers.

"To me," he said slowly, "the minister is a servant of God. I believe, of course, that whatever work a man does in life he must do as his service to the race and in that sense he serves God. But the ministry—" he reached for another flower, choosing his words carefully, "the ministry is, to me, the highest service to which a man may be called."

She did not reply but looked away over the valley.

"Tell me," he said, "is it not so?"

"If you believe it, then to you it is so," she answered.

"But you—" he urged, "how do you look upon the minister?"

"Why should I tell you? What difference does it make what I think? You forget that we are strangers." She smiled. "Let us talk about the weather; that's a safe topic."

"I *had* forgotten that we are strangers," he said, with an answering smile. "But I am interested in what you have said because you—you have evidently thought much upon the matter, and your profession must certainly give you opportunities for observation. Tell me, how do you look upon the minister and his work?"

She studied him intently before she answered. Then—as if satisfied with what she found in his face, she said calmly: "To me he is the most useless creature in all the world. He is a man set apart from all those who live lives of service, who do the work of the world. And then that he should be distinguished from these world-workers, these servers, by this noblest of all titles—*a minister,* is the bitterest irony that the mind of the race ever conceived."

Her companion's face was white now as he answered quickly, "But surely a minister of the gospel is doing God's will and is therefore serving God."

She answered as quickly, "Man serves God only by serving men. There can be no ministry but the ministry of man to man."

"But the minister is a man."

"The world cannot accept him as such, because his individuality is lost in the church to which he belongs. Other institutions employ a man's time, the church employs his life; he has no existence outside his profession. There is no outside the church for him. The world cannot know him as a man, for he is all preacher."

"But the church employs him to minister to the world?"

"I cannot see that it does so at all. On the contrary a church employs a pastor to serve itself. To the churches Christianity has become a question of fidelity to a church and creed and not to the spirit of Christ. The minister's standing and success in his calling, the amount of his salary, even, depends upon his devotion to the particular views of the church that calls him and his ability to please those who pay him for pleasing them. His service to the world does not enter into the transaction any more than when you buy the latest novel of your favorite author, or purchase a picture that pleases you, or buy a ticket to hear your favorite musician. We do not pretend, when we do these things that we are ministering to the world, or that we are moved to spend our money thus to serve God, even though there may be in the book, the picture, or the music, many things that will make the world better."

The big fellow moved uneasily.

"But" he urged, eagerly, "the church is a sacred institution. It is not to be compared to the institutions of men. Its very purpose is so holy, so different from other organizations."

"Which of the hundreds of different sects with their different creeds do you mean by the church?" she asked quickly. "Or do you mean all? And if all are equally sacred, with the same holy purpose, why are they at such variance with each other and why is there such useless competition between them? How are these institutions—organized and controlled, as they are, by men, different from other institutions, organized and controlled by the same men? Surely you are aware that there are thousands of institutions and organizations in the world with aims as distinctly Christian as the professed object of the church. Why are these not as holy and sacred?"

"But the church is of divine origin."

"So is this tree; so is the material in that old building; so are those farms yonder. To me it is only the spirit of God in a thing that can make it holy or sacred. Surely there is as much of God manifest in a field of grain as in any of these churches; why, then, is not a corn field a holy institution and why not the farmer who tends the field, a minister of God?"

"You would condemn then everyone in the church?" he asked bitterly. "I cannot think that—I know—" he paused.

"Condemn?" she answered questioningly, "I condemn?" Those deep gray eyes were turned full upon him, and he saw her face grow tender and sad, while the sweet voice trembled with emotion. "Who spoke of condemnation? Is that just the question? Are you not unfair? In my—" she spoke the words solemnly, "my ministry, I have stood at the bedside of too many heroes and heroines not to know that the church is filled with the truest and bravest. And that—Oh! don't you see—that is the awful pity of it all. That those true, brave, noble lives should be the—the cloud that hides the sun? As for the ministry, one in my profession could scarcely help knowing the grand lives that are hidden in this useless class set apart by the church to push its interests. The ministers are useless only because they are not free. They cannot help themselves. They are slaves, not servants. Their first duty is, not service to the soul-sick world that so much needs their ministry, but obedience to the whims of this hideous monster that they have created and now must obey or—" she paused.

"Or what?" he said.

She continued as if she had not heard: "They are valued for their fidelity to other men's standards, never for the worth of their own lives. They are hired to give always the opinions of others, and they are denied the only thing that can make any life of worth—freedom of self-expression. The surest road to failure for them is to hold or express opinions of their own. They are held, not as necessities, but as a luxury, like heaven itself, for which if men have the means to spare, they pay. They can have no real fellowship with the servants of the race, for they are set apart by the church not to a ministry but from it. Their very personal influence is less than the influence of other good men because the world accepts it as professional. It is the way they earn their living."

"But do you think that the ministers themselves wish to be so set apart?" asked Dan. "I—I am sure they must all crave that fellowship with the workers."

"I think that is true," she answered. "I am sure it is of the many grand, good men in the ministry whom I have known."

"Oh," he said quickly, "then there are good men in the ministry?"

"Yes," she retorted, "just as there are gold and precious stones ornamenting heathen gods and pagan temples, and their goodness is as useless. For whether they wish it or not the facts remain that their masters set them apart and that they are separated, and I notice that most of them accept gracefully the special privileges, and wear the title and all the marks of their calling that emphasize the distinction between them and their fellow men."

"Yet you wear a distinguishing dress," he said. "I knew your calling the first time I saw you."

She laughed merrily.

"Well what amuses you?" he demanded, smiling himself at her merriment.

"Oh, it's so funny to see such a big man so helpless. Really couldn't you find an argument of more weight? Besides you didn't know my profession the first time you saw me. I only wear these clothes when I am at work, just as a mechanic wears his overalls—and they are just as necessary, as you know. The first time you—you bumped into me, I dressed like other people and I had paid full fare, too. Nurses don't get clergy credentials from the railroad."

With this she sprang to her feet. "Look how long the shadows are! I must go right back to my patient this minute."

As she spoke she was all at once painfully conscious again that this man was a stranger. What must he think of her? How could she explain that it was not her habit to talk thus freely to men whom she did not know? She wished that he would tell her his name at least.

Slowly—silently they walked together across the weed-grown yard. As they passed through the gap in the tumble-down fence, Dan turned to look back. It seemed to him ages since he had entered the yard.

"What's the matter, have you lost something?" she asked.

"No—that is—I—perhaps I have. But never mind, it is of no great importance, and anyway I could not find it. I think I will say good-bye now," he added. "I'm not going to town just yet."

Again she wondered at his face, it was so troubled.

He watched her down the street until her blue dress, with its white trimming became a blur in the shadows. Then he struck out once more for the open country.

CHAPTER XI.

REFLECTIONS.

> "And gradually, out of the material of his school experience, he built again the old bulwark, behind which he could laugh at his confusion of the hour before."

Since that first chance meeting at the depot when he had looked into the nurse's eyes and heard her voice only for a moment, Dan had not been able to put the young woman wholly out of his mind. The incident on the street when she had gone to Denny, and the scene that followed in Denny's home had strengthened the first impression, while the meeting at the old Academy yard had stirred depths in his nature never touched before. The very things she had said to him were so evidently born out of a nature great in its passion for truth and in its capacity for feeling that, even though her words were biting and stung, he could not but rejoice in the beauty and strength of the spirit they revealed.

The usual trite criticisms of the church Dan had heard, and had already learned to think somewhat lightly of the kind of people who commonly make them. But this young woman—so wholesome, so good to look at in her sweet seriousness, so strong in her womanliness and withal so useful in what she called her ministry—this woman was—well, she was different.

Her words were all the more potent, coming as they did after the disquieting thoughts and the feeling of dissatisfaction that had driven him from his study that afternoon. The young minister could not at first rid himself of the hateful suggestion that there might be much truth in the things she had said. After all under the fine words, the platitudes and the professions, the fact remained he *was* earning his daily bread by being obedient to those who hired him. He had already begun to feel that his work was not so much to give what he could to meet the people's need as to do what he could to supply the wants of Memorial Church, and that his very chance to serve depended upon his satisfying these self-constituted judges. He saw too, that these same judges, his masters, felt the dignity of their position heavily upon them, and would not be in the least backward about rendering their decision.

They would let him know what things pleased them and what things were not to their liking. Their opinions and commandments would not always be in definite words, perhaps, but they would be none the less clearly and forcibly given for all that.

He had spoken truly when he had told Miss Farwell, as they parted, that he had lost something. And now, as he walked the country road, he sought earnestly to regain it; to find again his certainty of mind; to steady his shaken confidence in the work to which he had given his life.

Dan's character was too strong, his conviction too powerful, his purpose too genuine, for him to be easily turned from any determined line of thought or action. Certainly it would require more than the words of a stranger to swing him far from his course, even though he felt that there might be a degree of truth in them. And so, as he walked, his mind began shaping answers to the nurse's criticism and gradually, out of the material of his school experience, he built again the old bulwark, behind which he could laugh at his confusion of the hour before.

But withal Dan's admiration of the young woman's mind and character was not lessened. More, he felt that she had in some way given him a deeper view into her life and thoughts than was due a mere stranger. He was conscious, too, of a sense of shame that he had, in a way, accepted her confidence under false pretense. He had let her believe he was not what he was. But, he argued with himself, he had not intentionally deceived her and he smiled at last to think how she would enjoy the situation with him when she learned the truth.

How different she was from any of the women he had known in the church! They mostly accepted their religious views as they would take the doctor's prescription—without question.

And how like she was to his mother!

Then came the inevitable thought—what a triumph it would be if he could win such a character to the church. What an opportunity! Could he do it? He must.

With that the minister began putting his thoughts in shape for a sermon on the ministry. Determined to make it the effort of his life, he planned how he would announce it next Sunday for the following week, and how, with Dr. Harry's assistance, he would perhaps secure her attendance at the service.

Meanwhile Hope Farwell passing quickly along the village street on her way home from the old Academy yard, was beset by many varied and conflicting emotions. Recalling her conversation with the man who was to her so nearly a total stranger, she felt that she had been too earnest, too frank. It troubled her to think how she had laid bare her deepest feelings. She could not understand how she had so far forgotten her habitual reserve. There was a something in that young man, so tall and strong, and withal so clean looking, that had called from her, in spite of herself, this exposition of her innermost life and thoughts. She ought not to have yielded so easily to the subtle demand that he—unconsciously no doubt—had made.

It was as though she had flung wide open the door to that sacred, inner chamber at which only the most intimate of her friends were privileged to knock. He had come into the field of her life in the most commonplace manner—through the natural incident of their meeting. He should have stopped there, or should have been halted by her. The hour should have been spent in conversation on such trivial and commonplace topics as usually occupy strangers upon such occasions, and they should have parted strangers still. She felt that after this exhibition of herself, as she termed it in her mind, she at least was no stranger to him. And she was angry with herself, and ashamed, when she reflected how deeply into her life he had entered; angry with him too, in a way, that he had gained this admittance with apparently no effort.

She reflected too, that while she had so freely opened the door to him, and had admitted him with a confidence wholly inexcusable, he had in no way returned that confidence. She searched her memory for some word—some expression of his, that would even hint at what he thought, or believed, or was, within himself; something that would justify her in feeling that she knew him even a little. But there was nothing. It was as though this stranger, whom she had admitted into the privacy of the inner chamber, had worn mask and gown. No self-betraying expression had escaped him. He had not even told her his name. While she had laid out for his inspection the strongest passions of her life; had felt herself urged to show him all, and had kept nothing hidden. He had looked and had gone away making no comment.

"Of course," she thought, "he is a gentleman, and he is cultured and refined, and a good man too." Of this she was sure, but that was nothing. One does not talk as she had talked to a man just because he is not a ruffian or a boor. She wanted to know him as she had made herself known to him. She could not say why.

The nurse's work in Corinth was nearly finished; she would probably never meet this man again. She started at the thought. Would she ever meet him again? What did it matter? And yet—she would not confess it even to herself, but it did, somehow, seem to matter. Of one thing she was sure—he was well worth knowing. She had felt that there was a depth, a richness, a genuineness to him, and it was this feeling, this certainty of him, that had led her to such openness. Yes—she was sure there were treasures there—deep within, for those whom he chose to admit. She wished—(why should she not confess it after all)—she wished that she might be admitted.

Hope Farwell was alone in the world with no near living relatives. She had only her friends; and friends to her meant more than to those who have others dearer to them by ties of blood.

That evening when Dr. Harry was leaving the house after his visit to his patient, the nurse went with him to the door, as usual, for any word of instruction he might wish to give her privately.

"Well, Miss Hope," he said, "you've done it."

"What have I done?" she asked, startled.

"Saved my patient in there. She would have gone without a doubt, if you had not come when you did. It's your case all right." "Then I'm glad I came," she said quietly. "And I may go back soon now, may I not, Doctor?"

He hesitated, slowly drawing on his gloves.

"Must you go back Miss Farwell? I—we need you so much here in Corinth. There are so many cases you know where all depends upon the nurse. There is not a trained nurse this side of St. Louis. I am sure I could keep you busy." There was something more than professional interest in the keen eyes that looked so intently into her own.

"Thank you Doctor, you are very kind, but you know Dr. Miles expects me. He warned me the last thing before I left, that he was only lending me to you for this particular case. You know how he says those things."

"Yes," said the man grimly, "I know Miles. It is one of the secrets of his success, that he will be satisfied with nothing but the best. He warned me, too."

He watched her keenly. "It would be just like Miles," he thought, "to tell the young woman of the particular nature of the warning." But Miss Farwell betrayed no embarrassing knowledge, and the doctor said, "You did not promise to return to Chicago did you?"

She answered slowly, "No, but he expects me, and I had no thought of staying, only for this case."

"Well won't you think of it seriously? There are many nurses in Chicago. I don't mean many like you—" interrupting himself hastily—"but here there is no one at all," and in his low-spoken words there was a note of interest more than professional.

She lifted her face frankly and let him look deep into her eyes as she answered—"I appreciate your, argument, Dr. Abbott, and—I will think about it."

He turned his eyes away, and his tone was quite professional as he said heartily, "Thank you, Miss Farwell. I shall not give up hoping that we may keep you. Good night!"

"Isn't he a dear, good man?" exclaimed the invalid, as the nurse re-entered the sick room.

"Yes," she answered, "he is a good man, one of the best I think, that I have ever known."

The patient continued eagerly, "He told me the ladies could come here for their Aid Society meeting next week, if you would stay to take care of me. You will, won't you dear?"

The nurse busy with the medicine the doctor had left did not answer at once.

"I would like it so much," came the voice from the bed.

Hope turned and went quickly to her patient saying with a smile, "Of course I will stay if you wish it. I believe the meeting will do you good."

"Oh thank you, and you'll get to meet our new minister then, sure. Just to think you have never seen him, and he has called several times, but you have always happened to be out or in your room."

"Yes," said the young woman, "I have managed to miss him every time."

Something in the voice, always so kind and gentle, caused the sick woman to turn her head on the pillow and look at her nurse intently.

"And you haven't been to church, since you have been here, either."

"Oh, but you know I am like your good doctor in that, I can plead professional duties."

"Dr. Harry is always there when he can possibly go. I never thought of it before. Will you mind, dearie, if I ask you whether you are a Christian or not? I told Sapphira this afternoon that I knew you were."

"Yes," said Hope, "you are right. I cannot often go to church, but—" and there was a ring of seriousness in her voice now, "I am a Christian if trying to follow faithfully the teachings of the Christ is Christianity."

"I was sure you were," murmured the other, "Brother Matthews will be so glad to meet you. I know you will like him."

To which the nurse answered, "But you will be in no condition for the visit of the ladies, if I don't take better care of you now. Did you know that you were going to sleep? Well you are. You have had a busy day, and you are not to speak another word except 'good night.' I am going to turn the light real low—so—And now I am going to sit here and tell you about my walk. You're just to shut your eyes and listen and rest—rest—rest."

And the low, sweet voice told of the flowers and the grass and the trees, the fields lying warm in the sunlight, with the flitting cloud-shadows, and the hills stretching away into the blue, until no troubled thought was left in the mind of the sick woman. Like a child she slept.

But as the nurse talked to make her patient forget, the incident of the afternoon came back, and while the sick woman slept, Hope Farwell sat going over again in her mind the conversation on the grassy knoll in the old Academy yard, recalling every word, every look, every expression. What was his work in life? He was no idler, she was sure. He had the air of a true worker, of one who was spending his life to some purpose. She wondered again at the expression on his face as she had seen it when they parted. Should she go back to the great city and lose herself in her work, or—she smiled to herself—should she yield to Dr. Abbott's argument and stay in Corinth a little longer?

CHAPTER XII.

THE NURSE FORGETS.

"He seemed so made for fine and strong things."

The affairs of Memorial Church were booming.

Or, in the more orthodox language of Elder Jordan, in an article to the official paper of the denomination, "the congregation had taken on new life, and the Lord's work was being pushed with a zeal and determination never before equaled. The audiences were steadily increasing. The interest was reviving in every department, and the world would soon see grand old Memorial Church taking first place in Corinth, if not in the state. Already Reverend Matthews had been asked to deliver a special sermon to the L. M. of J. B.'s, who would attend the service in a body, wearing the full regalia of the order. Surely God had abundantly blessed the brethren in sending them such an able preacher."

The week following Dan's talk with Miss Farwell in the old Academy yard, the ladies of the Aid Society assembled early, and in unusual numbers, for their meeting at the home of Judge Strong. As the announcement from the pulpit had it—there was business of great importance to transact; also there was work on hand that must be finished.

The business of importance was the planning of a great entertainment to be given in the opera house, by local talent, both in and out of the church, for the purpose of raising money that the church still owed their former pastor. The unfinished work was a quilt of a complicated wheel pattern. Every spoke of each wheel contained the name of some individual who had paid ten cents for the honor. The hubs cost twenty-five cents. When finished this "beautiful work of the Lord" (they said their work was the Lord's work) was to be sold to the highest bidder; thereby netting a sum of money for the pulpit furniture fund, nearly equal to the cost to anyone of the leading workers, for the society's entertainment, in a single afternoon or evening, for what would appear in the Sunday issue of the Daily Corinthian as a "social event."

It must not be understood that all the women enrolled as members of Dan's congregation belonged to the Ladies' Aid. Only the workers were active in that important part of the "Body of Christ." Many there were in the congregation, quiet, deeply—truly—religious souls, who had not the time for this service, but in the scheme of things as they are, those were not classed as active members. They were not of the inner circle on the inside. They were reckoned as counting only on the roll of membership. But it was the strength, the soul, the ruling power, the spirit of this Temple of God that assembled that afternoon at Judge Strong's big, brown house, on Strong Avenue, just beyond Strong Memorial Church.

The Ally came also. The Ally, it is said, never misses a Ladies' Aid meeting in Corinth.

Miss Farwell was there with her patient as she had promised, and Mrs. Strong took particular care that as fast as they arrived each one of her guests met the young woman. To some—women of the middle class—the trained nurse, in her blue dress with white cap and apron, was an object of unusual interest. They did not know whether to rank her with servants, stenographers, sales-ladies or teachers. But the leading ladies (see the Daily Corinthian) were very sure of themselves. This young woman worked for wages in the homes of people, waited on people; therefore she was a working girl—a servant.

No one wasted much time with the stranger. The introduction was acknowledged with a word or a cool nod and an unintelligible murmur of something that meant nothing, or—worse—with a patronizing air, a sham cordiality elaborately assumed, which said plainly "I acknowledge the introduction here, because this is the Lord's business. You will be sure please, that you make no mistake should we chance to meet again." And immediately the new arrival would produce the modern weapon of the Christian warfare, needle, thread and thimble; and—hurrying to the side of some valiant comrade of her own set—join bravely in the fray.

That quilt was attacked with a spirit that was worth at least a half column in the denominational weekly, while the sound of the conflict might almost have been heard as far as Widow Mulhall's garden where Denny was cheerily digging away, with his one good side, while the useless, crippled arm swung from the twisted shoulder.

To Miss Farwell sitting quietly—unobserved, but observing—there came a confused sound of many voices speaking at once, with now and then a sentence in a tone stronger than the common din.

"She said the Memorial Church didn't believe in the Spirit anyhow, and that all we wanted was to get 'em in ... I told them that Brother Matthews would surely be getting some of their folks before the year was out, if they kept on coming to our services ... I says, says I—'Brother Matthews never said that; you'd better read your Bible. If you can show me in the Book where you get your authority for it, I'll quit the Memorial Church right then and join yours' ... Yes, all their people were out ... Sure, he's their church clerk. I heard him say with my own ears that Brother Matthews was the biggest preacher that had ever been in Corinth ... I'll venture that sermon next Sunday on 'The Christian Ministry' will give them something to think about. The old Doctor never misses a service now. Wouldn't it be great if we was to get him? Wasn't that solo the sweetest thing? Wish he would join; we'd be sure of him then ... They would like mighty well to get him away from us if they could. He'll stay fast enough as long as Charity plays the organ!"

There was a laugh at this last from a group near the window and Miss Charity blushed as she answered, "I've worked hard enough to get him, and I certainly intend to keep him if I can! I've been urging all the girls to be particularly nice to him."

Someone nearer to Miss Farwell said, in low tone—"Of course there's nothing in it. Charity's just keeping him in the choir. She wouldn't think of anyone but the preacher. I tell you if Brother Matthews knows what's best for him, he won't miss that chance. I guess if the truth was known old Nathan's about the best fixed of anyone in Corinth."

Sometimes a group would put their heads closer together and by the quick glances in her direction the nurse felt that she was contributing her full share to the success of the meeting. On one of these occasions she turned her back on the company to speak a few words to her patient who was sitting in an easy chair a little apart from the circle.

The invalid's face was all aglow. "Isn't it fine!" she said. "I feel as if I had been out of the world. It's so kind of these dear sisters to have the meeting here today so that I could look on. It's so good of you too, dear, to stay so they could come." She laughed. "Do you know, I think they're all a little bit afraid of you."

The nurse smiled and was about to reply when there was a sudden hush in the room and her patient whispered excitedly, "He's come! Now you'll get to meet our minister!"

Mrs. Strong's voice in the hall could be heard greeting the new arrival, and answering her the deeper tones of a man's voice.

Miss Farwell started. Where had she heard that voice before? Then she felt him enter the room and heard the ladies greeting him. Something held her from turning and she remained with her back to the company, watching her patient's face, as the eyes of the invalid followed the minister about the room.

Charity alone was noting the young woman's too obvious lack of interest.

The hum had already commenced again when Mrs. Strong's hand was placed lightly on the nurse's arm.

"Miss Farwell, I want you to meet our minister, Reverend Matthews."

There was an amused smile on Dan's face as he held out his hand. "I believe Miss Farwell and I have met before."

But the young woman ignored the out-stretched hand, and her voice had an edge, as she answered, "It is possible sir. I am forced to meet so many strangers in my profession, you know, but I—I have forgotten you."

Charity was still watching suspiciously. At the minister's words she started and a touch of color came into her pale cheeks, while at Miss Farwell's answer the look of suspicion in her eyes deepened. What could it mean?

Dan's embarrassment was unmistakable. Before he could find words to reply, the sick woman exclaimed, "Why, how strange! Do tell us about it, Brother Matthews. Was it here in Corinth?"

In a flash the minister saw his predicament. If he said he had met the young lady in Corinth they would know that it was impossible that she should have literally forgotten him. He understood the meaning of her words. These women would give them a hundred meanings. If he admitted that he was wrong and that he had not met her, there was always the chance of the people learning of that hour spent on the Academy grounds.

Meanwhile the young woman made him understand that she realized the difficulties of his position, and all awaited his next words with interest. Looking straight into her eyes he said, "I seem to have made a mistake. I beg your pardon, Miss Farwell."

She smiled. It was almost as good as if he had deliberately lied, but it was the best he could do.

"Please do not mention it," she returned, with a meaning for him alone. "I am sorry that I will not be here next Sunday to hear your sermon on 'The Christian Ministry!' So many have urged me to attend. There is no doubt it will be interesting."

"You are leaving Corinth, then?" he asked.

At the same moment her patient and Mrs. Strong exclaimed, "Oh Miss Hope, we thought you had decided to stay. We can't let you go so soon."

She turned from the man to answer the invalid.

"Yes I must go. I did not know the last time we talked it over, but something has happened since that makes it necessary. I shall leave tomorrow. And now, if you will excuse me please, I will run away for a few moments to get my things together. You are doing so nicely, you really don't need me at all, and there is no reason why I should stay longer—now that I have met the minister." She bowed slightly to Dan and slipped from the room.

The women looked significantly at one another, and the minister too came in for his full share of the curious glances. There was something in the incident that they could not understand and because Dan was a man they naturally felt that he was somehow to blame. It was not long until Charity, under the pretext of showing him a sacred song which she had found in one of Mrs. Strong's books, led him to another room, away from the curious crowd.

All the week Dan had looked forward to this meeting of the Ladies' Aid

Society for he knew that he would see the nurse again. Charmed by the young woman's personality and mind, and filled with his purpose to win her to the church, he was determined, if chance did not bring it about, to seek another opportunity to talk with her. He had smiled often to himself, at what he thought would be a good joke between them, when she came to know of his calling. Like many such jokes it was not so funny after all. Instead of laughing with him she had given him to understand that the incident was closed, that there must be no attempt on his part to continue the acquaintance—that, indeed, she would not acknowledge that she had ever met him, and that she was so much in earnest that she was leaving Corinth the next day because of him.

"Really, Brother Matthews, if I have offended you in any way, I am very sorry." Dan awoke with a start. He and Charity were alone in the room. From the open door, came the busy hum of the workers in the Master's vineyard.

"I beg your pardon, what were you saying?" he murmured.

"I have asked you three times if you liked the music last Sunday."

Apologizingly he answered, "Really I am not fit company for anyone today."

"I noticed that you seemed troubled. Can I help you in any way? Is it the church?" she asked gently.

He laughed, "Oh no, it's nothing that anyone can help. It's myself. Please don't bother about it. I believe if you will excuse me, and make my excuses to the ladies in there, I will go. I really have some work to do."

She was watching his face so closely that she had not noticed the nurse who passed the window and entered the garden. Dan rose to his feet as he spoke.

"Why, Brother Matthews, the ladies expect you to stay for their business meeting, you know. This is very strange."

"Strange! There is nothing strange about it. I have more important matters that demand my attention—that is all. It is not necessary to interrupt them now, you can explain when the business meeting opens. They would excuse me I am sure, if they knew how important it was." And before poor Charity had time to fairly grasp the situation he was gone, slipping into the hall for his hat, and out by a side door.

Miss Farwell from meeting the minister, had gone directly to her room, but she could not go about her packing. Dropping into a chair by the window she sat staring into the tops of the big maples. She did not see the trees. She saw a vast stretch of rolling country, dotted with farm-buildings and stacks, across which the flying cloud-shadows raced, a weed-grown yard with a gap in the tumble-down fence, an old deserted school building, and a big clean-looking man standing, with the sun-light on his red-brown hair.

"And he—he was that." She had thought him something so fine and strong. He seemed so made for fine and strong things. And he had let her go on—leading her to talk as she would have talked only to intimate friends who would understand. She had so wanted him to understand. And then he had thought it all a joke! The gray eyes filled with angry tears, and the fine chin quivered. She sprang to her feet. "I won't!" she said aloud, "I won't!"

Why should she indeed think a second time of this stranger—this preacher? The room seemed close. She felt that she could not stay another minute in the house, with those people down stairs. Catching up a book, she crept down the back way and on out to a vine covered arbor that stood in a secluded corner of the garden.

Miss Farwell had been in her retreat but a few minutes when the sound of a step on the gravel walk startled her. Then the doorway was darkened by a tall, broad-shouldered figure, and a voice said, "May I come in?"

The gray eyes flashed once in his direction. Then she calmly opened her book, without a further glance, or a sign to betray her knowledge of his presence.

"May I come in?" he asked again.

She turned a page seeming not to hear.

Once more the man repeated the same words slowly—sadly.

The young woman turned another page of her book.

Then suddenly the doorway was empty. She rose quickly from her place and started forward. Then she stopped.

Charity met him on his way to the gate.

"Have you finished that important business so soon?" she asked sharply. Then with concern at the expression of his face she exclaimed, "Tell me, won't you, what is the matter!"

He tried to laugh and when he spoke, his voice was not his voice at all.

The daughter of the church turned to watch her minister as he passed through the gate, out of the yard and down the street. Then she went slowly down the path to the arbor, where she found a young woman crouched on the wooden bench weeping bitter tears;—a book on the floor at her feet.

Quickly Charity drew back. Very quietly she went down the walk again. And as she went, she seemed all at once to have grown whiter and thin and old.

CHAPTER XIII.

DR. HARRY'S CASE.

"'Whatever or whoever is responsible for the existence of such people and such conditions is a problem for the age to solve. The fact is, they are here.'"

The meeting of the Ladies' Aid adjourned and its members, with sighs and exclamations of satisfaction over work well done, separated to go to their homes—where there were suppers to prepare for hungry husbands, and children of the flesh.

Thus always in the scheme of things as they are, the duties of life conflict with the duties of religion. The faithful members of Memorial Church were always being interrupted in their work for the Lord by the demands of the world. And as they saw it, there was nothing for them to do but to bear their crosses bravely. What a blessed thought it is that God understands many things that are beyond our ken!

The whistles blew for quitting time. The six o'clock train from the West pulled into the yards, stopped—puffing a few moments at the water tank—and thundered on its way again. On the street, business men and those who labored with their hands hurried from the scenes of their daily toil, while the country folk untied their teams and saddle-horses from the hitch-racks to return to their waiting families and stock on the distant farms.

A few miles out on the main road leading northward the home-going farmers passed a tired horse hitched to a dusty, mud-stained top-buggy, plodding steadily toward the village. Without exception they hailed the driver of the single rig heartily. It was Dr. Harry returning from a case in the backwoods country beyond Hebron.

The deep-chested, long-limbed bay, known to every child for miles around, was picking her own way over the country roads, for the lines hung slack. Without a hint from her driver the good horse slowed to a walk on the rough places and quickened her pace again when the road was good, and of her own accord, turned out for the passing teams. The man in the buggy returned the greetings of his friends mechanically, scarcely noticing who they were.

It was Jo Mason's wife this time. Jo was a good fellow but wholly incapable of grasping, single-handed, the problem of daily life for himself and brood. There were ten children in almost as many years. Understanding so little of life's responsibilities the man's dependence upon his wife was pitiful, if not criminal. With tears streaming down his lean, hungry face he had begged, "Do somethin', Doc! My God Almighty, you jest got to do some-thin'!"

For hours Dr. Harry had been trying to do something. Out there in the woods, in that wretched, poverty-stricken home, with only a neighbor woman of the same class to help he had been fighting a losing fight.

And now while the bay mare was making her tired way home he was still fighting—still trying to do something. His professional knowledge and experience told him that he could not win; that, at best, he could do no more than delay his defeat a few days, and his common sense urged him to dismiss the case from his mind. But there was something in Dr. Harry stronger than his common sense; something greater than his professional skill. And so he must go on fighting until the very end.

It was nearly twilight when he reached the edge of the hill on the farther side of the valley. He could see the lights of the town twinkling against the dark mass of tree and hill and building, while on the faintly-glowing sky the steeple of Memorial Church, the cupola of the old Academy building, and the court-house tower were cut in black. Down into the dusk of the valley the bay picked her way, and when they had gained the hill on the edge of town it was dark. Now the tired horse quickened her pace, for the home barn and Uncle George were not far away. But as they drew near the big brown house of Judge Strong, she felt the first touch of the reins and came to a walk, turning in to the familiar hitching post with reluctance.

At that moment a tall figure left the Judge's gate to pass swiftly down the street in the dusk.

Before the bay quite came to a stop at the post her master's hand turned her head into the street again, and his familiar voice bade her, somewhat sharply, to "go on!" In mild surprise she broke into a quick trot. How was the good horse to know that her driver's impatience was all with himself, and was caused by seeing his friend, the minister coming—as he thought—from the Strong mansion? Or how was Dr. Harry to know that Dan had only paused at the gate as if to enter, and had passed on when he saw the physician turning in?

Farther down the street at the little white cottage near the monument, the bay mare was pulled again to a walk, and this time she was permitted to turn in to the curb and stop.

The old Doctor was sitting on the porch. "Hello!" he called cheerily, "Come in."

"Not tonight, thank you Doctor, I can't stop," answered the younger man. At his words the old physician left his chair and came stiffly down the walk to the buggy. When he was quite close, with one hand grasping the seat, Dr. Harry said in a low tone, "I'm just in from Mason's."

"Ah huh," grunted the other. Then inquiringly—"Well?"

"It's—it's pretty bad Doctor."

The old man's voice rumbled up from the depth of his chest, "Nothing to do, eh? You know I told you it was there. Been in her family way back. Seen it ever since she was a girl."

"Yes I knew it was of no use, of course. But you know how it is, Doctor."

The white head nodded understandingly as Dr. Harry's hand was slowly raised to his eyes.

"Yes I know Harry. Jo take it pretty bad?"

"Couldn't do anything with, him, poor fellow, and those children, too—"

Both men were silent. Slowly the younger man took up the reins. "I just stopped to tell you, Doctor."

"Ah huh. Well, you go home and rest. Get a good night whatever you do. You'll have to go out again, I suppose. Call me if anything turns up; I'm good for a little yet. You've got to get some rest, Harry, do you hear?" he spoke roughly.

"Thank you, Doctor. I don't think I will need to disturb you, though; everybody else is doing nicely. I can't think of anything that is likely to call me out."

"Well, go to bed anyway."

"I will, good night, Doctor."

"Good night, Harry."

The mare trotted on down the dark street, past the twinkling lights. The Doctor stood by the curb until he heard the buggy wheels rattle over the railroad tracks, then turned to walk stiffly back to his seat on the porch.

Soon the tired horse was in the hands of old Uncle George, while Mam Liz ministered to the weary doctor. The old black woman lingered in the dining room after serving his dinner, hovering about the table, calling his attention to various dishes, watching his face the while with an expression of anxiety upon her own wrinkled countenance. At last Harry looked up at her with a smile.

"Well Mam Liz, what is it? Haven't I been good today?"

"No sah. Mars Harry yo ain't. Yo been plumb bad, an' I feel jest like I uster when yo was er little trick an' I tuk yo 'cross my knee an' walloped yo good."

"Why, Mammy, what have I done now? Wasn't that new dress what you wanted? You can change it, you know, for anything you like."

"Law, chile, 'tain't *me*. Yo ole Mammy mighty proud o' them dress goods—they's too fine fo ole nigger like me. 'Tain't nothin' yo done to other folks, Mars Harry. Hit's what yo all's doin' to yoself." A tear stole down the dusky cheek. "Think I can't see how yo—yo plumb tuckered out? Yo ain't slep in yo bed fo three nights 'ceptin' jest fo a hour one mo'nin' when other folks was er gettin' up, an' only the Good Lawd knows when yo eats."

The doctor laughed. "There, there Mammy, you can see me eating now all right can't you?" But the old woman shook her head mournfully.

Harry continued, "One of your dinners, you know, is worth at least six of other folks' cooking. Fact—" he added grimly, "I believe I might safely say a dozen." Then he gave her a laughing description of his attempt to cook breakfast for himself and the ten children at the Masons that morning.

The old woman was proudly indignant, "Dem po'r triflin' white trash! To think o' yo' doin' that to sech as them! Ain't no sense 'tall in sech doin's, no how, Mars Harry. What right dey got to ax yo', any how? Dey shore ain't got no claim on yo'—an' yo' ain't got no call to jump every time sech as them crooks they fingers."

Dr. Harry shook his head solemnly.

"Now Mam Liz, I'm afraid you're an aristocrat."

"Cos I's a 'ristocrat. Ain't I a Abbott? Ain't I bo'n in de fambly in yo' grandaddy's time—ain't I nuss yo' Pa an' yo? 'Ristocrat! Huh! Deed I is. No sah, Mars Harry, yo' ought to know, yo ain't got no call to sarve sech as them!"

"I don't know," he returned slowly, "I'm afraid I have."

"Have what?"

"A call to serve such as them." He repeated her words slowly. "I don't know why they are, or how they came to be. Whatever or whoever is responsible for the existence of such people and such conditions is a problem for the age to solve. The fact is, they are here. And while the age is solving the problem, I am sure that we as individuals have a call to personally minister to their immediate needs." The doctor had spoken half to himself, following a thought that was often in his mind.

It was a little too much for the old servant. She watched him with a puzzled expression on her face.

"Talkin' 'bout ministers, de Pa'son was here to see yo' yest'day evenin'."

"Brother Matthews? I am sorry I was not at home."

"Yes sah, I was sorry too; he's a right pious-lookin' man, he sho is. I don tole him de Lawd only knowed whar yo' was or when yo'd git back. He laughed an' says he sho de Lawd wasn't far away wherever yo' was, an' that I mus' tell yo' hit was only a little call, nothin' of impo'tance—so's yo wouldn't bother 'bout it, I reckon."

Dr. Harry rose from the table. "Perhaps he will run in this evening. No, this is prayer meeting night. Heigh-ho!" He stretched his tired body—"I ought—"

The old woman interrupted him. "Now look a here Mars Harry, yo' ain't goin' to leave this yer house tonight. Yo' goin' jest put on yo' slippa's an' jacket an' set down in thar an' smoke yo' pipe a lille an' then yo' goin' to bed. Yo' ain't et 'nough to keep er chicken 'live, an' yo' eyes like two holes burned in er blanket. Won't yo' stop home an' res', honey?" she coaxed, following him into the hall. "Yo' plumb tuckered."

The weary physician looked through the door into the library where the lamp threw a soft light over the big table. The magazines and papers lay unopened, just as they had been brought from the office by Uncle George. A book that for a month, Harry had been trying to read, was lying where he had dropped it to answer a call. While he hesitated, the old negro came shuffling in with the doctor's smoking jacket and slippers.

"Yes sah, here dey is—an' de mare's all right—ain't hurted a bit—takin' her feed like er good one. Oh, I tell yo' der ain't no betta on de road dan her."

Dr. Harry laughed. "Uncle George, I give you my honest professional opinion—Mother Eve was sure a brunette." As he spoke he slipped out of his coat and Mam Liz took it from his hand, while Uncle George helped him into the comfortable jacket.

"He—he—he—" chuckled the old servant. "A brunette, he—he. That air's yo Liz, ol' 'oman, yo' sho brunette. Yes sah, 'pon my word, Mars Harry, I believe yo'. He—he—"

And the black woman's deep voice rolled out—"Yo' go on now—yo' two, 'tain't so—'cause Adam he sho po'r white trash. Ain't no decent colored body goin' to have no truck wid sech as him."

With the doctor's shoes in his hand the old servant stood up, "Anythin' else, sah? No? Good night, sah! Good night, Mars Harry!" They slipped noiselessly from the room.

Is there, after all, anything more beautiful in life than the ministry of such humble ones, whose service is the only expression of their love?

Many of the Master's truths have been shamefully neglected by those into whose hands they were committed. Many of His grandest lessons are ignored by His disciples, who ambitious for place and power—quarrel among themselves. Many of His noblest laws have been twisted out of all resemblance to His spirit by those who interpret them to meet the demands of their own particular sects and systems. But of all the truths the Master has given to men, none, perhaps, has been more neglected, or abused than the simple truth He illustrated so vividly when He washed His disciples' feet.

Left alone Dr. Harry picked up one magazine after another, only to turn the leaves impatiently and—after a moment—toss them aside. He glanced at his medical journal and found it dull. He took up his book only to lay it down again. Decidedly he could not read. The house with its empty rooms was so big and still. He seated himself at his piano but had scarcely touched the keys, when he rose again to go to the window.

"After all," he thought, "it would have been better to have gone to prayer meeting. I am not fit to be alone tonight. If I could only go to bed and sleep, but I feel as if I had forgotten how. Those Masons certainly got on my nerves." Indeed, the strain was plainly visible, for his face was worn and haggard. In his ears poor Jo's prayer was ringing, "Do somethin' Doc! My God Almighty, you jest got to do somethin'!"

Turning from the window the doctor's eyes fell on his medicine case, which Uncle George had brought in from the buggy and placed near the hall door.

"Why not?" he thought.

Picking up the case he went to the table, where he opened it hesitatingly.

"After all, why not?" he repeated half-aloud. "I would give it to a patient in my condition."

"But the patient wouldn't know what it was," a voice within himself answered.

"I need something. I—" his hand went out toward the case—"I have never done it before."

"You have seen others who have," said the voice again.

"This is an exceptionally trying time," he argued.

"There will be many more such times in your practice."

"But I must get some rest!" he cried, "I must!" He reached again for the open case but paused—startled by the ringing of the door-bell.

Obeying the impulse of the moment he dropped into his chair and caught up a paper.

Mam Liz's voice, in guarded tones came from the hall, "Yes marm, he's to home, but he's plumb tuckered out. Is yo' got to see him? Yo' ain't wantin' him to go out agin is yo'?"

Another voice answered, but the listening doctor could not distinguish the reply.

"Oh sho mam. Come in, come in. He's in the library."

A moment the nurse stood, hesitating, in the doorway.

Dr. Harry sprang to his feet. "Miss Farwell! I'm glad to see you. I—" Then he stopped looking at her in astonishment.

Very softly she closed the door behind her, and—going to the table—closed the medicine case. Then lifting her eyes to him with a meaning look she said simply, "I am glad, too."

He turned his face away. "You—you saw?"

"The window shades were up. I could not help it."

He dropped into the chair. "I'm a weak fool, Miss Farwell. No man in my profession has a right to be so weak."

"Yes, that's it," she said gently. "Your profession—those who depend upon you for their own lives and the lives of their dear ones—you must remember that always. Your ministry."

He raised his face and looked at her squarely. "I never did this before. You believe me, Miss Farwell, that this is the first time?"

She returned his look frankly. "Yes," she said. "I believe you, and I believe it will be the last."

And it was.

For there was something in that voice, something in the calm still depth of those gray eyes that remained with Dr. Harry Abbott and whenever afterwards he reached the limit of his strength, whenever he gave so much of himself in the service of others that there was nothing left for himself—this incident came back to him, that something held him—kept him strong.

Very quickly the nurse changed the subject and led the physician's mind away from the sadness and horror of his work that had so nearly wrought such havoc. The big empty house no longer seemed so big and empty. She made him light his pipe again and soon the man felt his tired nerves relax while the weary brain ceased to hammer away at the problems it could not solve.

Then at last she told him why she had come—to bid him good-bye.

"But I thought you were going to stay!" he cried.

"I had thought of doing so," she admitted. "But something—something makes it necessary for me to go."

His arguments and pleadings were in vain. Her only answer was, "I cannot, Dr. Abbott, truly I cannot." Nor would she tell him more than that it was necessary for her to go.

"But we need you so. I need you; there is no one can take your place—Hope—" Then he stopped.

She was frankly permitting him to look deep into her eyes. "I am sorry, Doctor, but I must go." And the strength of her held him and made him strong.

"Just one thing, Miss Farwell. You are not going because of—because of me?"

She held out her hand. "No indeed, Doctor. Whatever you think, please don't think that."

He would have accompanied her home but she would not permit it and insisted so strongly that he retire at once, that he was forced to yield. But he would not say good-bye, declaring that he would be at the depot in the morning to see her off.

Mrs. Oldham, coming home from prayer meeting, found her husband still sitting on the porch. When she could not force him to listen to reason and go to bed, she left him to his thoughts. A little later the old Doctor saw the tall form of the minister turn in at the gate opposite. Then the light in the corner window flashed brightly. A few moments more, and he saw a woman coming down the street, going toward Judge Strong's. Nearing the house across the way, she slackened her pace, walking very slowly. Under the corner window she almost stopped. As she went on she turned once to look back, then disappeared under the trees in the dusk.

It was almost morning when Miss Farwell was awakened by a loud knocking at the front door. Then Mrs. Strong came quickly up stairs to the nurse's room. The young woman was on her feet instantly.

"That old negro of Dr. Abbott is here asking for you," explained Mrs. Strong. "He says Dr. Harry sent him and that he must see you. What in the world can it mean?"

CHAPTER XIV.

THAT GIRL OF CONNER'S.

"'You will tell the people that this poor child wanted to kill herself, and the people will call it suicide. But, by God—it's murder! Murder—I tell you!'"

Slipping into her clothing the nurse went down to the front door where Uncle George was waiting. A horse and buggy stood at the front gate.

"Evenin' mam, is yo' de nurse?" said the old negro, lifting his cap.

"Yes, I am the nurse, Miss Farwell. Dr. Abbott sent you for me?"

"'Deed he did, mam, 'deed he did—said I was to fetch yo' wid big Jim out dar. Tol' me to say hit was er'mergency case. I dunno what dat is, but dey sho needs yo' powerful bad over in Old Town—'deed dey does."

The latter part of this speech was delivered to the empty doorway. The nurse was already back in her room.

The old negro rubbed his chin with a trembling hand, as he turned with a puzzled look on his black face from the open door to the horse and buggy and back to the door again.

"Dat young 'oman run lak a scared rabbit," he muttered. "What de ole scratch I do now?"

Before he could decide upon any course of action, Miss Farwell, fully dressed was by his side again, and half way to the gate before he could get under way.

"Come," she said, "you should have been in the buggy ready to start."

"Yas'm, yas'm, comin' comin'," he answered, breaking into a trot for the rig, and climbing in by her side. "Come Jim, git! Yo' black villen, don' yo' know, dis here's er'mergency case? Yo' sho got to lay yo' laigs to de groun' dis night er yo' goin' to git left sartin! 'Mergency case!" he chuckled. "Dat mak him go, Miss. Funny I nebber knowed dat 'fore."

Sure enough, the black horse was covering the ground at a pace that fairly took Miss Farwell's breath. The quick steady beat of the iron-shod feet and the rattle of the buggy wheels echoed loudly in the gray stillness. Above the tops of the giant maples that lined the road, the nurse saw the stars paling in the first faint glow of the coming day, while here and there in the homes of some early-rising workers the lights flashed out, and the people—with the name of Dr. Harry on their lips—paused to listen to the hurried passing of big Jim.

"Can you tell me something of the case?" asked the nurse.

"Case? Oh you mean de po'r gal what tried to kill herse'f. Yes, Miss, I sho can. Yo' see hit's dis away. Hit's dat po'r Conner gal, her whose Daddy done killed Jack Mulhall, de town marshal yo' know. De Conners used to be nice folks, all 'ceptin' Jim. He drink a little sometimes, an' den he was plumb bad. Seems lak he got worse dat way. An' since dey took him off an' Mrs. Conner died de gal, she don't git 'long somehow. Since she left de hotel she's been livin' over in Old Town along some colored folks, upstairs in de old town-hall building. I knows 'bout hit 'y see, coz Liz an' me we all got friends, Jake Smith an' his folks, livin' in de same buildin', yo see. Wal, lately de gal don't 'pear to be doin' even as well as usual, an' de folks dey got plumb scared she ac' so queer like. Sometime in de night, Jake an' Mandy dey waked up hearin' a moanin' an' a cryin' in de po'r gal's room. Dey call at de door but dey ain't no answer an' so dey stan 'round for 'while 'thout knowin' what to do, till de cryin' an' screechin' gits worse, an' things 'pears to be smashin' round lak. Den Mandy say to de folks what's been waked up an' is standin' 'round de door she ain't goin' to stan dare doin' nothin' no mo', an' she fo'ce open de door an' goes in.

"Yes sah, Miss Nurse, Mandy say dat gal jest throwin' herself 'round de room an' screechin', an' Mandy grab her jest as she 'bout to jump out de winder. She won't say nothin' but how she's burnin' up an' Mandy she send Jake to me quick. I sho don' want to wake Dr. Harry, Miss coz he's done tuckered out, but I'se scared not to, coz once 'fore I didn't wake him when somebody want him an' I ain't nebber done hit no more. Go on dar, Jim. Yes sah, Mars Harry Abbott he's a debbil, Miss, when he's mad, 'deed he is, jest lak de old Mars—he's daddy. So I calls him easy-like but Lawd—he's up an' dress 'fore I can hook up big Jim here, an' we come fer Old Town on de run. Quick as he get in de room he calls out de winder fo' me to drive quick's I can to de Judge's an' fotch yo. An' dat's all I know—'ceptin' Dr. Harry say hit's a'mergency case. We most dare now. Go on Jim—go on sah!"

While the old negro was speaking the big horse was whirling them through the quiet streets of the village. As Uncle George finished they reached the top of Academy Hill, where Miss Farwell saw the old school building—ghostly and still in the mists that hung about it like a shroud, the tumble-down fence with the gap leading into the weed-grown yard, the grassy knoll and the oak—all wet and sodden now, and—below, the valley—with its homes and fields hidden in the thick fog, suggestive of hidden and mysterious depths.

"Is yo' cold, Miss? We's mos dar, now." The nurse had shivered as with a sudden chill.

Turning sharply to the north a minute later they entered the square of Old Town where a herd of lean cows were just getting up from their beds to pick a scanty breakfast from the grass that grew where once the farmer folk had tied their teams, and in front of the ruined structure that had once been the principal store of the village, a mother sow grunted to her squealing brood.

Long without touch of painter's brush, the few wretched buildings that remained were the color of the mist. To the nurse—like the fog that hid the valley—they suggested cold mysterious depths of life, untouched by any ray of promised sun. And out of that dull gray abyss a woman's voice broke sharply, on the stillness, in a scream of pain.

"Dat's her, dat's de po'r gal, now, nurse. Up dare where yo' sees dat light."

Uncle George brought the big black to a stand in front of the ancient town-hall and court-house, a two-story, frame building with the stairway on the outside. A group of negroes huddled—with awed faces—at the foot of the stairs drew back as the nurse sprang from the buggy and ran lightly up the shaky old steps. The narrow, dirty hallway was crowded with more negroes. The odor of the place was sickening.

Miss Farwell pushed her way through and entered the room where Dr. Harry, assisted by a big black woman, was holding his struggling patient on the bed. The walls and ceiling of the room—stained by the accumulated smoke of years, the rough bare floor, the window—without shade or curtain, the only furniture—a rude table and a chair or two, a little stove set on broken bricks, a handful of battered dishes and cooking utensils, a trunk, and the bed with its ragged quilts and comforts, all cried aloud the old, old familiar cry of bitter poverty.

Dr. Harry glanced up as the nurse entered.

"Carbolic acid," he said quietly, "but she didn't get quite enough. I managed to give her the antidote and a hypodermic. We better repeat the hypodermic I think."

Without a word the nurse took her place at the bedside. When the patient, under the influence of the drug, had grown more quiet, Dr. Harry dismissed the negro woman with a few kind words, and the promise that he would send for her if she could help them in any way. Then when he had sent the others away from the room and the hallway he turned to the nurse.

"Miss Farwell, I am sorry that I was forced to send for you, but you can see that there was nothing else to do. I knew you would come without loss of time, and I dared not leave her without a white woman in the room." He paused and went to the bedside. "Poor, poor little girl. She tried so hard to die, nurse; she will try again the moment she regains consciousness. These good colored people would do anything for her, but she must see one of her own race when she opens her eyes." He paused seemingly at a loss for words.

Miss Farwell spoke for the first time, "She is a good girl, Doctor? Not that it matters you know, but—"

Dr. Harry spoke positively, "Yes, she is a good girl; it is not that, nurse."

"Then how—" Miss Farwell glanced around the room. "Then why is she here?"

No one ever heard Dr. Harry Abbott speak a bitter word, but there was a strange note in his voice as he answered slowly, "She is here because there seems to be no other place for her to go. She did this because there seemed to be nothing else for her to do."

Then briefly he related the sad history of this good girl with a bad reputation. "Dr. Oldham and I tried to help her," he said, "but some ugly stories got started and somehow Grace heard them. After that she avoided us."

For a little while there was silence in the room. When Dr. Harry again turned from his patient to the nurse, Miss Farwell was busily writing upon his tablet of prescription blanks with a stub of a pencil which she had taken from her pocket. The doctor watched her curiously for a moment, then arose, and taking his hat, said briskly: "I will not keep you longer than an hour Miss Farwell. I think I know of a woman whom I can get for today at least, and perhaps by tonight we can find someone else, or arrange it somehow. I'll be back in plenty of time, so don't worry. Your train does not go until ten-thirty, you know. If the woman can't come at once, I'll ask Dr. Oldham to relieve you."

The nurse looked at him with smiling eyes, "I am very sorry, Dr. Abbott, if I am not giving satisfaction," she said.

The physician returned her look with amazement, "Not giving satisfaction! What in the world do you mean?"

"Why you seem to be dismissing me," she answered demurely. "I understood that you sent for me to take this case."

At the light that broke over his face she dropped her eyes and wrote another line on the paper before her.

"Do you mean—" he began, then he stopped.

"I mean," she answered, "that unless you send me away I shall stay on duty."

"But Dr. Miles—that case in Chicago. I understood from you that it was very important."

She smiled at him again. "There is nothing so important as the thing that needs doing now," she answered. "And," she finished slowly, turning her eyes toward the unconscious girl on the bed—"I do seem to be needed here."

"And you understand there will be no—no fees in this case?" he asked.

The color mounted to her face. "Is our work always a question of fees, Doctor? I am surprised, cannot I collect my bill when you receive yours?"

He held out his hand impulsively.

"Forgive me, Miss Farwell, but it is too good to be true. I can't say any more now. You are needed here—you cannot know how badly. I—we all need you." She gently released her hand, and he continued in a more matter-of-fact tone, "I will go now to make a call or two so that I can be with you later. Your patient will be all right for at least three hours. I'll send Uncle George with your breakfast."

"Never mind the breakfast," she said. "If you will have your man bring these things, I will get along nicely." She handed him a prescription blank. "Here is a list that Mrs. Strong will give him from my room. And here—" she gave him another blank, "is a list he may get at the grocery. And here—" she handed him the third blank, "is a list he may get at some dry goods store. I have not my purse with me so he will need to bring the bills. The merchants will know him of course—" Dr. Harry looked from the slips in his hand to the young woman.

"You must not do that, Miss Farwell. Really—"

She interrupted, "Doctor, this is my case, you know."

"It was mine first," he answered grimly.

"But Doctor—"

"Shall I send you my bill, too?" he asked.

A few moments later she heard the quick step of big Jim and the rattle of the wheels.

Two hours had passed when in response to a low knock, the nurse opened the door to find Dr. Oldham standing in the narrow hall. The old physician was breathing heavily from his effort in climbing the rickety stairs. His arms were full of roses.

Miss Farwell exclaimed with delight, "Oh Doctor, just what I was wishing for!"

"Uh huh," he grunted. "I thought so. They'll do her good. Harry told me what you were up to. Thought I better come along in case you should need any help."

He drew a chair to the bedside, while the nurse with her sleeves rolled up returned to the work which his knock at the door had interrupted.

Clean, white sheets, pillows and coverings had replaced the tattered quilt on the bed. The floor was swept. The litter about the stove was gone, and in its place was a big armful of wood neatly piled, the personal offering of Uncle George, who had returned quickly with the things for which the nurse had sent. The dirt and dust had vanished from the windows. The glaring light was softened by some sort of curtain material, that the young woman had managed to fix in place. The bare old cupboard shelves covered with fresh paper were filled with provisions, and the nurse, washing the last of the dishes and utensils, was placing them carefully in order. She finished as Dr. Oldham turned from the patient, and—throwing over the rough table a cloth of bright colors—began deftly arranging in such dishes as the place afforded, the flowers he had brought. Already the perfume of the roses was driving from the chamber that peculiar, sickening odor of poverty.

The old physician, trained by long years of service to habits of close observation, noted every detail in the changed room. Silently he watched the strong, beautifully formed young woman in the nurse's uniform, bending over his flowers, handling them with the touch of love while on her face, and in the clear gray eyes, shone the light that a few truly great painters have succeeded in giving to their pictures of the Mother Mary.

The keen old eyes under their white brows filled and the Doctor turned hastily back to the figure on the bed. A worn figure it was—thin and looking old—with lines of care and anxiety, of constant pain and ceaseless fear, of dread and hopelessness. Only a faint suggestion of youth was there, only a hint of the beauty of young womanhood that might have been; nay that would have been—that should have been.

Miss Farwell started as the old man with a sudden exclamation—stood erect. He faced the young woman with blazing eyes and quivering face—his voice shaken with passion, as he said: "Nurse, you and Harry tell me this is suicide." He made a gesture toward the still form on the bed. "You will tell the people that this poor child wanted to kill herself, and the people will call it suicide. But, by God—it's murder! Murder—I tell you! She did not want to kill herself. She wanted to live, to be strong and beautiful like you. But this community with its churches and Sunday schools and prayer meetings wouldn't let her. They denied her the poor privilege of working for the food she needed. They refused even a word of real sympathy. They hounded her into this stinking hole to live with the negroes. She may die, nurse, and if she does—as truly as there is a Creator, who loves his creatures—her death will be upon the unspeakably cruel, pious, self-worshiping, churchified, spiritually-rotten people in this town! It's *murder!* I tell you, by God—it's *murder!"* The old man dropped into his chair exhausted by his passionate outburst.

For a few moments there was no sound in the room save the heavy breathing of the physician. The nurse stood gazing at him—a look of mingled sadness and horror on her face.

Then the figure on the bed stirred. The sick girl's eyes opened to stare wildly—wonderingly, about the room. With a low word to the Doctor, Miss Farwell went quickly to her patient.

CHAPTER XV.

THE MINISTER'S OPPORTUNITY.

"He saw only the opportunity so mysteriously opened to him."

When Dan left Miss Farwell in the summer house at Judge Strong's he went straight to his room.

Two or three people whom he met on the way turned when he had passed to look back at him. Mrs. James talking over the fence with her next door neighbor, wondered when he failed to return her greeting. And Denny from his garden hailed him joyfully. But Dan did not check his pace. Reaching his own gate he broke fairly into a run, and leaping up the stairway, rushed into his room, closing and locking his door. Then he stood, breathing hard, and smiling grimly at the foolish impulse that had made him act for all the world like a thief escaping with his booty.

He puzzled over this strange feeling that possessed him, the feeling that he had taken something that did not belong to him, until the thought struck him that there might, after all, be good reason for the fancy; that it might indeed be more than a fancy.

Pacing to and fro the length of his little study he recalled every detail of that meeting in the Academy yard. And as he remembered how he had consciously refrained from making known his position to the young woman—not once, but several times when he knew that he should have spoken, and how his questions, combined with the evident false impression that his words had given her had led her to speak thoughts she would never have dreamed of expressing had she known him, the conviction grew that he had indeed—like a thief, taken something that did not belong to him. And as he realized more and more how his silence must appear to her as premeditated, and reflected how her fine nature would shrink from what she could not but view as a coarse ungentlemanly trick he grew hot with shame. No wonder, he told himself, that he had instinctively shrunk from looking into the faces of the people whom he had met and had fled to the privacy of his rooms.

Dan did not spare himself that afternoon, and yet beneath all the self scorn he felt, there was a deeper sub-conscious conviction, that he was not—at heart—guilty of the thing with which he charged himself. This very conviction, though felt but dimly, made him rage the more. He had the hopeless feeling of one caught in a trap—of one convicted of a crime of which in the eyes of the law he was guilty, but which he knew he had unwittingly committed.

The big fellow in so closely analyzing the woman's thoughts and feelings, and in taking so completely her point of view, neglected himself. He could not realize how true to *himself* he had been that afternoon, or how truly the impulse that had prompted him to deny his calling was an instinct of his own strong manhood—the instinct to be accepted or rejected for what he was within himself, rather than for the mere accident of his calling and position in life.

One thing was clear, he must see Miss Farwell again. She must listen to his explanation and apology. She must somehow understand. For apart from his interest in the young woman herself, there was that purpose of the minister to win her to the church. It was a monstrous thought that he himself should be the means of strengthening her feeling against the cause to which he had given his life. So he had gone to Judge Strong's home early that evening determined to see her. But at the gate, when he saw Dr. Harry turning in as if to stop, he had passed on in the dusk. Later at prayer meeting his thoughts were far from the subject under discussion. His own public petition was so faltering and uncertain that Elder Jordan watched him suspiciously.

It would be interesting to know just how much the interest of the man in the woman colored and strengthened the purpose of the preacher to win this soul so antagonistic to his church.

The next day, Dan was putting the finishing touches to his sermon on "The Christian Ministry" when his landlady interrupted him with the news of the attempted suicide in Old Town. Upon hearing that the girl had at one time been a member of his congregation, he went at once to learn more of the particulars from Dr. Oldham. He found his old friend who had returned from Old Town a half hour before, sitting in his big chair on the front porch gazing at the cast-iron monument across the way. To the young man's questions the Doctor returned only monosyllables or grunts and growls that might mean anything or nothing at all. Plainly the Doctor did not wish to talk. His face was dark and forbidding, and under his scowling brows, his eyes—when Dan caught a glimpse of them—were hard and fierce. The young man had never seen his friend in such a mood and he could not understand.

Dan did not know that the kind-hearted old physician had just learned from his wife that the girl with the bad reputation had called at the house to see him a few hours before she had made the attempt to end her life, and that she had been sent away by the careful Martha with the excuse that the doctor was too busy to see her. Neither could the boy know how the old man's love for him was keeping him silent lest, in his present frame of mind, he say things that would strengthen that something which they each felt had come between them.

Suddenly the Doctor turned his gaze from the monument and flashed a meaning look straight into the brown eyes of the young minister. "She was a member of your church. Why don't you go to see her? Ask the nurse if there is anything the church can do." As Dan went down the walk he added, "Tell Miss Farwell that I sent you." Then smiling grimly he growled to himself, "You'll get valuable material for that sermon on the ministry, or I miss my guess."

The nurse! The nurse! He was to see her again! The thought danced in Dan's brain. How strangely the opportunity had come. The young minister felt that the whole thing had, in some mysterious way, been planned to the end he desired. In the care that the church would give this poor girl the nurse would see how wrongly she had judged it. She would be forced to listen to him now. Surely God had given him this opportunity!

What—the poor suicide?

Oh, but Dan was not thinking of the suicide. That would come later. Just now his mind and heart were too full of his own desire to win this young woman to the church. He saw only the opportunity so mysteriously opened to him. Dan was thoroughly orthodox.

So in the brightness of the afternoon the pastor of Memorial Church went along the street that, in the gray chill of the early morning, had echoed the hurried steps of the doctor's horse. The homes—so silent when the nurse had passed on her mission—were now full of life. The big trees—dank and still then, now stirred softly in the breeze, and rang with the songs of their feathered denizens. The pale stars were lost in the infinite blue and the sunlight warmed and filled the air—flooding street and home and lawn and flower and tree with its golden beauty. At the top of Academy Hill Dan paused. For him no shroud of mist wrapped the picturesque old building; no fog of mysterious depths hid the charming landscape.

Recalling the things the nurse had said to him there under the oak on the grassy knoll, and thinking of his sermon in answer—he smiled. It was a good sermon, he thought, with honest pride—strong, logical, convincing.

And it was—*at that moment.*

With a confident stride he went on his way.

CHAPTER XVI.

DAN SEES THE OTHER SIDE.

"'What right have you, Mr. Matthews, to say that you do not understand—that you do not know? It is your business to understand—to know.'"

Miss Farwell was alone with her patient. Dr. Harry, who had returned soon after the girl regained consciousness, had gone out into the country, promising to look in again during the evening on his way home, and the old Doctor finding that there was no need for him to remain had left a few moments later.

Except to answer their direct questions the sick girl had spoken no word, but lay motionless—her face turned toward the wall. Several times the nurse tried gently to arouse her, but save for a puzzled, half-frightened, half-defiant look in the wide-open eyes, there was no response, though she took her medicine obediently. But when Miss Farwell after bathing the girl's face, and brushing and braiding her hair, dressed her in a clean, white gown, the frightened defiant look gave place to one of wondering gratitude, and a little later she seemed to sleep.

She was still sleeping when Miss Farwell, who was standing by the window watching a group of negro children playing ball in the square, saw a man approaching the group from the direction of the village. The young woman's face flushed as she recognized the unmistakable figure of the minister.

Then an angry light shone in the gray eyes, and she drew back with a low exclamation. As in evident answer to his question, a half dozen hands were pointed toward the window where she stood. Watching, she saw him coming toward the building.

His purpose was clear. What should she do? Her first angry impulse was to refuse to admit him. What right had he to attempt to see her after her so positive dismissal? Then she thought—perhaps he was coming to see the sick girl. What right had she to refuse to admit him, when it could in no way harm her patient? The room, after all, was the home of the young woman on the bed—the nurse was only there in her professional capacity.

Miss Farwell began to feel that she was playing a part in a mighty drama; that the cue had been given for the entrance of another actor. She had nothing to do with the play save to act well her part. It was not for her to arrange the lines or manage the parts of the other players. The feeling possessed her that, indeed, she had somewhere rehearsed the scene many times before. Stepping quickly to the bed she saw that her patient was still apparently sleeping. Then she stood trembling, listening to the step in the hall as Dan approached.

He knocked the second time before she could summon strength to cross the room and open the door.

"May I come in?" he asked hat in hand.

At his words—the same that he had spoken a few hours before in the garden—the nurse's face grew crimson. She made no answer, but in the eyes that looked straight into his, Dan read a question and his own face grew red as he said, "I called to see your patient. Dr. Oldham asked me to come."

"Certainly; come in." She stepped aside and the minister entered the sickroom. Mechanically, without a word she placed a chair for him near the bed, then crossed the room to stand by the window. But he did not sit down.

Presently Dan turned to the nurse. "She is asleep?" he asked in a low tone.

Miss Farwell's answer was calmly—unmistakably professional. Looking at her watch she answered, "She has been sleeping nearly two hours."

"Is there—will she recover?"

"Dr. Abbott says there is no reason why she should not if we can turn her from her determination to die."

Always Dan had been intensely in love with life. He had a strong, full-blooded young man's horror of death. He could think of it only as a fitting close to a long, useful life, or as a possible release from months of sickness and pain. That anyone young, and in good health, with the world of beauty and years of usefulness before them, with the opportunities and duties of life calling, should willfully seek to die, was a monstrous thought. After all the boy knew so little. He was only beginning to sense vaguely the great forces that make and mar humankind.

At the calm words of the nurse he turned quickly toward the bed with a shudder. "Her determination to die!" he repeated in an awed whisper.

Miss Farwell was watching him curiously.

He whispered half to himself, wonderingly, "Why should she wish to die?"

"Why should she wish to live?" The nurse's cold tones startled him.

He turned to her perplexed, wondering, speechless.

"I—I—do not understand," he said at last.

"I don't suppose you do," she answered grimly. "How could you? Your ministry is a matter of schools and theories, of doctrines and beliefs. This is a matter of life."

"My church—" he began, remembering his sermon.

But she interrupted him, "Your church does not understand, either; it is so busy earning money to pay its ministers that it has no time for such things as this."

"But they do not know," he faltered. "I did not dream that such a thing as this could be." He looked about the room and then at the still form on the bed, with a shudder.

"You a minister of Christ's gospel and ignorant of these things? And yet this is not an uncommon case, sir. I could tell you of many similar cases that have come under my own observation, though not all of them have chosen to die. This girl could have made a living; I suppose you understand. But she is a good girl; so there was nothing for her but this. All she asked was a chance—only a chance."

The minister was silent. He could not answer.

The nurse continued, "What right have you, Mr. Matthews, to say that you do not understand—that you do not know? It is your business to understand—to know. And your church—what right has it to plead ignorance of the life about its very doors? If such things are not its business what business has this institution that professes to exist for the salvation of men; that hires men like you—as you yourself told me—to minister to the world? What right I say, have you or your church to be ignorant of these everyday conditions of life? Dr. Abbott must know his work. I must know mine. Our teachers, our legal and professional men, our public officers, our mechanics and laborers, must all know and understand their work. The world demands it of us, and the world is beginning to demand that you and your church know your business." As the nurse spoke in low tones her voice was filled with sorrowful, passionate earnestness.

And Dan, Big Dan, sat like a child before her—his face white, his brown eyes wide with that questioning look. His own voice trembled as he answered, "But the people are not beasts. They do not realize. At heart they—we are kind; we do not mean to be carelessly cruel. Do you believe this, Miss Farwell?"

She turned from him wearily, as if in despair at trying to make him understand.

"Of course I believe it," she answered. "But how does that affect the situation? The same thing could be said, I suppose, of those who crucified the Christ, and burned the martyrs at the stake. It is this system, that has enslaved the people, that feeds itself upon the strength that should be given to their fellow men. They give so much time and thought and love to their churches and creeds, that they have nothing left—nothing for girls like these." Her voice broke and she went to the window.

In the silence Dan gazed at the form on the bed—gazed as if fascinated. From without came the shouts of the negro boys at their game of ball, and the sound of the people moving about in other parts of the building.

"Is there—is there no one who cares?" Dan said, at last in a hoarse whisper.

"No one has made her feel that they care," the nurse answered, turning back to him, and her manner and tone were cold again.

"But you" he persisted, "surely you care."

At this the gray eyes filled and the full voice trembled as she answered, "Yes, yes I care. How could I help it? Oh, if we can only make her feel that we—that someone wants her, that there is a place for her, that there are those who need her!" She went to the bedside and stood looking down at the still form. "I can't—I won't—I won't let her go."

"Let us help you, Miss Farwell," said Dan. "Dr. Oldham suggested that I ask you if the church could not do something. I am sure they would gladly help if I were to present the case."

The nurse wheeled on him with indignant, scornful eyes.

He faltered, "This is the churches' work, you know."

"Yes," she returned, and her words stung. "You are quite right, this is the churches' work."

He gazed at her in amazement as she continued hotly, "You have made it very evident Mr. Matthews, that you know nothing of this matter. I have no doubt that your church members would respond with a liberal collection if you were to picture what you have seen here this afternoon in an eloquent public appeal. Some in the fullness of their emotions would offer their personal service. Others I am sure would send flowers. But I suggest that for your sake, before you present this matter to your church you ask Dr. Oldham to give you a full history of the case. Ask him to tell you why Grace Conner is trying to die. And now you will pardon me, but in consideration of my patient, who may waken at any moment, I dare not take the responsibility of permitting you to prolong this call."

Too bewildered and hurt to attempt any reply, he left the room and she stood listening to his steps as he went slowly down the hall and out of the building.

From the window she watched as he crossed the old square, watched as he passed from sight up the weed-grown street. The cruel words had leaped from her lips unbidden. Already she regretted them deeply. She knew instinctively that the minister had come from a genuine desire to be helpful. She should have been more kind, but his unfortunate words had brought to her mind in a flash, the whole hideous picture of the poor girl's broken life. And the suggestion of such help as the church would give now, came with such biting irony, that she was almost beside herself.

The situation was not at all new to Miss Farwell. Her profession placed her constantly in touch with such ministries. She remembered a saloonkeeper who had contributed liberally to the funeral expenses of a child who had been killed by its drunken father. The young woman had never before spoken, in such cruel anger. Was she growing bitter? She wondered. All at once her cheeks were wet with scalding tears.

Dan found the Doctor sitting on the porch just as he had left him. Was it only an hour before?

CHAPTER XVII.

THE TRAGEDY.

"Now, for the first time, he was face to face with existing conditions. Not the theory but the practice confronted him now. Not the traditional, but the actual. It was, indeed, a tragedy."

Dan went heavily up the path between the roses, while the Doctor observed him closely. The young minister did not sit down.

"Well?" said the Doctor.

Dan's voice was strained and unnatural. "Will you come over to my room?"

Without a word the old man followed him.

In the privacy of his little study the boy said, "Doctor, you had a reason for telling me to ask Miss Farwell if the church could do anything for—for that poor girl. And the nurse told me to ask you about the case. I want you to tell me about her—*all* about her. Why is she living in that wretched place with those negroes? Why did she attempt to kill herself? I want to know about this girl as you know her—as Miss Farwell knows."

The old physician made no reply but sat silent—studying the young man who paced up and down the room. When his friend did not speak Dan said again, "Doctor you must tell me! I'm not a child. What is this thing that you should so hesitate to talk to me freely? I must know and you must tell me now."

"I guess you are right, boy," returned the other slowly.

To Big Dan, born with the passion for service in his very blood and reared amid the simple surroundings of his mountain home, where the religion and teaching of the old Shepherd had been felt for a generation, where every soul was held a neighbor—with a neighbor's right to the assistance of the community, and where no one—not even the nameless "wood's colt"—was made to suffer for the accident of birth or family, but stood and was judged upon his own life and living, the story of Grace Conner was a revelation almost too hideous in its injustice to be believed.

When the Doctor finished there was a tense silence in the minister's little study. It was as though the two men were witnessing a grim tragedy.

Trained under the influence of his parents and from them receiving the highest ideals of life and his duty to the race, Dan had been drawn irresistibly by the theoretical self-sacrificing heroism and traditionally glorious ministry of the church. Now, for the first time, he was face to face with existing conditions. Not the theory but the practice confronted him now. Not the traditional, but the actual.

It was, indeed, a tragedy.

The boy's face was drawn and white. His eyes—wide with that questioning look—burned with a light that his old friend had not seen in them before—the light of suffering—of agonizing doubt.

In his professional duties the Doctor had been forced to school himself to watch the keenest suffering unmoved, lest his emotions bias his judgment—upon the accuracy of which depended the life of his patient. He had been taught to cause the cruelest pain with unshaken nerve by the fact that a human life under his knife depended upon the steadiness of his hand. But his sympathy had never been dulled—only controlled and hidden. So, long years of contact with what might be called a disease of society, had accustomed him to the sight of conditions—the revelation of which came with such a shock to the younger man. But the Doctor could still appreciate what the revelation meant to the boy. Knowing Dan from his childhood, familiar with his home-training, and watching his growth and development with personal, loving interest, the old physician had realized how singularly susceptible his character was to the beautiful beliefs of the church. He had foreseen, too, something of the boy's suffering when he should be brought face to face with the raw, naked truths of life. And Dan, as he sat now searching the rugged, but kindly face of his friend, realized faintly why the Doctor had shrunk from talking to him of the sick girl.

Slowly the minister rose from his chair. Aimlessly—as one in perplexing, troubled thought—he went to the window and, standing there, looked out with unseeing eyes upon the cast-iron monument on the opposite corner of the street. Then he moved restlessly to the other window, and, with eyes still unseeing, looked down into the little garden of the crippled boy—the garden with the big moss and vine-grown rock in its center. Then he went to his study table and stood idly moving the books and papers about. His eye mechanically followed the closely written lines on the sheets of paper that were lying as he had left them that morning. He started. The next moment, with quick impatient movement, he crushed the pages of the manuscript in his powerful hands and threw them into the waste basket. He faced the Doctor with a grim smile.

"My sermon on 'The Christian Ministry.'"

CHAPTER XVIII.

TO SAVE A LIFE.

> "It was not Hope Farwell's way to theorize about the causes of the wreck, or to speculate as to the value of inventions for making more efficient the life-saving service, when there was a definite, immediate, personal something to be done for the bit of life that so closely touched her own."

"Nurse!"

Miss Farwell turned quickly. The girl on the bed was watching her with wide wondering eyes. She forced a smile. "Yes, dear, what is it? Did you have a good sleep?"

"I was not asleep. I—oh nurse, is it true?"

Hope laid a firm, cool hand on the hot forehead, and looked kindly down into the wondering eyes.

"You were awake while the minister was here?"

"Yes I—I—heard it all. Is it—is it true?"

"Is what true, child?"

"That you care, that anyone cares?"

Miss Farwell's face shone now with that mother-look as she lowered her head until the sick girl could see straight into the deep gray eyes. The poor creature gazed hungrily—breathlessly.

"Now don't you know that I care?" whispered the nurse, and the other burst into tears, grasping the nurse's hand in both her own and with a reviving hope clinging to it convulsively.

"I'm not bad, nurse," she sobbed. "I have always been a good girl even when—when I was so hungry. But they—they talked so about me, and made people think I was bad until I was ashamed to meet anyone. Then they put me out of the church, and nobody would give me work in their homes, and they drove me away from every place I got, until there was no place but this, and I was so frightened here alone with all these negroes in the house. Oh nurse, I didn't want to do it—I didn't want to do it. But I thought no one cared—no one."

"They did not mean to be cruel, dear," said the nurse softly. "They did not understand. You heard the minister say they would help you now."

The girl gripped Miss Farwell's hand with a shudder.

"They put me out of the church. Don't let them come, don't! Promise me you won't let them in."

The other calmed her. "There, there dear, I will take care of you. And no one can put you away from God; you must remember that."

"Is there a God, do you think?" whispered the girl.

"Yes, yes dear. All the cruelty in the world can't take God away from us if we hold on. We all make mistakes, you know, dear—terrible mistakes sometimes. People with the kindest, truest hearts sometimes do cruel things without thinking. Why, I suppose those who crucified Jesus were kind and good in their way. Only they didn't understand what they were doing, you see. You will learn by-and-by to feel sorry for these people, just as Jesus wept over those who he knew were going to torture and kill him. But first you must get well and strong again. You will now, won't you dear?"

And the whispered answer came, "Yes, nurse. I'll try now that I know you care."

So the strong young woman with the face of the Mother Mary talked to the poor outcast girl, helping her to forget, turning her thoughts from the sadness and bitterness of her experience to the gladness and beauty of a possible future, until—when the sun lighted up the windows on the other side of the square with flaming fire, and all the sky was filled with the glory of his going—the sick girl slept, clinging still to her nurse's hand.

In the twilight Miss Farwell sat in earnest thought. Deeply religious—as all true workers must be—she sought to know her part in the coming scenes of the drama in which she found herself cast.

The young woman felt that she must leave Corinth. Her experience with Dan had made the place unbearable to her. And, since the scene that afternoon, she felt, more than ever, that she should go. She had no friends in Corinth save her patient at Judge Strong's, Mrs. Strong, the two doctors, Deborah and Denny. At home she had many friends. Then from the standpoint of her profession—and Hope Farwell loved her profession—her opportunities in the city with Dr. Miles were too great to be lightly thrown aside.

But what of the girl? This girl so helpless, so alone—who buffeted and bruised, had been tossed senseless at her very feet by the wild storms of life. Miss Farwell knew the fury of the storm; she had witnessed before the awful strength of those forces that overwhelmed Grace Conner. She knew, too, that there were many others struggling hopelessly in the pitiless grasp of circumstances beyond their strength—single handed—to overcome.

As one watching a distant wreck from a place of safety on shore, the nurse grieved deeply at the relentless cruelty of these ungoverned forces, and mourned at her own powerlessness to check them. But she felt especially responsible for this poor creature who had been cast within her reach. Here was work to her hand. This she could do and it must be done now, without hesitation or delay. She could not prevent the shipwrecks; she could, perhaps, save the life of this one who had felt the fury of the storm. It was not Hope Farwell's way to theorize about the causes of the wreck, or to speculate as to the value of inventions for making more efficient the life-saving service, when there was a definite, immediate, personal something to be done for the bit of life that so closely touched her own.

There was no doubt in the nurse's mind now but that the girl would live and regain her health. But what then? The people would see that she was cared for as long as she was sick. Who among them would give her a place when she was no longer an object of ostentatious charity? Her very attempted suicide would mark her in the community more strongly than ever, and she would be met on every hand by suspicion, distrust and cruel curiosity. Then, indeed, she would need a friend—someone to believe in her and to love her. Of what use to save the life tossed up by the storm, only to set it adrift again? As Miss Farwell meditated in the twilight the conviction grew that her responsibility could end only when the life was safe.

It is, after all, a little thing to save a life; it is a great thing to make it safe. Indeed, in a larger, sense a life is never saved until it is safe.

When Dr. Harry called, later in the evening as he had promised, he handed the nurse an envelope. "Mr. Matthews asked me to give you this," he said. "I met him just as he was crossing the square. He would not come in but turned back toward town."

He watched her curiously as she broke the seal and read the brief note.

> "I have seen Dr. Oldham and he has told about your patient. You are right—I cannot present the matter to my people. I thank you. But this cannot prevent my own personal ministry. Please use the enclosed for Miss Conner, without mentioning my name. You must not deny me this."

The "enclosed" was a bill, large and generous. Miss Farwell handed the letter to Dr. Harry with the briefest explanation possible. For a long time the doctor sat in brown study. Then making no comment further than asking her to use the money as the minister had directed, he questioned her as to the patient's condition. When she had finished her report he drew a long breath.

"We are all right now, nurse. She will get over this nicely and in a week or two will be as good as ever. But—what then?"

CHAPTER XIX.

ON FISHING.

> "'It is not for you to waste your time in useless speculation as to the unknowable source of your life-stream, or in seeking to trace it in the ocean. It is enough for you that it is, and that, while it runs its brief course, it is yours to make it yield its blessings. For this you must train your hand and eye and brain—you must be in life a fisherman.'"

"Come boy," said the Doctor at last, laying his hand upon the young minister's shoulder. "Come, boy—let's go fishing. I know a dandy place about twelve miles from here. We'll coax Martha to fix us up a bite and start at daylight. What do you say?"

"But I can't!" cried Dan. "Tomorrow is Saturday and I have nothing now for Sunday morning." He looked toward the waste basket where lay his sermon on "The Christian Ministry."

"Humph," grunted the Doctor. "You'll find a better one when you get away from this. Older men than you, Dan, have fought this thing all their lives. Don't think that you can settle it in a couple of days thinking. Take time to fish a little; it'll help a lot. There's nothing like a running stream to clear one's mind and set one's thoughts going in fresh channels. I want you to see Gordon's Mills. Come boy, let's go fishing."

The evening was spent in preparation, eager anticipation and discussion of the craft, prompted by the Doctor. And as they overhauled flies and rods and lines and reels, and recalled the many delightful days spent as they proposed to spend the morrow, the young man's thoughts were led away from the first real tragedy of his soul. At daylight, after a breakfast of their own cooking—partly prepared the night before by Martha, who unquestionably viewed the minister's going away on a Saturday with doubtful eyes—they were off.

When they left the town far behind and—following the ridge road in the clear wine-like air of the early day—entered the woods, the Doctor laughed aloud as Dan burst forth with a wild boyish yell.

"I couldn't help it Doctor, it did itself," he said in half apology. "It's so good to be out in the woods with you again. I feel as if I were being re-created already."

"Yell again," said the physician with another laugh, and added dryly, "I won't tell."

Gordon's Mills, on Gordon's creek, lay in a deep, narrow valley, shut in and hidden from the world, by many miles of rolling, forest-covered hills. The mill, the general store and post office, and the blacksmith shop were connected with Corinth, twelve miles away, by daily stage—a rickety old spring wagon that carried the mail and any chance passenger. Pure and clear and cold the creek came welling to the surface of the earth full-grown, from vast, mysterious, subterranean caverns in the heart of the hills—and, from the brim of its basin, rushed, boiling and roaring, along to the river two miles distant, checked only by the dam at the mill. For a little way above the dam the waters lay still and deep, with patches of long mosses, vines and rushes, waving in its quiet clearness—forming shadowy dens for lusty trout, while the open places—shining fields and lanes—reflected, as a mirror, the steep green-clad bluff, and the trees that bent far over until their drooping branches touched the gleaming surface.

As the two friends tramped the little path at the foot of the bluff, or waded, with legs well-braced, the tumbling torrent, and sent their flies hither and yon across the boiling flood to be snatched by the strong-hearted denizens of the stream, Dan felt the life and freshness and strength of God's good world entering into his being. At dinner time they built a little fire to make their coffee and broil a generous portion of their catch. Then lying at ease on the bank of the great spring, they talked as only those can talk who get close enough to the great heart of Mother Nature to feel strongly their common kinship with her and with their fellows.

After one of those long silences that come so easily at such a time, Dan tossed a pebble far out into the big pool and watched it sink down, down, down, until he lost it in the unknown depths.

"Doctor, where does it come from?"

"Where does what come from?"

"This stream. You say its volume is always the same—that it is unaffected by heavy rains or long droughts. How do you account for it?"

"I don't account for it," grunted the Doctor, with a twinkle in his eye, "I fish in it."

Dan laughed. "And that," he said slowly, "is your philosophy of life."

The other made no answer.

Choosing another pebble carefully, Dan said, "Speaking as a preacher—please elaborate."

"Speaking as a practitioner—you try it," returned the Doctor.

The big fellow stretched himself out on his back, with his hands clasped beneath his head. He spoke deliberately.

"Well, you do not know from whence your life comes, and it goes after a short course, to lose itself with many others in the great stream that reaches—at last, and is lost in—the Infinite." The Doctor seemed interested. Dan continued, half talking to himself: "It is not for you to waste your time in useless speculation as to the unknowable source of your life-stream, or in seeking to trace it in the ocean. It is enough for you that it is, and that, while it runs its brief course, it is yours to make it yield its blessings. For this you must train your hand and eye and brain—you must be in life a fisherman."

"Very well done," murmured the Doctor, "for a preacher. Stick to the knowable things, and don't stick at the unknowable; that is my law and my gospel."

Dan retorted, "Now let's watch the practitioner make a cast."

"Humph! Why don't you stop it, boy?"

"Stop what?" Dan sat up.

The other pointed to the great basin of water that—though the stream rushed away in such volume and speed—was never diminished, being constantly renewed from its invisible, unknown source.

The young man shook his head, awed by the contemplation of the mighty, hidden power.

And the Doctor—poet now—said: "No more can the great stream of love, that is in the race for the race and that finds expression in sympathy and service, be finally stopped. Fed by hidden, eternal sources it will somehow find its way to the surface. Checked and hampered, for the moment, by obstacles of circumstances or conditions, it is not stopped, for no circumstance can touch the source. And love will keep coming—breaking down or rising over the barrier, it may be—cutting for itself new channels, if need be. For every Judge Strong and his kind there is a Hope Farwell and her kind. For every cast-iron, ecclesiastical dogma there is a living, growing truth."

Dan's sermon the next day, given in place of the one announced, did not please the whole of his people.

"It was all very fine and sounded very pretty," said Martha, "but I would like to know, Brother Matthews, where does the church come in?"

CHAPTER XX.

COMMON GROUND.

"'But we will find common ground,' he exclaimed. 'Look here, we have already found it! This garden—Denny's garden!'"

The following Tuesday morning Dan was at work bright and early in Denny's garden. Many of the good members of Memorial Church would have said that Dan might better have been at work in his study.

The ruling classes in this congregation, that theoretically had no ruling classes, were beginning to hint among themselves of a humiliation beyond expression at the spectacle, now becoming so common, of their minister working with his coat off like an ordinary laboring man. He should have more respect for the dignity of the cloth. At least, if he had no pride of his own, he should have more regard for the feelings of his membership. Besides this they did not pay him to work in anybody's garden.

The grave and watchful keepers of the faith, who held themselves responsible to the God they thought they worshiped, for the belief of the man they had employed to prove to the world wherein it was all wrong and they were all right, watched their minister's growing interest in this Catholic family with increasing uneasiness.

The rest of the church, who were neither of the class nor of the keepers, but merely passengers, as it were, in the Ark of Salvation, looked on with puzzled interest. It was a new move in the game that added a spice of ginger to the play not wholly distasteful. From a safe distance the "passengers" kept one eye on the "class" and the other on the "keepers," with occasionally a stolen glance at Dan, and waited nervously for their cue.

The world outside the fold awaited developments with amused and breathless interest. Everybody secretly admired the stalwart young worker in the garden, and the entire community was grateful that he had given them something new to talk about. Memorial Church was filled at every service.

Meanwhile wholly unconscious of all this, Big Dan continued digging his way among the potatoes, helping the crippled boy to harvest and prepare for market the cabbages and other vegetables, that grew in the plot of ground under his study window, never dreaming that there was aught of interest either to church or town in the simple neighborly kindness. It is a fact—though Dan at this time, would not have admitted it, even to himself—that the hours spent in the garden, with Denny enthroned upon the big rock, and Deborah calling an occasional cheery word from the cottage, were by far the most pleasant hours of the day.

Every nerve and muscle in the splendid warm-blooded body of this young giant of the hills called for action. The one mastering passion of his soul was the passion for deeds—to do; to serve; to be used. He had felt himself called to the ministry by his desire to accomplish a work that would be of real worth to the world. He was already conscious of being somewhat out of place with the regular work of the church: the pastoral calls, which mean visiting, day after day, in the homes of the members to talk with the women about nothing at all, at hours when the men of the household are away laboring, with brain or hand, for the necessities of life; the meetings of the various women's societies, where the minister himself is the only man present, and the talk is all women's talk; the committee meetings, where hours are spent in discussing the most trivial matters with the most ponderous gravity—as though the salvation of the world depends upon the color of the pulpit carpet, or who should bake a cake for the next social.

For nearly a week now, Dan had found no time to touch the garden; he was resolved this day to make good his neglect. An hour before Denny was up the minister was ready for his work. As he went to get the garden-tools from the little lean-to woodshed, Deborah called from the kitchen, "'Tis airly ye are this mornin' sir. It's not many that do be layin' awake all the night waitin' for the first crack o' day, so they can get up to somebody else's work fer thim."

The minister laughingly dodged the warm-hearted expressions of gratitude he saw coming. "I've been shirking lately," he said. "If I don't do better than this the boss will be firing me sure. How is he?"

"Fine sir, fine! He's not up yet. You'll hear him yelling at you as soon as he sees what you're at."

"Good," ejaculated the other. "I'll get ahead of him this time. Perhaps I can get such a start before he turns out that he'll let me stay a while longer, as it would not be pleasant to get my discharge."

Passing laborers and business men on the way to their daily tasks, smiled at the coatless figure in the garden. Several called a pleasant greeting. The boy with the morning papers from the great city checked his whistle as he looked curiously over the fence, and the Doctor who came out on the porch looked across the street to the busy gardener and grunted with satisfaction as he turned to his roses.

But Dan's mind was not occupied altogether that morning by the work upon which his hands were engaged. Neither was he thinking only of his church duties, or planning sermons for the future. As he bent to his homely tasks his thoughts strayed continually to the young woman whom he had last seen beside the bed of the sick girl in the poverty-stricken room in Old Town. The beautiful freshness and sweetness of the morning and the perfume of the dewy things seemed subtly to suggest her. Thoughts of her seemed, somehow, to fit in with gardening.

He recalled every time he had met her. The times had not been many, and they were still strangers, but every occasion had been marked by something that seemed to fix it as unusual, making their meeting seem far from commonplace. He still had that feeling that she was to play a large part in his life and he was confident that they would meet again. He was wondering where and how when he looked up from his work to see her coming toward him, dressed in a fresh uniform of blue and white.

The young fellow stood speechless with wonder as she came on, picking her way daintily among the beds and rows, her skirts held carefully, her beautiful figure expressing health and strength and joyous, tingling life in every womanly curve and line.

There was something wonderfully intimate and sweetly suggestive in the picture they made that morning, these two—the strong young woman in her uniform of service going in the glow of the early day to the stalwart coatless man in the garden, to interrupt him in his homely labor.

"Good morning," she said with a smile. "I have been watching you from the house and decided that you were working altogether too industriously, and needed a breathing spell. Do you do everything so energetically?"

It is sadly true of most men today that the more you cover them up the better they look. Our civilization demands a coat, and the rule seems to be—the more civilization, the more coat. Dan Matthews is one of those rare men who look well in his shirt sleeves. His shoulders and body needed no shaped and padded garments to set them off. The young woman's eyes, in spite of her calm self-possession, betrayed her admiration as he stood before her so tall and straight—his powerful shoulders, deep chest and great muscled arms, so clearly revealed.

But Dan did not see the admiration in her eyes. He was so bewildered by the mere fact of her presence that he failed to note this interesting detail.

He looked toward the house, then back to the young woman's face.

"You were watching me from the house," he repeated. "Really, I did not know that you—"

"Were your neighbors?" she finished. "Yes we are. Grace and I moved yesterday. You see," she continued eager to explain, "it was not good for her to remain in that place. It was all so suggestive of her suffering. I knew that Mrs. Mulhall had a room for rent, because I had planned to take it before I decided to go back to Chicago." She blushed as she recalled the thoughts that had led her to the decision, but went on resolutely. "The poor child has such a fear of everybody, that I thought it would help her to know that Mrs. Mulhall and Denny could be good to her, even though it was Denny's father, that her father—you know—"

Dan's eyes were shining. "Yes I know," he said.

"I explained to Mrs. Mulhall and, like the dear good soul she is, she understood at once and made the poor child feel better right away. I thought, too, that if Grace were living here with Mrs. Mulhall it might help the people to be kinder to her. Then someone will give her a chance to earn her living and she will be all right. The people will soon act differently when they see how Mrs. Mulhall feels, don't you think they will?"

Dan could scarcely find words. She was so entirely unconscious of the part she was playing—of this beautiful thing she was doing.

"And you?" he asked, "You are not going away?"

"Not until she gets a place. She will need me until she finds a home, you know. And Dr. Harry assures me there is plenty of work for me in Corinth. So Grace and I will keep house at Mrs. Mulhall's. Grace will do the work while I am busy. It will make her feel less dependent and," she added frankly, "it will not cost so much that way. And that brings me to what I came out here to say." She paused. "I wish to thank you, Mr. Matthews, for your help—for the money you sent. The poor child needed so many things, and—I want to beg your pardon for—for the shameful way I treated you when you called. I—I knew better, and Mrs. Mulhall has been telling me how much you have done for them. I—"

Dan interrupted, "Please don't, Miss Farwell; I understand. You were exactly right. I know, now." Then he added, slowly, "I want you to know, though, Miss Farwell, that I had no thought of being rude when we talked in the old Academy yard." She was silent and he went on, "I must make you understand that I am not the ill-mannered cad that I seemed. I—You know, this ministry"—he emphasized the word with a smile—"is so new to me—I am really so inexperienced!"

She glanced at him quickly.

He continued, "I had never before heard such thoughts as you expressed, and I was too puzzled to realize how my silence would appear to you when you knew."

"Then this is your first church?" she asked.

"Yes," he said, "and I am beginning to realize how woefully ignorant I am of life. You know I was born and brought up in the backwoods. Until I went to college I knew only our simple country life; at college I knew only books and students. Then I came here."

As he talked the young woman's face cleared. It was something very refreshing to hear such a man declare his ignorance of life with the frankness of a boy. She held out her hand impulsively.

"Let's forget it all," she said. "It was a horrid mistake."

"And we are to be good friends?" he asked, grasping her outstretched hand.

Without replying the young woman quietly released her hand and drew back a few paces—she was trembling. She fought for self-control. There was something—what was it about this man? The touch of his hand—Hope Farwell was frightened by emotions new and strange to her.

She found a seat on the big rock and ignoring his question said, "So that's why you are so big and strong, and know so well how to work in a garden. I thought it was strange for one of your calling. I see now how natural it is for you."

"Yes," he smiled, "it is very natural—more so than preaching. But tell me—don't you think we should be good friends? We are going to be now, are we not?"

The young woman answered with quiet dignity, "Friendship Mr. Matthews means a great deal to me, and to you also, I am sure. Friends must have much in common. We have nothing, because—because everything that I said to you at the Academy, to me, is true. We do not live in the same world."

"But it's for myself—the man and not the minister—that I ask it," he urged eagerly.

She watched his face closely as she answered, "But you and your ministry are one and the same. Yourself—your life is your ministry. You are your ministry and your ministry is you."

"But we will find common ground," he exclaimed. "Look here, we have already found it! This garden—Denny's garden! We'll put a sign over the gate, 'No professional ministry shall enter here!'—The preacher lives up there." He pointed to his window. "The man, Dan Matthews, works in the garden here. To the man in the garden you may say what you like about the parson up there. We will differ, of course, but we may each gain something, as is right for friends, for we will each grant to the other the privilege of being true to self."

She hesitated; then slipping from the rock and looking him full in the face said, "I warn you it will not work. But for friendship's sake we will try."

Neither of them realized the deep significance of the terms, but in the days that followed, the people of Corinth had much—much more, to talk about. The Ally was well pleased and saw to it that the ladies of the Aid Society were not long in deciding that something must be done.

CHAPTER XXI.

THE WARNING.

"From God's sunny hillside pastures to the gloom and stench of the slaughter pens."

It happened two weeks to the day after Dan and Miss Farwell met in Denny's garden.

The Ally had been busy to some purpose. The Ladies' Aid, having reached the point of declaring that something must be done, did something. The Elders of Memorial Church, in their official capacity, called on their pastor.

Dan was in the garden when the Elders came. The Doctor's wife declared that Dan spent most of his time in the garden now, and that, when there, he did nothing because that nurse was always helping him. Good Martha has the fatal gift of telling a bit of news so vividly that it gains much in the telling.

Miss Farwell was in the garden that afternoon with the minister and so was Denny, while Grace Conner and Deborah were sitting on the front porch of the little cottage when the two church fathers passed. Though neither of the men turned their heads, neither of them failed to see the two women on the porch and the three friends in the garden.

"For the love of Heaven, look there!" exclaimed Deborah in an excited whisper. "They're turnin' in at the minister's gate, an' him out there in the 'taters in his shirt, a-diggin' in the ground an' a-gassin' wid Denny an' Miss Hope. I misdoubt there's somethin' stirrin' to take thim to his door the day. I must run an' give him the word."

But Dan had seen and was already on his way to the front gate, drawing on his coat as he went. From the other side of the street the Doctor waved his hand to Dan encouragingly as the young man walked hastily down the sidewalk to overtake the church officials at the front door.

Truly in this denominational hippodrome, odd yoke-fellows are sometimes set to run together; the efforts of the children of light to equal in wisdom the children of darkness leading the church to clap its ecclesiastical harness upon anything that—by flattery, bribes or intimidation, can be led, coaxed or driven to pull at the particular congregational chariot to which the tugs are fast! When the people of Corinth speak of Judge Strong's religion, or his relation to the Memorial Church they wink—if the Judge is not looking. When Elder Jordan is mentioned their voices always have a note of respect and true regard. Elder Strong is always called "The Judge"; Nathaniel Jordan was known far and wide as "Elder Jordan." Thus does the community, as communities have a way of doing, touch the heart of the whole matter.

Dan recognized instinctively the difference in the characters of these two men, yet he had found them always of one mind in all matters of the church. He felt the subtle antagonism of Judge Strong, though he did not realize that the reason for it lay in the cunning instinct of a creature that recognized a natural enemy in all such spirits as his. He felt, too, the regard and growing appreciation of Elder Jordan. Yet the two churchmen were in perfect accord in their "brotherly administration."

When the officials met in Dan's study that day, their characters were unmistakable. That they were both in harness was also clear. The minister's favorite chair creaked in dismay as the Judge settled his heavy body, and twisted this way and that in an open effort to inspect every corner of the apartment with his narrow, suspicious eyes; while the older churchman sat by the window, studiously observing something outside. Dan experienced that strange feeling of uneasiness familiar to every schoolboy when called upon unexpectedly for the private interview with the teacher. The Elders had never visited him before. It was too evident that they had come now upon matters of painful importance.

At last Judge Strong's wandering eye came to rest upon Dan's favorite fishing-rod, that stood in a corner behind a book-case. The young man's face grew red in spite of him. It was impossible not to feel guilty of something in the presence of Judge Strong. Even Elder Jordan started as his brother official's metallic voice rang out, "I see that you follow in the footsteps of the early disciples in one thing, at least, Brother Matthews. You go fishing." He gave forth a shrill, cold laugh that—more than anything else—betrayed the real spirit he laughed to hide.

This remark was characteristic of Judge Strong. On the surface it was the mild jest of a churchman, whose mind dwelt so habitually on the sacred Book, that even in his lightest vein he could not but express himself in terms and allusions of religious significance. Beneath the surface, his words carried an accusation, a condemnation, a sneer. His manner was the eager, expectant, self-congratulatory manner of a dog that has treed something. The Judge's method was skillfully chosen to give him this advantage: it made his meaning clear while it gave no possible opening for a reply to the real idea his words conveyed, and forced his listener to an embarrassed silence of self-condemnation, that secured the Judge in his assumed position of pious superiority.

Dan forced a smile. He felt that the Judge's laugh demanded it. "Yes," he said, "I am scriptural when it comes to fishing. Dr. Oldham and I had a fine day at Gordon's Mills."

"So I understand," said the other meaningly. "I suppose you and the old Doctor have some interesting talks on religion?"

It was impossible not to feel the sneering accusation under the words. It was as impossible to answer. Again Dan's face flushed as he said, "No, we do not discuss the church very often."

"No?" said the Judge. "I should think you would find him a good subject to practice on. Perhaps, though, he practices on you, heh?" Again he laughed.

"Ahem, ahem!" Elder Jordan gave his usual warning. Dan turned to the good old man with a feeling of relief. At least Nathaniel Jordan's words would bear their face value. "Perhaps, Brother Strong, we had better tell Brother Matthews the object of our call."

The Judge leaned back in his chair with the air of one about to be pleasantly entertained. He waved his hand with a gesture that said as plainly as words, "All right, Nathaniel, go ahead. I'm here if you need me, so don't be uneasy! If you find yourself unequal to the task, depend upon me to help you out."

The minister waited with an expectant air.

"Ahem, ahem! You must not think, Brother Matthews, that there is anything really wrong because we called. But we, ahem—we thought best to give you a brotherly warning. I'm sure you will take it in the spirit in which it is meant."

The Judge stirred uneasily in his chair, bending upon Dan such a look as—had he been a real judge—he might have cast upon a convicted criminal. Dan already felt guilty. He signified his assent to the Elder's statement and Nathaniel proceeded:

"You are a young man, Brother Matthews; I may say a very talented young man, and we are jealous for your success in this community and, ahem—for the standing of Memorial Church. Some of our ladies feel—I may say that we feel that you have been a little, ah—careless about some things of late. Elder Strong and I know from past experience that a preacher—a young unmarried preacher cannot be too careful. Not that we have the least idea that you mean any harm, you know—not the least in the world. But people will talk and—ahem, ahem!"

Dan's face was a study. He was so clearly mystified by the Elder's remarks that the good man found his duty even more embarrassing than he had anticipated.

Then Judge Strong threw a flood of light upon the situation in a characteristic manner. "That young woman, Grace Conner, has a mighty bad name in this town; and the other one, her friend the nurse, is a stranger. She was in my house for a month and—well, some things about her look mighty queer to me. She hasn't been inside a church since she came to Corinth. I would be the last man in the world to cast a suspicion on anyone but—" he finished with a shake of his head, and an expression of pious doubt on his crafty face that said he could, if he wished, tell many dark secrets of Miss Farwell's life.

Dan was on his feet instantly, his face flaming and his eyes gleaming with indignation. "I—" then he checked himself, confused, as—in a flash—he remembered who these men were and his relation to them in the church. "I beg your pardon," he finished slowly, and dropped back into his chair, biting his lips and clenching his big hands in an effort at self-control.

Elder Jordan broke in nervously. "Ahem, ahem! You understand, Brother Matthews, that the sisters—that we do not think that you mean any harm, but your standing in the community, you know, is such that we must shun every appearance of evil. We, ahem—we felt it our duty to call." Big Dan, who had never met that spirit, the Ally, knew not how to answer his masters in the church. He tried to feel that their mission to him was of grave importance. He was tempted to laugh; their ponderous dignity seemed so ridiculous.

"Thank you, sir," he at last managed to say, gravely, "I think it is hardly necessary for me to attempt any explanation." He was still fighting for self-control and chose his words carefully. "I will consider this matter." Then he turned the conversation skillfully into other channels.

When the overseers of the church were gone the young pastor walked the floor of the room trying to grasp the true significance of the situation. Gradually the real meaning of the Elders' visit grew upon him. Because his own life was so big, so broad, because his ideals and ambitions were so high, so true to the spirit of the Christ whose service he thought he had entered, he could not believe his senses.

He might have found some shadow of reason, perhaps, for their fears regarding his friendship for the girl with the bad reputation, had the circumstances been other than they were, and had he not known who it was gave Grace Conner her bad name. But that his friendship for Miss Farwell, whose beautiful ministry was such an example of the spirit of the Christian religion; and that her care for the poor girl should be so quickly construed into something evil—his mind positively refused to entertain the thought. He felt that the visit of his church fathers was unreal. He was as one dazed by an unpleasant dream.

To come from the pure, wholesome atmosphere of his home and the inspiring study of the history of the Christian religion, to such a twisted, distorted, hideous corruption of the church policy and spirit, was, to Dan, like coming from God's sunny hillside pastures to the gloom and stench of the slaughter pens. He was stunned by the littleness, the meanness that had prompted the "kindly warning" of these leaders of the church.

Slowly he began to see what that spirit might mean to him.

No man of ordinary intelligence could long be in Memorial Church, without learning that it was ruled by a ring, as truly as any body politic was ever so ruled. Dan Matthews understood too clearly that his position in Memorial Church depended upon the "bosses" then in control. And he saw farther—saw, indeed, that his final success or failure in his chosen calling depended upon the standing that should be given him by this, his first charge; depended at the last upon these two men who had shown themselves, each in his own way, so easily influenced by the low, vicious tales of a few idle-minded town gossips.

As one in the dark—stepping without warning into a boggy hole—Dan groped for firmer ground.

As one standing alone in a wide plain sees on the distant horizon the threat of a gathering storm, and—watching, shudders at the shadow of a passing cloud, Dan stood—a feeling of loneliness and dread heavy upon him.

He longed for companionship, for someone to whom he could speak his heart. But to whom in Corinth could he go? These men who had just "advised him" were, theoretically, his intimate counselors; to them he was supposed, and had expected, to look—in his inexperience, for advice and help. These men, old in the service of the church—how would they answer his troubled thoughts? He shrugged his shoulders and smiled grimly. The Doctor? He smiled again.

Dan little dreamed how much that keen old fisherman already knew, from a skillful baiting of Martha, about the visit of the Elders that afternoon; while his knowledge of Dan's character from childhood, enabled the physician to guess more than a little of the thoughts that occupied the young man pacing the floor of his room. But the Doctor would not do for the young man that day.

Dan went to the window overlooking the garden. The nurse was still there, helping crippled Denny with his work. The minister's hoe was leaning against the big rock, as he had left it when he had caught up his coat. Should he go down? What would she say if he were to tell her of the Elders' mission?

Something caused Miss Farwell to look up just then and she saw him. She beckoned to him playfully, guardedly, like a schoolgirl. Smiling, he shook his head. He could not go.

More than ever, then, he felt very much alone.

CHAPTER XXII.

AS DR. HARRY SEES IT.

> "Thus Dr. Harry presented another side of the problem to his bewildered friend—a phase of the question commonly ignored by every fiery reformer, whose particular reformation is the one—the only way."

The friendship between Dan and Dr. Abbott had grown rapidly, as was natural, for the two men had much in common. In a town as small as Corinth, there are many opportunities for even the busiest men to meet, and scarcely a day passed that the doctor and the preacher did not exchange greetings, at least. As often as their duties permitted they were together; sometimes at the office or in Dan's rooms; again, of an evening, at Harry's home; or driving miles across country behind the bay mare or big Jim—the physician to see a patient, and the minister to be the "hitchin' post."

Harry was just turning from the telephone that evening when Dan entered the house.

"Hello, parson!" he cried heartily. "I was just this minute trying to get you. I couldn't think of anything to do to anybody else, so I thought I'd have a try at you. That wasn't such a bad guess either," he added, when he had a good look at his friend's face. "You evidently need to have something fixed. What is it, liver?" He led the way into the library.

"Not mine," said Dan shortly. "I don't believe I have one."

He pushed an arm chair to face the doctor's favorite seat by the table.

Harry chuckled as he reached for his pipe and tobacco. "You don't need to have one yourself in order to suffer from liver troubles. Speaking professionally, my opinion is that you preachers, as a class, are more likely to suffer from other people's livers than from your own, though it is also true that the average parson has more of his own than he knows what to do with."

"And what do you doctors prescribe when it is the other fellow's?" asked Dan.

The other struck a match. "Oh, there's a difference of opinion in the profession. The old Doctor, for instance, pins his faith to a split bamboo with a book of flies or a can of bait."

"And you?" Dan was smiling now.

The answer came through a cloud of smoke. "Just a pipe and a book."

Dan's smile vanished. "I fear your treatment would not agree with my constitution," he said grimly. "My system does not permit me to use the remedy you prescribe."

"Oh, I see. You mean the pipe." A puff of smoke punctuated the remark. The physician was watching his friend's face now, and the fun was gone from his voice as he said gravely, "Pardon me. Brother Matthews; I meant no slur upon your personal conviction touching—"

"Brother Matthews!" interrupted Dan, sharply, "I thought we had agreed to drop all that. It's bad enough to be dodged and shunned by every man in town without your rubbing it in. As for my personal convictions, they have nothing to do with the case. In fact, my system does not permit me to have personal convictions."

Dr. Harry's eyes twinkled. "This system of yours seems to be in a bad way, Dan. What's wrong with it?"

"Wrong with it! Wrong with my system? Man alive, don't you know this is heresy! How can there be anything wrong with my system? Doesn't it relieve me of any responsibility in the matter of right and wrong? Doesn't it take from me all such burdens as personal convictions. Doesn't it fix my standard of goodness, and then doesn't it make goodness my profession? You, poor drudge; you and the rest of the merely humans must be good as a matter of sentiment! Thanks to my system my goodness is a matter of business; I am paid for being good. My system says that your pipe and, perhaps your book, are bad—sinful. I have nothing to do with it. I only obey and draw my salary."

"Oh, well," said Harry, soothingly, "there is the old Doctor's remedy. It's probably better on the whole."

"I tried that the other day," Dan growled.

"Worked, didn't it?"

Dan grinned in spite of himself. "At first the effects seemed to be very beneficial, but later I found that it was, er—somewhat irritating, and that it slightly aggravated the complaint."

The doctor was smiling now. "Suppose you try a little physical exercise occasionally—working in the garden or—"

Dan threw up his hands with a tragic gesture. "Suicide!" he almost shouted.

Then they both lay back in their chairs and fairly howled with laughter.

"Whew! That does a fellow good!" gasped Dan.

"I guess we have arrived," said Harry, with a final chuckle. "Thought we were way off the track once or twice; but I have located your liver trouble, all right. When did they call?"

"This afternoon. Did you know?"

The doctor nodded. "I have been expecting it for several days. I guess you were about the only person in Corinth who wasn't."

"Why didn't you tell me?"

"If I can avoid it, I never tell a patient of a coming operation until it's time to operate; then it's all over before they can get nervous."

Dan shuddered—the laugh was all out of him now. "I have certainly been on the table this afternoon," he said. "I need to talk it out with someone. That's what I came to you for."

"Perhaps you had better tell me the particulars," said Harry, quietly.

So Dan told him, and when he had finished they had both grown very serious.

"I was afraid of this, Dan," said Harry. "You'll need to be very careful—very careful."

The other started to speak, but the doctor checked him.

"I know. I know how you feel. What you say about the system and all that is all too true, and you haven't seen the worst of it yet, by a good deal."

"Do you mean to tell me that Miss Farwell will be made to suffer for her interest in that poor girl?" demanded Dan warmly.

"If Miss Farwell continues to live with Grace Conner at Mrs. Mulhall's, there is not a respectable home in this town that will receive her," answered the doctor bluntly.

"My God! are the people blind? Can't the church see what a beautiful—what a Christ-like thing she is doing?"

"You know Grace Conner's history," replied Harry, coolly. "What reason is there to think it will be different in Miss Farwell's case, so far as the attitude of the community goes?"

Dan could not keep his seat. In his agitation he walked the floor. Suddenly turning on the other he demanded, "Then I am to understand that my friendship with Miss Farwell will mean for me—"

Dr. Harry was silent. Indeed, how could he suggest, ever so indirectly, that the friendship between Dan and Miss Farwell should be discontinued. If the young woman had been anyone else, or if Dr. Harry himself had not—But why attempt explanation?

The minister continued tramping up and down the room, stopping now and then to face the doctor, who sat still in his chair by the library table, quietly smoking.

"This is horrible, Harry! I—I can't believe it! So far as my friendship for Miss Farwell goes, that is only an incident. It does not matter in itself."

Dr. Harry puffed vigorously. He thought to himself that this might be true, but something in Dan's face and voice when he spoke—something of which he himself was unconscious—made Harry glad that he had not answered.

"It is the spirit of it all that matters," the minister continued, pausing again. "I never dreamed that such a thing could be. That Grace Conner's life should be ruined by the wicked carelessness of these people seems bad enough. But that they should take the same attitude toward Miss Farwell, simply because she is seeking to do that Christian thing that the church itself will not do, is—is monstrous!" He turned impatiently to resume his restless movement. Then, when his friend did not speak he continued slowly, as though the words were forced from him against his will: "And to think that they could be so unmoved by the suffering of that poor girl, their own victim, and so untouched by the example of Miss Farwell; and then that they should give such grave consideration and be so influenced by absolutely groundless and vicious idle gossip! And that the church of Christ, that Christianity itself, should be so wholly in the hands of people so unspeakably blind, so—contemptibly mean and small in their conceptions of the religion of Jesus Christ!"

He confronted the doctor again and his face flushed. "Why, Doctor, my whole career as a Christian minister depends upon the mere whim of these people, who are moved by such a spirit as this. No matter what motives may prompt my course they have the power to prevent me from doing my work. This is one of the strongest and most influential churches in the brotherhood. They can give me such a name that my life-work will be ruined. What can I do?"

"You must be very careful, Dan," said Dr. Harry, slowly.

"Careful! And that means, I suppose, that I must bow to the people of this church—ruled as they are by such a spirit—as to my lords and masters; that I shall have no other God but this congregation; that I shall deny my own conscience for theirs; that I shall go about the trivial, nonsensical things they call my pastoral duties, in fear and trembling; that my ministry is to cringe when they speak, and do their will regardless of what I feel to be the will of Christ! Faugh!" Big Dan drew himself erect. "If this is what the call to the ministry means, I am beginning to understand some things that have always puzzled me greatly."

He dropped wearily into his chair.

"Tell me, Doctor," he demanded, "do the people generally, see these things?"

"It seems to me that everyone who thinks must see them," replied the other.

"Then why did no one tell me? Why did not the old Doctor explain the real condition of the church?"

"As a rule it is not a safe thing to attempt to tell a minister these things. Would you have listened, Dan, if he had tried to tell you? Or, because he is not a church man, would you not have misunderstood his motives? The Doctor loves you, Dan."

"But you are a church man, a member of the official board of my congregation. If men like you know these things why are you in the church at all?"

Silently Dr. Harry re-filled and lighted his pipe. It was as if he deliberated over his reply. The membership of every church may be divided into three distinct classes: those who are the church; those who belong to the church;

and those who are members, but who neither are, nor belong to. Dr. Harry was a member.

"Dan," said the physician, "I suppose it is very difficult for such men as you to understand the religious dependence of people like myself. We see the church's lack of appreciation of true worth of character, we know the vulgar, petty scheming and wire-pulling for place, the senseless craving for notoriety, and the prostitution of the spirit of Christ's teaching to denominational ends. We understand how the ministers are at the mercy of the lowest minds and the meanest spirits in their congregation; but, Dan, because we love the cause we do not talk of these things even to each other, for fear of being misunderstood. It is useless to talk of them to our ministers, for they dare not listen. Why man, I never in my life felt that I could talk to my pastor as I am talking to you!" He smiled. "I guess that I was afraid that they would tell Judge Strong, and that the church would put me out. And, with most of them, that—probably, is exactly what would have happened. I am not sure but you will consider me unsafe, and avoid me in the future," he added whimsically.

Dan smiled at his words, though they revealed so much to him.

Dr. Harry went on, "We remain in the church, and give it our support, I suppose, because we are dependent upon it for our religious life; because we know no religious life outside of it. It is the only institution that professes to be distinctively Christian, and we love its teaching in spite of its practice. We are always hoping that some one will show us a way out. And some one will!" He spoke passionately now, with deep conviction: "Some one must! This Godless mockery cannot continue. I have too much faith in the goodness of men to believe otherwise. I don't know how the change will come. But it will come and it will come from men in the church—men like you, Dan, who come to the ministry with the highest ideals. But you must be careful, mighty careful, not for your own sake, alone, but for the sake of the cause we both love. Some operations are exceedingly dangerous to the life of the patient; some medicines must be administered with care lest they kill instead of cure. Men like me, from long experience with professional reformers, look with distrust upon the preacher who talks about his church, even while we know that there is a great need."

Thus Dr. Harry presented another side of the problem to his bewildered friend—a phase of the question commonly ignored by every fiery reformer, whose particular reformation is *the* one—the only way.

Later Dan asked, "Do you think Miss Farwell understands what her course means, Doctor?"

Harry shook his head. "I wish I knew how much she understands. Already two or three people who expected to call her have told me they would find someone else. I have several cases now that need a trained nurse, but they won't have her because of what they have heard. And yet I promised her, you know, that she should have plenty of work."

"Have you told her this?" asked Dan.

Again Harry shook his head. "What's the good?"

"But she ought to be told," exclaimed the other.

"I know that, Dan. But I can't do it, after urging her, as I did, to stay in Corinth. You are the one to tell her, I am sure."

Then, as if to avoid any further discussion of the matter he rose. "You certainly have had enough of this for today, old man. I think I'll prescribe a little music, now, and, if you don't mind, I'll take some of my own prescription. I feel the need."

He went to his piano, and for an hour Dan was under the spell.

When the last sweet harmony had slipped softly away into the night, the musician sat still, his head bowed. Dan went quietly to his side, and laid a hand on the doctor's shoulder.

"Amen!" he said, reverently. "It is a wonderful, beautiful ministry, Doctor. You have given me faith and hope and peace. Thank you!"

When his friend had gone, Dr. Harry went back to the piano. Softly, smoothly his fingers moved over the ivory keys. He had played for Dan—he played now for himself. Into the music he put all that he dared not put into words: all the longing, all the pain, all the surrender, all the sacrifice, were there. For again, when the minister had spoken of Miss Farwell the doctor had seen in his friend's face and heard in his voice that which Dan himself did not yet recognize. And Harry had spoken the conviction of his heart when he said, "You are the one to tell her, I am sure."

Of this man, too, it might be written, "He saved others; himself he could not save."

CHAPTER XXIII.

A PARABLE.

> "'And do you think, Grace, that anything in all this beautiful world is of greater importance—of more value to the world—than a human life, with all its marvelous power to think and feel and love and hate and so leave its mark on all life, for all time?'"

"Miss Farwell!"

The nurse looked up from her sewing in her hands.

"What is it, Grace?"

"I—I think I will try to find a place today. Mrs. Mulhall told me last night that she had heard of two women who want help. It may be that one of them will take me. I think I ought to try."

This was the third time within a few days that the girl had expressed thoughts similar to these. Under the personal care of Miss Farwell she had rapidly recovered from her terrible experience, both physically and mentally, but the nurse felt that she was not yet strong enough to meet a possible rebuff from the community that, before, had shown itself so reluctant to treat her with any degree whatever of consideration or kindness. The girl's spirit had been cruelly hurt. She was possessed of an unhealthy, morbid fear of the world that would cripple her for life if it could not somehow be overcome.

Miss Farwell felt that Grace Conner's only chance lay in winning a place for herself in the community where she had suffered such ill-treatment. But before she faced the people again she must be prepared. The sensitive, wounded spirit must be strengthened, for it could not bear many more blows. How to do this was the problem.

Hope dropped her sewing in her lap. "Come over here by the window, dear, and let's talk about it."

The young woman seated herself on a stool at the feet of her companion who, in actual years, was but little her senior, but who, in so many ways, was to her an elder sister.

"Why are you so anxious to leave me, Grace?" asked the nurse with a smile.

The girl's eyes—eyes that would never now be wholly free from that shadow of fear and pain—filled with tears. She put out a hand impulsively, touching Miss Farwell's knee. "Oh, don't say that!" she exclaimed, with a little catch in her voice. "You know it isn't that."

The eyes of the stronger woman looked reassuringly down at her. "Well, what is it then?" The low tone was insistent. The nurse felt that it would be better for the patient to express that which was in her own mind.

The girl's face was down-cast and she picked nervously at the fold of her friend's skirt. "It's nothing, Miss Farwell; only I feel that I—I ought not to be a burden upon you a moment longer than I can help."

"I thought that was it," returned the other. Her firm, white hand slipped under the trembling chin, and the girl's face was gently lifted until Grace was forced to look straight into those deep gray eyes. "Tell me, dear, why do you feel that you are a burden upon me?"

Silence for a moment; then—and there was a wondering gladness in the girl's voice—"I—I don't know."

The nurse smiled, but there was a grave note in her voice as she said, still holding the girl's face toward her own, "I'll tell you why. It is because you have been hurt so deeply. This feeling is one of the scars of your experience, dear. All your life you will need to fight that feeling—the feeling that you are not wanted. And you must fight it—fight it with all your might. You will never overcome it entirely, for the scar of your hurt is there to stay. You will always suffer at times from the old fear; but, if you will, you can conquer it so far that it will not spoil your life. You must—for your own sake, and for my sake, and for the sake of the wounded lives you are going to help heal—help all the better because of your own hurt. Do you understand, dear?"

The other nodded; she could not speak.

"You are going out into the world to find a place for yourself, of course, for that is right," Hope continued. "And it will be best for you to find a place here in Corinth, if possible. But it is not going to be easy, Grace. It's going to be hard, very hard, and you will need to know that, no matter what other people make you feel, you have a place in my life, a place where you belong. Let me try, if I can, to tell you so that you will never, never forget."

For a little the nurse looked away out of the window, up into the leafy depths of the big trees, and into the blue sky beyond, while the girl watched her with a look that was pathetic in its wondering, hungering earnestness. When Miss Farwell spoke again she chose her words carefully.

"Once upon a time a woman, walking in the mountains, discovered by chance a wonderful mine, of such vast wealth that there was nothing in all the world like it for richness. And the mine belonged to the woman because she found it. But the wealth of the mine went out into the world for all men to use, and thus, in the largest sense, the riches the woman found belonged to all mankind. But still, because she had found it, the woman always felt that it was hers. And so, through her discovery of this vast wealth, and the great happiness it brought to the world, the mine became to the woman the dearest of all her possessions.

"Tell me, Grace, do you think that anyone could ever replace the mountains, the ocean or the stars, or any of these wonderful, wonderful things in the great universe, if they were to be destroyed?"

"No." The answer came in a puzzled tone.

"And do you think, Grace, that anything in all this beautiful world is of greater importance—of more value to the world—than a human life, with all its marvelous power to think and feel and love and hate and so leave its mark on all life, for all time?"

"No, Miss Farwell."

"Then don't you see how impossible it is that anyone should ever take your place? Don't you see that you have a place in the world—a place that is yours because God put you in it, just as truly as he put the mountains, the seas, the stars in their places? And don't you see why you must feel that you have a right to your own life-place, and that you must hold it, no matter what others say, or do, or think, because of its great value to God and to the world? And Grace—look at me, child! do you think that anything in all the universe is dearer to the Father than a human life, that is so wonderful and so eternal in its power? So life should be the dearest thing in all the world to us. Not just the life of each to himself, but every life—any life, the dearest thing to all. I think this was true of Christ; I think it should be true of Christians. I believe this with all my heart."

There was silence for a little while; then Hope said again: "Now tell me, Grace, ought the mine to have felt dependent upon the woman who found it, and who valued it so highly, do you think? Then why should you feel dependent upon me? Why, you belong to me, child! Your life, the most wonderful—the dearest thing in all the world, belongs to me; just as the mine belonged to the woman and brought her great joy because it blessed the world. When others threw your life aside, when you yourself tried to throw it away, I found it. I took it. It is mine! And it is the dearest thing in all the world to me, because it is so great a thing, because no other life can take its place, and because it is of such great worth to the world. Don't you see?" The calm voice was vibrant now with deep emotion.

Looking into those gray eyes that shone with such loving kindness into her own, Grace Conner realized a mighty truth; a truth that would mould and shape her own life into a life of beauty and power.

"So, dear," the nurse continued, "when you go out into the world again, and people make you feel the old hurt—as they will—you must remember the woman who found the mine; and, feeling that you belong to me and to all life, you will not let people rob you of your place in the world. You will not let them rob me of my great wealth. And now you must try the very best you can to get work here in Corinth, but if you should fail to find it, you won't let that matter too much. You'll keep your place right here with me just the same, won't you, Grace, because you are my mine, you know?"

Long and earnestly the girl looked into the face of the nurse, and Miss Farwell understood what the other could not say. Suddenly the girl caught her friend's hand and kissed it passionately, then rushed from the room. Miss Farwell wisely let her go without a word, but her own eyes were full.

She turned to the open window to see her neighbor, the minister, coming in at the gate.

CHAPTER XXIV.

THE WAY OUT.

"'You see you will need to find a way out for yourself.'"

Deborah was in the rear of the house, busily engaged with a big washing. Denny had gone up town on some errand. Much to Miss Farwell's surprise Dan did not, as usual, take the path leading to the garden, but kept straight ahead to the porch, and his face was very grave as he asked if he might come in. She welcomed him with frank pleasure, and took up at once the thread of conversation which the visit of the Elders had interrupted the day before. But it was clear that her big friend's mind was busy with other thoughts, and soon they were facing an embarrassing silence. The young woman gazed thoughtfully at the monument across the street, while Dan moved uneasily. At last the man broke the silence.

"Miss Farwell I don't know what you will think of me for coming to you upon the errand that brought me, but I feel that I—I mean, I want you to believe that I am trying to do what is best."

She looked at him questioningly.

Dan went on. "I learned something yesterday, that I am sure you ought to know, and there seems to be no one else to tell you, so I—I came."

Miss Farwell's cheeks and brow grew crimson, but in a moment she was her own calm self again.

"Go on, please."

Then he told her.

While he was speaking of the Elders' visit and his talk with Dr. Abbott, she watched him closely. Two or three times she smiled. When he had finished she asked with a touch of sarcasm in her voice, "And do you wish to see my letters of recommendation? Shall I give you a list of people to whom you might write?"

"Miss Farwell!" Dan's voice brought the hot color again to her cheek.

"Forgive me! That was unkind," she said.

"Well rather. You might see that I did not come to you with this for—well for fun," he finished with a grim smile.

"You don't seem to be enjoying it greatly," she agreed critically. "I can easily understand how this talk might result in something very serious for you. You will remember, I think, that I warned you, you could not leave the preacher on the other side of the fence." She was deliberately trying him. "But of course you can easily avoid any trouble with your people, you have only to—"

She stopped, checked by the expression on his face.

His voice rang out sharply with a quality in its tone that sent a thrill to the heart of the woman. "I did not come here to discuss the possibility of trouble for me. Please believe this—even if I am a servant of the church."

He spoke the last words with a shade of bitterness, she thought, and as she looked at him—his powerful form tense for a moment, with firm-set lips and square jaw and stern eyes—she found herself wondering what would happen if this servant should ever decide to be the master.

"Don't you see how this idle, silly, wicked talk is likely to harm you?" he asked almost roughly. "You know what the same thing did for Grace Conner. It is really serious, Miss Farwell—believe me it is, or I should not have told you about it at all. Already Dr. Harry—" He checked himself. His reference to his friend was unintentional.

She finished the sentence quietly, "—has found some people who will not employ me because of the things that are being said. I knew something was wrong, for—instead of telling me of possible cases and assuring me of work, he has been saying lately, 'I will let you know if anything turns up.'"

Dan broke in eagerly, "Dr. Abbott has done everything he could, Miss Farwell. I ought not to have mentioned him at all. You must not think—"

She interrupted him with quiet dignity. "Certainly I do not think of any such thing. You and Dr. Abbott are both very kind to consider me in this way, but really you must not be troubled about this silly gossip. I am not exactly dependent upon the good people of Corinth, you know. I can go back to the city at any time. Perhaps," she added slowly, "considering everything that would be the wisest thing to do, after all. It was only for Grace Conner's sake I have remained."

Dan spoke eagerly again, "But you do not need to leave Corinth. This talk you know, is all because of your companion's reputation."

"You mean," she said quietly, "the reputation that people have given my companion."

"So far as the situation goes it amounts to the same thing," he answered. "It is your association with her. If you could arrange to board with some family now—"

Again she interrupted him. "Grace needs me, Mr. Matthews."

"But it is all so unjust," he argued lamely. "The sacrifice is too great. You can't afford to place yourself before the community in such a wrong light."

The young woman's face revealed her surprise and disappointment. She had grown to think of Dan as being big and fine in spirit as in body, and now, to hear him voice, what she believed to be the spirit and policy of his profession, was a shock that hurt. She would have flashed out at him with scornful, cutting words, but she felt, intuitively, that he was not being true to himself in this—that he was forced, as it were, into a false position by something deep down in his life. This feeling robbed her of the power to reply in stinging words, and instead gave her answer a note of sadness.

"Are you not advocating the doctrines and policy of the people who are responsible for the 'wrong light' rather than the teachings of Christ? Are you not now speaking professionally, having forgotten our agreement to leave the preacher on the other side of the fence?"

The big fellow's embarrassment was evident as he said, "Miss Farwell, you must not—you must not misunderstand me again. I did not mean—I cannot stand the thought of your being so misjudged because of this beautiful Christian service. I was only seeking a way out."

"No," she said gently, "I will not misunderstand you, but there is only one way out, as you put it."

"And that?"

"My ministry."

Dan sprang to his feet and crossed the room to her side.

"What a woman you are!" he exclaimed impulsively.

She arose, trembling; always when he came near—something about this man moved her strangely.

"But my way out will not help you," she said. "You must think of your ministry."

"I thought we agreed not to talk of that," he returned.

"But we must. You must consider what the result will be if you are seen with me—with Grace and me." She caught herself quickly. "Can the pastor of Memorial Church afford to associate with two women of such doubtful reputation? What will your church think?" She was smiling as she spoke, but beneath the smile there was much of earnestness. She was determined that he should know how well she understood his position. She wondered if he himself understood it. "You see you will need to find a way out for yourself," she insisted.

"I am not looking for a way out," he growled.

"Ah, but you should. You must consider your influence. Consider the great harm your interest in Grace Conner will do your church. You must remember your position in the community. You cannot afford to—to risk your reputation."

Under her skillfully chosen words, he again assumed an air of indignant reserve. She saw his hands clench, and the great muscles in his arms and shoulders swell.

Unconsciously—or was it unconsciously?—she had repeated almost the exact words of Elder Jordan. The stock argument sounded strange coming from her. Deliberately she went on. "Really there is no reason why you should suffer from this. It is not necessary for you to continue our little friendship. You can stay on the other side of the fence. I—we will understand. You have too much at stake. You—"

He interrupted. "Miss Farwell, I don't know what you think of me that you can say these things. I had hoped that you were beginning to look upon me as a man, not merely as a preacher. I had even dared think that our friendship was growing to be something more than just a little friendly acquaintance. If I am mistaken, I will stay on the other side of the fence. If I am right—if you do care for my friendship," he finished slowly, "I will try to serve my people faithfully, but I will not willingly shape my life by their foolish, wicked whims. Denny's garden may get along without me, and you may not need what you call 'our little friendship' but I need Denny's garden, and—I need you."

Her face shone with gladness. "Forgive me," she said. "I only wished to be sure that you understood some things clearly."

At her rather vague words, he said, "I am beginning to understand a good many things."

"And understanding, you will still come to—" she smiled, "to work in Denny's garden?"

"Yes," he answered with a boyish laugh, "just as if there were no other place in all the world where I could get a job."

She watched him as he swung down the walk, through the gate and away up the street under the big trees.

And as she watched him, she recalled his words, "I need you;—just as though there were no other place in all the world." The words repeated themselves in her mind.

How much did they mean, she wondered.

CHAPTER XXV.

A LABORER AND HIS HIRE.

> "But it was a reaching out in the dark, a blind groping for something—Dan knew not exactly what: a restless but cautious feeling about for a place whereon to set his feet."

It was the Sunday evening following the incidents just related that Dan was challenged.

His sermon was on "Fellowship of Service," a theme very different from the subjects he had chosen at the beginning of his preaching in Corinth. The Doctor smiled as he listened, telling himself that the boy was already beginning to "reach out." As usual the Doctor was right. But it was a reaching out in the dark, a blind groping for something—Dan knew not exactly what: a restless but cautious feeling about for a place whereon to set his feet.

With the sublime confidence of the newly-graduated, this young shepherd had come from the denominational granary to feed his flock with a goodly armful of theological husks; and very good husks they were too. It should be remembered that—while Dan had been so raised under the teachings of his home that, to an unusual degree his ideals and ambitions were most truly Christian—he knew nothing of life other than the simple life of the country neighborhood where he was born; he knew as little of churches. So that—while it was natural and easy for him to accept the husks from his church teachers at their valuation, being wholly without the fixed prejudice that comes from family church traditions—it was just as natural and easy for him to discover quickly, when once he was face to face with his hungry flock, that the husks were husks.

From the charm of the historical glories of the church as pictured by the church historians, and from the equally captivating theories of speculative religion as presented by teachers of schools of theology, Dan had been brought suddenly in contact with actual conditions. In his experience of the past weeks there was no charm, no glory, no historical greatness, no theoretical perfection. There was meanness, shameful littleness—actual, repulsive, shocking. He was compelled to recognize the real need that his husks could not satisfy. It had been forced upon his attention by living arguments that refused to be put aside. And Big Dan was big enough to see that the husks did not suffice—consistent enough to cease giving them out. But the young minister felt pitifully empty handed.

The Doctor had foreseen that Dan would very soon reach the point in his ministerial journey where he was now standing—the point where he must decide which of the two courses open to him he should choose.

Before him, on the one hand, lay the easy, well-worn path of obedience to the traditions, policies and doctrines of Memorial Church and its denominational leaders. On the other hand lay the harder and less-frequented way of truthfulness to himself and his own convictions. Would he—lowering his individual standard of righteousness—wave the banner of his employers, preaching—not the things that he believed to be the teachings of Jesus—but the things that he knew would meet the approval of the church rulers? Or would he preach the things that his own prayerful judgment told him were needed if his church was to be, indeed, the temple of the spirit of Christ. In short Dan must now decide whether he would bow to the official board, that paid his salary, or to his God, as the supreme authority to whom he must look for an indorsement of his public teaching.

In Dan's case, it was the teaching of the four years of school against the teaching of his home. The home won. Being what he was by birth and training, this man could not do other than choose the harder way. The Doctor with a great amount of satisfaction saw him throwing down his husks, and awaited the outcome with interest.

That sermon was received by the Elders and ruling classes with silent, uneasy bewilderment. Others were puzzled no less by the new and unfamiliar note, but their faces expressed a kind of doubtful satisfaction. Thus it happened that, with one exception, not a person of the entire audience mentioned the sermon when they greeted their minister at the close of the service. The exception was a big, broad-shouldered young farmer whom Dan had never before met.

Elder Strong introduced him, "Brother Matthews, you must meet Brother John Gardner. This is the first time he has been to church for a long while."

The two young men shook hands, each measuring the other with admiring eyes.

The Judge continued, "Brother John used to be one of our most active workers, but for some reason he has dropped behind. I never could just exactly understand it." He finished with his pious, patronizing laugh, which somehow conveyed the thought that he did understand if only he chose to tell, and that the reason was anything but complimentary to Brother John.

The big farmer's face grew red at the Judge's words. He quickly faced about as if to retort, but checked himself, and, ignoring the Elder said directly to Dan, "Yes, and I may as well tell you that I wouldn't be here today, but I am caught late with my harvesting, and short of hands. I drove into town to see if I could pick up a man or two. I didn't find any so I waited over until church, thinking that I might run across someone here."

Dan smiled. The husky fellow was so uncompromisingly honest and outspoken. It was like a breath of air from the minister's own home hills. It was so refreshing Dan wished for more, "And have you found anyone?" he asked abruptly.

At the matter-of-fact tone the other looked at the minister with a curious expression in his blue eyes. The question was evidently not what he had expected.

"No," he said, "I have not, but I'm glad I came anyway. Your sermon was mighty interesting to me, sir. I couldn't help thinking though, that these sentiments about work would come a heap more forceful from someone who actually knowed what a day's work was. My experience has been that the average preacher knows about as much about the lives of the laboring people as I do about theology."

"I think you are mistaken there," declared Dan. "The fact is, that the average preacher comes from the working classes."

"If he comes from them he takes mighty good care that he stays from them," retorted the other. "But I've got something else to do besides starting an argument now. I don't mind telling you, though, that if I could see you pitch wheat once in a while when crops are going to waste for want of help, I'd feel that we was close enough together for you to preach to me." So saying he turned abruptly and pushed his way through the crowd toward a group of working-men who stood near the door.

The Doctor had never commented to Dan on his sermons. But, that night as they walked home together, something made Dan feel that his friend was pleased. The encounter with the blunt young farmer had been so refreshing that he was not so depressed in spirit as he commonly was after the perfunctory, meaningless, formal compliments, and handshaking that usually closed his services. Perhaps because of this he—for the first time—sought an expression from his old friend.

"The people did not seem to like my sermon tonight?" he ventured.

The Doctor grunted a single word, "Stunned!"

"Do you think they will like it when they recover?" asked Dan with an embarrassed laugh.

But the old man was not to be led into discussing Dan's work.

"In my own practice," he said dryly, "I never prescribe medicine to suit a patient's taste, but to cure him."

Dan understood. He tried again.

"But how did *you* like my prescription, Doctor?"

For a while the Doctor did not answer; then he said, "Well you see, Dan, I always find more religion in your talks when you are not talking religiously."

Just then a team and buggy passed, and the voice of John Gardner hailed them cheerily.

"Good night, Doctor! Good night, Mr. Matthews!"

"Good night!" they answered, and the Doctor called after him, "Did you find your man, John?"

"No," shouted the other, "I did not. If you run across anyone send 'em out will you?"

"There goes a mighty fine fellow," commented the old physician.

"Seems to be," agreed Dan thoughtfully. "Where does he live?"

The Doctor told him, adding, "I wouldn't call until harvest is over, if I were you. He really wouldn't have time to give you and he'd probably tell you so." Which advice Dan received in silence.

The sun was just up the next morning when John Gardner was hitching his team to the big hay wagon. Already the smoke was coming from the stack of the threshing engine, that stood with the machine in the center of the field, and the crew was coming from the cook-wagon. Two hired men, with another team and wagon, were already gathering a load of sheaves to haul to the threshers.

The house dog barked fiercely and the farmer paused with a trace in his hand when he saw a big man turning into the barn lot from the road.

"Good morning!" called Dan cheerily, "I feared I was going to be late." He swung up to the young fellow who stood looking at him—too astonished to speak—the unhooked trace still in his hand.

"I understand that you need a hand," said Dan briefly. And the farmer noticed that the minister was dressed in a rough suit of clothes, a worn flannel shirt and an old slouch hat—Dan's fishing rig.

With a slow smile John turned, hooked his trace, and gathered his lines. "Do you mean to say that you walked out here from town this morning to work in the harvest field—a good eight miles?"

"That is exactly what I mean," returned the other.

"What for?" asked the farmer bluntly.

"For the regular wages, with one condition."

"And the condition?"

"That no one on the place shall be told that I am a preacher, and that—for today at least—I pitch against you. If, by tonight, you are not satisfied with my work you can discharge me," he added meaningly. As Dan spoke he faced the rugged farmer with a look that made him understand that his challenge of the night before was accepted.

The blue eyes gleamed. "I'll take you," he said curtly. Calling to his wife, "Mary give this man his breakfast." Then to Dan, "When you get through come out to the machine." He sprang on his wagon and Dan turned toward the kitchen.

"Hold on a minute," John shouted, as the wagon began to move, "what'll I call you?"

The other answered over his shoulder, "My name is Dan."

All that day they worked, each grimly determined to handle more grain than the other. Before noon the spirit of the contest had infected the whole force. Every hand on the place worked as if on a wager. The threshing crew were all from distant parts of the country, and no one knew who it was that had so recklessly matched his strength and staying power against John Gardner, the acknowledged champion for miles around. Bets were freely laid; rough, but good natured chaff flew from mouth to mouth; and now and then a hearty yell echoed over the field, but the two men in the contest were silent; they scarcely exchanged a word.

In the afternoon the stranger slowly but surely forged ahead. John rallied every ounce of his strength but his giant opponent gained steadily. When the last load came in the farmer threw down his fork before the whole crowd and held out his hand to Dan.

"I'll give it up," he said heartily. "You're a better man than I am, stranger, wherever you come from." Dan took the offered hand while the men cheered lustily.

But the light of battle still shone in the minister's eyes.

"Perhaps," he said, "pitching is not your game. I'll match you now, tonight, for anything you want—wrestling, running, jumping, or I'll go you at any time for any work you can name."

John slowly looked him over and shook his head, "I know when I've got enough," he said laughing. "Perhaps some of the boys here—" He turned to the group.

The men grinned as they measured the stranger with admiring glances and one drawled, "We don't know where you come from, pardner, but we sure know what you can do. Ain't nobody in this outfit hankerin' to tackle the man that can work John Gardner down."

At the barn the farmer drew the minister to one side.

"Look here, Brother Matthews," he began.

But the other interrupted sharply. "My name is Dan, Mr. Gardner. Don't go back on the bargain."

"Well then, Dan, I won't. And please remember after this that my name is John. I started to ask if you really meant to stay out here and work for me this harvest?"

"That was the bargain, unless you are dissatisfied and want me to quit tonight."

The other rubbed his tired arms. "Oh I'm satisfied all right," he said grimly. "But I can't understand it, that's all."

"No," said the other, "and I can't explain. But perhaps if you were a preacher, and were met by men as men commonly meet preachers, you would understand clearly enough."

Tired as he was, the big farmer laughed until the tears came.

"And to think," he said, "all the way home last night I was wondering how you could stand it. I understand it all right. Come on in to supper." He led the way to the house.

For three days Dan fairly reveled in the companionship of those rough men, who gave him full fellowship in their order of workers. Then he went back to town.

John drove him in and the two chatted like the good comrades they had come to be, until within sight of the village. As they drew near the town silence fell upon them; their remarks grew formal and forced.

Dan felt as if he were leaving home to return to a strange land where he would always be an alien. At his door the farmer said awkwardly, "Well, goodbye, Brother Matthews, come out whenever you can."

The minister winced but did not protest. "Thank you," he returned, "I have enjoyed my visit more than I can say." And there was something so pathetic in the brown eyes of the stalwart fellow that the other strong man could make no reply. He drove quickly away without a word or a backward look.

In his room Dan sat down by the window, thinking of the morrow and what the church called his work, of the pastoral visits, the committee meetings, the Ladies' Aid. At last he stood up and stretched his great body to its full height with a sigh. Then drawing his wages from his pocket he placed the money on the study table and stood for a long time contemplating the pieces of silver as if they could answer his thoughts. Again he went to the window and looked down at Denny's garden that throughout the summer had yielded its strength to the touch of the crippled boy's hand. Then from the other window he gazed at the cast-iron monument on the corner—gazed until the grim figure seemed to threaten him with its uplifted arm.

Slowly he turned once more to the coins on the table. Gathering them, one by one, he placed them carefully in an envelope. Then, seating himself, he wrote on the little package, "The laborer is worthy of his hire."

CHAPTER XXVI.

THE WINTER PASSES.

"And, as the weeks passed, it came to be noticed that there was often in the man's eyes, and in his voice, a great sadness—the sadness of one who toils at a hopeless task; of one who suffers for crimes of which he is innocent; of one who fights for a well-loved cause with the certainty of defeat."

The harvest time passed, the winter came and was gone again, and another springtime was at hand, with its new life stirring in blade and twig and branch, and its mystical call to the hearts of men.

Memorial Church was looking forward to the great convention of the denomination that was to be held in a distant city.

All through the months following Dan's sermon on "The Fellowship of Service," the new note continued dominant in his preaching, and indeed in all his work. Even his manner in the pulpit changed. All those little formalities and mannerisms—tricks of the trade—disappeared, while the distinguishing garb of the clergyman was discarded for clothing such as is worn by the man in the pew.

It was impossible that the story of those three days in John Gardner's harvest field should not get out. Memorial Church was crowded at every service by those whose hearts responded, even while they failed to grasp the full significance of the preaching and life of this manly fellow, who, in spite of his profession, was so much a man among men.

But the attitude of the church fathers and of the ruling class was still one of doubt and suspicion, however much they could not ignore the manifest success of their minister. In spite of their misgivings their hearts swelled with pride and satisfaction as, with his growing popularity they saw their church forging far to the front. And, try as they might, they could fix upon nothing unchristian in his teaching. They could not point to a single sentence in any one of his sermons that did not unmistakably harmonize with the teaching and spirit of Jesus.

It was not so much what Dan preached that worried these pillars of the church; but it was what he did not preach, that made them uneasy. They missed the familiar pious sayings and platitudes, the time-worn sermon-subjects that had been handled by every preacher they had ever sat under. The old path—beaten so hard and plain by the many "bearers of good tidings," the safe, sure ground of denominational doctrine and theological speculation, the familiar, long-tried type of prayer, even, were all quietly, but persistently ignored by this calm-eyed, broad-shouldered, stalwart minister, who was often so much in earnest in his preaching that he forgot to talk like a preacher.

Unquestionably, decided the fathers, this young giant was "unsafe"; and—wagging their heads wisely—they predicted dire disasters, under their breath; while openly and abroad they boasted of the size of their audiences and their minister's power.

Nor did these keepers of the faith fail to make Dan feel their dissatisfaction. By hints innumerable, by carefully withholding words of encouragement, by studied coldness, they made him understand that they were not pleased. Every plan for practical Christian work that Dan suggested (and he suggested many that winter) they coolly refused to endorse, while requesting that he give more attention to the long-established activities.

Without protest or bitterness Dan quietly gave up his plans, and, except in the matter of his sermons, yielded to their demands. Never was there a word of harshness or criticism of church or people in his talks; only firm, but gentle insistence upon the great living principles of Christ's teaching. And the people, in his presence, knew often that feeling the Doctor was conscious of—that this man was, in some way, that which they might have been. Some of his hearers this feeling saddened with regret; others it inspired with hope and filled them with a determination to realize that best part of themselves; to still others it was a rebuke, the more stinging because so unconsciously given, and they were filled with anger and envy.

Meanwhile the attitude of the people toward Hope Farwell and the girl whom she had befriended, remained unaltered. But now Deborah and Denny as well came to share in their displeasure. Dan made no change in his relation to the nurse and her friends in the little cottage on the other side of the garden. In spite of constant hints, insinuations and reflections on the part of his church masters, he calmly, deliberately threw down the gauntlet before the whole scandal-loving community. And the community respected and admired him—for this is the way with the herd—even while it abated not one whit its determination to ruin him the instant chance afforded the opportunity.

So the spirit that lives in Corinth—the Ally, waited. The power that had put the shadow of pain over the life of Grace Conner, waited for Hope and Dan, until the minister himself should furnish the motive that should call it into action. Dan felt it—felt his enemy stirring quietly in the dark, watching, waiting. And, as the weeks passed, it came to be noticed that there was often in the man's eyes, and in his voice, a great sadness—the sadness of one who toils at a hopeless task; of one who suffers for crimes of which he is innocent; of one who fights for a well-loved cause with the certainty of defeat.

Because of the very fine sense of Dan's nature the situation caused him the keenest suffering. It was all so different from the life to which he had looked forward with such feelings of joy; it was all so unjust. Many were the evenings that winter when the minister flew to Dr. Harry and his ministry of music. And in those hours the friendship between the two men grew into something fine and lasting, a friendship that was to endure always. Many times, too, Dan fled across the country to the farm of John Gardner, there to spend the day in the hardest toil, finding in the ministry of labor, something that met his need. But more than these was the friendship of Hope Farwell and the influence of her life and ministry.

It was inevitable that the very attitude of the community should force these two friends into closer companionship and sympathy. The people, in judging them so harshly for the course each had chosen—because to them it was right and the only course possible to their religious ideals—drove them to a fuller dependence upon each other.

Dan, because of his own character and his conception of Christ, understood, as perhaps no one else in the community could possibly have done, just why the nurse clung to Grace Conner and the work she had undertaken; while he felt that she grasped, as no one else, the peculiarly trying position in which he so unexpectedly found himself placed in his ministry. And Hope Farwell, feeling that Dan alone understood her, realized as clearly that the minister had come to depend upon her as the one friend in Corinth who appreciated his true situation. Thus, while she gave him strength for his fight, she drew strength for her own from him.

Since that day when he had told her of the talk of the people that matter had not been mentioned between them, though it was impossible that they should not know the attitude of the community toward them both. That subtle, un-get-at-able power—the Ally, that is so irresistible, so certain in its work, depending for results upon words with double meanings, suggestive nods, tricks of expression, sly winks and meaning smiles—while giving its victims no opportunity for defense, never leaves them in doubt as to the object of its attack.

The situation was never put into words by these two, but they knew, and each knew the other knew. And their respect, confidence and regard for each other grew steadily, as it must with all good comrades under fire. In those weeks each learned to know and depend upon the other, though neither realized to what extent. So it came to be that it was not Grace Conner alone, that kept Miss Farwell in Corinth, but the feeling that Dan Matthews, also, depended upon her—the feeling that she could not desert her comrade in the fight, or—as they had both come to feel—their fight.

Hope Farwell was not a schoolgirl. She was a strong full-blooded, perfectly developed, workwoman, matured in body and mind. She realized what the continued friendship of this man might mean to her—realized it fully and was glad. Dimly, too, she saw how this that was growing in her heart might bring great pain and suffering—life-long suffering, perhaps. For—save this—their present, common fight, the life of the nurse and the life of the churchman held nothing in common. His deepest convictions had led him into a ministry that was, to her, the sheerest folly.

Hope Farwell's profession had trained her to almost perfect self-control. There was no danger that she would let herself go. Her strong, passionate heart would never be given its freedom by her, to the wrecking of the life upon which it fixed its affections. She would suffer the more deeply for that very reason. There is no pain so poignant as that which is borne in secret. But still—still she was glad! Such a strange thing is a woman's heart!

And Dan! Dan was not given to self-analysis; few really strong men are. He felt: he did not reason. Neither did he look ahead to see whither he was bound. Such a strange thing is the heart of a man!

CHAPTER XXVII.

DEBORAH'S TROUBLE.

"'Oh, I don't know what he'd do, but I know he'd do something. He's that kind of a man.'"

When the first days of the spring bass-fishing came, the Doctor coaxed Dan away for a three days trip to the river, beyond Gordon's Mills, where the roaring trout-brook enters the larger stream.

It was well on toward noon the morning that Dan and the Doctor left, that Miss Farwell found Deborah in tears, with Denny trying vainly to comfort her.

"Come, come, mother, don't be takin' on so. It'll be all right somehow," Denny was saying as the nurse paused on the threshold of the little kitchen, and the crippled lad's voice was broken, though he strove so bravely to make it strong.

The widow in her low chair, her face buried in her apron, swayed back and forth in an agony of grief, her strong form shaking with sobs. Denny looked at the young woman appealingly as—with his one good hand on his mother's shoulder—he said again, "Come, mother, look up; it's Miss Hope that's come to see you. Don't, don't mother dear. We'll make it all right—sure we will though; we've got to!"

Miss Farwell went to Denny's side and together they managed, after a little, to calm the good woman.

"It's a shame it is for me to be a-goin' on so, Miss Hope, but I—but I—" She nearly broke down again.

"Won't you tell me the trouble, Mrs. Mulhall?" urged the nurse. "Perhaps I can help you."

"Indade, dear heart, don't I know you've trouble enough of your own, without your loadin' up with Denny's an' mine beside? Ain't I seen how you been put to it the past months to make both ends meet for you an' Gracie, poor child; an' you all the time fightin' to look cheerful an' bright, so as to keep her heartened up? Many's the time, Miss Hope, I've seen the look on your own sweet face, when you thought nobody'd be noticin', an' every night Denny an' me's prayed the blessed Virgin to soften the hearts of the people in this danged town. Oh, I know! I know! But it does look like God had clean forgotten us altogether. I can't help believin' it would be different somehow if only we could go to mass somewhere like decent Christians ought."

"But you and Denny have helped me more than I can ever tell you, dear friend, and now you must let me help you, don't you see?"

"It's glad enough I'd be to let you help, an' quick enough, too, if it was anything that you could fix. But nothin' but money'll do it, an' I can see by them old shoes you're a-wearin', an' you goin' with that old last year's coat all winter, that you—that you ain't earned but just enough to keep you an' Gracie alive."

"That's all true enough, Mrs. Mulhall," returned the nurse, cheerfully, "but I am sure it will help you just to tell me about the trouble." Then, with a little more urging, the nurse drew from them the whole pitiful story.

At the time of Jack Mulhall's death, Judge Strong; had held a mortgage on the little home for a small amount. By careful planning the widow and her son had managed to pay the interest promptly, and the Judge, though he coveted the place, had not dared to push the payment of the mortgage too soon after the marshal's death because of public sentiment. But now, sufficient time having elapsed for the public to forget their officer, who had been killed on duty, and Deborah, through receiving Grace Conner and Miss Harwell into her home, being included to some extent in the damaging comments of the righteous community, the crafty Judge saw his opportunity. He knew that, while the people would not themselves go to the length of putting Deborah and her crippled boy out of their little home, he had nothing to fear from the sentiment of the community should he do so under the guise of legitimate business.

The attitude of the people had kept Deborah from earning as much as usual and, for the first time, they had been unable to pay the interest. Indeed it was only by the most rigid economy that they would be able to make their bare living until Denny's garden should again begin to bring them in something.

Their failure to pay the interest gave the Judge added reason for pushing the payment of the debt. Everything had been done in regular legal form. Deborah and Denny must go the next day. The widow had exhausted every resource; promises and pleadings were useless, and it was only at the last hour that she had given up.

"But have you no relatives, Mrs. Mulhall, who could help you? No friends? Perhaps Dr. Oldham—"

Deborah shook her head. "There's only me an' Brother Mike in the family," she said. "Mike's a brick-layer an' would give the coat off his back for me, but he's movin' about so over the country, bein' single, you see, that I can't get a letter to him. I did write to him where I heard from him last, but me letter come back. He don't write often, you see, thinkin' Denny an' me is all right. I ain't seen him since he was here to help put poor Jack away."

For a few minutes the silence in the little room was broken only by poor Deborah's sobs, and by Denny's voice, as he tried to comfort his mother.

Suddenly the nurse sprang to her feet. "There is some one," she cried. "I knew there must be, of course. Why didn't we think of him before?"

Deborah raised her head, a look of doubtful hope on her tear-wet face.

"Mr. Matthews," explained the young woman.

Deborah's face fell. "But, child, the minister's away with the Doctor. An' what good could he be doin' if he was here, I'd like to know? He's that poor himself."

"Oh, I don't know what he'd do, but I know he'd do something. He's that kind of a man," declared the nurse, with such conviction that, against their judgment, Deborah and Denny took heart.

"And he's not so far away but that he can be reached," added Hope.

That afternoon the dilapidated old hack from Corinth to Gordon's Mills carried a passenger.

CHAPTER XXVIII.

A FISHERMAN.

> "'Humph!' grunted the other, 'I've noticed that there's a lot of unnecessary things that have to be done.'"

In the crisis of Deborah's trouble, Hope had turned to Dan impulsively, as the one woman turns to the one man. When she was powerless in her own strength to meet the need she looked confidently to him.

But now that she was actually on the way to him, with Corinth behind and the long road over the hills and through the forests before, she had time to think, while the conscious object of her journey forced itself on her thinking.

The thing that the young woman had so dimly foreseen, for herself, of her friendship with this man, she saw now more clearly, as she realized how much she had grown to depend upon him—upon the strength of his companionship. How she had learned to watch for his coming, and to look often toward the corner window of the house on the other side of the garden! But, after all—she asked herself—was her regard for him more than a natural admiration for his strong character, as she had seen it revealed in the past months? Their peculiar situation had placed him more in her thoughts than any man had ever been before. Was not this all? The possibility had not yet become a certainty. The revelation of Hope Farwell to herself was yet to come.

The hack, with its one passenger, arrived at Gordon's Mills about four o'clock, and Miss Farwell, climbing down from the ancient vehicle in front of the typical country hotel, inquired for Dr. Oldham.

The slouchy, slow-witted proprietor of the place passed her inquiry on to a group of natives who lounged on the porch, and one, whose horse was hitched in front of the blacksmith shop across the way, gave the information that he had seen the Doctor and the big parson at the mouth of the creek as he came past an hour before. He added that he "reckoned they wouldn't be in 'til dark, fer they was a-ketchin' a right smart of bass."

"Is it far from here?" asked the nurse.

"Somethin' less than a mile, ain't hit, Bill?"

Bill "'lowed hit war about that. Mile an' a quarter to Bud Jones', Bud called hit."

"And the road?"

"Foller the creek—can't miss it." This from the chorus. And Miss Farwell set out, watched by every eye on the place until she disappeared around the first bend.

As she drew near the river, the banks of which are marked by a high bluff on the other side, the young woman felt a growing sense of embarrassment. What would Mr. Matthews think of her coming to him in such a way? And Dr. Oldham—. Already she could feel the keen eyes of the old physician, with their knowing twinkle, fixed upon her face. The Doctor always made you feel that he knew so much more about you than you knew about yourself.

Coming to the river at the mouth of the creek, she saw them, and half hidden by the upturned roots of a fallen tree, she stood still. They were on the downstream side of the creek; Dan, with rubber boots that came to his hips, standing far out on the sandy bar, braced against the current, that tugged and pulled at his great legs; the Doctor farther down, on the bank.

Miss Farwell watched Dan with the curious interest a woman always feels when watching a man who, while engaged in a man's work or play, is unconscious of her presence.

She saw the fisherman as he threw the line far out, with a strong, high swing of his long arm. And as she looked, a lusty bass—heavy, full of fight—took the hook, and she saw the man stand motionless, intent, alert, at the instant he first felt the fish. Then she caught the skillful turn of his wrist as he struck—quick and sure; watched, with breathless interest as—bracing himself—the fisherman's powerful figure became instinct with life. With the boiling water grasping his legs, clinging to him like a tireless wrestler seeking the first unguarded moment; and with the plunging, tugging, rushing giant at the other end of the silken line—fighting with every inch of his spring-steel body for freedom, Dan made a picture to bring the light of admiration to any woman's eyes. And Hope Farwell was very much a woman.

Slowly, but surely, the strength and skill of the fisherman prevailed. The master of the waters came nearer the hand of his conqueror. The young woman held her breath while the fish made its last, mad attempt, and then—when Dan held up his prize for the Doctor, who—on the bank—had been in the fight with his whole soul, she forgot her embarrassment, and—springing into full view upon the trunk of the fallen tree—shouted and waved her congratulations.

Dan almost dropped the fish.

The Doctor, whose old eyes were not so quick to recognize the woman on the log, was amazed to see his companion go splashing, stumbling, ploughing through the water toward the shore.

"Hope—Miss Farwell!" gasped Dan, floundering up the bank, the big fish still in his hand, the shining water streaming from his high boots, his face glowing with healthful exercise—a something else, perhaps. "What good fortune brings you here?"

At his impetuous manner, and the eagerness that shone in his eyes, and sounded in his voice, the woman's face had grown rosy red, but by the time the fisherman had gained a place by her side the memory of her mission had driven every other thought from her mind. Briefly she told him of Deborah's trouble, and a few moments later the Doctor—crossing the creek higher up—joined them. As they talked Hope saw all the light and joy go from Dan's face, and in its place came a look of sadness and determination that made her wonder.

"Doctor," he said, "I am going back to Corinth with Miss Farwell tonight. We'll get a team and buggy at the Mills."

The old man swore heartily. Why had not the foolish Irishwoman let them know her situation before? Still swearing he drew from his pocket a book and hastily signed a check. "Here, Dan," he said, "use this if you have to. You understand—don't hesitate if you need it."

Reluctantly the younger man took the slip of paper. "I don't think it will be needed," he responded. "It ought not to be necessary for you to do this, Doctor."

"Humph!" grunted the other, "I've noticed that there's a lot of unnecessary things that have to be done. Hustle along, you two. I'm going back after the mate to that last one of yours."

On the way back to the hotel Dan told the nurse that the check would mean much to the Doctor if it were used at this particular time. "But," he added thoughtfully, again, "I don't think it will be used."

They stopped long enough at the hotel for a hurried lunch, then—with a half-broken team and a stout buggy—started, in the gathering dusk for Corinth.

As the light went out of the sky and the mysterious stillness of the night came upon them, they, too, grew quiet, as if no words were needed. They seemed to be passing into another world—a strange dream-world where they were alone. The things of everyday, the common-place incidents and happenings of their lives, seemed to drift far away. They talked but little. There was so little to say. Once Dan leaned over to tuck the lap robe carefully about his companion, for the early spring air was chill when the sun went down.

So they rode until they saw the lights of the town; then it all came back to them with a rush. The woman drew a long breath.

"Tired?" asked Dan, and there was that in his voice that brought the tears to the gray eyes—tears that he could not see, because of the dark.

"Not a bit," she answered cheerfully, in spite of the hidden tears. "Will you see Judge Strong tonight?" She had not asked him what he was going to do.

"Yes," he said, and when they reached the big brown house he drew the horses to a walk. "I think, if you are not too tired, I had better stop now. I will not be long."

There was now something in his voice that made her heart jump with sudden fear, such as she had felt at times when Dr. Miles, at the hospital, had told her to prepare to assist him in an operation. But in her voice no fear showed itself.

He hitched the team, and—leaving her waiting in the buggy—went up to the house. She heard him knock. The door opened, sending out a flood of light. He entered. The door closed.

She waited in the dark.

CHAPTER XXIX.

A MATTER OF BUSINESS.

'You say, sir, that some things are inevitable. You are right.'"

At the church prayer meeting, that evening, Judge Strong prayed with a fervor unusual even for him, and in church circles the Elder was rated mighty in prayer. In fact the Judge's religious capital was mostly invested in good, safe, public petitions to the Almighty—such investments being rightly considered by the Judge as "gilt-edged," for—whatever the returns—it was all profit.

Theoretically the Judge's God noted "even the sparrow's fall," and in all of his public religious exercises, the Judge stated that fact with clearness and force. Making practical application of his favorite text the Judge never killed sparrows. His everyday energies were spent in collecting mortgages, acquiring real estate, and in like harmless pursuits, that were—so far as he had observed—not mentioned in the Word, and presumably, therefore, were passed over by the God of the sparrow.

So the Judge prayed that night, with pious intonations asking his God for everything he could think of for himself, his church, his town and the whole world. And when he could think of no more blessings, he unblushingly asked God to think of them for him, and to give them all abundantly—more than they could ask or desire. Reminding God of his care for the sparrow, he pleaded with him to watch over their beloved pastor, "who is absent from his flock in search of—ah, enjoying—ah, the beauties of Nature—ah, and bring him speedily back to his needy people, that they may all grow strong in the Lord."

Supplementing his prayer with a few solemn reflections, as was expected from an Elder of the church, the Judge commented on the smallness of the company present; lamented the decline of spirituality in the churches; declared the need for the old Jerusalem gospel, and the preaching of the truth as it is in Christ Jesus; scored roundly those who were absent, seeking their own pleasure, neglecting their duties while the world was perishing; and finished with a plea to the faithful to assist their worthy pastor—who, unfortunately, was not present with them that evening—in every way possible. Then the Judge went home to occupy the rest of the evening with some matters of business.

In the Strong mansion the room known as the library is on the ground floor in a wing of the main building. As rooms have a way of doing, it expresses unmistakably the character of its tenant. There is a book-case, with a few spick-and-span books standing in prim, cold rows behind the glass doors—which are always locked. The key is somewhere, no doubt. There are no pictures on the walls, save a fancy calendar—presented with the compliments of the Judge's banker, a crayon portrait of the Judge's father—in a cheap gilt frame, and another calendar, compliments of the Judge's grocer.

The furniture and appointments are in harmony; a table, with a teachers' Bible and a Sunday school quarterly, a big safe wherein the Judge kept his various mortgages and papers of value, and the Judge's desk, being most conspicuous. It is a significant comment on the Elder's business methods that, in the top right-hand drawer of his desk, he keeps a weapon ready for instant use, and that the window shades are always drawn when the lamps are lighted.

Sitting at his desk the Judge heard the front doorbell ring and his wife direct someone to the library. A moment later he looked up from his papers to see Dan standing before him.

The Judge was startled. He had thought the young man far away. Then, too, the Judge had never seen the minister dressed in rough trousers, belted at the waist; a flannel shirt under a torn and mud-stained coat; and mud-spattered boots that came nearly to his hips. The slouch hat in the visitor's hand completed the picture. Dan looked big in any garb. As the Judge saw him that night he seemed a giant, and this giant had the look of one come in haste on business of moment.

What was it that made the Judge reach out impulsively toward that top right-hand drawer.

Forcing his usual dry, mirthless laugh, he greeted Dan with forced effusiveness, urging him to take a chair, declaring that he hardly knew him, that he thought he was at Gordon's Mills fishing. Then he entered at once into a glowing description of the splendid prayer meeting they had held that evening, in the minister's absence.

Ignoring the invitation to be seated, Dan walked slowly to the center of the room, and standing by the table, looked intently at the man at the desk. The patter of the Judge's talk died away. The presence of the man by the table seemed to fill the whole room. The very furniture became suddenly cheap and small. The Judge himself seemed to shrink, and he had a sense of something about to happen. Swiftly he reviewed in his mind several recent deals. What was it?

"Well," he said at last, when Dan did not speak, "won't you sit down?"

"Thank you, no," answered Dan. "I can stop only a minute. I called to see you about that mortgage on Widow Mulhall's home."

"Ah! Well?"

"I want to ask you, sir, if it is not possible for you to reconsider the matter and grant her a little more time."

The man at the desk answered curtly, "Possibly, sir, but it would not be business. Do you—ah, consider this matter as coming under the head of your—ah, pastoral duties?"

Dan ignored the question, as he earnestly replied, "I will undertake to see that the mortgage is paid, sir, if you will give me a little time."

To which the other answered coldly, "My experience with ministers' promises to pay has not been reassuring, and, as an Elder in the church, I may say that we do not employ you to undertake the payment of other people's debts. The people might not understand your interest in the Widow's affairs."

Again Dan ignored the other's answer, though his face went white, and his big hands crushed the slouch hat with a mighty grip. He urged what it would mean to Deborah and her crippled son to lose their little home and the garden—almost their only means of support. But the face of the Judge expressed no kindly feeling. He was acting in a manner that was fully legitimate. He had considered it carefully. As for the hardship, some things in connection with business were inevitable.

As the Elder answered Dan's arguments and pleadings, the minister's face grew very sad, and his low, slow voice trembled at times. When the uselessness of his efforts were too evident for him to continue the conversation he turned sadly toward the door.

Something caused the Judge to say, "Don't go yet, Brother Matthews. You see, being a minister, there are some things that you don't understand. You are making a mistake in—" He caught his breath. Instead of leaving the room, Dan was closing and locking the door.

He came back in three quick strides. This time he placed his hat on the table. When he spoke his voice was still low—intense—shaken with feeling.

"You say, sir, that some things are inevitable. You are right."

There was that in his manner now that made the man in the chair tremble. He started to speak, but Dan silenced him.

"You have said quite enough, sir. Don't think that I have not fully considered this matter. I have. It is inevitable. Turn to your desk there and write a letter to Mrs. Mulhall granting her another year of time."

The Judge tried to laugh, but his dry lips made a strange sound. With a quick movement he jerked open the top right-hand drawer, but before he could lay hand on the weapon, Dan leaped to within easy striking distance.

"Shut that drawer!"

The Judge obeyed.

"Now write!"

"I'll have the law on you! I'll put you out of the Christian ministry! I'll have you arrested if you assault me. I'll—"

"I have considered all that, too," said Dan. "Try it, and you will stir up such a feeling that the people of this community will drive you out of the country. You can't do it and live in Corinth, Judge Strong. You have too much at stake in this town to risk it. You won't have me arrested for this; you can't afford it, sir. Write that letter and no one but you and I will ever know of this incident. Refuse, or fail to keep the promise of your letter, and no power on earth shall prevent me from administering justice! You who would rob that crippled boy of his garden—"

The man shuddered. Suddenly he opened his mouth to call. But Dan, reading his purpose in his eyes, had him by the throat before he could utter a sound.

This was enough.

With the letter in his pocket Dan stood silently regarding his now cowering victim, and his deep voice was full of pain as he said, in that slow way, "I regret this incident, Brother Strong, more than I can say. I have no apology to make. It was inevitable. You have my word that no one shall know, from me, what has occurred here this evening. When you think it all over you will not carry the matter further. You cannot afford it. You will see that you cannot afford it."

When the Judge lifted his head he was alone.

"Did I keep you waiting too long?" asked Dan, when he had again taken his place by Miss Farwell's side.

"Oh no! But tell me: is it all right?"

"Yes, it's all right. Judge Strong has kindly granted our friends another year. That will give us time to do something."

Arriving at the house he gave Hope the letter for Deborah. "And here," he said, "is something for you." From under the buggy seat he drew the big bass.

When Dan returned to Gordon's Mills with the team the next morning, he gave back the Doctor's check, saying simply, "The Judge listened to reason and decided that he would not press the case." And that was all the explanation he ever made though it was by no means the end of the matter.

Dan himself did not realize what he had done. He did not realize how potent were the arguments that he had used to convince the Judge.

The young minister had at last furnished the motive for which the Ally waited!

CHAPTER XXX.

THE DAUGHTER OF THE CHURCH.

"Thus the Ally has something for everybody."

Dan was right. Judge Strong could not afford to make public the facts connected with the young man's visit to him that evening. He could not afford it for more reasons than Dan knew. The arguments with which the minister had backed up his personal influence were stronger than he realized. The more the Judge thought about the whole matter the more he was inclined to congratulate himself that he had been saved from a step far more dangerous than he had ever before ventured. He saw where, in his desire to possess all, he had come perilously near losing everything. But these reflections did not make the Elder feel one whit kindlier towards Dan.

While the Judge was held both by his fear of Dan and by his own best interests, from moving openly against the man who had so effectually blocked his well-laid plans for acquiring another choice bit of Corinth real estate, there were other ways, perfectly safe, by which he might make the minister suffer.

Judge Strong had not been a ruling elder in the church for so many years without learning the full value of the spirit that makes Corinth its home.

While the Elder himself feared the Ally as he feared nothing else, he was a past master in the art of directing its strength to the gaining of his own ends. His method was extremely simple: the results certain.

When he learned of Hope's trip to Gordon's Mills and the long ride in the night alone with Dan, the Judge fairly hugged himself. It was all so easy!

In the two days preceding the next weekly meeting of the Ladies' Aid Society, it happened, quite incidentally, that the Elder had quiet, confidential talks with several of the most active workers in the congregation. The Judge in these talks did not openly charge the minister with wrong conduct, with any neglect of his duties, or with any unfaithfulness to the doctrines. No indeed! The Judge was not such a bungler in the art of directing the strength of the Ally in serving his own ends. But nevertheless, each good sister, when the interview was ended, felt that she had been trusted with the confidence of the very inside of the innermost circle; felt her heart swell with the responsibility of a state secret of vast importance; and her soul grow big with a righteous determination to be worthy.

That was a Ladies' Aid meeting to be remembered. There had been nothing like it since the last meeting of its kind. For of course, every sister who had talked with the Judge was determined that every other sister should understand that she was on the innermost inside; and every other sister who had talked with the Judge was equally fired with the same purpose; and the sisters who had not talked quietly with the Judge were extraordinarily active in creating the impression that they knew even more than those who had. So that altogether things were hinted, half revealed and fully told about Dan and Miss Farwell that would have astonished even Judge Strong himself, had he not known just how it would be.

The Sunday following it seemed almost as if Dan had wished to help the Judge in his campaign, for while there was much in his sermon about widows and orphans, there was not a word of the old Jerusalem gospel.

Monday evening Judge Strong and his wife called upon Elder Jordan and his family, and the two church fathers held a long and important conference, with the church mothers and the church daughter assisting.

The Judge said very little. Indeed he seemed reluctant to discuss the grave things that were being said in the community about their pastor. But it was easy to see that he was earnestly concerned for the welfare of the church and the upbuilding of the cause in Corinth. Nathan himself was led to introduce the subject. The Judge very skillfully and politely gave the women opportunities. He agreed most heartily with Elder Jordan that Dan's Christian character was above reproach, and that it was very unfortunate that there should be any criticism by the public. Such things so weakened the church influence in the community! He regretted, however, that their pastor in his sermons did not dwell more upon first principles and the fundamental doctrines of the church. His sermons were good, but the people needed to be taught the true way of salvation. Dan was young: perhaps he would learn the foolishness of taking up these new ideas of the church's mission and work, that were sapping the very foundations of Christianity.

Nathaniel Jordan, because of the very goodness of his heart and his deeply religious nature, had learned to love Dan, and to believe in him, even while he was forced—by his whole life's training—to question the wisdom of the young man's preaching. And while he was deeply pained by the things the sisters reported, he found, as the Judge intended, that Elder Strong's attitude was in close harmony with his own.

Thus the Ally has something for everybody. Those who did not doubt Dan's character questioned his preaching; and those who cared but little what he preached found much to question in his conduct.

But there was one in the company that evening who contributed nothing to the discussion, save now and then a word in defense of Dan. And everything that Charity said was instantly and warmly endorsed by the Judge.

When Judge and Mrs. Strong at last bade their friends good night and left Nathaniel and his wife to cultivate the seed the Ally had so skilfully planted, Charity retired at once to her room, but not to sleep. Not for nothing had this young woman been reared in such close touch with the inner circle of the ruling classes in Memorial Church. This was by no means the first conference of its kind that she had been permitted to attend. Her whole life experience enabled her to judge to a day, almost, the length of any minister's stay in Corinth. Few had stayed more than a year.

There was Rev. Swanson—who was too old; and Rev. Wilson—it was his daughter; and Rev. Jones—it was his wife; and Rev. George—it was his son; and it was Rev. Kern—who did not get on with the young people; and Rev. Holmes—who was too young, and got on with the young people too well. Charity always thought that she might have—. If he had only been permitted to stay another three months! And Rev. Colby—it was because he had neither wife nor sons nor daughters. Charity was sure she might have—. If only he had been given more time! And now—Dan!

The poor girl cried bitterly in the dark and in her tears determined upon desperate measures.

CHAPTER XXXI.

THE REALITY.

> "'Faith,' said Deborah, who, in the kitchen, heard their merry talk and laughter. 'It must be the garden as does it.'"

"Who shall say that the Irishwoman had not the truth of the whole matter?"

The incident of Deborah's trouble brought Hope to a fuller dependence upon Dan than she had ever before known. The long ride alone in the hack, with her mind so filled with thoughts of her big friend, his greeting of her and his quick response to her appeal in Deborah's behalf, with the drive home in the night by his side, and the immediate success of his call upon the Judge had all led the young woman much nearer a full realization of herself and a complete understanding of her feeling for Dan than she knew. But one touch more was needed to make the possibility which she had long foreseen a reality.

The touch needed came early in the afternoon of the day following the Judge's call upon Elder Jordan. Miss Farwell, with Grace and Denny, was in the garden, making ready for the first early seed. At Dan's urgent request a much larger space had been prepared this year and they were all intensely interested in what was to be, they declared, the best and largest garden that Denny had ever grown.

Denny with his useless, twisted arm swinging at his side, and his poor, dragging leg, was marking off the beds and rows, the while he kept up a ceaseless, merry chatter with the two young women who assisted him by carrying the stakes and lines.

Any one would have thought they were the happiest people in all Corinth, and perhaps they were, though from all usual standards they had little enough to be joyous over. Denny with his poor, crippled body, forever barred from the life his whole soul craved, yearning for books and study with all his heart, but forced to give the last atom of his poor strength in digging in the soil for the bare necessities of life, denied even a pittance to spend for the volumes he loved; Grace Conner marred in spirit and mind, as was Denny in body, by the cruel, unjust treatment of those to whom she had a right to look first for sympathy and help; and the nurse, who was sacrificing a successful and remunerative career in the profession she loved, to carry the burden of this one, who in the eyes of the world, had no claim whatever upon her. What had they to be joyous over that sunny afternoon in the garden?

"Faith," said Deborah, who, in the kitchen, heard their merry talk and laughter. "It must be the garden as does it."

Who shall say that the Irishwoman had not the truth of the whole matter?

The three merry workers were expecting Dan. But Dan did not come. And it may have been because Hope turned her eyes so often toward the corner window, that she failed to see the young woman who turned in at their own gate. Then Deborah's voice called from the kitchen for Miss Hope, and the nurse went into the house.

"It's someone to see you," said the widow with an air of great mystery. "I tuck her into your room, where she's waitin' for you. Dear heart, but the day has brung the roses to your cheeks, and the sunshine is in your two eyes. Sure, I can't think what she'd be wantin'. I hope 'tis nothin' to make ye the less happy than ye are."

"Oh you, with your blarney!" returned the young woman playfully, and then, with a note of eagerness in her voice, "Who is it, do you know her?"

"Sure I do, and so will you when you see her. Go on in child; don't be standin' here, maybe it's the job you've been lookin' for come at last. I can't think that any of them would be sendin' for you, though the good Lord knows the poor creature herself looks to need a nurse or somethin'."

She pushed Hope from the kitchen, and a moment later the young woman entered her own room to find Miss Charity Jordan.

Hope Harwell was a beautiful woman—beautiful with the beauty of a womanhood unspoiled by vain idleness, empty pleasures or purposeless activity. Perhaps because of her interest and care for the girl, to whom she was filling the place of both mother and elder sister, perhaps because of something else that had come into her life—the past few months, in spite of her trials, had added much to that sweet atmosphere of womanliness that enveloped her always. The deep, gray eyes seemed deeper still and a light was in their depths that had not been there before. In her voice, too, there was a new note—a richer, fuller tone, and she moved and laughed as one whose soul was filled with the best joys of living.

Charity arose to her feet when Miss Farwell entered. The nurse greeted her, but the poor girl who had spent an almost sleepless night, stood regarding the woman before her with a kind of envying wonder. What right had this creature to be so happy while she a Christian was so miserable?

To Charity there were only two kinds of people—those who belonged to the church and those who belonged to the world. Those of the world were strangers—aliens. The life they lived, their pleasures, their ambitions, their loves, were all matters of conjecture to this daughter of the church. They were, to her, people to save—never people to be intimate with; nor were they to be regarded without grave suspicion until they were saved. She wondered, sometimes, what they were like if one were to really know them. As she had thought about it the night before in the dark, it was a monstrous thing that a woman of this other world should have ensnared their minister—her minister.

Charity was a judge of preachers. She saw in Dan the ability to go far. She felt that no position in the church was too high for him to reach, no honor too great for him to attain, if only he might be steadied and inspired and assisted by a competent helper—one thoroughly familiar with every detail of the denominational machinery, and acquainted with every denominational engineer.

Thus to be robbed of the high place in life for which she had fitted herself, and to which she had aspired for years, by an alien to the church was maddening—if only Charity had possessed the capacity for being maddened. What right had this creature who never entered a church—what right had she even to the friendship of a minister—a minister such as Dan? And to ruin his reputation! To cause him to be sent away from Corinth! To wreck his career! To deprive him of a companion so fitly qualified to help him realize to the full his splendid ambition! Small wonder that the daughter of the church had determined upon a desperate measure.

Left alone when Deborah had gone to call Miss Farwell, Charity had examined the nurse's room with interest and surprise. The apartment bore no testimony to an unholy life. Save that it was in every way a poorer place than any room in the Jordan house, it might have been Charity's own. There was even a Bible, well worn at that, lying on a table by which a chair was drawn as if the reader had but just laid the book aside.

And now this woman stood before her. This woman with the deep, kind eyes, the soft, calm voice, her cheeks glowing with healthful outdoor exercise, and her air of sweet womanliness.

The nurse spoke the second time.

"I am Miss Farwell. You are Miss Jordan, I believe. I see you pass the house frequently. Won't you be seated, please, you seem to be in trouble."

Poor Charity! Dropping weakly into a chair she burst into bitter tears. Then before Miss Farwell could recover from her surprise, the caller exclaimed, "I came to see you about our minister, Reverend Matthews."

The color in the nurse's cheeks deepened.

"But why should you come to me about Mr. Matthews? I know nothing of your church affairs, Miss Jordan."

"I know that you do not," the other returned bitterly. "You have never been to hear him preach. You know nothing—nothing of what it means to him—to me, to all of us, I mean. How could you know anything about it?"

This passionate outburst and the sight of Charity's crimson face and embarrassed manner caused the color to disappear from the nurse's cheeks. After a moment she said coolly, "Do you not think it would be well for you to explain clearly just what you mean and why you come to me?"

In her effort to explain Charity's words came tumbling recklessly, impetuously out, in all sorts of disorder. She charged the nurse with ruining the minister's work, with alienating him from his people, with injuring the Memorial Church and the cause of Christ in Corinth, with making him the talk of the town.

"What is he to you," she finished. "What can he ever be to you? You would not dare to think of marrying a minister of the gospel—you a woman of the world. He belongs to us, he does not belong to you, and you have no right to take him from us." Then she pleaded with her to—as she put it—let their pastor alone, to permit him to stay in Corinth and go on to the great future that she was so sure awaited him.

As the girl talked the other woman sat very still with downcast face, save now and then when Charity's disordered words seemed to carry a deeper meaning than appeared upon the surface. Then the gray eyes were lifted to study the speaker's face, doubtfully, wonderingly, questioningly.

In her painful excitement Charity was telling much more than she realized. And more, Charity was not only laying bare her own heart to the nurse, but she was revealing Hope Farwell to herself. That young woman was stirred as she had never been before.

When her visitor had talked herself out the nurse said quietly, "Miss Jordan, it is not at all necessary that I should reply to the things you have said, but you must answer me one question. Has Mr. Matthews ever, either by word or by his manner towards you, given you reason to feel that you, personally, have any right whatever to say these things to me?"

It was so frank, so direct, and withal so womanly and kind, and so unexpected—that Charity hung her head.

"Tell me please, Miss Jordan. After all that you have said, you must."

The answer came in a whisper. "No."

"Thank you." There was that in the nurse's voice that left the other's heart hopeless, and robbed her of power to say more. She rose and moved toward the door.

The nurse accompanied her to the porch. "Miss Jordan." Charity paused. "I am very sorry. I fear you will never understand how—how mistaken you are. I—I shall not harm either your church or—your minister. Believe me, I am very, very sorry."

Miss Farwell could not return to the garden. He would be there. She could not meet him just yet. She must be alone. She must go somewhere to think this thing out.

Stealing from the house, she slipped away down the street. Without her conscious will, her feet led her toward the open country, to Academy Hill, to the grassy knoll under the oak in the old Academy yard.

The possibility had become a reality, and all the pain that she had foreseen, was hers. But with the pain was a great gladness.

Miss Farwell need not have fled from meeting Dan in the garden that afternoon. Dan was not in the garden. While the nurse, in her room, was greeting Miss Charity, Elder Jordan, who had stopped on his way home from the post office was knocking at the door of the minister's study.

CHAPTER XXXII.

THE BARRIER.

> "As he looked at the figure so immovable, so hideously rigid and fixed in the act of proclaiming an issue that belonged to a dead age, he felt as if his heart would burst with wild rage at the whole community, people and church."

The Elder's visit to Dan was prompted not alone by the church situation, as he had come to look upon it in the conference with Judge Strong the evening before, but by the old man's regard for the young minister himself. Because of this he had said nothing to his brother official of his purpose, wishing to make his visit something more than an official call in the interest of the church. Nathaniel felt that alone he could talk to Dan in a way that would have been impossible in the presence of Judge Strong, and in this he was not mistaken.

In the months of his work in Corinth, Dan had learned to love this old church father, whose faithfulness to the dead past and to the obsolete doctrines of his denomination, was so large an element in his religion. It was impossible not to recognize that, so far as the claims of his creed would permit, Elder Jordan was a true Christian man—gentle, tolerant, kind in all things, outside the peculiar doctrine of the founders of his sect.

It was impossible for the minister and his Elder to see life from the same point of view. They belonged to different ages. The younger man, recognizing this, honored his elder brother for his fidelity to the faith of his fathers, and saw in this very faith, a virtue to admire. But the older man saw in Dan's broader views and neglect of the issues that belonged to the past age, a weakness of Christian character—to be overcome if possible, but on no ground to be tolerated, lest the very foundation of the church be sapped.

Elder Jordan's regard for Dan was wholly personal, entirely aside from the things of the church. The Elder was capable of sacrificing his own daughter if, in his judgment, it was necessary for the good of the cause, but he would not have loved her the less. There was that inhuman something in his religion that has always made religion a thing of schools and churches, rather than a thing of farms and shops; a thing of set days, of forms, rites, ceremonies, beliefs—rather than a thing of everyday living and the commonplace, individual duties, pleasures and drudgeries of life.

The old churchman did not spare Dan that afternoon. Very clearly he forced the minister to see the situation, making him understand the significance of the gossip that had been revived, and the growing dissatisfaction of the church leaders with his sermons. Dan listened quietly, with no lack of respect for the man who talked to him so plainly—for, under the sometimes harsh words, he felt always the true spirit of the speaker and his kindly regard.

Touching his preaching Dan could make no reply, for he realized how impossible it was for the Elder to change his point of view. The young minister had, indeed, neglected the things that, to the Elder and his kind, were the vital things. That he had taught the truths that to him seemed most vital made no difference in the situation. The fact remained that he was the hired servant of Memorial Church and was not employed by that body to preach what he considered the most vital truths.

But touching his friendship with the nurse, Dan spoke warmly in defense of the young woman—of himself he said nothing. As the Elder listened, he thought he saw how Dan had been influenced in his ministry by this woman who was not of the church, and the idea that had sent Charity to Miss Farwell took possession of him. Even as his daughter pleaded with the nurse to set the minister free, Nathaniel pleaded with Dan to free himself. Inevitably the results were exactly the same.

"Think of your ministry, my boy," urged the old man, "of the sacred duties of your office. Your attitude towards this woman has been, in every way, just what the people expect the conduct of a man to be toward the one he is seeking to make his wife. Yet no one for a moment thinks you expect to marry this woman, who is known to be an alien to the church. What success could you hope to have as a minister if you take to wife one who would have nothing to do with your church? What right have you, then, to be so intimate with her, to seek her company so constantly? Granting all that you say of her character, and all that Dr. Miles has written, why does she stay in Corinth, where no one will employ her, when she could so easily return to her work in the city, taking that Conner girl with her?"

Dan could find no words to answer the Elder. He was stunned by the situation to which he had been so suddenly awakened by the old man's plain words. But there were elements in the problem unknown to Nathaniel Jordan, though the old man felt that somehow his lance had gone deeper than he intended.

When the Elder was gone Dan's mind and heart clutched those words, "No one believes for a moment that you expect to marry this woman."

"To marry this woman—to marry—to marry!" He thought of his father and mother, and their perfect companionship. "What right have you in this case, to be so intimate with her, to seek her company so constantly?"

He started to go to the window that looks down on the garden, thinking to see her there, but checked himself. He knew now why the garden had grown to mean so much to him. He tried to realize what his life would be without this woman who had so grown into it.

Dan Matthews was no weakling who could amuse himself with a hundred imitation love affairs. In his veins ran the fierce, red blood of a strong race that had ruled by the simple strength of manhood their half-wild mountain wilderness. As the tiny stream, flowing quietly through peaceful meadow, still woodland, and sunny pasture—growing always broader and deeper as it runs—is unconscious of its quiet power until checked by some barrier, and rising, swelling to a mighty flood—seeks to clear its path; so Dan's love had grown. In the fields of friendship it had gained always depth and power until now—coming to the barrier—it rose in all its strength—a flood of passion that shook every nerve and fibre of the man's being, a mighty force that would not be denied.

Going to the other window he saw the cast-iron monument. And as he looked at the figure so immovable, so hideously rigid and fixed in the act of proclaiming an issue that belonged to a dead age, he felt as if his heart would burst with wild rage at the whole community, people and church.

"What right had he to the companionship of this woman?"

"The right that God has given to every man—nay to every beast and bird—the right to seek his mate; the right of the future. What right, indeed, had anyone to challenge him, to say that he should not win her if he could? If he could—"

As suddenly as the rage had come it left him, and he shrank hopeless within himself, cowering before the thought of his position in life, and of her attitude toward the church and its ministers.

"The Elder and his people need give themselves no uneasiness," he thought. "The barrier was too well-built to be swept aside by love of man and woman."

He saw that now, even the old friendship between them would be impossible. He wondered if his going out of her life would make any ripple in its calm, even current; if she would care very much?

The Elder had asked, "Why has she remained in Corinth?"

"Could it be—No, no! That would be too much. It was her interest in Grace Conner alone that held her."

So Big Dan faced this thing against which the very strength of his manhood was his greatest weakness, and facing it he, too, was afraid to go into the garden—as he thought—to meet her. He must gain a little self-control first. He must grow better acquainted with this thing that had come upon him so quickly.

Following the instinct of his ancestors to face trouble in the open, he, too, set out, bound for a long tramp across the country. Perhaps he would go as far even as John Gardner's, and spend the night there. He went up the street for a block before turning north, lest his friends in the garden hail him. Then walking quickly he pushed on towards the outskirts of town, on the old Academy Hill road.

CHAPTER XXXIII.

HEARTS' TRAGEDIES.

"So she sent him away to fight his battle alone, knowing it was the only way such a battle could be rightly fought."

When Miss Farwell, under the oak tree in the Academy yard, turned her eyes from the far blue roll of hills to see Dan Matthews coming through the gap in the tumble-down fence, it was as if he had appeared in answer to her thoughts, and the intensity of her emotions at the moment, frightened her.

Her first impulse was to escape. Then she sat still, watching him as if fascinated, while her trembling fingers picked at the young grass by her side. With his face turned toward the valley below, Dan came slowly across the weed-grown yard, unconscious of the presence of the young woman on the knoll. Then he looked in her direction. With her face turned quickly half-aside, she saw him stop suddenly as if halted by the same feeling that had so moved her.

For a full minute he stood there as if questioning his senses. The girl sat very still. Once she thought he would turn back—then he came on eagerly, as he had come that day from the water when he had looked up to see her on the river bank. And then he stood before her as he had stood that other day long weeks ago, with the sunlight on his red-brown hair.

There was now no word of formal greeting. None was needed. Each seemingly knew the travail of soul of the other.

Dropping down on the grass by her side he said quietly, as if it were unnecessary that he should speak at all, "I thought you were in the garden this afternoon."

"And I thought you were in the garden," she returned.

He looked at her in wondering gladness, saying, "I had a caller. After that I could not go."

"And I—I too had a caller; and after that I—I could not go." The words were spoken almost in a whisper. Her trembling fingers were picking again at the short young grass; she was looking far away beyond the sweeping line of blue. One foot had slipped a little from under the protecting shelter of the blue skirt. He saw with a flush of anger that the shoe was very shabby. The skirt, too, showed unmistakable signs of wear. He controlled himself with difficulty, saying, "Your caller was—?"

"Miss Charity Jordan. And yours?"

"Elder Jordan." Dan looked away, and when he spoke again he said bitterly, "Then I suppose you know?"

At his tone and manner she turned her face quickly to his, permitting him for the first time to search her eyes. It was as if she wanted to comfort him, to reassure him.

"Yes!" she said softly, gladly, triumphantly, "Yes, I know!"

Something in her confident reply caused the minister to forget all his half-formed resolutions. His work, his life, the possible outcome, the world itself—were lost in the overpowering rush of the passion-flood that swept his being. His deep voice trembled. "Then you know that I love you—love you!"

He repeated the simple words as if laying his whole self—body, soul and spirit, at her feet.

And the woman, in very wonder at the fullness of the offering, was as one transfixed and could find no word fit to express her acceptance of the gift.

"It is my right to tell you this," he said proudly—defiantly almost, as though challenging some unseen spirit or power. "And it is your right to answer me."

"Yes," she said, "it is our right."

"Then you do care for me, Hope? I am not mistaken—you do?"

"Can you doubt it?" she asked.

He moved quickly toward her but she checked him, and while the love in her eyes answered to the mastering passion in his, she seemed in some subtle manner to build up a protecting wall between them, a wall to guard them both.

"I do not understand," he faltered.

"You must think," she bade him quietly, firmly. "Don't you see that, while it is right for you to tell me what you have, and right for me to tell you how proud—how glad your words have made me, and how with all my heart and life I—I—love you, this—," her voice faltered now, "don't you see that this must be all?"

"All?" he questioned.

"All," she answered. "Everything that I said to you the first day that we met here is still true. Don't you see that I can never, never be more to you than I am now?"

As one who hears himself sentenced to life-exile Big Dan dropped his head, burying his face in his hands.

And seeing him so, such a figure of helpless strength, the woman's gray eyes filled with tears, that were not yet permitted to fall. In his presence she would be strong—afterwards her own heart should have its way.

Once her hand went out, slowly towards the shaggy red-brown hair, but was silently withdrawn, and the trembling white fingers again plucked the young blades of grass.

So they sat, these two—face to face with their hearts' tragedy, each—for the other's sake—striving to be strong.

"Tell me," he said at last, raising his head but not looking her in the face, and speaking in tones that were strained and hard, "if I were anything else, if I were engaged in any other work, would you be my wife?"

"Why do you ask that?"

"Because I must know," he answered almost harshly.

"If you were a common laborer, a business or professional man, if your work was anything honorable and right, save what it is—yes, gladly; oh, how gladly!"

"Then," he burst forth hotly, "I will give up my work. I will be something else!"

"You would give up your ministry for me?" she questioned doubtfully; "your chosen life work?"

His voice sank to a hoarse whisper. "Yes, and if it need be—my religion, my God."

As he finished speaking she laid her hand on his arm. "Hush, oh hush! That is not worthy of you; it is not true to our love. You are beside yourself."

He continued eagerly, "But I have learned that other work is just as holy, just as sacred, as the work of the preacher and the church. You do not know how in the past months I have been teaching this. Why should I not give my life to some of these other ministries?"

"Because it is not some other work that calls you now. These other ministries are not yours," she answered gently. "I have learned to love you because you are so truly yourself, because you are so true to yourself. You must not disappoint me now. And you will not," she continued, confidently, "I know that you will not."

At last when he had argued, protested and pleaded until she was so beset by both his passion and her own that she felt her strength going, she said: "Don't, oh please don't! I cannot listen to more of this now. It is not fair to either of us. You must have time to think alone. I believe I know you even better than you know yourself. You must leave me now. You must promise that you will not try to see me again until tomorrow afternoon at this same hour. I will be in the garden with the others until four o'clock, when I will go to the house alone. If then you have decided that you can, with all truthfulness to yourself and me, give up your ministry, come to me and I will be your wife. But whether you come or not you must always believe that I love you, that I shall always love you, as my other self, and that I shall never, never doubt your love for me."

So she sent him away to fight his battle alone, knowing it was the only way such a battle could be rightly fought, and because she wanted him, for his own sake, to have the certainty of a self-won victory, never doubting in her own heart what that victory would be or what it would mean to her. She indeed knew him better than he knew himself.

CHAPTER XXXIV.

SACRIFICED.

"Standing in the midst of these things, so much a part of his chosen life that they seemed a vital part of himself, he heard the voices in the garden."

Alone in his little study—the door locked—Big Dan battled with himself. Everywhere in the room were things that cried aloud to him of his ministry; his library—books of peculiar interest to ministers, papers and pamphlets filled with matters of the church, written for church men, his sermons—one lying half-finished on the study table, the very pictures on the walls and the unanswered letters on his desk. Standing in the midst of these things, so much a part of his chosen life that they seemed a vital part of himself, he heard, the voices in the garden. He knew that she was there.

Since the beginning men like Dan Matthews have fought for women like Hope Farwell. For such women such men have committed every crime, endured every hardship, braved every danger, made every sacrifice, accomplished every great thing. Few of the race today are strong enough to feel such passion. It was primitive—but it was more. For there had been bred into this man something stronger than his giant physical strength—a spirit, a purpose, fitting such a body.

The little clock on the mantel struck the hour. Softly, slowly, the sweet-toned notes rang out:

One! Two! Three! Four!

With face white and drawn Dan went to the window. All that afternoon, knowing that she was there, he had denied himself even the sight of her. Now he would see her.

He watched as, without a glance toward his window, the young woman left her friends and went slowly into the house. Five—ten—fifteen—twenty minutes! The ticking of the little clock seemed to beat on Dan's brain with sledge-hammer blows.

Then he saw her come out on the front porch of the cottage. Slowly she walked out into the yard, until screened from the street by the big lilac bush. Turning she faced toward his window. She waved a greeting. She even beckoned to him to come. The man swayed and put out his hand to grip the window casing. Again she beckoned him—come. When he did not leave his place and only waved a hand in return, she went slowly back into the house.

Then Dan Matthews, minister—man, staggered back from the window to fall on his knees in prayer.

It was perhaps two hours before sunrise when Dr. Harry's horse stopped suddenly in a dark stretch of timber six miles from town. Dimly the man in the buggy saw a figure coming toward him.

"Hello!" he said sharply; "what do you want?"

The man in the road laughed a strange, hoarse, mirthless laugh, saying as he continued to advance, "I thought it must be you. You nearly ran me down." And Dan climbed in by the physician's side.

The minister made no explanation, nor did his friend, after the first few surprised questions, press him. But when they were turning in towards Dan's gate the big fellow burst forth, "Don't stop, Harry—not here! For God's sake, if you love me, take me on to your house for a little while!"

Then did Dr. Harry guess the truth that later he came to know.

CHAPTER XXXV.

THE TIE THAT BINDS.

> "The Ally was there in power. The day of the rack, the thumbscrew and the stake, is long past: in place of these instruments of religious discipline we have—the Ally."

All the next day Dan remained at Dr. Harry's home, returning to his own rooms in the evening. Early the following morning he was to take the train for the annual gathering of the denomination, that was to be held in a distant city. He would be away from Corinth three days at least.

The minister's little study, when he had lighted the lamp that night, seemed filled with a spirit that was never there before. It was as if, during his absence, some unseen presence had moved in to share the apartment with him. The very books and papers impressed him as intimate companions, as if, in thus witnessing and—in truth—taking part in the soul-struggle of the man, they had entered into a closer relation to him, a relation sacred and holy. He was conscious, too, of an atmosphere of privacy there that he had never sensed before, and, for the first time in his life, he drew the window shades.

In the battle that Hope Farwell had set for him to fight Dan had sought to be frankly honest with himself, and to judge himself coldly, without regard to the demands of his heart. If he had erred at all it was in an over-sensitiveness to conscience, for conscience has ever been a tricky master, often betraying its too-willing slaves to their own self-injury. It is, a large question whether one has a greater right to injure himself than to harm another.

Dan could not admit, even to himself, that he had in any way neglected the church, or fallen short of his duties as a hired shepherd. But after all, was he not to some degree in error in his judgment of his people? Had he not, perhaps, misunderstood the spirit that moved them? He had come to Corinth from his school with the thought fixed in his mind that the church was *all* right. Had he not, by the unexpected and brutal directness of his experience, been swung to the other extreme, conceiving conditions as all wrong?

Groping in the dark of his ministry he had come to feel more and more keenly his inexperience. After all, was he right in taking the hard, seldom-traveled path, or was not the safe way of the church fathers the true way? Was not his failure to put himself in tune with things as he found them, only his own inability to grasp the deeper meanings of those things? He had come to doubt those leaders whom he had been taught to follow, but he had come to doubt more his own ability to lead, or even to find the way for himself. It was this doubt that had led him to decide as Hope Farwell knew he would.

For Big Dan could not turn from the church and his chosen work without the same certainty that had led him to it.

Least of all could he, after that which Hope had made so clear, go to her with a shadow of doubt in his mind.

His convictions were not, as yet, convincing. His new-born love for the woman bulked too large in his life for him to trust his own motives. So it came that he had chosen at such cost to himself, and—making the greatest sacrifice possible to one of his nature—turned to give himself wholly to that which he still felt to be his ministry.

He looked forward now with eagerness to the gathering of church men to which he was going on the morrow. There he would meet the great leaders of his church, those with life-long experience in the work to which he had given himself; those whose names were household names in the homes of his people. There he would come into touch with the spirit of the church as a whole, not merely the spirit of his own local congregation, and in the deliberations of the convention, in their reports of work accomplished, of conditions throughout the country, and in the plans for work to be done, he would find—he must find—the key that would put him in full harmony with those who were his fellow-workers.

Dan's thoughts were interrupted by a familiar knock at the door. The old Doctor entered.

Of the recently-renewed talk of the community regarding Dan and Hope, and of the growing sentiment of Memorial Church the Doctor knew all that Dan knew—with this more. From long observation he understood, as Dan did not, the real significance of this revival of activities by the Ally, and the part that Judge Strong had in its inspiration. Concerning Dan and Hope he could only conjecture, but the Doctor's conjectures amounted almost to certainties. That the lad so dear to him was passing through some tremendous crisis he knew, for he had talked with Dr. Harry that afternoon. Seeing by the light in the window that Dan had returned, he had run across the way to see if all was well with the boy. It was characteristic of the Doctor that, while he did not make known the object of his visit in words, he made the minister feel his sympathy and interest, and his readiness, as he himself would have said, "to stand by."

Grasping his young friend's hand in greeting and placing his other hand on Dan's shoulder, he studied his face as he would have studied a patient. "Come boy," he said, "don't you think we better go fishing?"

The minister smiled back at him. "I wish I could, Doctor; I need it, all right. But you see there's that convention tomorrow."

"Humph!" grunted the Doctor, as he seated himself. "Heard who's going?"

Dan named a few of his church people. The Doctor grunted again. They were nearly all of the inner circle, the Judge's confidantes in matters of the church.

"Judge Strong is going too," offered the Doctor.

Dan said nothing.

"Uh-huh; told me this evening." The old man chuckled. "I rather thought I'd go myself."

"You!" Dan said in surprise.

The other's eyes twinkled. "Yes, me; why not? I've never been to one of these affairs, but for that matter neither have you. I don't suppose they would put me out. Anyway I have some business in the city and I thought it would be fine for us to go up together. Martha's tickled to death! Thinks I'll get it sure if I can only hear some of the really *big* preachers."

Dan laughed, well-pleased. He could not know of the real motive that prompted the Doctor's strange interest in this great meeting of church men.

The next morning at an early hour they were off: Dan, the old Doctor, some six or eight of the active women leaders of the congregation, Charity, and Judge Strong. The Ally went also. There was no little surprise expressed, in a half-jesting manner, by the company, at the presence of Dr. Oldham, and there was much putting together of heads in whispered consultation as to what it might mean. The Judge and his competent associates, with the Ally, kept very much together and left Dan and his friend as much to themselves. Whenever the young minister, prompted by his thoughts of the last few hours, approached the group there was a significant hush, while his pleasantries were met by very formal, and as evidently forced, monosyllables, which very soon sent him back to his seat again with a face that made the old Doctor say things under his breath.

"Look here, Dan," said the old physician, as they neared their destination, "I understand that at these meetings the visiting delegates are always entertained at the homes of the local church people. I'm not a delegate, so I go to a hotel. You come with me; be my guest. Tell 'em you have already accepted an invitation to stop with a friend. Don't worry, they'll be glad enough to have one less to care for, and I want you."

The young man eagerly accepted.

At the meeting was the usual gathering of the usual types. There were the leaders, regularly appointed by the denomination, who were determined to keep that which had been committed to them, at any cost; and to this end glorified, in the Lord's service, the common, political methods of distributing the places of conspicuous honor and power, upon program and committee, among those friends and favorites who could be depended upon to respond most emphatically, or who were—in the vernacular—"safe." Equally active, with methods as familiar but not equally in evidence—for one must be careful—were the would-be leaders, who—"for the glory of Christ"—sought these same seats of the mighty, and who were assisted by those who aspired to become their friends and favorites—joint heirs in their success should they succeed. Then there were the self-constituted leaders who pushed and pulled and scrambled to the front; content if they could, only for the moment, be thought by the multitude to be something more than they were; who were on their feet instantly to speak upon every question with ponderous weight of words, and were most happy if they could fill some vacant chair on the platform. There were the heresy hunters who sniffed with hound-like eagerness for the scent of doctrinal weakness in the speeches of their brothers; and upon every proposed movement of the body, guarded with bulldog fidelity, the faith of their fathers. There were also the young preachers who came to look with awe on the doings of the great ones, to learn how it was done and to watch for a possible opening whereby they might snatch their bit of glory here on earth.

Many there were of this latter class who, from the highest religious motives, had answered the call to the ministry as to something sacred and holy, even as had Dan. These young men, though they knew it not, were there to learn how their leaders—while theoretically depending upon God for their strength and guidance in managing the affairs of the church—depended actually upon the very methods which, when used by the world in its affairs, they stamped ungodly.

The Ally was there in power. The day of the rack, the thumbscrew and the stake, is long past: in place of these instruments of religious discipline we have—the Ally.

Mostly those on the firing line were ministers, though here and there a prominent woman leader pushed to the front. The rest were brothers and sisters, mainly sisters; who like other mortals, always backed their favorites in the race that was set before them all. These prayed sincerely and devoutly that somehow, in ways beyond their bewildered ken, the good God would bless the efforts that were being made for righteousness and truth, hoping thus for heavenly results from very worldly methods.

Judge Strong was an old campaigner. A heavy contributor to the general work and missionary funds to which the leaders looked for the practical solution of their modest bread and butter problems, he had the ears of them all. Nor was the Elder slow to use his advantage. He could speak his mind with frankness here, for these great men of the church lived far from Corinth and, while knowing much of the Elder—the church man, knew nothing of the Judge—the citizen and neighbor. More than this such reports as the Elder had to make must, in the very nature of things, for the good of the cause, be strictly private.

While the Judge was holding these little confidential chats with the leaders, and the leaders were holding equally confidential chats with their friends and favorites, and these in turn were doing as they had been done by, the Elder's assistants, assigned to various church homes in the city, were confidentially exchanging confidences with their hostesses. And this is the simple truth of the whole matter, and the way it all came about.

Dan was introduced to the secretary. "Ah—yes, Brother Matthews of Corinth! Glad to meet you. Ah, excuse me I—ah, see a brother over there with whom I must speak."

Dan was presented to the treasurer. "Oh yes, I have heard of you—at Corinth. Why, hello, Brother Simpkins"—catching a passing preacher by the arm—"glad to see you! How are you and how is the work?"

Dan introduced himself to one or two of those whom he had hungered to see, those who were noted in the church papers for their broad wisdom and saintly character, and somehow Dan felt rebuked for his forwardness when each, from his pedestal, looked at him and said, "Oh yes; Brother Matthews! I have heard of you, Brother Matthews!"

During the forenoon session of the second day the order of business was reports of the churches. In response to roll call, one after the other, the representatives of the various congregations would tell what they had done and what they were going to do. Dr. Oldham remarked later, "No one told what they had failed to do, or what they were not going to do."

As a rule the ministers reported for their own churches, save when some delegate whom the pastor knew to be peculiarly qualified, was present. Generally speaking the ministers consider the value of such a report to be greatly increased if it can be given by some such member. The minister himself always sees that the report is properly prepared.

Judge Strong, without consulting Dan, responded to the call for the Memorial Church. There was a distinct hush, and heads went forward in interest. The Elder regretted to report that, while they had held their regular services every Sabbath, and their preacher was the most popular preacher in Corinth, the conversions for some reason had not been as numerous as in some previous years. But Memorial Church could be depended upon to remedy that very soon, for they were contemplating a great revival meeting to begin as soon as a competent evangelist could be secured. [Loud applause from the professional evangelists present.] They felt that a series of good old Jerusalem gospel sermons would put them again to the front in the matter of additions. [Loud applause from the defenders of the faith.]

Dan listened in silent amazement. This was the first he had heard of a meeting in Corinth. The Doctor saw the boy's face grow burning red.

The Elder continued his report, touching every department of the church in like vein, and finished by "regretting exceedingly that their offering for the missionary, and for the general work for the present year, had fallen short of previous years." The Judge did not explain that he had subtracted from his part in the church offering an amount exceeding the shortage, which amount he had added to his usual personal subscription. As for the regular expenses of the congregation, he went on, they had been cared for.

"And," remarked the state secretary in a loud voice, rising instantly as the Judge sat down, "I want you all to know that Judge Strong's personal contribution to our funds is larger this year than ever before. We who know Brother Strong's splendid Christian generosity will understand how the regular expenses of Memorial Church have been paid." Whereupon the leaders-who-were and the leaders-who-would-like-to-be joined with one accord in loud applause.

Not a preacher there but understood exactly what the Elder's report signified.

Following the reports of the churches came the introductions of the new pastors. Skilfully the preachers were marshaled upon the platform, Big Dan towering at the foot of the line. Stunned and embarrassed as he was by the Judge's report, the boy would not have gone forward at all, had not the Doctor fairly pushed him into the aisle. The old philosopher told himself grimly that the lad might as well get all that was coming to him. In the ceremony that followed Dan got it.

One after the other the ministers were introduced by the secretary, who had a glowing word for each. "Brother Williams who has done such marvelous work at Baxter." [Loud applause for Brother Williams.] "Brother Hardy who is going to do a wonderful work at Wheeler." [Louder applause for Brother Hardy.] And so on down the line. Not one, from big church or little, from city pulpit or country district, but secured the boosting comment and the applause; for this was Christian enthusiasm.

Dan's turn came at last. His face was now white.

"And this," shouted the secretary, "is Brother Matthews, the present pastor of our church at Corinth." There was a hush still and significant; for this was church policy.

After a moment's silence the secretary continued, "Please sing hymn three-hundred and one:

'Blest be the tie that binds
Our hearts in Christian love.'

Everybody sing!" And the denominational papers agreed that they made a joyful noise unto the Lord.

Were the high officials and their mates on this ship of salvation to be blamed? Not a bit of it! The Elder's report made Dan "unsafe"—and he was.

They were right. More than this, the Lord needed the Judge's influence—and money.

When the young minister came back to his seat his old friend thought his face the saddest he had ever seen.

At lunch the Doctor told Dan that he was going to call upon several friends that afternoon, and among them mentioned the superintendent of a famous steel plant in the city. Agreeing to meet at dinner in the evening they parted, Dan going alone to the convention building. At the door he paused.

Several ministers, chatting gaily with friends passing in for the opening of the afternoon session, looked curiously at the stalwart, irresolute figure standing there alone. Two or three greeted him with a word. All were sorry for him; for not one but understood the meaning of the incidents of the morning.

An hour later the superintendent of the great steel works greeted, with admiring eyes, the big clean-looking fellow and wondered at the look of sadness on his face.

"I am in the city with my friend, Dr. Oldham," explained Dan. "I expected to find him here. He told me at lunch that he was coming."

"Oldham in town? Good!" exclaimed the man of affairs. "Of course he would look me up, but he hasn't been here yet. Glad to meet any friend of the Doctor's. Sit down, Mr. Matthews; he'll be in presently, no doubt. Or perhaps while you're waiting, you would care to look about." At Dan's eager reply he touched a bell and, to the man who appeared, he said, "Jack, show Mr. Matthews around. A friend of my friend, Dr. Oldham."

And so the Doctor found the boy standing in the very heart of the great plant, where the brawny workmen, naked to the waist—their bodies shining with sweat and streaked with grime, wrestled with the grim realities of life.

For a little while the Doctor watched him; then, tapping him on the shoulder, shouted in his ear, above the roar of the furnace, the hissing of steam and the crash and clank of iron and steel. "Almost as good as a fishing trip, heh Dan?"

Back in the office again the superintendent introduced them to a gray-haired, smooth faced, portly gentleman—the president of the steel company, a well-known capitalist. The great man repeated Dan's name, looking him over the while.

"Matthews. By your name and your build, sir, you are related to the Grant Matthews who owns Dewey Bald."

"He is my father, sir," returned Dan, delighted.

"Ah yes. Through my interests in the lead and zinc industry, I am familiar with your part of the country, sir. I have met your father several times. It is not easy to forget such a man."

Dan now remembered the president's name, having heard it in connection with the mines on Jake creek, near his home.

The capitalist continued, "I have tried several times to persuade your father to open up that hill of his. He has a fortune in that mountain, sir, a fortune! Are you interested in mining, Mr. Matthews?"

"Not directly, sir."

"No? Well, if your people should ever decide to develop that property come to me; I know what it is. We would be glad to talk it over with you. Good-bye, sir; glad to have met you. Good day, Doctor." And he was gone.

The Doctor and Dan dined with the genial superintendent and his family that evening and the next morning set out for Corinth.

CHAPTER XXXVI.

GOOD-BYE.

> "But the big house for Dr. Harry is still empty when he returns from his long drives; empty save for his dreams."

When Hope Farwell dismissed Dan that afternoon in the old Academy yard, because she feared both for her lover and for herself, she had not for a moment questioned what Dan's decision would be. With all the gladness that their love had brought, there was in her heart no hope; for she exacted of herself the same fidelity to her religious convictions that she demanded of Dan. It would be as wrong for her to accept the church as for him to reject it. So she had gone to the limit of her strength for his sake. But when she reached again the privacy of her room, her woman nature had its way. With the morning, strength returned again—strength and calmness. Quietly she went about; for, while she had left the whole burden of decision upon Dan, her heart was with her lover in his fight.

At the appointed hour she left her friends in the garden and went into the house as she had planned. She did not expect him but she had said that she would wait his coming. Her heart beat painfully as the slow minutes passed, bringing by his absence, proof that she had not misjudged him. Then she went outside and looking up saw him standing at his window; smiling, she even beckoned to him. She wished to make the victory certain, final and complete. Very quietly she returned to her room. She did not again enter the garden.

And now the young woman was conscious that she also had a part to do. For every reason she must not remain in Corinth. She explained her plans to Grace, for she could not leave the girl, and the two commenced to make their simple preparations for the journey. Feeling that her strength was not equal to the strain which another meeting with Dan would occasion, there was no one left to bid good-bye save Deborah and Denny and—Dr. Abbott.

Dr. Abbott's faithful Jim was waiting, ready for a long trip into the country, when Miss Farwell reached the physician's home. Harry himself, dressed for the drive, met her at the door.

"You were just answering a call," said the nurse. "I will not keep you, Doctor."

"Not answering a call, just making a visit," he said, "and there is no need at all for me to hurry, Miss Farwell." He led her to the library.

"I came to tell you good-bye," she said. "I could not go away without thanking you, Dr. Abbott, for all your kindness to me."

The strong hands of the physician, so firm and sure in their professional duties, trembled, as the man placed his hat and gloves on the table.

"To tell me 'good-bye,'" he repeated blankly.

"Yes," she answered, "I cannot remain longer in Corinth."

Harry's face flushed.

"Miss Farwell you do not know how sorry I am for my failure to—"

She interrupted, "Please don't Doctor. I know how you have tried," her eyes filled, "and I know all that you have done. You understand it has been for Grace—" she paused. "Grace will go with me. I am sure Dr. Miles will find her a place in the hospital."

"Yes," he said, "I understand. I will—will see you again some day, Miss Farwell."

"I shall never return to Corinth, Doctor," she answered with a shudder. "If you come to the city, though, I shall always be glad to see you." The words were as frank as from one man to another.

Harry was thinking of his friend, the minister, of the meeting in the night, and Dan's plea to be taken to the doctor's home, where he had remained until late the evening before he left for the church convention. Why was she leaving Corinth while Dan was away attending the convention? Did she know that he was gone? What did it all mean? Could it be—! He started from his chair.

"I may see you again, then? You will be glad to see me, Miss Farwell? Hope—tell me, surely you know what I would say! I would have said it long ago but you would not let me. Tell me if there is any chance for me—ever?"

She had risen to her feet and into her face there came a look of tender sadness. She did not turn away, and the man, looking into those gray eyes, knew that she spoke truly when she said, "I am sorry, Dr. Abbott, oh so sorry! No, there can never be, for you more than my regard and friendship." Her voice trembled. "I know how it hurts because for me—for us—too, there is no chance."

Then Harry Abbott understood.

She left him in the library. Outside she paused a moment to bestow a good-bye caress upon the doctor's horse and then she quickly went away.

Other helpers have now taken the place of the faithful old Mam Liz and Uncle George, for these true souls have gone to the Master of all who truly serve. But the big house for Dr. Harry is still empty when he returns from his long drives; empty save for his dreams.

Dr. Harry will never leave Corinth. When the old Doctor berates him roughly for wearing himself out for those who never express their appreciation, and from whom he can never hope to receive a fee, he laughingly retorts in kind, charging the Doctor himself with having consigned to him such unprofitable patients. He will never give up his patients; neither will he give up his dreams.

Miss Farwell's plans for the girl, whose life she had reclaimed, did not fail. Dr. Miles, when he heard her story, gladly helped Grace to a place in the school where she might fit herself for her chosen ministry; for, said the famous physician, "The best nurses in the world are those who have themselves suffered. No amount of professional skill can make up for a lack of human sympathy and love."

As Dan, home from the convention, was turning wearily in at his gate, Deborah, from the garden, called to him. By her manner as she came slowly to the fence, Dan knew the good soul was troubled.

"It's a heavy heart I have, Mr. Matthews," she said; "for she's clean gone, an' Denny an' me's that lonesome we don't know what to do."

Dan's big hand gripped the fence.

"Gone," he repeated blankly. He did not need to ask who was gone.

"Yes sir, gone—yesterday evenin' be the train, leavin' her kindest regards and best wishes to you."

CHAPTER XXXVII.

RESULTS.

"When he had finished his letter, he bowed his face in his hands and wept."

Dan could not—or perhaps it should be written would not—understand rightly his experience at the church convention. Sadly puzzled and surprised by the spirit and atmosphere of that meeting to which he had gone with such confidence, and sorely hurt by his reception, he had no thought of the real reason for it all. He only blamed himself the more for being so out of harmony—for failing so grievously to find the key that should put him in tune.

In the great steel works among the sweating, toiling men; with the superintendent of the plant, under whose hand men and machinery were made to serve a great world's need; and with the president whose brain and genius was such a power in the financial and industrial world Dan had felt a spirit of kinship. Amid those surroundings he had been as much at home as if he were again in his native hills, and for the hour had forgotten his fellow churchmen and their ministries. But as their train drew nearer and nearer Corinth, the Doctor saw by his companion's face, and by his fits of brooding silence, that the minister was feeling again the weight of his troublesome burden.

By this and by what he had seen at the convention, the old physician knew that the hour in Dan's life for which he watched with such careful, anxious interest, was drawing near.

With Hope gone out of his life he turned to his work with grim, desperate, determination. What, indeed, had he now to which he might turn but his work? He realized that now he must find in this work for which he had made the supreme sacrifice of his life, the only thing that would, to him, justify his choice—the choice that had cost both him and the woman he loved so much suffering. His ministry had now become something more to him than a chosen life work. To those high motives that had led him to the service of the church, he added now the price he had paid in giving up the woman who had grown so much into his life. He *must* find that in his ministry which would make the great price paid, not in vain.

So, with all the strength of his great nature, he threw himself with feverish energy into what had, in spite of himself, come to be a too-empty ministry. Crushing every feeling of being misunderstood, and unjustly criticized; permitting himself no thought that there were under the surface treacherous currents working for his overthrow; blaming himself always and others never, when he felt a lack of warmth or sympathy in his people; yielding for the time even his own conviction as to his teaching, and striving to shape his sermons to the established lines of the Elders, he fought to put himself into his work.

And always, at the beck and call of Dan's real masters, that other servant of the church—that spirit that lives in Corinth—wrought the will of those whose ally it is.

That last meeting of Dan and Hope in the Academy yard, as if by appointment; the sudden departure of the nurse so soon after; and Dan's too-evident state of mind, were all skilfully used to give color to the ugly whispered reasons for the nurse's leaving town so hurriedly.

The old Doctor knowing, watching, waited for the hour he knew would come; understanding Dan as he had always understood him; wisely recognizing the uselessness of doing aught but let him go his own strong, hard, way. And Dr. Harry also, knowing the malignant power that was forcing the end, and conscious what the end would be, watched silently, hopelessly, helplessly, as many a time he had watched the grim drawing near of that one whose certain coming his professional knowledge enabled him to recognize, while giving him no power to stay.

Memorial Church was all astir, and on the tiptoe of expectancy, preparing—they said—for the greatest revival ever held in Corinth. The professional evangelist selected by the Elder, whose choice was, as a matter of course, approved by his fellow officials and congregation, had sent full instructions for the proper advertising of himself, and—as his instructions stated—"the working up of the meeting." Dan ignoring the slight to himself in the matter of calling the evangelist, did everything in his power to carry out his part of the instructions.

The evangelist arrived. Royally received by the Elders and the inner circle, he was escorted in triumph to the Strong mansion, which was to be his home during the meeting, and within the hour began his professional duty of "setting the church in order, and gathering a mighty harvest of souls."

This evangelist was a good one, of his kind. His kind is that type of professional soul-winner evolved by the system whereby the church pays for the increase of its flock at so much per head, inasmuch as the number of his calls, and the amount of his hire depend upon the number of additions per meeting to the evangelist's credit. A soul-winner with small meetings to his credit receives a very modest compensation for his services, and short notices in the church papers. But the big fellows—those who have hundreds of souls per meeting, come higher, much higher; also they have more space given them in the papers, which helps them to come higher still. Souls may have depreciated in value since Calvary, but one thing is sure, the price of soul-winners has gone away up since the days of Paul and his fellow ministers.

Preaching every night and conducting afternoon meetings, calling at the homes of the people, directing the efforts of the members of the inner circle, sometimes with Dan—oftener without him—fully informed and instructed by the Judge, whose guest he was and to whom he looked for a larger part of his generous salary, the evangelist made himself no small power in the church of Corinth. Assisted always by the skill and strength of the Ally, the effectiveness of his work from the standpoint of Elder Strong and the inner circle at least, was assured.

That was a great meeting; a mighty revival, far reaching in its influence and results! So the denominational papers had it from Judge Strong's report, written while the services were still in progress, and edited by the evangelist. And the papers published a greater truth than they knew. There were influences of which they were ignorant, and the results reached ends they dreamed not of.

Night after night—Dan heard the evangelist with harsh words and startling roughness of expression, declare the awful, eternal disaster that would befall every soul that did not accept the peculiar brand of salvation which he and his church alone offered. He listened to the long arguments planned to prove the rightness, and therefore righteousness, of the evangelist himself and his denominational way, and the equal wrongness, and therefore unrighteousness, of every other minister and church not of his way. Then as he heard these utterances most emphatically and enthusiastically indorsed by his Elders and people as the old Jerusalem gospel, the conviction grew upon him that his preaching would never be acceptable to Memorial Church.

And what place is there in the scheme of things as they are for the unacceptable preaching of any gospel? What gospel can a preacher deliver in order to be acceptable to his peculiar church save that church's peculiar gospel? Dan was not one to ask the oft repeated question of the ministry, "What must I preach in order that I may be saved?"

In the semi-secret workers meetings; in the still more private planning of the committees; in the jubilant reports of the uneasiness of the other churches; and in the satisfying accounts of the awakened opposition and answering sermons of the other preachers; in the evidence of the general stirring up of the community; and in the schemes for further advertising and boosting the evangelist and the cause, Dan felt himself growing ever more and more out of harmony—felt himself more and more alone.

In those days the sadness of his face grew fixed; his color lost its healthy freshness; strange lines, that did not belong to his young manhood, appeared; and the brown eyes that were wont to look at you so openly, hopefully, expectantly, with laughter half-hidden in their depths, were now doubting, questioning, fearful, full of pain.

The Doctor saw, and silently "stood by." Dr. Harry saw and wished that it was all over.

Then came a letter from the officials of the Chicago church of which Dr. Miles was a member. The letter asked if Dan would consider a call to that congregation. Again and again Dan read the letter. What should he do? He could not stay in Corinth. The sense of failure haunted him, while he was unable to fix upon the reason for it. He condemned himself for committing unknown offenses. Could he honestly go to another church? How should he answer the letter? He could not answer it at once—perhaps in a few days!

While he hesitated the meeting drew to its triumphant close. After one last, mighty, farewell effort, the evangelist departed to some other grand harvest of souls, to some other church that needed "setting in order." His work was well done! So well done that he was justified, perhaps, in making another substantial increase in his stated weekly "terms."

That night when the farewell meeting was over, and the last "good-bye" and "God bless you" had been said to the evangelist, Dan stood alone in his study, by the window that looked out upon Denny's garden. He was very tired. Never before in his life had he known such weariness. He felt that in the past few weeks he had neglected the garden down there. For Denny and Deborah he had planned that the little plot of ground should be more profitable that year than it had ever been before. He would not neglect it longer. There at least were visible, actual returns for his labor. Tomorrow he would spend in the garden.

But to-night—

Seating himself at his writing table he wrote the Chicago church that he could not consider their call. And then in that little room where he had made for his ministry the supreme sacrifice of his life; surrounded by the silent witnesses of his struggle and victory, he penned his resignation as the pastor of Memorial Church.

Dan Matthews will never outlive the suffering of that hour. He had lost the woman he loved with all the might of his strong passionate manhood. When she had waited and beckoned him to come, he had chosen his ministry. And now—God pity him!—now he had lost that for which he had sacrificed both himself and the woman he loved.

When he had finished his letter, he bowed his face in his hands and wept.

CHAPTER XXXVIII.

A HANDFUL OF GOLD.

"'I fear it is more his church than mine, sir.'"

Rising early the next morning Dan looked from his window to see a stranger already at work in the garden. He was tall, raw-boned, having the figure and dress of a laborer. A few minutes later Dan was introduced by the delighted Deborah to her brother Mike McGowan, who had arrived the afternoon before from somewhere in the west. All the morning the two men worked side by side with crippled Denny.

Returning to his self-appointed task in the afternoon, Dan was met by the brawny Irishman who in a towering rage, was just leaving the house.

"Parson," he roared, "'tis a good man ye are, if ye be only a protestant preacher—a damn good man sir, beggin' your pardon! But you've got a danged poor kind of a boss, thot'll be lookin' more like he ought to when I git through with him."

"Why, what's the matter?" asked Dan stopping with his back to the gate, thus blocking the way, for he saw that the stranger was bent on violence to someone. "Whom do you mean, by my boss?"

"Who do I mane? And who should I mane, but him that runs the thing yonder they call a church, beggin' your pardon, sir. 'Tis the Elder, as you call him—Judge Strong. I'll judge him, if I can coax him widin reach of my two hands." He shook his huge, hairy fists in the air. "It's not strong but wake he'll be when I git through wid him. Leave me pass, if you please, sir."

Dan held his place. "Come, come McGowan," he said, "let's go into the house and you tell me about this."

Deborah, who with Denny was standing in the doorway, called out to them, "That's right Mr. Matthews. Come on in Mike, and talk it over quiet like; let the minister tell ye what to do. It's him that'll save us a sight o' trouble that nobody wants. Come in sir! Come on Mike, come with the minister."

The wrathful Irishman hesitated. Dan laid a hand on his arm and together they went into the cottage.

"'Twas this way sir," said McGowan, "I was sayin' to Debby and Denny here at dinner what a danged fine man I took ye for after workin' wid ye all mornin' in the garden, an' then she up an' tells me 'bout you fixin' up the mortgage fer them an' how they niver could find out how you fixed it with the Judge. 'The mortgage' says I, 'what mortgage is that, Debby?' 'The mortgage on the place, of course,' says she. 'Don't you mind, I was tellin' you 'bout it when ye was here before?' 'Do I mind' says I, 'I should think I did,' and wid that it all come out sir, and this is the way of it.

"When I come from Colorado that time Jack was killed I found Debby here, widout even money enough to pay for a mass, to say nothin' of the buryin', bein' as they had put iverythin' into the little place here, d'ye see? Well I had a run o' luck the week before, which is neither here nor there, but I had money. I knowed from experience that it wouldn't shtay by me long anyway, an' so I thought I'd kinda fix things up fer Debby an' the kid here, while I could, d'ye see?

"Well when 'twas all over, I paid the undertaker's bills an' iverythin' like that, an' then the very day I left I went to that damn thief, beggin' your pardon, an' paid off that mortgage in good, hard cash. Explainin' to him, d'ye see, that I wanted the papers all fixed up straight and clear and turned over to Debby here, as a kind of a surprise, d'ye see, after I was gone an' she would be feelin' down-hearted bein' left by her man and me besides. The Judge bein', as I knew, the main guy in the big church, I niver thought but that'd be all right, d'ye see? Well sir, I went away that very day as tickled as a boy over the thing an' niver thought nothin' about not gettin' a letter about it from her, 'cause ye see wid me on the move so, most of the letters I git from Debby niver find me at all. An' here she's tillin' me now that she's niver heard nothin' 'bout it from the Judge an' she's been payin' the interest right along, an' would a been turned out by him if it han't a bin fer you, sir. An' me wid no writin' nor nothin' to show for the good money I paid him. Now, ain't that a hell of a thing, sir? What kin I do save bate the face off him onless he fixes it up right an' gives back ivery cint he's had off her besides?"

As he listened to the Irishman's story, the new, drawn lines in Dan's face deepened. He sat with bowed head as though he himself were being charged with theft. When the tale was finished there was silence in the little room for several minutes. Then Dan raised his head and the others saw that in his eyes, as though he had received a mortal hurt.

"Tell me, Mr. McGowan," he said. "Are you sure there is not some mistake somewhere? It is very hard for me to believe, that an Elder of the church—would—" his voice broke.

The Irishman's rough tones were softened as he answered, "An' how could there be any mistake, sir, wid me givin' him the hard cash out of me own pocket after his tellin' me how much it was, an' his promise to fix it up all right fer Debby when I'd explained the surprise I'd meant fer her?"

"You paid him the money, you say?"

"That I did sir—gold. Ye see I happened to have that draft—jest a thousand an' I turned it in here at the bank. I remember how the feller at the winder tried to make me take thim dirty bills an' I would not, as neither would you if you lived as long in the west as I have, sir, an' got used to the good, clean gold. 'It's the gold or nothin' I'll have' says I to him, 'clean money to pay a clean debt' an' we had some words over it—his bein' on the other side o' the winder, ye see, where he could talk to me. An even eight hundred and fifty I gave the Judge, one hundred and forty I paid the undertaker and the other tin I gave to Denny here as I was leavin'. The priest I paid out of some I had in me belt."

"Come," said Dan, "we must go to the bank."

In the rear room of the little country bank, Dan introduced the Irishman to the cashier, Colonel Dunwood.

"I think I have met Mr. McGowan before," said the Colonel with a smile. "Mrs. Mulhall's brother are you not? You were here when Jack was killed."

"I was, sir. Glad to meet you again, sir."

"Do you remember cashing a draft for Mr. McGowan, Colonel?" asked Dan.

The banker laughed heartily. "I should say I did—a thousand dollars in gold. I was glad the counter was between us, when I tried to persuade him to take paper. Why sir, not in twenty years in this state would you find a man who would even accept the gold, let alone fighting for it!"

Then Dan explained briefly the situation.

When he had finished the Colonel sprang to his feet with an oath. "And that explains something that puzzled us here in the bank, for many a day. Wait a minute."

He left the room to return with a slip of paper. "Can you tell me the exact date on which you cashed the draft?" he said to McGowan.

"It was the day after the funeral. I disremember the date, but 'twould be easy to find."

The banker nodded, "Our books show that I paid you the money the sixteenth. And here," he laid the slip of paper before them, "is a deposit slip made out and signed by Judge Strong dated the seventeenth, showing that on that date he deposited eight hundred and fifty dollars in gold. That is what puzzled us, Mr. Matthews—that the Judge should deposit that amount of gold, there being, you see so little gold handled here. It makes it very easy to trace. I'll illustrate." He turned to Mike. "Did you spend any more of the gold in Corinth?"

McGowan told him about paying the undertaker. After a moment the Colonel triumphantly laid before them a deposit slip made out by the undertaker dated a day later, showing an item of one hundred and forty dollars in gold.

"You see," he said, "how easy it is."

"Colonel Dunwood," said Dan, "would this be sufficient evidence before a jury to—" He hesitated.

The Colonel let fly another oath, "Yes sir, and before any jury you could get together in this county it wouldn't take half this to send that damned, long-faced, sniveling, hypocrite where he belongs. He is one of our best customers, too, but I reckon this bank can get along without his dirty money. I beg your pardon, sir; I forgot he is an Elder in your church."

Dan smiled sadly, "I fear it is more his church than mine, sir." And they left the banker to puzzle over the minister's remark.

That evening Dan went again to the home of Judge Strong. He had persuaded McGowan to let him act in the matter, for he feared that the Irishman's temper would complicate things and make it more difficult to secure Deborah's rights by creating some feeling in the community against the little family.

Dan found the Judge in his library. Very quietly, sadly indeed, he told the story. The Elder, righteously indignant, stormed at the minister, denying everything; accusing Dan of being an impudent meddler; threatening him with dismissal from, the church and the denomination; accusing him even, with unlawful interest in the affairs of the widow, and taunting him with the common reports as to his relations with Miss Farwell and her companion.

Dan with a look of sadness growing deeper on his face listened, without a word until the final insinuation; then he checked the other sharply, and his voice had the ring of metal in it as he said slowly, "Judge Strong you shall answer to me later for this insult to these good women. Just now you will not mention them again. I am here in the interests of Mr. McGowan. Confine your remarks to that subject."

Then he laid before the Judge the evidence he had obtained at the bank and pointed out its damaging strength. The man was frightened now, but still he obstinately denied having received any money in payment of the mortgage. Dan pleaded with him, urging even the cause of the church, telling also how McGowan had agreed to do nothing further if the Judge would simply make restitution.

The Judge answered arrogantly that he had been a faithful member, and an Elder in the Memorial Church, too long to be harmed by the charges of a stranger, a wandering ruffian, who had nothing but his word to show that he had paid him a sum of money. "And as for you, young man," he added, "I may as well tell you now that your time is about up in Corinth, and I'll take mighty good care that you don't get another church in our brotherhood either. I'll show you that preachers get along better when they attend to their own affairs."

Dan's final words, as he stood by the door, were, "I cannot believe Judge

Strong, that you will force my friends to take this matter into the courts. But we will certainly do so if I do not receive from you by tomorrow noon the proper papers and a check for every cent you have taken from Mrs. Mulhall."

Until late in the night after Dan's departure, Judge Strong still sat at his desk, deep in thought. Occasionally he rose to walk the floor.

When the Judge had received that money from McGowan he had had no thought but regret at losing the property he coveted. With Deborah and Denny left alone in the world, he knew that in time the place would be sure to come to him. He had only to wait. This wild Irish brick-layer—and who knows what beside—who was he to block the Elder's plans with his handful of gold?

The gold! How well the Judge remembered that day, and how when Mike was gone, he had sat contemplating the shining pieces! What a fool the man was to carry such stuff on his person! The careful Judge never dreamed that the money had come from his own bank. The Irishman was going away on the morrow. Planning gleefully to surprise his sister, he had told no one. He would wander far. It would be years before he would return, if he ever came back. By that time the property would be—

It was seemingly all too easy. The Judge's character was not a character to resist such an opportunity. The gold alone perhaps would not have won, but the gold and the place—the place he had planned for and felt so certain of owning—that was too much!

And now this big sad-faced preacher—the Irishman again, and the bank! The more the Judge thought over Dan's quiet words, the more he saw the danger.

So it came about, that the next morning Dan, waiting in his study, received a visitor—the good old Elder—Nathaniel Jordan.

CHAPTER XXXIX.

THE VICTORY OF THE ALLY.

"So the old Doctor found him in the late afternoon—his great strength shaken by rage and doubt; found him struggling like a beast in the trap."

Nathaniel was greatly agitated as he faced the minister in the doorway. He moved unsteadily across the room, stumbling toward the chair Dan offered, and his hand shook so violently that his cane rattled against the window ledge, where he attempted to lay it—rattled and fell to the floor. He jumped in his seat at the sound. Dan picked up the cane and placed it on the table. Then the Elder found his voice—thin and trembling—and said, "I came about—about Brother Strong, you know."

"Yes," said Dan, a great pity for this good old man in his heart. "Did Judge Strong send anything?"

The Elder fumbled in his pocket and drew out an envelope. He extended it with shaking fingers to Dan, who opened it and examined the contents. Slowly he replaced them in the envelope and, looking at his visitor, waited.

Again the Elder found his voice and said with a little more self-control, "A bad business, Brother Matthews; too bad, too bad; poor Brother Strong!"

He shook his head sadly. Dan looked at him curiously, but made no reply.

"Poor Brother Strong," the Elder repeated. "Brother Matthews, I want to ask you to use your influence with these people to keep this sad affair from getting out. Do you think they will insist on—ah, on bringing action against Brother Strong now—now that he has—ah, complied with your request?"

"And why," asked Dan, "should you wish the matter kept secret?"

The Elder gazed at him blankly. "Why? Why, on account of the church, of course. Judge Strong is one of our leading members—an Elder. He has been for years. It would ruin us—ruin us!"

"But," said Dan coolly, "he is a thief. You must know that he stole this money. Here—," he stretched forth his hand, holding the envelope, "here is his confession of guilt."

The Elder's voice trembled again. "Brother Matthews! Brother Matthews! I—I protest! Such language, applied to an Elder is unchristian; you know the scripture?"

"Is it not true?" persisted Dan.

"Ahem! Brother Strong may have made a mistake, may—ah, have done wrong, but the church—the church; we must think of the good name of the cause! Coming so soon after the revival, too!"

"Am I to understand, then, that the church will keep this man in his place as an Elder; that you will protect him when you know his true character?"

At the question the other stared blankly. "Why—why how could we get along without him?"

"How can you get along with him?" asked Dan.

"But there isn't a man in Corinth who has done so much for us and for the missionary cause! No, no, we must be more careful, Brother Matthews."

"Then for the sake of his contributions and his position in the community the church will shield him from the results of his crime?"

The Elder squirmed uneasily in his chair.

"Is that what you mean?" insisted Dan.

"Why—I—I don't think, Brother Matthews, for the good of our cause in Corinth, that it would be good policy to make this matter public and so create a great stir. Brother Strong has made restitution. We must be charitable, brother, and forgiving. You must not think too—too hard of him. Are these people determined to push this matter?"

"Oh, no," said Dan, "not at all. They want only that which belongs to them. You may rest easy; as I told the Judge last night, this will end the matter. It was under that promise that he made restitution, as you call it. I was simply asking to know how the church would look upon such a thing when it touches an Elder. You have explained it clearly—*policy!*"

The Elder stiffened. It was remarkable how quickly he revived under Dan's assurance that the danger was past! Very dignified now, as became one in his position, he said, "Ahem, ahem! I fear, Brother Matthews, that you are not—ah—not entirely in harmony with our brotherhood in many things."

Dan was silent.

"Ahem! The tone of your sermons has been I may say—ah, questioned by a good many of us, and your attitude toward the board has not been quite as cordial as we feel we have a right to expect."

"Do you speak from personal experience, sir?"

"Oh, no—no indeed, Brother Matthews; but—ah, Brother Strong has felt for some time past that you have treated him rather coldly."

Dan waited.

"A lack of harmony between a pastor and his Elder is very bad—ah, very bad. Ahem! Ahem! And so, considering everything we—Brother Str—that is the board have thought best that your relations with the Memorial Church should discontinue."

"And when was this action taken?" asked Dan quietly.

"The day before the meetings closed. We wished to have the benefit of Brother Sigman's advice before he left. He met with us and we considered the whole matter quite carefully and prayerfully. I was appointed to tell you. I should add that there is no doubt but the people will concur in the board's decision. Many of the members, I may say, were seen before we took action."

Dan glanced toward his desk where, in the envelopes, lay his resignation and his answer to the Chicago church. In the excitement of McGowan's trouble he had neglected to mail them.

"Of course," he questioned, quietly curious now, "the board will give me a letter?"

"Ahem! We—ah, discussed that also," said the Elder. "Brother Strong and the Evangelist—and, I may say, the entire board feel that we cannot consistently do so."

"May I ask why?"

"Ahem! Your teaching, Brother Matthews, does not seem to be in harmony with the brotherhood. We cannot endorse it, and the talk in the community about your conduct has been very damaging; very!"

"Is it charged that my teaching has been false to the principles of Christianity as taught by Christ?"

"I cannot discuss that part, Brother Matthews. It is not such teaching as the churches of our brotherhood want."

"Does the church, sir, believe that my character is bad?"

"No, sir—no, sir! No one really believes that, but you have been—ah, injudicious. There has been so much talk, you know—"

"Who has talked?" Dan interrupted.

The Elder continued, "These things follow a minister all his life. We cannot recommend a man of bad repute to our sister churches; it would reflect upon us."

"For the same reason that you keep in a high office in the church a man who is an unrepentant thief?" said Dan.

The Elder rose. "Really, Brother Matthews, I cannot listen to such words about our Elder!"

"I beg your pardon, sir," said Dan huskily. "I was thinking aloud. Please tell me one thing more. I have here a letter from a church in Chicago asking me to consider a call. Have the Elders received a letter from them?"

"Ahem! Yes, we considered it at that same meeting."

"And you have written them?"

"We could not recommend you. I am sorry, Brother Matthews."

"I believe you are," said Dan slowly. "Thank you."

When the Elder was gone Dan turned sadly back to his little study; the study that had come to stand so for everything to which he had devoted his life with such holy purpose, for which he had sacrificed so much.

Slowly he went to his desk and looked down upon the work scattered over it. Taking up the two letters he tore them slowly into fragments and dropped them into the waste basket. Then as slowly he turned to his books, touching many of the familiar volumes with a caressing hand. Then he went to the table where lay his church papers and the missionary pamphlets and reports. The envelope from Judge Strong caught his eye.

Mechanically he took his hat and went to carry the message to his friends on the other side of the garden. From across the street the old Doctor hailed him but he did not hear.

Delivering the envelope, with a few brief words, the minister left his friends and wandered on down the street in a bewildered, dazed fashion, scarce knowing where he went, or why; until he turned in through the gap in the tumble-down fence to the old Academy yard.

But he could not stay there. The place was haunted, he could not stay! He turned his face toward the open country, but the fields and woodlands had no call for him that day. It was his little study that called; his books, his work.

As one goes to sit beside the body of a dear friend, conscious that the friend he loved is not there, yet unable to leave the form wherein the spirit had lived, so Dan went back to his room, his desk, his books, his papers—that which had been his work.

And now the deep passions of the man stirred themselves—awoke. Wild anger, mad rage, seized and shook him. His whole sense of justice was outraged. This was not Christianity, this thing that had caught him in its foul snare! And if the church was not Christian what was Christianity? Was there, indeed, such a thing? Was it all such a hollow mockery?

So the Doctor found him in the late afternoon—his great strength shaken by rage and doubt; found him struggling like a beast in the trap.

And the Doctor saw that the hour for which he had waited had come.

Dan needed him—needed him badly!

CHAPTER XL.

THE DOCTOR'S GLASSES.

"'There is no hatred, lad, so bitter as that hatred born of a religious love; no falsehood so vile as the lie spoken in defense of truth; no wrong so harmful as the wrong committed in the name of righteousness; no injustice so terrible as the injustice of those who condemn in the name of the Saviour of the world!'"

When Dan, forced into something of his habitual self-control and calmness by the presence of his old friend, began telling the Doctor of the action of the church the other checked him abruptly with, "I know all about that, lad."

"You know!" ejaculated Dan.

"Certainly I know. Isn't Martha one of the elect? I reckon everybody in the whole town but you knew it before noon of the day after the meeting."

Dan muttered something about being a blind fool and the old Doctor answered, "Humph! The fools are they who see too much, boy. Such blindness as yours is a gift of the gods; for Heaven's sake don't let any quack fit you out with glasses!"

Dan threw himself wearily into a chair and there was a spirit of recklessness in his reply, as though he were letting go of himself again. "How is a blind man to recognize a quack? I would to God I had your glasses!"

"Perhaps," said the Doctor deliberately, "I might lend them to you, just for once, you know."

"Well then," said the other, sitting up suddenly, "let me have them! How do you see this thing? What have I done or not done? For what shall I blame myself? What fatal error have I made that, with the best of motives, with the—," he hesitated, then—"I can say it to you, Doctor, and I will—with the sacrifice of the dearest thing in the world to me, I am cast out in this fashion? If I can find a reason for it, I can bear it."

"It is your blindness, boy. You could not help it; you were born blind. I have always known this would come."

"You have always known this would come?" repeated Dan questioningly.

"Yes, I have always known, because for half a century, boy, I have observed the spirit of this institution. Mind, I do not say the spirit of the people in the institution. Strong people, Dan, sometimes manage to live in mighty sickly climates. The best people in the world are sometimes held by evil circumstances which their own best intentions have created. The people in the church are the salt of the earth. If it were not for their goodness the system would have rotted long ago. The church, for all its talk, doesn't save the people; the people save the church. And let me tell you, Dan, the very ones in the church who have done the things you have seen and felt, at heart respect and believe in you."

Dan broke forth in such a laugh as the Doctor had never heard from his lips. "Then why?"

"Because," said the old man, "it is their religion to worship an institution, not a God; to serve a system, not the race. It is history, my boy. Every reformation begins with the persecution of the reformer and ends with the followers of that reformer persecuting those who would lead them another step toward freedom. Misguided religious people have always crucified their saviors and always will!"

Dan was silent, awed by the revelation of his old friend's mind. Presently the Doctor continued, "There is no hatred, lad, so bitter as that hatred born of a religious love; no falsehood so vile as the lie spoken in defense of truth; no wrong so harmful as the wrong committed in the name of righteousness; no injustice so terrible as the injustice of those who condemn in the name of the Saviour of the world!"

"What then, as you see it—what can I do?" demanded Dan.

The Doctor changed his tone. His reply was more a question than an answer. "There are other churches?"

Dan laughed bitterly. "They have taken care of that, too." He began to tell of the call to Chicago and the Elders' refusal to give him a letter, but again the Doctor interrupted him. "Yes, I know about that, too."

"Well," demanded Dan almost angrily.

"Well," answered the other easily, "there are still other churches."

"You mean—."

"I mean that you are not the only preacher who has been talked about by his church, and branded by his official board with the mark of the devil in the name of the Lord. It's easy enough! Go farther, get a little obscure congregation somewhere, stay long enough to get a letter, not long enough to make another name; try another in the same fashion. Lay low, keep quiet, stay away from conventions, watch your chance, and—when the time is ripe—make a hit with the state workers in some other state. You know how! It's all easy enough!"

Dan leaped to his feet. "Good God, Doctor! I have done nothing wrong. Why should I skulk, and hide, and scheme to conceal something I never did, for the privilege of serving a church that doesn't want me? Is this the ministry?"

"It seems to be a large part of it," answered the other deliberately. "My boy, it's the things that preachers have not done that they try hardest to hide. As to why, I must confess that I am a little near-sighted myself sometimes."

"I can't, I can't do it, Doctor!"

"Humph! I didn't suppose you could," came dryly from the old man.

Dan did not heed but went on in a hopeless tone to tell the Doctor how he had written his resignation, and had declined to consider the call to Chicago. "Don't you see that I couldn't take a church if one were offered me now?" he asked. "Don't you understand what this has done for me? It's not the false charges. It's not that! It's—it's the thing, whatever it is, that has made this action of the church possible. I am forced to doubt, not alone the church, but everything—the people, myself, God, Christ, Christianity, life itself; everything! How can I go on with a work, in which I cannot say to myself with truth that I believe?" His voice ended in a groan.

And the old man, who knew the lad so well felt as though he were gazing upon the big, naked soul. Then, indeed, the Doctor knew that the hour had come.

There are those who, capable of giving but little to life, demand of life much in return. To such weak natures doubt means not much. But souls like this one, capable of giving themselves to the last atom of their strength, demand no small returns in convictions as to the worthiness of the cause to which they contribute. To such, doubt is destruction. It was because Dan had believed so strongly, so wholly in the ministry of the church that he had failed. Had he not accepted so unreservedly, and given himself so completely to the ministry as it was presented to him in theory, had he in some degree doubted, he would have been able to adjust himself to the actual conditions. He would have succeeded.

For while, theoretically, the strength of the church is in its fidelity to the things in which it professes to believe; practically and actually the strength of the church of today is in its tacit acceptance of its unbeliefs. Strange things would befall us if we should ever get the habit of insisting that our practice square with our preaching; if churches should make this the test of fellowship—that men must live their doctrines, rather than teach them—that they must live their beliefs rather than confess them—that they must live their faiths, rather than profess them.

Dan's was not a nature that could preach things in which he only half believed to a people whose belief he knew to be no stronger than his own. It was with these things in mind that the Doctor had waited for this moment in Dan's life, for the old man realized, as the young man could not, what such moments mean.

Rising and going to the window overlooking the garden the Doctor called to Dan, "Come here, boy!"

Together they stood looking down on the little plot of ground with its growing vegetables, where Denny, with his helpless, swinging arm, and twisted, dragging foot, was digging away, his cheery whistle floating up to them. The physician spoke with a depth of feeling he had never betrayed before, while Dan, troubled as he was, listened in wonder to his friend, who had always been so reticent in matters such as this.

"Dan," he said, "you wished for my glasses. 'Tis always a mighty dangerous thing to try to see through another man's eyes, but here are mine." He pointed below.

"Down there I see religion—Christianity—what you will, but religion; living, growing, ever-changing, through the season-ages; lying dormant sometimes, it may be, but always there; yielding to each season the things that belong to that season; depending for its strength and power upon the Great Source of all strength and power; depending as truly upon man's efforts, upon his cultivation and care. There is variety, harmony, law, freedom. There is God! Something for all—potatoes, peas, turnips, cabbage. If you do not care for lettuce, perhaps radishes will satisfy. And there, boy, in the midst of his church, ministering to the needs of his congregation, and thus ministering to men—is my minister: crippled, patient Denny, who gives his frail strength to keep the garden growing.

"And look you, boy, at the great rock in the very center of the field! How often Denny has wished it out of his way! I caught the poor lad digging, one time, to find, if he could, how deep it is in the earth, and how big. For three days I watched him. Then he gave it up. It is beyond his strength and he wisely turned to devote his energies to the productive soil around it.

"There is a rock in every garden, Dan. Religion grows always about the unknowable. But Denny's ministry has naught to do with the rock, it has to do with the growing things about it. So religion is in the knowable things not in the unknowable; there such men as you, lad, must find it. And the rock, boy, was not put in the garden by men. It belongs to the earth itself."

While the Doctor was speaking his eyes had been fixed on the crippled boy in the garden. He turned now, for the first time, to face the young man by his side. Dan's eyes had that wide, questioning look. The old physician moved to the other window.

"Now come, see what men have done." He pointed to the cast-iron monument. "These people will tell you that was erected to commemorate the life of my friend. His was a warm, tender, loving spirit—a great, ever-growing soul. What can that hard, cold, immovable mass tell of him? How can that thing—perpetuating an issue that belongs to a past age, that has nothing to do with the life of today—how can that thing speak of the great heart that loved and gave itself always to men?

"Through my glasses that is the church! How can an institution, or a system of theological beliefs—with cast-iron prejudices, cast-iron fidelity to issues long past and forgotten, cast-iron unconcern of vital issues of the life of today and cast-iron want of sympathy with the living who toil and fight and die on every side—how can such speak the great loving, sympathetic, helpful spirit of Him whose name only it bears, as that bears only the name of my friend?

"But would the people of this town, out of love for my dead friend, tear down that monument if Denny should leave his garden to argue with them about it? Why, they would tell him that it is because of their love for the statesman that they keep it there and they believe it—and it is true. Well, then, let them keep their monument and let Denny work in his garden! And don't you see, Dan, that the very ones who fight for the cast-iron monument must depend at last for their lives and strength upon the things that Denny grows in his garden. Now boy, that's the first and only time I ever preached."

CHAPTER XLI.

THE FINAL WORD.

"'This closes my ministry as you understand it. It by no means closes my ministry as I have come to understand it.'"

Dan's farewell sermon was to be given in the evening. John Gardner, who—true to the promise he had made when he challenged the minister, after that sermon on "Fellowship of Service"—had become a regular attendant, was present in the morning.

In the afternoon the farmer called on Dan in his study.

"Look here, Dan," he said. "You are making the mistake of your life."

"You're wrong, John. I made that mistake nearly two years ago," he answered.

"I mean in leaving Corinth as you are leaving it."

"And I mean in coming to Corinth as I came to it."

"But wait a minute; let me tell you! You have done a lot of good in this town; you don't know—."

"So have you done a lot of good, John; you don't know either."

The farmer tried again. "You have helped me more than you know."

"I'm glad, John, because you have helped me more than *you* know."

"Oh, come; you know what I mean!"

"Well, don't you know what I mean?"

"Yes, I think I do. I've been listening pretty close to your sermons and so have a lot of others. I have managed to talk with a good many church people since it was known that you were going; just common plugs in the congregation, like me, you know." Dan smiled. "We all understand what you have been driving at in your preaching, and we know pretty well what the bosses think about it, and why they have let you out. No one takes any stock in that foul gossip, not even Strong himself. Now what I came to say is this: a lot of us want you to stay. Why can't we have another church for our people right here in Corinth? There's enough of us to back you, and we mean business."

Dan shook his head sadly.

"Thank you, John," he said simply. "It is useless for me to try to tell you how much good this does me; but I can't accept. I have thought of the possibility you mention, but I can't do it. You do not need another church in Corinth. You have more than you need now."

Nor could any argument move him.

"Well," said the farmer, when at last he gave it up and rose to say good-bye, "I suppose I'll keep right on being a church member, but I reckon I'll have to find most of my religion in my work."

"And that," said Dan, as he gripped his friend's hand, "is the best place I know of to look for it. If you cannot find God in your everyday work, John, you'll not find Him on Sunday at the church."

That farewell sermon is still talked about in Corinth or rather—it should be said—is still remembered, for it was one of those sermons of which, while little could be said, much could never be forgotten. And the picture of the big lad, whose strong, clean-looking body drooped so as if in great weariness; whose frank open countenance was marked with drawn lines; in whose clear brown eyes were shadows of trouble and pain; whose voice betrayed the sadness of a mighty soul, will also remain long in the memory of those who were there that evening.

The place was crowded. The triumphant Judge and his friends of the inner circle were there in force, striving in vain to hide, with pious expression of countenance, the satisfaction and pride they felt in their power. The other members were there, curious to hear what Dan would say; wondering how much he knew of the methods that had brought about his dismissal; a little sorry for him; a little indignant; and with a feeling of impotence withal that made their sorrow and indignation of no worth whatever. With identically the same emotions as the members, except that it felt free to express them more freely, the world was there. To a portion of the congregation Dan stood in the peculiar position of a friend whom, as an individual, they loved and trusted, but whom, as a preacher, they were forced to regard as unsafe and dangerous.

It would not do to report all he said, for much of his sermon was not fashioned for the printed page.

But his final words were: "It is not the spirit of wealth, of learning, or of culture that can make the church of value, or a power for good in the world, but the spirit of Christ only. It is not in fidelity to the past but in fidelity to the present that the church can be Christian. It is not the opinion of man, but the eternal truths of God that can make it a sacred, holy thing. It is holy to the degree that God is in it. God is as truly in the fields of grain, in the forests, in the mines, and in those laws of Nature by which men convert the product of field and forest and mine into the necessities of life. Therefore these are as truly holy as this institution. Therefore, again, the ministry of farm, and mine, and factory, and shop; of mill, and railroad, and store, and office, and wherever men toil with strength of body or strength of mind for that which makes for the best life of their kind—that ministry is sacred and holy.

"Because I believe these things I am, from this hour, no longer a professional preacher, hired by and working under the direction of any denomination or church leaders. This closes my ministry as you understand it. It by no means closes my ministry as I have come to understand it."

When he had finished they crowded around him to express regret at his going—sorry that he was leaving the ministry; the church needed men of his great ability—prayed God to bless him wherever he should go—all this and much more, with hand-shaking and many tears from the very people who had made it impossible for him to stay. For this is the way of us all!

As quickly as he could Dan left the church, and with the Doctor walked toward home. The two made no exchange of words, until they reached the monument, where they paused to stand silently contemplating the cast-iron figure. At last Dan turned with a smile. "It is very good cast-iron, I suppose, Doctor."

Then, as if dismissing the whole matter, he took his old friend's arm and, with a joyous ring in his voice that had not been there for many months, said, "Doctor, you'll do me one favor before I leave, won't you?"

"What?"

"Go fishing with me tomorrow. There is something, still, before I can leave Corinth—. I do not know how—Will you go?"

CHAPTER XLII.

JUSTICE.

"The last shadow of his Corinthian ministry had been lifted from his soul."

Early the next morning Dan and the old Doctor set out for Wheeler's Ford. It was the nearest point, and while the fishing was not so good as at other places they knew the spot was what they wanted. This was one of the days when they would go fishing—but not for fish.

Leaving their rig by the roadside near the fence, the two friends wandered away up the stream; casting their hooks now and then at the likely places; taking a few fish; pausing often to enjoy the views of silver water, over-hanging trees, wooded bluffs, rocky bank or grassy slope, that changed always with the winding of the creek.

Returning to the rig for their lunch and to give the old horse his generous allowance, they went downstream in the afternoon, this time leaving their rods behind.

"Really, you know," said the Doctor, "the tackle is such a bother on this kind of a fishing trip." At which sage remark Dan's laugh rang out so freely that the woods on the other side of the little valley gave back the merry sound.

Dan felt strangely light-hearted and free that day. The Doctor thought the lad was more like himself than he had been for months. The truth is that Dan's gladness was akin to the gladness of home-coming. He felt as one who, having been for long years in a foreign land, returns to his own country and his own people. He was again a man among his fellow-men, with no barrier between him and his kind. Once more he was in the world to which he belonged, and it was a good world.

There was, too, a strange, delightful feeling of nearness to her—the woman he loved. He had had no word since she left Corinth, nor did he know where she was. He would never find her again, perhaps, but he no longer belonged to a world separate and apart from her world. He felt nearer to her even than when they were together that last time in the old Academy yard.

Dan was conscious, too, of a sense of freedom—of a broader, fuller life than he had ever known. Through the old Doctor's timely words, setting his thoughts into new channels, he had come out of his painful experience with a certain largeness of vision that made him stronger. He had found himself. He did not know yet what he would do; he had plans dimly formed, but nothing fixed. What did it matter? Somewhere he felt his garden waited for him; he would find his work. He was free from the deadening influence of the cast-iron monument and that, for the moment, was enough. So far as his Corinthian ministry was concerned only one shadow, out of all the dark cloud of his troubled experience remained. When that was lifted he would turn his back upon Corinth forever, but until then he did not feel free to go.

They were lying on the grassy bank of a woodland pasture, where a herd of cattle grazed or lay contentedly in the shade of the scattered trees.

"Heigh-ho," said the Doctor, "I believe I will go with you, lad."

For some time they had been silent and it was almost as though the old man had spoken to his companion's thoughts.

"Go where?" asked Dan, turning over on his side and half-raising himself on his elbow.

"Why home to Mutton Hollow, of course. You'll be leaving pretty soon now, I reckon."

"I suppose so," mused Dan vaguely. "But I'm not going home."

The old Doctor sat up. "Not going home!"

Dan smiled. "Not just yet," he answered. "I want to run about a little first."

"Uh-huh," the Doctor nodded. "Want to get your hair dry and your shirt on right side out before you face the folks."

Dan laughed. "Perhaps I want to look for my garden," he said.

"Good!" ejaculated the other, now very much in earnest. "Let me help you, lad. You know what I have always hoped for you. My profession needs—."

Dan interrupted gently, "No. No Doctor, not that. I have a notion—but there—it's all too vague yet to even discuss. When I am ready to go home I'll write you and you can meet me there. Will you?"

The old man hid his disappointment, answering heartily, "Sure I will! I'll be there when you arrive, to help kill the fatted calf." He did not tell Dan of a letter from his mother urging him, for certain reasons, to visit them, or that he had already promised her to be with them when Dan should return.

The shadows were beginning to stretch toward the river, and the cattle were moving slowly in the direction of the farmyard, hidden somewhere beyond the fringe of timber, when the two friends went leisurely back to the road to find their rig and start for home.

Climbing the fence they paused and—seated on the top rail—watched a team and buggy just coming down the opposite bank of the stream to cross the ford. Midway the horses stopped to drink.

"By George," muttered the Doctor, "it's our friend the Judge!"

The same instant, Dan recognized the man in the buggy. With the recognition all the brightness went out of his face—as a cloud, all the sadness returned.

"Doctor," Dan said, slipping down from the fence as he spoke, "excuse me a minute. I must speak to that man."

The Doctor kept his place on the fence, while Dan stepped into the road. The team, when they had left the ford, stopped as they reached him.

"How do you do, Doctor?" called the man in the buggy in a loud voice; then to Dan, "Well, sir, what do you want now?"

Dan stood near the horses' heads, his eyes fixed on their driver, and the Judge, seeing the sorrow in his face, misunderstood, as always.

"Judge Strong," said Dan. "You are the only man in the world with whom I am not at peace. I cannot be content to leave Corinth, sir, with anything between us."

The crafty Judge thought he understood. He took Dan's words, with his manner, as an acknowledgment of defeat; an act of submission. The Elder had not believed that the young man had really wished to leave the ministry. He was quite sure now that the preacher, recognizing at last the power that had thrust him from his position and place in the church, wished to sue for peace, that the same power might help him to another position. So this big upstart was tamed at last, was he?

The Doctor, sitting on the fence and hearing every low-spoken word, held a different view of the situation.

"Well," said the Judge haughtily.

Dan hesitated. "I—I wished to ask a favor, sir; one that I feel sure a Christian could not refuse."

Now the Judge was confident of his position and power. He grew still more dignified and looked at Dan with the eye of a master.

"Well, out with it. It is growing late and I must be going."

"You will remember, sir, that the last time I called on you in your home, you made certain grave charges against three women who are my friends."

"I repeated only the common—"

"Wait, please," interrupted Dan. "This is a matter between you and me. I understand that you were angry and spoke hastily. Won't you please retract those words now?" Dan's voice was almost pleading in its sad slowness; his eyes were on the Judge with an anxious, appealing look. Disappointed at the request so different from that which he had expected, the Judge angrily answered, "Stand out of my way; I have no time for this, sir!"

But quietly, carelessly it seemed, Dan laid one hand on the back of the nearest horse, almost touching the rein, and moved a step or two closer to the buggy.

"Sir, I am sure you do not understand. Miss Farwell and I—I had hoped to make her my wife. We—we parted because of the church."

The Doctor on the fence felt a lump in his throat at the pain in the boy's voice. Dan continued, "I am telling you, sir, so that you will understand. Surely you cannot refuse to take back your words under the circumstances."

"Oh, I see," sneered the Judge. "You lost the girl because of the church and then you lost the church! A fine mess you made of your pious interference with other people's business, didn't you?" And then he laughed. Looking straight into those sad, pleading eyes—he laughed.

"The damned fool," muttered the old Doctor on the fence.

"Am I to understand that you refuse to retract your words after my explanation?" Dan's tone was mildly doubtful.

The Judge was well pleased at what he had heard.

"I have absolutely nothing to take back, sir." He laughed again. "Now if that is all, stand aside!"

But suddenly the light in Dan's eyes flashed red.

"No!" he cried, "that is not all!" With a long step he reached the side of the buggy.

The next moment the Judge found himself on the ground.

"Wh—what do you mean sir?" he roared. "Take your hands off of me!"

Dan's voice was trembling with rage, but he spoke deliberately.

"You unspeakable cur, I have felt sorry for you because of your warped and twisted nature; because you seemed so incapable of being anything more than you are. I have given you a chance to act like a man, and—you—you laugh at me! You escaped punishment for your theft from that poor widow. You have escaped from God knows how many such crimes. But now, in the name of the people you have tricked and robbed under the cover of business, in the name of the people you have slandered and ruined under cover of the church, I'm going to give you what such a contemptible rascal as you are, deserves."

The Judge was a large man, in the prime of life, but his natural weapons of warfare were those of the fox, the coyote and their kin. Cornered, he made a show of resistance, but he was as a child in the hands of the young giant, who thrashed him until he lay half-senseless, moaning and groaning in pain, on the ground.

When Dan at last drew back the Doctor, who through it all had remained quietly seated on the fence—an interested spectator—climbed down from his position and came slowly forward. Looking the Judge over with a professional eye he turned to Dan with a chuckle.

"You made a mighty good job of it, lad; a mighty good job. Lord, how I envied you! Chuck him into his buggy now, and I'll take him home. You can follow in our rig."

So they went home in the dusk of the evening. And the old Doctor told around town a tale of how the Judge had met with an accident at Wheeler's Ford that would keep him in the house for quite a spell.

Dan spent his last evening in Corinth with Dr. Harry and the next morning he left. The last shadow of his Corinthian ministry had been lifted from his soul.

Corinth still talks of the great days that are gone, and the greater days that are to come, while still the days that are, are dead days—shadowed by the cast-iron monument which yet holds its place in the heart of the town, and makes of the community a fit home for the Ally.

Judge Strong has gathered to himself additional glory and honor by his continued activity and prominence in Memorial Church and in his denomination, together with his contributions to the various funds for state and national work.

Elder Jordan has been gathered to his fathers. But Nathaniel came to feel first, the supreme joy of seeing his daughter Charity proudly installed as the assistant pastor to the last of Dan's successors. They live at the old Jordan home and it is said he is the most successful preacher that the Memorial Church has ever employed, and the prospects are he will serve for many years to come.

Denny, through his minister friend, has received his education and—surrounded now by the books he craved—cultivates another garden, wherein he bids fair to grow food for men quite as necessary as cabbages or potatoes. Deborah is proud and happy with her boy; who, though he be crippled in body, has a heart and mind stronger than given to many.

The Doctor seldom goes fishing now, though he still cultivates his roses and, as he says, meddles in the affairs of his neighbors. And still he sits in his chair on the porch and watches the world go by. Martha says that, more and more, the world, to the Doctor, means the doings of that minister Dan Matthews.

It was a full month after Dan left Corinth when he wrote his old friend that he was going home. The Doctor carefully packed his fishing tackle and started for Mutton Hollow.

CHAPTER XLIII.

THE HOME COMING.

"Some things, thank God, are beyond the damning power of our improvements."

And now this story goes back again to the mountains to end where it began: back to where the tree-clad ridges roll, like mighty green billows into the far distant sky; where the vast forests lie all a-quiver in the breeze, shimmering in the sun, and the soft, blue haze of the late summer lies lazily over the land.

Beyond Wolf ridge, all up and down Jake and Indian creeks, and even as near as Fall creek, are the great lead and zinc mines. Over on Garber the heavily loaded trains, with engines puffing and panting on the heavy grades, and waking the echoes with wild shrieks, follow their iron way. But in the Mutton Hollow neighborhood, there are as yet no mines, with their unsightly piles of refuse, smoke-grimed buildings, and clustering shanties, to mar the picture. Dewey Bald still lifts its head in proud loneliness above the white sea of mist that still, at times, rolls over the valley below. The paths are unaltered. From the Matthews house on the ridge, you may see the same landmarks. The pines show black against the sunset sky. And from the Matthews place—past the deerlick in the big, low gap past Sammy's Lookout and around the shoulder of Dewey—looking away into the great world beyond, still lies the trail that is nobody knows how old.

So in life. With all the changes that time inevitably brings, with all our civilization, our inventions and improvements, some things must remain unchanged. Some things—the great landmarks in life and in religion, the hills, the valleys, the mists, must ever remain the same. Some things, thank God, are beyond the damning power of our improvements.

In minor things the Matthews home itself is altered. But Dan's father and mother are still—in spite of the years that have come—Young Matt and Sammy.

It was that best of all seasons in the Ozarks—October—the month of gold, when they were sitting on the front porch in the evening with the old Doctor, who had arrived during the afternoon.

"Now, Doctor," said the mother, "tell us all about it." There was no uneasiness in her calm voice, no shadow of worry in her quiet eyes. And the boy's father by her side was like her in serene confidence. They knew from Dan's letters something of the trials through which he had passed; they had assured him often of their sympathy. It never occurred to them to doubt him in any way or to question the final outcome.

"Yes, Doctor," came the deep voice of the father. "We have had Dan's letters of course, but the lad's not one to put all of his fight on paper. Let's have it as you saw it."

So the Doctor told them—told of the causes that had combined to put Dan on the rack, that had driven him in spite of himself to change his views of the church and its ministry; told of the forces that had been arrayed against him, how the lad had met these forces, and how he had battled with himself—all that the Doctor had seen in the months of watching; all that he knew of Dan, even to the time when Dan declared his doubt of everything, and to the chastising of Judge Strong. He omitted nothing except the declaration he had heard Dan make to the Judge.

Several times the narrator was interrupted by the deep-voiced, hearty laugh of the father, or with exclamations of satisfaction. Sometimes the Doctor was interrupted by a quick, eager question from the mother, that helped to make the story clear. Many times they uttered half-whispered exclamations of wonder, distress or indignation.

"When he left Corinth," said the Doctor in conclusion, "he told me that he had no clearly-defined plans, though he hinted at something that he had in mind."

"But, Doctor, haven't you forgotten a very important part of your story?" the mother asked.

"What have I forgotten?" he questioned.

"Why, the girl of course. What is a story without a girl?" she laughed merrily.

To which the Doctor answered, "I reckon Dan will tell you about that himself."

At this they all joined in a hearty laugh.

The next day Dan arrived and after a brief time, given up to the joy of family reunion, he took up the story where the Doctor had left off.

From Corinth Dan had gone directly to the president of the big steel works, whom he had met at the time of the convention. With the assistance and advice of this man of affairs he had been visiting the big mines and smelters and studying zinc and lead. He had worked out his plan and had interested capital and had come home to consult with his parents concerning the opening and development of the mine on Dewey Bald.

Then he talked to them of the power of wealth for good, of the sacredness of such a trust—talked as they had never heard him talk before of the Grace Conners, and the crippled Dennys, who needed elder brothers willing to acknowledge the kinship.

When he had finished his mother kissed him and his father said, "It is for this, son, that mother and I have held the old hill yonder. It is a part of our religious belief that God put the wealth in the mountains, not for us alone, but for all men. So it has been to us a sacred trust, which we have never felt that we were fitted to administer. We have always hoped that our first born would accept it as his life work—his ministry."

So Dan found his garden—and entered the ministry that has made his life such a blessing to men.

The next morning he saddled his mother's horse early. At breakfast she announced that she was going over to the Jones ranch on the other side of Dewey. "And what are you planning to do today?" she said to Dan as he followed her out of the house.

"I was going over to old Dewey myself," he answered. "I thought I would like to look the ground over." He smiled down at her. "But now I'm going with you. Just wait a minute until I saddle a horse."

She laughed at him. "Oh no, you're not."

"But, mother, I want to talk to you. I—I have something to tell you."

"Yes, I know," she nodded. "You have already told me—"

"Has Doctor—" he burst forth.

"No indeed! For shame, Dan. You know Doctor wouldn't. It was in your letters, and—But I have planned for you to tell me the rest this evening. Go with your father and Doctor to look at the stock this morning and write your business letters while I attend to *my* affairs. Then, the first thing after dinner, you slip away alone over to Dewey and do your planning. Perhaps I'll meet you on the old trail as you come back. You see I have it all fixed."

"Yes," he said slowly, "you always have things fixed, don't you? What a mother you are! There's only one other woman in all the world like you."

And at this she answered bravely, "Yes, I know dear. I have always known it would come, and I am glad, glad my boy—but—I—I think you'd better kiss me now." So she left him standing at the fence and rode away alone down the old familiar path.

After dinner Dan set out.

CHAPTER XLIV.

THE OLD TRAIL.

"... Those whose hearts and souls are big enough to follow the trail that is nobody knows how old."

Leaving the ridge just beyond the low gap, Dan made his way down the mountain side into the deep ravine, below Sammy's Lookout, that opens into the hollow.

For an hour he roamed about, his mind upon his plans for the development of the wealth that lay in the heart of the mountain. After a time, still intent upon his work, he scrambled up the end of the little canyon, regained the ridge near the mouth of the cave, then climbed up on the steep slope of Dewey to the top. From here he could follow with his eye a possible route for the spur that should leave the railroad on Garber to the east, round the base of the mountain and reach the mine through the little ravine on the west.

From the top he made his way slowly toward the Lookout, thinking from there to gain still another view of the scene of his proposed operations and to watch the trail for the coming of his mother.

Drawing near the great ledge of rock that hangs so like a cornice on the mountain side, he caught a glimpse—through the screen of trees and bushes—of a figure seated on the old familiar spot. His mother must have come sooner than she intended, he thought, or else he had been longer than he realized. He looked at his watch; it was early yet. Then going on a little, he suddenly stopped—that was not his mother! He drew nearer and pushed aside a bush for a better view.

His heart leaped at sight of the familiar blue dress and its white trimming! The figure turned slightly as if to look up the trail. The big fellow on the mountain side trembled.

"How like," he whispered half aloud, "God, how like—"

Softly as one fearing to dispel a welcome illusion he drew nearer—nearer—nearer. Suddenly a dry bush on the ground snapped under his foot. She turned her face quickly toward him.

Then, springing to her feet Hope Farwell stood waiting with joy—lighted face, as Dan went stumbling in wondering haste down the hill.

"I thought you were never coming," she said. "I have been waiting so long." And then for a little while there was nothing more said that we have any right whatever to hear.

When he insisted upon an explanation of the miracle, she laughed merrily.

"Why it's like most miracles, I fancy, if only one knew about them—the most natural thing that could happen after all. Dr. Miles came to me some two months ago, and said that he had a patient whom he was sending into the mountains with a nurse, and asked me if I would take the case. He said he thought that I would like to see the Mutton Hollow country, and—and that he thought that I needed the trip. You can imagine how quickly I said that I would go. I am living down at the Jones place."

"Where my mother went this morning?" Dan broke in eagerly.

She nodded, "Your mother and I are—are very good friends," she said demurely.

"Does she—"

Hope blushed. "I couldn't help telling her. You see she had your letters and she already knew a great deal. She—"

"I suppose she told you all about it—my finish at Corinth—I mean, and my plans?" interrupted Dan.

"Yes," Hope replied. "Then there's nothing more to do but—How is your patient?" he finished abruptly. "How long must you stay with the case?"

She turned her head away. "My patient went home three days ago."

When the sun was touching the fringe of trees on the distant ridge, and the varying tints of brown and gold, under the softening tone of the gray-blue haze that lies always over hollow and hill, were most clearly revealed in the evening light—Dan and Hope followed the same path that Young Matt and Sammy walked years before. In the edge of the timber beyond the deerlick, the two young lovers found those other older lovers, and were welcomed by them with the welcome that can only be given or received by those whose hearts and souls are big enough to follow the trail that is nobody knows how old.

THE END.

GOD AND THE GROCERYMAN

CONTENTS

GOD AND THE GROCERYMAN

CHAPTER I.

DAN MATTHEWS.

In a suite of offices high up in the Union Mining Building in Kansas City, an old negro janitor was engaged in his humble evening tasks. Save for this ancient colored man the rooms were deserted. The place was unmistakably a center of large business interests. The dark, rich woods of the paneled wainscoting, heavy moldings, polished desks, and leather upholstered chairs, the bronze fixtures, steel filing cases, and massive vault door, all served to create an atmosphere of vast financial strength.

It was an evening in spring—one of those evenings when the cold discomforts of winter are far enough in the past to be forgotten while the hot discomforts of summer are so far in the future that no one need think of them. From homes and hotels and boarding houses, from apartments and tenements and rooms, the people were going forth to their pleasures and their crimes or to the toil of those who must labor in the night. Roaring street cars, screeching fire engines, clanging gongs, blaring horns, heavy murmuring undertone of the city's life. Brilliantly illuminated restaurants, gleaming show windows, glittering, winking, flashing electric signs, dazzling arc lights, shadowy alleys, dark doorways, nooks and corners. Mighty rivers of hurrying, crowding, dodging pedestrians. Vociferous newsboys, furtive drabs with shame to sell, stolid merchants, slinking followers of nefarious trades, nurses, clergymen, sly beggars, laughing merrymakers, purveyors of vice, children, impassive policemen. As the old colored man with broom and dust cloth moved about the quiet office rooms he crooned the wailing melody of an old-time hymn.

Suddenly the old negro ceased his crooning song. Without straightening up from his stooping position over the desk which he was polishing he paused in an attitude of rigid alertness much like a good pointer dog, his gray woolly head cocked attentively to one side. It came again—the heavy, jarring rumble of distant thunder. Shuffling to the nearest window the old man looked into the night. Below him the city stretched away in the gloom like a dark, unfathomable sea. The shadowy masses of the higher buildings were misty headlands, the twinkling lights were stars reflected in the black depths, and the noise of the streets came up to him like the roar of the surf. A flash of lightning ripped the night and he saw the wind-tossed clouds.

"By Jack, hit sure am a-comin'," the old man muttered nervously. "Yas sah—reg'lar ol' ripsnorter—Bam! Lissen at dem hebenlly guns! Lawdy—Lawdy! Dem big black clouds am sure a-pilin' up—whoo-ee! Look lak de jedgment day am here right now—hit sure do. I knowed my ol' rheumatiz warn't lyin' nohow—*No* sah—No *sah!"* He turned from the window and as his eyes took in the familiar rooms a wide grin deepened the wrinkles in his old, black face. "Ol' man storm, he ain't nohow gwine come in dese here offerces though—no *sah!* Rumble an' grumble an' shoot yo' ol' lightnin' and blow yo' ol' wind twell yo'-all bus' yo'sef—yo'-all ain't gwine git ol' Zac in here—no *sah!* Dem pore folkses outside, dey sure gwine ketch hit, though—yas indeedee—dey sure *am!"* Wagging his head sorrowfully he again stooped over the desk.

But scarcely had the old negro resumed his work when again he was interrupted. This time he jerked himself erect and faced about with a quick movement surprising in one of his years. Some one had entered the outer office. A moment later a man appeared in the open doorway of the room where the janitor stood.

"Good evening, Uncle Zac." The man was smiling at the expression of the old servant's face.

"Ev'nin', boss—ev'nin', Mista Matthews, sah." He bobbed and grinned with genuine delight. "But what fo' de lan's sake fotches you down here at yo' offerces dis time o' night? An' hit a-fixin' to storm like all git out, directly, too. Lissen dar!" An ominous roll of thunder punctuated his remark.

"Does look like it meant business, doesn't it?" Dan agreed, moving to the nearest window.

"Hit sure do, sah—hit sure do. An' iffen you'll 'scuse me, sah, yo' ain't got no call to be a-comin' down town on er wil' night like dis gwine be. Yo' jes' better hustle 'long back home, right now, fo' de storm break. Yo' kin tell Missus Hope ol' Uncle Zac jes' naturally discharged yo'an yo' quit." He chuckled at the thought of discharging the boss, and Dan laughed with him.

"Why don't you run home before the storm breaks, Uncle Zac?"

"Me? Me go hom dis early? Why, Mista Matthews, sah, I ain't *near* finish ma work yet."

"My fix exactly," returned Dan.

Another blinding flash of lightning was followed by a crashing peal of thunder. The old negro regarded his employer with an expression of proud hopelessness, the while he nodded his head solemnly. "Man's work ain't nebbah gwine be finish, I reckon—no sah—not when he's that kin' of man."

Twenty years had passed since Judge Strong and his brother officials of the

Strong Memorial Church in Corinth drove Dan Matthews from the ministry because he would not preach the kind of Christianity they wanted. But the years had worked little outward change in this son of Young Matt and Sammy Lane. "Big Dan." he had been called in his backwoods home, and the name bestowed with so much admiration and affection by the Ozark mountaineers clung to him still. Not only to his intimate friends but to his employees—laborers, miners, officials, clerks, to the newsboys on the street, and to the kings of Big Business he was still Big Dan. True, there were touches of gray in the shaggy, red-brown hair. The sensitive mouth smiled not quite so readily, perhaps. But the brown eyes—his mother's eyes—were still clear and steady and frank, with Sammy's spirit looking out, questioning but unafraid. One knew instinctively that his nickname was not used in reference to his great body and powerful limbs, alone. The years had given him, too, a certain quiet air of authority—of responsibility and power. In that place of large business interests he was as a captain on the bridge of his ship, or a locomotive engineer in the cab of his engine.

"Missus Hope, she am well as allus, sah?"

"Very well, thank you, Uncle Zac." Dan came and seated himself on a corner of a desk near the janitor. "She was asking about you at dinner this evening. I expect she'll be going to see you and Aunt Mandy before long."

The old negro's face beamed with pride and delight. "Thankee, thankee, sah. Lawd bless her dear heart. Mus' be mighty lonesome fo' yo' an' Missus Hope, all 'lone in yo' big house wi' de boys a' lil' Missee Grace erway to dey schools an' colleges."

"It is that," agreed Big Dan, "but I guess we'll have to stand it, Uncle Zac. I suppose, next thing we know, we'll wake up some morning and find that we are grandparents."

"Go 'long wid yo'! Shoo! Hit warn't more dan yest'day yo' oldes', Masta Grant, war a-layin' in he cradle makin' funny faces at ol' Uncle Zac."

They laughed together. Then Dan, with the same courtesy he would have shown one of his business associates, asked: "How are your folks, Uncle Zac? Aunt Mandy feelin' pretty pert these days?"

"Sure am, sah. Ol' woman feelin' so persnickety almost kick up her heels an' prance roun' like yearlin' filly, sted o' behavin' like ol' work mare wid her chilluns all growed up an' mighty nigh ready to be gran'pappies an' gran'-mammies theyselves."

"Good for Aunt Mandy! And how are you making out with your old friend, rheumatiz?"

"Ben makin' out fine, sah, twell las' night, ol' man rheumatiz he come roun' prognosticatin' this here storm."

"That's too bad. I'm sorry, Uncle Zac. Perhaps you had better lay off for—"

"No, sah—no, *sah.* Ain't nobody gwine 'tend yo' offerces but me, Mista Dan. Rheumatiz, he ain't so *bad,* nohow—jes' sort o' weather projectin'. Ain't hurt *much.* No rheumatiz in ma soul yet. Everythin's all hunky-dory long's rheumatiz stay in man's lags. Rheumatiz gits in de soul—whoo-ee—look out *den! Yas,* sah—yas, *sah*—dat *am* bad!"

"Well, there is nothing the matter with your soul, Uncle Zac." Big Dan's hand dropped gently on the toil-bent shoulders and the brown eyes of the boss looked smilingly down into the janitor's wrinkled, upturned face. "It's one of the cleanest, truest, whitest souls I know."

"What's dat, sah?" The old negro gazed at his employer with startled eagerness. "What's dat yo' sayin', Mista Dan? White? Yo' reckon ol' negro man like me can hab white soul?"

"Why not, Uncle Zac?"

The old man wiped his eyes with a corner of his dust cloth.

"Lawdy, Lawdy, Mista Dan, to think o' yo' sayin' a thing like dat! White—Lawdy, Lawdy!"

"Well, Uncle Zac, I must get to work." Dan crossed the room toward his private office.

"Yas, sah—yas, sah—we bof o' us got to work." With sudden energy Uncle Zac applied his dust cloth to the nearest piece of furniture. "Ol' man storm, he gwine git to work too—mighty sudden now. Can't cotch us in dis here place, though—no indeedee!"

"Mr. Saxton will be along presently. Tell him to come right on in, please."

"Yas, sah—yas, sah."

As the door closed behind Big Dan, Uncle Zac stood looking after him. "Ain't dat jes' like him now," he muttered to himself. "Ain't dat jes' like him to think o' a thing like dat? White—white—Praise de Lawd!"

The old negro janitor stooped vigorously to his task and again the distant roar of the city was accompanied by the crooning melody of an old-time hymn.

CHAPTER II.

BIG DAN'S PROBLEM.

Dan Matthews, alone in his private office, did not sit down to any work. Standing before his big desk, he idly fingered a silver paper knife, pulled open a drawer, closed it again, pulled open another drawer and took out a paper, glanced at it and put it back. The flashes of lightning were almost continuous now while the jarring roar of the accompanying thunder told that the storm was near. Big Dan turned from his desk to pace thoughtfully up and down the heavily carpeted room. As he moved to and fro one might have thought that he was nervous because of the threatening elements. He went to the window and stood looking out over the city—homes, churches, dens of vice, shops and factories, stores, retreats where criminals hide, houses of shame, dance halls, theaters, night schools, police stations, tenements, the black night, the play of lightning, the crash of thunder, the fury of the wind-torn clouds.

The door opened.

Glancing over his shoulder, Dan greeted the man who stood on the threshold with a brief: "Hello, John," and absorbed in his thoughts, turned his face again toward the city and the storm. Evidently the relationship between himself and the newcomer was so close and so well established that a more elaborate welcome was unnecessary. The man closed the door behind him noiselessly.

John Saxton was about the age of his employer, and while he was not nearly so imposing in stature as Big Dan, his personality, in a way, was as striking. The quiet inner strength of the man was unmistakable. One felt instinctively that he was rich in experience beyond most men and that his judgments of men and events would always be governed by that large charity without which even justice is impossible. While in general appearance he was clearly a man of large business affairs, his face was the face of one who had suffered deeply and in his eyes there was that brooding look which is so characteristic of those who, even in a crowded world, live much alone.

Without turning his head, Dan called: "Come here, John—come look at this." And Saxton went to stand beside his chief.

For some time the two men watched in silence. Then Dan spoke. "I'm sorry, John, to bring you out on such a night; but I'm leaving for New York early in the morning and this is really my only opportunity to go over that business with you. It's lucky you returned to-day."

"I am very glad to come," returned the other quietly. He took a sheaf of papers from his pocket. "I have my report here, whenever you are ready."

Something in John Saxton's voice—a suggestion of loneliness, perhaps, seemed to touch Big Dan or it might have been that the storm had thrown him into a peculiar mood. Turning from the window, he looked full into his companion's face. "John, do you know that you are almost the only man left to keep my faith in humanity alive?" I have always found it easy to believe in God but these last few years it has been mighty hard, at times, for me to believe in men. You have always held me up. You are the only man who has never failed me. I am not speaking merely of business. John—you understand, don't you?"

The other fumbled over the papers which he held in his hands. "It is like you to forget the circumstances under which we met—I—it was just such a night as this"— His voice broke and he went quickly to a table where he spread out his papers and bent over them as if seeking a particular sheet. In reality he was trying to hide his deep emotion. When he spoke again his voice was steady. "I think I have everything you wanted me to get."

Dan, with an effort, returned in a matter-of-fact tone, "All right, John, we'll go over what you have there presently. But first, if you don't mind, there are some things I wish to say. Before we go any farther I must be dead sure that you understand exactly what it is that I want to do, and why."

Big Dan dropped into the chair before his desk and Saxton, seating himself, waited while his employer seemed to be arranging his thoughts.

Slowly, with long pauses at the end of every sentence, as if speaking more to himself than to the man who listened so intently, Dan began: "It was just twenty years ago this month that I decided to develop the mine in old Dewey Bald Mountain. We took out the first ore three months later. Father and mother owned Dewey Bald long before I was born. They knew that enormous deposit of mineral was there. It wasn't a guess, they could see it—thousands of tons—in the big cave where the Old Shepherd's son died. But they would never touch it for themselves.

"Father and mother had received from the Old Shepherd, my namesake, some ideas of life and Christianity that were different from the ideas of established church members generally. Born and raised as I was, it was natural, I suppose, that I should feel called to the ministry, but there were no churches in that section of the Ozarks in my boyhood days. The only Christianity I knew was the Christianity of the Old Shepherd of the hills—the Christianity of my father and mother. All my life, up to the time I entered college, mother was my only teacher.

"But in that denominational college I was taught, of course, the history and doctrines of the denomination with which I became identified. Then when I took up my work as pastor of the Memorial Church at Corinth I found that the church in actual operation was quite a different thing from the simple Christianity of my backwoods home and the theoretical church of the college and seminary. It is no wonder that Judge Strong and the others drove me from the ministry. I was a down-and-out failure." There was a note in Big Dan's voice which told how deep had been the hurt of that experience.

Saxton made as if to speak, but the other motioned him to wait.

"But, you see, I still had father and mother and Hope, and with them to help I simply couldn't let go of Christianity. And so, believing as I did that all work which truly serves humanity is God's work, and that a man's ministry is whatever he can do best for the best life of his fellow men, I entered what Hope calls the Ministry of Business. I undertook the development of the Dewey Bald Mine with the idea of making it my contribution to the welfare of my generation. I know to-night, John, that as I failed in my Ministry of Preaching I have, so far, failed in my Ministry of Business. I don't mean that I have failed in *business,*" he added with an odd smile, "I mean that I have failed to make my business a ministry; I have failed to accomplish in any large way the purpose of all Christian business, as I understand it."

Again, for a few silent moments, Big Dan seemed to be arranging his thoughts. When he spoke this time it was with the solemn earnestness of one laying bare the deepest convictions of his soul. "I tell you, John Saxton, if the business men of America do not somehow get a little Christian religion into the business of our country, and if the citizens of this nation do not get a little Christianity into their citizenship and into their everyday affairs, national destruction is inevitable. Since our survey of the political, economic and social conditions throughout the country was completed last month I have been making a careful study of the material gathered by our workers. The facts and figures submitted by these unprejudiced observers would convince any sane person that the United States of America is moving toward utter ruin. Unless this destructive trend of our national life is radically altered we will simply go to pieces. And the only force which can combat our present ruinous course is the religion of Jesus.

"Our survey shows that the annual cost of crime in the United States is over two and one half times the total ordinary income of our nation and over three times the national budget.

"The number of prisoners in our penal institutions has increased in seventeen years from one hundred and six-tenths prisoners for every one hundred thousand of our population, to one hundred and fifty out of every one hundred thousand.

"In the last twenty-four years the crime of murder has increased from two and one-tenth per one hundred thousand to eight and five-tenths per one hundred thousand.

"Throughout the whole country the percentage of illegitimate births has steadily risen, while the number of very young mothers is rapidly increasing. The great majority of mothers of illegitimate children are under twenty-one years of age. In 1920 the age of greatest frequency was twenty years, but in 1924 it stood at eighteen, with an alarming number at the ages of seventeen and sixteen. Children, John! The generation that is just coming into the motherhood and fatherhood of the nation!

"Approximately half the convicts in our penitentiaries are under twenty-five and eight out of ten are under thirty. It is estimated that eighty per cent of all crimes are committed by boys. Children, John, the generation that is just coming into the responsibilities of citizenship!

"With all this there is an astounding increase in degeneracy with all the horrors which that term, rightly understood, implies."

Turning to his desk Big Dan took up a book. "This is Frederick Pierce's *Mobilizing the Mid-Brain.* Listen to what he says of certain conditions which are inseparable from our national situation as a whole:

"In about seventy years from now, that is to say, within the lifetime of some of us and within the lifetime of almost all our children, unless the rate of increase of insanity and disabling neurosis in America is radically checked, it will be intolerable for those who remain in health to support the burden of those who are mentally or nervously ill. To make sure that we do not allow ourselves to escape the force of this fact let us consider the utterances of two alienists within the last year, reporting from widely separated sections of the country. Their published statements agree on the following point—that at the present rate of increase in insanity in the United States and Canada, the last sane person will have disappeared from the major portion of North America in two hundred years from this date. In a third of that time the burden of taxation to maintain the necessary institutions and sanitariums would become tremendous. Moreover, the average breeding strain of our grandchildren will be so impaired and deteriorated that the normal expectation in every family of father, mother and three children, will be at least two wholly or partially disabled by mental or nervous disease.'

"In a footnote, he says:

"'The figures are not taken merely from the period affected by the recent War, but go back through thirty years. For example, the six-year period of 1904-1910 shows increases, sectionally, of twenty-one percent to forty percent in enumerated hospital cases of insanity throughout the United States.'

"Dr. Pierce rightly adds: 'The effect of this condition upon the chances of our nation being able to survive politically or economically, I leave to the reader's imagination.'

"'Read the figures as we may, there is no possible escape from their meaning. We have the choice of facing the issue and taking the necessary measures to correct the situation or of letting our children and grandchildren face it when it will probably be too late. Compared to the impending menace of this situation, such calamities as the recent War, with its welter of slaughter and aftermath of ruin, appear as mere ripples in the stream of human history.'

"Dr. Pierce makes no observation, here, John, as to the relation of morals to mental and nervous health. That there is a very close relationship I think no one of average intelligence will deny. Mental and nervous diseases are fruits of immorality, and immorality roots in irreligion. Only by reestablishing the people's sense of God can our nation regain its moral, mental, and physical health and insure the future of the race.

"To show that I am neither an unbalanced pessimist nor a religious fanatic, and that I am not alone in my conclusions—do you remember the opening paragraph of that resolution which was passed by eight hundred business men at the luncheon of the Industrial Relations Committee of the Philadelphia Chamber of Commerce in 1922?

"'As Americans, we recognize that we face a crucial condition in our social, political and industrial life, which, if not corrected, can lead only to individual and national disaster."

"And Ernest T. Trigg in his address on that same occasion said:

"'There must be brought back into the situation a recognition of God and His divine guidance.'

"These eight hundred leading industrialists of the country are not wild-eyed alarmists, John. Mr. Trigg is not a religious fanatic. These men represent the best business intelligence of this nation and this is their sane and solemn opinion as to the industrial situation and its needs.

"You know what the National Economic League is. It is not too much to say that a list of members of the National Council of the League would be practically a list of the biggest brains in America—every leading thinker in the country, almost—and they represent every field of our country's interests: the Press, Law, Education, Government, Commerce, Labor. Well, the Council recently indicated the paramount problems of the United States by a preferential vote. The list of fifty-five subjects gives the comparative importance of these subjects as shown by the votes of eighteen thousand one hundred and seventy-six members of the Council. Now, if the votes had been equally distributed each subject would have received, in round numbers, three hundred and thirty votes. But, John, *three* subjects out of the fifty-five received *three thousand and seventy-seven votes.* These three problems are: Lawlessness, Respect for Law, Administration of Justice; Ethical, Moral and Religious Training. They are all embraced in one word RELIGION. Certainly no one would say that these eighteen thousand one hundred and seventy-six members of the Council of the National Economic League are unbalanced pessimists or religious cranks.

"You and I understand why these leading thinkers of our country consider these three problems of such relatively great importance to the nation. The most feeble-minded man or woman in the land ought to be able to grasp the fact that without respect for law; without justice; without moral and religious training, our nation cannot endure.

"I have failed in my Ministry of Business, John, because I have failed to make any real contribution to our one great national need, the need of Christian religion."

Big Dan was tremendously in earnest. As if half ashamed of his display of feeling he rose from his chair and turning away from his companion went again to the window where he stood looking down over the city which now lay under the full fury of the storm.

"I should think," said Saxton slowly, "that you would be the last man in the world to feel that you had failed in your Ministry of Business. As your confidential agent I know, better than any person living, the enormous sums of money you have given to all sorts of charity—to schools and hospitals and every kind of benevolent work—and to individuals as well. Haven't you, from the beginning, held the wealth of your mine as a trust to be administered by you?"

Big Dan answered with almost a touch of impatience:

"I have failed just the same."

"But how have you failed, when your work has been a Christian work?"

"I have failed because the one great need of the world is not the need of Christian work. As I have just said, it is the need of Christian religion.

"Why, John, the amount of money given to good works—I mean outside of churches—to charity, to schools and education, is enormous. If you look up the statistics you will find that in the last few years there has been, in the United States, an amazing development of interest in social-welfare work and in charities and benevolences of every kind. But it is of profound significance that as the public interest in good works has increased the religious spirit of the people has declined. Never in the history of mankind has so much been given to what we call good works—works I mean that are essentially Christian. And never in our own country, at least, have the people been so irreligious. And this collapse of Christianity has brought us to the verge of an appalling moral bankruptcy.

"I know, John, that we give also something over seven hundred million dollars annually to religion; but wait, I have a letter—here it is. After mother's death I found this among the things which she had treasured. It was written by the Old Shepherd, who was her only teacher, to his friend Dr.

Coughlan. At the time of Dad Howitt's death Dr. Coughlan gave this letter to mother. I have read it so many times that I know it by heart.

"'We build temples and churches but will not worship in them; we hire spiritual advisers but refuse to heed them; we buy Bibles but will not read them; believing in God we do not fear Him; acknowledging Christ we neither follow nor obey Him.'"

As Big Dan was putting the Old Shepherd's letter reverently away in his desk, Saxton said: "But I thought you were such a firm believer in the religion of good works."

"And I am," returned Dan, quickly, "but I have come to understand that while good works are the fruits of the Christian religion, they are no more Christianity itself than a barrel of apples is a tree.

"Our fathers worshiped God. Christianity grew from that worship as a tree grows from its roots, until in our generation it is bearing its legitimate fruit—good works. Can any one question that the marvelous growth of interest in charities and social-welfare work of every kind in this generation is the direct result of the Christianity of our fathers? But while we to-day are harvesting these fruits of Christianity, like the miserable farmers of life that we are, we are neglecting the tree which produces them. With no thought of the future we are permitting the roots of our religion to die for want of intelligent cultivation.

"Our great need in this generation is to see our good works not as religion but as the fruit of religion—to understand that the fruit is not the tree—that the tree is Christianity, and the root of the tree is the worship of God as He is revealed in the life and teaching of Jesus, in the teaching of all other great spiritual leaders, in the wonders and beauty of nature and, indeed, in all the miracles of life and the universe. If this generation neglects to cultivate the tree there will be no fruit for the generations that are to come.

"Religiously, John, we are a race of spiritual grocerymen. We traffic in the produce upon which the very life of our nation depends without a thought of the gardens and orchards which supply the stuff we buy and sell or a single care for the condition under which this food of the race is produced. To save America we must do more than deal in good works. To save America we must worship God."

John Saxton said slowly, "I think I understand, but just what do you mean by the worship of God?"

"I mean the recognition of God—the feeling of God—the acknowledgment of God. The groceryman, for example, must feel God in the produce which he buys and sells. He must be conscious of God as he is conscious of money. He accepts money as a vital element in his business; he must accept God as a vital element in his life. He looks upon a grocery store as a necessity in the community; he must look upon religion as a necessity in the nation. The groceryman, in his business dealings, recognizes his dependence upon the farmer from whom he buys. He must go a step farther and habitually acknowledge to himself that without God manifested in nature there would be no food with which to feed the people—that without God the combined strength and skill of all the agriculturists of the world could not produce so much as a single grain of wheat. Our modern civilization does not recognize God—it only uses Him."

"But do you mean to say that religious work—I do not mean distinctively church work, I mean any good work, Christian work—do you mean to say that such work is not a recognition of God, is not in fact worship?"

"It might be—it should be. If it were so conceived and so understood it would be. But only in exceptional cases is it so conceived, and certainly, by the people in general, it is not so understood. These enormous sums of money that are given annually to charity and social-welfare work, and to schools and education—are these gifts ever thought of definitely as offerings to God—as acts of worship? Would any one contend that the purpose of these good works is to bring the people to a recognition of God? The millions devoted to scientific research, the millions bestowed upon higher educational institutions—is the idea or spirit of worship in these great endowments and foundations? As for our civic charity organizations and that class of good works, they are merely business policies and are so presented to the people. These vast fortunes that are given to good works are not even given in the name of Christianity, but in the names of individuals and cities and various organizations!

"But, John, listen, *the majority of the people who give these millions to humanity are Christians, and they are intelligent, thinking Christians.* They see the disaster which menaces our country. They know that the only thing that can save America is religion. Why, then do they not give millions to religion? I'll tell you why: It is because *in this so-called Christian country there is no organization in existence through which one can spend a dollar for a purely religious purpose."*

"And that," Big Dan continued, "is my problem.

"When father and mother turned Dewey Bald Mountain over to me they expected me, in their simple Christian way, to use it religiously. From the first I have honestly desired to fulfill the trust. I have talked it all out with Hope and with the boys. Neither Hope nor I have any wish to leave a great fortune to the children. They have not been taught to expect it. She is with me heart and soul in what I propose to do. So are the boys. We haven't said anything to Grace yet because she is a little too young, and we don't like to disturb her just now with such questions. But the girl is too much like her mother, John, for us to have any doubts as to where she will stand.

"As I have told you, I am convinced that our country, because of its rapidly increasing wealth, together with the amazing growth of popular lawlessness, immorality, insane extravagance and cynical irreligion, is fast approaching a state of general anarchy, social degeneracy and political rottenness which can only result in our national downfall. I solemnly believe that the only thing which can save America is for us, somehow, to reestablish through worship the people's sense of God.

"They call me 'The Rockefeller of the lead and zinc industry—the Carnegie of mining,' and all that. You and I know, of course, that I am a long way yet from the Rockefeller-Carnegie class, but we know also that I am rated at several millions. John, I want to devote the millions I have taken from the Dewey Bald Mine to what I believe to be the one great vital need of the world to-day. I want, in a word, to give these millions to religion as other men have given millions to science and art and welfare-work and education. But, John, I don't know how to do it."

"You are a church man," said Saxton significantly. "It was as a church man that you—" he hesitated, "that you came into my life."

"Yes," said Big Dan.

Saxton continued: "During the fifteen years that I have known you, you have been an active member of the Old Commons Church, and you have given hundreds of thousands of dollars to the local work and to the missions and schools of your denomination. Don't you call that giving to religion?"

"I am a member of a church, John, and have contributed to its various denominational enterprises because it is the only organization I know which makes even a pretense of standing for and promoting the Christian religion. It is the only thing in sight. But we must face that fact that the Church of to-day is utterly unable to meet this national crisis of immorality and lawlessness which is the direct result of the irreligious spirit of the people.

"There must be a reason for this failure of the church," he continued. "Are we to believe that Christianity is less potent for righteousness to-day than it was in the days of our fathers? Or has the Church been rendered impotent through the dissipations of its energies in meeting the demands of innumerable activities which are not purely Christian? One thing is clear: We must either doubt the power of the Christian religion as a vital force in the life of the people or we must question the policies and methods of the Church.

"You and I are Christians, John—members of the same church. Which shall we do? Question the divine religion of Jesus or question the human efficiency of this institution which exists for the sole purpose of making Christianity a vital factor in the lives of men?"

"There can be only one answer to that," returned Saxton. "Between the teaching of Jesus and the wisdom of His human agents whose business it is to present Christianity to the world there can be no comparison."

"Well, then," said Big Dan, "suppose we, as business men, look into these human policies of the Church. It seems to me that the cause of this disastrous loss of efficiency is fairly obvious. I have realized for several years—as I believe the great majority of thinking church members realize—that a comparatively small portion of the enormous sum of money annually contributed to our churches is used for a purely religious purpose.

"The Bureau of the Census in 1916 lists one hundred and eighty-three different Christian denominations. Denominations are multiplied by dividing denominations into denominations. Think of it! One hundred and eighty-three separate and distinct Christian organizations to be maintained in the name of one Christ, for the sole purpose of teaching one Christianity!"

Saxton said thoughtfully: "I doubt if many people, to-day, believe that it makes any real difference as to which church one belongs."

"Exactly," returned Dan, "and that more than anything else perhaps proves the weakness of the denominational system. If the churches had not lost their grip upon their own members, even, it would make a tremendous difference as to which church one belonged. You are right, John, in the minds of the people it makes no difference. And, yet, the fact remains that it is impossible to give a dollar to any church and not support this denominationalism.

"The strength, energy and interest of the people, in these modern times, is most adequately represented in terms of money. Dollars stand for human power. Well, four-fifths, at least, of all the money contributed to the cause of Christian religion goes to maintain these denominational differences which we are told are of no importance. When, led by the religious desire of his heart to see the truths of Jesus' teaching made effective among men, a church member gives five dollars to his church, what happens? Four dollars out of that five are spent to maintain whatever it is that makes his denomination different from the one hundred and eighty-two other denominations, each of which is actively engaged in spending four out of every five dollars which it receives to maintain *its* distinguishing features. And yet we are asked to believe that these one hundred and eighty-three churches are all one in Christ and are all united in preaching one Christianity. Mathematically, the oneness of the churches is one to four in that they spend one dollar for the thing upon which they agree and four dollars for the things upon which they differ.

"Does such a state of affairs, in fact, make no difference to the people, John? Is it any wonder that the central idea of Christianity is lost—that the spirit of worship is lost—that religion has become a subject for our humorous magazines, our jokesmiths, cartoonists and funny papers? The wonder is that any one retains membership in a church. No one would, except, as I say, they want to do *something* and the Church is the only thing they know."

"But is there not a strong tendency among certain denominations to unite?" Saxton asked.

Big Dan answered: "In the years between 1906 and 1916—the last available figures—nine denominations consolidated with other bodies. In the same period twenty-two new denominations came into existence. It is true that there is something like an agreement between a few of the denominations as to a division of territory. In many communities churches have so multiplied that there are actually not enough people to maintain them all. But this agreement on the division of such territories is not primarily in the interest of Christianity; it is clearly an effort of the denominations to save themselves. Competition has simply reached a point where it is disastrous to all so they are uniting to maintain their differences."

Saxton smiled. "And yet you say the world has never before known such good works and that these good works are the fruits of the Christianity of our fathers. Well, our fathers worshiped God in denominational churches."

"Yes," replied Big Dan, "but the denominationalism of our fathers was born of their religious spirit. To-day, denominationalism is not the expression of a Christian spirit, but quite the contrary. To our fathers, the choice of a church was wholly a matter of religious conviction. To-day one joins this, that or the other church as one chooses a social club or a political order—the motive governing the choice is convenience, social, political or business policy, friendship or family. In our fathers' time a Christian character was necessary to membership in any church. To-day, under the competitive system of denominational churches, character is no longer a test of fellowship. If it were, the churches could not pay their running expenses. Denominationalism in the past stood in the minds of the people for Christianity. To-day the people think of Christianity—when they think of it at all—as something apart from denominationalism; and this is just as true of church members as it is of those who are not identified with any church."

Big Dan arose suddenly and went again to the window where he stood silently looking out into the night and the storm. For some time he stood there as if lost in contemplation of the scene. Then, still looking down upon the city, he spoke: "John, how many churches have we here in Kansas City?"

"You mean denominations?"

"Yes."

"I suppose we have most of them—there must be at least a hundred."

"They all say that Christ is coming again, do they not?"

"Practically all teach the coming of Christ, yes."

"Well, John, if Jesus had actually come in those clouds to-night, to which church would He call His followers? From which pulpit would He issue His divine proclamations? In the light of what you know of churches, would that particular church selected by Jesus rejoice that the Lord had come again to the world or would they not rather more rejoice that He had come to them and not to one of their rival denominations? In the rejoicing of the other ninety-nine would there be any note of regret that they must go to a rival denomination to meet their Lord? Would it be inconsistent with modern church methods if the pastor of the honored church were to rush to the newspapers with an announcement to the effect that his peculiar denominational doctrines were vindicated because among all the churches Jesus had come to them—that if the people wished to hear the Messiah they must assemble at his particular place of worship? Would any down-to-date minister overlook such an opportunity, do you think? John, if you will tell me to which church Jesus would come I will give all I have to that church."

John Saxton's voice betrayed the depth of his emotions as he answered: "You are right—there is no organization existing to-day through which one could spend a dollar for a purely religious purpose. And yet, no one—least of all the Christian ministry, I think—questions the desperate need of a great religious awakening. God only can save this country from the disastrous chaos toward which we are moving. But God has always worked through human agencies. God makes the wheat but the farmer must cultivate and harvest it, the miller grind it and your groceryman distribute the flour. We cannot doubt that God will do His part in supplying our need of religion. But what about the human agency? Where are we to look for our groceryman?"

"We will look to the Church, John."

"To the Church! But haven't you just been saying—"

Big Dan smiled. "I have been speaking of the one hundred and eighty-three different conflicting denominational organizations. I have said nothing of the great multitude of sincerely religious church members who are to be found in every denomination. If there were not in every church individual members who are far more Christian than the organization which they support the situation would be hopeless. These Christian church members, when the time comes, will rise superior to the worn out machinery of their ancient denominational creeds and reestablish their touch with God.

"Most Christian thinkers and many who make no profession of Christianity are saying that right now we are on the verge of the greatest religious revival known to history. The very fact that the nation is breaking down spiritually and morally predicates this revival of religion exactly as a man's hunger predicts that he will eat when food is placed before him. On every hand there is abundant evidence to show that there is already a widespread awakening interest. For instance, you can scarcely turn the pages of any one of our great popular magazines without coming upon an article on religion, or of a religious trend. Ten years ago no editor of such a publication would have dared give space to any one of these articles that are appearing now by hundreds. The sales of books on religion compared with the sales of even five years ago have increased enormously. Since the War, the people have been thinking and talking of religion with a freedom they, perhaps, have never before known. That this freedom is expressed so commonly in a spirit of contempt for existing religious forms no less clearly indicates the interest.

"And the most significant feature of this increasing popular interest in religion is that it is not of the Church. To an amazing degree it is independent of the Church. These great popular magazines are not church publications. The writers of these articles are not strictly religious writers. The publishers of these books are not denominational publishing houses that specialize in religious literature. Nor is this awakening interest turning *toward* the Church. In my opinion it is very clearly a turning *away* from the Church. The great body of Christian church members who see in business, in national government, in civic affairs, in courts of justice, and in our social life, the almost universal lack of honor and honesty, of respect for law, of right moral sense, and common decency—these Christian church members, I say, are not looking to their churches to remedy the situation. They are still aboard the old religious ship, yes, but they know that the ship is sinking. They recognize that their church ship has been in its day a safe and seaworthy craft and they love it for its honorable record—for its memories and associations, but they sadly recognize that the time has come when they must look elsewhere for a vessel adequate to these present-day religious needs."

For some minutes the two men, in that quiet room which was so charged with the feeling of great financial wealth and power, were silent. Each was absorbed in his own thoughts. Over the city the storm raged.

"Come," said Big Dan at last, "we must get down to our work. You have your reports ready, you say?"

John Saxton turned to the table and took up the sheaf of papers. For an hour or more they bent over columns of figures and tabulated statistics. Then Big Dan pushed back in his chair with a smile of satisfaction. "Very good, John," he said heartily. "Now for the place—you have located the city?"

Saxton unfolded a map and spread it on the table. "I have found that towns of less than twenty thousand population in general are not adequately representative. I have eliminated cities of over one hundred thousand for the same reason. In towns of the less-than-twenty-thousand class the rural element is too large. The great cities are too far removed from the country class; they are a world in themselves. By the census of 1920, there are in the

United States two hundred and eighty-seven cities with a population of from twenty thousand to one hundred thousand. The average population of these cities is forty thousand six hundred and ninety-eight. A city of this size, if located in the most American section of the country, would, I believe, in every phase of its political, social, business, civic and religious life, most fairly represent the American people."

"You have such a place in mind?" asked Dan.

Saxton indicated a point on the map. "The city of Westover."

Big Dan rose to his feet and placing his hands on the shoulder of his confidential agent said quietly: "You understand perfectly what you have to do, John?"

The man's dark eyes met his employer's gaze with a steady strength. "Perfectly."

"When will you start?"

"In the morning."

"Good! When you have something to report I will see you again—until then—"

"Until then," echoed John Saxton, gravely.

Big Dan looked at his watch. "My car is waiting. I'll drop you at your hotel."

The outer offices were deserted. Uncle Zac had long since finished his work and departed.

"By the way," said Big Dan as they stepped into the night elevator, "I know some people in Westover."

CHAPTER III.

THE GROCERYMAN.

Joe Paddock sat in the little office of his grocery store. The office was a tiny box-stall-like arrangement separated from the store proper by partitions of varnished Georgia pine and window glass. The woodwork was very shiny; that glass not too clean. The groceryman was seated in a golden oak chair at a golden oak desk. The top of the desk was protected by a large square of gray blotting paper stamped with the large black-lettered advertisement of an insurance company.

It was half past one; a slack hour in the grocery business. On the insurance company's advertisement over which the groceryman's head was bent industriously were neatly arranged stacks of silver dollars, quarters, dimes, nickels and pennies, a pile of paper money and another of checks. The groceryman was making up the cash to go to the bank. Evidently the morning trade had been good. Writing in the total on the deposit slip Joe dumped the coins and stuffed the bills and checks into a canvas sack and pushed back his chair. Presently he would walk down the street two blocks to the First National Bank on the corner of State and Washington.

In his general appearance, Joe Paddock was comfortable. His age was the comfortable age of, say forty-five. He was neither large and imposing nor small and insignificant—just average, with an average face of ordinary kindly intelligence. In short, the groceryman's countenance would have reminded one of those composite photographs which one sees in textbooks or magazine articles on physiognomy. But the groceryman's face, at the completion of his task, which by all the rules of the game should have been a most satisfying task, did not express satisfaction. With his well kept, well clothed body resting comfortably in his golden oak office chair and the prosperously filled canvas sack at his elbow he still gave the impression of one under the shadow of gloomy thoughts.

And Joe, himself, was conscious of this gloom. He felt it as distinctly as one feels the hush that comes before a storm. He was not expecting a storm of any sort. His life, so far as he could see, was all fair weather with no clouds even on the most distant horizon. Yet, with apparently no reason at all, he was feeling, as he would have said, "glum." Without any apparent cause, he was burdened with a sense of something wrong—a feeling of impending trouble.

For nearly twenty years now the groceryman had "made up the cash" at half past one and had walked to the bank. Joe was a director in the First National. The First National was as sound as old wheat. His business was as sound as the bank. Whatever the cause of his low spirits it was certainly not financial troubles. The only financial trouble the groceryman knew was the universal trouble of not having enough. As for that, Joe Paddock often reflected that *he* had all *he* wanted, and always he added, "for myself."

A clerk presented himself listlessly. "Mr. Paddock," he whined, "that Carlton woman wants us to charge another order—five dollars and thirty cents—says her old man is working again now and will pay week from Saturday. What'll I do?"

The groceryman did not look up.

The clerk raised his voice with a complaining note as if protesting at the unnecessary labor of repeating his question. "Mr. Paddock, that Carlton woman—"

"Heh— Oh, excuse me, Bill—sure—all right—give her what she wants."

The clerk turned wearily away.

"What in thunder is the matter with me" mused Joe uneasily.

Grasping the canvas sack as he rose, he stepped to the door of his office. In the doorway he paused and from long habit looked over the store. It was not a large store—just an ordinary, commonplace, well established grocery. Shelves behind the counters from floor to ceiling, filled with brightly labeled canned goods, packages of breakfast foods, boxes of pepper and spices, bottles of olives and pickles, jars of preserves. Show cases filled with candies, cigars and trinkets. A big red coffee mill, a cheese under a screen cover, a glass-doored cupboard for bread and cookies, a golden oak refrigerator. Crates of vegetables, apples, oranges, lemons, a hanging bunch of bananas. Stacks of flour in sacks, barrels and boxes. A mixed odor of everything edible flavored with every known spice, tea and coffee, coal oil, molasses and gasoline. That odor was as familiar and uninspiring to Joe Paddock as the smell of hay to a farmer, the tang of the sea to a sailor or the odor of a stable to a hostler.

Joe Paddock had no great absorbing interest in his grocery. It was a good business, as good as any other, better than some. He had become a groceryman for no particular reason; it had seemed a good thing. He accepted it as he accepted the other commonplaces of life such as family cares, taxes, politics, schools, religion. As his eye, directed by habit, took in this familiar scene of his everyday life he noticed the delivery boy, Davie Bates, staggering under a basket of groceries toward the rear door where a Ford delivery car was waiting. Davie was a pale-faced, thin-shouldered, weak-limbed lad, sadly underfed and pitifully overworked. The groceryman's kindly thought was that Davie really ought not to lift such a heavy load. But confound it, the boy was late. He should have been started with his first afternoon delivery a good hour ago. Joe Paddock and Davie's mother had been sweethearts in their boy and girl days. Then Joe had married Laura Louise Fields and become a groceryman and Mary had married a young carpenter, Dave Bates. "Darn those clerks—worthless, triflin' lot—can't keep their minds on their work a minute! Bill there's gassin' with that Susie Brown, flapper; Tom and Hank, they're visitin' with each other and three customers waiting!" He walked toward the front of the store and the clerks became attentive. When he reached the sidewalk he paused again and stood looking up and down the street. He seemed to be waiting for some one, or something. But he was not. He was merely standing there. And the groceryman, himself, curiously enough, had the feeling of waiting for some one or something.

Charlie Bannock, the druggist, on the southeast corner of the block, stopped. "Hello, Joe, goin' to the bank?"

"Hello, Charlie. Yep."

"I've just been. How's business, Joe?"

The groceryman answered with listless indifference: "Business? Oh, business is all right." Then, as if his dulled interest had suddenly kindled he repeated with a show of enthusiasm: "Business is fine, Charlie, *fine.*" The final word flamed out right heartily and in the glow of it he was able to ask with spirit: "How is it with you, Charlie?"

"Never seen it so good. Tell you, Joe, we're goin' to be a big town some day. Hear about the building permits? Increase already one hundred per cent over last year. Banks all show big increase in deposits, too. So long—must be gettin' back on the job."

"So long, Charlie."

The groceryman felt the flame of the moment flickering, dying. Already the chill of his unwarranted gloom was upon him. He looked carefully up and down the street. There was nothing wrong anywhere. State Street was a good street, best in town for the grocery store. Even at this hour of the day it was a scene of hustling activity, with clatter and rattle and roar enough to fully justify the druggist's optimism. The groceryman's nearest neighbor, Jim Hadley, came out to stand in front of his store—gent's furnishings—and Joe moved a few slow steps to the side of his brother merchant.

"Hello, Jim."

"Hello, Joe. How's business?"

"Business? Oh, business is all right—fine, Jim—business is *fine!* How's yours?"

"Great, Joe. Last month biggest month I ever had. Hear about the building permits? One hundred per cent increase. Bank deposits coming up all the time, too. Lots of strangers in town. All Westover needs now is some big capital—big factories, mills or automobile works or something. Missed you at the Booster's Club luncheon to-day, Joe. What's matter? You know our motto: 'Keep a-pushin'!' Got everythin' goin' our way now if we only just keep a-pushin'! Remember them two frogs that fell into the can of milk? One of 'em says 'It's no use' and sank to the bottom and drowned. T'other just kept a kickin' and kicked out a chunk of butter big enough to float around on till the farmer let him out in the mornin'." He slapped Joe on the back and laughed as heartily as though he had not told that old story a thousand and one times before.

At the corner, as the groceryman waited for an opening in the stream of traffic, a big, shiny car with a liveried chauffeur at the wheel and an imposing personage in the rear seat passed. The personage, seeing the groceryman, smiled and bowed. Joe returned the salutation in his best manner. Mrs. Jamison was his wealthiest customer. The Jamison's had a wine cellar—all pre-war stuff—so Joe had heard. Mrs. Jamison went every season to New York for grand opera. Joe's wife always called his attention to the news in the *Morning Herald* and in the *Evening Star.* Mrs. Jamison, it was generally understood, always ran over to Paris for her gowns. Mrs. Jamison never wore a dress, she always wore a gown. As her shining car was chauffeured proudly on down the street, Mrs. Jamison was thinking: "What an utterly commonplace man—good man, though, no doubt of that—real backbone-of-the country class. And what a commonplace business, a groceryman, ugh!" Mrs. Jamison's husband was a promoter of almost anything that could be promoted.

The glow of being recognized by Mrs. Jamison lasted Joe Paddock almost until he reached the First National Bank.

There were long queues of customers waiting their turns at the different windows. After all, to be a director of the First National of Westover was something. The groceryman really did not need to wait in the line at his window but he liked it. He liked the nods and smiles of greeting. He fancied they were thinking: "Joe Paddock is a director here," and it gave him a sense of importance which he never enjoyed in his store—nor, for that matter, anywhere else.

It was his turn at the window. As he plumped the canvas sack down on the marble slab he greeted the teller with a cheerful "Hello, Frank."

"Good afternoon, Mr. Paddock." (The groceryman was a director.) "How are you to-day?"

"Me? Oh, I'm all right—'bout as usual."

"Business pretty good?"

"Business? Oh, yes, business is good." He was watching the teller sort and stack the coins. "Business is very good, Frank—*fine.*"

As the groceryman, with his empty sack, turned from the window the teller glanced after him curiously.

The president's desk was at the far end of the room just inside the low wall of polished marble which separated the First National officials from the outer world. The open-and-above-board effect of this arrangement was supposed to engender a feeling of confidence in the financial heart of the public while at the same time the marble wall prevented the customers from intruding too far into the financial heart of the institution. The president beckoned to Joe and the groceryman went to lean on the marble wall with two of the bank's largest depositors. Ed Jones, real estate, and Mike Donovan, general contractor.

Before the others could speak, Jones, who always spoke first in any company, greeted the groceryman with: "What's the matter with you, Joe, you missed the Rotary Club again this week?"

"Couldn't help it, Ed," Joe answered with a feeble grin. "I was out of town, at the farm." He forced himself to meet the quizzical humor of Mike Donovan's keen Irish eyes. "How are you, Mike?"

The contractor's heavy voice rumbled up from the depths of his broad chest: "Purty good, Joe, purty good. I guess I'm gettin' *mine* all right."

The banker, the groceryman and the real estate man laughed.

As Donovan and Jones moved on the bank president murmured admiringly: "You bet your life, Mike is getting his." Then, with a friendly interest which was genuine and a smile of honest affection, he said: "Well, Joe, how are you anyway?"

The groceryman tried to smile. "Oh, I'm all right, I guess, Henry."

Joe Paddock and Henry Winton were born on neighboring farms. They had attended the same country school, fished and swum together in Mill Creek, hunted in the same woods, skated in winter and picnicked in summer with the same crowd. Together they had attended the State University at Westover and were graduated in the same class.

Banker Winton was shrewdly studying his old friend's face. "What's the matter with you, Joe? You don't act like yourself lately. What's the trouble, old man?"

The groceryman moved uneasily. "Oh, I don't know, Henry. Nothin', I guess, just feelin' sort o' grouchy."

Winton was sympathetic. "Liver out of order? Kidneys, maybe, when a man gets along our age, you know, Joe."

"Aw, there's nothing the matter with me physically. Doc Gordon says I'm sound as a nut—eat anything I want—sleep like a top—no ache nor pain nor anything. It's nothing like *that.* How are you, Henry?"

The banker's face seemed suddenly to reflect his friend's troubled spirit. It was almost as if he had for a moment, dropped a mask. "To tell the truth," he lowered his voice to a confidential pitch, "I've been feeling a little below par myself. I'm just like you, don't know what it is—it's not business—business couldn't be better. We're going to show darned near fifty per cent increase over this month last year, Joe. Your business all right, isn't it?"

"Business—oh, yes, business is good—fine, Henry—*fine!*"

They were silent for a moment as if they had unintentionally reached the end of the conversation.

Then the groceryman, with a painful attempt at casual cheerfulness, asked: "How's Mary these days? Haven't seen her for a coon's age. Laura and I were talking about it last night."

The banker lowered his eyes and turned his face a little to one side. "Mary's all right, Joe," he answered slowly, "that is, she would be if it wasn't for—well, she worries a lot—*you* know. How is Laura?"

"She's well—'bout as usual," the groceryman answered gravely.

"No need to ask about Georgia," said Winton, trying to smile, "she was in here this morning." Georgia was Joe Paddock's daughter.

The groceryman did not answer, neither did he smile. Then, lowering his voice and speaking as if the question had been in his mind all the time, he asked: "How is Harry doing lately, Henry?"

The banker again turned his face away and slowly shook his head. Harry was Henry Winton's son.

A brisk but suave voice broke the spell. The banker caught up his mask. The groceryman, who was leaning over the marble wall, jerked himself erect. "Good afternoon, gentlemen. How do you do, Mr. Winton? How are you, Mr. Paddock?" It was George Oskins, proprietor of the Palace Hotel.

"Hello, Oskins," returned Winton.

"How do you do, Mr. Oskins?" said Paddock.

It will be noted that the hotel man addressed the banker as *Mr.* Winton while the banker called him simply Oskins, which may be understood fairly to indicate their business relationship. The hotel man saying *Mr.* Paddock and the groceryman returning with *Mr.* Oskins shows as clearly that the supplies for the Palace were purchased wholesale in Kansas City.

"Didn't see you at the Chamber of Commerce luncheon Tuesday, Mr. Paddock," said Oskins in a tone of "My dear sir, how can you expect Westover to progress without your honored presence at the Chamber of Commerce luncheon?"

"No, I missed it," replied the groceryman dryly.

Henry Winton asked briskly: "How is the hotel business, Oskins?"

The proprietor of the Palace was eagerly and anxiously enthusiastic. "Wonderful, Mr. Winton. Every room in the house full. Had to turn down twenty reservations last week. By the way," he put his soft pudgy hand on the groceryman's arm to draw him closer and, leaning confidentially over the marble wall, spoke in a hushed tone, "we have a guest at the hotel that you gentlemen really ought to meet. Wonderful man! All kinds of money, I should say, or at least represents mighty big interests—impresses you that way. He's here for some time—wouldn't say how long—monthly rates—wonderfully interested in Westover. Just the kind of big business man we need. I recommended the First National."

"What's his name?" asked the banker.

"Saxton, John Saxton, registered from Kansas City."

"Saxton — Saxton—" the banker repeated thoughtfully. "Name sounds familiar. Ever hear of him, Joe?"

"Saxton?" The groceryman shook his head. "Don't recall that I have."

"He's somebody big all right," said Oskins. "The kind that you just naturally give the best room in the house, you know. If you gentlemen will drop around to the hotel this afternoon, say about four o'clock, I'll see that you meet him."

"I'm tied up this afternoon," said Winton. "How about you, Joe?"

The groceryman answered indifferently: "I guess I could make it."

"I'll be in the lobby at four," said Oskins, and bustled way.

"Oskins is a pretty good sort," remarked the banker as if some explanation were necessary. "We carry the hotel for a little more than we would ordinarily, but on the other hand he's in a position to do us a lot of good turns. Sends us a pretty good bunch of business altogether. You'd better drop around and meet this man Saxton, Joe. Can't tell what might come of it."

CHAPTER IV.

A STRANGER IN WESTOVER.

Joe Paddock was wholesomely aware of the hustling talents of his fellow townsmen. He loved Henry Winton and his business friends and admired them tremendously. Modestly, he felt himself inferior to these live wires—it was so often difficult for him to hold up his end in the game which they played with such tireless and brilliant enthusiasm.

But the groceryman was not at all pleased with the idea of going to the hotel at four o'clock to meet the gentleman who had so impressed Mr. Oskins. He grumbled that he wasn't going to push himself on a total stranger. It might be all right for people like Oskins and for newspaper reporters and promoters and such, but as for himself—well, he wasn't that kind—he had a little decent reserve, he did. If it wasn't for good old Henry Winton and the First National he'd not do it—not for all the boosters in Westover. Still, on the other hand, the boys were all pushing for Westover and whatever good came to Westover he would share. This Mr. Saxton might bring a manufacturing plant of some sort to Westover with hundreds—it might be thousands—of employees to rent houses and buy clothing and groceries, and a big banking business for somebody. You never could tell. Such things happened to other cities. Some one really ought to get in touch with him. For a man to accept his portion of whatever good came to his city without doing his share toward pushing the community interests was not exactly playing the game. Joe Paddock honestly wished to play the game. He guessed he'd just walk over to the hotel and maybe meet Mr. Saxton casually. No—he'd better take his car. Mr. Saxton might like to drive around for an hour or so. It would be a wonderful personal opportunity—being the first one to meet and show him around—if he should really be figuring on starting something big.

In the somewhat ornate lobby of the Palace, Joe tried to appear as if he had merely dropped in to purchase a cigar. He managed to spend some time at the cigar counter making a selection (his vest pocket was already full) and, while waiting for his change, looked indifferently over the guests in the lobby. Neither Oskins nor any one as imposing as Saxton was to be seen. The groceryman purchased a newspaper. He had already read it—and again waited for his change. The Mayor, George Riley, chanced to pass that way and Joe laid hold of him eagerly. They were exchanging the usual "How's business?" with the accepted formula on the increase of building permits and the growth of bank deposits, when Oskins appeared suddenly at the groceryman's elbow with: "Excuse me, gentlemen—Mr. Paddock, Mayor Riley—I want to introduce you to Mr. Saxton. Mr. Saxton is from Kansas City. He is spending some time in Westover. I am sure he will be glad to know you gentlemen. Excuse me please, they want me at the desk for something."

It seemed to Joe Paddock that the stranger was regarding him with rather more interest than the occasion warranted and he was struck by something familiar in the man's face—what was it—could he have met him somewhere?—those eyes, serene, kindly, shadowed with sadness.

He was distinctly conscious of a little thrill of pleasure when Saxton, instead of giving all his attention to the Mayor, said: "You are in the grocery business, I understand, Mr. Paddock."

The groceryman answered with pardonable pride: "Yes, sir, twenty years now—right here in Westover."

The stranger appeared unusually thoughtful. "Twenty years," he said, and his voice warmed the groceryman's heart.

Joe was about to ask, "Haven't I met you before?" when Mayor Riley broke in with: "Are you interested in the grocery business, Mr. Saxton?"

"Oh, no, not at all. That is, not directly, in the way that you mean. We are all of us bound to be more or less interested in the grocery business, don't you think—particularly at meal time?"

The Mayor and the groceryman laughed and the tiny flame in Joe's heart grew brighter.

Encouraged by the stranger's genial humor that Mayor asked courteously, "And what line of business *are* you particularly interested in, Mr. Saxton?"

Joe waited breathlessly for the answer.

Mr. Saxton replied carefully: "Just at present, Mayor Riley, I am making a study—I may say in fact a survey of certain conditions throughout the country. Frankly, it is for that purpose that I have come to your city."

The groceryman drew a long breath. Oskins was right in his estimate of the importance of this man's presence in Westover.

"Ah," said the Mayor, "speaking for the city, Mr. Saxton, we shall be very glad indeed to extend to you every courtesy—heh, Joe?"

"I should say yes," exclaimed the groceryman in his best boosting vein. "And we'll be mighty glad for the opportunity. What do you say to a little drive around this afternoon, Mr. Saxton? I have my car right here. You'll come, too, won't you, Mayor?"

"Sorry, Joe, but I can't this afternoon—council meeting to-night, you know."

"I shall be very glad to go, Mr. Paddock," said Saxton genially.

As he drove carefully down State Street toward his store with Mr. Saxton beside him, Joe Paddock was a different man from the gloomy creature who had so reluctantly entered the lobby of the Palace less than an hour before. The personality of the stranger—that impression of his wide experience and deep knowledge of men and affairs—the feeling of his inner strength and steadfast purpose, together with the thought of all that his presence in Westover might mean, quickened the groceryman's spirit to new life. "He's big," said Joe to himself, "just naturally big—you can't help feeling it every time he looks at you."

"Ever been in Westover before, Mr. Saxton?"

"I have passed through several times. That is all."

"Can't get over the impression that I have seen you somewhere."

The groceryman, because the State Street traffic demanded all his attention, did not see the stranger's eyes as he answered gravely: "Perhaps." Then he added the usual commonplace: "This is a small world, Mr. Paddock."

"You won't mind if I stop at the store? I'll only be a minute—want to tell 'em I won't be back."

"Certainly, I'll just wait in the car. Please don't hurry on my account." Mr. Saxton looked at the groceryman's place of business with an interest which pleased Joe mightily.

Hurrying through the store with an air of importance, the groceryman bustled into his office. Glanced at the unopened letters on his desk, hurried out to the cash register, opened the till, shut it again, spoke to the delivery boy, greeted customers with a hasty nod and briskly said to the listless clerk: "Bill, I'm goin' out—won't be back this afternoon—you see to things and close up. Got to show big business man from Kansas City around town. So long."

Bill gazed wearily after the retreating form of his energetic employer.

"I guess you've already seen the downtown district," said Joe, as he settled himself under the wheel beside his guest.

"This is State Street—principal business street—First National on corner two blocks west. I'm a director—Henry Winton's president. Be glad to do anything we can for you in the banking line, Mr. Saxton. Four new business buildings under construction right now. Two on State, one on Washington—Washington crosses State, next corner there—one on Hope. Hope is next street south. We'll start out Lincoln Avenue and go through the park. Building permits last month show one hundred per cent increase over last year. Bank deposits about doubled. Gosh! That fellow just missed us—traffic almost as badly congested as Kansas City."

They turned into Lincoln Boulevard and the going was easier. Joe relaxed his tense grip on the wheel.

"So you are interested in Westover, are you, Mr. Saxton—sort of looking us over, heh? Well, sir, you would go a long way to find a better town."

"Westover seems to be a very progressive city," agreed Mr. Saxton.

"Progressive is right," said Joe stoutly. "Wonderful opening for a big factory or manufacturing plant of any kind. That's what you're looking for, I suppose."

"You'll pardon me, Mr. Paddock," returned Saxton gently, "but I am not at liberty just at present to reveal the exact nature of the investment which I—I should say my principal—desires to make. I am only a confidential agent in the matter. I can assure you, however, that the interests which I represent are very large. You, as a business man, will understand of course why I cannot, at this time, go further. I am not ready yet to make even this much too generally known but I feel sure that you will respect my confidence."

The groceryman was deeply moved. He felt that such an expression from a man like Mr. Saxton was no mean compliment. And indeed he was right. Dan Matthews' confidential agent was not often mistaken in his judgments of men. Joe Paddock was worthy.

The groceryman answered with unassumed dignity: "Thank you, Mr. Saxton," while his honest heart swelled with pride.

"This is our park—Roosevelt Park. That building over there beyond the band stand is the armory. This one here on our right is the Public Library."

"Carnegie, I suppose?"

"Oh, yes, Westover could scarcely afford a library building like that, you know. Wonderful thing for a man to give his millions to such good works, Mr. Saxton."

The groceryman's guest agreed heartily. "It is a good work; Mr. Carnegie is worthy of every honor. You say that you have lived in Westover twenty years, Mr. Paddock?"

"I've been in business here twenty years. I was born and raised on a farm eight miles west of town. My father and mother settled here in the early days. They are living on the old place yet. When I finished my university course—our State University here in Westover, we'll drive around there presently—I married and started in the grocery business."

He paused and for some reason Saxton turned his head to look thoughtfully at his companion's face. When Joe continued, his voice seemed to drag a little. "My wife was a country girl—neighboring farm—we were classmates in the University. I always liked the farm myself but she—well, after finishing school she didn't care much for the country life and so we moved into town."

He suddenly brightened up. "This is our Masonic Temple—you're not a Mason, Mr. Saxton?"

"No. That is a beautiful building. How many children, Mr. Paddock?"

"Only one, a girl. She graduated from the University last year."

"You have brothers and sisters?"

"No, there were four of us, three boys and a girl. I am the only one left."

They saw the Odd Fellows' Hall. Mr. Saxton answered that he was not an Odd Fellow.

"You are a family man, are you, Mr. Saxton?"

And this time it was the groceryman who turned his head as Saxton answered: "I am alone in the world now, Mr. Paddock."

They had viewed the County Hospital, Court House, City Hall, ice plant, power house, sash and door factory, flour mills and elevators, cold storage plant, warehouse, high school and the University, and were driving down a wide avenue between trim, unfenced lawns shaded by stately trees when the groceryman, pointing, said: "That's my place—the house with the vines over the porch. We'll have you for dinner some evening soon."

"I should be delighted," returned Saxton, looking with interest at the groceryman's modest but substantial home.

"House is a little old," commented Joe, and again his voice dragged. "Built it the year we were married."

"That big show place, across the street in the next block, is Henry Winton's."

"You have many beautiful homes in Westover, Mr. Paddock."

"Yes, sir, we have some mighty fine places."

Saxton looked at his host. For some reason the groceryman was speaking with not quite the buoyant spirit which had marked his talk earlier in the drive. "I notice several fine churches, too."

"Churches? Oh, yes, we have them all. I'm a Presbyterian myself. Father and mother were just about the first Presbyterians in Westover County. Henry Winton, he's a Baptist. His folks started the Baptist Church same as mine did the Presbyterian. Mayor Riley and his folks are Congregationalists. What's yours, Mr. Saxton? I take it that you are a church member."

"I have been a member of the Old Commons Church in Kansas City for the last fifteen years. You consider that churches are a great asset to a town, do you not, Mr. Paddock? I mean from a purely business point of view?"

"No doubt about it, sir," returned the groceryman heartily. "And you'll find Westover as well fixed in that line as any city of its size in the country. We're mighty proud of our churches. Most of our civic leaders are members somewhere. And our preachers—take 'em as a whole—are a mighty practical and down-to-date bunch. Just as good rustlers—most of 'em—as the best of our live wires in business. Take my own pastor, Dr. Coleman, he's president of the Kiwanis Club. The Methodist minister, Reverend Wilson, he's a member of the board of directors of the Chamber of Commerce. The ministers have their ministerial association and take just as much interest in all sorts of civic affairs as if they were merchants, or real estate men, or bankers, or in any other business. Why, the Congregational pastor, Mr. Carter, he's chairman of the finance committee of our Boosters' club. He's starting a drive right now for a hundred thousand dollar advertising fund. Going to put the advantages of Westover in every high-class magazine in the country. It's just like Dr. Coleman said in his sermon last Sunday: 'The world demands a practical Christianity, and we've got to make religion pay, right here on earth, if we expect to interest people in it.' And then he went on to show how the money spent in Foreign Missions had opened up those heathen countries to our commerce until the returns in dollars and cents were already a thousand times more than the total cost of the work. Wish you would come around to our services, Mr. Saxton. You'd like Dr. Coleman. He's a regular he-man. Come next Sunday. He's goin' to preach on 'Fig Leaf Fashions.' How's that for a live one—nothing slow about that, heh? Perhaps you have noticed his ad in the papers."

"Yes," said Mr. Saxton, "I have. And is Westover well organized in community work?"

"We certainly are. There is the Chamber of Commerce, the Get-together Club, Rotary, Kiwanis, Lions, Boosters, beside our Merchant's Association, Wholesale and Retail, Board of Trade, Real Estate Board, Bar Association, Medical Association, Automobile Dealers' Association, Labor Council and a lot more."

"And your charities and welfare work, down-to-date too, I suppose?"

"Oh, sure—our Organized Charities has a big drive every year. You see, by putting the charities of the city in the hands of paid professionals we eliminate a lot of unworthy cases and cut the total cost down to the minimum. Our citizens are really generous in their subscriptions, Mr. Saxton. And beside this, almost every club and order and lodge has a benevolent fund, you know. Of course we have the Y.M.C.A., Y.W.C.A., Boy Scouts, Campfire Girls, and a host of other similar organizations that are supported by the town in one way or another and are all doing good work, too.

"Well, here we are at the country club. Thought you might like to drop in for a little while. We're likely to find some of the men you'll want to meet about this time of day."

As they walked toward the wide steps, leading to the main entrance, the groceryman remarked: "Not so grand as some of your big city clubs, Mr. Saxton, but we have the same spirit. We manage to give some mighty swell affairs occasionally at that."

"I have no doubt that you do. The club presents a very creditable appearance indeed. I have observed, too, that spirit is not at all dependent upon size. For instance, consider the flea."

The groceryman roared with laughter and slapped his guest on the back. "That's a good one—that's a dandy."

After registering Mr. Saxton, in due form, and directing that a visitor's card be mailed to him at his hotel, the groceryman, with an air of mystery, drew his guest to one side. "I don't know," he said in a low confidential tone, "perhaps I ought not to mention it, but—well, really I don't want to make a mistake—would you, ah, would you care for a little drink?"

"Thank you, no," replied Mr. Saxton, in exactly the courteous, matter-of-fact tone that he would have used in declining an offered cup of tea.

"It's the real stuff," assured the groceryman anxiously. "I almost never drink myself—just a little nip once in a great while, you know. But we have it here and if you like, don't hesitate."

"No, thank you."

Several men came in, greeted the groceryman, were introduced to Mr. Saxton and went on to the locker room. When the door at the end of a corridor leading to the locker room opened, shouts of boisterous laughter with a confusion of hearty voices reached the groceryman and his guest. Several of the members, after meeting the stranger, winked slyly at Joe and nodded toward the door at the end of the corridor with a significant look toward the politely unobserving man from Kansas City. But Joe always frowned a warning with a negative shake of his head.

The good fellows really wished to be hospitable to the groceryman's friend but if he would not—well, they guessed it was up to old Joe to entertain him. Mayor Riley came, inquired anxiously what Mr. Saxton thought of Westover, made the customary silent but significant signals to Joe, was frowned upon by the groceryman and went his way to the locker room. Henry Winton came. The banker acknowledged the introduction to the guest as if Mr. Saxton were an old friend of his old friend, Joe Paddock, discussed briefly the business situation in Kansas City, Westover and throughout the country, and went the way of his fellow club members. It was significant that Banker Winton needed no warning look from the groceryman.

And so, presently, the groceryman and Mr. Saxton were seated in a quiet corner of the veranda overlooking the tennis courts while, in the locker room and on the golf course, Mayor Riley and Banker Winton were making known to their club friends and fellow citizens the probably significance of Mr. Saxton's presence in Westover.

"Smoke?" inquired Joe, offering a cigar.

"Thank you— Oh, my favorite brand! Do you know, Mr. Paddock, every time I smoke a really good cigar I am nervous."

"That's too bad."

"Yes—you see, smoking makes me wonder how long it will be before the disciples of Volstead make my innocent pleasure illegal, and when smoking is made a crime I know that I shall develop criminal tendencies."

"Heh? Oh, I see," laughed Joe. "Well, I guess you have no cause to worry. They may succeed in prohibiting the use of tobacco but, law or no law, we'll smoke just the same."

"As long as they leave us our locker rooms," murmured Mr. Saxton in an odd tone.

And, for some reason, Joe Paddock did not laugh.

"Mr. Saxton," he said while they watched the tennis players, "I have been wanting to ask you all the afternoon—what, in your opinion, is the general effect of the Volstead Act? I mean, particularly, upon the home life and upon the characters of our young people?"

Mr. Saxton did not answer. He was watching two young people, a man and a woman, who were playing a vigorous game on the nearest court.

Joe was about to repeat his question when his guest exclaimed: "What a beautiful girl! Who is she?"

The groceryman promptly dismissed the prohibition question.

"That, Mr. Saxton, is my daughter, Georgia."

Mr. Saxton turned to his host with a hearty: "Indeed, sir, I congratulate you. She is a wonderful girl—such vigor, such grace, such spirit!"

Joe Paddock answered slowly, and there was that in his voice and in his face which deepened the shadows of sadness in the dark eyes of his guest. "Georgia and I have always been good pals. She's grown up now—finished university course last year. Can't seem to make myself believe it—don't see as much of her these days as I used to."

Presently he continued: "That chap with her is Jack Ellory. I want you to meet him. He is one of our most promising young business men—automobiles. Takes an active part in every progressive movement. President of our Organized Charities. A genuine public-spirited, up-and-coming citizen. Everybody says that Jack is bound to be a big man some day. He and Georgia have been chums since they attended kindergarten together. Good family, too. Parents both dead—has no one but himself—inherited enough to start him in business."

It was evident that the groceryman was making an effort to speak with enthusiasm. But, with his eyes fixed upon his daughter and her partner, his voice dragged into a dull spiritless monotone. "Georgia is a good girl, Mr. Saxton," he finished with a determined effort. "She and I have always been regular pals."

And the groceryman felt that this stranger, whose face, with the dark brooding eyes, seemed so hauntingly familiar, that the stranger somehow understood.

CHAPTER V.

THE GROCERYMAN'S DAUGHTER.

Morning—soft gray sky in the east. Starlight waning pale and dim. Lingering fragrance of the night. Cool earthy smell of growing things wet with dew. Clouds rose-pink and gold, purple-shadowed with edges of shining silver. Sunlight under the horizon. The day.

In a tree just outside the window of Georgia Paddock's room a mother bird perched on a twig close by her nest and surveyed her tiny brood. The fledglings, with wide-open mouths, clamored feebly for their breakfast. From the topmost bough the father sang his morning hymn. Then, together, the parents flew down to the lawn and began their day's work.

The milkman's Ford rattled down the street and stopped. The man's hurrying steps on the cement walk echoed around the silent house. The screen door of the back porch slammed. The sound of the hurrying feet was repeated—with a clattering whirr the Ford moved on.

Georgia turned her head on the pillow and opened her eyes. Dreamily she looked at the gray square of light between the window hangings, and through the open casement heard the song of the birds. With a slow luxurious movement of her body and a delicious yawn she turned her back to the window and nestled under the covers for another nap. And strangely enough, at that moment, while she lay half asleep and half awake, she thought of Mr. Saxton. Where had she seen that face before?

Her father had introduced her, with Jack Ellory, to Mr. Saxton at the club yesterday afternoon. They had chatted a moment with the groceryman and his guest and then had gone on to change after their somewhat strenuous hour at tennis. But the man's face had haunted her all that evening. She felt certain that somewhere, sometime, she had seen him before. Jack, too, had been struck with the same feeling that this was not the first time that he had stood face to face with the man who, so far as they knew, was a stranger. Who was he anyway? The name, Saxton, meant nothing. And why was he her father's guest? How had her father met him? When Jack returned from the locker room he had told her that Mr. Saxton was a big business man from Kansas City and that he was in Westover on a mission which might result in a good thing for everybody. But that information was of no particular importance to Georgia. It was of much greater importance that Jack Ellory, himself, was going to be a man of big business.

The girl moved uneasily and adjusted her pillow. When Jack was a big business man with whom would he share his success? At that moment—though Georgia would never have confessed it to any one and had she been more wide awake would not have admitted it even to herself—that question was, for her, the most important question in all the world. As one will in those half-dreaming moments, the girl drifted on the wide, sleepily flowing stream of memories.

It all started in those early years when she and Jack sometimes played at "keeping house." But, even then, the game was always of her choosing and he had made himself a stern papa to her dolls. At one period he had stoutly informed all the world that he was going to marry Georgia when they grew up. But the kindergarten had quickly put an end to all that and forced her to suffer tearfully his rude taunts, contemptuous sneers, and cruel teasing. What a masterful leader he had been in every sort of mischief—always bullying the other boys, always fighting, boasting, showing off. How he had scorned all games in which girls had a part. She wondered did he not, in his heart, scorn them still? She sometimes thought he did, but there were other times, when—grade school, high school and the University—from scorning the girls he came to tolerate, then to accept and, finally, to seek their company. He had been masterful always, but was less and less a bully—boasted not so openly, and showed off not quite so conspicuously as he moved up in life, grade by grade. Always they had gone with the same crowd. Nearly always he had preferred her. Since the period of their first going out together, she had felt toward him something very like fear. And he had seemed to feel the same toward her. It was strange—she wondered why. With other boys of her set she had been—well, no more a prude than other girls, and these other boys had taken what her grandparents would have called liberties. But with Jack there had been nothing of that sort though she knew—as girls know such things—that with the others he had been as bold as the boldest. With the passing of their university years her fear, if it was fear, of him had grown until now. She wondered what sort of a man Jack Ellory really was anyway. Her father thought highly of him as a business man. He was admired and praised by the community. But after business hours? There was nothing slow about their set. Some of their parties—had they gone too far last night? Harry Winton did drink too much—it was disgusting. Might there not be a very real danger in their boasted freedom? Danger of what? Jack went to parties where she was not invited. She had heard some things—why did she feel afraid when she was with him—if it was fear? She was not afraid—that was all nonsense, but if it was not fear what was it?

Not many of her girl friends who had married had escaped unhappiness. She thought of some of the confidences she had received. Were all men like that? She recalled the married men she had seen with women who were not their wives, at some of the places frequented by her set. Grandfather and Grandmother Paddock—what a dear, loving old couple! Fifty years together and sweethearts still. Was such happiness possible in this generation? Could such a home ever be, to her or to any one whom she knew, more than an idle dream? The plays that she saw, the motion pictures, the newspapers, magazines, novels, the popular songs, the jokes in the funny papers—was there anywhere in this modern world a love like that of her grandparents? If there *was* why didn't some one talk or write or sing about it? Why did everybody talk and write novels and stories and songs and make plays and pictures about the other thing?

The living room of the Paddock home was in keeping with the exterior. It was old-fashioned enough to have dignity but, with each progressing year, Mrs. Paddock had been careful that modern effects were not lacking. On the shelves of the bookcases Dickens and Ruskin and Hawthorne touched elbows with latest-born of the realists. On the fine old Steinway piano were sheets of popular songs. A mahogany library table of a past period held a magazine of the super-intellectuals, a novel of sex madness, a volume of Hindu poetry, a denominational church paper, the latest authority on bridge, and a Bible. The walls were hung with pictures—a landscape in oils, painted by Mrs. Paddock with the help of a teacher, from a study which she had received with an art magazine, two fine old engravings, three bargain counter etchings and an excellent reproduction of the head of Jesus from Hoffmann's "Jesus and the Rich Young Ruler." Directly under this picture of the lowly Nazarene a radio stood ready with an inexhaustible program of jazz.

When Georgia Paddock came down to the living room that morning her father, with an air of ominous self-control, was pretending to read the *Herald.* Mrs. Paddock stood before the gas log, glazed tile and golden oak fireplace. From her mother's somewhat martial attitude and the set expression of her rather classical countenance the daughter knew that the domestic barometer registered slightly colder.

People quite generally remarked that the beautiful daughter of the groceryman was exactly like her mother. And, in a way, the people were right. Laura Louise Paddock certainly was not fat. By unlimited worrying and the strenuous use of every known method—exercises, diets, treatments, salts, baths, massage, and mental suggestion—she still managed to look anything but matronly. That she managed, also, to look anything but motherly was quite beside the all-important question of the day.

But it must not be understood by this, that Georgia's mother was actually lacking in those finer qualities of motherhood which the world agrees are, after all, woman's most enduring charm. It was only that by certain well known, modern, intellectual processes this instinctive and natural motherliness in Mrs. Paddock had been refined to a point where it was almost invisible to the naked eye.

With an air of critical, if loving, authority Mrs. Paddock noted every detail of her daughter's appearance. Had she not been so unmistakably Georgia's mother one might have fancied that, in her expression of proud possession, there was a slight touch of envy—the girl's beauty was so fresh, and vigorous, and youthful.

"I'm sorry if I am late, Mother," said Georgia, and there was a wistful look in the frank, gray eyes as if the girl's early morning thoughts lingered with her still.

The groceryman dropped his paper and smiling cheerfully at his daughter rose from his chair.

Mrs. Paddock returned evenly: "It is of no importance, I suppose. The cook will probably give notice. Your father's business does not matter. As for *my* affairs—they, of course, are not to be considered."

The wistfulness vanished from the girl's face and in its stead came a look of proud rebellion. Her voice was coolly impudent. "Oh, bunk, Mother, it's not five minutes past our usual breakfast time."

Joe looked at his watch. "Four minutes exactly," he said with forced good humor. "Good morning, dear. You look fresh as a posy. Come on, Mother, let's eat."

He went to the girl and put his arm around her with a comforting little hug which she acknowledged with a kiss. Then they followed the wife and mother to the dining room.

Mrs. Paddock glanced competently over the details of the breakfast table. With the studied effort at calmness, of one announcing a national disaster, she spoke to the maid: "Ella, there are no fruit knives."

A moment later she addressed her husband in exactly the same tone: "Joe, this fruit is simply impossible! I should think that, as long as you are in the grocery business, you might at least supply your own family with decent food!"

"It's hard to find any good fruit just now," Joe answered mildly, "between seasons, you know."

"Others seem to know where to find it. The fruit salad at Mrs. Gordon's luncheon last Thursday was simply perfect. What have you been doing since yesterday morning, Georgia? I never see you any more except at breakfast."

"Dad and I lunched at home—strikes me you are the one to give an account of yourself, Mother dear."

"You dined at the country club, I suppose?"

"Not much! Catch me feeding on the junk they serve there, if I can help!

Jack and I had some tennis, then we went to Tony's Place for eats, danced a while and played around with the bunch till quittin' time. How did you and dad spend your evening? Did you foregather with some of the elect to sample their home-brew and discuss the morals of the younger generation—or did you fight peacefully at home?"

"Georgia!"

"Yes, Mother dear."

Mrs. Paddock loftily withdrew into her superior self. The groceryman was mutely feeling inferior and hopelessly wondering what was wrong. Georgia was thinking of Grandpa and Grandma Paddock.

"You'll have to walk down town this morning, Joe," said Mrs. Paddock as her husband pushed back his chair. "I want the car."

"All right," Joe returned heartily. "Exercise will be good for me."

"And you must put some money in the bank for me—I have overdrawn my account."

"All right, Mother, I'll fix you up. By the way, I'd like to ask Mr. Saxton for dinner some evening soon—if it's convenient."

"And who is Mr. Saxton?"

"You know—the man I told you about last night—from Kansas City—represents big interests. He's looking into Westover with a view to establishing an industrial plant of some sort. I thought—"

"Why don't you take him to the Palace or to your club?"

"Well, I thought—well, you see, he's the sort of a man who would really enjoy a simple home dinner."

"Well, I wouldn't particularly enjoy entertaining some one we know nothing about. Besides, if he really *is* a man of any importance and you are trying to impress him with your position in Westover it would be a sad mistake to try to entertain him in *this* house—it's quite impossible."

"Oh, Mother," cried Georgia. "Be a good spot—if dad wants to bring a friend to dinner—"

"Georgia! How many times have I assured you that I have no ambition to be, what you call, a good sport?"

The groceryman was already on his way to the front door.

Georgia caught him as he was going down the steps.

"Dad, let me drive you down to the store. I'd love to—it's such a glorious morning. I'll bring the car straight home."

"Never mind, daughter, I'd just as soon walk—exercise do me good."

"Please let me, Daddy," she urged.

"Nope—need the exercise—by-by."

She stood in the doorway watching him down the street.

The telephone rang. The instrument was in the hall and Georgia turned from the door to answer the call. As she took down the receiver her back was toward the living room so that she did not notice her mother, who had also heard the bell and was coming to answer. Mrs. Paddock, seeing her daughter at the phone, paused in the living room door and waited, unnoticed by the girl, who was speaking into the instrument.

In the customary, matter-of-fact, impersonal voice: "Hello—"

A shade of doubtful recognition—not at all glad to hear the voice at the other end of the line: "Who is speaking, please?"

With a touch of mocking surprise: "Oh-h, it is? Well—" sarcastically, "not exactly."

Cheerfully: "No, I'm not the maid—I'm not the cook either. Father has just left the house. You can get him at the store in half an hour, ring 702—"

Impudently: "Oh, you do—well, I don't think she is in."

With positive disapproval: "Oh, she did—well, you can't talk to Mrs. Paddock just now. She is—"

A furious exclamation caused the girl to look hastily over her shoulder. Her mother was upon her with: "Georgia Paddock! I never heard such impudent rudeness in all my life— Give me that receiver!"

The daughter spoke into the instrument with mocking sweetness: "I'm sorry, Mr. Astell, I find that mother is here after all."

With her lips still close to the instrument she added: "Mother, dear, Mr. Astell wishes to speak to you—Mr. Edward Alton Astell."

The daughter stood aside but did not leave the hall while her mother spoke over the wire.

"Yes, Mr. Astell—

"Good morning, isn't it rather early for you?—

"Oh, how *perfectly* charming of you—yes, indeed, it is *perfectly* beautiful—

"Oh, but you know I *love* to rise at an early hour when nature is so fragrant and cool and sweet—

"Yes—yes—how perfectly *wonderful*—

"You should hear the birds in our trees. The air fairly rings with their music, and the flowers are so wonderful in their dewy freshness—

"Yes—

"Yes—

"Oh, yes—

"How wonderful—so few men are able to appreciate such things. I don't wonder that you find your greatest inspiration in the early morning—

"At eleven o'clock—

"Oh, thank you—thank you so much. It is so generous of you to give poor little me so much of your valuable time—

"How charming of you to say that—

"I only wish it *were* true—

"Until eleven—good-by."

She hung the receiver gently on the hook and whirled on her daughter: "Now, young lady, perhaps you will be good enough to explain how you dare to treat a man like Mr. Astell with such unheard of rudeness?"

Georgia stood her ground with the frank contempt of parental authority so characteristic of her generation. "Perhaps *you* will explain why that darned snob calls you up and you make appointments with him when he wouldn't even speak to father on a bet."

"Mr. Astell is one of our few real gentlemen. It is a privilege to have his friendship. I'm consulting him about our Literary Club program. He is not only an authority on art and literature, he is, himself, a distinguished author. He lives in a world very different from the world in which your father moves. You can't expect a genius of Mr. Astell's standing to have anything in common with mere grocerymen."

"Distinguished author! Your foot! Why, you know, he never wrote but one fool novel and had to pay to have that published. No one outside of Westover ever even heard of the silly indecent thing—and no one here ever read it, except a bunch of half-baked women that he gave autographed copies to. Genius—my eye! He's a common, nasty-minded snob who would be cleaning cuspidors for his living if his father hadn't left him enough money to keep him."

The girl caught her breath with a choking sob and her angry eyes filled with tears. "Oh, Mother—Mother, what's the matter with us all? You're not a bit like you used to be when I was little—and I—I guess I'm going crazy too, chasing around day and night. Nobody seems to want the simple, honest, unpretentious, decent things any more. Why can't we be like Grandpa and Grandma Paddock? Poor dad looks so old and worried and lonesome and discouraged. And you—you—you don't care for anything but your rotten old culture. I—I tell you, I can't stand it, Mother! I can't stand it!"

She rushed upstairs and Mrs. Paddock heard the door of her daughter's room slam.

For several minutes Mrs. Paddock stood as motionless as a woman carved in wood.

Slowly the strained, shocked expression of her face changed and the light of motherhood came into her eyes. Slowly, almost reluctantly, as if forced by some inner power that was stronger than her will, she went up the stairway.

Georgia, who had thrown herself on the bed with her face buried in the pillow of her morning dreams, heard a knock at the door. She did not answer. Then a voice—a gentle voice—called: "Georgia—it is mother—may I come in, dear?"

"No," cried the girl, "I don't want to see you. I don't want to see any one!"

The girl felt, rather than heard, the door open quietly. She felt some one softly crossing the room. Then an arm encircled her trembling shoulders. She turned her head impatiently on the pillow. Her mother was kneeling beside the bed. Her mother's face was close beside her own. Her mother's cheeks were wet.

CHAPTER VI.

PAST AND PRESENT.

The groceryman, on his way down town, was physically conscious of the morning and walked briskly enough, but his spirit dragged miserably along, unmoved by the familiar objects and incidents of the friendly street.

Sam Gordon's new house was nearly finished. Joe wondered dully if Sam and his wife would be happy there. Sam had appeared sort of glum and worried lately—not like his old jolly self. His business was all right—Sam banked at the First National and bought his groceries at Joe's store—could it be the family—there had been some talk—too bad if there was anything really wrong—with their new house so nearly ready. Jim Watson hailed the groceryman with an invitation to ride. Joe forced a cheerful return to the neighborly greeting and declined—he needed exercise. Watson and his wife put on some lively parties at their home. Joe wondered if there was anything in the whispered report that they were going to separate. The new Congregational Church was a mighty costly-looking edifice. He wondered how much they owed on it. He guessed George Riley had been forced to put up a good share of the money and would likely have to come across with a lot more before they finished. The groceryman, himself, had made a generous contribution to the rival house of God—didn't want to—had to support his own church; but Riley and a number of other Congregationalists traded at his store and banked at the First National. That man Saxton, yesterday—unusual sort of man, big though, almighty big—not often a man of his caliber is so interested in churches, that is, not in exactly the way that Saxton was. Joe wished that he had gotten Saxton's views on the effect of prohibition on the homes and the young people. The bunch that Georgia ran with were setting a good pace. The girl was all right though; she knew when to stop—no danger for her. These modern girls knew a lot about things. How much did they really know anyway? He wished he hadn't offered Saxton a drink. What in thunder did he want to go and pull a bonehead like that for anyway? Saxton's friendship might easily result in big money—perhaps—perhaps—if he played his cards just right he might be able to give Laura some of the expensive things she was always wanting. He didn't care for expensive things himself. A quiet farm home life such as father and mother lived—that was the thing for him. The noisy activity of State Street annoyed him. He didn't want to go to the store to-day. He believed he would run out to the farm and see the old folks. No, Laura wanted the car. He'd call up Saxton and ask him to lunch. Why the dickens didn't Jack Ellory ask Georgia to marry him? In his day, no young couple could be together as much as Georgia and Jack without something coming of it.

The groceryman walked briskly through the store to his office where he sat down to his desk and pretended to read his letters. In the old days he used to spend the busy hours of the morning in the store greeting his customers and helping the clerks serve them. He didn't seem to want to meet people lately. Glad he met Saxton though—Saxton was different. Funny how sure he felt that he had seen him somewhere before. He wished Laura would let him invite Saxton to dinner. What in thunder was the matter anyway? With sudden determination he pulled open a drawer in his desk and took from it a photograph. It was the portrait of a beautiful young woman with a baby in her arms and the woman's face was glorified by the holy passion of her motherhood. His wife and baby, Georgia.

With the bustling activity of his business on the other side of the glass partition, his morning mail lying on the desk before him, and the ringing of the cash register in his ears, the groceryman gazed at the old photograph and searched the years that had passed since the camera made that record of his happiness.

Their sweetheart days—their engagement—the first years of their married life. Surely if ever there was a marriage for love, theirs had been—and was yet—he assured himself stoutly. If a man of forty-five is not quite so demonstrative in his affections does that mean that his love is less sincere and true? No, no—it means, rather, that the current of his passion has deepened and broadened. If the stream of his love runs with less noise, it as surely flows with more strength. The groceryman knew that his love for his wife was all that it had ever been—all and more. He was almost, if not quite, as sure of his wife's love. In spite of the cloud which had come over their home there were occasions—less and less frequent, he feared—when Laura was the wife and mother of that old photograph. How then had they come to such a pass? Perhaps if their boy had lived—the groceryman's eyes grew misty. The boy had come to them two years after Georgia's birth. He was just beginning to walk alone when he left them.

It was soon after the boy's death that Mrs. Paddock had developed an absorbing interest in church affairs. For a year or more, night and day, she had gone about what her pastor assured her was her Master's business—sewing circles, bazaars, rummage sales, socials, entertainments, raising money for the minister's salary, for a new carpet, for pulpit furniture. Then, with a change of pastors, her religious fervor cooled and she had entered upon a period of scholarship. She again attended the university classes—economics, astronomy, chemistry, French—until a sudden interest in civic clubs and politics left her not a moment for things academic. This political period, in turn, gave way to a program of welfare work—organized charities, hospitals, health centers, surveys, and social science. And then came art, with lectures to attend, exhibitions to manage, courses of study, and lessons in painting. Music followed next with more club courses of study—long hours at the piano, recitals to attend and recitals to give, programs and conventions. And so they had arrived by easy stages at her present absorbing interest in literature and what she called "the higher culture." Devotedly, now, she worshiped at the shrines of the intellectuals. She aspired to be one of the few. She read the unexpurgated ancients and those moderns of whom if they were expurgated there would be nothing left. She talked bravely and broadly of all matters pertaining to sex and discoursed at length upon the new freedom. Between club programs, lectures, studies, and talks, she was herself writing a book—a fearless novel for the very few who could understand.

And through all these changing periods of Mrs. Paddock's progress toward the higher things of life, Joe had gone every morning to his grocery store. Year in and year out, he had lived between the producers of food and the consumers of food. Day by day, he had helped to answer the universal prayer, "Give us this day our daily bread." The groceryman burned no incense before the altars of intellectuality. The only incense he knew was the perfume of coffee and tea and spices and fruits and vegetables. He worshiped at no shrine of Art or Letters; he bought and sold groceries. He bowed before no god of the superior culture; he paid his bills. And the reward of his labor was his home. For his devotion to the lowly business of answering the common prayer of the people, the groceryman had received for his wife and daughter and himself—bread.

That reminded him—Laura had told him that her account was overdrawn. He must write a check. And Georgia's allowance, too. He might as well write a check for that while he was about it. With his problem still unsolved, Joe Paddock laid the old photograph reverently back in the drawer and from another drawer took his checkbook. As he opened the book and wrote he was oppressed with the burden of his failure—for the groceryman knew, in his heart, that he had failed.

The protesting whine of the listless clerk came from behind his chair: "That darned kid is late again this morning—just got here—what'll I tell him?"

Joe carefully laid a blotter on the checks. "Send him in here to me."

The delivery boy came and stood before his employer.

His thin, undernourished body with its narrow shoulders and scrawny limbs was clothed in garments patched and faded. His colorless hair was unkempt, his face gaunt and old. He nervously fingered an old rag of a cap and his deep, somber, hollow eyes were sullenly fearful.

The groceryman looked the lad over—not unkindly. He was thinking: "Poor boy, he doesn't look very happy, either."

"Well, Davie," he said at last, "what's your trouble?"

"Bill said you wanted to see me." The lad's voice was thin and frightened, with an undertone of desperate antagonism. His manner was that of a trapped animal—wary, ready to fight if he must, but wanting most of all to escape.

"You are late again this morning, Davie."

The lad fingered his cap in silence.

"You realize, don't you, that I must have some one who will get out these morning deliveries on time?"

Davie did not speak.

"Well," Joe demanded, sharply, "what have you to say? Can't you talk?"

"Please, Mr. Paddock, for Christ's sake don't fire me. I can't—I can't lose my job now—" The boy's words seemed literally torn from him. His features worked in an agony of fear, his eyes were wild and pleading, his bony fingers twisted his old cap with desperate strength. "I'll do better, honest to God I will. It would be murder—plain murder—if you was to fire me now!" His words ended in a chocking sob.

The groceryman suddenly remembered—he had heard somewhere that Davie's mother was not well. The clerk, Bill, had said something about it a week or so back. Two years ago the carpenter-father had fallen from a scaffold while working on the Presbyterian Church and had never stood on his feet since. The carpenter and his wife, Mary, were both members of the church and the man had been donating his work when the accident occurred. Since he was hurt, they had not attended services and had failed to pay their dues. Those morning deliveries must be sent out on time. Oh, hang the morning deliveries!

"How is your father these days, Davie?"

The boy answered in a sullen monotone as if his outburst had left him weak and hopeless: "He's just the same."

"Can't the doctors do anything?"

"Doctors! Where'd we get money enough for a big hospital job like that? We're lucky if we eat."

The desperate brutality of the boy's reply startled the groceryman. "Your mother is pretty well, is she?"

"She—she's been in bed for a month past."

"Oh, that's too bad, Davie. Why didn't you tell me?"

"I told Bill."

"I'm sorry I didn't know—didn't realize, I mean—What's the trouble?"

"I don't know—just clean worn out, I guess. There ain't nobody to do nothing but me—Jimmie and Maud, they's too little."

"You have some one to stay with them during the day?"

"The neighbor women, they look in when they can. She's worse nights—I—I—that's what makes me late sometimes. I don't dare lose my job now, sir. I'll do better, honest to God I will."

The groceryman was thinking. "Organized Charities, I must report it. Don't know though—the boy is working." "Davie," he said suddenly, "go and tell Bill I want to see him. You come back with him."

"Are you going to fire me?"

"No, Davie, we'll manage somehow. Go and fetch Bill."

When Davie returned with the clerk Mr. Paddock said: "Bill, I want you to give Davie, every day, everything he needs from the store. Charge it to me, but don't get the orders mixed up with my family account. He is to have anything he wants from our stock every day until I tell you different. Do you understand?"

"Yes, sir."

And Bill went to tell his fellow clerks: "Pretty soft for that darned kid, pretty soft, I'd say. The old man ought to 'a' tied the can on him—he would have, too, if it'd been one of *us.*"

When the delivery boy, after trying with halting, stumbling, sobbing words to thank his employer, had gone to the waiting Ford, the groceryman was shocked to find himself thinking: "Suppose Laura Louise had married the young carpenter, Dave Bates. Would Laura now be 'just clean worn out' with no one but that slip of a boy to provide for her and her helpless husband and their little ones? Suppose Mary Graham—suppose I, Joe Paddock, had married Mary—would I be here in the grocery business with Laura's son working for me? Suppose—oh, what's the use supposing anything."

Life to the groceryman, just then, was a hopeless tangle with no beginning and no end to anything. He decided he would call up the house and ask Laura to drive out to the farm with him. Perhaps Georgia would go, too. If he could he would coax Laura to go with him for a walk in the woods, they would slip away and leave Georgia with the old folks. Perhaps, if they should go together to the old tree beside the pond in the heart of the woods where they had spent so many happy hours—where he had asked her to be his wife—perhaps—

He called his home.

The maid answered that Mrs. Paddock was out. Miss Georgia was in—did he wish to speak to her?

"No, never mind."

He hung up the receiver.

Where was Laura anyway? Of course, he remembered now, she had wanted the car. Great Scott, it was eleven o'clock.

The groceryman and Mr. Saxton lunched together.

Joe would have liked to talk to his new friend, if he had dared, about some things which he could not mention even to Henry Winton. Winton and Riley and nearly everybody that Joe knew had things of their own which they did not talk about. It was odd how the groceryman felt that he had known Saxton for many years.

CHAPTER VII.

ONE EVENING.

That small group of Westover men who were popularly said to be on the inside of every important financial enterprise and who were thus privileged to know well in advance every contemplated move in the progress of their city, lost no time in cultivating the acquaintance of Mr. Saxton. The information first passed in the locker room was amplified by conjectures in snatches of confidential talk during business hours, confirmed by Mr. Saxton's unmistakable interest in Westover, and certified by the personality of Mr. Saxton himself. But no one, so far, was sufficiently on the inside to know the exact nature of the large investments which the unknown powerful interests represented by Mr. Saxton were contemplating. They knew only that it was a big thing for Westover. That a big thing for Westover might also be a big thing for the individual who was sufficiently in with the man who held the whole matter in his hands was understood.

Aside from this—which, after all, was no more selfish than was necessary—the members of the inner circle had come to regard Mr. Saxton for something quite apart from the financial interests and the material hopes which he represented. The groceryman's feeling that he had seen the man before, that he had met him somewhere, was shared by Joe's friends, and each in his own way and time mentioned the fact that Saxton impressed him with a sense of something that was more than just business. As Judge Burnes said: "I don't know why, but he makes me think of religion."

The judge was a pillar in the Methodist Church North. And Ed Jones, who was an official in the Methodist Church South, said practically the same thing. As for Banker Winton, Baptist, and Mayor Riley, Congregationalist, they also agreed with Presbyterian Joe Paddock that this newcomer was an unusually fine Christian character, who, even apart from business considerations, would be a real asset to the community. Quite consistently, too, each individual pillar was careful to assure his own particular pastor that Mr. Saxton would be a member well worth having.

As a result of the competition thus engendered Mr. Saxton received attentions not unlike a college fraternity rush. In due time he was even invited to the groceryman's home—*that* was after he had dined with the Jamison's. But, with it all, no one could say that the deservedly popular subject of these special efforts was drawn more to one church than another. He was interested in all; but his interest remained decidedly impersonal.

A month had passed since Mr. Saxton's first appearance in Westover.

Georgia Paddock was in the living room, that afternoon, reading *Life* and waiting for Jack Ellory to pick her up on his way to the country club.

She looked at the clock. A quarter past four. If Jack expected to play much tennis he's better be coming along. Father would be home from the store presently. Mother had been out since just before lunch. Oh, darn! Why couldn't mother at *least* manage to be around the house when dad got home at the end of the day?

The girl tossed her magazine fretfully aside and wandered uneasily out to the front porch. She was just in time to see an automobile stopping in front of the house. The car was an expensive roadster, one of those machines which, more than any other piece of property, advertises its owner's excessive material wealth. Any one would have known that the man at the wheel was the owner. Fat, florid, forty, he was dressed in keeping with his car—not loud, but with a shade *too much* good taste.

The face of the groceryman's daughter set and her eyes were hard as she saw her mother step from the car and stand as if continuing a most interesting conversation with the gentleman who had brought her home. With an angry swing the girl fled into the house where she was not above watching the little scene from one of her living room windows.

When the shining roadster finally moved on with its radiant owner, Mrs. Paddock came up the walk with the step of a woman half her age. There was color in her cheeks, her eyes were bright, and a faint smile lingered on her lips as if her mind dwelt on pleasant thoughts. As she entered the living room and met her daughter's level gaze of cool and knowing appraisement the color in her cheeks deepened. At the moment, one might easily have thought her an older sister to the girl, and Georgia, always proud of her mother's beauty, paid her the tribute of involuntary admiration, while the stern judgment in the daughter's eyes gave way to a look of troubled affection.

Mrs. Paddock spoke with nervous excitement. "Oh, Georgia, my dear, I *do* wish you had been at the club this afternoon. My program was *such* a success. Mr. Astell was *wonderful.* His address on the 'Courage of Realism' was simply *marvelous,* quite the most *exquisite* thing I ever heard. As Mrs. Brownell said, when she congratulated me on my program, 'We are so fortunate in having a man of Edward Alton Astell's culture living right here in Westover!'" She glanced at the clock. "My goodness, I did not dream it was so late."

Georgia said dryly: "You held an unusually long *session* to-day—the club I mean."

Mrs. Paddock missed it. "Your father is not home yet, is he?"

The girl smiled. "No, he's just a *little* late. There he is now—no, it's Jack. Good-by Mother, I'm off."

"Good-by, dear. The country club, I suppose?"

"Yes—tennis."

The mother's voice was vaguely troubled. "And after that? Oh, Georgia, do be careful. The girls of your age these days—"

The daughter interrupted with a mocking laugh: "You should worry, Mother dear—you should worry!"

"Now what," thought Mrs. Paddock, as the girl ran lightly from the house, "did Georgia mean by that?" And Georgia's mother moved restlessly about the living room which was so filled with the memories of all her married years. Every piece of furniture, every ornament, picture, book, the very rugs on the floor and the paper on the walls, were associated with some home-making incident, some domestic joy, sorrow, disappointment or achievement. There was a little of the wife and mother soul in everything. Husband and daughter and the baby son who had stayed so short a time—they were always there in that room.

Mrs. Paddock paused before the painting which was the sole relic of her interest in art. She never looked at that picture without thinking, "If I had only gone on with my studies I might have won a place among the people who are known." And she would see as in a vision a studio, like the studios of famous painters that she had read about in illustrated magazines. She would see great galleries with throngs of people viewing the work of her brush. She would see the Sunday papers with pages devoted to her life and her art—with reproductions of her pictures, and photographs of herself. Seating herself at the piano she dreamily touched the keys and thought, "If I had continued with my music I would now be at the height of my fame." And she visioned herself playing to vast audiences in the great cities of the world, being honored by royalty, her picture on the billboards, her name in electric lights, and pages and pages in the newspapers and magazines about her career. She turned from the piano and her restless glance fell upon a row of books. If only she had kept up her work along social welfare, economics or political lines. And she saw herself the center of public interest, lecturing to crowded houses, leading important movements, discussing great issues, a representative in Congress, a famous authority featured in the magazines and headlined in the daily papers. Her thoughts turned to the novel she was writing and she visioned the finished book, with her name—her name on the cover, her name in the advertisements everywhere—the reviews, the praise, the articles about her in the magazines, her photograph in the papers. She *must*—she *would* make it all come true. And all the while she was hearing her daughter's mocking voice: "You should worry, Mother dear—you should worry." Should she really worry?

What did Georgia mean? What should Laura Louise Paddock—wife and mother—worry about?

When the groceryman reached home a half hour later he found his wife in their bedroom. She was seated before her dressing table and greeted him without turning her head: "You know we are going to the Winton's for dinner to-night, Joe."

"Gosh, I *had* forgotten," he returned. "But there's lots of time. We don't need to start for a couple of hours yet."

He stood just inside the door looking at her thoughtfully. He was wishing she would turn away from her own image in the glass and come to him. He could see her face in the mirror. She did not even look at him. She was looking at herself. He crossed the room and, stooping, kissed her bare shoulder. She gave no sign that she knew he was there.

Joe spoke to the face in the mirror: "Have you had a good day, dear?"

Her eyes met his for an instant, then with an indifferent shrug she continued doing things to her hair.

The groceryman, with what might have been a sigh, dropped wearily into a chair.

"Where is Georgia?" he asked presently.

Mrs. Paddock's answer sounded like an accusation. "She is at the country club with Jack Ellory, I suppose. She *said* she was going there. Where they will go between now and midnight, goodness knows. I think the way girls like Georgia go to all sorts of questionable places, with any man who will take them, is perfectly dreadful."

"I know it is, Laura. Nothing seems to faze this younger generation. I wish"—he paused as if he could not express exactly what it was that he wished—then he said reassuringly: "Georgia is safe enough with Jack though. Why, they've been playmates all their lives."

"Exactly. But you don't seem to realize how easy it would be for them to be something more than playmates."

"You mean they might marry?"

"That or something worse."

"You seem to have a lot of confidence in your daughter, I must say."

"Oh, Joe! How *can* one have confidence in anybody these days? Think of Marjory Jones! Everybody knows the *real* cause of her *death!* And Maud Riley—away on a *visit.* How would you like for *our* daughter to go away on that kind of a visit?"

When the groceryman replied, his voice was not as confident as his words.

"She's all right as long as she is with Jack, Laura. Jack is a mighty fine chap—really—and you know how fond he has always been of Georgia. I admit, though, I wish they would marry and settle down and have done with it."

"Joe Paddock! Would you actually be satisfied to have our daughter married to *him?*"

"Why not? Everybody says Jack is one of our most promising young business men. He's bound to be a big man some day. There is no better family than his in Westover. And he's a lot steadier than most of the men of his age. Look at Henry Winton's boy, Harry, for instance. And those two Burnes boys—I'm darned if I see how the Judge ever gets a night's sleep. Jack may chase around some and enjoy a good time occasionally, but you bet your life he is wise enough not to let it interfere with his business! That boy keeps his head working all the time."

"That may all be true, but I have heard some things just the same. He doesn't share all his good times with Georgia—I *hope*. But even if you are right, after all, what *is* he? The automobile business! Could anything be more deadly commonplace? Unless it was the grocery business. I want my daughter to have some sort of a future, a future worth while, I want her to get something out of life—to *be* somebody."

The groceryman slumped down in his chair. With a retort on his lips he thought: "What's the use?" and remained silent. Presently he stole a look at his wife as she stood, now, before the long mirror in the door of their bathroom. Keenly alive to her beauty, he thought of their courtship days in the country and how, for her, he had given up the farm life that he loved and had moved to the city.

When Mrs. Paddock had given the last final pat and twitch to her dress and the last lingering touch to her hair she went to a small desk in one corner of the room, and from a little pile of monthly statements selected a single sheet.

"Joe," she said in a cool, competent tone, "I wish you would instruct your clerks to be more careful. Look at this." She handed the statement to her husband.

Joe glanced at the printed form with the itemized entries. "Well, what's the matter with it? It's the regular monthly statement of our account at the store. Have you checked it with the sales slips?"

"Certainly I have checked it. That is how I know it is wrong. None of those entries which I have marked were delivered to us. I am very careful to have cook save every slip and, besides, I know what I order. Some one is charging to you groceries which we never received."

For some time the groceryman's eyes were fixed on the statement as if he were studying the problem. Then returning the paper to his wife he said: It's all right, Laura—Davie Bates got these groceries. I told Bill to charge them to me but to keep the account separate from our house account. The fool has mixed things up, as usual."

But in spite of his effort to appear at ease, the groceryman exhibited all the symptoms of a schoolboy called unexpectedly to account by his teacher. Mrs. Paddock's lips curved in a little smile which her husband, whose eyes were downcast, did not see.

"So *you* are taking care of that wretched Bates family, are you?"

"It doesn't amount to anything, Laura— And they are terribly up against it. Dave, you know, has been a helpless cripple for two years, and now Mary is down in bed. They haven't a cent except what little Davie earns and there are two other kids younger than he. I don't see why our church can't do something for them. The man was giving his work to us when he was hurt. I tried to put it up to the board at our last meeting but they wouldn't even listen to me."

"Our church, Joe," said Mrs. Paddock thoughtfully, "needs more money for its own work, right now, than we can possibly raise. With the Congregationalists completing their beautiful new building only a block away, and the Methodists putting in that wonderful new pipe organ, and the Baptists adding that new wing with those lovely social parlors, I'm ashamed to be seen going to our services. We simply *must* do something!"

"That's what our board said," returned Joe, gloomily.

"Why don't the Organized Charities take up the case?" asked Mrs. Paddock.

"They can't. They haven't anywhere near funds enough to meet all the charity needs of the city, and because Davie has a job they say the case is not desperate. By the way, Laura, I spent some time this afternoon with Mr. Saxton."

"Yes?"

"I took him out to see that tract of ours on the east side. I'm almost sure he has made up his mind to locate in Westover. If I could only sell him that land you could have your new house and your big car with a chauffeur and go to New York and abroad with Mrs. Jamison and the best of them."

"Oh, Joe! Is there *really* a chance?" She moved quickly behind her husband's chair; two cool arms encircled the groceryman's neck; a perfunctory kiss dropped on the groceryman's bald spot, and a gentle voice soothed the groceryman's troubled heart. "Joe, you are the dearest, kindest man in the all the world."

The groceryman and his wife were quite happy that evening with the little group of their most intimate friends who met at the Winton's home. The Judge Burneses were there and the Ed Joneses and the Mayor Rileys, and the fact that each family represented a different church in no way marred the pleasures of the occasion, which, of course, was exactly as it should have been. Joe Paddock, himself, was in unusually good spirits. Whether it was the good company or the excellent cocktails and wines (Banker Winton enjoyed the luxury of a most competent bootlegger) or whether it was because his wife was in a kindly mood, Joe could not have said. He only knew that he, as he would have expressed it, was feeling fine—*fine.*

It was nearly twelve o'clock. The party was at its best, when, in a distant part of the city, the poorest and most squalid section, the clanging bell of an ambulance rang through the darkness of the night and Davie Bates started from his sleep.

The place called home by the Bates family was a three-room shack of unpainted boards and a roof that leaked. The neighboring homes were of similar construction, which gave that quarter of Westover its local name of "Shack Town." Here and there a house gave shabby evidence of having once been painted, but these feeble attempts at decency were so ancient that the improvement had long since become questionable. There were a few families that, with good reason, held themselves superior to the prevailing tone of the community. Their roofs did not leak.

Davie's father slept in the room where Davie had his own rickety old cot. Every morning the delivery boy half carried the helpless carpenter from his bed to an old rocking chair, every night be half carried his father back again from the chair to the bed.

The sound of the passing ambulance died quickly away. Seated on the edge of his cot, Davie listened. From the sound of heavy breathing he knew that his father was asleep. The two younger children occupied a bed in the kitchen. Davie tiptoed to the door. The little ones were safe in slumber land. Stealing quietly to the door of the only remaining room, the delivery boy paused a moment on the threshold, then crept softly to the side of his mother's bed. The form under the ragged coverlid stirred. A skeleton-like hand reached out.

"Do you want anything, Mother?" Davie whispered anxiously.

"Oh, Davie, dear, I was having such a beautiful dream! We were all back in the country—the woods and orchards and flowers and birds—and fields of corn all tasseled out—and wheat and oats and meadow grass waving in the wind. And everything was so fresh and shining and clean—like—like it is in the country when the sun shines out after a summer shower. There was a creek, too, and the water was clear and sparkly. And all the houses were white and clean and not crowded close together but scattered here and there among the green trees and fields. Oh, Davie, it was so beautiful! And your father was well and strong like he used to be, and I wasn't sick, and Jimmie and Maud were so clean and neat and rosy-cheeked and happy, and you with the books you love. And our house seemed to be on a hill like—under some big trees, and not very far across a little valley there was a white church and while were all there together waiting, the church bell rang—and I woke up—"

"'Twas that damned ambulance bell," muttered the delivery boy, under his breath, so that his mother could not hear.

"But, Davie boy, I must not keep you from your sleep— Go back to bed, son, you need your rest."

"Can't I do something for you, Mother? Don't you want a drink?"

"No, dear, there is nothing. It was such a lovely dream. Kiss me now and run along."

The delivery boy was going softly from the room when the sound of his mother's low, weak voice came again, and he paused just outside the open door. Standing there in the darkness he heard:

"Dear God, our Heavenly Father, I thank Thee for Thy wondrous kindness, for a husband's love, for the children Thou hast given me, for the roof that shelters us, and for our daily bread. I praise Thy name in thankfulness, oh God, for the church and its ministries, and for the blessed gospel of Jesus— As our Lord taught us to ask of Thee, our Father, I pray, oh God, give my dear husband strength to bear his affliction, and if it be Thy will make him well. Safeguard my little ones, oh God— They have no place to play but in the streets, and no one to watch over them through the long day— In Thy infinite mercy keep them safe from harm. Bless all the churches and the pastors who labor in Thy vineyard and grant that from their toil and sacrifice they may reap a mighty harvest of souls. And, dear God, be very close to my boy Davie. Keep him strong and well. Make him honest and upright; give him a clean mind and a kind heart; guard him from every temptation. And Thine shall be the honor and the glory and the praise forever. In the name of Jesus Christ, Thy Son, Amen."

The delivery boy, lying on his cot, gazed with wide eyes into the darkness of the night. *He* did not pray. He considered ways and means by which he might possibly bring an answer to his mother's prayer. That is, he considered how parts of her prayer might be answered. He was not much concerned about the answer to her prayers for the churches and the ministry. And if some of the ways and means considered by Davie were lawless it was only because, for him, there were no ways and means within the law. Beside Davie's devotion to his mother, the law was a little thing. Beside the desperate need of the delivery boy's family, the salvation of souls seemed of little importance.

When the groceryman and his wife said "good night" to the Winton's and their friends they fervently expressed their appreciation of the pleasant evening which they had so heartily enjoyed. But somewhere between the banker's residence and the Paddock home the happy spirit of the occasion deserted them. By the time Joe had unlocked and opened the front door they were as joyful as two people paying a visit to the family tomb.

When the daughter of the house came in an hour later the groceryman was alone in the living room.

"Why, Daddy, what's the matter?" cried Georgia from the doorway.

"Nothing," returned Joe, laying aside the church paper which he had not been reading.

"But don't you know that it is hours past your bedtime?"

"Is it?"

The girl came into the room and stood looking down at her father with an expression half smiling, half anxious. "Daddy, I believe you have actually been sitting up here alone waiting for me!"

"Well, why not? You—you don't mind, do you?"

"Oh, how funny!" laughed the girl.

The groceryman tried to smile but failed miserably.

Instantly, she was serious. "Surely you were not worried about me, Daddy? I was with Jack. Didn't mother tell you?" She dropped into the chair with an air of being quite willing to talk frankly about whatever it was that troubled him.

At this her father smiled successfully. "I knew you were all right, of course, dear." Then he continued soberly, almost as if in apology: "It was rather late when your mother and I cam home from the Winton's and when you were not here I got to thinking about you, Marjory Jones, and Maud Riley, and Harry Winton, and Judge Burnes's boys, and—well—"

Georgia gazed thoughtfully at the toe of her slipper. "Jack and I went to the club. We nearly always play tennis on Thursdays, you know. Then we had dinner at Tony's and after that went out to the Sundown Inn. Our crowd was there and we danced."

"I suppose you know, Georgia, that both Tony's and Sundown Inn are likely to be raided any night?"

"Yes, and they have just as good reason for raiding a lot of the parties that are pulled in the best homes in Westover," retorted the girl indignantly. A moment later she added, with characteristic frankness, "I know you are right, Daddy, they are not decent places. All sorts of people go there—fast women and sports—even women from the red light district—but what is a girl to do? All of my crowd—the bunch I have run with all my life, go. We try not to mix with the others more than we can help, but I'll admit we do get a little gay sometimes—Harry Winton is a beast. But gee! I can't cut all my friends and settle down for an old maid future just yet!"

"I would trust you with Jack anywhere," said the groceryman helplessly.

The girl answered bitterly: "Of course *you* would. And I—I wouldn't trust *any* man anywhere. There's one thing I like Jack for, though," she continued, "no matter how wild the others get *he* never loses *his* head—he always knows exactly what he's doing. Sometimes I think he knows too darned well what he's doing—I don't believe there is a woman in the world that *he* would trust."

"Why, Georgia, I thought—that is—I have sort of halfway had the idea that you and Jack—"

She laughed recklessly. "Forget it, Dad, forget it. We know too much about each other. I used to think—but never mind *that.* Homes like Grandma and Grandpa Paddock's are all out of date, Dad. None of the girls I know ever think of such a home. We don't marry to make homes anymore, we marry for fun—because we want to be married. When it comes to that, why should we want homes? Good gosh! Look at the homes in which most of us were born! Are our respected parents so wonderfully happy in their married state these days? I'll tell the world they are not!"

The groceryman, watching his daughter's face, tried to speak lightly. "Oh, I guess there are a few people left in the world who are happy though married."

To which the girl retorted: "Sure there are. But I am farmer enough to know that when you size up a field of corn you don't pick out a few individual hills that happen to be Class A. I'm talking about the present-day human crop, as a whole, Daddy dear, and I must admit that we don't look very promising. By the way, Dad, do you know that Astell man very well?"

"Who, Edward Astell? Yes, I know him—that is, I have met him a few times—why?

"Oh, nothing—only he is considered to be the one grand prize catch of Westover."

"I suppose so, but what of it?"

"Well, he was at the Sundown Inn to-night with that she-sport, Mrs. Waldmire. They were both more than loaded."

"That doesn't concern me, Georgia. I'm not interested in Astell and his women. I'm interested in my daughter and her friends and her future."

"I understand, Daddy. I only mentioned Astell because—well—because you see, there's not a dear mama of our acquaintance who wouldn't give a leg to have her daughter married to the beast. And then you all wonder why the girls of to-day don't look upon marriage as something holy and sacred. Daddy, dear, you are a lot too good and trusting for us moderns. You really should have stayed on the farm like grandpa and grandma."

"Young people certainly have a lot more freedom now than they did in my day," murmured Joe.

"Freedom!" cried the girl, "freedom! Huh! We brag about it a lot but that's all bunk. There is no such thing as freedom. We do what we *have* to do—

what we are *expected* to do, exactly as the young people of your day did. If our ideas and ideals and standards and customs are different it's because our fathers and mothers have changed theirs."

The groceryman was studying his daughter with a puzzled expression as if he were mentally groping for some half-revealed truth.

"When your mother and I were your age," he said slowly, "Nearly every one in our crowd was interested in the Church. We all attended church services as a matter of course." He paused doubtfully and his daughter smiled much as a kindly scientist might smile at the quaint observations of a child. But the groceryman was either too dense or too occupied with his mental effort to get hold of that shadowy truth to notice. "You and Jack are both members of the Church," he continued. "You used to be active in the Christian Endeavor work."

The girl rose quickly and went to sit on the arm of his chair. "Oh, Daddy dear, don't make me laugh! You are so old-fashioned, and I love you for it. But for Jack and me and our crowd the Church is simply impossible. It just doesn't fit into our lives anywhere. You and mother, when you were young, didn't believe in all the old church stuff—like witchcraft, for instance—that your great-grandparents had to swallow when they boys and girls—did you?"

"No, of course we didn't."

"Well, then, what right has the Church to expect my generation to hang on to all the denominational bunk that you and mother, when you were young, took from your preachers as the one and only Simon pure, eighteen carat, A-1 religion?"

"W-e-ll—" said the groceryman.

"As a matter of fact, Daddy dear, you don't believe half that's in our church creed yourself. And you know darned well that you don't really get any kick out of the antediluvian drivel that Parson Coleman calls a sermon. Why, if that reverend fraud should happen to have a real honest-to-goodness thought he wouldn't dare mention it for fear some of his denominational bosses might hear about it and fire him. It's just as Jack says, 'Our preachers don't *preach*—they just stand up there and dodge—like the poor cuss in the street fair who sticks his head through a hole and lets people throw at him for so much a shot.'"

"Oh—come now, Georgia."

"It's so, Daddy—why, just let me tell you— One evening about a month ago Jack and I tried to go to church. Do you know what happened? Well, it was like this—you see I got to thinking that it might be better for us if we were to slow down a little, and after Jack and I had talked it over like we do most everything, we decided we'd try it. We didn't want to go to church for *fun,* Dad, we weren't hunting amusement, we honestly wanted to hear a good, straight, religious sermon because—well—because way down deep inside we were both feeling that way.

"First, we naturally went to our own church. It was the night that woman missionary gave her illustrated lecture on China—you remember. It was good stuff, I suppose. I guess she knew what she was going to talk about. But information about China didn't seem to be what Jack and I wanted, so we went over to the church on the next corner. There was a distinguished agriculturist there who was going to talk about the Philippines, with pictures, of course. The speaker didn't even pretend that he was going to preach. The Philippines didn't appeal to us, so we went on a few blocks to another place of worship, and there the preacher was just beginning a review of the latest popular novel. We had both read the book so we beat it to a church farther down the street and, Dad, we ran slap into the dinkiest sort of a picture show. Oh, they were Bible pictures, all right, all about the Holy Land, with tombs and camels and donkeys and everything. And the reverend D.D.—a great big good-looker he is, too, with all his university and football and theological seminary training—was going to explain the pictures—so we could tell the difference between the camels and the donkeys. I suppose. *That* finished us. We sneaked out and went down town to a real movie house where we saw 'Flaming Youth.' Jack said it was no wonder youth flamed, and we have never tried to spend an evening in a house of God since."

Joe's arm was around his daughter and he gave her a little hug. "Georgia, dear, will you tell me something?"

"Sure, Daddy, anything you want to know."

"It's about Jack."

"All right, what about him?"

The girl's utter frankness touched her father's heart and gave him such confidence that he changed the form of his question to: "Do you love Jack, Georgia?"

"What do you mean by love, Daddy? Can two people who don't trust each other really love?"

"Not the kind of love I mean, Georgia."

"That's what I thought. Well, I can tell you one thing for sure—no matter how much I loved Jack Ellory I wouldn't dare marry him—and I suspect he feels exactly that way about me. I don't believe a single one of the girls of my set who has married ever really trusted her man. She only thought maybe she could somehow manage to hold him. I don't care for any of that in mine, thank you. Nice situation, isn't it, Daddy? So full of promise for the future—and all that!

She suddenly released herself from his arm. "Good night now, Daddy. It's really late. You should have been in bed hours ago." She stooped and kissed him. "And please don't worry about me. I can take care of myself. I think a lot about religion—I really do—and so does Jack. We talk about it a lot too. But what is that old line, 'Youth will be served'? You pull that on your preacher and see if he can find anything in it."

When she was gone the groceryman sat very still. He was not mistaken—he *could* not be mistaken—when his daughter kissed him he caught the unmistakable odor of liquor. Slowly he arose and, crossing the room, he stood before the picture of Jesus which hung above the radio. For a long time he gazed upon the countenance of the Great Teacher.

CHAPTER VIII.

THE FARM.

The Paddock farm was eight miles west of town on the state highway. Grandpa and Grandma Paddock had settled in the new county of Westover the year they were married, coming with other adventurous families in covered wagons from the more crowded districts farther east. Their first home was a log cabin down by the spring at the foot of the hill. Their first crops were planted among the stumps of the newly cleared lands in fields fenced with brush and rails. Westover was a general store, a sawmill, a blacksmith shop, a gristmill, and five houses. The post office, with mail by stage every two weeks, was in the store. The highway was two deep rutted wheel tracks wandering erratically through the forest, fording the creeks, and climbing laboriously over the hills.

The farmhouse, which was built the year Joe was born, stood on the brow of a long, low hill overlooking the broad, gently rolling fields, the meadow lands and pastures of the Paddock acres and the neighboring farms from which the stumps and the primitive brush fences had long since disappeared. From the kitchen door one looked across the garden to the orchard. Beyond the orchard a cornfield extended along the crest of the ridge to the woods which rose gently to the highest point of the hill.

Grandpa Paddock was a lover of trees, and so he had retained not only this bit of the virgin forest but here and there over the entire farm were beautiful individuals which he had saved from the ax. Some were old giants of the original army which occupied the land before the day of the conquering white man. Others were the children of that ancient race. The house itself, placed well back from the road, was guarded by a goodly company of these gnarled and leafy old warriors whose protecting arms defied the impudent irreverence of the modern state highway and thus preserved, in a world of restless change and ill-considered hurry, an atmosphere of old-time peace and quiet. A two-story frame, with wide verandas on two sides, white with green shutters, a shingled roof grayed by the weather and the lichens, and honeysuckles and climbing roses and morning-glories—it was something more than just a house to rent or to sell. It was never a mere residence for a swiftly passing year or two. It was a home to be born in—to live in—to die in. Even the big red barn seemed to have gathered the surrounding smaller buildings to its protecting wings like a mighty mother watching over her brood.

For nearly fifty years this house had shared the most intimate joys and sorrows of the man and woman who together planned and built it. For nearly half a century this husband and wife, this father and mother, had enriched this home with their deepest and most sacred experiences, and glorified it with their steadfast love. To these walls they had confided all their secret hopes and fears, all their trials and triumphs—their struggles, their victories, their temptations, their defeats, In these rooms their children were begotten and born. In these rooms their little ones had been nursed, had learned to laugh and cry, to talk and walk. In these rooms they had watched two sons and a daughter die. The house, the trees, and the man and woman had grown old together, but as their fields were ever young with the new life of each springtime, so the hearts of Grandpa and Grandma Paddock were young.

In the early morning, following that night when the groceryman and his daughter talked together, Grandpa Paddock came out from the house to see the new day. Standing on the veranda he viewed the countryside, looked at his trees, studied the sky, felt the early morning air, and heard the familiar voices of the farm. And Grandpa, himself, was like a tree. His old trunk and limbs, though gnarled and roughened by the marks of many storms, were still sturdy and strong. There was sunlight in his eyes, and kindly shadows in his face. There was the sheen of shining leaves on his white hair, and in his voice there was the sound of the gentle breeze.

Grandma joined him a minute or two later and standing close by his side remarked on the beauty of the morning with an enjoyment not in the least dulled by nearly eighty years of mornings. Then she went to look into the family affairs of a pair of wrens who, having nested in the honeysuckle vines, were "expecting." Grandma Paddock was one of those women (God give us more of them) who manage to carry the everyday burdens of wifehood and motherhood as if they were treasures beyond price, and so inevitably the accumulated experiences of her years made the last of her life the richest and the best. All that she had lived she still possessed, but that which had been crude was refined—that which had been raw was softened; all that once was new had gained the flavor and the mellowness that comes with time.

The farmhouse bell, outside the kitchen door, rang. They saw the hired man, Henry, coming from the barn with his pails of milk. Henry had been with them twenty years. The other hands, with their families, lived in two cottages under the hill. Arm and arm they went into the house.

Grandpa found his "specs," took the big family Bible from its place of honor on the center table in the sitting room and, seating himself in his old armchair, reverently opened the book. Grandma, in her favorite rocker by the window, rocked gently and looked out and away across the fields, and if the dear old lady's thoughts strayed from the moment into the years that were gone it was with no irreverence. Hetty came from the kitchen rolling her bare arms in her apron. Hetty had been grandma's "girl" for nearly forty years. Then Henry found a seat on the edge of the chair nearest the dining-room door. Dandy, the collie dog, walked sedately to grandpa's side and the house cat, Peter, arched his back and rubbed against Henry's boots, favored Hetty with purring attention, and crossed the room to settle down in grandma's lap.

Slowly and reverently grandpa read the morning lesson, his kindly voice caressing every word. "Come unto me, all ye that labor and are heavy laden, and I will give you rest." The quiet was broken by the raucous shriek of an automobile that, with wide open exhaust, thundered along the state highway at seventy miles an hour. . . . "And learn of me for I am meek and lowly in heart; and ye shall find rest unto your souls."

The prayer which followed, while the members of the household knelt beside their chairs, was as unpretentious as their lives. As the grain in the fields, the grass in the meadows and the mighty trees looked to heaven for the needed sunshine and rain, so this old-fashioned household, without show or ceremony, looked to God for their daily need.

Then they all went in to breakfast.

The groceryman was not surprised that morning when his daughter appeared at his office in the store and begged him to go with her to the farm. The groceryman, himself, was feeling the need of something which he never failed to find at his old home in the country. He never realized what it was that he wanted, or what it was that he always, without fail, received. He only knew that at certain times—when life drove him with such pitiless haste that he became confused and distracted—the farm called to him as a well of water calls to one who thirsts.

"Perhaps mother would like to go too," he said, and before Georgia could reply called for the house number on the telephone.

The girl watched him while he was hearing from Ella that Mrs. Paddock was not in. He hung up the receiver and for almost a minute sat as if lost in thought, his hand still on the instrument.

"Mother has a luncheon engagement," said Georgia. "I heard her telephoning about it to someone just before I left the house. They are to call for her. That's how I knew we could have the car. Come on, Daddy, let's go. If I don't get away from this town right now I shall scream."

They exchanged scarcely a word until, as they reached the crest of the hill in front of the house, the girl, drawing a full, deep breath, exclaimed: "Oh, Daddy, look! How beautiful! Everything is so—so *clean.*"

It was strange that the groceryman's daughter should have used the same word that the delivery boy's mother had repeated so often in telling Davie of her dream.

The collie welcomed them joyously; Hetty started for the barnyard to tell Henry to kill a chicken; grandpa came from the orchard and grandma appeared on the veranda.

"Hello."

"Howdy."

"How's everything?"

"Time you was coming."

"Haven't seen you for a coon's age."

"Where's Laura?"

"Why didn't she come too?"

They sat on the veranda, "just visiting," as grandma would have said, until Hetty came to tell them dinner was ready. But when the midday meal was over Georgia must go with grandpa to see the bran' new colt, the baby pigs, and the week-old calf whose mother took the premium at the last fair and whose father was a grand champion.

When grandma and her son were alone the old lady, with no preliminary verbal skirmish, asked gently: "What's the trouble, my boy?"

"Oh, nothing," said Joe.

"Business going pretty well?"

"Well enough—first rate in fact."

"That's good, but of course it would 'cause you'll always do your part and the folks are just bound to eat. Your father was saying last night your grocery business ain't like those stores that sell nothing but luxuries. I told him that was all right as far as it went but sometimes people got their necessities and their luxuries so mixed that they couldn't tell which was which. What is Laura busying herself with these days?"

"Oh, she has her clubs and social duties."

"That's nice. Laura takes a lot of comfort in such things. I've often had a notion that I'd like to join a club or something. Your father and I thought we saw her go past in an automobile day before yesterday, but we decided it couldn't 'a' been her 'cause Laura would never 'a' gone right by without even waving to us and she wouldn't 'a' been riding along with a man in a roadster, neither."

Grandma watched Joe's hands as he cut the end from a cigar and searched every pocket in his clothing, except the right one, for a match.

"What's the matter with Georgia, Joe?"

"What makes you think there is anything the matter with her, Mother?"

"'Cause there *is*. Is she in love?"

"I don't know."

"What does Laura think about it?"

"I don't know that either."

"Well, son, you and Laura had better be finding out, 'cause there is nothing more important that can happen to the child. If she *ain't* in love it's time she was. For a girl her age there's only one thing worse than being in love, and that's not being. She and Jack Ellory come out here every now and then. Jack's a fine boy—no better bred lad in Westover County. And, if my old eyes ain't fooling me, they think a lot of each other. They always have as I remember. It's against nature, son, that they should go as far as they have and not go farther. It's time they was making up their minds to marry or quit."

And then grandma made one of her characteristic observations which at the moment seemed to have no bearing upon the topic of the conversation, but was sometimes found, later, to be the root of the whole matter: "It takes a lot of religion, son, for two people to love and marry and live together long enough to raise children and be grandparents."

Joe rose hurriedly. "Father and Georgia are coming yonder. If you don't mind, Mother, I'll slip away for a little while—I want to go for a walk."

He went quickly through the house and out by the kitchen door, swiftly crossed the garden to the orchard, hurried on under the trees and climbing the fence made his way through the cornfield toward the woods. Any one watching his movements might easily have thought him a fugitive from the law. Indeed, the groceryman, himself, felt that he was trying to escape, that he *must* escape from—what?

But having gained the cover of the woods he moved with less haste. The cool and shadowy quiet closed about him as if an unseen hand had drawn a curtain to shut out the noisy troubled world. The column-like trunks of the great trees defined dim, temple aisles and corridors that led to distant mysteries, while over head their mighty limbs, like cathedral arches, supported the roof of shimmering leaves. Here and there, though windows screened by fretwork of twigs and branches, the sunlight streamed in shafts of gold upon the living green of wall and floor. The carpet of moss and fern yielded kindly to his feet. He felt a solemn presence. Instinctively he uncovered his head and moved softly. The sweet, earthy fragrance, the songs of birds, the murmur of the gentle wind in the tree tops, and the soft rustle of leaves were as the incense, the music, and the prayers of a religious service. Somewhere near, before an unseen altar, true priests were worshiping a living God.

And then, almost before he realized where he was, the groceryman was sitting under an old tree on the bank of a pond which lay in a little hollow in the very heart of the woods. From his earliest childhood that spot had been to Joe Paddock a place of refuge—a retreat, a sanctuary. That ancient tree, with its branches overhanging the still amber water of the leafy pool, had always shared his secret troubles, and helped him in those spiritual and emotional experiences which every boy and man must undergo without help from his fellows. It had witnessed his decisions and been the confidant of his most precious dreams. It had heard his faltering declaration of love to his girl neighbor and schoolmate, and had seen the kiss which sealed their betrothal. Here, if anywhere, the groceryman felt that he could find himself. Here he might glimpse a way through the confusing fog that enveloped him. Here, if anywhere, he might hope to feel the presence of his God.

There are few of us, I think, for whom there is not somewhere a place that is sacred. But rarely in these restless, modern times is one privileged to go to his spot of holy ground.

When the groceryman left the woods an hour or two later he was still depressed by that feeling of impending evil. Returning by the lane which led to the barnyard he saw another automobile parked with his own machine near the house. From the barnyard gate he saw a stranger sitting on the veranda with his father and mother and daughter. And then as he drew nearer he discovered to his amazement that the fourth member of the group was John Saxton.

Grandpa was about to introduce Joe to Mr. Saxton when that gentleman said with a laugh: "Oh, but your son and I are already very good friends, Mr. Paddock." And then, as he shook hands with the groceryman, he added, still smiling: "I certainly chose the right day to call upon your father and mother. To find *three* generations at home is rather better luck than I hoped for."

"Joe," cried grandma, eager as a child, "did you know that Mr. Saxton is a friend of Dan Matthews? You remember how often you have heard us talk about Dan Matthews, the big mining man who used to preach in Corinth where your Aunt Nellie lived, and your cousin John Gardner and Mary, his wife?"

"Yes, Mother, I know who Dan Matthews is, of course, but I—", He looked inquiringly at Mr. Saxton, "and you are really representing the Matthews interests?"

"Yes."

"Well, I'll be hanged!"

They all laughed at the groceryman's expression.

Saxton explained: "When Mr. Matthews sent me to Westover he told me to be sure and call on your father and mother. I wanted to come long before this," he continued to grandpa and grandma, "but circumstances have prevented."

The groceryman understood as clearly as if the man had spoken the words, that for some reason this representative of Dan Matthews had wished to become acquainted with *him* before making himself known to his parents.

Big Dan had said to his confidential agent, before leaving him at his hotel that night in Kansas City, "John, I want you to know the Paddocks—the old people, I mean. They will show you how the Christian religion worked in a typical American home of the last generation. I shall be surprised if you do not find their son mighty helpful when the time comes."

In the hour that followed grandma told once more the story of her visit to her sister Nellie on the Gardner farm near Corinth when Dan Matthews was pastor of the Memorial Church. She had first seen Big Dan that day when the minister walked out from town to work with Nellie's son John, in the harvest field. The Gardners were members of Dan's church. The incident of the harvesting contest between the young farmer and his pastor had resulted in a close friendship between the two men. So Grandma Paddock came to know all about the trouble in the Corinth church—how the minister had befriended crippled Denny and his mother, the tragedy of Grace Connor's life, and how Big Dan had met and loved Hope Farwell who became his wife.

Joe Paddock had heard the story many times for grandma, confirmed hero worshiper that she was, never missed an opportunity to tell it, but he listened now with new and excited interest.

Mr. Saxton, in his turn, answering their many questions told them of his employer's home and family—of his activities in the church and his generous contributions to every good cause. But of his mission in Westover Dan Matthews' confidential agent did not speak.

And all the while the groceryman was thinking what this financially powerful mining man's friendly interest in his family, together with his own well established friendship with the representative of Dan Matthews, might mean to him. Surely *now* he would be given an opportunity to get in on the ground floor of whatever enterprise Mr. Saxton was sent to inaugurate in Westover. So intent was the groceryman on his own thoughts that he scarcely heard his daughter's comment when Saxton told them of the Matthews' home.

"Is it really true that there are homes like that these days?"

Saxton's grave eyes, with their shadows of sadness, met the girl's frank look. "Are you really such a skeptic, Miss Paddock?"

"How can any one be anything but skeptical?" the girl returned boldly. "Don't you read the papers? Don't you read magazine stories and novels and see plays and pictures? And can't you see what is going on all around you? Your Dan Matthews and his wife may be as happy as you picture them, Mr. Saxton, but if they are, they are decidedly old-fashioned."

Saxton asked gently: "And do you think, then that for the men and women of this day the happiness of home and family love is impossible?"

The groceryman's daughter answered with a shockingly frank statement of her unwholesome convictions: "The men of this generation don't want wives, Mr. Saxton, they want women. People have forgotten how to love."

"If they have," returned Saxton, "it is because they have forgotten how to worship."

And Georgia, with her eyes fixed on the speaker's countenance, wondered, "Where *have* I seen that face before!"

Grandpa, who was sitting close beside the girl, gently touched her arm.

Grandma said with her quiet smile: "I guess you had better stay out here on the farm for a few days, dearie. You are needing a change and rest."

"I was hoping you would ask me," the girl answered with a troubled laugh. "You won't mind, will you, Father?"

"It will do you good," returned Joe.

Only Georgia had noticed the roadster which passed the house at terrific speed while Mr. Saxton was telling them about the Matthews' home. And the girl, with eyes so much younger than the eyes of her grandparents, had seen clearly the man and woman who rode in the expensive machine.

At Joe's suggestion Mr. Saxton sent his car home and returned to town with the groceryman. But when Joe, highly elated over his discovery of the financial interests represented by his friend, tactfully sought further information, Saxton as tactfully told him that he was not at liberty to divulge the nature of Mr. Matthews' contemplated investment in Westover. He asked, too, that for a little while Joe hold what he had learned as confidential. The groceryman, of course, readily agreed.

As Saxton was alighting from the car in front of the Palace, he said: "I am having a few men for dinner, here at the hotel, this coming Thursday evening. I would be delighted if you will come."

CHAPTER IX.

MR. SAXTON'S DINNER PARTY.

The more Joe Paddock thought about it the more clearly he saw how fortunate he was in his friendship with Mr. Saxton. Or rather, to be exact, the groceryman saw how his friendship with Mr. Saxton might lead to his good fortune. Joe had a very high regard for Dan Matthews' confidential agent. He was not lacking in sincere appreciation of the man's unusual personality and character. He often spoke to others of his admiration for him. He realized that he always received something from Saxton which he did not receive from any other friend. It was a something, rather vague and indefinite, which he could not have explained but which was nevertheless very real. It steadied and comforted him and gave him hope and courage when he was depressed by that feeling of impending evil. But always, in the back of the groceryman's head, or underneath his thoughts, or deep somewhere inside of him, there was the possibility that out of this friendship might come large material gains. There are so few of us who can worship even God without asking a very material return for our adoration.

The friendship between Joe's parents and Dan Matthews had been for years a matter of pride in the Paddock family. Indeed, it was well on the way of becoming one of those treasured traditions which are to be found in every family. For twenty years or more, Joe had listened to that story of Big Dan's experience in Corinth and had watched his progress from the pulpit of the obscure country town church to his present position of financial power. That this great millionaire mining man still held memories of his Corinth friends and that his regard for the Paddocks still lived, was proved by Saxton's call at the farm. The groceryman knew the value of right connections in business. Friendship has often been the foundation of a fortune.

Never before had the groceryman looked forward to a dinner party with such eager interest. It was evident, to him, that the event was to be no mere social affair. There were no ladies invited. It was not even mentioned in the social columns of the paper. While it was true that Saxton had accepted invitations to several Westover homes, those occasions had always been without social significance. Dan Matthews' representative, Joe assured himself, was merely taking this way of assembling a few chosen men to whom he would reveal Big Dan's plans for his contemplated enterprise in Westover. As Joe explained to his wife, whatever Dan Matthews was planning to do in Westover, he would want a few local men associated with him. He hoped Saxton would make no mistake in choosing his men. He wondered who were the others invited to the dinner. He wished that Saxton had consulted him.

But with all his interest in the approaching event, the groceryman was very careful not to tell any one, except his wife, of course, that he knew who it was that Saxton represented. And he cautioned Laura, explaining that the value of Dan Matthews' friendship must not be lessened by any betrayal of Saxton's confidence. Nor did he mention the dinner party to any of his friends. He feared that to do so might appear as indiscreet and, in a way, disloyal to Saxton. It is safe to say, too, that the others invited—whoever they were—were looking forward as eagerly as the groceryman and for exactly the same reasons. Mrs. Paddock, with her mind on New York opera and Paris gowns, was exceedingly gracious to her husband and when the evening arrived helped him to look his best. It is to be supposed that the other wives interested were as helpful to their representatives.

When the groceryman arrived at the Palace and met his fellow guests he knew that Mr. Saxton had made no mistake. Only five men were present but they were the acknowledged leaders of the largest business interests in Westover and, in all civic affairs, the most influential citizens. Intimately associated in matters of finance and friends of long standing, they were the innermost circle of the inner circle. And each man, when he saw the others and noted the limited number of the company, was confirmed in his opinion as to the importance of the occasion. They greeted one another by their given names and, without putting their thoughts into words, managed to congratulate one another and express their common gratification.

Mr. Saxton met them all with a quiet, genial greeting, with no excessive good spirits or overdone cordiality, but with that genuineness which ever marks the perfect host. But to his guests the personality of the man, perhaps because of the very keenness of their interest in the occasion, was even more impressive than usual. They sensed a power back of him. He was as one of authority. Yet they were drawn to him as to a close friend. They felt his strength and were won by his kindliness. They admired him for his broad knowledge of men and events, and were charmed by his gentle courtesy. In spite of the prevailing custom at such occasions in Westover, no liquor was served, nor did Mr. Saxton apologize for the omission. Possibly because they needed no stimulant other than the occasion itself, the guests were not disappointed. On the contrary, each man's confidence in his host was strengthened. In fact, they would have been disappointed had Saxton offered them drink.

The company was soon seated at the table in a private dining room. The usual commonplaces, light laughter, and small talk, passed around the board. But in the mind of every guest the real purpose of the gathering was uppermost. Joe Paddock was thinking of his land which he hoped Dan Matthews would buy, of Laura's ambitions and Georgia's future. Perhaps he could give his daughter a home for her wedding present. He wondered if he could ask Dan Matthews to let Jack Ellory come in with them. Henry Winton was thinking of the building he hoped to erect on his lot at the corner of State and Washington. The ground floor would be leased by the bank. Saxton's company could have offices above. Their business would mean a great deal to the First National. He must try and place Harry with them. George Riley's mind was on the Governorship of the state. With the Saxton interests back of him he could hope. It would mean much to his daughter. Ed Jones, with the help of the Saxton connections, could swing the new subdivision he had planned. A big industrial company would boom the sale of lots and the building of homes. Judge Burnes realized that Saxton's company would need counsel. It might easily be the realization of his wife's dream of a new house on the avenue, and perhaps he might be able to establish the boys in some business that would steady them down.

It was Winton who made the first tentative approach. "Well, Mr. Saxton," he said, with just the right touch of familiar good fellowship, "how do you like Westover now that you have been with us long enough to get around a little?"

The general conversation died away. Every eye was turned toward the host.

"I like Westover very much, Mr. Winton," Saxton answered. "The more I see of it the more I am convinced that you have everything with which to create an ideal American city. I must confess, though, I often wonder how many of your taxpayers ever consider the *real* possibilities of Westover."

The guests glanced at one another with pleased expressions.

Lawyer Burnes followed the banker's lead: "May we ask, sir, if you are finding here the particular advantages, or perhaps I should say opportunities, for which you are looking?"

Again every eye was upon the gentleman at the head of the table. The silence was significant.

Mr. Saxton smiled. "I'm afraid I can't answer that, Judge—not just now. I am not yet at liberty to discuss the business which brought me to Westover. As men of affairs you all must recognize the danger of premature announcements."

A wave of disappointment swept over the company like a chilling draft.

With the evident purpose of tempering the coolness, Saxton continued: "I may say, however, that I am finding everything here most favorable to the enterprise which the interests I represent are contemplating. I can also assure you that this enterprise will be of the greatest value to Westover and to every one who is in any way interested in the future of this city."

This at least was *something.* They all felt, from Saxton's manner that he was not speaking lightly. They realized they must not press him further. They felt, too, that their host understood their disappointment and sympathized with them. The groceryman was more cheerful than the others because he, alone, knowing who it was that Saxton represented, could gauge the real value of their host's assurance. He was so elated that he could not resist venturing a knowing smile as he met Saxton's look of understanding.

Returning the groceryman's smile, Saxton, with the air of helping the company out of a conversational difficulty, said: "Do you not think, gentlemen, that as men of business—from a purely business point of view, I mean—we often underrate the value of a city's general character?"

His guests gave him polite attention but were slow to follow.

Smiling, he continued persuasively: "Our friend, Joe Paddock, here, would not pick a cannibal island as a good location for a grocery store."

They all laughed at this and Mayor Riley said: "You are right, sir, cities do have character the same as individuals and the civic character of a community is a great factor in its business interests."

"Personal character," remarked Judge Burnes, somewhat heavily, "is unquestionably a great asset in any profession or business."

"We certainly have no use for check raisers and forgers in the First National," laughed Banker Winton.

The host carried them a step farther with: "And individual character, Judge, is the basis for community character, just as the character of a business of any kind is fixed by the personal characters of those interested in it. For several years now my work has been largely that of finding the right men for the right places, and we have made it our invariable rule that whatever the nature of the position to be filled the first qualification is personal character. And mark you, this is purely a business policy. It is a policy that is recognized in big business everywhere."

When Mr. Saxton said that his work was to find the right men, his guests did not miss the significance of his remark. They leaned forward in their chairs and looked toward the head of the table with renewed interest.

It was Judge Burnes who said: "Speaking of character, Mr. Saxton, I don't know whether you are aware of it or not but this gathering here to-night might well be a religious meeting. Joe Paddock is a pillar in the Presbyterian Church that was established by his parents. Winton is an official in the Baptist church which his family built. Riley is a Congregationalist—a deacon, or trustee, or something. Ed Jones is Methodist South, and I am Methodist North. By all the laws of our churches, Ed and I ought to be at swords' points, but you can see we are not, which fact, I think, fairly indicates the religious spirit of Westover."

The five Westover citizens silently agreed that the Judge had very tactfully presented their qualifications to the gentleman whose work was to find the right men.

"Judge," said Mr. Saxton, "you have raised a great question! To many of our foremost thinkers, it is the one great question of the age." He paused while his guests exchanged looks of inquiry. They were well aware that the lawyer member of their circle had not spoken to raise a question, but rather to answer one.

Saxton continued: "Why is it, gentlemen, that Christian business men never get together, regardless of their denominational affiliations, to inquire into and discuss matters of the Christian religion? You meet to discuss your common interests in various business enterprises, in civic affairs, in social clubs, in community welfare, and in your public schools. You realize that Christianity touches every phase of life—society, business, politics, art, education, homes—and to say that it is the most important and vital factor in the futures of your children is no exaggeration of fact. You must realize that your interests in the Christian religion are mutual, and that the great problems of Christianity are not peculiar to any one of the several denominations which you represent, but are problems of all. I venture to say that, in your own minds, the value of your individual denominational interests, compared to the common cause of Christianity, is as a drop of water to a heavy rainfall. And yet, while you have each no doubt often met with your respective pastors and fellow officials to discuss your own peculiar denominational affairs, you have never met to consider ways and means for your vast and common interests in Christianity as a whole."

There was silence for a little, but it was not for lack of interest in what their host had said:

Mayor Riley spoke slowly: "I suppose it is because we leave the ways and means of Christianity to the preachers."

"You mean," said Jones dryly, "that we leave the ways to our preachers—we dig up the means."

They laughed.

Then the Judge spoke: "I suppose the reason is that the average lay member doesn't know enough about church matters to consider them intelligently. I'll bet Ed, here, can't give a Christian reason for the difference between his church and mine."

The groceryman grinned. "I'll bet Ed can't even tell what the difference is."

"You win, Joe," returned the real estate man. "I couldn't even tell why I am South. Why are you North Judge?"

"I don't know," admitted the lawyer," and, what's more, I don't care."

"I couldn't give a real reason for being a Baptist," said Winton. "Father and mother were, that's all."

"And that's all I know about Presbyterianism," admitted the groceryman.

And Mayor Riley confessed: "I'm a Congregationalist by accident—they all look alike to me."

Mr. Saxton said with quiet meaning: "And the amazing fact is that you gentlemen have fairly expressed the attitude of fully ninety per cent of the present-day church members, and, I should say, very close to one hundred per cent of all the Christians who are not identified with any denominational organization."

Judge Burnes asked thoughtfully: "Does any one here know how many denominations there are?"

Ed Jones answered promptly: "I don't."

Said Joe Paddock: "I know there are a lot of different kinds of Presbyterians."

"And a lot of Baptists," echoed Winton.

"I haven't a ghost of an idea," said the Mayor, "there must be fifty, at least. We have fifteen or twenty right here in Westover.

With one accord they looked at the man at the head of the table.

"Do you know how many denominations there are, Mr. Saxton?" asked the lawyer.

Mr. Saxton answered gravely: "In the United States, in 1906 there were one hundred and eighty-three. There are more now. I can't give the exact figures for this year."

"You mean one hundred and eighty-three different *religions,* Mr. Saxton? Said the Mayor doubtfully.

"No, one hundred and eighty-three separate and distinct denominational organizations of one religion—Christianity. Judge, you and your friend Jones represent only two out of seventeen different kinds of Methodists. Mr. Paddock, you are one of ten kinds of Presbyterians. As a Baptist, Mr. Winton, you have your choice of seventeen varieties. There is a Church of the Universal Messianic Message, a Pillar of Fire, and a Reformed Zion Union Apostolic Church. There the Defenseless Mennonites, the Christadelphians, the Two-Seed-in-the-Spirit Predestinarian Baptists, and the General Six Principle Baptists. There are twenty-one kinds of Lutherans. I really can't remember all of the others."

"I'll say you have done pretty well," muttered Joe Paddock grimly.

"Do you know," said Judge Burnes, "I have often thought that when they say 'God moves in mysterious ways his wonders to perform' they must be referring to theology."

"Our theologians have certainly devised ways enough to spend the money we give in the name of one Lord," remarked the banker. "What do you suppose it costs the Church, as a whole, to maintain these one hundred and eighty-three competing roads to the same place?"

"Yes," cried Jones, "can't you see a railroad company building, equipping, maintaining and operating one hundred and eighty-three parallel lines, through the same territory, to one terminal station?"

"The waste of money must be enormous," observed Winton. "Does any one know what these one hundred and eighty-three denominations cost the people—taking them all together as one church, I mean?"

"You can't measure the value of the church in money, Henry," protested Judge Burnes.

"Of course you can't," echoed Joe Paddock. "Christianity isn't a matter of dollars."

With one accord they looked expectantly toward their host.

Mr. Saxton, with a smile, asked: "Is education a question of money?"

"Not in the sense that you can buy it as you would purchase a hat or a pound of steak," answered Jones.

To which Winton retorted: "Somebody has to pay for it."

"You bet they do," echoed Riley. "Our children go to school free, but what about ours taxes?"

Mr. Saxton said gravely: "Jesus, Himself, made Christianity a matter of money, or its equivalent—goods, possessions, treasure, riches. Our church managers make Christianity a question of money when funds are needed for a new building, an organ, or the current expenses. Could our ministers minister without their salaries? If money has nothing to do with religion, why do some preachers receive ten and fifteen thousand dollars annually for the services which they render the Lord, while others, in the same service, receive only five and six hundred?"

"Big preach, big pay—little preach, little pay," murmured the groceryman.

"Is it not a fact," continued Mr. Saxton, "that the professional evangelist's salary is based upon his reputation as a soul winner—that the more souls he wins the more money he receives? Do our preachers, in their pulpit pleadings for money, ever hesitate to make contributions to the cause a gauge of religious sincerity? It is true that religion is not wholly a matter of dollars. Neither is Mr. Paddock's grocery business. The grocery business is a matter of hunger, good health, frosts and rain and labor. Real estate, Mr. Jones, is a matter of home making—of housing people. Your profession, Judge, is a matter of justice and protection of human rights. We are not putting a money value on education when we try to see that our educational funds are not misused and wasted. The very fact that Christian character is beyond price should force us to count the cost of our churches and watch the expense of their maintenance and operation with the greatest care. Jesus,

Himself, taught economy. Considered purely as a question of economics, universal irreligion would be ruinous. For every individual dishonest or criminal act, the people must pay many times the amount of money involved in the act itself. Our one great defense against the rapidly increasing immorality of our nation, and the consequent drain upon the strength of the people, is Christianity. Enormous sums are given to this holy cause, and the waste of this money by the preachers and managers of the Church in perpetuating their denominational differences—which the Church, as a whole, agrees are of no importance—is the greatest economic crime of the age. The spiritual and moral consequences are disastrous beyond calculation. The Church, itself, is breaking down under it. Our national, moral collapse is a direct result."

Mr. Saxton's words were followed by a solemn hush. It was as if, for the first time in their lives, these men glimpsed the real magnitude and importance of the religious problem.

Then Winton spoke: "Mr. Saxon, can you tell us what the Church, as a whole, represents in money?"

Saxton answered: "As nearly as can be ascertained, taking the figures given in the 1916 Bulletin of the Bureau of the Census as a basis, the total valuation of church property in the United states—edifices, lots, organs, bells, parsonages, and general equipment including schools, homes and institutions of various kinds—over three billion dollars. This amount, I am convinced, is too low. Church managers do not like to give figures—many churches refused—many protested against the inquiries, claiming that the United States Government had no constitutional authority to make an investigation of religious matters. One denomination refused outright to give any figures whatever. Many, who gave statements of their membership, preachers and other similar items, made no references in their reports to the money involved."

"This sum of three billion dollars is the money invested?" asked the banker.

"Yes."

"Can you tell us anything of the annual cost of operation?"

"The annual running expenses—and by that I mean salaries, fuel, lights, payments to maintain general denominational offices and secretaries, and so on, but not including denominational benevolences and missions—in round numbers is about three hundred million dollars. Our total yearly contribution to Christianity—new churches, running expense, missions and all—is around seven hundred million.

"You appear to have made a study of religious conditions, Mr. Saxton," said Judge Burnes thoughtfully.

Saxton replied: "I believe that the religious problem is so far more important than any other, that the very life of the nation depends upon it."

In support of his opinion, Dan Matthews' representative then gave his guests the results of his employer's investigation, as his chief had presented them to him that stormy night in Kansas City.

"And Christian business men, like you," he concluded, "are giving practically no thought whatever to this alarming state of affairs. The situation which we have developed here this evening is typical. Your city is a representative American city. You are business men, church men, men of families. You believe that, to yourselves, as individuals, to your children, your homes, to citizenship, business, government, education, religion is of supreme importance. And yet you have never given an hour to the consideration of this question, as you would consider other problems which are of individual and community interest. You know about your schools. You can give figures relating to your banks. You can tell the value of the building permits issued each month. You know the costs and efficiency of your police department and your fire department. You know the amount of money spent for cleaning your streets, for your sewer system, and for removing the city garbage. But this business of Christianity, which represents three billion dollars and a yearly cost of seven hundred million, which is life and character and happiness, and upon which the future of your country depends, you put into the hands of your preachers and church managers and never ask a question as to their management nor make an intelligent effort even to learn the facts.

"Let me prove that you gentlemen of Westover are not exceptions," continued Mr. Saxton. "We may assume, I think, that the Chambers of Commerce and similar organizations fairly represent the business men of our nation. Some time ago there was sent to a large number of these organizations, throughout the country, a letter asking for a few of the simplest facts and figures relating to the churches in their respective cities. Thirty-nine per cent of these business organizations ignored the request. Of those who replied sixty per cent gave no information, explaining, in nearly every case, that it was impossible for them to get the figures. Only fifteen per cent gave full answers. Forty-five per cent referred the questions to ministerial organizations or similar bodies, and of these only one answered. Think of it. A business, representing in money an investment of over three billion dollars, with an annual expenditure of seven hundred million, and which, in addition to these great sums involved, is conceded to be of vital importance to every business, every city, every home, and every individual in the land, and the business men of the nation know nothing about it!"

"I should like to know what community service our churches render," said Banker Winton thoughtfully.

"Outside of their denominational interest, you mean?" asked the Judge.

"Yes."

Mr. Saxton said earnestly: "You must not overlook the fact, gentlemen, that every individual Christian character is an asset to his community. In every denomination there are many splendid men and women who are genuine Christians in spite of their denominational handicaps, and these Christ-like spirits are of untold value of the country. They are, everywhere, the saving element in our social, business, civic and national life."

"Certainly, Mr. Saxton, I am not overlooking that. But the fact remains that the denominational churches do not make Christians without making Methodists, and Presbyterians, and Baptists, and Congregationalists, and all the other hundred and eighty varieties."

Mr. Saxton, nodding assent, returned: "Four-fifths of every dollar expended by the Church goes to maintain these denominational interests."

The banker persisted: "And what do the churches spend on community work—I mean work that is undenominational but Christian?"

"You are the treasurer of our Organized Charities, Henry," remarked the groceryman.

"That's why I raised the question," retorted Winton. "Our Westover churches, as churches, have never given a penny to our civic charities, nor to any other community welfare work. Is that the case throughout the country, Mr. Saxton?"

Saxton answered: "I have found that to be the case, almost universally."

"Our churches, under the present denominational plan then, do practically nothing that does not have their denominational interests in view?" asked the Judge.

"The further one goes in the study of this question, the more apparent that fact becomes," replied Saxton. "And this is in the face of the truth that the Christian members of the church, as a whole, almost universally consider their denominational interests of no importance when compared with Christianity, which is common to them all, and for which they give these enormous sums of money. You, gentlemen, are forced to give four dollars to support a system in which you do not believe, in order to give one dollar to the sacred cause of Christianity, in which you all believe. There is no place outside of a denominational church where a man can worship God. There is no organization through which one can spend a dollar for a purely Christian purpose."

"If such a state of affairs existed in any other institution in the world, the people would demand an investigation," declared Mayor Riley.

"You can't investigate the Church," said Jones.

"I'd like to know why not," retorted Riley. "We investigate everything else in which the public has an interest. I'm in favor of a national committee, made up of Christian business men appointed by our Chambers of commerce, to inquire into church finances and management. The people put up this three billion dollars and are putting up, every year, this seven hundred million. The Church wouldn't, necessarily, need to be less Christian to be more businesslike."

"It couldn't be done, George," said the Judge.

Said Ed Jones: "If a committee of business men *were* to take hold of the Church, the first thing they would do would be to consolidate and cut out all this ruinous waste of money in unnecessary buildings and equipment, and in the duplication of operating expense caused by denominational competition."

"I suppose something like five hundred million a year could be saved," suggested Winton. "Think of the good work that the Church could do with, say, even two hundred million a year. I mean charities, hospitals, homes and all that kind of work, which Jesus certainly made an essential party of Christianity, and which the Church is now forced for lack of funds, to leave to civic and fraternal bodies. Why, if our charities, instead of being done in the name of the city or Kiwanis or the Odd Fellows, could be carried on by the church, in the name of Christianity, the religious effect would be tremendous!"

"Consolidation of all the denominations is an idle dream, Henry," said the Judge. "For one thing, too many religious teachers and high salaried denominational officials would have to lose their jobs. The clergy has always controlled the Church—and always will. What would you do, for instance, with a billion dollars' worth of church property that would be rendered useless?"

"Turn it into better and more beautiful churches—into hospitals and homes and endowments," cried the groceryman.

"It could never be done," insisted the Judge.

Mr. Saxton asked: "What is the Church, gentlemen? In *our* language, I mean—not the language of theology."

"Legally"—Judge Burnes replied, "legally, well, it's hard to say exactly *what* the Church is, legally. Actually, the Church is the whole body of Christian believers."

"It is all the Christians, no matter to which of the one hundred and eighty-three denominations they belong," offered Joe Paddock.

"A church is any group of Christians banded together to promote Christianity," suggested Winton.

"And to worship God," added Riley.

"The membership of any given church is *that* church," said Jones. "And the combined membership of all the churches is *the Church.*"

Mr. Saxton smiled as he said: "It must follow, then, that the preachers and managers of our churches—or let me say of *the* Church—are the servants of the people who constitute the Church."

"Certainly no one could hold that the members are the servants of the preachers," agreed the Judge.

"Well," continued Mr. Saxton, "the Church exists for a very definite purpose, does it not?"

"To build Christian character," said the Judge.

"To teach the truths that Jesus taught," said the groceryman. "And to care for the sick and needy, to feed the hungry, clothe the naked, house the homeless, in His name, as He said we should do."

"Why, then," asked Mr. Saxton, "if the people are the Church, and the ministers and managers are the servants of the Church, and the Church exists for one definite purpose, why, if the people are not satisfied with the results obtained, may they not inquire into the reason for the failure?"

They all turned to the lawyer member of the circle.

Judge Burnes answered: "You overlook the fact, Mr. Saxton, that our church managers, who are directly responsible for the existing conditions, are also our spiritual leaders and teachers. The clergy is the highest religious court to which the people can appeal. If our ministers could be brought to bar for their management of these vast sums of money entrusted to them, they would necessarily be tried before themselves and would render a verdict in their own favor. The members of the Church—and the membership *is* the Church—are in a difficult position. To question the policies of the managers is to question their spiritual teachers; and to question their spiritual teachers, is to question the religion of the Church itself. One of Joe's customers can complain and it's up to Joe to do something or lose the customer. That is because Joe's customer *buys* something with the money he pays Joe. The clergy has taught the people to look upon their contributions to the church as gifts to God. When a church member pays money into the church treasury he, theoretically, *doesn't buy anything—he gives the money to the Lord.* When the people put up this three billion dollars they didn't invest it in church property—they gave it to the Lord. We don't receive anything in return for the millions which we pay out every year. That would be heresy. Whatever we receive from the Church *is given to us by the Lord.* We don't *employ* a pastor, we *call* him. We don't *pay* him for his services, we *give* his salary to the Lord. He doesn't serve us for *pay,* he gives his services to the Lord. I'd like to know how any committee of mere business men is going to investigate a situation covered up like that."

"They couldn't even find a place to start," said Paddock.

And Riley added: "If a group of business men, like us, should begin to ask questions the preachers would simply shift the inquiry to a theological discussion and *then* where would we be?"

"It seems to me, gentlemen, that you have at least fixed the responsibility," said Saxton.

"Upon the clergy?" asked Joe.

"No," said the Judge, "upon the membership."

"Exactly," said Saxton. "If the ministers are the servants of the Church, and represent the Church, and spend the Church's money, it is clearly the duty of the membership, which is the Church, to see that their preachers preach Christianity and spend the money they hold in trust for the Christian purpose for which it is given. If any one believed that the Christianity which Jesus gave to the world is dependent upon denominationalism the case might be different. But no one—certainly not the great majority—believes that, but quite the contrary, and, therefore, the money spent to maintain this denominationalism, which is defeating the cause of Christianity, is a misuse of the Church funds. The preachers ask the people to give money to the Lord and then use four-fifths of it for something which the Lord never contemplated."

"But, Mr. Saxton," said Judge Burnes, "my pastor argues that denominationalism is necessary to Christianity because people do not think alike and that we must, therefore, have a variety of churches in order to accommodate all."

"That's what my pastor argues," said Jones.

"And mine," echoed Riley.

Saxton replied gently: "And would your ministers contend that there are one hundred and eighty-three varieties of Christianity?"

The lawyer smiled. "I think not."

"Well, then, if Jesus gave to mankind only one Christianity, who gave us our one hundred and eighty-three denominations? Was Jesus such a failure, as a teacher, that we must rely upon our theologians to make His meaning clear? Do these theological confusions emphasize the simple truths of Christianity, or do they not so complicate and obscure Christianity that its directness and force are lost? Did Jesus know what He wanted when, in His prayer for His disciples, He said: 'Neither for these only do I pray, but for them also that believe on me through their word; that they may all be one; even as Thou, Father, are in Me, and I in Thee.' Would your ministers contend that there were one hundred and eighty-three varieties of Oneness between Jesus and the Father to whom He prayed? To say that these theologically devised divisions of the followers of Jesus are necessary to the Christian religion is nothing less than to question the wisdom of Him who gave us Christianity itself. A child can understand Jesus. But all the theological seminaries in Christendom can't make clear the complicated systems of denominational doctrines, which they call Christianity."

There was silence for a little as Mr. Saxton's guests sat with bowed heads, thinking. And the countenance of the man at the head of the table, as he looked upon them, was aglow with the light of his mission.

At last Mayor Riley spoke: "We hear a lot of talk, these days, about the failure of the Church."

"That's about all you do hear—about the Church," said Paddock sadly.

"And not only by nonchurch people, but by the members themselves," added Winton.

"Yes," agreed Jones, "and most of our ministers, even, admit it."

"What is your opinion, Mr. Saxton?" asked the lawyer. "Is the Church meeting the present-day religious need?"

For a long moment their host did not answer and they all saw the sadness which shadowed his eyes deepen. Then he said gently: "I am alone in the world. You, my friends, are men of families; you have homes and children. . . . What is your answer to that question?"

Again, at his words, a solemn hush fell upon the company. No man answered because each was thinking, now, things of which he could not speak. And yet, each knew that the others knew what it was that troubled him. And all were wondering if the man at the head of the table also knew why they were silent—if he understood. What had put those shadows of sadness in his eyes? Why was his voice so kind?

It was the groceryman who, at last, said slowly: "I confess that the Church doesn't mean to me what it did to my parents. I don't seem to get anything out of our services. I don't believe our young people get much out of the Church, either. I believe that is why they don't go more—because the Church means nothing to them."

Winton followed with: "There is no question but that the Church has lost its influence—upon the younger generation, at least."

"Our preachers are certainly not making themselves felt, religiously," Riley agreed.

And the Judge added: "The Church is failing even to hold its own membership to the fundamental teaching of Jesus—we all realize that in our own lives."

With one accord they turned their faces toward the man at the head of the table, and the groceryman spoke for all: "What is the result of your observation, Mr. Saxton?"

Mr. Saxton, in answering, spoke gently, sadly, but never had they felt so strongly the power of his character and personality. He spoke as one having authority. "You are agreed, friends, that the sole purpose, mission, or business of the Church is to teach the truths that Jesus taught, and to exemplify to the world the doctrines of the life which Jesus, Himself, lived among men. A Christian is one whose professions and life conform to the teaching and example of Jesus. By Christianity we, of the Church, mean, and the world means, the teachings of Jesus. Mr. Winton, you know the teachings of Jesus, and you know banking. Would you say that the banking operations of this country are Christian?"

Henry Winton shook his head.

"Mr. Paddock, would you hold that the mercantile interests, the business of clothing and feeding people, are governed by the teaching of Jesus?"

The groceryman did not need to answer.

"Mayor Riley, in your opinion, based upon your knowledge of the teachings of Jesus and your political experience, is the work of governing the people, of making and enforcing the laws of the country Christian?"

The Mayor did not reply.

"Mr. Jones, you have knowledge of lands and buildings—the housing and homing of people. Do the teachings of Jesus prevail in real estate and building deals?"

There was no answer.

"Judge, are our courts of justice, our penal institutions and the practice of law, governed by the principles of Christianity? Do our public schools and universities teach Christianity? Is the art or literature of our day Christian? Are our newspapers governed by the teachings of Jesus? Is our social life Christian? Is the policy of our theaters and motion-picture houses Christian?"

No one spoke.

Their host continued: "There are many *private* institutions and enterprises which do square with Jesus' teachings, but I can find nothing in any phase of our national life, nothing in our many and varied public interests, nothing in any field of public activity, that can, with reason, be called Christian."

Again Mr. Saxton paused, and the men who sat around the table felt, as they had never felt before, a sense of impending evil.

With solemn earnestness and with a sadness so poignant that his hearers were moved almost to tears, their host broke the silence: "Measured by the standard of Jesus' teaching and example—the only standard by which we can measure Christianity—the Church itself—is not to-day Christian. The Master could not have contemplated anything like this multitude of warring denominations which are bringing His teaching to naught. Under the competition engendered by this denominational policy of the Church's theological managers, which is contrary to that Oneness which Jesus taught, and for which He prayed, each separate organization is literally *forced* to put its own peculiar denominational interests above the common cause of Christianity. If a denominational organization failed to magnify its sectarian peculiarities it would cease to exist. Denominations live, not on the Oneness of Christianity, but on the differences of theology. Christianity is of Jesus. Denominational doctrines are of men. Therefore, the modern Church is not Christian.

"The preachers of every denomination, almost universally, preach things which they themselves do not believe but which they *must* teach to satisfy the theological requirements of their superior denominational officers—and thus hold their positions.

"You men know your churches. Consider some of the methods of raising money and try to square these with the spirit and teachings and example of

Jesus. You have often served on church finance committees, Mr. Winton. Were all the contributions you solicited, from your fellow business men, voluntary offerings—asked for and given on purely religious grounds?"

"Most of the contributions to our new church building were little short of blackmail," answered the banker. "And your church, Jones, held *me* up in the same fashion."

"We all do it," said Riley. "We put influential men, like Winton, on these money-raising committees because there are business, political, or social reasons why certain people can't refuse them."

"Churches are not, to-day, built in a religious spirit," said Judge Burnes. "The business houses of the community are forced to contribute or lose patronage. The preacher, in appealing to his membership, appeals to their pride and to the spirit of rivalry. I never could imagine Jesus selling memorial windows in his church to a few individuals who happen to have money to buy, while He gave no honor, whatever, to the thousands who, out of their little, contributed more, in proportion, than those whose names were thus heralded to the world."

"What of the arguments used to induce certain desirable people to join the Church?" asked Saxton.

"Mostly business or social," returned Riley.

Saxton continued: "Consider the methods of securing influence to gain a denominational advantage, and the methods and schemes by which ministers strive for personal honors, preferments, better positions, and higher salaries. What of the fact that the churches do nothing for non-sectarian charity and welfare work in their own communities, and even farm out their own needy members on civic organizations and fraternal orders. Consider that brotherly love in the churches is not even strong enough to unite two denominations when their own members can't tell what keeps them apart. Witness Judge Burnes and Mr. Jones.

"How can an institution which is not Christian—in spirit, in name, in policy, in teaching, or in example—produce Christian character in the world? As long as the Church makes a mock of its own religion it cannot expect the world to believe in, or even respect, it."

"No one can honestly deny the justice of your charge, Mr. Saxton," said Judge Burnes. "Most of the church members and many of the ministers would admit these things are true. But just the same, it is a terrible thing to say—terrible!"

"The time has come, Judge," answered Mr. Saxton, "when it is a terrible thing *not* to speak out on this subject. It is no longer a question of the Church saving the people—it has become a question of the people saving the Church. It is a question of saving Christianity, itself. The future of the Christian religion is in the hands of the sincere Christians who are to be found in the membership of every denominational church, and who are Christians in spite of denominationalism. The future of Christianity and, therefore, of your country, your homes, your children, is in the hands of capable Christian business men like you.

"Our ministers are powerless. They are the product of denominationalism; they are trained in denominational schools; they are controlled by their denominational higher-ups. They are in the grip of this great un-Christian machine, and no matter how sincere and godly they may be, as individuals, they must obey the powers or get out. That is why, too often in these modern times, the preacher is neither the intellectual, spiritual, nor moral equal of the majority of those who pay his salary.

"The modern, down-to-date clergyman, under the ruthless competition of this denominational system, has little time or strength or thought left for the Christian religion. He is ten percent social visitor, tea drinker and diner-out; five percent handy man and speaker for all kinds of boosting clubs; five percent political henchman; twenty percent denominational advocate; five percent protector and comforter of that portion of his membership who, because their deeds will not bear the light, must live under the cloak of the Church; and fifty percent public entertainer. The remaining five percent of him is teacher of the truths of Jesus, which, alone, constitute one hundred per cent of Christianity."

As Mr. Saxton's guests made their several ways home, late that evening, their minds were not so much occupied with the material gains which they still hoped to realize through Mr. Saxton's friendship. They thought of other things.

It may be assumed, too, that their waiting and anxious wives were disappointed when no material progress was reported.

CHAPTER X.

SUNDAY.

The work horses on the farm were in the pasture. They grazed leisurely. Now and then one would pause to stand with lifted head contentedly viewing the peaceful surroundings. Chickens moved sedately about the barnyard, selecting choice bits of food with lazy indifference, while the old Plymouth Rock rooster from the top of the fence surveyed the scene with quiet satisfaction. On the roof of the big barn pigeons made soft-voiced love. Swallows gossiped from nest to nest under the eaves. There were no men in the fields. The growing crops seemed to sleep in the sunshine. The orchard trees were dozing. The leafy giants that guarded the house rested. It was Sunday morning.

In town, the business streets, except for an occasional automobile, an empty street car, or a lone pedestrian, were deserted. Save at the post office, the cigar counters and newsstands there was no stir of life about the stores and office buildings. The homes on the avenue gave no sign that they were inhabited. The wretched dwellers in Shack Town had not yet issued from their squalid quarters. But in the restaurants, motion-picture theaters, night clubs and dance halls employees were actively engaged in removing the débris left by Saturday night crowds and preparing for the usual Sunday rush. The church janitors, too, were busy opening the houses of God—to air them out and rid them as much as it were possible of their musty, closed-up, weekday smell.

When the late breakfast at the Paddock home was over the groceryman went out on the front porch to find the Sunday paper. He picked up the *Herald* which was lying on the walk at the foot of the steps and with an impatient ejaculation collected three handbills, such as are commonly used by advertisers, of a sort, to litter well kept lawns and exasperate the citizens by the untidy appearance of their streets. Then, because he was not insensible to the beauty of the morning, he moved on to a rustic chair under one of the trees which shaded the generous yard. Seating himself, he leisurely lit his after-breakfast cigar preparatory to reading the Sunday morning news.

Following that Saxton dinner, the groceryman had held several interesting conversations with his fellow guests.

Henry Winton confessed that he had not slept well that night. He had never before heard religion discussed from Saxton's viewpoint. He was rather inclined to question some of Saxton's figures, and yet, he did not know, he certainly could not deny them. For a long time he had felt that there was something wrong with the Church. Saxton was a fine man, no doubt about that, sincere, genuine, and with unusual ability. The banker wished the Kansas City man would tell them something about his real business in Westover.

Judge Burnes felt that Saxton's presentation of the religious situation brought home the responsibility to the church members in a way that was difficult to escape. He hoped that things were not so bad as Saxton thought. After all, the denominations had accomplished much, but still, "The question is not what have they done; but, what are they doing now? Everybody knows that the Church is failing to meet the present-day religious needs." The Judge, too, wished that Saxton would make known his real business.

Ed Jones thought that Saxton was right but that nothing could be done about it. "There is waste in everything. Churches do a lot of good. We all know there is something wrong but what can we do?" Ed was disappointed that Saxton did not tell them about his contemplated enterprise in their city.

Mayor Riley found Saxton's arguments unanswerable. And yet never before had he considered religion from the economic side of the question. Of course, in a way, it *was* a question of economics. Character—morality—honesty—they are all questions which affect the people as a whole. Saxton's views of a national crisis were undoubtedly correct. There was a general feeling that something must be done and that the churches were doing nothing. He wondered what brought Saxton to Westover anyway.

The groceryman, himself, was bewildered. He felt that, so far as he was concerned, his old established mental attitude toward religion was upset forever. Christianity, the Church, religion could never again, in his mind, be held as something apart from the business, political and social life of the nation. But what to do about it! He doubted if the Church *could* change. Certainly it could not change without ceasing to exist as separate and distinct denominational institutions. It was unthinkable that the denominations would voluntarily close their doors—shut up shop—go out of business. He tried to talk it over with Laura but got nowhere. Of one thing he was sure, Dan Matthews' representative was a remarkable man, and his presence in Westover was a big thing for them all. But was the big thing a material thing? Of that he was not so sure. The groceryman was beginning to feel a significance—a meaning, a purpose—in Saxton's dinner party. Where had he seen the man before?

The groceryman was about to take up his paper when he glanced at those handbills—three typical examples of the job printer's art.

The first one announced: "The Greatest Sensational Motion Picture of the Year—'Red Hot Mamas'—At the Royal—The Most Popular House in Westover."

The second sheet implored him not to miss "The Biggest Feed and Dance of the Season—At Tony's To-night—The Famous Wild Boys' Jazz Band—The Prettiest Girls—Something Doing Every Minute—The Most Popular Place to Spend a Wide-awake Evening in Westover."

Joe grunted his disgust and read the remaining handbill. "Don't Go to the —— Church This Summer Expecting to Sleep—Pastor —— Will Preach a Great Wide-awake Series of Popular Sunday Night Sermons—This Church Is Famous for The Gospel."

The groceryman crumpled the handbills and, for several minutes, smoked thoughtfully. Then he opened his paper to the church section where the first thing to catch his eye was a picture of a group of grinning jazz musicians with their instruments.

He read: "An Up-to-date Jazz Band Furnishes the Music at Services in the Fashionable —— Church—on invitation of the pastor. Other jazz musicians will appear in the church during the year."

With awakened interest he proceeded to read the headlines of other church news items:

"Bible Class to Hear Eugenics Discussed."

"Ghastly Means of Ending Life—given in play to-morrow. A rope, a gun, a razor, a dagger, gas, a drink of poison—all means to an end—of life. The Christian Endeavor Society will present the play Thursday night."

"Bronco Jack, Here to Hog-tie Souls of Men—I will ride human herd here and I promise to rope, hog-tie, bull-dog, and scratch the Devil every evening."

"Church Crowds Fall Off As Bitterness Lessened—Reverend —— blames the increasing respect and cooperation between the different religious sects for lack of attendance at church services."

He read slowly every line of a long flamboyant blurb which closed with: "The public is cordially invited to hear this magnetic, humorous, young minister."

He thought over an announcement of Sunday worship which promised: The Meeting for Men and Boys will be a Thriller. There will not be a dull moment throughout the day."

There were more headlines: "Battling —— *vs.* Beelzebub—The Reverend ——, 'fighting parson,' cornered the Prince of Darkness, grabbed him by both horns and twisted his neck until the entire valley reverberated with the strident sound of Satanic screams."

"Pastor Seeking to Learn Life's Greatest Kick—offers cash awards for best answer to question, 'How is one to get a kick out of life?'"

"Varied Bill for Vaudeville—different features each evening will mark vaudeville performance at the —— Church fair—Oriental Stunt—Card Parties. There will be many parties of school children who will attend the Jitney Dance. Five or six cigarette girls will be in costume and sell the nicotine."

"What Is Wrong with the Church?"

Turning to the programs of the Sunday services, the groceryman found in the columns of feverish announcements of special attractions: "extraordinary tenors," "celebrated quartettes," "popular singers," "marvelous violinists," "unusual tableaux," "wonderful musical programs," the following invitations and sermon themes:

"Come and Hear Sunshine Jim."

"Our South American Neighbors—illustrated."

"The Fifth Sermon in a Series on Famous Characters in Classic Fiction."

"What I Saw at Third and Market Streets in San Francisco—He promises something of a most interesting nature."

"An Ex-Governor to Occupy Pulpit."

"Don't Die On Third—with a number of interesting baseball illustrations. It is doubtful if any preacher to-day has as many friends among baseball players as Doctor ——."

"Bleaching a Black Man."

"The Go-Getter Church."

"Presentation of Flag to Congregation by Elks—the Pastor being a member of the Lodge."

"How's Your Backbone? In this sermon he will tell how he knocked out Bob Fitzsimmons, the famous pugilist, in his pulpit. Tokens will be offered to the father whose boy looks most like him; to the newest newlyweds; to the oldest man; and to the one who comes the greatest distance."

"Standing On A Banana Peeling."

"Music As An Aid to Better Living."

"Why Johnny Fell Out of Bed."

"You've Got to Quit Kicking My Dog Around!"

"Traffic to Be Discussed As Sunday Sermon—Doctor —— will raise and discuss many pertinent questions in this sermon. What is the cause of our alarming increase of automobile accidents? Unreasonable and unenforced traffic ordinances. Irresponsible and careless drivers. Inadequate brakes and unsteady hands. Should citizens be informers."

"Why Go to Church?"

An automobile stopped in front of the house and the groceryman, looking up from his paper, waved a greeting to the young man who left the machine and came toward him across the lawn.

Georgia appeared on the porch. "Hello, Jack," she called, "be with you in a minute."

"No hurry," returned the young man. Then, as the girl disappeared again into the house, he said to her father: "I was hoping I would see you this morning, Mr. Paddock."

The groceryman was very fond of this fine young chap whom he had known since his birth.

"Business pretty good, Jack?"

"Growing all the time, sir. But I wanted to see you about our Organized Charities—the meeting of the directors and workers next Thursday, you know. It is mighty important that we have a full attendance. Everything is set to start the annual drive for funds. Wilcox, the expert from Cleveland, who is to have charge of the campaign, will arrive Thursday morning. You won't mix this meeting, will you, Mr. Paddock? I'm counting on you and Mrs. Paddock."

"Sure, we'll be there, Jack. How is everything lining up this year?"

The young president of the Civic Charity organization answered doubtfully: "I'm afraid it's not going to be so easy to raise the money we need this year."

"Why, what's the trouble? Westover has always, responded before."

"Up to last year our Charities' board always got what they asked for," returned Jack, "but you remember the last campaign finished about ten thousand dollars short. We've got to make the strongest drive we have ever made this year or we'll fall down worse than that. That's why I'm so anxious about this meeting, Thursday night. We've all got to be on our toes every minute—right from the start."

"But our people believe in the Organized Charities, Jack."

"Oh, the people are all right—they want to help—their hearts are in the right place. It isn't that."

For some reason young Ellory seemed reluctant to continue, but the groceryman was persistent.

"Times are good, Jack. Everybody is prosperous."

"Yes, sir, but—"

"But what?"

"You seem to forget, Mr. Paddock, that we have built four big new churches in Westover the last two years."

The groceryman, with the air of one who suddenly sees an old problem from a new angle, asked: "And do you think that has any bearing on the difficulty of raising funds for our charities? I always thought most of the subscribers to our Civic Charities were church members."

"That is just the trouble," retorted Jack. "The great bulk of our Civic Charity funds *does* come from church members. And practically all of the money raised to build these four new churches came from the same church members. There is a limit to the amount that even the most generous person can give, you know. No matter what they would like to do, people can't give beyond their means. It is because so much of the available money has gone into church building these last two years that we are short of the necessary funds for our Civic Charity."

The groceryman did not answer and Jack continued: "The worst of it is that even if we get all the money we are asking for we will not be able to do half what there is to do. Conditions in Shack Town are terrible. Our only hope is in educating the public. We must somehow sell Westover the idea of working together, as a community, for the good of the community as a whole. The people have scarcely begun to realize what this Civic Charity work really means. You know how it is."

The groceryman glanced down at his newspaper. "Yes," he said thoughtfully, "I know how it is."

Then as Georgia came toward them and he watched the faces of the two young people he thought how years ago Laura had come to him. The same glad eagerness, the same happiness, the bright eyes, the glowing color, the illuminated countenance, the impulsive gestures, the fond laughter, the gay voices. Suddenly he remembered his mother's words: "It takes a lot of religion, son, for two people to love and marry and live together long enough to raise children and be grandparents."

As he watched them crossing the lawn toward the waiting roadster he wondered if there could be anywhere in the world a finer couple. Why did they not marry and establish their home? More than anything else in life, the groceryman wanted to see his daughter in a home of her own. With a farewell wave to him they drove away. The church bells rang. The groceryman felt old and incompetent.

Mrs. Paddock's voice came from the front door: "Joe, if you're going to church you must hurry and get ready."

"I don't think I'll go this morning, Laura."

"Not go! Nonsense, of course you are going. Miss Gordon is to sing, Mrs. Trevor has a cornet solo, we have the Goodwin Male Quartette, and Professor Levinski gives a special organ number. I wouldn't miss it for the world. There is no finer program in any church in the city. Come on, you have just time to dress."

The work horses, in the barnyard, dozed peacefully after their day of rest in the pasture and their evening meal of grain. The chickens had gone to roost. The doves and swallows were fast asleep. Grandpa and grandma, from their easy chairs on the veranda, watched the colors of the sunset fade, the western sky grow dim and the dusk of twilight deepen into the darkness of the night. Overhead, the kindly stars; here and there, across the fields, a friendly light.

"Well, Mother," said the old gentleman, with a great yawn, "I don't know about you, but I'm ready to call it another day."

She answered with a little sigh of contentment: "I was just thinking it must be near bedtime."

They were about to enter the house when grandpa, who was holding the screen door open for his companion, heard a strange sound. He put his free hand on grandma's arm and she paused. The sound came again.

"What is it?" whispered the old lady.

"It's there at the end of the veranda, whatever it is," he whispered in return.

He quietly closed the door and they stood in the darkness listening.

Suddenly, as the sound came again, the old lady started forward. But grandpa held her back. "It's some one crying," she said in a low tone. "Some one is in trouble."

Grandpa went down the steps and around to the end of the veranda, with grandma following close behind.

Crouching on the round, almost hidden in the vines, they found a woman moaning, sobbing, almost delirious with fright or pain.

When grandpa spoke to her and touched her on the shoulder she cried out: "No—no—" and tried to drag herself deeper among the vines.

With a firm hand the old gentleman lifted the poor creature to her feet and together they tried, with gentle voices, to reassure and calm her as they helped her toward the door of the house.

Grandma turned on the light.

"Georgia!"

The girl's dress was soiled and torn, her stockings grass-stained and ragged, her hair disheveled, her eyes wild, and her face scratched and tear-washed. She was trembling, crying, laughing.

They helped her to a couch, and grandpa spoke firmly to steady her: "Georgia, you must control yourself. You are all right. Tell me, was it an automobile accident? Was any one else hurt? Where did it happen? You must tell me—there may be others needing help."

With an effort, the girl answered: "It was an accident all right—not automobile though—there's no one else—I— ran away from him."

The two old people looked at each other in horrified silence. The trembling girl, moaning and sobbing, hid her face in her arms. Then while grandma, kneeling beside the couch, soothed her with loving hands and low, gentle voice, grandpa went to the telephone.

"The Sheriff's office."

With a scream, the girl sprang from the couch and rushed across the room. "No—no—no—" she cried, snatching the receiver from grandpa's hand and replacing it on the hook. "You must not—you shall not—it was—it was Jack."

She clung desperately to her grandfather's arm, laughing and crying hysterically. "Don't you understand? It was Jack, I tell you—Jack Ellory! It was my fault! He's just like all the rest! I might have known! Oh, God—oh, God—what a fool I've been!"

They half carried her back to the couch.

Hetty appeared. Grandma explained briefly that there had been an accident, but that no one was hurt, and sent her to make tea.

Grandma was urging the girl to take the hot drink when they were startled by a knock at the door.

Georgia clung to her grandmother like a frightened child. Staring at grandpa, with terror-stricken eyes, she begged: "Don't let him in. Please don't let him in, I hate him—I hate him—don't let him come near me."

The old gentleman, kneeling, took her in his arms. "There, there, child. No one is going to get you here. You know you are safe with grandpa and grandma, don't you?"

The knock sounded again.

"Shall I go to the door?" whispered Hetty.

Grandpa shook his head. "No, I'll go." He patted the girl's shoulder. "Don't worry, honey, grandpa will take care of you all right. You just lie still here with grandma and Hetty."

He strode across the room, threw open the door, and stepping out, closed it behind him.

The girl watched the door with wide, terror-haunted eyes. Grandma murmured soothing, reassuring words, as she would have quieted a frightened child. At a signal from her mistress, Hetty slipped away upstairs to see that the guest room was ready.

"I—I ought to see him," the girl whispered. "I am to blame as much as he. I—I want to see him." She was trembling again. "Don't let him come—please don't let him in."

"There, there, dearie it'll be all right. It's just a neighbor, likely, or one of the men, or some automobile people wanting to ask the road to some place."

"No, no, Grandma, I know it's Jack—I know."

When grandpa appeared on the veranda, closing the door behind him, the figure of a man, vague and shadowy in the darkness, drew back toward the steps.

The old gentleman, with his back to the door, stood waiting.

The shadowy future spoke in a voice uncertain with emotion. "I am Jack Ellory, Mr. Paddock."

Grandpa returned coolly: "Well, what do you want?"

"Is Georgia here?"

"Yes."

The younger man's voice was not lacking in sincerity as he ejaculated: "Thank God!" He removed his hat and wiped his forehead. "I thought she might be here. I came round the hill by the east road. I thought if she wasn't here I could phone for help."

Grandpa was grimly silent.

Jack moved uneasily. "May I—could I see her?"

"No."

Another painful silence. Then: "Of course you are right, sir. It was foolish to ask. I—is she—I hope. . . ."

The old gentleman, standing so still with his back to the closed door, did not speak.

"I'll go, sir." The young man turned and started down the steps.

"Wait!" The word was a stern command.

Jack halted and in three long steps grandpa stood over him. "I want to know one thing, young man."

The one on the steps bowed his head. "I understand, sir. I have not harmed Georgia." He suddenly raised his head, and with a pleading gesture, continued: "Great God, Mr. Paddock, I've known her ever since we were little children. She's been the one girl to me always—since before we went to kindergarten together. She was never like the other girls to me. You know what I mean—you haven't forgotten your young days. But this afternoon I thought—I mean I lost my head—I misunderstood—I thought—oh, hell! How can I explain?" He choked, his voice broke with something very like a sob.

Grandpa's hand went out in the darkness to rest upon the younger man's shoulder, and grandpa's voice was gentle: "We'll take care of her, Jack."

A moment later Jack said: "Don't let her go home to-night, Mr. Paddock. Telephone her father that she is going to visit with you for a few days. Don't let them know about this. Home is no place for her just now."

"That's a good idea, Jack. I guess her grandmother is best for her right now."

"And will you call me up in the morning, sir? I'll not sleep till I know how she is. If she'll let me, I'll come for her and take her home when she is ready. But I don't suppose she will ever speak to me again. I don't blame her—she has always been different from the others—I never thought till this afternoon. . ." He turned suddenly and disappeared in the darkness.

Grandpa stood waiting—peering into the night. He heard the sound of the automobile. He waited while the sound grew fainter and fainter. When he could no longer hear the departing machine he still stood there peering into the darkness, listening, listening. Slowly he turned and reentered the house.

They watched silently as the old gentleman came across the room and stood looking down at the girl. He seemed to be trying to think out a difficult situation. At last, as if answering her unspoken question, he said quietly: "It was Jack."

"Oh, Grandpa, what—what did you do to him?"

"Nothing."

"Is he—is he gone?"

"Yes, he's gone. He is mighty sorry, Georgia—says for us not to let you go home for a day or two. Good idea, I'll phone your father and mother."

The girl laughed bitterly. "Why should I want to go home?"

The two old people looked at each other questioningly.

"Georgia," said grandpa firmly, "this is not quite clear to me. You must tell us—Jack says he did not harm you—that you are all right. Is that true?"

"Yes, that is true," the girl cried piteously. "I am not—harmed—not in the way you mean. Oh, Grandpa—Grandma—you *must* believe me!"

Again the old gentleman knelt beside the couch and took the overwrought girl in his arms. "There, there, honey—I think I begin to understand now. Of course you are not a bad girl. Grandma and I know all about it. You will just stay here with us for a few days. Henry is going to town in the morning and will bring what clothes you want. It will be all right. No one but grandpa and grandma will ever know about this. There, there. . . ."

A little later, when grandpa had telephoned to Georgia's parents, grandma helped the girl to a warm bath, and after robing her in one of her own old-fashioned nightdresses, tucked her, with many a motherly pat and caress, into the white bed in the cheerful guest room.

But when the old lady would have turned out the light the girl begged: "Please, Grandma, don't leave me. I can't sleep. I'm afraid—I—shall go mad if you leave me here alone to think. I must talk—I must tell you. . . ."

"Why, of course I'll not leave you, dearie, if you want me. I'll just go and tell grandpa that you are all right so he won't come blundering in on us when he is not wanted. I'll only be gone a minute."

When she returned she arranged the lights so that the room was almost in darkness, drew a chair close beside the bed, and, seating herself, took the girl's outstretched hand.

"Don't you think you could sleep, dear, if you were just to lie quiet a little and let me do the talking? Most people find it easy to sleep when grandma talks, you know."

The girl clutched the thin, old hand that had ministered to so many tired and troubled souls. "No—no—I must tell you."

"All right then." Grandma spoke cheerfully, in a matter-of-fact tone, that, while it lacked nothing in sympathy, was charged with comforting strength and assurance, "All right. If you want to tell me it is best that you should."

When Georgia did not speak for a little, the old gentlewoman added: "Start at the beginning, dearie. I don't mean the way back beginning—the real beginning I suspect is farther back than any of us realizes. Start, say, this morning, or last night maybe. You and Jack were out to a party somewhere last night, were you, and danced till pretty late?"

"Yes—it was late when I got home. He came for me again this morning."

"About church time, I guess that was," said grandma.

"Yes—well—we went first to the club as usual. Our crowd usually gets together there. And they were all planning for the afternoon and night. But I didn't want to go."

"Didn't you have a good time Saturday night?"

"Yes, I guess so—but somehow I was tired of it—so I suggested to Jack that we cut the bunch and go to the country for a quiet afternoon—just us two. He didn't seem to care for the crowd either, so he got a box of lunch, and. . ."

"And a bottle of liquor," said grandma, in her matter-of-fact tone.

"Yes—and we came out the state highway and turned off on the old east road that runs by the woods, you know."

"That old road was your father and mother's favorite drive of a Sunday afternoon," remarked grandma.

The girl continued as if she had not heard: "We left the automobile and went into the woods. It was so beautiful—so quiet and restful and—and solemn-like—like a church ought to be. Jack said the woods always made him feel that God was not so far away as He seemed in the city. And we talked a long time about religion, and life, and such things."

"Of course you did, dearie," said grandma, "and Jack said he worshiped God in nature, I suppose."

"Oh," exclaimed the girl, "did he ever tell you about what he believes?"

"No, but you see I was young once myself, child, and we are all nature worshipers at certain times. You had your lunch in the woods, did you?"

"Yes—in the loveliest spot—beside a little pond. I wonder if you know the place?"

"I know it very well, child. And you had a drink or two of liquor—with your lunch?"

"Jack drank more than I ever saw him drink before. I only took a little—I never was so happy and contented—no noisy crowd—no one to bother—just Jack and me."

"I know just how beautiful it was, dear, I know."

"And then," whispered the girl, "I—I don't remember how it happened—I was teasing Jack just for fun—and all at once he caught me in his arms. He never did that before. I—I was frightened. I tried to make him stop but he wouldn't. I fought him and broke away and ran. I didn't know where I was going—I just tore away through the woods and brush—I was crazy. He called and called and tried to follow me. But I hid and wouldn't answer, and yet, all the time, I could hardly keep myself from going back to him. And that frightened me more than ever. And so when he went another way I ran again. I felt I must get away from the sound of his voice. I ran and ran—until I couldn't hear him any more. Then it began to get dark, and I didn't know where I was. And then I saw the house, I didn't know until I was right in the yard that it was your house."

The girl was trembling again as if with a chill. "Oh, Grandma, Grandma, what is the matter with me? I don't want to be bad—I'm not bad. But when Jack came on the porch I knew who it was—and I wanted to go to him. If you and grandpa had not been with me I *would* have gone. I was afraid of him, too—but I was more afraid of myself."

"There, there, dearie—you mustn't let yourself get all worked up again. Of course you are not bad. Once we get some of your twisted thoughts straightened out, and some of your tangled emotions unsnarled, you will feel better."

"He said he wanted me," murmured the girl. "I thought he meant that he loved me, and I was glad. Then I knew that he only wanted me just as he wants other women. I always thought he was different with me. I know now he is just like all men and thinks of me just as they all think of all women."

"Yes, child, Jack is just like all men as you are like all women. That is the first thing that you must understand clearly. It is as Jesus said: 'He which made them at the beginning made them male and female.'"

"But, Grandma, Jack never treated me like that before."

"And was it all *his* fault, Georgia?"

The girl turned her face away.

The old lady continued: "I've noticed for a good many years now that men in general try to live up to what their woman expects of them."

Georgia's reply was a troubled confession: "When he didn't act like other men toward me I—I tried to see if I could make him."

"What fools we women be," murmured grandma. "What blessed fools."

The girl returned with more spirit: "It seems to me that if he really loved me he would not have taken advantage of me."

"And it seems to me," the old lady retorted, "that it was you who took advantage of him. You wanted him to do what he did, and you tempted him. And you would have despised him if he had not responded to your advances. If a girl invites a man she has no right to expect him to ignore her invitation."

Georgia was silent for a little after that and grandma wisely gave her time to think.

Then: "Is it wrong for me to want love, Grandma—I mean for me to want a home and children like you and grandpa have had?"

"That's all there is in life that is worth wanting, dear child."

"And did you want love when you were a girl?"

"Yes. And I had to fight to protect it too. Every woman, I think, for the sake of the children she hopes some day to mother, has to protect her love. But that doesn't mean that you must distrust all men, dear. Most men are as decent and true and good as the women will let them be."

"How can I help distrusting men?" cried the girl. "No woman, nowadays, believes in any man as you believe in grandpa. The men don't even try to hide from us what they do—they brag about it. They don't expect the girls to believe in or trust them."

"And don't you suppose that the men distrust the girls with as much reason?"

"They would be fools if they didn't."

"Of course. And you thought Jack was different from other men because he was different toward you. Well—don't you see that he was different toward you because he thought you were not like the other girls? Then all at once you acted just like the others. You let down the bars. You became common. You threw away the precious thing. *You* were to blame for what *he* thought, exactly as he is to blame for what you think."

The girl moved uneasily. "I think—" she began, then asked abruptly: "Did you and grandpa ever have such an experience?"

Grandma smiled. "It wouldn't be quite fair to grandpa for me to tell, would it, dearie?"

Georgia squeezed the old gentlewoman's hand and smiled in answer.

"I suspect," continued grandma, "that it has been the same since the time of Adam and Eve. I don't believe any cave girl was ever hit with a club and dragged away by the hair of her head when she did not invite the attack. Served her right—the hussy!"

"But it seems to me, Grandma, that the whole world has gone sex mad. You wouldn't believe the talk we hear—the things we say—the books we read and discuss. It's just sex, sex, sex. And the girls are that way because the men want us to be."

"My dear child, the love that brings a baby into the world is a good love. But like every good in life it must be kept from evil—it must be guarded and protected. And that, Georgia, is the woman's part. Because it is the woman who bears the children, the Creator has given to her the control of this mating love. Water is good. Without it all life would cease. But a great flood is destructive. Sex attraction is of God. It is good and beautiful and right. But nations have been destroyed by this same force when it was loosed beyond control. To keep this great creative force, sex, under control and make it a blessing rather than a curse, God has given us religion. Whenever in history the spiritual has been banished, licentiousness has ruled and ruin has followed."

"It's awfully hard for me to believe that grandpa and you were just like Jack and me," said the girl.

"Well, we were," returned the old lady stoutly, "we were just as human as you modern young folks dare to be."

"But men and women, when you were young, were not so—so—oh, dear, I don't know how to say it—I mean they were not so independent, so much alike, so promiscuous."

"I'll admit there was not so much of this new freedom that the women of to-day brag about," returned grandma. "You see, to us, God, spirituality, religion, morality, were real. Strange as it may seem, immorality was actually immoral. You and Jack have cut loose from those old-fashioned religious anchors. You are trusting to luck. You invite disaster. If you don't go to smash it will be an accident. Your grandfather and I had something beside sex attraction. You young people of to-day haven't anything *but* sex."

Georgia said thoughtfully: "I suppose the girls of to-day *could* be like the women of your day. We are physically strong; we are the stuff that pioneer mothers were made of—the War proved that."

"Yes," returned the old gentlewoman, "you modern girls have everything except the *one* thing to make your strength safe. I *know* it was my religion that made my love the safe and beautiful thing it has been all these years. The girls of my generation could have gone sex mad, too, but they had religion to keep them sane."

"But, Grandma," cried the girl, "how can we have a real religion? Where are we going to get it? Why, our own minister, even, is always making rotten *jokes* about love and marriage."

"I know, child, but we women who have to mother the race have always had to hold fast to religion in spite of the preachers. God is the same always. And preachers or no preachers, if the women of this generation let go their hold on God and the spiritual realities of religion they will breed a race of moral degenerates. Until these advanced thinkers, who sneer at religion, can produce a laboratory baby they better not loosen the world's grip on God. For human beings, sex love uncontrolled *is* degeneracy. And, so far, my dear child, the only control the world has ever known is spirituality."

Some time passed before the girl spoke. She lay so still that once grandma leaned forward over the bed to see if she were sleeping. Then she said: "Grandma, do you think Jack will every forgive me? Will he want me—I mean will he care for me as—as I want him to care—as he did before I let the bars down?"

"He will care more than ever, dear, because, you see, you put the bars up again. He knows it was an accident. But you must never lose control again."

Again there was a long silence. Then: "I wish mother would talk with me the way you do, Grandma. Perhaps if she had. . . ."

The old gentlewoman kissed her. I'm going to leave you now, dearie. If I were you I would just make a little prayer—ask God to bless your love for Jack—to be with you and make you strong for him and for the sake of the home and children you hope to have."

But to grandpa, a few minutes later, grandma said with amazing vigor for such a gentle old lady: "If Laura Louise Paddock, and all these other down-to-date mothers, would give half the thought to their daughters that they give to their new fangled culture our modern girls would have a chance."

CHAPTER XI.

GEORGIA RETURNS HOME.

It was not unusual for the groceryman's daughter to spend several days at the farm, so her parents thought nothing of it when grandpa phoned that she would stay with them. Henry brought the things she would need, and the girl seemed her usual self. But grandma knew that she was thinking. Jack Ellory called the second day, but she refused to receive him, though she watched from her room window as he returned to his car and drove away.

They were just finishing breakfast Thursday when the telephone rang.

Grandpa, who answered the call, said: "It's for you, Georgia."

The girl hesitated. "Is it Jack?"

"No—it's your father."

When she turned from the instrument a few minutes later she was very serious. "Daddy sounds awfully lonesome. He says if I don't come home to-day he's going to come out here to live, too. I guess I better go. He is coming for me late this afternoon—can't come earlier because he has an engagement with Mr. Saxton."

"He doesn't need to come for you." Said grandpa. "If you really think you ought to go home you can go in with me this afternoon. I'm going to town on business anyway." He stepped to the telephone. "I'll tell him—where did he call from, the house or the store?"

"The store."

When Georgia and her grandfather arrived at the girl's home the old gentleman refused to go in.

"Can't stop to-day, Georgia—haven't time—several things to see to, and you know I always have to get back to the farm before dark. It's dangerous enough for me to run this here machine in daylight. I don't know what would happen if I was to try drivin' it at night. Mother would be a-startin' out with a team to pick me up, I expect."

"But you can't go without even saying 'howdy' to mother," protested the girl. "Wait just a minute and I'll tell her you are here."

She ran into the house to return a few seconds later. "Mother is not home," she said. "She didn't know I was coming, I guess."

When grandpa had driven slowly and carefully away the girl went to her room.

As she moved about, unpacking her bag and preparing to change her dress, she hummed a little tune. Two or three times she paused before the photograph of Jack Ellory which occupied the place of honor on her dresser, and looking at the face of the man she loved, she smiled—as a woman always smiles at the man she loves. Should she telephone Jack, or write him, or wait for him to make another attempt to see her? She decided that it would be better to wait.

With grandma's help, the girl had freed herself from the tangle of unwholesome doubt and suspicion. She saw her feeling for Jack clearly—understandingly. There was no fog of sex madness, now, to obscure her love. She had thought it all out. She knew now what she would do.

She would tell him frankly that she was to blame for what had happened, and ask his forgiveness. Then she would cut out all the wild parties. She would go with him for tennis and decent dinners and dances whenever he wanted her, but there would be no more of Tony's Place and Sundown Inn. Her set would guy her; but grandma was right, if she wanted Jack's love she must fight for it. If she wanted a home and children she must prove to him that she was worthy to be a mother. She had been trying to win Jack by being what they called a good sport. She would try always to be a good sport, but not the kind that her crowd meant. No man like Jack would want that kind of a sport for a wife. As she kissed the picture of the man she loved the mother light was in her eyes and in her heart there was that feeling of motherliness which every good woman feels toward her husband. She would protect him and their future. She knew how fine he was. She was sure of his response to her new life. He always responded so readily to her moods—that was what had led them so near the wreck of their real and enduring happiness.

The front screen door slammed. The girl went to the open door of her room and heard her mother's voice in the hall below. She was about to step to the head of the stairs to call a greeting when she heard another voice. She put out her hand and caught the door frame to steady herself.

Her mother's voice came again. "No, really, you must not come in. There is not a soul in the house but cook. Georgia is at the farm, as I told you."

The other voice—a man's voice, answered: "Please don't be so hard-hearted, Laura. I promise to be good."

"But, Edward, think of the neighbors—what if some one should come?"

"Damn the neighbors! Think of us! Have we no rights?"

"You naughty man! Well then—but you must promise to go in half an hour."

"You darling!"

The door shut. "Edward!"

Georgia crept toward the head of the stairs and looked down to see her mother in the arms of Astell.

They moved on into the living room and the girl heard her mother's protesting: "No, no, Edward. You must not. You promised to behave."

Weak and trembling, the girl crept back to her room.

What should she do? What *could* she do? A few days ago she would have walked boldly down the stairs and confronted them. But with her own experience so fresh in her mind she could not. She recalled some of the things grandma had said. Some of her own thoughts came back to her. She felt her own guilt more keenly than ever. Queerly, she felt that she understood her mother as she had never understood her before. She felt a bond of sympathy with her—it was from her mother that she inherited evil desires. That her desires were evil there now could be no question. A voice within her cried exultingly: "You were right in your estimate of men and women. Grandma is all wrong. Grandma belongs to a past age. Your mother is a modern woman—so are you. Grandma's philosophy and beliefs are not for the women of to-day." She must do something—she *must.* She started toward the stairway determined to go down, but in the doorway of her room she hesitated. How could she face them? Sounds came from the living room. On a sudden impulse she slammed her room door. Then she stood trembling, listening.

Her mother called from the hall below.

She did not answer.

Her mother's voice came up from the foot of the stairs: "Is that you, Georgia?"

The girl opened the door noisily. "Did you call, Mother? I am dressing. I must have been in the bath when you came in. I'll be down in a few minutes."

"All right, dear—glad you're home."

The girl heard the front door open and shut.

Then her mother started up the stairs.

Fearfully, the daughter waited, half hiding herself in her closet as if searching for some article of clothing. Would her mother come to her room—would she dare?

Mrs. Paddock passed hurriedly on to her own room and shut the door.

The girl smiled grimly. "Oh, well," she said to herself, "I know exactly how she feels."

She looked at the photograph on her dresser and laughed. "Good old Jack."

Then in desperate haste she dressed.

When she was ready she knocked at her mother's door.

"You can't come in just now, Georgia," said Mrs. Paddock. "I'll be down presently."

The girl answered with a bitter smile. "Oh, all right, Mother. But I'm going out—have a date—so long—see you later—give my love to daddy."

She ran downstairs and out of the house.

Grandpa Paddock drove to his son's grocery store where he was told that the groceryman would not be in until evening. Leaving an order for groceries for which he would call later, the old gentleman went on to Jack Ellory's place of business. Jack chanced to be in the salesroom and, seeing him drive up, hurried out to the curb.

The young man, embarrassed and nervous, was stammering incoherent words of greeting when grandpa said anxiously: "There's something gone wrong with my car, Jack. Thought as long as I was in town I better find out about it or she might quit on me and make me walk most of the way home."

Jack felt the ground become steady under his feet. "How does she act, Mr. Paddock?"

"Acts all kinds of ways—like she had the heaves and stringhalt and spavin and mebby a touch of colic."

The automobile man laughed. "Run her into the shop, Mr. Paddock, and I'll have our veterinary look her over."

Leaving the car in the hands of the shop foreman grandpa and Jack retired to the private office, where the young man faced the old gentleman with a look of serious inquiry.

Grandpa smiled reassuringly.

"Well?" said Jack.

"I brought Georgia home this afternoon. She's all right."

Grandpa seated himself and the younger man dropped into a chair with a sigh of relief. "I certainly made an awful fool of myself, Mr. Paddock."

"I've made dozen of fools of myself, son," grandpa returned cheerfully, "it's easy."

"But it never happened with Georgia before, sir. You believe that, don't you?"

Grandpa nodded. "It was due to happen all right."

"Well, it has taught me a lesson. I'll never lose my head again."

"Didn't it teach you anything else, son?"

"Yes, sir, it did. But I guess I have learned my lesson too late."

Grandpa's keen old eyes twinkled. "Oh, I wouldn't be so sure of that, if I were you! There's only one thing harder to figure than a woman, and that's another woman."

Jack smiled ruefully. Then with a grim earnestness he said: "Most of the girls, these days, are all right to play around with but no man with any sense would marry one of them—I mean, no man with my ideas would take such a chance."

The old gentleman studied the young man's face with frank interest. "Just what are your ideas, Jack?"

"Well," said Jack slowly, "I was over there, you know, and tried to do my bit to make the world safe, and all that, by killing off as many of my fellow men as I could. But I've come to the conclusion that you can't make the world safe for anybody by turning it into a hell to start with. I'm no saint, Mr. Paddock, but after what I went through in France I don't believe that *any* country needs men to be killed for it as much as it needs men to live for it. And so I want to do my share of living for my country as I tried to do my share of drying for it."

"And that means . . .?" said grandpa.

"That means, as I understand it, Citizenship. It means taking my part in civic affairs right here in my home town, helping to make Westover a better place for everybody to live in. I want success in my business because my business is part of the great game. I want money—honest money, I mean—because I want the power to make myself felt. I want a home—every decent man does, I think. I mean an established home, not a one-night stand arrangement in an apartment house or hotel. I want children, and a place for them to grow into the right kind of men and women, and I want to help make the community the kind of community that will give the boys and girls a chance. I want grandchildren. Is that looking too far ahead, sir?"

"It's not so far ahead as it seems, son."

"Well, you can see that all means a wife—a mother, a real woman—not a sporting, feather-brained, fly-by-night, jazz-crazed, cocktail-drinking Jane that a man can take like he'd take a drink of moonshine, and forget all about it the next morning, except for the headache."

Grandpa nodded understandingly. "I suppose the average man wants something of almost any normally attractive woman, son, just because he is a man and she is a woman. But every man wants something of the woman he marries that he doesn't want from any of the others. He wants her to mother his children. I'm talking about decent men, Jack. I know you are decent or I wouldn't be talking to you like this. I'd be trying to run you out of the country."

The young man bowed his head.

"I guess there's no harm in my asking, Jack—doesn't Georgia come pretty close to filling the specifications for the sort of woman a man with your ideas would want?"

Jack Ellory raised his head and looked straight into the old gentleman's eyes. "She does, Mr. Paddock."

"That's *my* impression," murmured Georgia's grandfather.

"I have always felt that Georgia was different from other girls," the young man continued. "I'll admit I have been free with the others—but never with Georgia. Since I can remember, I have always liked her better and would rather be with her than any girl I ever knew, but I wasn't sure I wanted to ask her to marry me. Damn it all! I've always been afraid. You see, sir, all girls are pretty wise these days. They know life and—well. . . ."

"Do you mean, Jack, that you were afraid to trust Georgia?"

"I was afraid of the whole thing—of her—myself—and everybody. Georgia and I have both run with the same bunch, you know, and—well—while our crowd is not so bad as it might be, I'll not say that we would inspire much confidence. I can see now that the reason I never tried Georgia out was because I was afraid she would turn out like all the rest. Then came last Sunday, and I found that she was not like the others. And now it's too late—I have lost her."

Grandpa considered the matter for several minutes; then he said earnestly: "Georgia is not a girl who will marry a man just for fun, like so many appear to do. She'd never take you with the idea that if she got tired of you she could easy enough divorce you and get some one else."

"I know that is true, Mr. Paddock. That is, I know it *now.*"

"Hum! And now that you've settled your mind that you want her to help make your home, and mother your children, you're scared to death thinking that she's found *you* out and won't have you—is that it?"

"Georgia knows what men are, Mr. Paddock. She has had opportunities enough to find out. And even though she has never had reason to question my attitude toward her before, from now on, she'll lump me in with the rest."

Grandpa rose and crossed the room to look at a road map that hung on the wall. For some time he stood there, his back toward Jack, as if lost in the contemplation of state highways.

"'Tain't fair for me to tell nothing out of school, maybe," he said as he turned at last, "but us young men must stick together, Jack. The girls are bound to make fools of us any way we can fix it and I guess that justifies us in heading 'em off whenever we get a chance. So I'll just say—mind you I'm not telling anything—I'll just say from what *my* girl told me about her talk with *your* girl, you have no reason to worry *too* much."

Jack Ellory sprang to his feet. "Do you mean, sir—do you think I still have a chance?"

Grandpa Paddock answered earnestly: "I wish you were as sure of heaven as you are of Georgia's love."

Then, when the young man was calm enough to listen, he added: "But you've got to give her her head a little, son. Don't go rushing things like you were trying to sell her an automobile before some other live wire could beat you to it. She's all woman, Georgia is, and that means, if my seventy-odd years' experience counts for anything, that she'll exercise her right to make you suffer some for what she admits she's to blame for. When your suffering gets to the point where it hurts her worse than it does you, she'll forgive you for what she's done."

At that moment a boy came to say that Mr. Paddock's car was ready.

"What was the trouble?" Jack asked the foreman.

The mechanic grinned. "Not a thing."

"Now ain't that just like me?" said grandpa.

Jack looked at him with an understanding smile. "Yes, I'd say that was just exactly like you. Drop in again when you find anything you think needs attention."

They laughed together, and the shop foreman, without in the least understanding what it was all about, laughed with them.

Then the old gentleman, under Jack's watchful eye, backed his car carefully out of the shop. In the street he pulled up to the curb and stopped the engine to say casually: "I see by the papers that you are having a meeting of the Organized Charities to-night."

"Yes."

"Going to make the annual drive for money?"

"Yes, sir."

"Well, I never did much take to being driven," smiled grandpa, "so here's my check before you start."

The president of the Organized Charities thanked him for the generous contribution, adding: "If they would all come through like this it would save us a lot of work."

Grandpa looked at him thoughtfully. "You give considerable time to this sort of thing, don't you, Jack?"

"Yes, sir, between the Charities, the Boy Scouts, and three or four other welfare organizations, it takes something out of every day. But it all has to be done."

"You are not giving as much time to the Church as you used to a few years ago, are you?"

"No, Mr. Paddock, I am not. I give to the churches when they are raising money, because I have to. It would hurt my business if I didn't. And I try to make the business pay for it the same as I pay for advertising. I sold your church a car for the pastor the other day."

"Don't you ever go, any more, Jack?"

"No, sir, I won't go to church and pretend it means anything to me when it doesn't. My charity work is my religion. Whenever the Church functions in our community life—I mean, when it actually *does* some of the things the preachers are always talking about, when it takes hold of our problems and helps to care for our sick and needy—I am with it. Some one must do this charity work. If the Church won't we unregenerated outsiders must."

"Fair enough, son. But maybe if a bunch of live ones like you was to get together, you could make the Church 'function,' as you call it."

"Not a chance!" retorted Jack. "Things are moving too fast these days for anybody to accomplish anything with antediluvian, worn-out equipment. All the old carriage factories in the world, combined, couldn't make an automobile."

"That's right," agreed grandpa. "And automobiles and carriages were made for exactly the same purpose, too—to get people somewhere."

Jack laughed. "The automobile gets more people there and gets them there quicker, though. That's why the carriage works were scrapped or converted into automobile factories."

When grandpa was gone, Jack shut himself up in his private office. "What a wonderful old couple Grandpa and Grandma Paddock are," he thought. "When Georgia and I are grandparents. . ." He wondered if he dared to call her up.

He was reaching for the telephone when the instrument rang. It was Georgia calling him. She was at the club. He must come right away—she needed him.

"What's the matter?" he asked anxiously, for her voice sounded a little queer.

"I'll tell you when you get here," came the answer.

Jack caught up his hat and almost ran out of the building.

The girl was waiting for him, flushed and excited, on the veranda of the club house. How beautiful she was!

"Hello, old-timer," she cried as he ran up the steps. "I'll tell the world you didn't lose any time answering the call of the wild."

"Are you wild?" he asked, smiling—a little puzzled by her manner.

"I'll say I am—wild and rarin' to go."

He spoke seriously. "What's the trouble, Georgia?"

"No trouble at all." There was defiance in her voice. "I'm throwing a party, that's all. Harry Winton, the Burnes boys, Grace, Molly, and all the rest of the regular bunch. You are due to chaperon me. And believe me, boy, you're going to have your hands full. I got hold of Davie Bates and he's bringing us the hooch. I was afraid you might not have enough in your locker. Davie will be here any minute now. Nothing like having a groceryman papa with an understanding delivery boy, is there? What's the matter, old top?—you look funny."

"I'm afraid you'll have to count me out, Georgia."

"Count you out, nothing—where would I be without my little playmate?"

"But I have a meeting of the Organized Charities to-night. I can't cut that, you know."

"Aw, what's a charity meeting between friends—they'll get along without you. Don't kid yourself that you're so necessary, old dear—go get yourself a drink and you'll feel different. The bunch will be along any minute now."

"Georgia—I . . ."

"Yes, sir."

"I must tell you something, Georgia."

"You can't tell *me* anything, my boy; but if it will relieve your mind—shoot."

"Come, let' find a place where we can talk."

He led her to a secluded corner. "Have you forgiven me for what happened Sunday, Georgia?"

"Nothing happened, did it?"

"I love you, Georgia."

"My Gawd! And you haven't had the first drink yet!"

"Georgia, you must listen to me. I am serious. I love you."

"Of course you do, old dear. And I love you."

"Will you be my wife?"

"Your wife! Just like that! Don't make me laugh, boy. I'll get drunk with you, but I wouldn't marry anything that even looked like a man. Marriage is all out of date, old thing—didn't you know about that? It belonged to my grandmother's day. Marriage! Huh! I'll respect the dead and all that, but I won't stand having a funeral service read over me while I'm living. I'm yours if you want me, Jack dear—and I'm hoping you do, but don't ask me to be old-fashioned. I'm a free woman, I am, and so help me God, I'm going to *stay* that way. Now will you go and get us a shot of hooch? There's my sainted dad's delivery boy in his little old Ford, with the goods, right now."

CHAPTER XII.

TRAGEDY.

The meetings of the Organized Charities of Westover were held in one of the rooms in the City Hall. There were about thirty people—directors and workers, in the organization—present that evening. Because they were about to launch the annual drive for funds, and because the professional campaign director from Cleveland was on hand to take charge of their money-raising operations, the meeting was of more than usual importance. President Jack Ellory had personally urged each individual to be there. But when they were all assembled and the time set for the meeting had arrived, the president, himself, was not present.

Some of the company were church members, but with the exception of the treasurer, Banker Winton, the most active workers were not identified with any religious body. The Organized Charities did not represent the Church in any way. The organization represented Westover. The meetings were held without any kind of a religious note or suggestion and yet, the nature of the work was distinctively Christian in that it was taught by Jesus and, by Him, made an essential part of Christianity. The members of the board and the workers were not there as Christians, they were there as citizens. They were interested because they were intelligent enough to recognize the necessity of caring for the city's poor. It was not a sense of Christian but of civic duty which prompted them. They would have been surprised had any one thought of them as representing the Church. Many of them would have been indignant. Even those who were church members were not there in the name of their churches. They were there in the name of the city of Westover. And no one thought it strange that the Church, which exists for the sole purpose of teaching by preaching and by example the truths of Jesus, should have no part in this Christian work of ministering unto the city's sick and needy.

It was nearly an hour past the time for opening the meeting when the vice-president, urged by several members of the board, called the meeting to order.

The people were looking at their watches, whispering, wondering, and restlessly watching the door. There was a feeling of nervous tension in the room.

"I can't imagine," said the chairman, "what has delayed our president, Mr. Ellory. We all know how enthusiastic and faithful he is. Something very unusual must have occurred."

Mrs. Winton whispered to Mrs. Paddock: "What in the world do you suppose has happened?"

"I can't imagine," Laura returned.

"Where is Georgia, Laura?"

"I don't know. She left home about four o'clock—said she had a date."

The presiding officer rapped for silence.

The minutes of the previous meeting were read, the treasurer made his report, and some unfinished business was disposed of. Then Mr. Wilcox, the professional money raiser from Cleveland, was introduced.

"Mr. Wilcox," the chairman explained, "is to have entire charge of this campaign to secure funds for our city charities."

There was a round of applause and the company settled down to the important business of the evening.

But the expert charity worker had barely concluded his opening remarks, when he was interrupted by the hurried entrance of a motor-cycle policeman.

When the speaker paused and gazed toward the door every one in the room turned. A hush fell over the company as the man in uniform stood looking them over, evidently searching for some individual. Then the officer stepped forward and, with a motion of his hand, drew Banker Winton aside.

Mrs. Winton gasped, and Mrs. Paddock slipped a supporting arm around her.

With breathless interest the company watched while the policeman whispered to Mr. Winton. The banker caught the officer's arm as if to keep himself from falling.

Mrs. Winton screamed: "Harry—my boy, Harry!" and rushed to the two men who stood with bowed heads.

Mr. Winton, with an effort, mastered his emotion and supported his wife. The groceryman and his wife hurried to their friends. Others gathered round. The room was filled with whispers. White faces—frightened eyes—trembling lips.

Quickly, the awful word was passed: "Automobile accident—car went of the bluff curve a mile this side of Sundown Inn—young Winton killed. He was driving—no one else badly hurt—drunk! That's not a dangerous road. Speeding—drunk—wild party. Poor Mr. and Mrs. Winton. Everybody has been expecting it. Only child."

Tenderly they assisted the stricken parents to their automobile. Mrs. Paddock would go with them to their home. Joe would follow in the Paddock car.

And through it all, the groceryman's brain was hammering: "Georgia—Georgia—Georgia."

When the Winton's car pulled away, the groceryman drew the officer aside.

"Young Winton was drunk as usual," said the representative of the law. "There was a party—three cars. They had been at Tony's and were on their way to the Inn. Winton's car was last. They were speeding recklessly, and my partner and I were following them when it happened. We were on the lookout because we saw the bunch when they arrived at Tony's earlier in the evening. I didn't get the names of the others in the Winton car. My partner looked after that while I came to tell Mr. Winton."

"My—my—daughter?"

"She was with the party, Mr. Paddock, but not in the Winton car. She was ahead with Jack Ellory in his roadster."

The hour was late when the groceryman and his wife, after doing all they could for their stricken friends, left the Winton home.

As they drove down the silent street, Mrs. Paddock whispered: "Oh, Joe, I'm so frightened—Georgia. . . ."

Joe repeated what the officer had told him—their daughter was not hurt.

"But, Joe, she was in the party—the talk, it is terrible—the whole town will know. The newspapers! Poor Mary Winton! Can't you do something to keep Georgia's name out of it—can't it be hushed up? You must do something!"

As they turned into the driveway at their own home they looked for a light in the window of their daughter's room. There was no light.

The groceryman looked at his watch. "It's twenty minutes of two."

"She may be in bed," whispered Mrs. Paddock.

"If she were home she would be waiting for us," returned Joe.

They entered the silent house and Mrs. Paddock went up to the girl's room. She was not at home!

The mother returned to her husband in the living room and they looked at each other in frightened silence.

The groceryman paced up and down. Mrs. Paddock moved about wringing her hands.

"Can't we do something?" cried the distracted mother. "Call Sundown Inn—they will know her—ask for Jack Ellory."

The groceryman was about to act on her suggestion when they heard the front door open and close.

They waited—breathless.

Their daughter came and stood before them.

The girl's face was flushed, her eyes were bright and hard, she moved unsteadily, with an air of reckless abandonment. She was not at all the girl who had stood before them that morning of her dream. The groceryman moved closer to his wife. Father and mother and daughter!

With a mocking grin, and a playfulness which filled their hearts with ghastly fear, the girl said: "Oh, you spooners! Caught you in the very act, didn't I? Aren't you 'shamed? At your age—this time of night—I'm surprised—that's what I am—surprised!"

Too shocked to speak they could only gaze at her in horrified silence.

With exaggerated seriousness the girl continued: "Well, what you got to say for yourselves? What you looking at me like that for—I'm not a ghost. I'm flesh and blood girl, I am. Good flesh and blood, too—no spirit about me. Don't you know your darling daughter? What's wrong with you two, anyway?"

"Georgia—"gasped Mrs. Paddock. "What *is* the matter—what has happened to you?"

The groceryman, watching his daughter closely, did not speak.

"Matter?" returned Georgia. "Is anything the matter? Everything's lovely, far's I can see. Nothin' matter with me. You two 're havin' good time aren't you?" She laughed and walked unsteadily to a chair.

The mother uttered a low cry: "Oh Joe, Joe, she's *drunk!"*

The girl chuckled. "You should worry, Mother dear, you should worry!"

Then Mrs. Paddock arose to the occasion. In righteous indignation she stood over her daughter. "You dreadful girl! Have you no sense of decency—no shame? The idea of you, *my daughter,* brought up as you have been, in a Christian home, being in this disgusting condition."

The groceryman murmured warningly: "Go slow, Laura."

Georgia threw up her head and her eyes blazed quick defiance. "That'll be about enough from you, Mother dear—I've had all your lectures I'm going to stand for. I'm a free woman, I am. If daddy has anything to say, that's different. But before you preach to me about Christian homes and all that bunk, you'd better clean your own slate. That's what I mean. You know what I mean, too! A swell Christian you are! A swell mother, too, if you ask me!"

Mrs. Paddock, white with rage, shame and fear, dropped into the nearest chair.

The groceryman spoke: "Georgia—"

"All right, Daddy."

She seemed steadied a little, and he asked: "Have you heard what happened to-night?"

"I know what happened to me when I came home from the farm this afternoon." She faced her mother again.

Mrs. Paddock cried out: "Please, please, Georgia!"

The groceryman looked from his daughter to his wife, and back to his daughter, wonderingly.

"I mean about Harry Winton, Georgia. Do you know about him?"

The girl answered recklessly: "He was good and drunk, if that's what you mean. He and the Burnes boys were certainly lit up when we all left Tony's for Sundown Inn. That's the last I saw of Harry or any of the crowd. You see, Jack and I cut the bunch before we got to the Inn, and beat it into the country all by our lonesomes."

Mrs. Paddock exclaimed: "You went into the country, alone with Jack Ellory—at this time of the night—in your condition?"

"Well, what of it?" flamed Georgia. "If you are raising a moral question—well—I wouldn't if I were you. I don't mind telling you, though, that Jack asked me to marry him."

"And you—you accepted him?" gasped the mother.

"Accepted him—me? Well hardly—not in the way you mean," sneered the girl. "Don't make me laugh, Mother dear. I told the dear boy I'd get drunk with him."

Mrs. Paddock hid her face in her hands. The groceryman sat with bowed head.

Watching the effect of her words with a ghastly smile, the girl continued: "Think I'd marry any man after what I know about the sacred ties of matrimony? Not much! Marriage—love—and all that—seems to have worked all right in grandma's time. Perhaps it was, like grandma says, because they had religion to help. Maybe if we had a little religion we could make the grade, too. I don't know how anybody would go about getting religion these days, though. We're advanced—we are. We got improvements, and culture, and intellectuality, and art, haven't we, Mother dear? *You* know. Marriage for keeps is the bunk—it's—it's obsolete. That's good word 'obsolete'! Love 'em hard and leave 'em quick—that's down-to-date idea. Take your lovin' where you find it, but don't take it too seriously. That's my motto! We women have won our freedom—just as free as the men—aren't we, Mother dear? You know what I mean. Do you know what I mean, Daddy? Sometimes I think you do, and then again I think you don't. You're such an old-fashioned groceryman! Mother and I—we are modern—we know—bet your life we. . ."

The groceryman interrupted her: "Georgia, Harry Winton is dead."

She gazed at her father stupidly. "What's that you say? Harry dead?"

"He was killed in an automobile accident on the road to Sundown Inn."

As the girl grasped the fact, her eyes grew big with horror. "Dead!" she whispered hoarsely. "Jack tried to persuade him he wasn't fit to drive. Always was a reckless fool. He had it coming. Good boy at heart—just couldn't carry his liquor—dead!"

Suddenly she slumped down in her chair, crying, moaning, her body shaken with fear and grief.

They half carried the girl upstairs to her room.

Under the stress of the moment she was like a child and clung piteously to her father, who tried to soothe her.

"Oh, Daddy, Daddy—I'm so sorry—poor Harry—there wasn't a mean thing about him—as kindhearted a boy as ever lived. Oh, God, what a mess!"

Mrs. Paddock, kneeling, removed the girl's shoes. Then motioning Joe to leave them, she said: "Come, dear, let mother help you to undress."

At the head of the stairs the groceryman hesitated. It was no use to go to his own room—he felt he would never sleep again. He wanted to be near his daughter. He felt that she relied on him. But he was so helpless. He wanted to go back to her, but it was her mother's place. After she was in bed he would go to her.

He heard the girl crying. Then his wife's voice: "Come, Georgia, let me help you—you must get to bed."

"Oh, Mother, I can't believe it! Poor Harry—it isn't true—tell me it isn't true?"

Mrs. Paddock, at her daughter's collapse, seemed to have recovered her usual air of superiority. The groceryman heard her say sternly: "I certainly hope this will be a lesson to you and your crowd of hoodlums, Georgia. You must tell me—I must know—as your mother I have a right to know. You and Jack Ellory to-night—you say you went into the country with him—where did you do—what. . . ."

At the name of Jack Ellory the girl sprang to her feet and pushed her mother away. In a voice charged with scorn and fury she cried: "It's none of your business where Jack and I went or what happened. Don't you ever dare to mention his name to me again. He's too good—too-fine—too big—for you to understand if I were to try to tell you."

The groceryman grasped the stair rail for support. He suddenly felt weak and sick.

His wife was pleading: "Please don't, Georgia—I—I—am your mother, dear."

"You've said it," retorted the girl, with bitter cruelty. "You are my mother! Next you'll be reminding me that you are daddy's wife. Why don't you rub it in good while you're at it?"

Mrs. Paddock attempted to carry it off with a show of dignity, but her voice faltered: "I—I—hope you know what you are trying to say—I'm sure I don't."

"Oh, you don't! Well, in plain words, then, I saw you in the arms of your beloved Edward Astell this afternoon when you and he thought you were alone in the house."

Mrs. Paddock, with broken, frightened words, pleaded for mercy. Crushed with shame, terror-stricken, she begged the girl to stop.

But the daughter went on pitilessly while the groceryman heard every word.

"So you *do* understand what I'm talking about, after all, do you? Everybody in Westover, except poor daddy, knows how you have been chasing that low-down beast. You've told me many times that you had no desire to be a good sport. Well, I'll say you're not—you're a rotten cheap sport. You couldn't even pick out a regular man. If you had to have some one, besides daddy, why in God's name couldn't you fix on something better than that bloated, blear-eyed, flabby toad? You know, as everybody knows, the kind of women *he* gets drunk with! Of course you'd say we must forgive his rottenness because he's such a genius—the intellectual and artistic leader of Westover—the darling of your culture clubs. You are one of his women, I suppose, because you can't resist the charm of his marvelous mentality—because he is so understanding—so kind and thoughtful and attentive in all the little refinements that superior, sensitive souls like you need. And you have the nerve to pretend that you are horrified because I go for a ride with Jack Ellory! Well, you don't need to worry about me! Being only a girl, I haven't the protection that a respectable married woman like you enjoys, I know, but I can take care of myself just the same. You feel terribly sorry for Mr. and Mrs. Winton, don't you? And you'd like to make me feel that I am to blame for Harry's death because it was my party. Well, I am to blame. It was my liquor that made him drunk. But I'll tell you this—if I had actually killed him I wouldn't change places with you. You've killed something in daddy, and you've killed something in me, that's more than the death that came to Harry Winton!"

The groceryman never knew how he got downstairs and into the living room. He saw the familiar objects—the furniture— the books—the pictures—as in a dream. All the associations—the home memories of his years—crowded in upon him. The piano—his wife's music—that painting—her art. He was not conscious of having heard his wife leave Georgia's room, but he knew that she was in her own chamber. He could see her as clearly as if he were with her—she was frightened—she was hoping that he had not heard; she wanted to call him, but she dared not; she was wondering if he *had* heard, what he would do.

What should he do? Should he go to his wife and tell her that he had heard? Should he go to his daughter and try to comfort her? If he confronted his wife with what he knew, what would follow? Very clearly, the groceryman saw the ruin of his home—the home which they had built together through the years. He saw the separation—the scandal—the newspapers—their friends—the effect on Georgia's future. His daughter's future! The groceryman caught at that thought and held fast to it. For Georgia's sake, he must go carefully. He must think the thing out. He must consider every point—every move. If it were not for Georgia he could decide instantly. He loved his wife, but if she was not happy in his love, why—then. . . But he must do what was best for Georgia.

He was to blame, he supposed. He had really been too engrossed in his work of providing for his wife and daughter. He had been too ambitious for them. Perhaps if he had tried to keep pace with Laura's interests—if he had shared her ambitions—given more time to music, art, literature, the social life. She had found something in that fellow Astell which he, the commonplace groceryman, could not give. If it were not for Georgia. . . .

Suddenly it came to him that there was one thing he *must* do. No matter what he did after that, there was one thing which he must do first. He must kill Astell. Custom, tradition, his honor, demanded that. It would not be hard. He did not even think of it as murder. It was just one of those things that must be done. He did not particularly want to kill Astell, but he owed it to his own manhood. If he was ever to look men in the face again he must destroy this creature who had brought shame upon him. It was a duty he owed, not only to himself but to his friends—to other fathers and daughters—to other homes. The groceryman had always tried to do the things which he felt were his duty, like helping the Booster Club, acting on the Organized Charities Boards, going to church. He would kill Astell, then he would decide what was best to do next.

His revolver was in his dresser upstairs in his room. It was in the right-hand corner of the middle drawer. Deliberately he walked to the stairway. It was a relief to have something definite to do. But with his foot on the lower step he stopped. Georgia! To kill Astell would be to drag the whole shameful story into the light. His daughter would be branded as the daughter of a bad woman, and a murderer. But to kill a creature like Astell would not be murder! Georgia—his daughter—his pal—his little girl! He must go slow. He must think this thing out further. He must make no mistakes.

Back in the living room he sank into a chair. His head dropped forward—his eyes were fixed on a figure in the carpet. He tried to think. God, how tired he was! He must think. His thoughts went round and round in a circle, coming back always to what was best for Georgia.

Wearily, at last, he raised his eyes to that picture of Jesus which hung above the radio. He did not consciously look at the picture. But when his glance chanced to fall upon it he remembered that it was a wedding present from his parents. All his married life that picture had hung there in the living room. He remembered how the night Georgia was born he had sat before it as he was sitting now—waiting—waiting—and when their boy was born—and when he died. Because it seemed to afford him relief from the maddening tangle of his thoughts, he studied the pictured face. He wondered, if Jesus could speak, what would He advise? What nonsense—Jesus had never had a daughter like Georgia—Jesus had never had a wife to—to. . . . But Jesus was the wisest man the world had ever known. His wisdom was not of men. His teaching was of God.

And then a strange thing happened. As he gazed at the pictured countenance of the Master the groceryman suddenly realized that the face was the face of some one he knew. That feeling of calm, inner strength, the air of gentle authority, the expression of sympathy and understanding, those sorrow-shadowed eyes, they were real, living, familiar, in the flesh. It ceased to be the pictured face of a teacher who lived in the ages of the past. It was the face of a friend—an associate who was living now—a friend who was in touch with modern life as Jesus had been a part of the life in Galilee—one who knew all about *him,* the groceryman, and his troubles. Those eyes! Why—why—of course—how stupid not to have seen it long ago—John Saxton!

The groceryman understood now that it was his familiarity with this picture of Jesus that had made him feel that he had known Dan Matthews' confidential agent somewhere. It was strange that he had not thought of Saxton before. Saxton would know what he must do. So many times the groceryman had felt that Saxton understood and was waiting to help him. Saxton would help him now.

Very quietly the groceryman left the house.

CHAPTER XIII.

GETTING TOGETHER.

It cannot be said that the groceryman had definitely determined to go to John Saxton at that hour of the night. He had acted on the thought because he had reached a point where he must do *something* or go mad. The physical movement, to a degree, calmed his overexcited mind. The quiet night, the empty street which echoed this footsteps, the silent houses with here and there a lonesome light, soothed him. He wondered about the people sleeping in those dark houses. How many of them were hiding troubles and shame?

By the time he had reached State Street in the business district, the groceryman had decided that to call for Saxton at that unusual hour would not be wise. The night clerk at the hotel would be sure to comment. It might cause talk and, above all, Georgia's father must avoid talk—he must shun even the appearance of anything unusual. But what should he do? He could not bear the thought of returning home. He was not wanted. To be away from that house, in which he now felt himself a stranger, was a necessity.

In this mood he came to his grocery store with a feeling of relief. He belonged here. Here was his place. Here were the things about which he knew—about which he was sure. With a key, which he always carried, he unlocked the door and entered. The shelves of brightly labeled cans and bottles and boxes, the counters and cases and crates and barrels, in the soft glow of the night lights seemed to be waiting for him. The familiar smell of coffee and tea and spices was friendly greeting. The little office, with its varnished pine and window glass partition, made him welcome. His golden oak desk caused him to feel at home. Wearily he dropped into the hospitable arms of his golden oak chair.

And now, again, his thoughts went round the circle—Harry Winton's death—his daughter's condition, as one who had abandoned every pretense of decency—the fact that she had furnished the liquor for the party—her shocking expressions of her attitude toward marriage—her terrible arraignment of her mother—his daughter's relation to Jack Ellory—his wife's relation to

Astell. What—*what* should he do about Georgia and Jack? What should he do about his wife and Astell?

The groceryman was aroused from his thoughts by a sound at the rear door of the store. Some one was entering. He listened—sitting very still.

The intruder moved back of the counters toward one of the cash registers.

There was always some money in the till at the close of the day's business—that which was taken in after banking hours, and the change that would be needed for the early morning trade. He distinctly heard the prowler open the till.

Then the thief crossed the room toward the cash register on the other side. The groceryman slipped silently from his chair and, crouching low below the glass upper part of the partition, crept to the door of the office and peered out. Even in the dim night light he recognized Davie Bates.

The delivery boy was making his way back toward the rear door when the groceryman suddenly stepped from the office and confronted him.

The lad uttered a little cry of dismay.

"Well, Davie?"

The boy's manner changed to sullen defiance. "What are you doing here at this time of night?" he demanded. "You were laying for me, were you? Well, you can't take me." He drew a revolver from his pocket and covered his employer. "You make a move to touch me and I'll shoot—sure as hell I will."

Under normal conditions, the groceryman would have felt it his duty to turn the delivery boy over to the law. But that night, after his own shocking experiences, stealing seemed a very little thing. He rather welcomed the incident as a relief from the mental and emotional strain which had so nearly exhausted him. As for Davie's gun and the threat, which the boy, in his desperate state of mind might easily carry out, Joe was indifferent. He even smiled—a tired smile which puzzled the delivery boy.

"Would you really shoot me, Davie?"

"I will if you force me to. If you was to turn me over to the police, mother would know, and she'd die sure. I'd just as soon be hung for shooting you as to go to the pen knowing that I'd killed my mother, when I was only trying to help her." He started to back away. "I'm going now. Don't you make a move till I'm out of that door."

"Where are you going, Davie?"

Surprised at the groceryman's kindly tone, the boy stopped. Where *was* he going?

"You can't get very far, you know," continued Joe. "I could call the police and they would be after you before you could go a block. Perhaps you better kill me before you leave. But you must manage to do it without making a noise."

He was only a boy, and his voice trembled as he said: "I don't want to hurt you, Mr. Paddock. You've been mighty good to me. What did you have to go and show up here to-night like this for, anyway?"

"I know just how you feel about the shooting, Davie," remarked the groceryman sympathetically. "I thought, this evening, that I would have to kill a man. I didn't want to, but it seemed the only thing for me to do. Then I thought of something else. I didn't want my daughter to have a murderer for a father. You don't want your mother to have a murderer for a son. So you see, killing is not the way out for either of us. On the other hand, if you go and leave me free, you will probably run away and hide, and that would be almost as hard on your mother as shooting me."

The delivery boy groaned. "Oh, Christ! If you had only stayed away from here everything would have been all right."

"As for that," returned the groceryman, "I came here rather unexpectedly to my self. I certainly did not expect to meet you."

"You didn't?"

"I give you my word, Davie, I never thought of such a thing. But now that we are both here, suppose we go into the office where we can sit down and talk it over. Maybe we can find the best way out for both of us."

"Go into your office, where you can call the police? You can't put that over on me!"

"You have your gun, Davie. I am unarmed. If I try to phone you can stop me."

The groceryman turned and led the way to the office. The delivery boy followed.

Standing in the doorway with his weapon ready, the boy watched every move as his employer seated himself in his desk chair.

"Sit down, Davie, you look tired. I'm about all in myself."

As if struck by a sudden thought, the delivery boy stepped into the little room. "Look here, Mr. Paddock," he said with quick excitement, "you ain't going to have me arrested. You ain't even going to fire me. You ain't going to do nothing about this at all. Because if you *do,* I'll tell how I've been using your delivery car to peddle bootleg liquor, to a lot of your best store customers. I guess they wouldn't stay your customers long, if what I can tell was to come out in the papers."

The groceryman was interested. "You have been delivering bootleg liquor to my customers, Davie?"

"I'll say I have. And I've supplied a lot of people who are not your customers, too. It's easy—with the delivery car—just as if I was taking in groceries. You do anything to me and I'll give the names and everything. I'll show up some of these fine Westover swells! Church members, too, a lot of them, and most of them your friends. And that ain't all. I'll tell how I delivered liquor to your own daughter, at the club, this very afternoon."

"So *you* furnished the liquor for my daughter's party this evening." The groceryman's tone was still kindly.

The delivery boy seemed to feel that he was not making the impression he desired. "You can bet I did," he returned. "I know the crowd she runs with, too—a fine bunch they are! And I can tell some things about married men, with women they have no right to be with, and married women, with men who ain't their husbands that I've seen at the places where I've gone with booze. Sure as hell, I'll tell it all if you do anything to me. And—and there's your wife. I saw her at Astell's house the last time I was there. They didn't know I saw them, but I did—they have been chasing around together a lot."

"I have no doubt, Davie, that you could tell a great many things that people would not care to have known," said the groceryman calmly.

"You're dead right I can," returned the boy, "and that's why you ain't going to do anything to me."

The groceryman carefully thought over the situation, then he said: "As long as you already know so much about my daughter and my wife, Davie, I may as well tell you, that was what brought me down here to-night."

"How's that?"

"Why, I learned to-night how bad things were in my home. I was walking around, trying to think things out, you know, when I found myself near the store. I came in here to be alone so I could find out what was best for me to do. It was Astell that I was going to kill, when I thought of my daughter Georgia, and saw that wasn't the way out."

The delivery boy dropped into a chair. He sat there, a huddled heap, looking out at the groceryman from under his wrinkled brows. "Honest to God, Mr. Paddock, I'm sorry for you. I—I'd do anything to help you, if there was anything I could do."

"Thank you, Davie. It was like this: First Harry Winton, the son of my oldest and dearest friend, was killed. The liquor you sold my daughter did it. Then my girl came home drunk. And then I learned about my wife and Astell. It is all worked in together—don't you see, Davie?"

The groceryman leaned forward in his golden oak chair and buried his face in his hands.

The delivery boy slipped his revolver into his pocket. "Please, Mr. Paddock, don't let it get you down. Buck up, can't you? I'm not carin' much about Harry Winton but I feel like hell about Miss Georgia—yes, and Mrs. Paddock, too—because they're yours and you've been almighty good to me. Oh, Christ! I wish there was something I could do to help you!"

"It's a help, Davie, just to have some one to talk to about it. I can talk to you because you know."

"I hated to come here to-night, Mr. Paddock. You are the last man in the world I wanted to steal from—after all you've done for me. But you see, sir, it was my only chance. I just *had* to have the money for father and mother and the kids. And me having the key to the back door made it easy. I figured on paying it all back, soon as I could. Honest to God I did!"

"I understand, Davie."

The delivery boy continued desperately: "I hate the bootlegging, too. I don't guess there is anything meaner than that on earth. But, my God, sir, I tell you I just *had* to do something. When I heard mother praying for the Church and the ministers who wasn't turning a finger to help us—and a-thanking God for everything—and her a-going to die in that dirty hole if somebody didn't do something—I just couldn't stand it any longer. I tell you, I just couldn't stand it."

"I don't blame you, Davie. I can see just how it all happened."

"The groceries you've been giving us helped a lot," the boy went on. "But I figured if I could get hold of enough money to move mother and the children into the country somewhere, or anywhere out of Shack Town, and buy a hospital operation for father, we could pull through. Then I would quit peddling booze and pay back what I'd took from you. You see, if mother could get well and father could get fixed up so he could work again, we wouldn't ask nothing from nobody. We're not dead beats, nor lazy, nor nothing like that, Mr. Paddock."

The groceryman was thinking. His mind no longer went round and round that deadening circle. He recalled some of the things Saxton had said at that dinner. He thought of Saxton's resemblance to that picture of Jesus, and remembered the Master's words about "the least of these." He looked at Davie. Surely the delivery boy was one of those whom Jesus had in mind. And then, strangely, he saw Saxton and Jesus and Davie all as one, and felt that somehow in their oneness was salvation from that which had fallen upon his home and loved ones. "Davie," he said, "I am beginning to see deeper into all this trouble—your trouble and mine. You and I must help each other."

At the groceryman's words a light broke over the delivery boy's face. It was a good face, sensitive, intelligent. He straightened up in his chair. In spite of his half-starved body he seemed a man. It was as if his troubles had aged him by forcing him to think beyond his years, and his employer's kindness had brought his spirit into the light.

The groceryman continued: "It begins to look as though our troubles all led back to the same source. Perhaps if we get together we can work it out."

"Yes, sir," said the delivery boy, with eager readiness.

"Let's begin at the beginning, Davie. Where do you begin?"

The boy answered promptly: "When father got hurt. He was working on the church, you know. Before that, we were all right. We didn't live in Shack

Town. We had a good home, and I went to school. We all went to church and Sunday school, too."

The groceryman said slowly: "There was a time when Harry Winton and Jack Ellory and Georgia and their friends all went to Sunday school and church. Then as they grew up they lost interest in religion. The Church couldn't seem to hold them. Go on, Davie, what next?"

"Well, after father was hurt and couldn't work, I had to quit school and get a job. Mother and I kept things going but we had to give up our home and move to Shack Town. Then mother got sick and there wasn't any one but me. And then I—I had to take to bootlegging."

"Yes," said the groceryman. "And when the Church didn't seem able to do anything for Georgia and Harry and Jack, they found other interests that were closely related to what you were forced to do. Your father got hurt working on the church. That much is clear. My daughter got hurt by the Church, too, but just how is not so clear. Something must have happened to turn her against the Church, and because of *that* she turned to other things. Davie, did the Church ever help your family in any way?"

"No, nor any one else in Shack Town. When we couldn't pay church dues any more, and couldn't go, they dropped us."

"My daughter hasn't been going to church for a long time, but the church hasn't dropped *her.* Did the Organized Charities ever do anything for you?"

"No, sir, the Charities never did anything for us because I was working, you see. And anyway, if we was to starve to death we couldn't ask nothing from the city. The professional charity workers the city hires, don't care a damn about us. They come snooping into our homes asking all sorts of questions that ain't none of their business, like we was a lot of mangy dogs in the city pound 'stead of human beings just as good as they are. Of course there are lots of folks in Shack Town who do get help from the Charities and it is a good thing that the city does what the Church don't but generally those that need help the worst don't get it because they've got some pride left, even if they *are* down on their luck. The ones that get the most from the Organized Charities are the ones that make a business of working them. I tell you, Mr. Paddock, it's the help that is backed by the love, that the preachers are always talking about, that people like my father and mother need."

"You believe in Christianity, don't you, Davie?"

The delivery boy answered doubtfully: "I guess so—father and mother still hold to the Church."

"And yet you tried to help them by bootlegging and stealing. How about that, Davie?"

"Father and mother don't know nothing about that—that was just me. It would kill mother sure if she was ever to know. You see, I planned that when

I'd got enough I'd tell them that it came from the Church. That would make mother so happy she would be sure to get well. She would think God sent the money in answer to her prayers—so it would be all right."

"Tell me more about this bootlegging, Davie."

"Well, it was like this: I knew a bootlegger—one of the big ones—that is, I knew who he was. I went to him and told him how I needed the money and how easy it would be for me to deliver his stuff the same time I was delivering groceries for you. But there wasn't much in it for me. By the time the boss pays all he has to put up to the police and prohibition agents and others, there ain't so much left for delivering. The boss has to have a profit, of course, or he wouldn't be in the business. At the rate I was going it would take too long to get the money I had to have, so I—I—came here to-night. As God is my judge, Mr. Paddock, I don't want to be a bootlegger and a thief. But what could I do—with mother praying for help every night, and no help coming? It ain't fair—I mean mother praying for God to bless the preachers in their work of saving souls, while I got to peddle booze to church members and steal from you because the Church is letting mother die. And then they all wonder why fellows like me ain't Christians! You don't believe I wanted to do what I've done, do you, Mr. Paddock?"

"No, Davie, I don't believe you wanted to do it. I don't believe my girl really wanted to get drunk and do some of the things she has done. I don't believe my wife really wanted to ruin our home, and being shame on our daughter. I think, Davie, we are getting at the real cause of your trouble and of mine."

"What do you think it is?"

"Well, we know that you became a bootlegger and a thief because the Church did nothing to help your father and mother—as Jesus certainly meant that Christians should help people. I can't believe that Jesus would force a boy like you to answer your mother's prayer as you have been trying to answer it."

"That's the gospel truth about the Church and me, sir. But what has that got to do with your folks?"

"Why, you see, Davie, my wife, my daughter, the Winton's, all of us, are in trouble because the Church has lost its power to help us with a real religion. People loved Jesus and were influenced by His teaching because of what he was and did to help those who needed help. If the Church to-day was like Jesus people would love it and be influenced by its teaching. The Church is to blame for *your* trouble because it is not like Jesus—because it is not doing as Jesus did—because it is not Christian. And because it is not Christian itself, it has no influence over people—it has no power to make Christian character—it is not helping people like Harry Winton and my daughter and the rest of us to live right. You hate the Church and church people, don't you Davie?"

"You would, too, if you were in my fix."

"Yes, and my daughter despises the Church. Well—if the Church was helping people like your father and mother, boys like you would love it, and so would people like my daughter. It would help us all, because if the Church actually did what Jesus meant it should do, Christianity would be something real and vital to us, and not just empty form and ceremony and words that mean nothing."

"I tell you, Mr. Paddock, all the folks in Shack Town hate the Church. There is a man talks 'most every night down in our part of the city—he's an atheist and anarchist and all that—you ought to hear him go for the churches and preachers and them that's supposed to be Christian, and you ought to hear the people cheer what he says. He says the time is coming, sure, when all us poor people in Westover and all over the country will rise up and take the property away from the churches and the rich members, and that we'll run the government to suit ourselves, just like they've done in Russia. He says Jesus, Himself, wouldn't stand for no Shack Town in Westover. Does anybody have any use for the Church, sir? I mean, except the preachers who make their livin' that way, and people that belong because it makes them respectable, and folks like my mother, who are just naturally so good they can't help it?"

The groceryman smiled. "I am an officer in the church where your father and mother were members, Davie."

"Oh, gosh, I forgot!" exclaimed the delivery boy. "But you are a sure enough Christian, sir, or you wouldn't have helped us like you have, and you wouldn't be talking to me here to-night like you are. Yes, sir, you're a Christian all right. But if you're a *Christian* what are you a member of the *Church* for? Oh, hell, I don't know what's the matter! I can't help believing in religion because of mother and father and you. But I can't believe in the Church that mother prays for and you belong to. There must be something wrong somewhere!"

"You are right, Davie, there *is* something wrong. And somebody, somehow, must do something about it. You and I are only two out of millions—think of it, Davie—millions of people in trouble just as bad as ours, and nobody seems to know the real reason for it all or what to do about it! It is a big job, Davie, and I don't know how it is going to be done. But one thing is sure—you and I must stick together and help each other. Will you let me help you Davie? If I were to offer your father and mother help, in the name of Jesus and Christianity, they would accept it, wouldn't they?"

"I should say they would! Why wouldn't they? But I can't do anything to help you, Mr. Paddock."

"You *have* done a lot for me, to-night, Davie. And you are going to help me by letting me help you. That sounds funny but it is true. It is like the saying of Jesus that a man can save his life only by losing it."

"I think I understand, sir."

"All right. Then the first thing for us to do is to take care of your folks. I'm going to give you the money. By the way, you better put what you have there back where you got it, so that no one will know what happened here to-night."

With a choking sob, the delivery boy slipped out of the office and the groceryman heard him again at the cash registers.

When Davie returned his employer said: "And that's that! Now I'll tell you how we'll manage. You come to work in the morning as usual—just as if nothing had happened, see? Sometime during the forenoon I'll slip you the money. We'll get some one to take your place for a little while, so you'll have time to fix things up for your folks. Give your bootlegger boss notice that you have quit, so he can notify his customers."

I know a boy that can take my place delivering for you, Mr. Paddock. He's a good kid, too, and needs the job.

"Fine, Davie, bring him along when you come to work so you can teach him the ropes. Then you and I will run out to the farm and see my father and mother. I am sure they will know of a little place somewhere in that neighborhood that you can rent, and then you will move your mother and the children. In the meantime, I'll be finding out about doctors and a hospital for your father. There—there—Davie boy, don't cry like that—everything is going to be all right for us both—now that you and I have really got together."

The sky was just beginning to grow light in the east when the delivery boy crept, by way of the rear door, into his home in Shack Town.

He was stealing quietly to his cot when his mother called: "What are you doing, Davie? Is there anything the matter?"

"No, Mother, I was only getting myself a drink of water. Everything is all right. Can I do anything for you?"

"No dear, go to sleep. I'm sure that I shall be better in the morning.

The groceryman stole quietly into his home and went softly upstairs.

At the half-open door of his daughter's room he paused to listen. All was still.

He was preparing for bed when his wife spoke: "What in the world have you been sitting up all night for, Joe? It must be nearly morning. Is Georgia all right?"

The groceryman knew by her voice that she was frightened—wondering if he knew. "Georgia is sound asleep," he said.

"Oh, Joe—I—I—what in the world are we going to do? What *are* we coming to?"

"Don't worry, Laura. Everything is going to be all right."

Mrs. Paddock gave a sigh of relief. From her husband's matter-of-fact tone she was sure that he had not heard their daughter's terrible arraignment. When the groceryman slipped into his bed without coming to kiss her good night she thought it was because he was so preoccupied with Georgia's affair. She missed the customary little token of his love, but was rather glad, on the whole, that he had omitted it.

CHAPTER XIV.

NEW VALUES.

When the groceryman awoke the next morning his first thought was that it was strange he had slept. He had felt that he would never sleep or rest again. His next thought was that he must be careful. His wife and daughter must not know that he knew about Astell. He must manage, somehow, to hold things as they were until he could find a way to better the situation. If Laura and Georgia knew that he had heard the girl's arraignment of her mother, then he would be forced to make a decision—to act. He must not decide now—he must make no more until he could do so with a feeling of certainty that it was the best possible move to make. His talk with the delivery boy had helped him. It had shown him a light. But the light was still in the distance. He still was uncertain as to just what he should do about Laura. Until he could be sure he must do nothing.

Joe Paddock was not a great man. There was nothing heroic or unusual or superior about him. He was just an ordinary, everyday sort of person.

And so, in common with most of us, when given time to think, the groceryman wanted to do the right thing. The difficulty was to know the right thing to do.

Rising, he set about making himself ready for the day. He moved quietly, for his wife seemed to be asleep. Once he crept softly to the side of her bed to stand for a moment looking down at her and suddenly a wave of hatred for the other man swept over him. He felt weak and sick. To hold to his plan and for a time, at least, to do nothing, seemed literally impossible. All that he had loved most in life—all that he had worked for—all that he had dreamed, and hoped! His wife's love, his home, his daughter's happiness, his honor! How could he endure it in silence and go about as if nothing had happened? The horrid truth itself was forcing him to cry out that he knew. To kill Astell was a necessity. There was nothing that he could plan or do until he had done that one thing which was his right. After he had done that, then whatever followed would not matter.

But even as he turned away from the bed he seemed to hear Davie saying:

"Please, Mr. Paddock, don't let it get you down. Buck up, can't you? Oh, Christ! I wish there was something I could do to help you!"

Calmly he finished dressing. His hands were steady. He would see Saxton the first possible moment. But before he could do even that he would help Davie to get started. And he must do what he could for the Wintons. Davie's trouble and the Winton's grief would keep his mind from Astell, and Saxton would tell him what to do.

Then he was conscious that his wife was watching him. He felt her wondering, fearing, asking herself: "Does he know? What will he do?"

Mrs. Paddock was awake before her husband. When he stood beside her bed she was pretending to be asleep because she was afraid. She was dreading the moment when she must face him. What if he had heard Georgia's arraignment? If he chose, all her world would go to smash. She knew that she would find no refuge in Astell. And Georgia—what would become of her?

It was strange but at that moment Mrs. Paddock loved her husband with something of the love she had felt for him during those first happy years of their married life. Almost she hoped that he *did* know. She wanted to cry out—to tell him, to assure him of her love—to ask him for the sake of their love and for their daughter's sake to help her back to the realities of her wifehood and motherhood. Would he never finish arranging his tie? She had never known him to be so particular before.

"Good morning, dear," said the groceryman, in his usual calm, matter-of-fact tone. "The first bell rang ten minutes ago—I'll run on down and look at the paper."

The door closed behind him. He did not know—he did not know! Would Georgia tell? No, she decided, if the girl had wanted to do that she would have told long before last night. Georgia had said those terrible things last night because she had been beside herself with drink and the shock of Harry Winton's death. Poor Mary Winton—she must go to her the first thing after breakfast. But first, without another moment's loss of time, she must see her daughter. They must arrive at some sort of an understanding before the girl met her father.

Georgia did not come down to breakfast.

Mrs. Paddock said that the girl was sleeping.

The groceryman and his wife ate in silence save for an occasional word or two. They tried to appear natural—as if nothing had happened.

When they left the table Mrs. Paddock set out at once for the Winton home.

The groceryman went upstairs and stood at the door of his daughter's room.

He listened but could hear no sound.

He knocked gently.

There was no response.

Quietly he turned the knob and opened the door an inch or two.

With his lips to the opening he called softly:

"It is daddy, Georgia—may I come in?"

There was no answer.

He opened the door wider.

She was lying very still.

He entered, and tiptoed across the room.

She did not move.

He knelt beside the bed.

Two arms went round his neck and he held her close.

"Oh, Daddy, Daddy, what a mess," she sobbed.

He comforted her as he had comforted her so many times through all her childhood years.

But the daughter was not so easily deceived as her mother. She knew that her father knew, and she understood why he was pretending ignorance. She realized that for her sake he was playing a game to protect her mother.

And the groceryman saw that his daughter understood. He saw, too, that he could trust her to play the game with him.

There was no danger, now, that the groceryman would kill Astell.

Westover was shocked at the death of Harry Winton. Many who knew the banker's son shook their heads sadly and murmured they were not surprised. But they were depressed by the tragedy, just the same. The Winton family had been identified with Westover from pioneer days. Members of the most influential church, active in civic affairs, the leading banker—in a way, the Wintons were Westover. There had never been the least shadow of a cloud over Henry Winton's career—never a hint of scandal—never a suggestion of reproach. The community was sincere in its sympathy for the grief-stricken parents. The newspapers softened the account of the tragedy as much as possible. The ministerial association published resolutions boldly charging the officers of the law with the blame, and demanding that Tony's Place and Sundown Inn be closed and that whoever sold the liquor which caused the death of the banker's son be brought to justice.

In their haste to fix the responsibility upon some one, the ministers did not suggest that perhaps if the Church had not in some way failed to hold Harry Winton, the attractions which led to his death would have had no power over him. The boy was raised in the Sunday school and became a member of the church at an early age. It is significant, too, that the ministers, in their resolutions, made no mention of the country club where so many of their best paying members enjoyed the good fellowship of the locker room.

No one—not even the clergymen, themselves—really believed that the ministerial association would accomplish the closing of Tony's Place or the

Inn. No one believed it would make any difference if these places were closed. Everybody expected the ministers to make their charges and their demands. No one expected them to mention the country club. The ministers, themselves, understood exactly what was expected of them. All of which explains perfectly the power of the Church under the system.

The power of Jesus' teaching to build a Christian character strong enough to withstand Tony's Place and Sundown Inn—*that* is quite another question.

The community made ready for the largest funeral that Westover had seen for years. The prominence of the family and the story of the tragedy insured a record attendance. The undertaker congratulated himself, not only because of his large profits, but upon the advantage gained over rival establishments. The florists reaped abundant harvest, for no one among the banker's business associates cared to have his floral offering inconspicuous. Special singers were hired. In short, nothing was over looked—no expense was spared. The minister, keenly alive to the importance of the occasion, could be relied upon to do his eloquent best.

The groceryman attended that funeral in a state of mind very different from his usual mental attitude upon such occasions. He had done everything that a friend or a brother could do for Mr. and Mrs. Winton. Because of his lifelong, intimate friendship with Henry Winton, it was almost as if the banker's son were his own. He felt the more deeply, too, because of Georgia's part in the tragedy. But when all was done and they were assembled with the multitude in the church he found himself stepping aside, as it were, and viewing the whole affair impersonally.

The succession of events which followed so quickly that disturbing discussion of religion at Mr. Saxton's dinner had violently forced the groceryman out of his mental and emotional habits. His whole outlook on life was changed. Harry's death, his daughter's condition, his wife's betrayal of her home, the meeting with the delivery boy—it was as if a terrific explosion had totally wrecked the spiritual edifice which he had built up through the years. He stood on the bare ground amid the ruins of all his inherited and accepted religious conceptions. He saw life with startling clearness—not in the uncertain light of his old church conventions. He must begin all over again. His whole scheme of values was altered. Things which had been of first importance were now insignificant—things which had been trivial were now of vast importance.

As Joe Paddock saw it now, the pomp and show of this particular funeral were monstrous. What, he asked himself, had actually happened to cause this pretentious affair? A poor, worthless wreck of a man—a creature who had never been known to do a useful or unselfish thing, who had sacrificed home, parents and friends to his evil passions, and sunk his own manhood in the mire of sensuality—such a creature had, by his own gross indulgence, been removed from Westover. And the community, which his life had outraged, was now assembled to honor him—why? The worthless clay, from which the spirit was gone beyond all power of church or preacher, was now receiving their tenderest ministries. That theology, which by its confusions had robbed this boy of God, would now assure, the grief-stricken parents that all was well with his soul. Those teachers, whose holy privilege it had been to make Harry Winton's character strong with the bread of Jesus' truths but who had starved him with the stones of their silly contentions, would now pray for him.

As the groceryman looked at the wealth of flowers, the minister, the church, the people, and as he listened to the solemn tones of the organ and heard the sweet-voiced singers, he was thinking of the delivery boy and how Davie's crime had been born of his mother's prayer. He seemed to hear again the boy crying: "As God is my judge, Mr. Paddock, I don't want to be a bootlegger and a thief!"

The Church had forced the carpenter's son to become a bootlegger and a thief. The Church, that had neglected Davie, had in another way neglected Harry. And the minister, who was now so eloquently voicing beautiful sentiments over the empty husk of the rich man's drunken son, would howl like a wolf on the track of the poor delivery boy who, in his desperate need, had sold the liquor. Was the delivery boy, who did not want to be a bootlegger, in fact responsible for Harry Winton's death?

For the first time in his life the groceryman felt that he was seeing these things in their true proportions. As he had felt Davie's stealing to be a little thing in comparison with the tragedy in his home, he felt Harry Winton's death to be a little thing. Harry Winton's life—that was the terrible thing. His lack of character—the fact that in a Christian home and community and church such a lack of character could be possible—*that* was the real tragedy. That the delivery boy should violate the law was nothing compared to the violation of Jesus' teaching which had led to the Church's neglect and indifference and forced Davie into lawlessness. The money represented by the pomp and show of Harry Winton's funeral would have solved Davie's problem—restored his father to health, saved his mother, and permitted the boy to go on with his schooling—thus fitting him for a useful life.

"I am the resurrection and the life," intoned the minister. Life—life—life—the word echoed in the groceryman's mind. He wondered: "What is the speaker really thinking about? Is he actually so ignorant of the real values of life?"

As the preacher continued his sermon, eloquent with meaningless phrases and beautiful sentiments, skillfully avoiding facts, shunning the truth and shutting out reason in the name of Him who said: "Ye shall know the truth and the truth shall make you free," the groceryman thought: "Suppose the minister should suddenly cry out: 'Fathers and mothers of Westover, the death of this young man is of little consequence—it is for his life that we should mourn. Because Harry Winton was a weakling he did that which resulted in his death. He lacked strength to meet life because he was not well nourished with character-building food. We who profess the Christian religion are responsible for his weakness. The crime of this poor boy's life lies at the door of the Church whose mission it is to make men strong with the truths of Jesus' teaching. Stop this pomp and ceremony—this weeping over the dead clay—and let us mourn that which died while yet he lived. Let us place the blame for the terrible tragedy of his life where it justly belongs.'"

The hired singers sang "Nearer, My God, to Thee."

The groceryman looked around. Henry Winton's face was the face of a man of stone. Joe knew what his friend was thinking. Judge Burnes met his eye, and he knew that the lawyer's heart was filled with fear for his own boys. George Riley's thoughts were of the shame in his own home. Ed Jones was thinking of his daughter. These men, who had been with the groceryman at Mr. Saxton's dinner, were suffering through their homes and children even as the groceryman, himself, was suffering.

Suddenly the groceryman knew what he must do.

CHAPTER XV.

IN AN UPPER ROOM.

The evening of the third day following that funeral the five men who had been at Mr. Saxton's dinner met in an upper room in the Palace Hotel.

The groceryman received each man with a simple greeting and the words, "I have talked with him. He will be here presently."

They did not, as on that former occasion, appear to be congratulating one another. They spoke quietly, with an air of earnest purpose, as though they had come to some solemn and momentous decision. They seemed to be looking to one another for strength. They were as men resolved upon a great service. Their eyes turned often toward the door.

The groceryman answered a knock at the door, and John Saxton entered.

The men rose to their feet.

Slowly Mr. Saxton looked from face to face—searching, kindly, sympathetic—and they felt the inner strength of the man and sensed his unusual personality.

The groceryman indicated a chair and with a word of greeting to each, Saxton seated himself at the head of the circle.

When the others resumed their chairs, the groceryman remained standing. Without preliminary remarks he said: "We have come to you, Mr. Saxton, because there is no one else to whom we can go. We do not think, now, that it was chance which led you to invite only churchmen to your dinner, or that it was an accident that each man in the group represented a different church. We were deeply impressed on that occasion by your observations on the whole question of the Christian religion. Since then the community has been shocked by a tragedy which has forced us to realize as never before the imperative need of Christianity and the truth of your presentation of the church situation.

"The community will soon forget Harry Winton's death. Westover, and the Westover church, will go on in the same old futile way. But we, because of our meeting with you, cannot forget. We cannot go on in the same old way. We have each suffered in our homes and through our children. We are of five different denominational churches but we are one in our needs.

"We have agreed that we cannot go for advice to our ministers. They cannot tell us what to do. We already know exactly what they would say. We do not want soft words of comfort. We do not want theological argument. We want to find a way to make the Christian religion effective in the world of to-day. We are not asking what must we do to be saved, we are asking what can we do to save our homes, our children, our community and nation.

"We do not know how it is to be done, but one thing is clear to us: Before we can do anything we must stop pretending—stop covering things up, stop hiding the truth of things, stop looking at things through our personal prejudice glasses. We must seek facts—face facts—consider facts—and talk clearly and plainly of things as they actually are, before we can ever hope to even begin this work which we desire to undertake."

The groceryman paused. No one moved or spoke, for it was evident to all that the man was summoning all his strength for that which was to follow.

Then simply, quietly, with no unnecessary words, the groceryman told them what had happened in his home—how the discord and coldness had grown as he had been absorbed in his business and his wife had found other interests—how their daughter had drifted from the Church to follow dangerous ways—and how the crash had come the night of Harry Winton's death. He told them of Georgia's drunken condition, of her relation to Ellory, of his wife's affair with Astell, and how nearly he had come to an act of violence which would have resulted in utter and complete ruin.

It was a terrible thing to hear this man laying bare the shame of his home and loved ones. Often he paused, and seemed to gather strength to continue, while the others sat motionless in tense silence. John Saxton's countenance expressed his sympathy and understanding.

"I am telling you men nothing which you do not already know," the groceryman continued. "I have courage to say these things because I am aware of your secret troubles. I have pretended that you did not know my shame, and that I did not know of your troubles, and you have pretended with me. We have been telling polite lies to one another, knowing all the time that no one believed the lies and that every one knew the truth which we were trying to hide."

He then told how he had met the delivery boy in his store and related their conversation.

"And so I have come to face my personal responsibility," he continued. "I have pretended to believe that my church was all right, and the church has played the game of pretense with me. I can make believe no longer. I am faced with the fact that my church, by its neglect of Davie's father and mother, is responsible for Davie's crime, and that because we are not doing this work which Jesus made vital to the Christian religion, our preaching is vain and we have no power to influence our children or protect our homes. As surely as Jesus said, 'This do and thou shalt live,' so surely has the Church, by its failure to teach and l*ive* the Master's teachings, made the Christian religion a dead thing.

"My wife is not a bad woman—my daughter is not a bad girl. They have simply lost their grip on the realities of life. They are seeing things out of proportion. The teaching of their church is not vital to them because it does not emphasize the vital things. Religion is not, for them, a living force—it is not real. Therefore they have turned to other interests—interests, which, however right they may be when seen in proper proportion, do not in themselves have the character-sustaining power of the Christianity of Jesus.

"I, too, have been confused and have not seen clearly the real values of life. But I know now that it is not the Presbyterianism of my parents that can meet the present-day religious need. Nothing but the truths that Jesus taught can put the world again in touch with God. And so I am ready to throw aside everything but those simple truths. I am ready to abandon every nonessential, and to stand for Christianity with nothing less and nothing more."

When the groceryman had finished, Henry Winton rose to his feet. The banker's face was gray and worn. He fixed his eyes on John Saxton as if pleading for a measure of that strength which they all felt the man possessed. His voice was low and steady but they knew it was so by a supreme effort of his will.

"My son is dead. You all know how he died. You know the shame of his life. We have all pretended and lied about it. My wife and I, even, made believe and lied to each other and invented all sorts of excuses which we knew did not hide the truth.

"You were with me at the funeral. You saw the expensive flowers, the costly trappings. You heard the wonderful music and the eloquent sermon. I paid for the show. I hired the singers. I employed the preacher who so eloquently covered up and hid the terrible truth of the real tragedy. And all the while I sat there thinking—thinking—thinking. What a ghastly farce it all was!

"The sympathy of my friends is very dear to me but it is not the death of my boy that wrings my heart—it was the shame of his life. It is the awful realization that I am responsible. If my wife and I and our fellow church members had been living the teaching of Jesus, our boy would have found the Christian religion a sustaining influence in his life instead of a thing which he learned to hold in contempt. We of the Church are to blame because there is nothing vital, nothing real and genuine in our religion upon which boys, like Harry, and girls, like Georgia, can take hold. In our efforts to make our church attractive we have devitalized Christianity—we have made it insipid, tasteless, unattractive, meaningless.

"The ministers blame the prohibition officers and demand that the place where the fatal party was held be closed. Their demand is a confession of their weakness. It is a confession that Tony's Place exerts a more powerful influence than the teaching of the Church.

"We of the Church, I say, are to blame for what has happened in Joe's home. We are to blame for Davie's crime. You are all to blame, with me, for the death of my son. I am to blame for the trouble and shame in your homes. I, too, am ready to clear the decks of every hindering thing and to give the Christian religion a chance. I am hoping, sir, that you can help us to find a way at least to begin."

Judge Burnes, Mayor Riley and Ed Jones followed, each speaking frankly of the tragedy in his own home and family.

There was no exaggeration. No condoning arguments, no speaking in figures, no veiled allusions, no half-truths, no evasions, no emotional hysteria. Calmly, deliberately, as they might have bared bodily wounds to a surgeon, they stripped off the coverings of conventional pretense and falsehood. They said to one another: "Here is the hurt—this is the shame—this is my right to be included in the brotherhood of those who have suffered." They spoke with that straightforward reasonableness which would have characterized a discussion by business men of a national crisis or a financial catastrophe. Their spirit was that spirit in which good, capable men, of their type, faced the War. And with it all, though they spoke of personal things, there was an impersonal feeling. There was the feeling that they were not doing this for themselves, alone, but to help one another and to meet a world-wide need.

When the last man had spoken they waited for Saxton. And the interest with which they had hung upon his words at that former meeting, when they had hoped for material gains, was nothing to their interest now.

After all, we really care more for our homes and children than we do for business or possessions. If we seem not to, it is because, in our hearts, we carry on our business and strive for possessions for the benefit of those we love.

Mr. Saxton spoke with quiet meaning. "When Mr. Paddock told me why you wished me to meet with you to-night I felt that the hour for which I have been waiting was at hand."

At these strangely familiar words, the five Westover men looked at one another questioningly. But no one spoke.

The man at the head of the circle continued: "I confess that I did know you were church men when I asked you to dine with me. I had a definite purpose in bringing this particular group of men together and in provoking a discussion of religious conditions. I am satisfied to-night that I made no mistake. I am now ready to make known to you my mission in Westover—the mission in which you have manifested such kindly and patient interest."

Again he paused, and the men exchanged questioning looks. Did Mr. Saxton's words refer to those material interests which had so occupied their thoughts at the previous meeting?

It was Judge Burnes who finally said: "But, Mr. Saxton, is it possible you have misunderstood us? We have not met here to-night to ask you about whatever it was that brought you to Westover. We are here, and we asked you to meet with us, because of the things you said and made us think at our former meeting. You have led us to consider the whole religious question as we had never considered it before and we have come to you for advice on things which are much more vital to us and to our city than any business enterprise which you could possibly place before us. Forgive me, sir, but I do not think we, to-night, care to hear about the enterprise which brought you to Westover—we do not care to consider your plans for your contemplated Westover investment. Can you not help us in the things for which we have come to you?"

Mr. Saxton smiled. "Have no fear, gentlemen, I understand exactly why you are here. But the first principle of Jesus' teaching is that our material and our spiritual interests are one and inseparable. Life and religion are identical. The Christianity of Jesus is a religion of the plow, the office, the store, the bank, of government, laws and education. The Christian religion was born in a carpenter shop. It is quite impossible to separate the spiritual from the material and have anything like the religion of Jesus left. The failure of the theologian's church proves *that.* Denominationalism took religion out of the material affairs of life and made it a thing of sectarian seminaries and ecclesiastical forms. The Christianity of Jesus, for instance, would have saved the world millions of lives, billions of dollars, and all the incalculable suffering of the World War. Would any one contend that no material interests were involved in the War? If the world's peace is ever to be secured it will not be by courts of human law, leagues of nations, or the cunning of diplomacy, but it will come by this spirituality which was first taught in the terms of common, everyday, material things. Would any one hold that there are no material interests at stake in the question of the world's peace? There is not a problem touching the so-called worldly affairs of humanity which would not be solved by the application of the spiritual truths which Jesus gave to men."

The five men sat in amazed silence. All their lives they had been taught to mentally separate their material and spiritual interests. The theology of their denominations was not the religion of a carpenter's shop. They did not know what to say. The magnitude of the vision opened to them by John Saxton's simple words was overwhelming.

Saxton continued: "Because this is not the commonly accepted view of the Christian religion, the one whom I represent thought it would be best not to make the exact nature of his contemplated investment in Westover known until I had first found the men who would understand it. If I have permitted you to think that the proposed investment is of material value only, it was because I could not do otherwise until you were prepared to receive it.

"I represent Mr. Dan Matthews.

"Mr. Matthews plans to invest a considerable sum of money in Westover for the purpose of working out, or helping to work out, these very religious problems which we discussed at our former meeting, and which have now become so vital to you.

"At Mr. Matthews' request I invite you five gentlemen to be his associates—to work him. But before you accept that invitation it will be necessary for you to meet Mr. Matthews and to consider the plans which he will lay before you."

CHAPTER XVI.

THE PLAN.

It was early evening. In that suite of offices high up in the Union Mining Building in Kansas City, old Uncle Zac was busy with broom and dust cloth. Below, and extending mile after mile in every direction, the myriad lights of the city shone in the world of darkness—lights of homes, places of amusement, places of vice, schools, hospitals, police stations, factories—lights to attract, to repel, to warm—lights to lead astray, to confuse, to wreck—lights of hope and promise. And overhead the stars. The roar of the city's life came faintly up from the crowded streets below. Uncle Zac crooned his old-time hymn.

Except for the old negro janitor, the outer rooms of that home of the great Matthews' interests were deserted. But Uncle Zac, as he moved here and there among the desks and chairs and filing cabinets, looked often toward the door of Big Dan's private office. Once he interrupted his low crooning song to mutter: "hit sure must be mighty 'portant meetin' in thar—yas indeedee. Boss Dan ain't er comin' down here to his offerces, in de night time to meet dem stranger gentlemens, 'cept hit's somethin' big. No, sah—no, *sah!*"

In that inner office, where Big Dan had talked with John Saxton the night of the storm several months before, the groceryman and his four Westover friends were sitting with Saxton about a long table. Every eye was turned toward the man who stood at the head of the table. Dan Matthews was speaking. The faces of the men and their attitudes of rapt attention gave the impression that, as Uncle Zac conjectured, business of more than ordinary importance was being transacted.

Big Dan's manner was that of one accustomed to dealing with questions of large importance. He was making no effort to appeal to the emotions of his hearers. He spoke with the conviction of one who has arrived at his conclusions after an exhaustive study of facts. His voice was quiet, with no effort at persuasive eloquence.

"It would be impossible to overestimate the value of the contributions to our national life which the Church has made in the past. All that we know of the Christian religion we have received, directly or indirectly, from the Church. The heroism, the sacrifice, the achievements of the church fathers are among the most inspiring records of our country. But the fact remains that, as the Church has grown with the passing years, theological leaders have multiplied and other interests have intruded until to-day, with the greatest potential power in its history, it is less effective for Christianity in the affairs of men than in its early years of material weakness.

"The rapidly increasing irreligion with the consequent trend toward the moral bankruptcy of our nation, to which the Church so often calls our attention, is in itself conclusive proof that the Church is powerless to remedy the situation.

"If the Church denies that it is powerless to meet this crisis, then its denial is a confession of its guilt in permitting these conditions to exist.

"To say that existing immorality is to blame for the existing irreligion is to reverse cause and effect. Immorality follows irreligion as darkness follows the setting of the sun.

"To find the reason for the Church's failure, we decided to make a study of actual conditions in a representative American community. Then we would attempt to work out in that same community a remedy; thus making a demonstration which would be applicable to the country as a whole.

"Westover, with its population of 40,698, in its culture, traditions, civic, social, business and church life, fairly represents the average American community. Mr. Saxton finds that the alarming conditions resulting from the irreligion of the people in Westover are typical of the conditions throughout the nation. If you wish detailed and reliable information as to what is actually going on among your young people of the high-school age, read Judge Lindsey's *The Revolt of Modern Youth.* His findings are based upon actual cases which have passed through his court in Denver over a period of twenty-five years, and apply to every city in the land. Your churches, too, are fairly representative. The figures which I am about to submit to you check with the averages of all the cities between twenty-five and fifty thousand in the United States."

The groceryman and his friends leaned forward with intense interest.

Referring to the typewritten sheets on the table before him, Big Dan continued:

"The Christian religion is represented in Westover by eighteen separate and distinct denominations or sects. The combined membership of these eighteen denominations is 21,409. In other words, over fifty per cent of your population is identified with the various church organizations in your city.

"To put it another way, you have one church member for every individual nonchurch member in Westover. And this does not take into account the large number of professed Christians who are not identified with any denominational organization.

"Gentlemen, human nature is to-day what it was in the day of Jesus. Licentiousness, crime, political graft and injustice are not modern inventions. When the Christian religion was first given to men, twelve Christians upset the world and brought into human affairs a spiritual force which made its mark on every page of human history. With the simple truths of Jesus' teaching, twelve men stood against the world and won. The religion, which the man of Galilee taught by wayside well, in the fields, the village streets and on the mountain, became more potent in the world than the armies of Rome. Twelve Christians against the world! But to-day, in Westover, with twelve church members for every twelve people not identified with the church, the professed followers of Jesus cannot withstand or check the increasing irreligion of the people. The Church cannot, in fact, influence to any marked degree, the lives of its own members.

"The Church, itself, would scarcely hold that the teaching of Jesus is not a certain remedy for irreligion. Therefore we cannot escape the conclusion that for some reason the Westover church is not adequately presenting the Christianity of Jesus to the modern world."

Big Dan took another typewritten sheet from the pile on the table before him.

"Referring again to Mr. Saxton's report, and keeping in mind that these figures are the averages for cities of this class throughout the United States, consider first the strength of the Westover church as it is expressed in property.

"There are in Westover forty-four church edifices. With their furnishings, organs, lots, parsonages and so forth, the total property value is $2,559,494.08.

"The total seating capacity of these forty-four edifices is 20,321 or one edifice for every 461 possible worshipers.

"But, gentlemen, the total average attendance at the regular services of the church in Westover is 4,845. In these forty-four places of worship there are, at the average regular services, 15,476 empty seats.

"In other words, the Westover church has put $2,559,494.08 of its money strength into forty-four edifices in order that there might be one edifice for every 110 worshipers.

"Can you imagine any company of sane business men building, in your city, forty-four separate theaters to accommodate an average attendance of 110 persons each, and with a total seating capacity of only 461 each?

"As I shall show you later, these forty-four edifices represent a waste of $1,059, 494.08. Multiply this by the thousands of cities and communities throughout the country and the waste of the Church's money strength in useless property is appalling.

"Consider now the operating cost of the Westover church, under this system which furnishes one place of worship for every one hundred and ten worshipers. By operating cost, I mean, the local running expenses—janitor, fuel, lights, ministers' salaries and the general denominational organization expense, such as salaries of bishops and secretaries, office expense, and so forth. This operating cost throughout the country, by way, is eighty-five per cent of the total expenditures of the Church.

"The annual running expense of the Westover church is $137,732.19.

"This, as I shall show you later, is a total loss.

"Nearly one-half of the church's money strength, as it is represented in property, is wasted and every cent of the annual running expensed is literally thrown away.

"The preaching strength of the Westover church is more important than its property cost or running expense.

"The truths of Jesus, which constitute the Christian religion, must be taught. Jesus, Himself, was, first, last and always, a teacher. To all who accepted His teaching, He committed His truths in trust for the succeeding generations. The Church—that is, the whole body of Christians—has no other reason for existing save to teach, by its preaching and by its activities, those truths which Jesus gave to His immediate followers and through them to the world.

"The power of the Christian religion to lead mankind to a consciousness of God, and to engender and foster character-building principles and ideals, is in the personality, the teaching and the life of Jesus. Jesus, Himself, placed it there: 'I am the way, the truth and the life.' 'Learn of Me.' 'No man cometh unto the Father but by Me.' The emphasis is unmistakable.

"Well, forty-four ministers of the Westover church, at their average regular Sunday services, preach to 4,845 persons, which is an average of 110 souls for each teacher. And yet any one these ministers could easily preach to two or three times the entire church-going population of the city.

"But, gentlemen, these forty-four teachers of the Christian religion—each with his little company of one hundred and ten people who look to him for those living vitalizing truths which Jesus committed to his followers in trust for all mankind—these forty-four teachers represent eighteen denominations. *They must, therefore, deliver at least eighteen different messages.*

"It is idle to say that these preachers all teach the same thing, because if they all taught the same thing they could not represent eighteen separate and distinct denominations. It is as idle to say that these ministers do not represent their several denominations, because if that were true these eighteen different denominations would not exist.

"With the imperative needs of eighteen competing denominations demanding the largest possible audiences, the ministerial effort to draw a crowd of hearers results in a ruinous neglect of Jesus' teaching—the necessity of presenting these denominational differences leads to a substitution of theological views for Christian truths—the confusion, to those who would learn of Jesus, is disastrous—the result in irreligion is tragic.

"Mr. Saxton, in his report, gives a list of the subjects discussed by your religious teachers in Westover during the last six months. As these subjects were announced in the papers by the ministers themselves, we may assume that they consider them of religious importance. If a person advertises that he will lecture on, dogs, the people certainly have the right to assume that the lecturer will endeavor to teach them something about dogs.

"These subjects, which the preachers of Westover have presented to the public for their spiritual inspiration and guidance, range from baseball to traffic regulations. There are several discussions of evolution. There are many presentations of the various sectarian interests. There are sermons of historical, political, economic, artistic, literary and scientific interest. There are a number of Biblical subjects, such as, "Who wrote Isaiah?' and 'Where did Cain get his wife?" *Not one subject in five suggests that a preacher of the Christian religion will deal directly with the personality, the teaching, or the life of Jesus.*

"But even these advertised sermon subjects, calculated as they so evidently are to draw an audience at any cost, occupy an insignificant position in the general program of attractions offered. Jazz bands, instrumental solos, orchestras, singers, are all played up with portraits, headlines, and blurbs as the leading entertaining or amusing features offered by the various churches where the people theoretically gather to worship God as He is revealed in Jesus, and to receive from their spiritual teachers those truths which alone have power to build Christian character.

"Think what this means, gentlemen! With the God of Jesus to worship, the modern Church is offering jazz bands and motion pictures as its chief attraction! With Jesus, Himself, to present to men, the ministers advertise amusing, humorous and clever entertainments! With the happiness of our homes, the future of our children and the very life of the nation depending upon the saving, keeping powers of the Christian religion, our church teachers strive to make the people laugh!

"It is not difficult to account for those empty seats in the Westover churches. It is easy to understand why the people seek entertainment in those places which the ministers condemn as worldly.

"Men have always found God in the personality, teaching and life of Jesus. Men are not finding God in the preaching of the modern Church.

"Nothing could be farther from the spirit and example of Jesus than the spectacle of a down-to-date clergyman struggling to raise the money for his salary. Nothing could be less Christian than the antics of a modern pulpit entertainer striving, with thrills, sensationalism and humor, to draw a larger crowd with larger box-office returns than the other places of amusement against which he rails.

"The personality of Jesus compels respect, admiration, love. His teaching had the force and authority of eternal truth. The methods of our modern ministers breed contempt, disgust, and scorn. Their sermons have no more authority than a vaudeville performance.

"Take Jesus out of the Christian religion and your religion is no longer Christian. To the degree that our preachers magnify theology they belittle Christianity. In substituting their denominational interests for the simple teaching of Jesus, they have lost their power to bring their hearers face to face with God.

"In the bewildering maze of theological opinions, doctrinal discussions, sectarian interests, and denominational ambitions, the central idea—the strength and simplicity of Jesus' teaching—has been lost. The emphasis has been shifted from the living, eternal, character-building truths which the Master gave us, and placed upon theological nonessentials of which Jesus never spoke.

"These theological differences, which were never contemplated by Jesus and are not of His teaching, take ninety-five per cent of the preaching strength of the Church. And yet they have no more to do with the Christian religion than an electric eel has to do with an electric street car. You could as easily operate your Westover street car system by propagating electric eels as you can make the teaching of Jesus effective in your city by promoting denominationalism.

"The tragedy of this situation is that it is not chargeable to the ministers, themselves. In all the world, there is no body of men more Christlike, as a whole, than are these preachers of Christianity. They are, in general, fit and capable in natural endowments, in personal character, personal devotion and personal sacrifice. The fault lies not with the teachers but with the system under which they are compelled to teach. The ministers, themselves, are the helpless victims of their denominational machines.

"Many a minister faces his audience with a heavy heart because he longs to teach the simple, unassailable, character-building, saving truths which he has from his Master, and for which he knows the people hunger. But he cannot. The material needs of his denominational church are imperative. He must put the sectarian interests of his pulpit first or yield his pulpit to some leader who will. If the ministry of the Church were to concentrate upon the teaching of Jesus, denominationalism, with its wasteful and destructive competition, would cease.

"The people heard Jesus gladly. The people hear our modern teachers of religion laughingly. But show these teachers the way to freedom and they will lead the world to God. Set these same ministers free from the shackles of their denominationalism and they will present Jesus to the world to-day with the irresistible power which gave the twelve their victories."

"Consider another element of the Church's strength—the activities of the membership.

"No one of the most ordinary intelligence can fail to understand what Jesus taught as the essential activities which should engage the strength and time of Christians: 'For I was hungered, and ye gave me meat; I was thirsty, and ye gave me drink; I was a stranger, and ye took me in; naked and ye clothed me; I was sick and ye visited me; I was in prison, and ye came unto me. . . .' 'A cup of water in my name.' 'Sell and give to the poor.' 'The Good Samaritan'—these and many other sayings, with innumerable examples, reveal the mind of the Master with unmistakable clearness.

"The citizens of Westover last year, in the name of the city and of various clubs and lodges, gave nearly $100,000 to those of whom Jesus said: 'Inasmuch as ye have done it unto one of the least of these my brethren, ye have done it unto Me.' But your forty-four churches gave not one penny to minister unto those of whom Jesus said: 'Inasmuch as ye did it not to one of the least of these, ye did it not to Me.'

"But while the Westover Church, in the name of the Christian religion, had no part in ministering unto the poor with whom Jesus so unmistakably identified Himself, in the names of its eighteen denominations it spent the strength and time of its membership in activities to raise this sum of $137,732.10 for its running expenses, which, as I have shown, was worse than wasted.

"Mr. Saxton gives a list of these activities as they were extensively advertised in the papers and enthusiastically promoted by the ministers and church members—card parties, balls, entertainments, banquets, vaudeville shows, rummage sales, Oriental bazaars, fairs and lotteries were all carried on for the sole purpose of raising money to maintain the different denominational institutions.

"By no stretch of the imagination can we hear Jesus say: 'Come unto me and play a game of cards, for inasmuch as ye win ye glorify my name,' "Come all ye who desire a good time and join our jitney dance—the proceeds are to buy a pulpit carpet,' 'Come unto our Oriental bazaar and buy of the cigarette girls in costume, for the price ye give will help to pay our pastor's salary.' And in the meantime, *while the strength of the church membership is spent in these activities, the Church's own poor and needy are cared for by the civic charities, the Elks, the Kiwanis and other organizations.*

"The effect of this policy of the modern Church is obvious. If the $137,732.19, which the Westover church last year threw away on its denominationalism which is making the teaching of Jesus of no effect, had been used by the Christian workers in ministering to the city's poor, Westover would have no religious problem. As surely as the loving sympathy of Jesus for suffering humanity won the world to His teaching, so surely would the same sympathy and kindliness in His name win Westover to Christianity. If the membership strength of the Church were given to personally ministering to these sick and suffering ones the world would bow before the Church in love and adoration as it bows before Him who went about doing good.

"As in the waste of the teaching strength, the tragedy is that these silly, trivial, ineffectual activities use the best strength of the membership. It is not a weakness of the people; it is a misuse of their strength by denominationalism. Most often it is the Christian zeal of these workers which leads them to engage in these enterprises. *That this Christian zeal should be forced by denominationalisms to spend itself in such activities while the work to which Jesus committed Himself and His followers is undone—this is the tragedy.*

"This same waste is found in what is generally known as the 'young people's work.'

"The young people's societies, under the guidance of the church leaders, all stress loyalty to their parent denominations. The young people of the Church are taught that to serve Jesus they must serve a denomination. In all of their activities a good time is stressed, the argument being 'join our society because with us you will have more fun than you will otherwise.' The policy is to make the Christian religion attractive by emphasizing the good times of the social activities.

"Consider this full-page newspaper advertisement of what the Church is offering young people. It is headed: 'Flaming Youth. Get This New Thrill.' 'You say you are after the big time stuff. Then why don't you come into the main tent? . . . Be a sport and give Him a chance. He will not take the fun out of life. He will add to it. . . . If He should fail in your case *you will have lost nothing* and the experience will at least give your something to talk about. Come to Church. Come to Sunday school. Come to Young People's Meeting.'

"Certainly there is nothing in Jesus' teaching to take the joy out of life. But it is as certain that Jesus never based his appeal to the world upon social pleasures, good times, or fun.

"Our Young America of to-day is a remarkably keen, observing and wide-awake Young America. Its frankness is astounding. Its intolerance for sham and pretense is its greatest strength. With amazing impudence it questions everything. It is in active revolt against all authority that is not backed by reality. It may not know it but it is seeking everywhere and trying everything in an effort to find truth, in which alone is freedom.

"Make so mistake, Young America is rejecting the Church because it sees through the pretenses, shams and failures of denominationalism.

"The modern Church, by inviting Young America to accept the Christian religion for fun, has driven Young America to seek its fun elsewhere. Young America will be drawn to the Christian religion when the truths of Jesus are taught with the sincerity and simplicity of the Sermon on the Mount, and when the activities of the Church are those activities in which the Master, Himself, engaged.

"Under the stress of denominational competition, the Church has sought to make religion attractive by eliminating the elements of its strength. But the modern system has not made religion attractive, it has made it insipid."

'One other element of the Church's strength remains to be considered—worship.

"By worship we understand the act of adoration or homage toward the being worshiped; the contemplation of, surrender to and spiritual communion with God; a conscious yielding of the worshiper, a giving of one's self to the divine principle. Any candid, honest and unprejudiced observer will be forced to admit that worship, in this sense, has little place in our modern Church.

"At a cost of over two and a half million dollars, the Westover Church has built forty-four so-called places of worship. Forty of these temples to the God of the Christian religion have no beauty, no dignity, no distinction. They are as commonplace and lacking in architectural significance as your warehouses, coal sheds and lumber yards. They have no more religious meaning than your barber shops. They are fitting monuments to the denominationalism which built them.

"Under this system of ruinous competition, the modern church edifice is everything else but a place of worship. It is a place of entertainment, a social center, the headquarters of a theological camp, a parade ground for the display of denominational strength, an amusement hall, a show house. The spirit of the announcements and advertisements of the services is the spirit of the invitations to the motion-picture theaters, the dance halls and the restaurants. The spirit of the preaching is the spirit of entertainment, of seeking to please. The spirit of the music is the spirit of the concert hall or opera. The spirit of the church activities is the spirit of a social event, an afternoon tea, or a club affair. *To the degree that the material necessities of the competing theological systems have eliminated Jesus, the modern Church has banished the spirit of worship.*

"The essential element of worship is the offering. It has been so in all religions, whether the offering be fruit or flowers, an animal or a human being. Whether the offering was made by Aztec or Hottentot or Maori, the religious significance has been the same. It has remained for the modern denominational church to do away with offerings to God as acts of worship, and to substitute membership dues, pew rentals and public collections to pay the preacher and defray the expenses of the sectarian institution.

"The spirit which characterizes the taking of the so-called offerings at the typical church service to-day is not the spirit of worship. The act is more often comparable to the passing of the hat by a street performer following his free entertainment. If the person who has been drawn to the meeting by the advertisements is pleased with the program, he pays. If he is not pleased he does not pay. If a member likes the pastor he subscribes to his support. If the members are not pleased with their minister they withhold their subscription and the man of God answers a call to some other community.

"To see God through the personality, teaching and life of Jesus, and to see Jesus in that humanity with which He identified Himself—and then, in the spirit of Jesus' ministry, to give money for the relief of those who are naked and hungry and sick, as an offering to God—this is the essential element of Christian worship. But such worship, if restored to our modern religious gatherings, would wreck the denominationalism which lives on membership dues, the earnings of the church activities and the ability of the ministers to please their congregations and to draw pennies from the pockets of a more or less appreciative public."

"To sum up this analysis: The irreligion of the present day is directly chargeable to the lack of Christianity in the modern Church. This lack of Christianity is the result of the substitution of theological differences for the teaching of Jesus. The appalling immorality of our generation is chargeable to the denominationalism which rendered the Church powerless to meet our religious needs."

There was silence for a little, then Mayor Riley said: "But, Mr. Matthews, are not all the Christian denominations founded upon the Bible, or rather, I should say, upon the New Testament?"

Big Dan answered: "The theological differences, which constitute this denominationalism, have grown out of the teachings of men who wrote years after Jesus' death. They have not grown out of what Jesus, Himself, said, and, by personal example, taught. For instance, there are no divisions based upon Jesus' teaching: "Whatsoever ye would that men should do to you, do ye even so to them.'

"If this denominationalism is in fact a necessity of the Christian religion, then Jesus was incompetent and short-sighted, because nowhere, in all His teaching, is there a suggestion that His followers divide into one hundred and eighty-three sects. On the contrary, when His darkest hour was at hand and He summed up His personal ministry and teaching, He prayed that all who believed in Him might be one—'as thou, Father, art in Me, and I in Thee.' And He gave as a reason for this prayer *'that the world may believe.'* It follows that Jesus knew if Christians were not one, the world would not believe. The present-day irreligion, which results from the lack of Christian oneness, is proof again that Jesus was wiser than our theologians."

Said Judge Burnes: "Granting the accuracy of Mr. Saxton's observations and the justice of your analysis, is it not also true that, under all these differences of denominationalism, there is a oneness of spirit?"

"How is it possible, Judge, to have oneness of spirit without oneness in fact? The Westover Church is, *in fact,* not one but eighteen. How can these eighteen, in fact, result from anything but a corresponding lack of oneness in spirit?

"Devotion to Jesus, worship of God as He is revealed in Jesus, loyalty to the teaching of Jesus—these are not the tests of fellowship in any one of the denominations. A person is not received into a denominational church because he is a Christian, but because he is willing to accept the peculiar tenets of that sect. He may be ready to die upon a cross for the Christian religion, but that sacrifice would not admit him to membership in a denominational brotherhood. Therefore it is clear that the modern Church, in the essentials of Christianity, is not placing the emphasis where Jesus placed it.

"But let us assume that in some mysterious theological way these eighteen competing organizations in Westover, with their forty-four edifices and their forty-four ministers and their forty-four groups of one hundred and ten worshipers, are one in spirit. It still remains that it is not oneness of spirit which characterizes them before the world. *The world accepts or rejects the Church for what it is, not for what its theologians assume its theoretical invisible spirit to be. And mark you, the world accepts or rejects the Christian religion as it sees it in the Church. If that oneness in spirit did in reality exist, then that spirit of oneness would in itself do away with the existing fact differences which are so clearly making the Christian religion of no effect."*

"Do not all the churches engage in Christian work, Mr. Matthews?" asked the groceryman. "What about our benevolences, schools, orphans' homes, hospitals and such institutions?"

"I should have explained," returned Big Dan, "that the figures given apply to local work only. The benevolences, schools, missions and similar works of the Church are all denominational and are maintained in the name of, and in the interest of, the denomination. And at that, these benevolences throughout the country are only fifteen per cent of the total expenditures of the Church, as against eighty-five per cent for running expenses."

"We hear a great deal about church union," remarked Henry Winton. "Some of the denominations in Westover have been trying for years to get together."

"Yes," returned Big Dan, "but as I have said, the denominations are not built upon the teaching of Jesus, they are formed about various distinctive theological theories, views or central thoughts. These various sectarian institutions do not go directly to Jesus as the source of their distinctive doctrines. Taking them at their own terms, their origin is not Jesus; it is Calvin, or Wesley, or Luther, or Campbell. We cannot produce the Christianity of Jesus by union of all the theological differences which were not founded upon His teaching—we would still have only a compromise of Calvin, and Wesley, and Luther, and Campbell, and the rest of them.

"If you could have made all the tallow candles, and whale-oil lamps, and kerosene lamps, into one great lamp you still would not have produced an electric arc light. The electric light did not come by uniting the other lights. It came by applying a different principle of lighting. It came by going directly to the great source of electric light.

"No existing denomination can set the Christian religion free, because the moment it gave one hundred per cent of its strength in property, preaching, activities and worship to the teaching of Jesus, it would lose its denominational identity and cease to exist.

"Denominations will end, not by uniting them but by abandoning them. They will go as the candles and whale-oil and kerosene lamps went, when the electric light of Jesus' teaching is made available to the world.

"And this, gentlemen, is exactly the central idea of the plan which I have to propose."

"The only possible remedy for the increasing irreligion and the moral bankruptcy which threaten our country is somehow to ignore this denominationalism which has arisen, and make available to the world the full value of the Christian religion.

"Christianity is Jesus—nothing less, nothing more. Jesus made God understandable. The direct, simple, vital truths with which Jesus won men to Himself, and through Himself to God, will restore to the American people their consciousness of God.

"The hope of humanity is in the fact that the great majority of church members are already sick, tired and disgusted with denominationalism. We go on in the same old way, inadequate, as we know it to be, because we know no better way. Our church leaders and teachers are barred, by their training and their obligations to their denominational pulpits, from leading the people away from the cause of all the sectarian evils, from which to be released they pray. It is clear, therefore, that any movement away from denominationalism and toward a simple, direct and understandable Christianity must be inaugurated by the lay members and not by the clergy.

"Any plan to effect the freedom of the Christian religion must be, in a way, experimental, in that while it looks toward the ideal, it must never be held to be in itself ideal, or perfect, or final. Obviously, the experiment must be such that the plan will prove itself by actual, tangible results, and not rest its claim to recognition upon untried theories, unproved propositions, or intangible returns. The experiment must deal with actual conditions—normal conditions.

"As I have said, the first step was to find a community which would most adequately represent the conditions throughout the country as a whole. The second step was to find the men. I say men, because no one person, by setting himself up as an inspired reformer, could ever, in this enlightened day, accomplish the desired end.

"As the experiment requires a representative place, it calls for a representative group of men. These men must be Christians. They must be active members of different denominational churches—sufficiently prominent in church affairs to be well identified with their denominations by their fellow-citizens. They must be prominent in business, meriting the confidence of the people in matters or questions of judgment—leaders in civic affairs. They must, so far as possible, represent the different business, political and professional interests. They must be men of families—fathers. And 'last"—Big Dan's voice was gentle—"they must have suffered from the irreligion which is everywhere causing such suffering.

"To demonstrate how the Church's money strength is wasted in church property: The plan is to build, in Westover, three edifices which, it is hoped, will take the place of the forty-four now in use. To simplify the experiment, the plan is to start with one, in the district where the largest of your denominational houses are now located. The other two will be built later, where they will be most accessible to the remaining portions of the city.

"To make the experiment or demonstration most effective, each of these temples is to have a seating capacity of at least 5,000, which you will note, would give the three edifices a total seating capacity of *more than three times the total average attendance of the present forty-four places of worship. These three temples are to cost $1,500,000, or $500,000 each, which is more than eight times the cost of the average church edifice now in Westover.* They are to be architecturally worthy of their holy purpose—beautiful—significant—dignified—impressive—distinctive—not unsightly, ill-kept shacks—not cheap adaptations of the architecture of business.

"These temples must be as sacred to worship as the mosque of a Mohammedan, or the temple of a Hindu. They must never be closed, night or day, in order that those who feel the need of communion with God may enter at any time for meditation or prayer or relief from the rush and distractions of our modern life.

"These places of worship will not be identified by any names of denominational character. They will memorialize no one but Jesus. They will call to mind only the Christian religion. They will be holy ground—sacred to the worship of God as he is revealed in the personality, the teaching and the life of Jesus.

Of the $2,559,494.08 now represented by your present forty-four Westover church edifices, the $1,500,000 cost of these three proposed temples would save

$1,059,494.08. This amount invested at five per cent would yield an annual income of $52,974.70, which would give, for the annual operating expense of each temple, $17,658.23, or more than five times the annual running expense of each one of the forty-four edifices now maintained by the present system.

"This, you see, would effect a saving of the total annual running expense of the present denominational system, which is $137,732.19, and enable the Christian people of Westover to spend that amount annually for the relief of the poor, in the name of the Christian religion.

"Which would Jesus have His followers in Westover do—spend $137,732.19 every year to maintain eighteen divisions of His followers, or spend that amount annually in ministering to those who are naked and hungry and sick and homeless? Which plan would make the Christian religion most effective among men?"

"The temple ministers will be free to preach the teaching of Jesus only.

"These teachers of the Christian religion will not be dependent upon their congregations for their material needs because the endowment of $1,059,494.08 will provide for them and for all other running expenses. The people will understand clearly that neither the ministers nor the temples receive one penny from the public or from any individual. These preachers will feel no *financial* necessity for drawing a crowd. There will be no *temptation* or need for them to substitute anything as an attraction, either for personal or denominational interest, for the simple presentation of Jesus. With this freedom, they will face the wealthiest and the poorest, the most influential and the unknown, with a sense of independence which will enable them to present the Christian religion without hesitation or reservation, and with the authority of untrammeled truth. With no denominational masters or overlords to support and satisfy; with no personal money interest in his audiences; knowing that he is not dependent upon the favor of any one of his hearers, *each minister will be free to center his whole strength upon the one thing, and will teach nothing but the truths which Jesus taught.*

"Each temple minister will give all of his time and strength and talents to his ministry of teaching. He will not need to devise and promote schemes for raising money. He will not engineer campaigns and drives; he will not need to make himself a social favorite in certain circles; he will not be a booster for civic enterprises, or lend himself to politics. But in addition to his public preaching, this minister will be accessible to those who are in need of his counsel and advice—a spiritual leader, guide, counselor and teacher, in constant, intimate touch with the people's needs, as free to devote himself to this ministry as Jesus, Himself, was free—free to declare without fear or favor those truths which reveal God and which, if so declared, will make God a vital force in the lives of the people.

"The only way to free Christianity from the theological machines is to have no machine. Therefore these temples and these ministers will represent no organization.

"There will be nothing for any one to join; nothing for any one to support; nothing for the people to run or operate. With no membership dues, no allegiance to any organization, there will be no prominent members, no personal influence, no rich, no poor. These temples and their ministers will be as free from any spirit of denominationalism as the Christian religion itself.

"Do you think that the people of Westover would go, under such conditions, to hear such preaching?"

"In these temples—through the teaching of these ministers—the spirit of worship will be restored and the offering given its rightful place as an act of worship.

The people will be taught, as Jesus taught them, to make their offerings to God as he is represented in humanity. They will give to this essential act of worship the significance and meaning which Jesus gave to it, and make it again a vital thing in the Christian religion.

"With the endowment providing for the minister and the temple, *every penny of the offerings will be used in ministering to those with whom Jesus identified Himself,* and the people, knowing that their gifts are used to relieve the city's sick and suffering poor in the name of the Christian religion, will attach a new and deeper meaning to their contribution to Christianity.

"Under this plan the Christian people in Westover will not waste their strength and time in activities for the purpose of raising money to support competing denominational institutions, but they will engage in administering the temple offerings. They will go among the needy ones of Westover, not as hired agents of the city, but as representatives of Jesus, with personal Christian interest, engaging in the work which Jesus made so essential to Christianity.

"With houses of worship worthy of the Christian religion, sacred to the cause which they represent, and free from the atmosphere of sectarianism; with a teacher free to teach, without fear or favor, the truths of Jesus, and with time to minister to the spiritual needs of the people; with the spirit of worship restored and the offerings given their rightful place in that worship; with the poor of the city cared for in the name of Christianity; and with the Christian people free to do a Christian work in the community, the oneness of Jesus' followers in Westover would become a fact—the religion which Jesus gave to the world would become real and effective."

"I believe," said Judge Burnes, "that such a demonstration of Christianity would be irresistible—it would Christianize Westover in a year—it would make itself felt in *every life, every home, every business, every school in the city.*"

The groceryman added thoughtfully: "If, under such conditions, the people failed to respond then we would be forced to conclude that Christianity itself is a failure."

"Every sincere Christian, I think, dreams of such a place of worship, longs for such teaching, and hopes for such a Christian work," said Banker Winton. "We cannot question the result of such an enterprise. But, Mr. Matthews, your own analysis shows that it would not be humanly impossible to persuade all of the Westover churches to abandon their separate organizations and unite in such a movement. And even if the local organizations, by some miracle, *could* be persuaded, their denominational organization would not permit it."

"That is true, Mr. Winton. Therefore, to make this experiment possible and so demonstrate to the world the real power of the Christian religion when freed from denominationalism, I propose to establish in Westover a foundation." He smiled. "This is the investment which I wish to make in your city, gentlemen, and you are all invited to come in on the ground floor. In short, as others have established foundations in the interest of art, and science, and education, I desire to establish this foundation in the interest of the Christian religion.

"To make this experiment a real demonstration, the amount of the foundation will be the exact sum now represented by the cost of the forty-four edifices and their properties now operating in Westover. As I have shown, this sum will be sufficient to build the temples and to furnish ample income to provide for their running expenses for all time to come.

"I have asked you gentlemen to consider these things which I have put before you, because it is my wish that you will act as trustees of this foundation, which must not even bear my name. I suggest that it be called simply the Westover Church Foundation."

There was no mistaking the answer which the five Westover men were ready to make. They sat in silence, with bowed heads, too deeply moved for words.

"Before you accept this work, gentlemen," continued Big Dan, "it would be well, I think, for us to take up some of the objections to the plan which are sure to be raised."

Judge Burnes asked: "Might not the plan be, in effect, only another denomination? Other movements for undenominational Christianity have been inaugurated in the past, but they have always resolved themselves into distinct sects with all the effect of the denominationalism from which they proposed to be free."

"That is true, Judge," returned Big Dan, "but those movements, or as they are more often termed, 'reformations,' have always centered about the personality and leadership of some individual. They have taken the leader's name, or the name of the particular doctrine which he championed. They became distinct denominations because they organized and made membership in the organization necessary. As separate bodies, they entered into competition with other denominations in order to promote their particular views, and so they became, as you say, only other denominations.

"This plan is not a reformation; it is not coming out of any of the existing organizations; it is not to be built around the ideas of any individual; it calls for no distinctive body of worshipers; it will have no distinctive name; there will be no organization formed about any one or anything; there will be nothing for any one to join, nothing to support, nothing distinctive; it will antagonize no existing order—it will simply present to the world the teaching of Jesus, and it will present nothing else. It will be no more sectarian than the Sermon on the Mount."

"But how can it be managed without organization?" asked Mayor Riley.

"How was the Christian religion which Jesus gave to the world managed in His day?" returned Dan. "Very few of the denominational churches to-day contend that one must be a Methodist, or a Presbyterian, or a Congregationalist in order to be Christian. Do you five men, of five different denominations, not recognize one another as Christians? One is a Christian because one worships God as he is revealed in Jesus, which means, if it means anything, accepting the teaching of Jesus as the guiding principle in all the affairs of life. Jesus set up no human organization which men must join. He devised no machine to which men must belong and which they must support. All Christians are certainly free to hold individual ideas, but no man is free to make his individual ideas necessary to the Christian religion, or to build about himself a separate and distinct organization which makes the teaching of Jesus of no effect, and defeats the end for which Jesus came."

"How would it be possible, without organization, to conduct the necessary business?" asked Banker Winton.

Dan answered: "The Foundation would, of course, be a legal corporation. The trustees or stewards would administer the funds. They would, for their business operations, provide whatever organization was necessary. That is why the plan calls for experienced and skillful business men to serve in that capacity. *But such organization would not in any way be a denomination which people would be asked to join, to which they would pay dues, or with which they would become identified as members.* It would be a business, not a theological organization."

The groceryman asked: "And where would we find such a minister?"

Big Dan's answer came heartily: "Thousands of our most able and talented ministers in all denominations would gladly preach Jesus only. I doubt if there is a true minister of the Christian religion to-day who does not feel the burden of his sectarian obligations. Certainly the more Christ-like—the more zealous and best-fitted to teach the truths of Jesus—would rejoice to be set free. If the Christianity of denominationalism has not produced religious leaders who would be happy to preach nothing but Jesus, and to devote all their time and strength to a spiritual ministry, then indeed is the modern church system condemned. In fact, the great majority of the ministers themselves, so far as they dare, are saying that denominationalism is doomed."

"But how could the temple minister be controlled?" asked Riley. "Would he not set up his own individual ideas and rally about himself a group of personal followers?"

Dan smiled. *"You forget that the five trustees are members of five different denominations.* These trustees will undertake this work because they have come to realize the tragic failure of denominationalism, and because they understand that the teaching of Jesus alone can make the Christian religion effective. These men, from five different denominations, would select the minister. *The Board of Trustees would be self-perpetuating, which means that as vacancies occur, the trustees will fill them with men like themselves in ideals and purpose.*

"Furthermore, the minister who undertakes this ministry will of necessity throw aside every denominational interest. No denomination will recognize him. He will be ostracized by all sectarian organizations, branded as unorthodox and shunned by his fellow ministers. It will be quite impossible for him to have any sectarian interests even should he be so inclined. He will have nothing to do with the business management of the trustees, no necessity to raise money, no need to bid for social favors, no hope of denominational preferments or honors, no incentive to raise theological questions—theological questions do not grow out of Jesus' teaching. There will be nothing for him to argue about. The very nature of his position, his freedom and the nature of his teaching will keep him close to the Master, and single-minded in His service."

"Will there be organization of the workers who engage in the activities of which you speak?" asked the Judge.

Dan answered: "I suppose that will work out as a necessity, but there will be no denominational guilds, or aids or societies for the purpose of making money for denominational ends. The only organization will be that which is necessary to make the ministry of the people to the poor most effective, and to prevent confusion and duplication of effort."

"What provision will be made for the social life?" asked the groceryman.

"None, in the sense of the present denominational churches' efforts," Dan answered. "Because there will be, as I have said, no distinctive organization. The preaching, the worship, the activities, will all center on the one purpose of the Christian religion, which is *to build Christian character.* If the people are Christians, in deed and in truth, can we doubt that their social life will be Christian? With the principles which have been outlined once established, we may safely leave the social activities of the people to take care of themselves. There will be no need for church balls to raise money and no need for Young People's Societies to perpetuate denominationalism."

"I can see how the experiment endowed by you would work in Westover," said Judge Burnes, "but the demonstration will have a comparatively small national value unless it can be extended to other parts of the country."

Big Dan returned: "My belief is, Judge, that this Westover Foundation will merely open the way.

"I have faith that when the plan is established the most Christian members of all denominations will be drawn to the movement. The best paying members of the denominations—I mean those who pay most in proportion to their means—are the most Christian. You will find it is these same Christian members who are also the most generous supporters of your city charities. Because these Christian men and women already recognize the waste and inefficiency of the denominations, and deplore the Church's indifference to charity, they will be first to see the value of the temple plan. The temple worship, the preaching of Jesus only; the activities, ministering to the poor; the offerings, one hundred per cent given to the needy—all this will make a strong appeal to the most sincere, most intelligent and most Christian members of all denominations, and they will drop their denominationalism just as all sensible people cast aside their candles and whale oil and kerosene lamps when the electric light was put within their reach.

"The denominational churches will be abandoned as the old carriage and buggies were discarded when automobiles became possible. *When the strength of the present forty-four churches in Westover is concentrated upon the Christian religion, and the money which now pays the running expenses of these forty-four organizations all goes through the temple offerings to the poor, denominationalism in Westover will go out of business.*

"The two and a half millions now in useless church property will then be converted in a Foundation similar to the Westover Foundation to set Christianity free in some other community.

"In addition to this, millions will be given to religion when religion is made effective. Millions will be available for Christian work when the donors know that the money will not be used to keep alive these divisions in which the people, as a whole, no longer believe."

Said Mayor Riley: "There is no doubt that the plan would make great inroads upon the strength of denominationalism. At the same time there are many of the older members who would never change."

"Certainly," returned Dan, *"but what about the younger generation?* Our young people, in their revolt against the present church system, have proved quite conclusively that they would not be bound by the sectarian prejudices of their parents.

"It is this generation which is just coming into power in the country that is most important to our national future. I am convinced that the youth of the land, in their daring independence, their intolerance of sham and in their insistence upon realities, would be irresistibly drawn to such a presentation of the Christian religion as this plan proposes."

"These trustees," said the groceryman doubtfully, "would need to be men above reproach."

"No man is above reproach," answered Big Dan. "One of the most beautiful and vital truths of Jesus' teaching is that, while it sets up an ideal and makes that ideal possible for humanity, Christianity does not rest upon the perfection of its followers, but upon the truth of its principles. Christianity is not in attaining a perfect ideal but in the effort put forth to attain. It is not in a victory gained, it is in the strength and valor of the battle waged. Of the twelve chosen by Jesus to be His personal companions and disciples, and to whom He committed His teaching, not one was above reproach. They had all the characteristic weaknesses of human nature. There certainly would be less chance for mistakes under this simple plan than under the competitive system now in vogue.

"There are in every denomination thousands of men qualified to serve on such a board of trustees. The many who are already filling like positions of trust prove that there is no lack of fitting material. It is the opportunity to serve that is lacking.

"And this," added Big Dan in conclusion, "brings us again to my request that you five men undertake this work in Westover. And again I urge—before you accept, count well the cost.

"You will be subjected to the bitter attacks of your denominations. You will be called renegades—disloyal to your churches. You will be held up to scorn and ridicule. You will be charged with all sorts of motives. You will be called fanatics, fools. Business pressure will be brought to bear. You will lose friends, patrons, customers, votes. Indeed, you should count well the cost before you undertake the task.

"You should look also to the end to be gained for your homes, for your children, for your country, and for humanity."

CHAPTER XVII.

MOTHER AND DAUGHTER.

When Jack Ellory talked to Grandpa Paddock that afternoon, about his hopes for a home with all that the word implies, he had been very much in earnest. Men of his stamp are not generally given to talking about such things, but he was really in a state of mind over the affair in the woods and grandpa had made it easy for him to speak.

Jack's love for Georgia had come as a natural, almost unnoticed development of their childhood intimacy. He had grown into his love as he had grown into manhood. As he had passed from early childhood into adolescence and from youth to full manhood, his feeling for his little girl playmate had changed from childhood affection to the fully matured love of a man for his mate.

But with the slow and natural development of this mating love, young Ellory had been subjected to all the influences which operate to form those unwholesome conceptions of life which so sadly characterize our modern youth. With his physical development and the changing quality of his love for this girl had come a mental development—had come views, mental attitudes, habits of thought, contacts, experiences. As he gained knowledge of the ways of men and women, he acquired that cynical disbelief in womanly virtue which is the seed of racial degeneracy. Almost before he knew the *quality* of his love for Georgia, he was *afraid* to believe in her as a man must of necessity believe in his mate. The instinct of self-protection led him to defend himself against his developing love. He felt instinctively that if Georgia was what his set commonly assumed all women to be, he must not permit himself to think of her as his wife. The same instinct operated in all his association with this girl, to protect her from that which he feared by guarding her even against himself.

Then came that incident in the woods. Because the girl had been strong enough to resist him, his doubt of her had been swept away; his love had triumphed over his fears and had become the dominant thing in his life. But with this awakening had come realization that the girl, in her love, had been subjected to the same forces which had inhibited him. The very incident, which had convinced Jack that Georgia was *not* like all the others, had brought with his wakened love for her a new fear. *He feared, now, that her doubt of him had been so confirmed that she would not dare accept him.*

Then grandpa's visit had brought relief and in answer to Georgia's call he had hurried to her in the spirit of one who loves and is loved and who in his love has found realization of his best ideals and fulfillment of his fondest dreams.

He had been shocked by the girl's greeting, but his mood had served to carry him on to the declaration of his love. The utter recklessness and apparent lack of decent love ideals in her answer to his proposal had crashed all his awakened hopes, but his old habit of instinctively protecting her had caused him to yield to her mood and to go with her that night. And yet, even under the shock of his disappointment and his reawakened fears, he seemed to sense that the girl's desperate recklessness was a result of some experience of which she could not speak. He felt that the girl needed him—that in her state of mind she was not safe without him. His instinct to protect the woman he loved was strong enough to cause him to act for her, even while his hopes were apparently destroyed by the nature of her refusal of his proposal.

With the news of the tragic results of that wild party came afterthoughts of Georgia's apparent surrender to the standards which prevailed among their set. Even had he known that the girl would accept him now, he would not have dared ask her again to marry him.

Did he still love her? Yes, he admitted to himself, he did. And that, he added in the vernacular of his day, "was the hell of it." Had he not loved her as he did, he could have enjoyed making the most of the opportunities offered by her abandonment of those standards which had, so far, protected them. But Jack Ellory's love for Georgia was not the kind of love which would permit him to accept her reckless offer of herself. He wanted her for a wife, not a mistress. Because he might have her for a mistress made it impossible for him to ask her to be his wife. Because he loved her as his wife made it as impossible for him to take her as his mistress.

And yet, while sober thought compelled him to accept her refusal as final, he still could not accept the situation. He felt baffled. He sensed something behind the apparent facts. The conviction that she loved him persisted. He felt that there was a reason for her refusal which he must know, and that he could not surrender all hope until he had seen her again. He must know why she had so changed from the girl who had withstood him, that afternoon in the woods, to the girl who had offered herself to him, the night of that wild party.

He sent a little note to her asking if she would see him.

The answer came—a pitiful, broken-hearted letter, but so final that he was compelled to accept it as the end.

Mrs. Paddock had lied to her husband that morning when she told him that their daughter was sleeping. She had talked with the girl in her room—had begged her to keep silent about the Astell affair, and Georgia had promised to say nothing more about it because she was indifferent now to anything that might happen. All her love hopes, which grandma had built up for her, were gone. She realized that in refusing Jack, as she had, she had destroyed his belief in her, without which their happiness was impossible. Nothing now mattered. While the groceryman and his wife were miserably pretending over their breakfast, their daughter was lying in her bed, staring wide-eyed at the ceiling—trying not to think—trying not to feel.

But when the girl's father came to her later and she saw that he knew about Astell, her love for him stirred her sympathies. The tragedy of her own love drove her very close to him in the tragedy of his love. And then, when she understood that to protect her, to save her mother, and their home, her father would endure his shame in silence and pretend not to know, she realized that she must help him. For her mother she would do nothing. She cared as little for what might happen to her mother as she cared for what might happen to herself. Why, she asked herself, *should* she care? But for her father—her pal, her dear old groceryman daddy!—she would play the game. They had not played together lately as they used to do. It would be her part to reestablish their old comradeship. He needed her even as she needed him.

During the days which followed, when the community interest in Harry Winton's death and funeral was at its height, the girl did not leave the house. She refused to see any one except her parents. Had it not been for her father's dependence upon her, the situation would have been intolerable. In this crisis, through which the groceryman and his daughter were passing, it was their loving companionship which saved them both.

Then the groceryman went to Kansas City, and left his daughter alone with her mother. The girl did not know why he had gone. With only the companionship of her mother, the days dragged miserably. Mrs. Paddock scarcely spoke to her, and was absent from the house most of the time—Georgia did not know where. The girl's attitude toward her mother bordered on a contemptuous indifference.

Then, one morning, a telegram came. The groceryman would return home the following day.

Mrs. Paddock, without comment, handed the message to her daughter.

The girl read it silently.

After waiting in vain for Georgia to speak, the mother asked uneasily: "Have you any idea why your father went to Kansas City?"

The girl shook her head. "No."

Mrs. Paddock, watching her daughter closely, said: "It is strange that Henry Winton, Ed Jones, Judge Burnes and Mayor Riley should all go with him—and that their wives know no more about it than I."

The girl made no reply.

"Your father used to talk with me about his affairs," complained the older woman.

Georgia did not speak.

"He evidently thinks I am not to be trusted," added Mrs. Paddock, bitterly.

The daughter was silent.

"For heaven's sake, say something," cried the mother; "you sit there like a graven image!"

"I am sorry," returned Georgia calmly, "but there doesn't seem to be anything for me to say. You surely can't expect me to sympathize with you because father does not trust you?"

At this, Mrs. Paddock was silent for some time and the girl could see that she was debating some question in her own mind. Then hesitatingly, as if reaching a doubtful conclusion, she said: "Mary Winton asked me to spend the day with her. She is lonely and wants me to drive out to their old home. I shall be away until dinner time this evening. Why don't you run out to the farm for the day? It will be good for you. You can't spend the rest of your life shut up here in this house."

The girl felt a sudden longing to see her grandparents. She saw that for some reason her mother wanted her to go. She hesitated a brief moment, then answered with sudden decision that she would spend the day in the country.

A half hour later Georgia bade her mother a perfunctory good-by and went to the garage for the car. She looked at the indicator on the gasoline tank, consulted the oil gauge, saw that there was water in the radiator and was about to step into the car when she remembered an article in the last issue of the *Literary Digest* which she had thought grandpa would enjoy.

Returning to the house and entering through the kitchen, she was just in time to hear her mother's voice at the telephone.

"No, he is still in Kansas city. I have a telegram that he will return home to-morrow. . . .

"Of course not—she has gone to spend the day at the farm. . . .

"No, no, you can't come this forenoon. . . .

"No, I must go down town—-I am sorry, but I *must*. . . .

"Oh, Edward, you know better. . . .

"Yes—yes—this afternoon. . . ."

Georgia went back through the kitchen, and out to the garage.

What should she do? It was evident that her mother had deliberately planned for this meeting with Astell. The girl did not believe that they had seen each other since that terrible night of Harry Winton's death. She had hoped that in spite of her promise not to tell her father about Astell, her mother's fear of exposure would force her to drop the affair. If her mother continued to see Astell—if she even saw him once more—the situation might easily develop beyond the point where it would be possible to avert irretrievable disaster. For her father's sake, if not for her mother's she must do something.

Mechanically she stepped into the car and started the motor.

As the girl turned into the street from the driveway and passed the house, Mrs. Paddock appeared on the porch. Halfway down the block the girl glanced back and saw her mother leaving the house.

Still with no definite plan, but feeling that she must do something, Georgia drove around a few blocks and returned to the garage.

Reentering the house, she moved nervously about the living room, then with a sudden desperate resolution, she went to the phone and called Astell's number.

When the answer came she said hurriedly, in a voice which might easily be mistaken for her mother's carefully cultured tones: "I have changed my mind, Edward—I'm not going out this morning after all. . . .

"Yes—yes—oh, wonderful. . . .

"Come at ten. . . .

"Yes—yes—and leave your car somewhere a block or two away."

In her room upstairs, the girl watched from a window which gave a view of the street in front of the house.

Would her mother or Astell arrive first? What if they should approach the house at the same moment?

It was half past nine when Mrs. Paddock returned to her home.

The girl, listening at her door which she had set ajar, heard her mother come up the stairs and go to her room.

Fifteen minutes later she saw Astell coming up the street.

Quietly, she stole from her room and down the stairs. Careful to make no sound, she opened the front door.

Georgia was right in thinking that her mother had not seen Astell since that meeting which she had witnessed. The truth is that Mrs. Paddock had not arranged this interview from any real desire to be with the man. She was not capable of a passion strong enough to drive her to such risk.

The groceryman's wife had been terribly frightened by her daughter's arraignment and was still afraid. She bitterly resented her daughter's discovery of her conduct. As she saw the old companionship between her husband and her daughter being reestablished and, with some reason, perhaps, felt herself left out and, to a degree, ignored, the situation for her, too, became almost unbearable. She had been driven to attempt this interview with Astell by her feeling that things could not continue as they were—that the crash might come at any moment.

But most of all, perhaps, the groceryman's wife felt that the change in her husband's attitude toward her was ominous. In spite of his resolution to act as if nothing had happened until, for Georgia's sake, he could be sure of doing the right thing to save their home, Joe Paddock could not play the game beyond a certain point. Mrs. Paddock was puzzled and anxious. If her husband knew, why did he remain silent? If he did not know, what had changed him? She had always thought that she dominated her commonplace, groceryman husband by virtue of her intellectual superiority. Like many women of her type, she was incapable of understanding that she ruled her mate, not by right of *her* superiority, but by the grace of *his* love. Suddenly, with no apparent reason, she had lost her power over him. She, all at once, discovered in this man, who had always been so pliant to her will, a rocklike quality against which she felt herself helpless.

It should be said, too, that Georgia's mother bitterly regretted her affair with Astell. After all, her husband and her daughter were more to her than this man. But she lacked that strength of character which might have enabled her to extricate herself from the situation into which she had drifted. If the crash should come, as it might any day, she would be left helpless. Her husband and daughter would have each other. Who would take care of her?

By this it will be understood that Mrs. Paddock was born with a not unusual feminine complex which led her to assume that, though the heavens fall, some one must take care of her. She felt that she had paid all her obligations to life by being born a female. She fulfilled her mission on earth by permitting some man to provide for her. She loved her groceryman husband, yes, but she expressed that love by accepting all that his love prompted him to do for her as her right. The more she loved him the more he was obligated to do for her. She instinctively sought to absorb him. Because she loved him he was her personal property—he had, in her mind, no existence except as he existed for her. She recognized that as husband and wife, in theory, they were one but she never failed to remember that, in fact, she was *the* one. Her love sought fulfillment not in what she could be to him, but in which he could do for her. This arrangement had worked because, while the only expression of love which she knew was to *take,* it was the groceryman's nature to express his love by *giving.*

And now something had happened—her commonplace, groceryman husband was no longer her personal property. She did not ask herself if she had lost his love; she was too much alarmed that she had lost *him.* He had for so many years yielded himself to her that she was frightened to find that he could so calmly and quietly become his own master. To establish dominion over some man became an immediate necessity, to be left without a man to provide for her was a fate too horrible to contemplate. She much preferred to keep her husband and daughter and home, but if the situation developed to make that impossible, then she must be assured of some other man's support. Astell, of course, was the logical candidate.

Mrs. Paddock heard the front door close. Surprised, wondering, she stepped into the upper hall and listened.

It—she could not be mistaken—it was Georgia's voice. The girl seemed to be entertaining some one. Why was she at home? She had gone to the country for the day! And Astell was coming! He must not come—he must be warned—he—good heaven! That other voice—a man's voice! It was Astell! Astell was there with Georgia! And Georgia believed that her mother was with Mary Winton—and Astell thought that Mrs. Paddock was down town—and they were there together! Her daughter and Edward Astell!

The groceryman's wife forced herself to listen. She could not distinguish their words, for the two had gone into the living room, but the tone of her daughter's voice was unmistakably teasing—and she laughed. The man's voice was as clearly pleading. Then their voices sank to low confidential murmurs.

The woman, in the hall above, was almost beside herself with anger, humiliation and fear. She pictured the scene which, she believed, was being enacted in the living room. One moment she wanted to shriek—to rush in upon them—denounce them—upbraid them—to strike—to hurt them physically. The next moment she wanted to crawl away somewhere, anywhere, and hide her shame. If only she could disappear and never be seen again by any one who knew her.

When Astell was gone, the groceryman's daughter came slowly up the stairs and found her mother waiting for her. For what seemed a long time they stood looking at each other in a dead silence. The mother's face was white with anger. The girl's face was pale, but serene.

The older woman spoke first: "I thought you were at the farm?"

"And I thought you were spending the day with Mrs. Winton," the girl returned calmly.

"Will you explain the meaning of this?" demanded Mrs. Paddock. "How dare you receive that man here, in this house, when you believe yourself alone?"

"I have a better right to Edward than you have," the girl retorted. "You seem to forget that I was present when you thought *you* were alone with him. You told me you were not going to be here to-day. I drove away to make you think that I was going to the country. Then I came back and phoned him. Surely you don't think that you are the only woman in the world for him. Edward and I have often met at Tony's and the Inn and other joints."

Mrs. Paddock gasped. "Do you mean—is it possible—" she faltered, "that you phoned and asked him to come to you—this morning?"

"It was easy," returned the girl, impudently. "When he knew you were away he came running. He would have spent the day with me if he had not had important business this afternoon. And why should I not invite him—why should he not come? We are both free souls, you know. Am I so ugly and ill-formed and unattractive that you wonder a man of Edward's taste would want me?"

Laura Louise Paddock was crushed. Her punishment was almost too cruel. Her face was haggard and old. Her eyes were pleading—filled with shame. Her form relaxed and drooped.

The daughter's eyes filled with tears, but the mother did not see.

As the older woman bowed her head and turned away she said, with a faltering whimper: "I could not have believed it—I shall never, never see that man again."

"Just a minute," cried the girl.

Mrs. Paddock halted on the threshold of her room.

"You are right that you will never see Edward Astell again," Georgia said and paused, as if to give full emphasis to her words. Then she continued deliberately: "Astell is leaving Westover this afternoon. It will be a long, long time before he dares return. I warned him that when father came home tomorrow I was going to tell him about you two, and that daddy would certainly kill him as any decent man would kill such a dirty rat."

Again she paused, then: "Of course, with Astell gone, I shall not tell father, and you will go on as if nothing had happened."

The girl's voice faltered, and the tears came: "Oh, Mother, Mother, for daddy's sake, let's help him to save us and our home.

Mrs. Paddock, without a word, without a look toward her daughter, closed the door of her room.

CHAPTER XVIII.

BUILDING THE TEMPLE.

The groceryman arrived home from Kansas City on the morning train. That afternoon he went to the farm.

When grandpa and grandma had heard from their son the reason for his visit to Kansas City, with the details of the proposed Westover Church Foundation and the temple plan, grandma looked at grandpa with a knowing smile. The old gentleman smiled back at her and moved his chair closer to her side, and the groceryman was surprised and relieved to see that his parents were not nearly so shocked at his new religious views as he had feared they would be.

"Son," said grandpa slowly, "your mother and I love this farm. It has been our life. It seems like, sometimes, that every square foot of it is associated with some precious memory.

"When we first settled here in the wilderness, I cleared the land and plowed the ground for our first crops, with oxen. We thought a lot of those oxen." He looked at grandma. "'Member old Buck and Red and Baldy and Jerry, Mother?"

Grandma chuckled and wiped her eyes.

Grandpa continued: "But when the land was all cleared and the stumps gone and we could work horses to better advantage, we gave up using oxen. 'Cause why? 'Cause it was the *farming* that counted most.

"And then we got to be mighty fond of our horses— 'Member Tom and Nelly and Dick and Sally, Mother?"

Grandma nodded and smiled, with misty eyes.

"Why, we *raised* those horses, son," continued the old gentleman. "They were almost like our children. Even *you* can remember Prince and Joe, our carriage team, and old Kate, that your mother used to drive. I never *could* learn to love a piece of machinery like I love a horse, nohow. But, just the same, we're doing most of our farming with tractors now, 'cause farming, you see, is the *main* thing.

"I suspect, if mother and I keep staying on a few years more, we'll be farming with flying machines, or maybe I'll just sit up here on the porch and push a 'lectric button and the plows and harrows and cultivators and mowing machines and reapers will run themselves, without me ever gettin' out of my chair. I'm dead sure of one thing—if I'm here and can *farm* better by changing from tractors to something else, *I'll change* just like I always have, 'cause it's the *farming* that's always been most important.

"There's another thing—with all the changes we've made in our ways of farming, I notice that we're plowing and planting the same old ground, and that it's the same old sun and rain that makes the seed grow and the harvest ripen in the same old way.

"Well, your mother and I love the old Presbyterian Church that we helped to start in Westover. We've seen some wonderful crops of Christian character planted and cultivated and harvested by that old church. But our love for the church we helped to build has never blinded us to the truth that it was the Christianity of Jesus that counted most. For a good many years, when this country was *new,* our church was all there was to work with, and that was all right. But anybody can see that this denominationalism of to-day is just as inadequate in religion as our old oxen would be, now, in farming.

"As I see it, this plan that you've been telling us about can't in any way change Christianity, any more than our using a tractor instead of oxen or horses changes the ground or the sun and rain. It's the same old Christianity that you're proposing to teach, only you're going to teach it with modern efficiency, just as we're working the same old farm with modern machinery.

"If this new plan can teach Christianity better than our old denominational methods—and I believe it can—why then if we're *really Christians we're bound to use it.*"

The old gentleman reached out to pat grandma's hand reassuringly. "That's the way we feel about it, isn't it, Mother?"

"That's the only way we *could* think about it without putting our Presbyterianism above our Lord and Master," returned the old lady bravely. "And your father and I have *never done that,* Joe. But there's some of us old ones will cry over it a little, I suspect.

"I remember that when we first moved into this house from the little log cabin that we'd built with our own hands, and that we started housekeeping in the year we were married, I used to go back down the hill to the old cabin every day and cry a little 'cause I was so lonesome and strange in this big new place. But shucks, I wouldn't near have gone back down there to *live.* And even *now,* when there's nothing left of the old log cabin, I *love the spot where it stood.*

"We didn't build this big house 'cause we weren't *happy* in our log cabin. If it had been just for your father and me we'd *never* have moved. But we needed this house 'cause you see we was countin' on having a big family. We *had* to have this house to raise the children right. The cabin wasn't going to be big enough.

"If it could be done, I'd like to see all God's children gathered together under one roof. You can't raise a real family by scatterin' 'em around in so many different homes. If Christianity hasn't outgrown its little old denominational log cabins, it ought to. Those cabins—taking them any way you please—are too small for the religious family that the Church has got to raise, if it expects to cut much of a figure in the world to-day. It's time the Church was moving into a bigger house, I say. There's a lot of us will cry over the move, I suspect, *but we'll move just the same, 'cause we love the family more than we do the house, after all.*"

The papers announced the Westover Church Foundation in rather a light vein, as if it did not matter much what a millionaire did with his money provided he spent it. The bare facts were given, with no remarks except the suggestion that the chief value of the project would be more or less publicity for Westover. The names of the five trustees were given without comment.

Mrs. Paddock read the announcement and demanded an explanation.

Georgia was interested.

The groceryman told them about the plan.

Georgia asked many questions.

Mrs. Paddock waxed more and more indignant. She protested against *her* husband having anything to do with such a ridiculous affair. She feared for her standing in the community. It would be vulgar for them to countenance such a religious fad. The *best* people were always conservative. "Think how your father and mother will feel, with the church that they founded depending upon your support! If you have so much influence with Dan Matthews why did you not interest him in your *own* church? I'm sure we could use the money. Everybody will be disgusted with you. As if your grocery business were not humiliation enough—now *this!*"

But the groceryman's daughter, glimpsing the deeper truths of the plan, supported her father with eager loyalty.

The church people received the announcement with great interest. The ministers were mildly alarmed. Five different pastors interviewed the five trustees.

The general public, as a whole, was amused.

The friends of the trustees advised, joked and asked questions. When the groceryman and his associates explained the purpose of the experiment, the questioners became thoughtful. One group of the younger business men, headed by Jack Ellory, was bitterly opposed to the movement. The city, they said, was already dunned to death by the churches and could not stand another. Several of those who were most opposed went privately to the trustees in hopes of selling them a lot. But Saxton already held an option on the most desirable property. The disappointed ones became more outspoken in their opinions that this new-fangled religious scheme would be a bad thing for Westover.

It had been decided, by Dan Matthews and the trustees, that Mr. Saxton would remain in Westover and have active charge of the work until the plan was fully established and the first move of the Westover Church Foundation was to open an office in the business district.

The day that the office furniture was being moved in Mr. Saxton received an applicant for a position.

"I have had no experience," the applicant admitted frankly, "but I am sure I could learn to be useful, and I want very much to try."

Mr. Saxton smiled at her earnestness. "Have you talked with your father about it, Miss Paddock?"

"No, sir, but I don't think daddy would object. Do you?"

Saxton replied gravely: "No, child, I don't think he would object." Then he added: "The trustees permit me to employ my own assistants, of course. I am quite sure you could, as you say, learn to be useful. As to salary. . . ."

She interrupted him eagerly: "Oh, Mr. Saxton! But I would not expect a salary! Don't you understand? Father has told me all about the plan. I believe in it. It is wonderful! It is Christianity—*real* Christianity, I mean! And I want to help. Please let me come! I so want to do something!"

"You are hired," cried Saxton promptly.

"But, about that salary," he said when her rejoicing had calmed so that he could speak. "This Foundation, you understand, is a *business* organization. The trustees, Georgia (I really must call you Georgia now that I am your boss), the trustees have decided on the policy of paying regular salaries to their regular office force. You expect to consider this a regular job, do you not?"

"Yes, sir—just as though I were working in a bank."

"Well, then, you must accept a salary. If you wish to turn your salary in at the temple services as your offering, that is your own private affair."

Mrs. Paddock was completely overcome when she learned that her daughter—*her* daughter—was to work in an office like a common stenographer. Georgia's old crowd hard the news with amazement, laughter and mourning. A few were thoughtful. The groceryman's happiness over the girl's resolution may be imagined.

With the passing months, the work of building the temple progressed steadily. There were no blurbs in the papers. There was no drive for funds. If Dan Matthews ever came town it was not known. The newspapers, after that first announcement, never mentioned his name. Indeed, the general public soon ceased to connect Big Dan with the Foundation, for the trustees, understanding that the effectiveness of the plan demanded that no man's name be glorified by this temple, were careful never to refer to him when speaking of the work.

As the building went forward in an orderly and efficient manner, the people were not long in discovering that there was nothing in Westover to compare with the temple in architectural beauty. Interest in the movement grew. The public looked upon the Foundation with increasing respect. While the plan of the experiment was not yet generally understood, Westover was beginning to feel that something of more than ordinary religious significance was taking place.

With this change in the attitude of the people toward the experiment, the apprehension of the churches increased. The denominational "higher-ups" gave the matter their attention and advised the local ministers. The preachers, with more or less wit, began to ridicule this latest freak religion. The sinful waste of money was deplored. Efforts to strengthen denominational pride became more strenuous; exhortations to loyalty to the faith of the fathers more fervid. Sermons, to demonstrate the fallacy of thinking that Christianity could possibly endure without denominations, were frequent. The pastors labored with their errant members and with those influential one whom they had reason to fear might be tempted to become errant.

The trustees, in answer to all this, said nothing. To the attacks of the ministers they made no reply nor did they in any way retaliate. When questioned directly by some interested one, they simply explained the plan.

The inevitable followed. The very people whom the ministers tried to turn against the movement, were aroused by the criticisms of the clergy to a still greater interest in the Foundation and its plan. Because human nature is what it is, the increasing opposition of the churches served to turn the tide of sentiment toward the temple.

As popular opposition to the temple became less active Mrs. Paddock became more lenient. She was not slow in interpreting the signs that her groceryman husband's connection with the Foundation might turn out a distinction instead of a dishonor. There were indications, in certain circles, which led her to comment with more caution. So far as it was possible, she held to her old place of superiority in her home. The Astell affair was a closed incident. But the feeling between mother and daughter persisted.

Georgia was absorbed in her work under Mr. Saxton in the Foundation office. She attended no more parties at Tony's and Sundown Inn. She saw Jack occasionally, by chance, but when possible they avoided each other.

The groceryman, grimly determined to follow the way he had chosen, quietly declined to come again under the rule of Mrs. Paddock. With his daughter's interest in the Foundation work, and their old companionship restored, he was happier than he had been for several years. As for the rest—with Astell out of the way, he was content to wait developments.

CHAPTER XIX.

WORSHIP.

The temple was placed well back from the street, in grounds spacious enough to set it apart from all neighboring buildings. This, in itself, gave the edifice a distinction, a dignity and a value which was sadly lacking in most of the denominational churches in Westover.

Wedged in as they usually are, on lots scarcely large enough to hold them, with other buildings crowding close to their walls, and nothing but the side-walks to separate them from the gutters of the streets, our modern houses of worship do not signify that the religion, which they visibly represent, occupies a place of much importance in the lives of the people who build them. In the pinching economy of space, and in the cheap, materialistic or trivial and showy spirit of the architecture, one feels the denominationalism which grudges room for its neighbors, builds on selfishness, and seeks to attract rather than deeply to impress.

The temple grounds were ample for effective planting which would add to the simple dignity of the building that quiet beauty which is the handmaiden of all true religion.

If it be said that Christianity needs no distinctive edifice with beautiful surroundings—that, perhaps, is true. Certainly, Jesus needed no pulpit other than a mountainside, a fishing boat, a lowly home or a seat beside the road. But if Jesus *were* to build a place of worship in Westover, can any one doubt that he would give to it that importance among the common buildings of the city which he would have his religion occupy in the thoughts of the people? Why should our public libraries and state universities be made so imposing and beautiful, and our places of worship so commonplace and ugly? Why should the animal houses in our zoological parks be set amid gracious tree and shrubs and generous lawns and lovely flowers, and our houses of God built so close to the gutters of our streets and the back yards of our dwellings?

For the architecture of the temple, it is enough to say that it was Christian. There was a tower for the bells and, high above all, softly lighted by subdued rays from some hidden source, quietly glowing against the dark night sky, a cross.

During the week before the opening service in the temple, every citizen of Westover received, through the mail, a pamphlet setting forth the plan of the Westover Church Foundation—much as Dan Matthews had presented it to the groceryman and his friends. The reason for the experiment was given with no unkindly criticism of the churches and with genuine appreciation of the good accomplished by the denominations in the past. But facts and figures were presented frankly. The endowment, in relation to the present expenditures of the forty-four Westover churches, was explained. The offering to the poor, the activities, and the character of the teaching were stressed. The name of the temple minister was given, with the hours when he would be at the temple to receive those who might wish to counsel with him. The name of Dan Matthews did not appear in the pamphlet, nor was any reference made to the man who had established the Foundation.

The newspapers took their stories from the pamphlet. There was no long and elaborate program of special music and exceptional singers. There were no flamboyant promises of eloquent preaching. There was no extravagant write-up of the minister. There was no advertising of a sensational sermon subject. The announcement of the hours of the service and the place was as simple as sincere as the invitation given by Jesus: "Come unto me, all ye that labor and are heavy laden, and I will give you rest."

Sunday came, and with the beginning of the day the temple bells were heard—clearly, sweetly, in the quiet of the early morning, the beautiful music of the chimes floated over the city—"Nearer, My God, to Thee." In hundreds of homes the people listened, and many hearts, which commonly held no thought of the day, involuntarily echoed the familiar words of that prayer as it was sung by the sweet-toned bells.

When the hour for worship arrived, the bells summoned the people. From every quarter of the city they came: the curious, the seekers after the new and unusual, the lovers of the sensational, those who hungered for religion, those who hoped for something to criticize or ridicule, and those who had grasped the meaning of the plan and were praying for its success.

The groceryman's emotion was too deep for words. If there had been in his heart a faint, lingering question as to the outcome of this religion experiment, it had vanished with that morning prayer of the bells.

Georgia, close by her father's side, shared his emotion as they now shared most of their thoughts and interests.

Mrs. Paddock, who had decided to attend this first service because she was told that many of the best people would be there, was very quiet and walked beside her husband with not quite her usual air of ownership. She, too, had heard the early morning bells.

As the three arrived at the broad walk which led from the street to the temple doors, the groceryman felt his daughter's arm tremble, and drew her closer with a comforting little movement. Jack Ellory was only a few paces ahead.

Then, just as they were about to turn from the street toward the temple entrance, an automobile drew up to the curb and they saw Grandpa and Grandma Paddock, Davie Bates and his father and mother.

The groceryman and his daughter greeted them joyously. Mrs. Paddock was more reserved. She was annoyed that the Jamison's should have happened along at the very moment when the groceryman was shaking hands with the delivery boy and his parents. Davie's face was beaming with happiness. His mother's eyes were shining with gratitude and thanksgiving. The carpenter's deep voice trembled a little as he told them that he was going back to work Monday morning! In spite of Mrs. Paddock's annoyance, they waited until Davie had parked the car and then all went up the walk and into the temple together.

As the throng of people streamed toward the place of worship there was much talk and laughter. Neighbors, friends and acquaintances greeted one another with comment and joke. But as they drew near the entrance and heard the music of an organ, soft and low, the laughter died away—voices were hushed.

There are few natures that do not respond instantly to an atmosphere of sincere and true religion. It would have been a strange person who could have entered through the portals of that temple of Christianity without being instantly impressed by the spirit of the place. The great room, softly lighted, was beautiful in the simple dignity of its proportions and quiet coloring. There was no attempt at elaborate decoration; no display of costly carvings and expensive windows; no glittering chandeliers. But while this place of worship was without a suggestion of theatrical showiness, on the one hand, it was as far from cheapness and bad taste, on the other.

Except for a simple reading desk there was no "pulpit furniture." There was no organ in sight. There was no choir, no chorus, no singer, to be seen. On either side of the rostrum and from the main floor, there were arched openings of passageways, leading evidently to other rooms. There were no doors except the great doors at the entrance. The seats were as comfortable as the seats in the best motion-picture theaters.

On the back of each chair was a receptacle to receive the offering of the person occupying the seat next in the rear. There was an inscription on this receptacle: "Your offering made in the name of Jesus for the relief of those of whom He said "Inasmuch as ye have done it unto one of the least of these, my brethren, ye have done it unto me.'"

There was also a small rack with a supply of cards and a pencil. On each card was printed: "If you wish to make an offering of personal service, write your name and address in the space below." On the same card was another line: "If you know of any person in need, write the name and address in the space below and deposit this card with your offering."

There were no racks filled with assorted hymn books and church literature.

With the subdued tones of the unseen organ trembling on the air, and with nothing to distract their attention, the people became very quiet. Many heads were bowed in prayer.

The minister entered from the archway on the right of the pulpit, and going to the reading desk stood before the people. He was dressed in no distinctive robe or garb.

With no organist in sight, mysteriously working his stops and keys; with no elaborately gowned and hatted soprano; no choir fussing with their music; no distinguished tenor; no cornet soloist tinkering with his instrument; the attention of the audience was fixed upon the teacher.

The music of the organ died softly away. There was a moment of silence. The minister raised his hands and the great audience arose to stand, with bowed heads, for the invocation prayer.

Again the organ was heard, and as the melody of one of those grand old hymns which are common to all denominations, and which for generations have been woven into the religious life of the nation, was recognized, the words of the hymn appeared in letters of light in a panel above the pulpit. There was no announcement of the hymn or number. There was no noise and confusion of books being taken from the racks; no searching for number or page; no helping a neighbor find the place. The people, as they stood, merely lifted up their eyes and sang.

When the hymn was ended and the congregation seated, the minister, without preliminary remark or announcement, read a brief saying of Jesus.

Another of the Master's sayings appeared in letters of light on the panel, and the people, with uplifted faces, read in unison.

The minister read another of those truths which Jesus gave to men, and the congregation responded with another as it appeared on the panel.

"I am the way, the truth and the life," read the minister.

"I am the vine, ye are the branches," came the response.

"If ye love me, keep my commandments," read the minister.

"This is my commandment that ye love one another as I have loved you," came the answer.

At the close of the reading the organ sounded with another hymn, and as the words appeared on the panel the multitude caught up the song in a great swelling chorus.

The minister, in a few simple words, spoke of the offering as an act of worship, and led the people to see their gifts in the light of Jesus' teaching. He made no appeal for funds. He called attention to no deficit in the treasury. He mentioned no overdue bills or back salaries. This was followed by a prayer, made in the spirit of surrender to God and of giving to his service.

With the closing words of the prayer the organ tones, soft and low, again filled the room. The people sat or knelt with bowed heads. They were very still. The worshipers saw in their offerings that which represented their human strength, talents, possessions. They knew that every penny they gave would be used in the relief of those in their own community who were sick or hungry or naked or homeless or wretched. There were neither ushers nor deacons passing boxes, plates or baskets, to break the feeling of the moment. There was no soloist to demand attention with an elaborate vocal effort. In the solemn hush, with only the low murmuring music of the organ, in the spirit of prayer and meditation the people laid their gifts before their God. In true homage and adoration to the Father of all they offered that which represented themselves, for the relief of those with whom Jesus identified Himself.

Presently, without a break in the music—with no announcement or fumbling for books—the tones of the organ swung into another hymn. The minister raised his hand and again the people stood, and with upturned faces sang.

With no announcement of any kind; no calling attention to special services; no urging of attendance at Ladies' Aid meeting; no stressing of social events; no urging that the people support this or that political or civic cause; the opening words of the sermon followed.

Intellectually, the thought of the sermon commanded the attention of the best minds in the audience. In simplicity, it was like the sermons of the Master whose teaching it presented. The feeling was deeply religious; as tender as it was strong, as sincere as it was uncompromising. There was no effort to amuse or to entertain. There was no straining for pulpit oratory. With the unassuming directness and authority of the Sermon on the Mount, it was an interpretation of the spirit of Jesus in the terms of to-day—a translation of the world-old truths which Jesus taught into the language of modern life.

If there were those who expected the minister to answer the attacks of the clergy or to criticize the Church, they were disappointed. Those who came to criticize found something which awakened them to the realities of religion. Those who came from curiosity or for sensationalism were shamed. Those who came to laugh found nothing to ridicule. Those who came merely to hear the new preacher forgot the minister in the message from Jesus which came through him.

There was not a feature of that service which would not have been endorsed by *all* churches. There was not a word of the sermon which would not have been endorsed by *all* ministers. It was simply Christianity in spirit and in fact—and it was nothing else.

Grandpa and Grandma Paddock sat hand in hand. Grandma's lips moved often, as if in prayer. Now and then grandpa raised a hand to his gentle old eyes.

The delivery boy sat on the edge of his chair in rapt attention. His mother's face was glorified. The carpenter's strong countenance, lined with suffering, was lighted with new courage and hope.

The groceryman's daughter knew that here was strength and that safe refuge, which in her heart she had always felt must be, if only one knew where to look for it.

Mrs. Paddock was awed by the spirit of eternal truth, beside which her shifting intellectual ideals were as nothing.

The groceryman and his four friends knew that they had made no mistake.

With the closing words of the sermon, the minister raised his hands and the people stood during the short prayer and benediction which followed.

Once more the sweetly solemn tones of the organ filled the building which was sacred to the God of all Christians.

The minister left the rostrum through the arched way.

Slowly the people filed from the temple.

There was no effusive and perfunctory hand-shaking by an appointed committee at the door. There was no laughing, chattering, or exchange of gossip. Quietly, under the spell of the truths of Jesus' teaching and the spiritual atmosphere of the place, the people went out from the house of worship.

CHAPTER XX.

HAPPINESS.

The denominational ministers of Westover planned a united campaign. They joined forces in a great union revival, with a revivalist of national reputation as a fighter. They held union prayer meetings. They appointed committees of workers to labor with the brethren who were going astray. In short, the churches united in opposition to the temple plan as they had never united in Christianity. It seemed almost as if they hated the sight of that cross against the sky. It was as if the music of the temple bells aroused in them only anger. Through the newspapers, the ministers made it known that their association would not recognize the temple preacher as a minister of the gospel.

To all of this the temple minister answered not a word. Never, in his sermons, was there the slightest allusion to the churches. The trustees of the Foundation quietly refused to even discuss the action of the clergymen. But the membership of the churches and the people, generally, were aroused by the bitterness of the preachers and began to ask: "To what do the churches object? If this worship in the temple is not Christian, what is Christianity? Are these ministers opposed to the teaching of Jesus? Do they object to the people meeting for worship in one house instead of forty-four? Do they object to the offerings begin used to relieve the suffering of the poor in Westover?"

To those who expressed a wish to join the temple, the minister said simply: "If you wish to become a follower of Jesus, follow Him. To accept the teaching and example of Jesus as the guiding principle of one's life, is to be a Christian. If you are a *Christian* you certainly must *by virtue of your Christianity be a member of the Church.* What more do you want? No one can join the temple, because there is nothing to join. The temple is a place where the people may, if they desire, worship God as He is revealed in the life and teaching of Jesus, and it is nothing else. Is there any organization, with laws as and salaried secretaries and learned counsels, which one must join in order to observe Christmas? Love needs no organization."

As the people came more and more to understand the principles of the temple plan, the spirit of the movement gained irresistible force. Saxton reported to Dan Matthews that the temple was filled at every service. The offerings were increasing steadily. Many were giving themselves to the work among the poor. The doors of the temple were never closed, and at almost every hour of the day people might have been seen in this house of God, sitting quietly in meditation, or kneeling in prayer. Every morning and every evening the music of the chimes floated over the city. Every night, high against the sky, the people saw the cross.

Lacking the denominational prejudices of their parents, the young people of Westover were quick to sense the reality of this worship, the spirit of the service, the authority of the preaching, and they responded with an eagerness which was amazing to the churches which had failed to interest them. Boys and girls from the high school and young men and women from the University came in increasing numbers to talk with the temple minister of religion and life, and to lay their problems before him.

As the weeks passed, the leaders of the Ladies' Aid Societies and similar denominational organizations complained to their pastors that their best workers were no longer attending their meetings. The treasurers of the various churches reported that the collections were decreasing at an alarming rate, and that many of their largest contributors were not renewing their subscriptions. Then the groceryman and his friends were expelled from their respective churches.

Mrs. Paddock went with her husband and daughter to every service at the temple. Gradually, in ways unmistakable, this apostle of what she had called "the higher culture" revealed an awakening interest in the Christian religion. As the teachings of Jesus and the spirit of the temple worship impressed her with the *realities* of Christianity, she sought with increasing earnestness to reestablish the home spirit of her early married years.

The groceryman, watching the change, waited the *fulfillment* of that which it promised. His old restless foreboding of evil was gone.

There was a new delivery boy at the store now—a man. Davie was in high school, with the promise of the groceryman's help when he should be ready for the University.

Georgia continued her work with Mr. Saxton in the office of the Foundation. She often went to the club in the afternoon for an hour of tennis, but she never played with Jack—though she knew that he sometimes watched her from a distance. Often, on Saturday, she would go to the farm to spend the night with grandma and grandpa, returning to town with them in time for the Sunday morning services.

But between the girl and her mother there was a wall which seemingly could not be broken down. They both wished to overcome the barrier but neither could bring herself to make the advance.

Then one day at dinner, the groceryman told his wife and daughter a bit of business news: Tony's Place was closed. "He has been falling behind for some time," Joe explained. "He blames what he calls 'this new religious craze.'" The groceryman smiled. "He tried to borrow from the First National to tide him over but we were forced to refuse the loan on the ground that this was not a temporary revival in which people would soon lose interest, but a very definite awakening which would continue to make his business unprofitable. The other banks turned him down on the same grounds—so Tony has gone out of business."

"Poor old Tony," murmured Georgia.

Mrs. Paddock started to speak, but changed her mind and remained silent.

"I hear the Sundown Inn people are having hard work meeting their bills, too," said the groceryman. "This is confidential, of course, but the merchants are going to refuse to extend their credit after first of the month."

They were silent for several moments, then the girl said: "By the way, Daddy, at the office to-day we figured, if the temple offerings continue at the present rate they will actually exceed the annual Organized Charity expenditures."

"Fine," cried the groceryman. Then he added confidently: "The offerings will continue, all right—and increase."

Mrs. Paddock's face was eloquent but she did not speak.

Georgia continued: "And Mr. Saxton thinks that we should start work on the other temples at once. He is going to recommend it to the trustees at their meeting to-morrow night."

"So he told me," returned the groceryman. "He is right, of course."

Mrs. Paddock rose suddenly. "Will you excuse me, please," she faltered. "I—it—it is all so wonderful. . . ." Her voice broke and she hurried from the room.

The afternoon of the following day, the groceryman's wife was among those who sought the temple minister's counsel.

The minister received those who came to him in rooms which were reached through one of the archways and passages from the main floor. Mrs. Paddock was met by a motherly woman, whose face under her silvery white hair was beautiful with that beauty which comes only to those who have passed through the fires of suffering. She explained that because so many called to see the minister it was necessary to have an attendant. She had volunteered for that service. If Mrs. Paddock would be seated in the main room she would call her when the minister was at liberty.

The groceryman's wife thanked the woman, then added: "Haven't we met somewhere before? Your face is strangely familiar."

The other answered gently, with a kindly smile: "No, Mrs. Paddock, we have never met, but I have been a member of your church for several years. You have, no doubt, seen me at the services. My husband died ten years ago; I lost my three sons in the War; I am alone in the world now."

In the quiet of the temple Mrs. Paddock waited. And as she sat there in that beautiful room where, during the months just passed she had come under a religious influence which had reawakened in her those deep and true emotions of wifehood and motherhood so long neglected and denied for lesser interests, she lived again the years that were gone. Her girlhood days—her farm home—Sunday school—the country church—the neighbor boy who won her heart—their university years together—the pond in the woods where he asked her to be his wife—their home-making in the city—the coming of their daughter—the baby son who stayed with them such a little while—the slow drifting from the home anchorage—the intrusion of other interests—the near, oh, so near, tragedy! Could she ever win back that which she had lost? Would her daughter ever forget—?

The woman with the silvery hair came to tell her that the minister could see her now, and she went to ask his advice and help. Could he help her?

Mrs. Paddock did not spare herself. She told the minister everything. Nor did she attempt to excuse or explain or justify what she had done.

When she had finished the minister spoke a few kindly, reassuring words and rose as if to end the interview.

The woman's heart sank with disappointment. "But what shall I do?" she faltered. "Can you not advise me? Is there—is there no hope that I can ever win back my place in my husband's life? Have I lost my daughter forever? Must I go on like this always?"

When the minister did not reply she started blindly toward the door through which she had entered.

Then he said quietly: "Not that way, Mrs. Paddock."

She paused and looked at him questioningly.

He stepped to another door and opening it, motioned her to pass through. As she crossed the threshold he smiled, and softly closed the door behind her.

"Georgia!"

"Mother!"

It was some time later when the daughter explained how she too had come to the minister for advice. When she had told him the whole pitiful story, he had asked her to remain for a little while. Then he had asked the silvery haired woman to send for Mrs. Paddock and was told that Georgia's mother was already there, waiting to see him.

The groceryman dined with Mr. Saxton at the hotel that evening, and then spent the hours until midnight at the meeting of the Foundation trustees.

The next morning it happened that Georgia was a few minutes late for breakfast.

While he waited, Joe picked up the morning paper to glance at the head-lines. Mrs. Paddock, standing by the fireplace, was smiling happily to herself as if anticipating a pleasure.

Then their daughter appeared in the doorway and at her cheery "Good morning, folks," the groceryman looked up and saw the girl go to her mother, who received her with a kiss. Laughing at the expression on his face, Georgia pulled her father to his feet, and the three went in to breakfast.

The maid had not forgotten the fruit knives that morning. The fruit, apparently, was very satisfactory. But the groceryman was puzzled. Something had happened—or was going to happen. His wife and daughter seemed to be sharing a secret and judging from their faces, they were having a lot of fun out of it.

Presently Mrs. Paddock asked: "Joe, have you anything of particular importance for this afternoon?"

"Why?"

"I'd like to go to the farm."

He stared at her in blank amazement. Laura Louise Paddock had not for many years suggested that she would *like* to do anything. She had merely announced what she was going to do, and ordered her groceryman husband to make his plans accordingly.

"Well?" he said at last.

"I thought," murmured Mrs. Paddock, while Georgia hid a smile in her napkin, "that you might like to take me. It's such a beautiful day and—and there will be a lovely moon."

"Fine," said the groceryman, meeting the situation heartily. "If Georgia can get off we'll all go. I'll phone mother to have Hetty fry us a couple of chickens. There are some that ought to be about ripe now."

Georgia looked at her mother and deliberately winked—a wink which caused Mrs. Paddock to blush like a girl.

"Sorry, Daddy, but you'll have to excuse me to-day."

As soon as their midday meal was over, the groceryman and his wife started for the country, and their daughter, as she watched them go, thought her mother the most beautiful woman in Westover.

Georgia felt a little lonely as she set out for the office. Considering everything it was not strange that the girl's thoughts were of the man she loved, and that her heart should be filled with a great longing. Nor was it strange that in her mood she should stop at the temple.

For some time she was alone in the great room. The solemn beauty of the place—the soft light—the shadowy arches—the lovely color—the stillness—soothed and comforted her. The spirit of the temple gave her strength and courage and hope. Something seemed to whisper a promise.

Presently, she felt that she was not alone. Some one had entered the temple and was sitting not far away. She did not move—not even to turn her head—but she knew who it was.

After a little, she felt him coming slowly toward her. She sat very still, with her head bowed—her face hidden.

Then he was in the chair beside her.

And then. . . .

The late afternoon sun that day made lanes of gold between the trees in the Paddock woods and shot arrows of light through the leaves and branches, while the pond in the hollow was a moss green cup of liquid amber.

Under the old tree, which had heard their first love vows, the groceryman and his wife put away their mistakes of the years that were past, and together began a new and more abundant life. They were so engrossed in their happiness that they did not hear the automobile which had stopped at the edge of the woods on the old East Road.

Then the sound of some one approaching startled them, and, as they might have done when they were boy and girl, they slipped away through the bushes to hide from the curious gaze of whoever it was that had chanced to come upon that sacred spot at the wrong moment.

Mrs. Paddock suddenly caught her husband's arm with a little gasp of happy amazement.

The groceryman, manlike, laughed—but softly—so as not to disturb those younger lovers to whom also that place was holy ground.

THE END.